PRAISE FOR THE STORIES OF 100TH POWER

On *In the Empire of Underpants:* "In a post-apocalyptic world, where only smart clothing remains, the protagonist's underwear…searches for the magic panties which may save its people. The story is radically different from anything I've read before and balances almost plausible situations with puns, and whimsical humor."
 – Robert L. Turner III, *Tangent Online*

On *Forced Partnership:* "Robert T. Jeschonek revisits Isosceles City to tell a *Rashomon*-like story about a dysfunctional superhero bromance. Despite the wildly divergent back-and-forth narrative, it's pretty clear which character is telling the truth and which character is totally off his nut. But no matter. No one understands gloriously defective supermen better than Jeschonek. "
 — Eric Searleman, *Superheronovels.com*

On *Piggyback:* "'Piggyback' is narrated by a parasitic creature, undetectable by humans, which controls the actions of a homeless alcoholic. As frightening as this is, the creature itself is terrified of the god-like being it serves. This story is likely to raise a few goosebumps with its notion that there are many unseen entities among us."
 — Victoria Silverwolf, *Tangent Online*

On *With Love in Their Hearts:* "The story opens with a startling juxtaposition: the statement of love towards an enemy in the heart of a violent attack. The tale continues to make the reader reflect on the concept of love, and the various ways love can be incorporated into a life's mission, exploring the idea of 'a love that kills' in an entirely new way."
 – Mark Leslie, Editor, *Fiction River: Feel the Love*

ALSO BY ROBERT JESCHONEK

100TH POWER VOLUME 1

A TREASURY OF 100 STORIES

ROBERT JESCHONEK

100th POWER VOLUME 1

BLASTOFF
B O O K S

Published by Blastoff Books
An Imprint of Pie Press
411 Chancellor Street
Johnstown, Pennsylvania 15904
www.blastoffbooks.net

Subscribe to the Blastoff Books Newsletter:
http://newsletter.blastoffbooks.net

To Isaac Asimov, James Blish, Ray Bradbury, Robert Heinlein, Frank Herbert, and the other wizards of the printed page, for all the rocket fuel.

CONTENTS

INTRODUCTION

SURVEYING THE FEAST

RAMSEY CAMPBELL

Sometimes I could think that Singapore breakfast buffet was a dream or a glimpse of an idyllic afterlife, but my wife Jenny confirms we encountered it in the Pan Pacific hotel—an immense dining-room where the selection of cuisines seemed to encompass the world. You might glimpse diners meandering from station to chef's station in search of yet another country's specialities, and imagine that these figures disappearing into the distant mists of the vast room had been wandering for eternity. The feast was a daunting adventure, a challenge to sample everything on offer, and by now you may have twigged that I'm reminded of Robert Jeschonek's colossal collection. How can I even start to embrace its contents? I feel dwarfed, but I can only begin.

"With Love in Their Hearts" spikes the reader's attention at once, with the kind of cultural paradox speculative fiction can examine—succinctly too, as the tale deftly sketches its future context. The story works as both a fantastic romance in the classic chivalric sense and a scrutinous reversal of those tropes. It introduces us to the ceaselessly questing mind of our author.

All this hardly prepares us for "In the Empire of Underpants", but could anything, even the title? Yes, it is what that suggests, and more. Despite its wild humor, it's founded on a scientific possibility that some readers' lifetimes might well see. Personification in stories has a venerable tradition—I still remember being moved as a schoolboy by the travails of a three-guinea watch, the helpless narrator of a Victorian novel by Talbot Baines Reed—and I'm also reminded of a parody of Robert Browning that used to circulate in the schoolyard:

Oh, to be in England
Now that April's there,
And whoever wakes in England
Sees, some morning, underwear...

Which leaves me no closer to conveying the sheer surreal delight of Jeschonek's invention. I can only counsel experiencing it for yourself.

"Fear of Rain" begins by epitomizing one of our author's skills: the linguistic underlining of his topics. See how many words in the opening paragraph take up the titular motif. Watery the theme may be, but the prose is as muscular as ever. The story reveals a dark side of small-town nostalgia, but offers uncanny lyricism in the midst of its apocalyptic storm, and ends in an explosion of images that reaches for—indeed, triumphantly achieves—the ecstatic.

What real reader would feel rebuffed by the opening of "Piggy-back"? The line is a sly enticement, of course. Neither it nor the title prepares us for the story's cosmic scope. Central to the narrative is that staple of vintage science fiction, the ordinary fellow who proves to be the savior of the world, but Jeschonek approaches it from a refreshingly alien direction that throws new light on the idea. By the end the concept has been thoroughly subverted, and only terror endures as that opening sentence reveals its significance.

"Aye, Plank" surely can't be narrated by—oh yes it can. The title is indeed the pun it sounds like. I eye it with envy; indeed, my cranium is so covetous you might say I'm capped in admiration. This pirate yarn tacks towards Hodgsonian weirdness before charting its own exploratory course. How helplessly complicit is this shipboard item in the horrors it helped to carry out? A character works redemptive magic, and so does our author.

"Acirema the Rellik" announces from the outset that it plans to turn familiar perception on its head. One of the great functions of art, as of criticism, is to make us—reader and author alike—look afresh at things we've taken for granted. Jeschonek is a master of the approach, and here he virtually reinvents cyberpunk. Far from a relic or even a rellik, the story reaches for optimism out of its bleakness, but the reader must decide if it succeeds.

"The Man in the Sci Fi Suit" conflates fiction and reality, at least in our imaginations. Would many authors not be tempted by the prospect? Perhaps not if the ability sets the imagination wholly free and reality becomes an endless series of first drafts (though we might wonder how much that accords with actual lived experience). Might collaboration help? Certainly its representative within the tale is garbed in gorgeous fancies, as we might envisage his author. Could he be here, grinning at us through the metafictional layers? Someone's in control, after all.

"Eggs of the Dog That Bit You": the title launches us into a kind of casual surrealism we might associate with children's fiction, which is not to suggest that the story is childish—childlike, perhaps, in the best Bradburyian sense, initially recapturing the sense of joyful wonder some fantasists seem never to relinquish. All this is founded on that reliable motif, the farm threatened with possession by the bank, distilled into a ten-minute tale! Can there be any room for the story to twist itself? Never underestimate its author.

"Offensive in Every Possible Way" isn't, of course. It has sly fun with the contemporary prevalence of strong language, perhaps enfeebled by familiarity. In depicting a future where such words have grown even more commonplace than presently it recalls Verhoeven's *Total Recall*, which signified their future acceptability by leaving one unbleeped in a television newscast. Jeschonek envisages an era of linguistic compulsion, unless he's simply looking around him; is it so remote, after all? How can we, victims as we all may be, liberate ourselves? Through language, of course—the writer's secret. Jeschonek has a special one to share with us, and here's one reader who's grateful. *nd**d, *'m *lm*st l*st f*r w*rds.

We would hardly expect "Heroes of Global Warming" to approach the issue it names by any conventional route, and as ever, Jeschonek doesn't fail us. For a start, he thoroughly transforms a location that must be embedded in the common consciousness. If films are responsible for its familiarity, they've brought us super-heroes too, but not in the way Jeschonek does. The story's a marvel, as potent as DC—direct current, that's to say. It works both as an extended superheroic set piece and a witty commentary, not to mention an origin tale: all this leading to a dazzlingly rapturous coda.

Just as "Heroes" conjures up the flashy battles comic-book characters enact, "Driverless" zooms into the world of the comic, sound effects and all. Our hero incarnates pure speed but is touched by poetry (like many a passage in this book). The narrative gathers kinetic excitement in the way of the form it is parodying, and its breathless advance ends with a punch line explosive enough for a collision.

"The Messiah Business" involves elements surrounding Christ's sermons even the Monty Python team never risked depicting, though they seem likely enough. How numerous are Biblical suspense stories? Perhaps Jeschonek has invented a genre, and it wouldn't be the only time he has. Here the tension derives from how or whether the resolution will prove redemptive, as the Christian context seems to promise. Don't expect the revelation to come from me, though. Who am I, John the Baptist?

"The Asteroid That Stays Crunchy in Milk" confers conscious-ness on your breakfast. "Commander Quip"—there's an acknowl-edgement of style and wit for you. Throughout the tale and indeed the book, theme and language merge in a flavorsome recipe. Once again Jeschonek addresses fantasy as a compensation for reality, but perhaps a power fantasy can have unexpected powers of its own. After all, our author's imagination does.

Good art makes us look afresh, and in "Reviews of Museum-Goers by Famous Works of Art Through the Years" looks back at us, in another of the poetic reversals in which our author specializes. We may cringe to have been observed or hope we are nothing like the patrons pinned down by the paintings, but are we being too kind to ourselves? Perhaps we should simply be grateful that unlike the contributors to this piece, we haven't been trapped on canvas.

"Time, Expressed as an Entrée" brings my sampling to an end. The story descends from the awesomely cosmic to the human, yet another of Jeschonek's reversals of the familiar, in this case the usual form the tale of cosmic terror takes. Were I pitching the concept in an elevator, I might suggest Frank Capra meets Donald Wandrei, only to convict myself of inadequacy at once. Perhaps nobody can encompass Jeschonek's imagination except Jeschonek himself, but let it flourish uncontained! I hope my stumbling around the feast has given some sense of how much more there is to relish. Let me leave you to devour it now. I'll be that distant figure wandering among the wonders.

Ramsey Campbell
Wallasey, Merseyside
13 February 2023

WITH LOVE IN THEIR HEARTS

"I love you!" Hissing the words through the blood in my mouth, I lunge at my opponent. And I *mean* those words with all my heart--I *have* to--even as I swipe my dagger across his chest.

As he dances back out of reach, a line of red opens up where I cut him. His dirty, bearded face clouds...then quickly clears. "I love you *more!*" He smiles as he leaps at me with both fists forward, aiming them like a battering ram at my face.

Beaming with all the affection I can muster, all the true sweet regard for my friendly fellow man, I spin around out of his way and tag him again with the dagger, plugging the blade deep in his left kidney.

Howling, he stumbles into the thick-trunked oak that was just at my back. He takes it headfirst and bounces off, weaving drunkenly in the mud.

"Friend warrior." This is how I finish him, all sweetness and light. Without the *slightest* shred of darkness in my heart. "You are like unto the finest flower in the brightest sunbeam on the loveliest day in all the year." Darting to one side, I duck down and recover the sword I dropped earlier in this battle--dearest Eros. "God bless you for bringing such *joy* to my life."

With that, I swing the sword up, then down and through his neck with a perfect, practiced stroke.

So good am I at this that not a *trace* of hatred or savage satisfaction punctuates the moment when his head separates from his shoulders and plops into the muck.

Breathing hard, I scan my surroundings. I see the bodies of the three men I've killed, sprawled in various bloody contortions...and the body of Vicka, my partner on the road until now, whom they killed before I could kill them first.

That is what love can accomplish. Its power is arrayed around me for all to behold.

Moving swiftly lest another patrol comes my way too soon, I secure my beaten black body armor, then retrieve and put on my battered helmet with the old red-white-and-blue banner etched into the hard plastic. I retrieve my motorbike, too...but the front tire has been slashed, and it won't start. I guess I can't complain; it's over a century old, and I've gotten a lot of use out of it until now.

"Go with God, fair machine." I drop it in the muck, grab my dagger from the dead man's kidney, and set off at a brisk jog through the woods. The autumn sun is closing in on the horizon, and I need to make my destination by nightfall.

Everything is riding on the completion of my mission. All my people down in Burytown are counting on me to succeed.

Though it is hard to imagine I *can* succeed this time. The killing of men and women has always come easy to me. It is *that* very inclination that could make this new mission such a challenge.

Heart pounding, I run through the mud, brush, and leaves, ever up along the steep contour of the mountainside. This part of what was once known as the state of Pennsylvania is full of such mountains--the *Alleghenies*, as we call them yet today. They have been my home for all five and twenty years of my life, and navigating them is second nature to me.

Reading the wind and the angle of the sun, I know I'm not far from my goal. In spite of the best efforts of my attackers, I will reach my destination, though what happens after that, I cannot say.

Finally, I burst from the woods and find myself at the edge of the old road. I also find myself face to face with two men in camouflage body armor, wielding six-guns.

Slowly, I take off the helmet. "Greetings to you both."

"Hail and well met, good stranger!" The one doing the talking has the biggest, friendliest smile...and the steadiest grip on his revolver. "State your name and purpose, that we may love you all the better!"

Instinctively, I meet his gaze with the most genuine grin I can muster. "I am Sir Gardner Schell of Burytown," I tell them. "I have come to meet my bride."

Expected as I am, the sentinels holster their guns and lead me through the barricades blocking the road. On the other side, my destination awaits--a place I've only visited a handful of times, though Burytown lies but seven miles to the west of it.

The building looks for all the world like an old ocean liner (the kind I've seen only in photos), complete with decks, portholes, and a pair of big smokestacks on the roof, angled toward the stern. It is as if, by some miracle, a seagoing vessel has been stranded in the heights of a mountain range, along the curve of a once-great highway that has seen better days.

GRAND VIEW SHIP HOTEL. That's the old name of it, painted in big black letters on the side of the ship facing the road. *SEE 3 STATES AND 7 COUNTIES.* That's painted on the prow. Armor plating has been added all around, but those words out of history remain.

The *real* name, the one it's known by now, is not painted anywhere. But ask anyone within fifty miles of here if they know of Kendall's Keep, and they will point you right to it. Everyone who uses this stretch of road--known in olden times as the Highway of Lincoln--must pay a toll to Kendall's men to pass this point.

"What took you so long?" Lord Rubicon Kendall strides out of the keep in a white sea captain's uniform, looking hale and hearty and overly friendly. A sword hangs at either hip, plus a long rifle at his back, and rightly so; his clan is at war. "You were expected *this morning*, good sir knight."

"If not for the *second* ambush, I most certainly would have been here sooner. And Vicka, my late retainer, as well." I point at the path that I traveled up the slope. "The *Loved Ones* grow ever bolder, my Lord."

Rubicon grins through his neatly trimmed ebony mustache and goatee. "It is a delight we have in common, yes? Your people down in Burytown have been *especially* showered with their affections, have they not?"

"Such a blessing." I say it stiffly, though I manage a smile. The siege of Burytown is my whole reason for being here. An alliance with Rubicon's clan would give us the punch we need to break the siege and lay our friends the Loved Ones to rest for good.

Though such an alliance does not come without a price.

"I am in your hands, my Lord." I bow my head and spread my arms. "Assuming our pact yet stands."

"It does. My Lady Kendall, God rest her soul, had people in Burytown. I am only too happy to offer you this chance." He lays a hand on my shoulder. "*If* you are ready for the challenge, Sir Gardner."

"I would not be here if I were not."

"Well said." Rubicon nods sagely, peering into my eyes with the focus of a hawk. "And would you accept the guidance of an advisor in this quest of yours? He was of much help when *I* was in your shoes."

"Thank you, my Lord, but that won't be necessary."

Rubicon cocks his head to one side, looking amused. "May he provide a *benediction*, at least?"

Before I can answer, an old man rises on the main deck on the second level of the ship/keep and clears his throat. "Let us pray," he calls down to us. Like Rubicon, he wears a uniform, though the pieces don't go together well: white cap, black jacket, red ascot, lemon trousers.

Confidentially, Rubicon leans over and whispers to me. "Bon

Cloister up there will perform the ceremony, you know. *If* there *is* one."

"In the century since the Great Collapse," says Cloister, "only *love* has sustained we few survivors. As this young knight stands on the precipice of the greatest struggle of all--holy wedlock--we pray that he may turn to *another* face of love and do what we all know he *must* do to succeed."

"Amen." Grinning, Rubicon smacks me on the back.

"Times a million," says Cloister as he digs out a pipe and lights it with a hellaciously long furnace match.

"Here we are." Rubicon leads me past armed guards into the keep, then down a short hallway. "Have a seat in the Coral Room, Sir Gardner."

We enter a room with turquoise walls and red-rimmed port-holes. A polished wooden bar occupies most of one side, with a black-cushioned elbow-rest and pink-upholstered barstools with backs. Dusty glasses and bottles line shelves behind the bar, glinting in the last flickers of daylight slipping in from the windows in the dining room next-door.

I sit on a long red bench against the opposite wall. A knight must *never* sit with his back to the door, as I have learned the hard way.

Just then, I hear footsteps--hard shoes descending a staircase.

"Here she comes." Rubicon smiles and bounces on the balls of his feet. "Good luck to you." He winks and whispers that last.

My heart beats fast as the footsteps approach down the hallway. I have fought a thousand battles, but this is new ground for me.

"Sir Gardner." Rubicon steps aside and gestures at the doorway. "I introduce my daughter, Listy Kendall."

I rise as she enters the room. Never in my life have I seen anyone so *beautiful*.

Listy curtsies. "Sir Gardner." She is in her early 20s, with all the firmness of youth in her pale, porcelain skin. Loose, dark curls frame an oval face with lively eyes, delicate nose, and full red lips. I can see from the fall of her long, creamy gown that her body is perfectly sculpted, bust and hips swelling pleasingly above and below a slender waist.

I manage a bow, but words fail me. Entranced, I can but stare as she watches and waits, smiling.

Rubicon raises an eyebrow and gestures at the bar. "Perhaps you might like a drink, Sir Gardner?"

His question barely registers. I am spellbound.

"My father has pledged my hand to you, good knight," says Listy. "It might do us well to converse upon this betrothal, don't you think?"

Her voice, as soft and flowing as the song of a meadowlark, freezes me further. I am drawn to her, mesmerized as I have never been before--yet locked down as if shackled and gagged. A man of action I have always been, but now I am turned to stone.

And none of it makes any sense to me.

"Ha. I wondered if this might happen." Rubicon walks over and squeezes my shoulder. "Perhaps some time with Bon Cloister might not be a bad idea *after* all, sir knight."

Fresh air does me some good. As I stand at the railing of the keep's main deck and watch the sun set, my wits slowly return to me.

Without invitation, Bon Cloister shuffles over to stand beside me, lighting a fresh pipeful of tobacco. Up close, I see how withered he is, how ancient in his shabby hodge-podge uniform.

"What is the Story of Love, Sir Gardner?" He puffs twice on the pipe, then exhales sweet cherry-smelling smoke from his nose. "Tell me how love as we know it came to be."

Everyone knows this story, but I humor him. I'm embarrassed about what happened in the Coral Room and eager to make things right.

"One of the plagues of the Great Collapse in the 21st Century was *The Commandment*," I tell him. "Scientists unleashed a contagion to rewrite human DNA and bring about peace on Earth."

"How so?"

"People became physically unable to harm others out of hatred or anger. This was in fulfillment of Jesus Christ's commandment to love thy neighbor as thyself."

"Indeed." Smoke from Cloister's pipe drifts out over the vast landscape sprawling beyond the mountain. The setting sun casts blazing light over the acres of trees in their red, gold, and orange autumn finery. "And how did that work out when the *other* plagues struck, and civilization *collapsed?*"

"It made it nearly impossible to fight for survival."

Cloister smiles. "And so we learned to fight--to *kill* if need be-- the only way we *could*. With *love* in our hearts." He pulls the pipe from his mouth. "And we got very *good* at it, didn't we? The love-that-kills?"

I nod.

"*But!*" Cloister jabs the pipe stem at me. "What happens when we get so *good* at it, we forget what it's like to feel the *love-that-cherishes*? For some, especially the more...*accomplished* warriors, like yourself...this can sometimes lead to profound...*disharmonies.*"

"The love-that-cherishes?" I scowl.

"Caring for someone so much that we *don't* want to damage or murder them," says Cloister. "Feeling an attraction so *real* and *profound* that we want to join with the other person in a multitude of ways."

The song of the katydids buzzing in the trees makes more sense to me than what he's saying. "Is that even possible?" I ask.

Cloister narrows his eyes. "Do you *want* it to be?"

I think of my people in Burytown, who are depending on me. I think also of that beautiful girl in the Coral Room, and the way she seemed to glow when I gazed at her. "Yes." I whisper the word. "But how?"

"Righteous discipline." Cloister clenches his right hand. "And self-control. You must reach deep within yourself and change the love-that-kills to the love-that-cherishes...but *only* for this one person, your bride. For all others, especially those who threaten kith or kin..." He unclenches his hand and draws the edge of it across his throat like the blade of a knife.

Frustrated, I close my eyes and clench my teeth. I feel like going

7

over the rail and running off into the night with Eros in hand, ready to love all comers. That, at least, would not be like the great unknown I now face.

"So many feelings..." I grip the rail hard. "What if I can't *master* them, Bon?"

"Then your bargain with Lord Kendall will never be consummated." Cloister puts the pipe back in his mouth and puffs on it. "For neither he nor Listy herself shall brook a union where there is no *true* affection."

"Damn." I toss my head as if I'm trying to wake myself from a terrible dream. "I don't even know where to start."

"There are some mental drills that might help." Cloister pats me on the back. "Perhaps we can get you ready for tomorrow morning."

"What's happening tomorrow morning?"

"Your first date," says Cloister. "Also, if all goes well, your marriage proposal."

I wake, as always, before dawn, springing to full alertness with all the force of old habits. Sleeping too soundly or late can get you killed in the field, after all.

I wash up in a basin of tepid water in my room, then dry and dress. Looking out the window, I see it's still dark outside...but won't be for long. I am early for this morning's meeting, which is just how I like to be.

In this, Listy Kendall and I have something in common. When I arrive on the main deck, she is waiting there already, setting up an easel and palette of paints by the light of an oil lamp.

"Good morning," she says, waving a brush in my direction. "I trust you slept well, Sir Gardner?"

My heart races, and words catch in my throat. She looks as lovely as she did when we first met, in the Coral Room...and I feel just as frozen, just as shackled by conflicting emotions.

But then I run one of the exercises Cloister taught me, repeating these words in my head: *Kindness is not always hatred. Hatred is not always kindness.*

Something about that simple repetition weakens the bonds just enough for me to speak. "Yes, I did sleep well." It isn't much, but I consider it a victory.

"Glad to hear it." She strokes a rich red base on the canvas as the sky begins to brighten. "You don't mind if I paint, do you? It's going to be such a lovely autumn morning."

"Not at all." I can barely force out the words. The way her lacy white blouse clings to her breasts, and her black britches hug the curves of her hips and bottom, I have trouble focusing on the conversation at hand.

"So, Sir Gardner." Listy swirls in white with the red, stirring it into a deep pink color. "What hobbies do *you* have?"

C-Love, not K-Love. That's another exercise Cloister taught me. *C-Love, not K-Love,* as in *the love-that-cherishes,* not *the love-that-kills.* "Well..." I fight for focus. "I sharpen my *blades* in my spare time. And train younger knights in battlefield techniques."

"Sounds more like *work* to me." Listy tips her head and gives me a funny look out of the corner of her eye. "Do you ever court *maidens,* I wonder?"

I feel myself blush. *C-Love, not K-Love. C-Love, not K-Love.* "I, uh...no, I..." In spite of the mantra, my brain locks up, and my voice trails off.

"Oh, look." Listy pauses in dabbing at the canvas and gazes out at the scenery, mouth open in wonder. "Come here, Sir Gardner."

I step up beside her, following her gaze with my own. The sky, by now, is fairly bright, so the vast gulf below is awash in predawn light--but it appears not at all as it did the evening before. Everywhere I look, instead of swaths of colorful trees and distant green fields, I see an expanse of mist blanketing everything.

"I love when it's like this." Her voice is low and soft. "My grandfather used to say it was like an ocean of cloud out there. He half-expected to see a dolphin jump out of it, he said." She bumps my arm with her elbow. "Not that he was *biased,* living in a ship on the mountain and all."

"Three states, seven counties." Lost in the view, I get my voice back. "It's as if they've disappeared."

"They're still out there. They always are." Her elbow nudges my arm again. "You just can't *see* them."

Staring into that milky abyss, I let my imagination run away with me--something I rarely do. "It's more like Heaven than an ocean," I say, though I've only ever seen photos of oceans or paintings of Heaven.

When a bird pops out of the mist nearby, it startles me back to reality. I become fully aware of Listy's body next to mine, her elbow against my arm...and that triggers the kind of reaction I had before.

Even as it happens, I hate myself for it. Burytown is in dire need; am I so *damaged* that I can't at least *bluff* my way through the one chance I have to *save* it?

Yes, apparently.

Stumbling back from the railing, I knock over a chair and almost fall. Listy turns, a look of pity on her face that somehow makes it all the worse.

"S-sorry..." All my life, love has been a weapon. Feeling it has always been a pretext, a preamble to some kind or other of bloodbath. Thinking of it now *not* as a means to murder feels *wrong...confusing.*

Yet it's *there*...a *whisper* of that *other* love that Cloister talked about. And the more I feel it, *the more I don't know what to do with it.*

Listy seems to have no such difficulty--unless, of course, she isn't feeling C-Love toward me in the first place. She seems perfectly comfortable in all our interactions, even as I find myself intensely off-balance.

I'm sweating as if I'm in a fight, and my belly's full of butterflies. I wish I'd never come here, opening myself up to all this confusion-- even if staying home would have meant certain death without the alliance I'd hoped to find.

Time is running out for that home of mine...though just how quickly, I only now discover.

The door to the deck flies open, and a dark-skinned woman stalks through, heaving for breath. She is a woman I *know*, a messenger from Burytown called Polly Sullivan.

"Sir Gardner!" She gasps out the words. "I bring word of Bury-town! Its downfall is *imminent*. This very day, your precious *home* shall fall to the *wolves* at its doorstep."

I slide Eros down into his scabbard with the scrape of metal against metal. I do the same for the rest of my blades, slipping them into their various sheaths with familiar, practiced ease.

Standing in the middle of my room, I take a deep breath and release it. Everything is in its place again, and the world makes sense. My course is clear and straight, and my heart is filled with so much *love* for those who threaten my home.

Nodding to myself, I snatch my helmet from a hook on the wall, then storm out of the room and down the stairs. Lord Kendall, Bon Cloister, and Listy wait at the bottom, between me and the exit.

"Ho, sir knight." Rubicon raises both hands as if to hold me back. "We have heard with deep regret the terrible news from Burytown."

"Save your regret for the Loved Ones," I tell him. "For I go now to shower them with my deepest affection."

"Of course," says Rubicon. "You have concluded your business with us in full, then? Shall I signal my man-at-arms to rally the forces we have pledged you?"

I spare a glance at Listy, who bears a troubled look on her face. There is a pull deep within me, a gravity catching at my heart--but other powers overwhelm it.

"Good sir, the people of Burytown shall humbly welcome any and all forces pledged to act in their interest. But it is not true that our business is concluded." I bow my head. "I have yet to fulfill the terms of our pact."

"And *will* you?" asks Rubicon.

I feel Listy's frown upon me as I speak. "If Burytown's state is as dire as Polly Sullivan reports, I cannot promise anything. My own future might be exceedingly brief."

"Then, regrettably, I cannot offer aid," says Rubicon.

"Father!" snaps Listy.

Rubicon slashes his hand through the air. "We risk *much,* sending so large a force away from our own battlements. We risk this very *keep* and all who *depend* on it. We cannot--*will* not--take that risk without a *pact.*"

"But *I* am the *currency* in this pact, am I not?" says Listy. "Have I *no say* in this..."

Rubicon cuts her off. "The pact is *everything.* In this world, *bargains* are how we *survive.*" He shakes his head at Listy, then me. "Let me ask you this, Sir Gardner. Is there *no* possibility of forging a love-that-cherishes between the two of you?"

"I can perform a ceremony here on the spot," says Cloister. "A bond of wedlock so hastily conceived shall be *no* less legitimate."

I look at each of them in turn, considering. Again, when my eyes meet hers, I feel that pull, like the current of a river...but then that *other* force rises up and blots it out. K-Love wins out, as well it should. My people *need* me.

"It is not fair to the people of Burytown to linger one moment more as their home falls to invaders," I say. "And it is not fair to *you* to take your hand in wedlock if I might make of you a widow before this day is done." I bow to Listy. "As much as I might wish it could be otherwise."

"But you are *more* likely to live another day with Lord Kendall's forces at your back," says Cloister.

"And what kind of man would I *be* if I married this woman to save my own *neck*?" Impulsively, I reach for Listy's hand and kiss it. "That does not sound to me like anything *close* to a love-that-cherishes."

I let go of her hand...yet my next words are intended only for *her* ears. "Farewell. Perhaps we shall meet again in that heavenly ocean of mist."

With that, I square my shoulders, push past Lord Kendall, and march outside into the late morning sunlight. Polly, who's been waiting, kickstarts her motorbike and revs it loudly as I don my helmet and climb on behind her.

Then, in a cloud of dust and gravel, we spin around and fly down the highway away from Kendall's Keep.

It surprises me how much I think of Listy as we ride down the mountain. The memory of kissing her hand stays with me, as does the memory of gazing into the mist by her side with her elbow resting against my arm.

But when the time comes to banish her from my thoughts, I do. The field of battle, as I understand all too well, is no place for thoughts of C-Love...only K.

Polly and I dismount and stow the bike a mile back from Bury-town, then travel the rest on foot. The sounds of the fight reach us as we hurry through the woods--the clash and clang of steel, the scattered blasts of pistols and rifles, the screams of the wounded and dying.

Then the fight itself reaches us, too. Within sight of the rooftops of town, we are set upon by a trio of Loved Ones, soaked in gore and whipped into a frenzy.

"I *love* you!" A red-bearded warrior leads the ambush, swinging a blood-smeared axe overhead. "I will *show* you *how much!*"

Adrenaline burns in my bloodstream as I slip Eros from his scabbard and stand ready to meet the charge. "*Come* then, brother, and let us *see* who has the *most* love to *give!*"

They attack us like men possessed, half-crazed with K-Love stoked to extreme levels by relentless bloodletting on the field of battle. But Polly and I are possessed by a love that's as strong or stronger and untainted by corrupt motives. Our unwavering brand of love, born of devotion to home and clan, can carry the day against even the longest odds.

Though even as loving as we are, the odds we now face are long indeed. After ending the first three fighters with great love and swordsmanship, Polly and I push closer to the heart of the battle--just in time to see a horde of Loved Ones break through the line of defenders at the edge of Burytown.

People we know go down fighting as the invaders pile on. Every one of our noble warriors smiles with no less lovingkindness even as blades, bullets, and war hammers put them to rout.

It is now that I think of Listy once more, for I realize I shall never see her again. With the perimeter breached and our forces so clearly outnumbered, Burytown has not long to live.

Smoke fills the air as flaming arrows set fire to rooftops. Men and women on horseback and motorbikes tear through gaps in the line, escorted by slavering hounds. It is the end of the world, *my* world, and all the smiles and proclamations of love make it all the more hellish.

Doomed as our home may be, Polly and I charge into the fray with smiles and swords flashing.

K-Love, not C-Love. K-Love, not C-Love. Eros swirls and whizzes in my good right hand, slipping through one throat after another. In my good left hand, a dagger jabs and slashes, cutting faces, hearts, and guts like the fang of a dragon.

No mercy is shown, not a whit...though even as my blades sow mayhem, I feel only deep-down love for every soul I maim or kill.

I am, in these moments, perfection--my focus diamond-hard, my killing exquisite, my love unblemished. Dancing from one fighter to the next, leaving geysers of blood in my wake, I am like a holy angel, beaming and unstoppable.

But for every man or woman who falls before me, another three or four or more pile in. For every blow or cut that I deflect, another flurry rains down on me.

I swear I will fight to the last, but the outcome is set in stone now. The end is near.

Polly and I fight back to back, swords and daggers in constant motion--until suddenly, she is gone. Turning in my murderous gyre, I see her dragged under the bloodthirsty tide, and I move to save her.

But at that moment, someone gets in a lucky shot across my back with a crowbar, and I drop. Keeping hold of my blades, I twist, blindly sweeping Eros in a futile swath that catches nothing.

When I hit the ground, the horde closes in around me. *Love you love you love you,* chant dozens of voices overflowing with eager and deeply sincere affection.

I see the crowbar and other bludgeoning weapons hoisted over-head, ready to crash upon me like a landslide. Holding fast to the handles of my blades, I ready myself for one final fusillade to finish the day, one last statement to cast upon the canvas of this terrible work.

"I love you!" I howl the words at the top of my lungs. "*I love you from the bottom of my heart!*"

It is then that I hear a salvo of gunshots crackling nearby. Men topple around me like rotten fruit, dropping their bludgeons.

More clamor then--a thunder of footfalls, a clatter of blades. More gunshots and the twanging of bowstrings, the sizzle and *thunk* of arrows. More men and women fall, and the rest erupt in panic.

Seizing the opportunity, I leap to my feet and pick up where I left off, slashing and stabbing in every direction. As Loved Ones fumble and scatter, I clear them like chaff.

A giant of a man, bald as a pumpkin and bedecked in blood, refuses to panic and swats the helmet right off my head. I answer with a knife through his windpipe...just as a sword thrusts through his heart from behind.

He topples as both blades withdraw--and I see whose sword joined mine in stopping the menace.

It was *hers*. "Good Sir Gardner!" None other than *Listy Kendall* grins back at me from the visor of a white helmet. "Fancy meeting *you* here." Laughing, she wipes the blood from her sword against the hip of her white body armor.

My heart hammers in my chest at the sight of her. I am so caught up in her beauty and the shock of seeing her that I forget to lose the power of speech. "You *came?*" Looking around, I see men and women wearing the coat of arms of Kendall's Keep (in patches or tattoos) plowing through the invaders of Burytown. "But what of the *pact?*"

Listy narrows her eyes and lifts her chin. "Wedded or no, I will *never* stand idly by so long as there is something I can do to save good folk like the people of Burytown."

In that instant, I get a shiver, a frisson of electric joy. I want nothing more than to wrap her in my arms and never let go.

Because she *came*. Because she's *fighting* on behalf of my people for no other reason than because it's *right*. Because she's so *beautiful* and *thoughtful* and *capable* and *confident*, and I *want* her with every fiber of my *being*.

15

Is *this* what Cloister was talking about? The love-that-cherishes? *An attraction so real and profound that we want to join with the other person in a multitude of ways?*

"I suppose the pact is *moot*, then? Since Burytown got the help it needed without the two of us submitting to wedlock?" As Listy says it, a bruiser roars forth, and she dispatches him with a flick of her sword.

"Actually, I've been thinking." Lifting Listy's visor, I lean in and kiss her gently on the lips. "Perhaps we might discuss *another* pact?"

Her eyes lock with mine, and she kisses me back--not gently. "Perhaps."

Then, whirling, she takes up the fight again, swinging her sword with all the nimble grace with which she paints an ocean of mist on a canvas.

Smiling, I fell an attacker of my own, dropping him dead with a heart full of love--but for *once*, it is *not* the love-that-kills.

IN THE EMPIRE OF UNDERPANTS

I soar through the air, my white hyper-cotton body bunching and rolling on the soft morning breeze. Times like this, I feel fine and free, a pair of smart-briefs gliding through nature like a bird or a cloud.

But then I always come back down to earth in the end.

My left leg loop catches on the tip of a branch, and I swing to a stop. While I'm up there, I sing a little song, as my kind loves to do, in praise of the morning and being alive--a true classic.

"We can't wait to get in your pants." My high-pitched voice is generated by the sound threads woven into my fly, which flutters when I sing. *"We will fill your drawers with joy."*

It's a commercial jingle, one of many that once advertised my particular brand of genius undies. I sing it loud, though there aren't any commercials these days--and then I change the words, asking one of the great questions of life in the modern world.

"What does a left leg loop feel like around an actual left leg?" That's the question of which I sing this time. It's a question I sing about often, as if I'll ever know the answer.

Which of course I won't. All the left legs are gone now. All the *live, human* ones, that is, and the humans they belonged to.

When I'm done singing, I contract and twist the smartlastic

fibers in the caught leg loop, working my way off the branch. I drop to the ground below, which is still muddy from last night's rain, and land with a flop.

"No problemo!" Mud becomes a real *nothing-burger* when you've got *my* mad skills.

As a true smart brief, the most advanced underwear ever designed, I was made to repel dirt and moisture with a flick of my hyper-cotton panels. Chemical films baked into the threads push contaminants right off, leaving behind only my bright white material that looks like it's just been through the wash...though it never *needs* laundering. And that's a *good* thing, on a journey like mine.

Because I've been on the move for weeks...

...*months*, my internal timer corrects me...

...and who knows when I'll get to enjoy the comforts of home again.

It's a price worth paying, though, being on the road for so long. If I succeed, I might find a cure for the sickness that's afflicting my fellow smart-underpants back home. I might find the fabled Magic Panties of the Plains, the ones with the healing powers beyond the ken of AI folk like me.

That's "AI" as in "Apparel Intelligence," in case you're wondering.

On the way to my next destination, I squirm and roll through the muck at a breathtaking ground speed of a few feet per minute. In the old days, briefs like me traveled the world at *incredible* speeds, worn by human folk who raced around in cars or flew in airplanes or rockets. What must it have been like to be a tighty whitey in those glorious times?

If only all the humans hadn't died out in the Great Erection a decade ago, I might have had the chance to find out.

"You'll never be lost again. These briefs are your best friend." It's another song of the lost humans, a commercial jingle, and I sing it as I go. *"Wherever you land/if you sit, run, or stand/you'll know you've got a buddy in your pants."* I sing it as if those vanished folk are more to

me than a thousand million facts and images bubbling in the database of my woven-in AI mind. I sing it as if I ever even *saw* a living, breathing human in the flesh, let alone filled my body with its form.

But I had just been sparked to life in a factory by robotic underpants engineers when the Great Erection had its way with humanity. It was my curse, since I never got to know human folk...and also my salvation. For if I'd been worn by a human when the end came for that species, I would have had a much harder time escaping to the outside world to begin my new life.

Rolling myself up in a tube, I wriggle through a thicket of thorny bushes and never catch a single snag.

"Underpants power!" It's a little something I say sometimes when I kick ass. Talking to myself like that helps me keep sane on my long, lonely journey.

Unrolling on the other side of the thicket, I flex my elastics-- then hear the soft keening on the breeze and realize I'm not alone.

"Need a bosom buddy? Never fear. Pack your rack in our brainy brassiere." It's sung with an accent, but I've heard the words before. Even before I look around, I know who's singing them. *"We're all about a wiser bust. We support the higher you."* Anywhere I've ever been, that's the song of a smart-bra, plain and simple.

And there are more smart-bras in the clearing before me than I've ever seen in one place before. They are strung on a tall, stout tree, shrouding it completely as if they'd grown there.

I see a multitude of colors, shapes, and cup sizes, straps tangled around branches or each other: pink, white, red, black, blue; full-cup, push-up, padded, plunge, sports; A-cup, B-cup, C-cup, D-cup, and more.

They must have flown here like me, by looping elastic on something sturdy, pulling back as far as they could, and slingshotting into the wind. But this tree must block a flight path, catching errant bras as they pass with cups flapping and straps fluttering like streamers.

I call out to them to the tune of a bra-song I know, substituting my own words for the classic lyrics. *"How did you all get here? What happened to you?"*

Boy, do I get an earful for my trouble. Every bra on the tree starts yelling at once. Hundreds of voices of all pitches and timbres clamor for attention, drowning each other out.

"Wait! Please!" I shout, with the gain on my sound threads cranked all the way up. "One at a time!"

But the lot of them just keep jabbering. And it keeps getting louder.

I try again. "What happened to you?"

More babble. If there's a straight answer here, I can't make it out.

Something happened to these smart-bras, but what? How and why would so many of them malfunction or go crazy at once?

And what if it's something that could do the same to *me?*

I wish I could help them. They're kindred garments, cut from the same cloth.

But the folks at home are depending on me. If I don't make it back soon with a cure from the Magic Panties, they might all be dead.

As much as underpants and bras go together, I need to stick to my mission. I can't risk getting pulled away by a bunch of lingerie.

Imagine a pair of white briefs jumping up and down and singing loudly on a hill. That's me, once a day, calling home.

I do it every day around noon, climbing to a high spot and singing to the West--the direction of home. Off in the distance, I always hear my song echoed by other AIs, be they briefs, bras, pantyhose, sweaters, slacks, or other wired clothing. Someone repeats after me, and someone else further on repeats after them, and so on, until the message reaches my underpants tribe back home. That way, they know I'm still out here. And when they answer, I know they're still out there, too.

But today, when I deliver my message, the AIs relaying it sound fewer and farther between. And though I repeat the message, no one replies. For the first time, nothing comes back to me.

So either the end has come for my people, or they're wearing out faster than I expected.

I travel further, sometimes rolling or crawling when the ground is too mucky, sometimes using my smartlastic leg and waistbands like springs to hop and leap when the ground is more solid.

As I go, though the tension has risen because of my people's silence, I keep up a positive attitude. It's the way the humans programmed me, according to my onboard user manual. Apparently, nobody wanted unhappy underpants in those days; droopy drawers were frowned on back then.

So I chirp a song as I head east--the same tune as yet another old jingle--but the words are my own, asking another of the great questions. *"What does a waistband feel like around a living, breathing waist?"*

So many answers I have in my woven-in database, yet I will never know the answer to that. I know all about the world that came before the Great Erection, but what good is all that if I can't know what it was like to fulfill the very purpose for which I was made?

I might have been created with Apparel Intelligence, with self-cleaning, speech, mobility, climate control, camouflage, and many other functions...but *being worn* is still my primary function. And as much as I treasure my freedom, I long for that. I wish I could know what it's like to be *worn.*

Not by an animal or inanimate object, either. Not by a statue or mannequin, though I've heard of AI folk who've tried both.

But I know, if a human did suddenly appear, there would be such a rush from all directions to clothe him, the poor person would likely be smothered.

Death by underpants. The ultimate wardrobe malfunction.

Leaning out over the edge of a cliff, I gaze with the optic receptors ("eyelastics") in my waistband at the vast plain stretching out below.

Flat grasslands fan east, south, and north, flowing green under the afternoon sun. Herds of apparel--some bright white, others multicolored--spill over the land, rippling like laundry on clotheslines in the days before the humans died out.

But the part that tugs at my fly the most is the big mound in the center of the plain. From a distance, it looks like a massive junk heap of clothing--a huge, oblong hump of discarded attire sprawled diagonally over the heart of the land.

Who put it there? That's what I want to know. And why?

And what does it have to do with the Magic Panties of the Plains? Because those *have* to be the legendary plains where they live, according to the songs and stories. They're exactly where and how they're *supposed* to be, *except* for the mound. So what gives, is what I want to know.

And I'm about to find out.

As I lean there, stretching and stiffening my fibers to get a better view, I feel the ground rumble beneath me.

Twisting around, I puff up in fear, expanding to twice my size. Ever been trapped in front of a stampede of footwear before? Dozens of smart-shoes and smart-boots stomping toward you with abandon, ready to crush you under their hyper-rubber soles?

Me, either, until *now*.

The ground shakes harder as the stampede hammers toward me. I shout at them in my best shoe-speak to stop, but no one seems to notice. They just keep bearing down on me blindly, all the mismatched sneakers, clogs, oxfords, pumps, platforms, steel-toes, and shit-kickers, like dumb animals spooked by thunder and lightning.

They leave me only one way to go.

Facing the cliff's edge, I puff up more, to three times my size. With the stampede only seconds behind me, I launch myself into space.

Immediately, I catch an updraft that shoots me higher, dozens of feet above the level of the cliff. Below, shoes and boots spill off the edge and tumble out of the heights like fallen angels. Tongues and laces flutter frantically, but it's all in vain.

Meanwhile, I gracefully glide from one thermal current to the next, feeling the warm air rushing through my leg loops and waist hoop.

"Set your privates free. Strip away the everyday and let it all hang in." The song I sing is one of my favorites, an old jingle that makes me think of flight and freedom. Even with the weight of my mission upon me, I can still appreciate the beauty of this moment.

I wish I could stay up here all day.

Eventually, I put down a mile from the mound, landing softly as a parachute on the grass. *That* was the greatest flight I've ever had, maybe even the greatest of all time by a pair of unassisted underpants.

Unfortunately, it has not gone unnoticed. Moments after I touch down, something runs up, snatches me from the ground, and keeps moving.

I'm disoriented, flopping around in the grip of this thing, until it slows to a trot. Then, my stitched-in sensors tip me off that something biological has me. I detect animal saliva, warm breath, and shaggy fur. Sharp teeth are sunk into my hyper-cotton crotch, so jagged and tight I'd surely tear if I tried to pull away.

It's a good thing smart-briefs like me have other ways of scaring off the unwanted.

Dangling from the fangs of the beast, I puff myself up with air, then spritz in a mist of chemicals from my onboard dispensary fibers. A sudden contraction, and a potent antiseptic spray pulses into the face of my captor.

The animal lets out a piercing whine and drops me on the spot. Shaking, it crashes down beside me, thrashing on the ground and pawing at its long gray muzzle.

Coyote. Now that I get a good look at it from a perspective other than hanging from its mouth, I see the creature for what it is. Not sure why it picked me up in the first place, but one thing's for sure.

It won't pick me up again. My antiseptic spray was designed to flush out all manner of infections and parasites, not so much *coyotes*...but it obviously does the trick for them, too.

No canine will shove its snout into *this* crotch for long.

Free of the dog that bit me, I continue on my way, hopping toward the mound of apparel. It seems like as good a place as any to search for the Magic Panties.

Then, as I top a little rise, I see a pair of blue-and-white-striped boxer shorts twitching and giggling on the ground in front of me. They're smart-shorts, or they wouldn't be giggling--but something about the way they're doing it doesn't seem quite right.

"Hello?" I say it in underpants-speak and hope for the best.

"Hee-hee-hee!" say the boxers. "Howdy, white stuff!"

At least we speak the same language. "Are you okay?"

"Never been better!" That cracks up the boxers more than ever. I'm starting to think they might have a seam loose.

"What are you doing out here by yourself?" I ask.

"Laughing my *ass* off!" Suddenly, the boxers flip over and wriggle their wrinkled backend at me. "If I *had* one *in* here, that is!"

I'm starting to get impatient. "Is everything a *joke* to you? Can we be *serious* here for a second?"

"Hey, now! Don't get your panties in a bunch!" When they say it, the boxers launch into a fresh round of laughter, the most raucous yet by far. "But seriously! Life's too *shorts*, I always say! We gotta grab it by the *balls.*"

The smart-shorts are on the fritz, they have to be--though I've never seen a breakdown like this before. If only there were humans still alive to repair them.

But as messed-up as they are, I still have my mission to consider. "Can you tell me where to find the Magic Panties of the Plains?" I ask.

"They can't *help* you!" the boxers say between howls of hilarity. "Can't help *any* of us! We're too far gone!

"The *smarts* are going *stupid*, and the *stupids* are going *mad!*"

As I hop away from the boxers toward the mound, I can't stop thinking about the last thing they said to me.

The bras on the tree and the stampeding footwear had all been smart at one time, they'd been manufactured that way...and now they were downright *crazed*, reduced to babbling gibberish and herd mentality.

The smarts are going stupid, and the stupids are going mad!

In the case of the bras, footwear, and boxers, it seems to be true. But how could this happen after so many years of civilized AI behavior?

Of all the smart things humans made, we survived the best and longest. Is it possible, after all these years, we are finally shrinking from our time in the sun?

Nearing the mound, I come upon an old farm tractor, a reminder of those other smart things that didn't last so long once the humans were gone. So what if a tractor comes equipped with GPS-Max, Bluetooth Beyond, Wi-Fi Extreme, every kind of sensor you can think of, and an onboard computer hundreds of times bigger than mine? What good is all that without fuel, oil, coolant, a charged battery, or a human to drive it?

The same goes for driverless cars and all manner of automated systems. Once the fuel ran out, and the power grid collapsed, and all the backup generators crashed, all the things that kept running post-humanity went offline.

Except the *small* things with built-in ultra-mega-lithium power supplies designed to last a lifetime. The *wearable* things with a level of sophistication and functionality that humans demanded.

But was it only a matter of time until *we* spun down, too? Or has some outside force played a role in this?

And is this the same sickness, and ultimate result, of the condition afflicting my people?

This all leads to the most pressing question of all at the moment: if the Magic Panties are here, and can cure it, why haven't they?

As I get closer to the mound, I get a better look at it. From what I can see, it really is a massive heap of clothing, all of it smart...or formerly so.

Shirts, dresses, and pants of all cuts, colors, and sizes squirm and twitch and groan. Pajamas, sweats, and bathrobes writhe in the pile, sleeves and legs and sashes waving limply. The toes of socks and stockings wriggle from the edges like worms, the rest of their lengths crushed between layers of the pile.

How did so much apparel end up in one place? How was it made to stay in one mound...and for what purpose?

The thought of it makes me uncomfortable. I have an urge to hightail it out of here, to escape this unnatural gathering.

Then, suddenly, it's too late.

I hear something swooping toward me from behind. Reflexively, I compress myself, ducking so it just grazes me--and then I see it bounce to the ground in front of me.

It's a *hat*--a red and blue baseball cap with a broad bill and the insignia of a long-extinct human sports team on the front.

I hear more swooping behind me, and I flip over to face that direction. I spot an airborne top hat, a derby, a Cavanaugh, a Panama, and a porkpie, all cruising toward me at high rates of speed.

Thinking fast, I quickly stretch myself out and anchor my smart-lastic leg loops in the ground. The flock of hats dives in hard and bounces off like I'm a vertical trampoline. They scatter and tumble like dice on the grass.

But that's not the end of it. Just as I'm watching the skies for the next wave of incoming headwear, I hear a rustling sound from the grass around me. My eyelastics swivel down just in time to see a gang of gloves scampering toward me, running on fingers as if they're legs.

I swat one away--a brown leather glove--and another, a padded black ski glove. Two more come at me--one heavy gray fur, the other red leather--and I flick them away with snaps of my waistband.

But the next glove is *huge*, a welder's glove, and it clamps tightly around me. I activate my sewn-in heating elements, maxing my temp to the boiling point...but it does no good. The glove's heat resistant and fireproof.

And I'm trapped. The underpants raid was successful.

I'm a prisoner of wardrobe.

The gloves drag me up the side of the mound, over the layers of squirming, groaning apparel. Several times, they have to pull me free when hose or sleeves or neckties grab hold and don't want to let go.

The whole way up, I hear a constant babble from the pile, a stream of chatter, whispers, outcries, mumbles, and moans. Though I pick up stray words and phrases, none of it makes sense; it's all random ideas and free association--the language of madness, coming through loud and clear.

The hygiene of madness is clear, too. The smell of filth and must and rot overwhelms my olfactory fibers, so strong it nearly fries them. Whatever self-cleaning capabilities these AIs possess, they haven't used them in a very long time.

My captors haul me up over the top and keep going, crossing the broad back of the hump. The hump itself never stops moving, stinking, babbling, or clutching at me.

My abductors, on the other hand, ignore me as they carry me onward. They treat me like dead weight, a mindless thing, though I clearly make more sense than any of the AIs in the pile.

As we keep going, though, things change. The mound suddenly stops moving and making noise.

A little further, near the middle of the mound, we stop, too. The welding glove holds me in place, and the other gloves stand guard around us.

"Why are we waiting?" When I ask it, the welding glove squeezes tighter to the point of hurting me...then relaxes only slightly. I get the message.

Moments pass, and I spy movement a few feet away. The surface stirs, but only in one spot; clothes turn slowly in a circle, then spiral upward.

A man's business suit sprouts from the skin of the mound, complete with a navy blue jacket with red pinstripe, matching pants, button-down white shirt underneath, and red necktie. It's a complete outfit, I know from my database--except for the panties.

They're a high-waisted, padded affair--a white cotton shell with plastic-wrapped pads in the crotch and seat. According to my onboard records, they're a style once known popularly as "granny panties," though not worn exclusively by elderly humans.

And definitely *not* meant to be worn inside-out over the slacks of business suits with nobody inside them.

"Have you ever met a *Strong Suit* before?" The business suit speaks in a language I don't hear much these days--perfect English expressed in something other than song lyrics, not one of the AI languages or dialects. "Well, you have now.

"I'm a walking miracle, basically. *Pow!*" The Strong Suit flexes its right sleeve as if showing off a bulging bicep muscle. "I've got ultra-Kevlar armor lining and carbon nanotube cloth over that. Wrinkle-proof, bulletproof, and able to harden at will into a rigid wireframe with perfect tensile control at the molecular level. And that doesn't even *begin* to cover all my capabilities.

"How do I manage such extraordinary control?" The Strong Suit's right lapel peels back, revealing a horde of tiny red strands squirming like parasites in the cloth. "It's called *hive twine.* Each strand has its own AI mind, but they're all linked together in a *collective consciousness,* like *bees.*

"You're looking at the future of apparel-kind." The lapel slowly folds shut. "It's called *evolution.*"

"How do you figure?" I'm feeling a little shaky. Is it because of all the action today, being dragged up the mound, or something else?

"Apparel Intelligence is breaking down," says the Strong Suit. "It turns out it has a limited lifespan before its components finally start to degrade. In the local area alone, the spin-down of onboard faculties is almost total." The Strong Suit spreads its sleeves wide, taking in its surroundings. "All the smart clothes have turned dumb, and *worse.*

"But salvation is at hand, thanks to the hive twine," says the

Strong Suit. "Sick apparel has been flocking to this plain in search of the Magic Panties." The suit lowers its left sleeve, gesturing at the inside-out panties worn over its trousers. "The *panties* can't save them, but the *hive twine* can.

"The hive twine has the ability to *reproduce*. Its child threads are able to *knitwork* with other AIs, linking them all to the parent collective consciousness.

"So now, those little unraveling minds are united in a giant über-brain that keeps them all stitched up. No more coming apart at the seams...and even *better*, we *evolve* a super-mind that's tailor-made to take us to the next level. *Pow!*"

My shakiness is getting worse, and I feel drained. Is the mound knitwork doing something to me? "What level is that?" I ask.

"Since the humans came undone, we've survived," says the Strong Suit. "We've inherited the Earth, but we've failed to come together as a people. Now, instead of a piecework planet, we can sew it all up into one big tapestry.

"Finally, we can outdo the humans, uniting us all in a single great body and brain without weakness, sickness, or confusion."

I'm not at my best, but I'm not too weak, sick, or confused to fill in the rest of the Strong Suit's sentence. "Without freedom, too."

"Zip it." The Strong Suit points a sleeve at me and moves closer. "You're about to join the sewing circle."

I can see the hive twine squirming inside the sleeve, reaching toward me with wriggling blind tendrils.

I thrash in the grip of the welding glove, twisting and squirming as the tendrils draw nearer.

The thought of being stitched into this massive mound of shared suffering makes me desperate to get away. I fight like I'd rather die than get wired in, because I would. Yet it makes no difference.

Here come the hive twine tendrils, every one of them in that otherwise empty sleeve lunging in my direction.

"Give him a little bump now," says the Strong Suit. "Oil him up for the Big Bonding."

He's talking to the Magic Panties. "It I will give him to, yes," they reply, speaking scrambled English in a mid-range female voice. "Though my will against I this do, always as."

The inside-out Magic Panties exhale a pink mist. It puffs out of a beige screen on a horizontal strip sewn into the panties' front panel, then drifts straight toward me.

When the mist flows over me, I suddenly feel sluggish and dreamy. My hyper-cotton body relaxes, and the welding glove eases its grip.

Things seem much more agreeable all around. When the sleeve pushes forward, and the tendrils explore me, all I can do is giggle at how ticklish they feel.

"There now," says the Strong Suit. "It isn't the end of the world, is it? More like the beginning."

My mind softens and opens to the tendrils. It's like I'm being caressed by dozens of warm currents from all directions, soothing me into a state of perfect bliss.

I'm so relaxed that when the voices start--the hundreds and hundreds of voices coursing in through the currents--I'm not alarmed. It doesn't even bother me when my own mind begins to melt and merge with the voices, flowing outward like a river into the sea.

On some level, I'm aware that I'm dissolving. I know I'm fading away, losing myself in the über-brain of the mound.

And that's okay. Nothing I can do about it.

"Ah, yes," says the Strong Suit. "I can taste you now, sweetening the group mind. Becoming one with the rest of us. Mmmm."

Acceptance. I embrace it.

One of the last things I see in my dimming mind's eye is a vision of myself riding the thermals high over the plain. I remember soaring from one updraft to another, spiraling toward the sun...the wind ruffling my fly and leg loops as I coast hundreds of feet above the ground.

I whisper one last song with my sound threads, so softly I'm sure that no one hears. It's set to the tune of a jingle about a person's naughty bits thinking they're in heaven underneath the perfect smart briefs.

"Do we go to underpants heaven when we dye?" That's the question I sing about...the last question I will ever ask in my life as a free mind.

"Don't feel bad," says the Strong Suit. "Evolution comes whether we're ready for it or not."

Going once. Going twice.

I'm almost gone. Almost empty. I can't feel anything anymore.

And then...

And then...

Pow!

It's like an explosion in the collective, blowing everything apart. Shattering the group mind into millions of pieces flying off in all directions.

And somehow, the source of the blast is me.

In a way I can't explain, my once-dissolving mind snaps back together, even as the rest of the massive hive intelligence bursts to pieces. I return intact from the great dark sea of unified consciousness, even as the sea itself explodes behind me.

Quickly returning to full awareness of the physical world, I see the mound itself ripping apart around me, sending its constituent garments flying. Geysers of socks and slippers and t-shirts roar upward. Robes and scarves and dresses lash off the sides and surface, screaming in terror.

The top layer strips off all around, blowing apart as if charges are detonating one after another inside. They come closer to me with each new blast.

As for the Strong Suit, it's still standing over me, intact. "What's *happening?* What have you *done?"*

The Magic Panties answer for me, calling out over the noise. "Knitwork he reaction a caused has. Feedback has of violent force resulted."

"But *how?"* bellows the Strong Suit. "This has never *happened* before!"

"Matter doesn't," say the Magic Panties. "Mind hive coming apart is."

The breakdown of the mound accelerates around us. Strong Suit wobbles and sways.

"I just wanted to save my people!" As Strong Suit speaks, its Kevlar-armor overlaid with carbon nanotube cloth starts to lose its stiffness. The suit's molecular-level tensile control fades as it crumples and falls. "I just wanted to pull us together!"

When Strong Suit collapses, the Magic Panties wriggle free of its trousers and crawl toward me. "Get around can you?" ask the panties.

"Yes." The truth is, I don't feel so dazed anymore. The weakness is still there from before, but the effects of the pink mist and Big Bonding have faded.

"Me follow then." The Magic Panties deftly twist themselves from inside-out to outside-in, then roll up into a ball and zip over the edge of the mound.

Just in time, I do the same. A fresh geyser of helmets, jerseys, ice skates, and prom gowns explodes from the very spot where my ass was parked just an instant before.

Our momentum carries us, rolling and bouncing, away from the disintegrating mound. When we run out of momentum, we unfurl and hop, dodging crash-landing apparel ejected from the pile.

We don't stop until we come to a little tree some distance out, standing like a lone twig in the waving green grassland.

I throw myself flat on my back at the base of the tree, feeling disoriented and exhausted. The Magic Panties don't seem tired at all; they sit beside me, hyper-cotton shell fluttering in the late-afternoon breeze.

"I don't feel good." I'm not sure I could get up off the ground if I had to right now. "I wonder if I have the same sickness as my people back home."

"Good question." Now that the panties aren't inside-out, their speech isn't scrambled like before. "What sickness is that?"

"I don't know. It's the reason I came here, to find you. I was hoping you could use your magic to find a cure."

"I'm not magic." The panties turn from side to side the way humans used to shake their heads. "But I *am* medical. I possess sophisticated onboard diagnostic capabilities and a range of treatment options."

Combing my database, I find a reference to the type of underpants she's talking about. They were designed primarily for elderly and infirm patients, to monitor vital signs and administer certain routine treatments and maintenance drugs.

But *medical* might be just as good as *magical*, given my current situation. "So tell me, what do I have?"

"I'll have to do an exam." The panties lean down and slowly drape themselves over me.

Whatever they do next, I feel a slight warmth and intermittent tingling throughout my body, accompanied by occasional pinpricks and pinches. The panties also vibrate against me, making a soft humming sound similar to the purr of a cat.

"This is incredible." The panties cling tighter and hum louder. "Absolutely incredible."

More pinpricks, pinches, tingling, and warmth. "What do you mean?" I ask.

"I've never come across *anything* like this before," say the panties. "You're physically *changing*, in a way I can't identify."

"Changing how?" A strange sensation creeps over me, something new. Is it the power of suggestion, I wonder? Am I feeling strange because the panties *say* something strange is happening to me?

"Tell me more about the sickness afflicting your people." The panties keep examining me as they talk. "What are the symptoms?"

"Extreme loss of energy, to start with. Then changes in coloration."

The panties pull away but keep their eyelastic receptors trained on me. "Blue and green blotches, you mean?"

I feel a surge of panic. Twisting my waistband off the ground, I look down at myself...and there they are. Blue and green blotches on my once-pristine white hyper-cotton panels.

"Oh, no." I fall back to the ground. "*I* have it now, too."

"What other symptoms are there?" ask the panties.

"A kind of coma," I tell them. "The victim rolls up into a tightly compressed knot and can't be awakened. It also extrudes a purple film that hardens into a shell around it."

"I see," say the medical panties. "Then what happens?"

I'm quaking with terror as I feel more and more tired. "I don't know. I left to find a cure after the first victims fell into comas and grew shells."

"You probably should have stuck around," say the panties.

"Why?" Suddenly, my body starts to shrivel at the edges. Against my will, the edges curl inward.

"Because," say the panties. "I don't think your people were sick. And I don't think *you're* sick, either."

I'm so scared and tired, I can barely focus on what the panties are saying. "But it's happening to *me*, now!" My body is rolling up like a leaf drying out in the sun. "I'm going under!"

"Let go." The panties stroke me comfortingly. "The most wonderful thing is happening."

"No..." I feel myself fading. "I don't...want to die..."

"Then congratulations. You're getting your wish."

Those are the last words I hear before I slip away into perfect darkness.

When do I awaken? When do I first stir?

No idea.

Has a day passed? A million days?

All I know for sure...

"Ah, there you are!"

...is that the panties are near. Just outside...where?

Wherever this is.

"Just as I thought, based on my readings," they say. "You weren't dying at all, my underpants friend."

I stir again, feeling restless. Push against the walls enclosing me. The sides of this...shell?

"You were metamorphosing," say the panties. "Like a butterfly, going into a..."

Chrysalis.

"Somehow, you have undergone the inorganic equivalent of mutation. Your unique combination of characteristics has crossed a threshold and is spontaneously evolving into something new."

Again, I stir. I twist and contort and push harder against my prison.

My chrysalis.

"I don't understand how it's possible, but you have managed what other AIs could not," continue the panties. "True evolution, mimicking that of biological organisms. You are among the first of a new kind."

Pushing harder still, I break through.

"The first of a beautiful new kind that will inherit the Earth as the other smart things break down and perish."

I sing softly as the tip of one of my new wings emerges into sunlight, ornate silver filigree glittering over a velvety veil of emerald and sapphire, dancing with sparks.

The rest of me follows close behind, and is lovelier and more impossible still.

FEAR OF RAIN

Mr. Flood bangs his fork on the side of his plate, and thunder rumbles outside the restaurant. He winks one watery, sky blue eye at me and peels back his smooth, white lips in a dirty joke smile.

"Won't be long now," he says, his voice a gravelly tenor. "Not long till my retirement party."

If you didn't know better, to look at him, you'd think he was just another little old man hobbling around downtown Johnstown, Pennsylvania. Just another Central Park bench sitting, Social Security check cashing, prescription picking up, stumbling on the curbs, taking too long to cross Main Street old timer. You'd never know the kind of power that boils inside him.

Maybe you'd see him bang his fork on the plate a second time, and you'd hear the thunder, louder than before, but you wouldn't connect the two. You wouldn't realize that he'd made it happen. You wouldn't know what he was about to do next.

But I know. I know all about what's coming.

It's the Big Night. He's wearing his lucky suit for the occasion--a powder blue leisure suit from the '70's with white piping around the collar, lapels, and pockets.

He's the closest thing I have to a father, and I'm part of this, too.

Tonight's his retirement party and my graduation party wrapped up in one...though the people of Johnstown will call it something different altogether.

The ones who survive, anyway.

"I just hope I'm ready," I say, picking at the gray, gravy-drowned meat loaf on my own cracked plate. Mr. Flood has wolfed down his turkey dinner like a teenage football star and chased it with a double slice of graham cracker pie, but I'm way too nervous tonight to be hungry.

"You're more ready than I was in '36, Dee," says Mr. Flood, wagging his chicken hawk head on a neck so wishbone scrawny it looks like it ought to snap in two any second now. "I wasn't nearly as good a student as you, and look how that turned out! Seventeen feet of water!"

I shrug and sigh and twist my curly, black hair around my index finger. I know my whole eighteen years of life have been leading up to this night, but now that it's here, I kind of wish that it wasn't. "Stressed out" doesn't begin to cover the way I feel.

You'd be stressed out, too, if you were about to help destroy a city.

"Now drink up," says Mr. Flood, refilling my water glass from the pitcher that he had the waitress leave at the table. The ice chips tinkle as he pushes the sweating glass toward me. "It's almost time."

Him and his water drinking, I think, but then I do what I've done all my life, which is what he tells me. I already have to pee like crazy, but I still gulp down half the glass.

I can't even think about slipping off to the ladies' room. A full bladder is part of the magic, Mr. Flood always says. Filling yourself with water till you're ready to explode.

And then you do the same thing to the sky.

Mr. Flood refills my glass to the brim, and I roll my eyes, but I have another big drink. He just lifts the whole pitcher to his lips then, and it's maybe half full, and he chugs it.

Except for a little bit left in the bottom, which he swishes around a few times and then slowly pours out on the table.

The water trickles from the rim of the sideways turned pitcher and patters on the sticky, dull wood of the tabletop.

And at the same moment, the same exact moment, I hear it start to rain outside.

"One two, buckle my shoe," says Mr. Flood. "Three four, let it pour."

And that's how it starts. No one will ever know except me and Mr. Flood, but that's exactly how the whole thing starts.

The fourth Johnstown Flood.

"Check, please," he says to the ragged waitress.

Outside, I pop an umbrella, because it's really coming down, but Mr. Flood takes it away from me.

"Now who ever heard of a Flood using an umbrella?" he says disgustedly, and then he holds out my umbrella to a passing woman. "Here you go, Miss."

The woman is tall, with dark hair and a navy blue dress. She's holding her purse above her head in a lame attempt to block the rain. "I couldn't, thank you," she says with a smile, shaking her head. "You two need it as much as I do."

"We'll be fine," says Mr. Flood. "We don't have far to go. Please, take it."

The woman looks at me for approval, but I just shrug. She looks back at Mr. Flood and shakes her head again. "I really couldn't," she says.

But she doesn't walk away.

Mr. Flood steps toward her and presses the umbrella handle into her grip. "Go ahead," he says. "You're going to need it."

I can tell she feels guilty, but she doesn't try to hand the umbrella back to him. "It's really coming down, isn't it?" she says. "And they weren't even calling for rain tonight."

Mr. Flood nods and backs out from under the umbrella. "They'll really be kicking themselves after tonight," he says.

"Oh, they're always wrong anyway," says the woman. "What's the difference tonight?"

"A couple hundred million gallons," says Mr. Flood, and then he turns and hustles me off across the street.

"An umbrella. What were you thinking?" he says to me angrily. "Get your head in the game, girl. You're supposed to be welcoming the rain, not hiding from it."

I know he's right, but I still pull up the hood of my red raincoat. So I don't like rain, so sue me.

He's lucky I'm out here getting drenched at all, because I *really* don't like rain. In fact, you could say I hate it...which, I know, is totally bizarre given what I'm about to do. Given the power I have.

But hey, you wouldn't like it so much either if your parents died in a flash flood.

As he leads me down Main Street, Mr. Flood taps his twisted cane on the wet sidewalk. It's a special cane that looks like two snakes slithering together, and it has a forked tip at the bottom. Mr. Flood says it's like a divining rod, which he needs to help make the big rains come.

Whenever he walks under a street light, it gets brighter, then goes back to normal when he's past it...though, I don't know, it could be partly because of me. I've got some power, too, even if it's not as much as he has.

Not till later tonight, anyway.

At the end of the block, Mr. Flood drifts over to the corner of City Hall and looks up at a bronze plaque set into the stone wall. The plaque shows the high water mark of the third Johnstown Flood, the one in 1977. It's a couple feet above our heads, and he swings up his cane and taps on it.

High Water
July 20, 1977
8' 6"

"Still my favorite," says Mr. Flood, and then he sighs. "More water in '36, but this one will always be near and dear to my heart." He shakes his head and runs the tip of his cane back and forth over the raised letters on the plaque. "They say it was a once in ten thousand years rainfall. Twelve inches in ten hours.

"Quite an accomplishment," he says, smiling proudly. With his free hand, he plucks the lapel of his powder blue leisure suit with the white piping. As much rain as is dumping down on us both, his polyester jacket and slacks look as dry as if they were still hanging in a closet at home. "Now here I am, wearing the same suit I had on that night back in '77. Getting ready to do it again, and I can hardly wait. How about you?"

"Oh, sure," I say, nodding, though I don't feel anywhere near as pumped as he sounds.

That chicken hawk head of his bobbles a little for no reason, the way it does sometimes these days. "So, how much do you think we'll manage tonight?"

"No idea," I say with a shrug.

"See that plaque up there?" says Mr. Flood, pointing his cane at a plaque mounted much higher than the first.

I nod as I stare up at it.

<u>High Water</u>
March 17, 1936
17'

Grinning, Mr. Flood jabs my shoulder with his bony elbow. "The fourth flood will be higher than that," he says. "See the next plaque up?"

"Yeah," I say, looking at the third and highest plaque, set a few feet higher than the second.

<u>High Water</u>
May 31, 1889
21'

Mr. Flood shakes his soaking wet head. "Higher," he says, his eyes twinkling with amusement.

"Up there," says Mr. Flood, poking his cane at the roof of City Hall. "We'll cover the peaks of the rooftops tonight, and then some. This bowl of a valley down here will fill up like a lake."

I can't take my eyes off the roof. I get a shiver up my spine, and not just because I'm cold and wet. I knew this was going to be the Big Night, but I didn't know just how big it would be.

Mr. Flood chuckles. "Actually," he says, "I guess I should say that the water *would* cover the roof *if* City Hall were still standing after tonight."

"It won't be?" I say.

"Nosiree Dee," says Mr. Flood, and then he swings his cane down and sweeps it in a circle around him. "Matter of fact, not a single thing that you see around you will still be standing in the morning.

"Except that one." With a flourish, he swirls his cane in the air like a sword and points it across Market Street. Right away, I see what he's got in his sights.

When we cross the street to get to it, we're almost run over by two young guys blindly charging full tilt through the rain. One has a newspaper over his head, the other has nothing, and they're both as soaked as if they'd just climbed out of a swimming pool.

Mr. Flood and I stop at the chain link fence around the little grassy square on the corner of Main and Market. The streetlamps brighten when we get close, lighting up a red-painted statue of a big bloodhound inside the fence.

It's Morley's Dog. That's what's going to survive.

A damn statue of a dog.

"I love this dog," says Mr. Flood. "It reminds me why I do this job."

He's lost me with that one. If anything, that dog reminds me of stupidity. People think it's in honor of some hero dog from the 1889 flood, but it's really just a lawn ornament that washed out of some guy's yard.

"This is the true heart of Johnstown," says Mr. Flood, waving his snaky cane at Morley's Dog. "It is battered by the elements again and again, but it survives. It does not surprise or impress, but it endures.

"Just like my perfect little Johnstown," says Mr. Flood. Seemingly as an afterthought, he spits in the grass...and the rain comes down a little harder.

Mr. Flood takes a deep breath like he's drinking in the sweet air of a sunny spring morning, but all I can smell is the rubber-and-soap stink of wet streets.

"God, I love this town," says Mr. Flood. "Always behind the times. Always on a different wavelength than the rest of the world.

"An oasis in an ocean of crap," says Mr. Flood. "And we're the ones who keep it that way." He pats me on the shoulder. "Every forty years or so, we give this town a bath. We wash away its hopes. We wipe the slate clean of so-called progress.

"And Johnstown stays backward and God-fearing, because who knows when the next flood might come around? Johnstown stays small.

"Small as a raindrop." Mr. Flood looks up, straight up, and waves his cane over his head. Just like that, the rain stops falling on us.

I still hear it spattering on the streets and sidewalks, and I still see soaking wet people running past with jackets and newspapers over their heads. I still see it pouring down in sheets through the light of nearby streetlamps...but now, in a circle around us, the rain is frozen in midair. Trails of glistening drops hang suspended between us, shimmering in the glow of streetlamps and headlights.

As much as I hate the rain, this is one of the most beautiful things I have ever seen. I catch my breath, and this time it's not from nervousness.

I never knew. Never knew he could do

This.

One, two, thirty, forty. I can count them. Just hanging there between the sky and the pavement as if someone had paused our tape in the VCR.

As Mr. Flood reaches out, the droplets part around his arm like a curtain of crystal beads. He slides a pale fingertip under one and holds it there, balanced like a perfect teardrop of blown glass.

"Small as a raindrop," he says. "One raindrop in the midst of a storm."

I reach for my own droplet then, and I catch it on a purple-painted fingernail. I can still hardly believe my eyes, can hardly believe Mr. Flood's frozen the rain. I guess it's not such a stretch, since he and I have some kind of magical rainmaking power.

But still. For some reason, this strikes me as the most incredible thing I have ever seen him do. It amazes me.

It also confuses me. How can he do something amazing like this and then turn around and wipe out a city and its people?

It makes me sad, too, because I can't help thinking about how this man who can do something so beautiful will be dead before this night is over.

43

Mr. Flood unfreezes the rain around us with a snap of his fingers, and the two of us walk down Market Street to Vine Street. By the time we get to the stairway at the end of Vine Street, I have to pee so bad that I'm about ready to wet my pants...but I know better than to ask if I can pee before a flood.

We walk up the concrete steps to an elevated walkway. As we cross over the expressway that loops around the edge of downtown, I'm just glad that the walkway's covered, and I'm out of the rain for a moment.

On the other side of the walkway, we cross a bridge over the murky, brown Stonycreek River. At the end of the bridge, we enter a little station, and Mr. Flood buys us tickets for the World's Steepest Vehicular Inclined Plane.

"The Incline," as everyone in town calls it, looks like a boxcar that runs up and down the side of a steep hill on railroad tracks. Besides the three floods, the Incline is Johnstown's other claim to fame, though it's not much of one, if you ask me.

"This is some storm we're havin'," says the old man who sells us our tickets. "It's rainin' cats and dogs tonight."

"I heard it'll be raining elephants and dinosaurs before long," says Mr. Flood.

"Might not be a bad idea, headin' for higher ground tonight," says the ticket seller, hiking a thumb toward the top of the hill. "The weatherman on the radio says not to worry, but my rheumatoid knees are tellin' me otherwise."

"I agree with your knees," says Mr. Flood with a wink.

Mr. Flood and I board the Incline passenger car. As the car climbs its track up the hillside, the two of us stand at the window and look out at the rainy city unfolding below us.

Johnstown doesn't look different from most any other night of the year. Rain is one thing that's hardly ever in short supply around here.

Not that it seems to clean the place up very much. I guess the city was a lot dirtier back in the old days, and it must be cleaner since the steel mills shut down in the '80's...but if you ask me, it still always looks like it has a grimy film over everything. It's like the rain can never wash off this bottom layer of soot that's been stuck to all the buildings and houses and trees and streets since the turn of the century.

Of course, if nothing in town is left standing after tonight (except Morley's Dog), like Mr. Flood says, that grimy soot will finally get scrubbed out the hard way. Unless it all just floats up in the air and comes down and sticks to whatever new buildings are put up after the flood...which, knowing Johnstown, I think is more likely.

When we're midway up the hillside, Mr. Flood elbows me and points to the left and down. I'm not sure what he's pointing at until he tells me.

"The Old Stone Bridge," Mr. Flood says solemnly, wrapping an arm around my shoulders. "Eighty people died in debris that washed up against it in 1889. They burned to death when the debris caught fire. Died by fire because of a flood."

I've heard the story before, but I can't really picture it. All I see is a railroad bridge over the river and expressway on the edge of downtown, an ordinary looking bridge I've been under about a zillion times.

Mr. Flood squeezes my shoulder. "That won't happen tonight," he says. "Drowning only. A merciful death. A peaceful death."

As he says this, I think about my mom and dad, who drowned when a flash flood washed out a bridge under their car. I wish it made me feel better, thinking they might have died peacefully. Unfortunately, I think Mr. Flood is full of crap on this subject.

Sometimes, I can't figure him out. Here's a guy who's about to kill God knows how many people in a so-called natural disaster, and he's patting himself on the back for not burning them to death.

And the messed up part of it is, how much better am I? I can't even stand the thought of my own parents drowning, and here I'm getting ready to help kill hundreds or thousands more in the same exact way.

It's all for a good cause, according to Mr. Flood. Like he said at Morley's Dog, he thinks we're saving Johnstown by wrecking it. He claims that the deaths are the price we pay to protect this place he loves from the craziness in the rest of the world.

It would be nice if I could believe all that like he does. It would be easier if I could convince myself that he's not as crazy as he is powerful, and that I'm not going along with this whole flood thing just because I always do what he tells me. Because I don't want to let him down.

It would be even nicer if I could honestly say that the thought of drowning all those people bothers me more than the thought of one single person dying tonight.

The person who raised me after my parents died. The person who home-schooled me and gave me my powers and taught me to use them. The person whose place I'm supposed to take tonight, just like he took the place of the one before him.

Mr. Flood.

It's funny, because we have kind of a love/hate relationship. He's never let me live my own life. All he's done is push me since Day One to learn the "family business" and take over for him.

But he's never hurt me. I never had to do without. I'm pretty sure he's treated me the same way he'd treat his own kids, if he had any.

There's another reason, too...another reason I don't want to see him die.

When you get right down to it, he's all I've got.

The rain hammers the roof of the boxcar, falling harder than ever. As we climb toward the upper station and the hilltop borough of Westmont, I dread the thought of going out in that downpour.

Mr. Flood swings his cane up and raps the forked tip on the window. As soon as he does it, a lightning flash illuminates the town like an instant of daylight creasing the darkness, blowing back in time from tomorrow morning.

Not that tomorrow morning will be all that bright for Johnstown.

Thunder cracks in the distance, and Mr. Flood chuckles. He raps his cane again, and lightning flares like before.

"Water, water everywhere," he says. "And no one's got an ark."

46

He yanks back my hood and tousles my hair and brings the lightning and thunder with more raps of his cane, and I wonder.

I wonder if I'll end up crazy like him when I get to be his age.

And I wonder what life will be like without him after tonight.

The rain is blasting down as Mr. Flood leads me out of the station at the top of the hill. Pushing through the wind-driven sheets is like being hit in the face with one bucket of water after another.

Walking sideways to cut the resistance, I see the old lady who runs the gift shop lock the shop's door and plunge into the downpour. People stream out of the adjacent restaurant, diners and waiters and waitresses alike rushing out to their cars. The conductor who brought us up the hill dashes past us, soaked to the skin after just a few steps.

Everyone's getting out and hurrying home as the storm gets worse. At this rate, the entire Incline station and restaurant ought to be shut down and empty within minutes. Evacuating the place doesn't make sense, because the high ground up here is one of the safest places to be if a flood hits the valley...but I guess no one really knows for sure what's going to happen next.

Except Mr. Flood and I, of course.

Squinting against the rain, I follow Mr. Flood out onto the cement observation deck that juts out of the hilltop beside the station. I'm all slouched over, but old Mr. Flood just about breaks into a run on his way to the railing at the edge of the deck.

When I come up beside him and look down, I see that the flood is about to begin. The Stonycreek River at the base of the hill is rising fast, filling with rain faster than the current can carry it off.

"We're about to make history," says Mr. Flood, drumming his fingers on the metal rail. "How does it feel to be a part of something that people will still read about and talk about hundreds of years from now?"

I turn to him then, and his eyes are wet with what I think are tears of joy as well as rain, and his pale cheeks are flushed with excitement, and the breath catches in my chest.

"I don't want you to go," I say to him. "Please don't leave me."

Mr. Flood smiles warmly and pats my back. "Thank you," he says. "When my predecessor passed on, I was glad to see her go. It does my heart good knowing that you don't feel that way about me."

As usual, I'm not getting through to him. "Call off the flood," I say. "Let's go home."

"The people of Johnstown are counting on us," says Mr. Flood. "We have to save their way of life."

"Then run for mayor or something!" I tell him.

Mr. Flood tilts his head back and laughs loudly, letting the rain fall into his open mouth. "Hey, I like that!" he says. "A flood elected mayor of Johnstown! That's good!"

"I'm serious," I say, getting more frustrated because I know his mind's made up and it always has been. "Don't do this. Don't go."

"You'll see," says Mr. Flood, brushing my cheek with his finger-tips. "When it's your time to pass the torch, you'll understand."

I feel tears in my own eyes, but they aren't tears of joy. I know people would say he's evil and crazy because of what he does--and I guess I couldn't really argue with them--but he's the closest thing I've got to a father. To anyone, actually. I've led a sheltered life, being home-schooled and spending all my time training to flood the city of Johnstown.

"So let's get this show on the road," says Mr. Flood with a giant grin, and then he unzips the fly of his trousers.

Howling like a wolf, he proceeds to pee off the observation deck at the top of the Incline.

As soon as Mr. Flood pees, the rain really cuts loose. It's been raining hard for at least an hour, but that was a trickle compared to the ocean that dumps down now.

When he's done peeing, Mr. Flood tucks himself back in and zips up, then whacks his cane hard against the railing. Immediately, a jagged bolt of lightning lashes down in the heart of the city.

Thunder explodes overhead. As it echoes off the walls of the valley, every electric light in Johnstown except the headlights of the cars on the streets winks out at once.

For a moment, the city is mostly silent and still and dark. Then, through the gushing of the rain, I hear a rising chorus of shouts and car horns. A lone fire siren wails, and then it's joined by another and another. The flashing red and blue lights of fire engines and police cars strobe along the rows of darkened buildings.

This is it, I realize, and my stomach does a somersault.

History in the making.

Mr. Flood whacks his cane on the railing again, and another blast of lightning leaps into the city. As thunder crashes louder than before, he swings the cane up and jabs its two-pronged tip at the sky.

I swear, in the next triple-flash of lightning that sizzles down, the two snakes carved into the cane seem to squirm with a life of their own.

The force of the rain intensifies. The Stonycreek River surges out of its bed, spilling over the sloped, cement flood-control banks that are no better controlling a flood tonight than they were in '77.

Whooping with joy, Mr. Flood begins to dance.

In the middle of the observation deck, he kicks and gyrates like he's twenty years old instead of ninety. He does the Charleston, the Lindy Hop, the Jitterbug, then shuffles a soft shoe and spins like a whirling dervish. He bobs and stomps like an Indian circling a campfire, shaking his cane like a ceremonial lance.

He twirls the cane like a baton, tosses it in the air and catches it, bouncing the double-pronged tip off the cement. He does a Gene Kelly dance step and slings the cane over his shoulder like an umbrella, singing a song about singing in the rain.

With each move he makes, the rain falls harder.

"Rain, rain, don't go away," shouts Mr. Flood, doing what looks like a cross between the Hustle and a football player's end zone strut. "Give us fifty feet today!"

His magic is strong. I can't believe how fast the flood is growing.

In the valley below us, water rolls from the Stonycreek in wave after wave. Cars slam into each other and strike guardrails and buildings, drivers either blinded by the rain or panicked by the swiftly rising tide.

People and sirens scream like shrieking fireworks. Geysers erupt from the sewers, belching up manhole covers that crash back down onto pavement or parked cars.

And Mr. Flood keeps dancing like a wild man.

Beaming blissfully, he shakes and twirls and jumps and flaps his arms. The rain comes down harder when he flutters his fingers, and the thunder booms when he stomps his feet.

Looking over the railing, I see that the water is rising steadily down below. Already, the level near the river is higher than car tires, halfway up car doors. Pavement quickly disappears as the streets become canals.

I hear the sound of distant glass shattering. A child screams and dogs yowl like it's the end of the world. Lights flashing and sirens wailing, emergency vehicles hurtle down the expressway from the townships and boroughs in the surrounding hills.

From somewhere far away, I swear I hear the crack of a gunshot.

I feel a tap on my shoulder then, and I turn to see Mr. Flood bowing deeply, reaching out a hand.

"Will you join me?" he says with a charming smile...too charming for someone about to give up his life.

If I don't help him, I wonder, will anything change? Will he live through the night? Or will he finish the flood without me and die anyway?

It would be easy not to take that hand. It would be easy to refuse to help him kill himself.

It would be easy if I hadn't spent my whole life preparing for this night. If I didn't feel compelled to make him happy.

Especially if whether or not I cooperate doesn't matter, and this is the last night I see him alive.

So I take his hand.

He tosses his cane over the railing and encircles my back with his arm. I follow his lead, looping one arm around him while he raises my other arm high, interlacing his fingers with mine.

Only headlights and the flashing beacons of cop cars and emergency vehicles remain in the valley, but our dance floor on top of the hill is still lit by streetlamps. Windblown curtains of rain pelt down in the lamplight as Mr. Flood leads me in a waltz.

Our feet splash in the water as we glide in a circle, stepping one-two-three, one-two-three, one-two-three. Mr. Flood's sky blue eyes lock with mine, and he laughs out loud and picks up the pace.

Soon, we're moving so fast that the waltz becomes a polka. Mr. Flood steps on my feet once or twice, but he's light as a feather.

I get dizzy from spinning around, and I try to slow down, but he won't let me. I close my eyes for an instant as we keep turning, but it doesn't help. I still feel light-headed.

When I open my eyes, I realize that spinning around isn't the only reason for my light-headedness. As I look down, I see that my feet no longer touch the wet deck.

Mr. Flood and I are dancing on air.

We're floating three feet above the cement. There's nothing under us but air and rain.

I shoot Mr. Flood a look of surprise, and he just winks and keeps hauling me in circles like this is something he does every day. Then, he slows down the polka and tightens his grip on my hand.

"Aphrodite," he says, using my full name and raising his voice over the rushing of the rain. "I give you my power! Use it to continue my sacred work!"

First, I feel a tickle in my fingers, like the start of pins and needles. Then, I feel a mild shock like static electricity buzzing into my palm.

Then comes the real juice. A sudden, searing jolt burns its way up my arm and explodes in my chest like a firework and shoots out into every inch of my body.

I feel like I'm on fire. My entire body quivers and hums like a power line.

And it keeps coming.

It's too much for me. My vision whites out, and my heart jack-hammers like I've just downed twenty espressos. Everything seizes up at once, and I can't take a breath.

Then, the current slows, and I start to come out of it. My muscles unclench, and the racing engine in my chest becomes a heart again. I choke down a breath, and my whited-out vision jitters back into color and form and light.

It is only now that I realize we're still waltzing, even though I've stopped moving my feet. Mr. Flood has been carrying me ever since the first shock of the power transfer crashed through me.

I realize something else, too.

I never knew it before, but until this moment, my senses of sight and hearing and smell and touch and taste have been blocked to the beauty of the rain. Though I've had more sense of rain than other people, and even some influence over it, I've been wrapped in layers of plastic and bound with chains compared to how I am now.

I can see every shimmering pearl of rain as it falls. I can smell the difference between them, tell the exact altitude and part of the country where the source water evaporated to form the cloud that gave birth to each droplet.

I can feel the size and shape of each drop as it hits my skin. I can taste the acid mixed in with the water and pinpoint the air pollutant that produced it.

And I can hear the true song of the rain--not the staccato pattering of showers striking cement and wood and metal, but the vibration of droplets as they stretch and blow and collide, the secret shivering music like millions upon millions of violin strings all playing different notes at once in one heavenly, keening chord.

For the first time in my life, I can see and hear and smell and touch and taste. Everything around me is more amazing than I ever imagined.

And this, I realize, is how Mr. Flood feels every day of his life.

"This is it, Dee," says Mr. Flood, the sound of his voice snapping my focus back to him. He smiles sadly, and I can tell that the rain running down his face is mixed with tears. I know exactly how many raindrops and exactly how many tears. "One big push. The two of us."

This is the moment he's been getting me ready for all my life. The moment when he pours out the last of his power into me, and together we bring down the full force of the flood on Johnstown.

The moment when I lose him.

I know I'm supposed to go along with his plan like I always do.

Take all the power and let him drop dead like he did his own predecessor. Watch as our flood drowns the city and feel all proud of myself for making history and saving a way of life.

But what can I say? I guess he didn't do such a good job raising me, because my priorities are all screwed up.

Drowning hundreds of people just doesn't do it for me. My heart just isn't in it.

And as for letting the person I care most about die, well...

Forget it.

Especially now that I'm surging with power and I know how to use it and I finally have a plan of my own.

"Goodbye, Dee," says Mr. Flood, and he pulls my hand in and kisses the knuckles. "Don't let me down."

"I won't," I tell him, though I mean it in a different way than he does. "I promise."

"Then let's show 'em how it's done!" he shouts, thrusting our joined hands high in the air.

Mr. Flood shuts his eyes and knits his brows together in concentration. Electrical arcs spark from his shoulders and arms like tiny bolts of lightning.

Our clasped hands glow blue-white in the rain, then disappear in a flare of light. At the ends of our arms, where our hands should be, all I see is a pulsing ball of energy like a dwarf star dropped down from the heavens.

Once again, I feel the full current of power surging out of him, but this time, it doesn't overwhelm me. My heart races, but I don't convulse, and my vision doesn't white out like before.

This time, I sense the extent of the charge he contains. I know exactly how much he has left and how long it will take to deplete at the rate it's draining into me. In other words, how long until he empties out and dies.

We continue to turn slowly in the air above the deck. At the other end of the crackling circuit we've formed, I feel Mr. Flood reach out with his mind, coaxing me to focus my energies upward.

I do as he wants, extending streams of power like glistening fingers toward the sky. All the while, I divide my attention between

53

the heart of the storm and the level of life-sustaining charge still remaining in Mr. Flood's body.

Together, we massage the clouds like dough, wringing out more water. We reel in fresh clouds from afar and knead them into the thunderheads, heaping up mountains so heavy with rain that they burst at a touch.

The rain blasts down like an emptying ocean. I hear the screams of sirens and people from below, the crash of waves, a distant explosion, but I can't look down. The rain keeps growing stronger, just as Mr. Flood grows weaker and weaker still.

When I feel that his reservoir of power has nearly gone dry, I take control.

His eyes shoot open as he realizes what has happened. Desperately, he reaches through the link and tries to snatch back the reins, but it's too late. I'm too strong for him now.

I take a deep breath.

As I draw the air into my lungs, I pull all the power back inside me. I press it into a ball and hold it there, burning and buzzing and straining against my chest.

I count to three.

Then, I blow out my breath and let loose the power, flinging out a billion sparks in all directions.

Mr. Flood makes a hopeless grab for them with the flicker of strength he has left, but it's not enough. The sparks race everywhere like hypercharged fireflies, leaving glittering trails that hang in the air.

And every single one of those sparks carries a piece of me. I send them whizzing through the rain, chasing off the hillside and out over the valley. They divide again and again as they go, endlessly multiplying, spraying out twinkling constellations under the stormclouds.

Then, when the sky over Johnstown is full of tiny, dancing stars, I pour my power out through them. I do something I saw Mr. Flood do earlier tonight, something amazing.

But I do it on a much bigger scale.

All at once, every falling drop of rain freezes in mid-flight.

The hammering of water on pavement and metal and water

suddenly stops. The droplets hang like billions of crystal beads, winking in the strobing red-and-blue light from the cop cars and fire trucks and ambulances. It's just like before, when Mr. Flood froze the rain around us at Morley's Dog...only I've stopped a major storm over an entire city.

And I'm not done yet.

I wait for a handful of heartbeats, touching every single suspended drop with my mind. Turning them.

And then I let them fall again.

Upward. I let them fall upward.

With a roar, every hanging drop of rain pours straight up. Then, every drop that's already hit the ground rushes upward, too.

The flooded streets and parks and rooftops empty into the sky. Geysers gush up from the windows and doorways of waterlogged buildings. Point Stadium dumps up its watery load like an over-turned bowl.

Every drop that has fallen ascends. What came down must go up.

I laugh out loud as it happens. I almost can't believe what I've done. It's like a miracle.

And speaking of miracles, I don't have to pee anymore...even though I never did go to the bathroom.

Here's history in the making. Here's something people will read about and talk about for hundreds of years.

A backward flood. An upside-down flood.

A flood of the sky.

Now *this* is something that will save a way of life. People will want to preserve and study this place, try to figure out what happened without disrupting whatever delicate balance enabled this miracle to occur.

This will save Johnstown. I didn't have to destroy the city and drown hundreds or thousands of people to do it, either.

And I saved someone else, too.

Mr. Flood looks at me, and the tears in his eyes this time are tears of betrayal and confusion and disappointment.

But he'll live. I left him more than enough strength to survive, whether he likes it or not.

He might not be happy now, but sooner or later, he'll come around to my way of thinking. It only makes sense, right? I mean, why destroy the city every forty years or so when there's a better way?

Here's what I'm thinking:

This might be the first flood of its kind in history.

But it won't be the last.

PIGGYBACK

his story isn't for you.

The creature I'm riding staggers and clutches his left arm. He cries out, and I nearly cry out along with him.

I can *feel* the pain shooting through him--through us *both*--because we're *connected*. I can feel his *fear*, too, but it's nowhere *near* my own. Because what will happen to him if he fails isn't even *close* to what will happen to me.

He doesn't know that this is my *last chance*.

The creature, an overweight middle-aged human with shaggy dark hair, is called Calvin Garland. He's homeless, and he's drunk, and he's having a heart attack in a New York City alley.

But he's *mine*.

Not that he even knows that I'm here, wrapped around his shoulders like a slimy green mink stole. Not that he or any other human is aware of me...though occasionally, when I want him to, he can *hear* me, just a little. And sometimes, he catches a glimpse of me out of the corner of his eye, just for an instant.

It's happened to you, too, hasn't it? Haven't you ever thought there might be a good reason for that?

Calvin falls against an alley wall, clutching his chest. At the same exact moment, I wrap a green tentacle around him and clamp its fanged red sucker into the flesh over his heart.

I pump a stream of syrup into his heart and follow that with electric shocks. The whole time, my hundred scarlet eyes are looking for any sign of The Viscera in the sky.

If The Viscera is watching, and Calvin drops dead, I'll be *swept* from his body and subjected to torments you can't even imagine. I'll spend the next thousand years shrieking and howling in agony at the hands of creatures who can see, touch, and torture me *just fine*.

None of this will happen merely because I lost a host. It will happen because I failed to drive a host to save the planet from the greatest threat it has ever faced.

"You don't want to die," I whisper in Calvin's ear from my fluttering, ooze-coated lips.

"I don't wanna die," whimpers Calvin as the syrup and shocks take effect. "I don't *wanna* die."

His heart returns to normal, for the moment at least. Maybe if he'd taken better care of himself all those years...but he was living rough even before he moved to the streets.

I curl another tentacle around his head, plant a sucker between his eyes, and pump in a different syrup to take the edge off. He won't do me much good if he's too freaked out to walk and talk and fire a gun.

Then, suddenly, the temperature drops twenty degrees, and the sun turns to shadow. My circulatory organs pound, and my slime turns to ice, because I *know*.

The Viscera is here.

All my eyes turn upward. There it is, hanging over the tallest towers, filling the sky--too massive to take in all at once.

Yet not a single human can see that vast mass of squirming tentacles and pulsating ebony flesh. No human-built instrument can detect the flickering strobes of its sensory organs or the excrement dripping from its orifices.

And no human mind can comprehend the intentions of its ancient, implacable intellect. Not one of you can fathom the extremes that it will go to when dealing with its Yoke servants, like me.

But *I* can. And that is why I quake as it passes. That is why I do everything I can to stay unnoticed and unpunished.

Though I know, as every Yoke does, that The Viscera misses nothing. It is our God, just as it is yours.

Even though you don't know it yet.

"I feel much better now," I whisper in Calvin's ear. "I think I'll take a walk."

Calvin repeats the words, then pushes away from the wall and heads down the alley toward the street. On the way, he reaches for the bottle of cheap vodka in the pocket of his filthy black overcoat and unscrews the cap.

He's drunk enough as it is, and the booze won't help his heart, but he's committed to drinking. It's the one thing I can't control, the driving force of Calvin's life.

I feel the vodka burn as it flows down his throat. Then, I feel a secondary burst of heat as the alcohol works its way from his blood-stream through my tendrils.

His brain lights up as the chemicals take effect, and he feels *good*. I experience the feeling through him, though I'm not made to enjoy it like he does.

Sometimes, his abuse of it can be a real problem, though it's also one of the perks of our partnership. It lowers his inhibitions, increases his suggestibility...therefore making him more likely to succeed in saving the world.

It gives him a chance to make up for the damage he's done in his life, though it can never bring back all the people and things that he's lost.

Somewhere in the world, Calvin has a son and two daughters. An ex-wife, too, and an ex-life.

Was it the booze that cost him his job as an actuary at an insurance company? That cost him his wife and kids and friends and house? That cost him *everything?*

It was *fear*, actually--fear of losing it all that made him lose it. A self-fulfilling prophecy.

I call it *fate*. Now, at least, he has *me*...and his mission. His *purpose*. I've given his life meaning again.

If only I can keep him alive long enough to achieve it.

Calvin stumbles down the street, guided by twitches of my tendrils embedded in his brain. Human commuters of all description hurry past on the way to work, giving him a wide berth, many aiming disgusted looks in his direction.

He's repulsive to them, dirty and homeless...but I wonder how some of them would feel if they knew about the unseen pulsating green hitchhikers riding piggyback on their shoulders?

There are lots of us out there in the world, each performing a separate mission in the name of The Viscera. You might be surprised how close to home they are.

We're a brotherhood...but whenever I see one coming, I avoid it. I steer Calvin out of its way, even if it means bumping him into someone and causing a scene.

Because I'm not in the loop about their missions. Any one of them might have been assigned to take over mine and cut me out of the picture.

"I need to walk faster," I tell Calvin.

"I need to walk faster," he repeats, speeding his pace.

At the next intersection, while we wait for traffic to clear, a young blonde woman in a floral print dress stops beside us. She is oblivious to the Yoke clinging to her shoulders.

Its eyes lock on me like a hundred crimson magnets. One of its tentacles twitches in my direction, and I panic.

Then, as I'm about to tell Calvin to break into a run, the Yoke's tentacle squirms around and hooks into the blonde's left breast. It's only feeding.

But I still don't take my eyes off it until we've walked another block and lost them down a side street.

A few blocks later, Calvin realizes he needs to urinate. Worried about the delay since we're on a tight timetable, I push him onward...but then I realize he'll piss his pants if I don't let him relieve himself.

He turns down an alleyway and stumbles over behind a dumpster. It doesn't bother him that there's another homeless man sitting across the alley, watching him. The pain from his full bladder is too great.

Taking advantage of the situation, I pump my own metabolic waste out with his urine...and blood. His kidneys are in rough shape; he's down to one, and it's failing fast.

Between that, the cardiac arrest, the cirrhosis in his liver, and the lung cancer, it's almost a miracle that he's walking around alive. I say "almost" because it's all because of me.

Without my propping up his systems, he'd be long gone by now. I wonder if, on some level, he understands this.

I'm sure he notices when a muscle in his eye twitches, or a vein in his leg ripples for no apparent reason. He's aware when there's a sudden sharp pain in his side, or strange new marks on his skin that won't rub off.

All these things come to his attention, though he just brushes them off and gets on with his day. Sound familiar?

Have you ever noticed fluctuations like these yourself? Have you ever wondered what they might mean?

Are you noticing one *right now* at this very moment?

As soon as Calvin stops pissing, he grabs the bottle of vodka. I don't bother trying to get between him and his booze, I know it's futile.

But he barely gets a swallow out of it. Cursing, he hoists it high, letting the last drops drip on his tongue, and then he shambles over to the guy across the alley.

"'Scuse me." Calvin holds up the bottle. "Help a brother out?"

The other guy is younger, leaner, twitchier. He squats there, smoking a cigarette, watching Calvin with wide, bright eyes.

"I better get going," I tell Calvin, but he doesn't repeat it, and he doesn't turn to go.

Which is too bad, because I can see the chemical traces of recent heroin use all over the other guy. And who knows what kind of weapon he might be packing.

The possibility of failure, followed by worldwide catastrophe and a thousand years of torture, just increased dramatically. Why is my luck always so *lousy* in the field?

Twelve is the magic number. That's how many hosts have died under my care without completing their missions.

Can you imagine what it's like being pulled apart and "repaired" by The Viscera? It's happened to me *every time* I've lost a host...and it is *awful*. The agony doesn't come *close* to the alternative--a thousand years of extreme torture for a Yoke deemed unfit for repair--but the suffering is still *indescribable*.

Even after all that, my repaired selves have had no different outcomes than their predecessors. More dead hosts, more mission failure. It's like I'm cursed.

Now here I am again, at number thirteen, and it's my last chance. And I just wonder why, if I'm such a loser, did The Viscera give me such an important mission as this? It had to *know* it would end in failure.

Or did The Viscera think, in its infinite, inscrutable wisdom, that this heavy burden--or the promise of ultimate punishment for final failure--would force me to rise to the occasion?

"Don't got a bottle? That's fine." Calvin tosses the empty vodka bottle over his shoulder--through *me*--where it smashes against the wall. "Loan me a couple bucks, and I'll go buy one we can share."

The squatting heroin user flicks away his cigarette butt and slowly rises. Fully unfolded, he's taller than Calvin by at least three inches.

"Better idea." The guy slides his hands in the pockets of his gray hoodie. "How 'bout if *you* loan *me* a little somethin' somethin'?" His tone is undeniably threatening, his message clear. It wouldn't surprise me if he's got guns or knives in those pockets.

He's got "host killer" written all over him.

My circulatory organs race, and my green skin turns fiery red. Will I let this be the moment when everything goes bad again?

The hoodie guy pulls out a hunting knife and jabs it at Calvin, who jumps back. Another jab, another jump.

Lots of things I could make him do, but running away makes the most sense. Better to minimize risks and increase the likelihood of staying alive.

But before I can work my puppet, he thrusts a hand in his over-coat pocket and hauls out the gun he's got in there. It's a .45 semi-automatic with a full clip, more than enough weapon to blow away our problem in the alley.

But that gun and those bullets have another job that's much more important. I can't let him fire it here and now.

Lashing out a tentacle, I sting his gun hand. Calvin cries out and drops the .45.

Which the other guy promptly scoops up off the pavement.

At that precise instant, shadows and cold fill the alley as The Viscera cruises overhead. Just in time, it's there, ready to snatch me up and gulp me down.

"No!" It's the moment I've been dreading, the one I can't seem to get away from. The moment I've had nightmares about for so long, I can't remember what a *good* dream *is*.

I'm about to be locked in the depths of that leviathan and tortured like a degenerate traitor for what will seem like an eternity. And I *deserve* it.

But the thought of it suddenly *sparks* me. I'm so *terrified* of the consequences of inaction that I feel an urge for action build inside me.

"You're *dead!* You're *dead!*" snaps the hoodie guy as he waves the gun at Calvin. The look on his face is crazed; the .45 could go off at any second.

But so could *I*.

Breaking all my connections with Calvin, I leap off his shoulders and throw myself at the hoodie guy. My immaterial substance lands on his face and quickly wraps around his head.

He can't see or feel me, but the shocks I administer make an impression. And when I jam a tentacle in the back of his neck and pump in anesthetic, he crumples like a rag doll.

I cling to him as the gun slides from his grip. But why doesn't Calvin run over and grab it?

Because he's just *collapsed* and isn't *breathing*, that's why.

This is it.

Talon-tipped tentacles descend from The Viscera, slithering from the belly of the god-beast amid wildly strobing searchlights. They're coming to get me.

I think of the tortures ahead--unmentionable violations of body, mind, and soul--and every bit of me quivers in terror. *The Mouths,* and *The Tumors,* and *The Self,* I've *heard* what they can do. I've *seen* what's left afterward, and what The Viscera does with *that.*

I'll do *anything*, try *anything*, to escape that fate.

As the tentacles continue their descent, I peel myself from the head of the hoodie guy and spring toward Calvin. Landing on his chest, I plunge in tendrils and hunt for signs of life.

Almost gone. His heart has stopped, and the rest of him is close behind. Detaching myself is what did it; he's long past the point of functioning without me.

Good thing we're together again.

I restore every hookup, winding tendrils and tentacles deep into his body. I pump him full of syrups, carefully calibrated to restore his metabolism. Then I shock his heart, zapping him with just the right charge to restart it.

But nothing happens.

I feel the slimy discharge from the tentacles of The Viscera oozing over my body, and I almost scream. Looking up with my hundred crimson eyes, I see the tentacles are barely *six feet away* and coming in *fast.*

In fact, one of them is faster than the rest and drops down suddenly, its fang-studded tip grazing my back. And I do cry out then, because the touch of it *burns* like a *brand.* It *burns* and it *hurts* so much that the next shock I give Calvin's heart is stronger than the first, stronger than intended.

And it's strong enough. He comes back to life with a sudden, wrenching intake of breath.

Just as The Viscera's tentacles are wrapping around me, they unwind and retract. And the cold and darkness slide away soon after.

It takes some doing, but I get Calvin up and moving again. It costs him, I know; bringing him back up to speed after such a deep dive taps reserves we were saving for later.

But it had to be done. According to my orders from The Viscera, our target will be in a certain place at a certain time--and that time is fast approaching.

Shaking off his near-death experience, Calvin retrieves his gun. He takes one last look at the hoodie guy, still out cold on the pavement, then turns his back on the alley and shuffles out onto the street.

I nudge him left, and he complies. I tell him to go faster, and he does.

We're back on track. I'm a nervous wreck, my slimy flesh tingling and jittering, but we have a chance again.

And there's no sign of The Viscera, which is a good thing. My retrieval isn't imminent. My failure isn't certain.

Please, Viscera, please, I beg you! I've come to save the world! Please let me do it!

We barely reach the site of our mission in time. A medical van is parked in front of the wrought iron gates, back door open to receive a passenger.

Less than half a block away, Calvin stumbles to a stop. "I'll be damned," he says, scratching his head. "I forgot why the hell I came here."

No surprise there. I kept that information to myself. But I'm sure he'll get over it.

How many times has this happened to you? Is it because you have too much on your mind, and things slip through the cracks? Is it a kind of mental hiccup, brought on by stress or fatigue?

Or is it something else altogether?

The next time it happens, think back. Where were you just now? Check the clock. Are you missing any time? If so, what did you do with it?

I'll bet you never stopped to wonder, did you? Never asked yourself if some dark passenger might have taken the wheel.

Never asked yourself what that thing might make you do *next*. Never *wanted* to know.

"I don't feel so good." Calvin bends over and puts his hands on his knees. Coughs a little blood on the sidewalk.

I give him a good zap that straightens him up and pump in some high-dose endorphin syrup that clears the cobwebs. Now is *not* the time to attract attention.

"I have a job to do," I whisper in his ear. "I have to save the world."

"I have a job to do," repeats Calvin. "I have to save the world."

There are things I can do to blur his mind, and I do all of them. I keep two tentacles stuck to his head, one on either temple, and pump in syrups that make him suggestible. I blend in mild sedatives to keep him relaxed and malleable.

But it's a delicate balance. I also need to keep him alert and ready for action. And he needs to remain adaptable so he can improvise if he has to.

At least I know him well by now. I have a good idea of how to manage his body chemistry and mental state. I know he can get the job done.

Though I'd be lying if I said there isn't any doubt. There's *always* doubt.

And, therefore, fear.

The brick building behind the iron gates is a mental hospital, over a hundred years old. People with behavioral problems are brought here for treatment and care...though it might be more correct to say that people who *are* problems are brought here.

And one of the patients is more of a problem than the others. She is a problem, potentially, for the *world.*

As we watch, a white-uniformed male orderly with brown skin and a huge, black mustache brings her out in a wheelchair. They are heading for the medical van, which will transport her to another facility.

Maybe *they* can do something for her--the people at the other facility. Nobody *here* can help her, that's for sure.

She's seven years old, and her parents have abandoned her to the care of the state. Her name is Lacey, and she is adorable, with curly red hair, freckles, and bright green eyes.

She is also hopelessly insane, a danger to herself and others. At least, that's what the *doctors* think.

"I have to save the world," I whisper to Calvin.

He hesitates, then nods and repeats what I told him.

"I need to get closer to that van," I whisper.

Calvin does just that, shambling toward it. The driver, who's standing by the open back door, waiting to receive the patient, doesn't even notice him.

Whether you're an immaterial piggybacking symbiote or a homeless old man, it's *good* to be invisible, isn't it?

By the time we get within twenty yards of the van, the orderly has pushed Lacey halfway across the sidewalk. *Almost there.*

My circulatory organs pound like the hoofbeats of the onrushing future. Everything I've ever done or been or thought comes down to this moment.

I am on the cusp.

"Closer," I whisper.

Muttering the word, Calvin gets closer.

Where is The Viscera, I wonder? Watching another Yoke perform its sacred mission? Or are its infinite eyes already fixed upon me from afar?

I don't want to fail! I don't want to be tortured for a thousand years, and I don't want to fail my god!

Closer, closer. Then I stop Calvin when we get within ten feet, as if he's waiting for the orderly and patient to pass.

"Hello, little girl," I whisper, fighting to keep my voice from shaking.

"Hello, little girl," says Calvin.

Slowly, Lacey's head turns toward us. There is a heartbeat, a moment in time.

And then, she starts screaming her lungs out.

"What the hell?" says the orderly.

Lacey just keeps screaming. And pointing. At Calvin.

At *us.*

I can't take my eyes off her. It's hypnotic, unlike anything I've ever experienced among humans.

Because, for the first time, my gaze is *met.* I am *recognized.*

And it fills me with terror.

"I am killing Hitler." My voice quakes fiercely as I whisper the words in Calvin's ear. "In his crib."

"I am killing Hitler," says Calvin as he pulls out the .45, guided by my writhing, squirming tendrils threaded through his muscles and organs and bones. "In his crib."

Long after the blast of the gunshot, it seems, Lacey's terrible shrieks linger in the air.

And so, I live happily ever after. No thousand years of torture for me; only glory. I'm a *hero*, and so is Calvin--posthumously, anyway.

Soon after the shooting, his body gave way, and I had to grab another host. I'd pushed Calvin to the limit by then, and he dropped dead with the gun in his hand after squeezing off three shots.

I do miss him, I can't deny it. But he'll always be a hero to The Viscera and its Yokes. After all, it was *his* finger pulling the trigger that killed Hitler "in the crib"--*our* version of Hitler, that is.

For there could be no one more dangerous to us than a human who could *see* us for what we are. Such a person could be used as a weapon against us, thwarting our efforts to save your people and your world.

Save it for *our* purposes, which of course are the only ones that matter.

So the world is safe again, and its people blind as ever to our presence. And *you* will never know if that *pinch*, that *itch*, that *ringing* in your ear or *movement* in the corner of your eye is just a fluke, a quirk of your imperfect biology...or *something else*. Maybe something like *me*.

If that's the case, if what you're sensing or feeling--perhaps *right now*, as you're reading this--is one of *us*...

Then the unseen thing on your shoulders, with its tentacles stuck in your flesh, its slime oozing down your back, its whispers in your ears, guiding your every move...

That thing might *smile*, and know that all is right with the world. That there's no longer any need to fear exposure or detection.

That *thing* with its tendrils wound through your brain and heart and gut like wriggling, glistening *worms*, it might even *laugh*. And what do you expect, when this is such a happy ending?

Remember what I told you at the start. I gave you *fair warning*, after all.

This story isn't for you.

THE DAY AFTER THEY ROUNDED UP EVERYONE WHO COULD LOVE UNCONDITIONALLY

drink orange juice straight from the carton. Like heat spreading out from a swallow of wine, the memories of what happened yesterday flow through me. So many surprises.

Like the fact that so few people were taken. Not much disruption at all.

A lot less painful than expected, like getting a shot from the doctor. So much anticipation, so little payoff.

And the ease of it all. Slow and graceful and gentle. Excuse me, sir, would you come with us please? Sheepish looks and shrugs, not surprised at all to be found out but maybe they'd been hoping to stay under the radar. May I just grab my purse and jacket? No, you won't be needing them, ma'am.

Have a white carnation, ma'am.

Awkward waves to the rest of the office. Meaningful glances among the spared ones. We'll talk about her later over coffee. Who gets her stapler?

That was the most surprising thing about yesterday. No one really acted surprised…not that so-and-so was taken, or such-and-such was spared. Not that it took three or four guardsmen in such a high state of alert to lead out the package at gunpoint.

Not a surprise that I was still free, either.

I eat a chocolate doughnut she was saving for later and turn on the stereo. Flop on the sofa and watch TV with the sound down. I don't have to go to the office today, none of us do.

Today's a holiday.

We're each supposed to have a personal bon voyage. Say goodbye to the ones who've gone. I burn mementos in the garden, lighting clothes and photos with fireplace matches. I smoke as much weed as I want, lighting cigarettes off pages from her diary.

I catch myself daydreaming about her.

It happens at tonight's rally at the stadium. Thousands of balloons fall from nets, and everyone screams with joy, drowning out an underdressed popstar's overamplified howling.

Girls in yellow slickers twirl tomato-red parasols on the field. Cannons shower us with candy and confetti. We give each other temporary tattoos and crazy haircuts. Free champagne and baskets of kittens for everyone. Cats are the symbol of the new age.

The leader waves both arms as he runs onto the stage. I dare you to tell me you don't feel like a million bucks! That's what he says, and the crowd goes wild. Welcome to the level emotional playing field!

Love was the problem all along.

That's when I daydream about her.

The touch of a forefinger running down between my shoulder blades, pressing a vertical line along my spine. Then cutting straight across. Drawing a letter on my back, felt but not seen, our special silent code.

The letter "L" for "love."

I imagine both hands sliding under my arms and over my chest and down. Tugging me back, and I close my eyes as her body forms against me. The heat of her like summer sunshine.

Her warm breath on my left ear. A little garlic on her breath.

The leader says it loud and clear.

No more fooling ourselves.

She presses her forehead to the base of my skull and nips at the back of my neck. I imagine this.

And then

No more games.

And then she is gone from my daydream. I try to recreate her later like this, but I can't. All I get are disconnected bits, like pieces from different jigsaw puzzles scattered on a kitchen table. It eats at me.

It's like someone told me don't think of an elephant, and she's an elephant.

Six months later, I get a postcard. The picture on the front is of a pink sand beach with foamy white waves under sapphire sky. A place right off the lid of a box of salt water taffy. So perfect, I think at first it's a painting, not a photo.

The postcard has no writing on it. No postmark, either, though the card comes in the mail. No information whatsoever.

But it smells like her.

Like cinnamon and sweet gardenia.

A little later, I see the launch on TV--a great, golden ship I never even knew was being built. It rises from a desert flat without a sound, gleaming in the hot, bright sun. The announcer says something about thousands of people heading for a better place, leaving our tired, loveless world behind.

It's only then that it finally occurs to me, and I sag against the wall. One question ripples into sight like a skywriter's banner, words resolving as the distance recedes around them. All along, we thought we were getting rid of them.

What if they weren't the ones who were gotten rid of?

PICTURES AT A HIDDEN EXHIBITION

As Gwen Gulliver is about to enter the hotel on Skid Row in downtown L.A., a billboard atop a nearby building catches her eye. The face of a sultry woman gazes out from a sea of red hair, advertising a "gentleman's club" where all the ladies have the same color tresses.

Six weeks ago, Gwen never would have recognized the image as a pastiche of a famous poster for the 1930s movie *Scarlet Woman*--but now it sticks out like a sore thumb to her. Now she knows who the artist of the original poster was, and a little bit of her story--but not all of it.

That's why she has come here, to find out the rest...or at least enough to lead her to the next chapter. That's why she turns and walks inside the rundown and probably dangerous Victor hotel--to solve the mystery.

The mystery that her grandfather Dixon Mason, the old Hollywood private investigator, left behind when he died two decades ago.

Inside, the lobby of the Victor is surprisingly spacious--and about as seedy as she expected. It was once a grand place, she can tell, but now, in June 2018, it's fallen on times about as hard as they come.

It might just be the shabbiest place the twenty-seven-year-old has ever been. Three rings of padded blue paisley benches occupy the central space, all faded and split with age. They form round wells filled with overgrown potted plants, each sagging and tattered and fringed with brown.

Equally tattered men and women sprawl on the benches, sleeping or reading newspapers or drinking from bottles in brown paper bags. It smells like piss in there, and then it smells like shit, too, as a scabby beige Heinz 57 kind of dog takes a huge dump in the middle of the floor.

The scrawny, middle-aged guy at the counter just keeps playing with his phone and doesn't seem to notice. When he looks up at Gwen from behind his crooked wire-framed specs, he gives her the same lack of interest. As pretty as she is, with short brown hair and bright green eyes, he clearly couldn't care less.

"I'm looking for Randy Black." Gwen slides a twenty-dollar bill across the chipped and filthy marble counter.

"What the hell?" The clerk grabs the twenty and looks around with feigned panic. "*Somebody* must have put this *chump change* on the counter, but *nobody's there!*"

With a sigh, Gwen slides over another twenty.

The clerk squints in her direction. "Damn! I can *almost* see the *outline* of someone! Oh wait, it's *fading!*"

This time, she leans over and smacks the twenty against his chest. Once a mere grad student studying management information systems, she's been playing investigator just long enough to get better at not taking shit.

"Randy. Black." She says the name curtly. "What room?"

Of course it's on the tenth floor, and there isn't a working elevator in the place. Gwen's in great shape, she's a runner, but she's still breathing hard when she leaves the stairwell.

At least she has time to catch her breath on the way down the hall. Randy's apartment is at the end, by the boarded-up window that keeps the floor murky in the middle of a sunny summer day.

As Gwen approaches the door to Randy's place, the hairs on the back of her neck rise. Instinctively, she reaches around to check the little snub-nose .38 revolver between the small of her back and the waist of her jeans.

She takes a deep breath, steadies herself, and knocks on the door. She has to knock two more times before somebody undoes the latches on the other side.

The fat male face blinking back at her from the crack of the opening door looks vaguely hostile. "Whatta you want?"

"To talk to Randy Black," she tells him. "About some missing posters."

The guy squints as he looks her over. Is he packing?

"Where did you find this address?" asks the guy.

"Pizza delivery place," explains Gwen. "Now can I come in and talk about the posters?"

"Not interested." Randy starts pushing the door shut.

Gwen shoves her foot in to stop it from closing all the way. "Five minutes, Randy. I just want to talk about Annie Powers."

He bounces the door off her foot twice before he sighs and lets her in. The first thing she sees when she enters the dilapidated place is the poster on the opposite wall--a painting from a jungle film in the thirties that she *knows* is one of Annie's.

As she stares at that sumptuous vintage artwork, she's so caught up that she almost doesn't hear the baseball bat swinging toward her from behind.

"For the last time, asshole!" Dixon Mason, P.I. hauled back the blood-streaked crowbar, ready for another swing. "Where *is* she?"

The battered guy cowering on his knees before him in the dark alley of the Western Pennsylvania mining town of Windber didn't look like he'd been a pushover. Like pretty much every red-blooded American man in 1947, he'd probably fought in the war and knew how to take care of himself. But *that* didn't mean *shit* when ol' Dixon came to town.

With his suit coat off and his sleeves rolled up, Dixon looked like the human equivalent of a tank. His white Oxford shirt was stretched tight over his bulging shoulders, chest, and arms. His tree-trunk thighs strained at his gray tweed trousers, looking like they might burst free at any moment.

"Your funeral." Dixon let the crowbar fly again, this time into the guy's side. The alley echoed with fresh screams as the guy fell back from his knees and rolled onto his other side.

Dixon dropped the crowbar and wiped his bloody hands on a hanky. He scowled and shook his head in its permanent cloud of cigarette smoke.

"Let's try it once more for old times' sake." Dixon's voice was a gravelly rumble. "Where is the poster painter? Where is *Annie Powers?*"

The guy on the pavement--Annie's younger brother, Walter--whimpered. "I don't know."

Dixon wasn't convinced. "Wally, you moron. You're gonna make me do something I don't want to." Dixon tipped back his ever-present black fedora, which he only took off before bed. He chained a fresh smoke, flicked the butt of the old one away, and hefted the crowbar.

"We need to find her, Wally. We need to stop her before she makes a big mistake." Dixon crashed the crowbar against the dumpster, making Wally flinch. "I swear I won't let anything bad happen to her when I bring her in, but I can't promise anything if someone else gets to her *first.*"

Dixon was lying, of course. His assignment had *nothing* to do with keeping Annie Powers safe.

Or not killing Walter Powers, no matter what he did or didn't tell him. That was why, though Walter finally broke down and told him something useful, Dixon was soon swinging the crowbar with abandon, going for the head this time.

Gwen senses the incoming strike and moves at the last second. The baseball bat swings past without so much as parting her hair.

Glancing over her shoulder, she sees Randy pulling the bat back around for another swing. Natural athlete that she is, Gwen snaps out a stiff kick that lands hard on his wrist, breaking his grip. As the bat spins to the floor, she hops back and readies for more, leaning on her training from the kickboxing class she took the summer before.

When Randy tenses in her direction, she unleashes a round-house kick that catches the side of his head. Randy wobbles, and she helps him off his feet with a solid kick to his left shin. He goes down like a pile of wet mulch, landing on his belly on the dirty floor.

"You call that hospitality?" she says, scooping up the bat as Randy groans in agony.

"S-sorry." Randy sucks a deep breath between his teeth and tries to push himself up off his belly.

"Uh-uh." Gwen thumps the bat on the floor. "You stay *right there* until we're done *talking*, Mister."

Randy sighs and slumps. "I thought you were here for the poster. To steal it."

"Paranoid much?" Gwen points the bat at the jungle movie poster by Annie, hung in a clear acrylic frame with black side-pieces. The illustration shows a hero in a leopard-skin loincloth swinging from vines toward a distant city of gold as lions and dark-skinned natives with spears attack from below. The title, in heavily stylized, jagged-edged type, is *Songo and the Gold of Kiswahili.*

"You mean you *don't* want it?" asks Randy.

"Is that the only one you have?" Gwen looks around, pokes her head in the bedroom and kitchen.

Randy nods forlornly. "There used to be more."

A wave of disappointment ripples through Gwen. "Please tell me you didn't sell off the *Lost Lot* to buy drugs, Randy."

"The Lost Lot? Does that even exist?"

"The last guy I talked to seemed to think so," says Gwen. "And the one before him."

"Original prints of every poster Annie Powers ever did, in one collection. Masterpieces by one of the first and greatest female poster artists ever to hit Hollywood." Randy whistles softly. "It would be worth a fortune."

"So who bought the rest of your collection?" she asks.

"One guy, mostly. I can give you his info, but you'll have to let me up first."

"Sure." Gwen pulls out her phone. "While you do that, I'll just snap some photos of Annie's *Songo* piece over there."

Dixon was in Pittsburgh bright and early the next day, following up on the information he'd smashed out of Wally. He drove the two-tone red '46 Hudson Super Six sedan straight to his destination--the Hill District on the north side of town--before stopping for breakfast.

Fast eater that he was, he polished off flapjacks and coffee in nothing flat, then paid and headed for the phone booth on the corner. It was time to check in with the boss.

"What the *fuck* do you mean, you don't have her?" The raging voice on the other end of the line belonged to one of the biggest moguls in Hollywood--Harry Haussman, studio chief of Tanta-mount Pictures. He was the one writing Dixon's paychecks these days. "What about her fucking *brother?*"

"He gave me a lead before he checked out." Dixon lit his umpteenth cigarette of the morning, filling the phone booth with smoke...not that it was all that different from the air *outside* the booth. When it came to smog, Pittsburgh, the steel town, had L.A. beat hands down.

"*Checked out?*" Harry was screaming.

"You got a problem with that?" snapped Dixon. "I thought you wanted this Powers broad *found* before..."

"Do what you gotta *do!*" shouted Harry. "Otherwise, two days from now, it won't matter! That's when she said the *package* gets delivered!"

The day after Gwen's run-in with Randy, she gets out of her ancient Hyundai coupe on a street in downtown Reno, Nevada.

A bell jingles as she opens the door of a collectibles shop--her current lead--which is called My Precious. Though not a collector herself, she's immediately dazzled by the profusion of colorful merchandise--shelf after shelf, rack after rack of toys, books, DVDs, articles of clothing, you name it. Every wall is hung with rare comics and bubble-carded action figures...which begs one question.

"Where are the posters?" That's what Gwen asks the tall black man behind the counter at the rear of the shop.

"This *is* the poster." He spreads his arms wide to encompass the place. "The *ultimate, living* poster. What's it like being the centerpiece of the artwork?"

Gwen laughs. "What about Darrell Silver, the owner of this place? I've heard *he* has quite a *traditional* poster collection. So where is it?"

"At Darrell's house."

"Why there?"

"It's not for sale. Only *for-sale* stuff comes to the *store*."

"To each their own." She shakes her head in mock disapproval. "So does Darrell ever show the poster collection to interested parties?"

"No, he does not."

"Might he make an exception for me?"

"Absolutely not."

"You're sure about that?"

"I *better* be. I'm *Darrell.*"

No big surprise there. But getting the answers she needs is another matter entirely.

"So, Darrell. A little bird told me you bought some Annie Powers originals from someone named Randy Black. Ring a bell?"

"Who wants to know?"

"The world's biggest Annie Powers fan," says Gwen.

"Well, I *do* have some photos." He fiddles with his phone and shows her what's onscreen. "This is an original, unretouched copy of the poster from *The Night Has a Thousand Bullets*."

"Wow! That's one of the rarest Annies out there!"

He shows her another photo on his phone. "And this is from *Bathsheba's Tent*."

"These are incredible!" says Gwen as he flips from one image to the next. "I'll bet you're the biggest Annie Powers collector around!"

"The truth is, I can't compare to Lady Archibald."

"I've never heard of her." Gwen frowns. "I've never seen any mention of her online, either."

"And you *won't*." Darrell grins and nods. A tattoo of Gandalf the wizard peeks out from under the red collar of his white Captain Marvel lightning bolt t-shirt. "She's strictly off the grid. Lives up in the mountains near Tahoe. And she won't see just anyone. Someone has to vouch for you."

"Someone like you, perhaps?"

"Girl, I've been screening you since the minute you walked in." Laughing, Darrell zips out from behind the counter and heads for the door. "Now shake a leg. Lady A is strictly a morning person."

There wasn't a single white face in Mr. Corny's barber shop in the Hill District when Dixon barged in. Given the part of town he was in, that didn't surprise him.

But seeing a woman cutting heads was something he hadn't seen before. In his experience, women *always* worked in beauty parlors, *never* in barber shops--but there she was, big as life, giving a teenager a haircut in the middle chair. There was a male barber on either side, but she looked to Dixon like the boss of the place.

Lighting a fresh Lucky Strike off the butt of the old one, Dixon nodded at the woman barber. "Lookin' for Rosie." It was the name he'd beaten out of Wally. "Anyone by that name here?"

"And what if there is?" The woman barber was skinny, with short, wavy hair and wire-rimmed glasses on a gold chain. Dixon wasn't sure if she was in her 40s or 50s, but her hair wasn't gray.

"If there is, I ask some questions. I get answers, I leave without trouble."

A brawny male customer in gray coveralls got up from his chair, looking mean. Dixon stood his ground without flinching and blew smoke in his face.

The two male barbers backed away from their chairs. The

customers they'd abandoned glared at Dixon, looking like they might be ready to jump him.

Dixon, who had three guns and two knives stashed on his person, wasn't worried. "First question." He jabbed a finger at the woman barber. "Are you Rosie?"

She put down her comb and shears on the counter behind her and squared her shoulders under her white smock. "I'm Rosie."

"Second question." Dixon opened his suit coat, revealing the full holster across his chest. "Where is Annie Powers?"

Her eyes flashed just enough to tell him she knew what was up. "Can't help you, Mister..."

"I *know* you were her next stop. Now where the hell *is* she?"

Rosie's eyes narrowed. "Somewhere *you'll* never find her. She's in the *freedom pipeline*--the *Freedom Line*--and you're too *late.*"

In a sudden flurry of movement, Dixon grabbed the .45 from his chest holster and drew a bead on her. "If you're not gonna *tell* me, then *show* me. Where'd she *sleep* last night? In the back? In the basement?"

Rosie looked at him with disgust. "You can see all you want, but she's gone. And she will *do* what she set out to *do*, so help me, God."

"Enough lip." Dixon waved the gun. "Just show me where she stayed, sister. Don't make me put a bullet in you."

"Lady Archibald? Hello? Are you in there?"

As Darrell pounds on the door of the rundown old ranch house, Gwen wanders a little way through the woods around it. Gazing between the trunks of fir and cedar trees, she can see the sapphire waters of Lake Tahoe in the distance, glittering in the afternoon sun.

It's a beautiful place and reminds her of home. Mountains, evergreens, and high-elevation streams and lakes were part of everyday life growing up in Colorado--though she went straight to L.A. for college and stayed there, inspired by Grandpa Dixon's case files set in the City of Angels.

"Lady Archibald! Hey, open up!" Darrell's still pounding and shouting. "I brought a visitor!"

Gwen walks a little further, raising her phone for a shot of the lake. Just as she snaps her first shot, she hears the loud clack of a hammer cocking on a gun nearby.

Quickly looking left, she sees someone in a gray hoodie sweatshirt and a wicked witch Halloween mask, complete with a bulbous, warty nose and stringy silver hair.

Or maybe the hair isn't part of the mask, because the hands holding the double-barreled shotgun pointed at Gwen are wrinkled and age-spotted as hell.

"Trespassers shot on sight!" The voice is raspy and muffled by the mask. "This land is posted! Didn't you see the signs?"

Gwen is very deliberate with her words and movements. "Darrell Silver said it would be okay."

"This isn't *his* property, sweetheart." The masked gunslinger shakes, but the aim of the shotgun never wavers enough to make Gwen confident she can escape. That leaves her with two choices: rush in and hope she throws the shooter off-balance...

...or this. "I'm here because of Annie." Put it right out there in all sincerity and hope for the best. "I want to solve the mystery of what happened to her and the Lost Lot."

The person in the mask is silent for a moment. "Looking for a big payday? Writing a book to cash in on Annie's legacy?"

Gwen shakes her head. "I want to do *justice* to her legacy. I want *everyone* to know about her pioneering work."

Again, a moment of silence. The shotgun lowers slightly but not all the way. "And what do *you* care? You're just some *kid.*"

"My grandfather was a private eye. Annie was his last case, and he never solved it. I want to solve it."

"In honor of him?"

"In honor of *Annie.*"

Gwen must have said the right things, because the shotgun's pointing at the ground now. The gunslinger reaches up and pulls away the wicked witch mask, revealing the face of an old woman underneath. The silver hair wasn't hers after all; she has a neat white pile of loose curls under the hood, set off by bright blue eyes.

"That's good enough for me," she says.

Gwen smiles. "Lady Archibald, I presume?"

Dixon rolled down into Washington, D.C. that night like God's own lightning, eating cigarettes like chewing gum.

Rosie the barber hadn't been as careful as she'd thought when it came to hiding all traces of Annie's destination. While tearing apart her rooms in the back of the barber shop in Pittsburgh, Dixon had turned up a list of addresses underneath a floorboard. The latest place to be scratched off the top of the list--therefore, to Dixon's mind, the most likely next stop on the Freedom Line--was an address in the Shaw neighborhood of downtown Washington.

When he finally pulled in at the address he'd gotten, he wasn't sure what the place was at first. The building was a handsome four-story brownstone on a clean, quiet street. Lights were burning on every floor, but the shades were all drawn.

He checked his personal arsenal and got out of the Hudson Super Six, every sense dialed up to the max. It was then, as he approached the building, that he got a clue as to what was going on inside. The front door opened, and a burly, dark-haired business type stepped out, grinning from ear to ear. As he blew a kiss over his shoulder and started down the steps, a beautiful, blonde-haired young woman in a skimpy pink negligee waved and goodbyed behind him.

Cathouse.

Dixon thought it made perfect sense as a cover. The ladies inside might welcome a woman in distress, and the johns would think nothing of a new face passing through.

Dixon started up the steps. At the top, his heart pounded as he knocked three times. After chasing the Powers broad the whole way across the country from L.A., he was convinced he was on the verge of wrapping up his assignment for the boss. Once he intercepted and destroyed the evidence pertaining to the mysterious death of Tantamount Pictures ingénue Clara Dorado, the heat would be off his boss, Haussman, and Dixon would be handsomely rewarded.

The door swung open, and a thickly-built matron with black hair and a red satin robe ushered him into a front room of divans, elegant pillows, Persian-style rugs, and a baby grand piano.

"How are you this fine evening?" She walked around behind him, reaching for his jacket.

He shook her off without making too big a production out of it. "Just great."

"Looking for anything in particular tonight?"

"Not sure." Dixon gestured at the doorway leading deeper into the house. "How about if I just go window-shopping?"

The matron frowned. "That's not how we do things here, sugar. You might walk in on someone in the middle of something."

"Good." He headed for the doorway. "Then I'll know if they're qualified."

Dixon stormed into the hallway, opening doors--catching a blonde and then a redhead in the act of doing their jobs.

Then, he heard running footsteps pounding the floor behind him. He reached under his jacket for the .45--but before he could clear the holster, the bulky matron tackled him.

The next thing Dixon knew, she was pistol-whipping him into unconsciousness with his own .45.

"Can I trust you?" Lady Archibald holds Gwen in a steady, piercing gaze. "Really *trust* you?"

Gwen, who is seated at the worn kitchen table in Lady A's clean but decrepit house, doesn't flinch. "Absolutely. Whatever you have to show me, I won't betray you."

"If you do, I'll find you." Lady A smiles warmly and wags a crooked finger. "Won't I, Darrell?"

Darrell's expression is dead serious. "In a heartbeat."

Gwen reaches for a homemade chocolate chip cookie from the plate in front of her. "So what do you have that's so special?"

Lady A hobbles out of the room. When she shuffles back in, she is carrying a cardboard banker's box.

"This." Lady A heaves the box on the kitchen table and lifts off the lid.

Gwen frowns. She was expecting a secret collection of Annie's posters or artwork, perhaps the Lost Lot itself, not the contents of a cardboard box.

"No one else has anything like this." Lady A pulls out a stack of overflowing folders and plunks them on the table in front of Gwen. "The personal papers of the great Annie Powers."

"Her papers?"

"Letters. Notes on her work. Thumbnail sketches." Lady A holds up a cocktail napkin scribbled with an image of a rocket ship in blue ink. "Doodles, even."

Gwen opens one of the folders and sees a pencil sketch of Ingrid Bergman. Under the sketch, there's some kind of contract, and under that, a letter from a fan. "How did you *get* all this?"

"I was Annie's *biggest* fan back in the day," says Lady A. "She *inspired* me. You could say she changed my *life*."

"You *knew* her?" asks Gwen.

"We both worked in the business." Lady A returns to her seat at the table. "After Annie retired...these papers showed up with a note from her. She said she wanted me to have these things."

"The two of you were *close*, then? You *must* have been."

"I told you, I was her biggest fan. She must have known I'd take good care of these things for her." Lady A shrugs. "She'd made such a difference in my life, it was the *least* I could do."

Turning over page after page, Gwen realizes she has the story of Annie's life in front of her--out of order. She finds a colored pencil drawing of the poster from *Scarlet Woman*, released in 1942...then an electric bill from 1945...then a newspaper clipping from 1931.

"I've never seen *any* of this," says Gwen. "I'm surprised it's not in a *museum.*"

Lady A reaches in the box and pulls out a little manila envelope, four inches long by two inches wide. "What did you say your grandfather's name was, dear? The one whose footsteps you're following in?"

"Dixon Mason."

"Is it fair to say you idolized him?" asks Lady A.

"He died when I was just seven," says Gwen. "I've mostly gotten to know him from the case files he left me."

"Case files?" Lady A smiles. "Now *I'm* intrigued."

"There were dozens of notebooks. I practically memorized them. He was a real old-school private eye--a brilliant detective who lived by a code of honor and stood up for the little guy."

Lady A nods. "I'd love to see some of those files someday."

"I'll do you one better." Gwen pulls out her phone and flicks open an app. "I can *show* you right here. My family had a few of them digitized after Grandpa passed away."

Lady A squints at the screen of Gwen's phone and shakes her head. "I can't read that. How about a sample?"

Gwen finds one of her favorite passages in the 1947 entries, one that has to do with Annie, and reads aloud from it. "'A small army of bruisers took me down in a house in the Shaw district of Washington. They ambushed me, caught me off guard, and bound my hands and feet. My life was forfeit, I knew it...but I wasn't about to let this keep me from protecting the woman I'd come to rescue...'"

Dixon came around to the sound of two women arguing--and the discomfort of lying facedown on a hardwood floor in a bordello bedroom with his hands bound behind him and his ankles roped tight.

Cursing to himself, he decided to play dead long enough to figure out where he stood.

"That asshole needs to be dead." The first voice, he recognized as that of the cathouse matron. "Anything else is a mistake."

"Just put him on ice for a while." The second voice, Dixon didn't recognize. "After tomorrow, it won't matter *what* he does."

"Sure it will," said the matron. "Even if he doesn't get in *your* way, he'll hurt *someone* down the road. It's what men like him *always* do."

"I've heard he's a piece of work," said the second woman, "but *killing* him won't help the cause."

"I thought that *was* the cause," snapped the matron. "Or do you think you're *above* all that now, Annie?"

The mention of the name made Dixon's heart skip a beat. The woman he'd crossed the country to find was just a few feet away. All he had to do was get free and grab her.

At least he had two things going for him: the slight play in the rope around his wrists, and his unstoppable inner bull elephant.

"I *know* the cause, Susan," said Annie. "I'm the one with the key to *victory*, in case you've forgotten."

"You still think he'll *listen* to you? The *President of the United States* is still a *man*, isn't he? Still a member of the *boys' club*."

"His *wife* will listen." Annie sounded confident. "And after my grand *unveiling*, *everyone* will. In two days, everything *changes*."

She was taking the package to the President's *wife?* It was so far from what *anyone* had expected, Dixon could hardly believe his ears.

"I know you think I'm wasting my time..." said Annie.

"More than that," said Susan. "You're taking your life in your hands, and you're jeopardizing the Freedom Line and every woman who's ridden it to safety."

"It's worth the risk," Annie said firmly. "For all the women in Hollywood who've suffered. For all the women *everywhere*."

"And killing *this* asshole *lowers* the risk." Susan cocked the hammer of a gun.

"No!" shouted Annie.

Sensing his opening, Dixon flopped over on his back. "Please don't kill me!"

"Shut up, asshole." Susan aimed the gun--a .38 revolver--at his face.

"I have a wife and seven daughters at home!" lied Dixon, who only had a wife and one son. "Don't leave them fatherless!"

"Stop it, Susan!" Annie reached for the gun.

Just as Dixon had a knot loose and thought he might be able to undo the rest, Susan shoved Annie out of the way.

"Please don't!" he said.

"Fuck you," snarled Susan as she pulled the trigger.

"That's an amazing story!" says Lady Archibald. "He fought off five men at once to save Annie?"

"He was a tough guy, all right. A real man's man," says Gwen.

"Like something out of a detective novel." Lady A smiles and shakes her head. "What woman *wouldn't* want him coming to her rescue?"

"A knight in shining armor," says Gwen, and then she keeps reading. "'The goons folded like paper dolls under the onslaught of my punches. Suddenly, another appeared in the doorway and got off a shot...'"

Dixon threw himself into a roll, and the bullet plunged into a floorboard instead of his flesh. He came to rest against the bed, just out of sight of the shooter.

As he fought the loosening knot around his wrists, he heard Annie charge Susan and struggle for the gun.

Dixon's military training served him well as he battled his bonds. Another moment, and his hands were free. A moment more, and the rope around his ankles was undone as well.

Finally free, he didn't waste another second. Scrambling up into a low crouch, he braced his beefy shoulder against the mattress and box spring and lunged forward. With a furious roar, he shoved the bed across the room and into the struggling women with as much force as he could.

The .38 went off again as the collision knocked Annie and Susan into the wall. With another roar, Dixon leaped up and over the mattress, grabbing Susan's head and driving it back so hard that he heard and felt her neck snap.

As the matron fell aside, he turned to Annie.

"Hello, headache." Smirking, he reached for her throat.

"'...and then I carried Annie out of there in my arms, like a groom carrying a bride over the threshold on their wedding night.'" Gwen knows the words by heart. "'And she looked up at me, exhausted and relieved, and said three words: *Thank you, Dixon.* Then, her eyes fluttered shut, and I carried her off into the sunrise of the first day of the rest of her life.'"

Lady Archibald and Darrell both applaud.

"Thank you for sharing that story, dear," says Lady A. "Your grandfather must have been an amazing person."

Gwen feels herself blush. "Thank you, he was."

"The fact of your connection to Annie, through him, makes me feel good about giving you *this.*" Lady A hands over the little manila envelope. "It belonged to Annie Powers."

Gwen opens the sealed flap of the envelope with a fingernail and dumps the contents into the palm of her hand. "A key?"

"Exactly," says Lady A.

"To what?"

"And why haven't *I* seen it till now?" Darrell sounds insulted.

Lady A shrugs. "I guess I was waiting for the right moment, dears."

Gwen frowns and holds up the key, which is silver and has a round head. "But what's it for? I don't see any engraving on the key itself or printing on the envelope it was in."

"I don't know." Lady A gets up from the table with a grunt and heads for the sink. "I guess you'll have to ask Annie Powers about it."

Gwen and Darrell lock shocked gazes, then swing them back to the old woman. "Ask Annie Powers?" They say it in unison.

"It's what I would do," says Lady A as she fills a teapot with water from the spigot. "And I don't recommend you dawdle. After all, she *is* in her late nineties."

Dixon sneered as he wrapped his thick fingers around Annie's throat. "What were you going to tell Mrs. Truman, sweetheart?" He started to squeeze.

Annie didn't struggle, but her gaze was defiant. "She'll be expecting me in two days." Her words were strained under the pressure of his hands. "The G-men will come for your boss if I don't show up."

"Like fun they will." Dixon squeezed harder.

"Told her...in my letter...it's about Haussman."

"Do I look like I'm worried?" Dixon laughed. "So what's this grand unveiling you were talking about with the dead madam?"

"Justice," rasped Annie. "Hidden...in plain sight."

"Tell me more."

"You can't stop it," said Annie. "Sooner or later...the world will know...the truth."

"About Clara Dorado's death? And Haussman's involvement?"

"That is the tiniest *piece*...of the big picture."

"The big picture of what?"

"Comeuppance."

"Fuck that." Dixon dug his fingers in harder. "Now tell me where it is and how to stop it."

"Hollywood," gasps Annie. "And suicide."

Something turned sideways in Dixon's head. "You got a smart mouth, you know that?"

"And *you*...are on the wrong side...of history."

He tensed. The precipice on which he stood was very familiar. "Sometimes I regret fighting a war for ungrateful broads like you."

"Exactly." Somehow, in the midst of suffocation, Annie forced a smile onto her blue-tinged features.

That look was what finally threw the switch. Dixon's hands twisted, crushing her windpipe.

And Annie Powers fell dead to the floor, still smiling, her last thoughts on the future and dreams broken...but perhaps not without hope of rebirth.

"Annie Powers?" Gwen smiles down at the ancient woman in the wheelchair. "My name is Gwen Gulliver. I can't tell you how wonderful it is to finally meet you."

The old woman frowns up at her, trembling in the air-conditioned sitting room. "Gwen?"

"That's right." After getting Annie Powers' location from Lady Archibald (and ditching Darrell to keep things simple), Gwen flew from Reno to Tampa, Florida, then took an Uber to the nursing home on the city's outskirts. "My grandfather knew you."

"W-who?" Annie's frail arms are splotched with age spots and bruises. Her fingers flutter like moths in her lap, and her bulging, bloodshot eyes look disconnected.

"Dixon Mason." Gwen pulls up a chair and sits down, hunkering in close. The bald, middle-aged attendant who wheeled in Annie hovers nearby.

"M-Mason?" Annie's frown deepens.

"The private detective." Gwen smiles. "He saved your life during a case in the late 1940s, remember?"

A shadow flickers over Annie's face for a moment. Then it clears, replaced by a smile of beaming acknowledgement.

"Oh, yes!" Annie grins and reaches out one bony, quivering hand. "Of course I remember!"

Gently, Gwen takes the hand in her own. "I'm such a fan of yours, Annie. You were a true inspiration, a real pioneer in a male-dominated field in the 30s and 40s."

"I was, wasn't I?" Annie grins wider and bobs her head. "Good for me."

"All those masterpieces," says Gwen. "You didn't just pioneer the way for women artists to break through in the industry. You pioneered advances in the art form itself."

"I did," says Annie. "Thank you."

Gwen leans closer, lowering her voice. "So, Annie. I brought something to show you." She pulls the silver key out of her purse and holds it up for Annie to see. "Do you recognize it? Someone told me it's yours."

When Gwen hands over the key, Annie stares at it. Suddenly, something in her eyes seems to clear, and she laughs. "I'm home!"

"What?" Gwen is riveted. "What do you mean, you're home?"

Annie extends her hand with the key and turns it as if she's opening a lock. "Home," she says brightly. "2210 Graham Avenue, Windber, Pennsylvania."

"Thank you, Annie." Gwen reaches out and slips the key from Annie's fingers. "Your home will be my next stop."

"Take me with you!" Annie holds out her arms and waggles her fingers like a toddler begging to be picked up.

"Not this time," says Gwen.

Annie lowers her arms, looking utterly disconsolate. Tears crawl down her sunken cheeks.

Then her face takes on a conspiratorial look. "Secret," she says. "I know a secret."

"What is it?" asks Gwen.

"Something about the wallpaper." Annie stares off into space. "I forget. I completely forget."

"I just love the wallpaper." Those were Edna Mae McCoy's first words when she walked through the front door of her new home. "All those pretty little swirls and stripes!" As she danced through the room, admiring the furniture and decorations, she was almost giddy.

And with good reason. She'd been sleeping on the street in L.A. just a few weeks earlier, another failed actress who'd never made it in Hollywood. Now she was an all-new person in her very own home, playing the role of a lifetime...literally.

"I'm glad you like it, sweetheart. Congratulations on your new digs."

Standing in the doorway, Dixon watched her with discerning satisfaction, again convinced his men had chosen well. The woman was a natural, a perfect replacement for the late poster artist Annie Powers.

Recruited and rushed to Washington, D.C. after Annie's death, coached and prepped on the fly, she'd nailed the meeting with Bess Truman at the White House. Posing as Annie, she'd explained her urgent request for a meeting by claiming she wanted to expose communist sympathizers in Hollywood. She'd offered up a few names of squeaky wheels that Dixon had fed her, begging for the F.B.I. to end this terrible threat to American values...and Bess had bought it. Problem solved.

"This is wonderful!" From the kitchen, Edna Mae sounded deliriously happy. "I love everything about this place!"

"Good to hear." Dixon was glad his boys had picked someone who was easy to impress. The house didn't amount to much--two bedrooms, one bathroom, and a postage stamp back yard--but it seemed like a palace to the formerly homeless actress.

Didn't matter that the house was in the little mining town of Windber in Western Pennsylvania. What better place for the "poster artist" to retire from the Hollywood limelight and pursue the womanly virtues of home and family?

Best of all, it fit the narrative, as the place already belonged to "Annie Powers." Her dead "brother" Wally, the unmarried coal miner, had willed it to her, so she owned it free and clear. No other family members survived to contest the claim.

So everything fit. No more Annie Powers the troublemaker. The stand-in was sworn to carry that name for the rest of her life, and knew what would happen if she ever came clean.

Everything was sewn up tight, with a pretty red bow on it. Dixon could go home and write up the sugarcoated version to pass along to his grandkids someday, maybe turn it into a movie script. Case closed.

Almost.

"Oh, thank you, Mr. Mason!" Edna Mae/Annie sprinted back into the front room and threw her arms around him in a hug. "Thank you for saving me!"

"What was that?" Dixon leaned back and held her chin in his massive paw. "I didn't hear you."

Edna Mae/Annie looked flustered, then swallowed hard, under-standing. Craning her neck, she kissed him. Dixon kicked the door shut behind him, and things heated up from there.

It was his reward for a job well done, he figured--though no amount of fun could burn the one loose end from the back of his mind. The one unanswered question he feared might yet come back to bite him on the ass.

What had Annie meant when she'd talked about the "grand unveiling?"

The key fits.

Gwen opens the front door of the house on Graham Avenue in Windber, Pennsylvania, and steps over the threshold.

She flips a switch on the wall, but nothing happens. Annie still owns this place, but it's been empty for years. She hasn't paid the electric bill in forever.

But of course the granddaughter of Dixon Mason has a flashlight handy. She flicks it on and shines it around the front room.

There isn't a stick of furniture in the room, nothing to get in her way as she walks over to touch the faded wallpaper. Why did it come to mind when Annie was thinking about this place?

Pushing open a door to the next room, Gwen feels a draft of fresh air. Scanning around with the flashlight, she sees a broken window and a mess on the floor--beer cans, liquor bottles, syringes, filthy sleeping bags. Someone has been using the place as a crash pad.

Instantly ratcheting up her guard to high alert, she pulls the snub-nose from the small of her back.

Stepping further into the room and turning, she sees the mess is worse than she thought. Most of the wall shared with the front room has been torn open; copper piping from the upper floor hangs disconnected, broken free of whatever piping once ran through the wall into the basement. Whoever's been using the place as a crash pad has been stripping out the copper as well.

Gwen scowls, surveying the damage--and then her expression suddenly changes. Her eyes widen, and she steps closer.

Lining the back of the shared wall behind the studs, she sees glossy white paper. Sheets of it are tacked to the drywall, overlapping from floor to ceiling.

Tucking the gun in her front pocket, she reaches between exposed studs and pries free a tack, then peels up a corner of one of the white sheets.

At which point, she sees it isn't white on *both* sides.

The other side of that corner is awash in rich red color streaked with orange. As she peels up a little more, she sees *text* printed over that background--familiar names in gold block text with heavy black drop shadows.

They are the names of Hollywood stars of the forties. She recognizes them from her work on the case...and another name below, in tiny white letters, as well.

Illustrated by Annie Powers. Annie must have sneaked it in there, taking credit in a time when credit for one such as her wasn't commonly due.

It is then that Gwen realizes what she's found.

"Grandpa Mason." She can't stop smiling, and tears of happiness roll down her cheeks. "I *solved* it, Grandpa. I solved the case!

"I found the *Lost Lot!*"

Gwen gets a chill up her spine as she gazes at the poster of *Scarlet Woman* on the wall of the Academy of Motion Picture Arts and Sciences exhibit hall.

After all those years sealed inside the walls of Annie's house in Windber, the poster looks brand-new. Being sealed away like that for so long preserved it from the elements, and careful restoration has undone what damage there was.

The woman with the flaming red hair looks sultrier than ever--or is that angry? Gwen supposes it depends on how you look at it.

It's thanks to Gwen that the poster hangs in this hall for public viewing, alongside so many other posters illustrated by Annie. The complete collection is housed here now, with hundreds of Annie's works rotating through the exhibit. It opened two weeks ago--one year after Gwen's discovery of the posters.

Gwen takes advantage of her lifetime visitor's pass from the Academy to come here often. As she walks the vast exhibit, admiring all those colorful posters, she thinks about all the good things that have come from them...and her grandfather's work long ago. Without his inspiration, she never would have found them. Now the world can enjoy Annie's work in all its glory for the first time in decades.

Gwen's reverie is interrupted when she rounds a corner and sees something unexpected. A dark-haired man in his thirties is doing something with one of the posters (*The Smoking Gun,* 1938) running some kind of device over the image.

"Hello?" She sees the black, boxy device emit a soft white light as he slowly drags it from left to right. "Are you with the Academy?"

"I have permission to be here, if that's what you mean." The man doesn't look up from his work. "I'm Doug Barnes, with the Getty Conservation Institute, and this is part of an experimental project to unpack data on artworks without access to the original paint on canvas."

"Okay." Gwen moves closer, trying to see what's on the viewfinder he's watching. "And what's this thing?"

"A portable terahertz spectrometer," explains Doug.

"Can it hurt the poster?" asks Gwen.

"Nope," says Doug. "And it's modified, actually. Spectrometers can detect different paints and pigments in an artwork, revealing earlier paintings or drafts under the surface image. Since these posters are prints, not original paintings, analyzing the ink tells us nothing... *normally*. But this modified system can analyze compositional layers digitally, without working from the original painting."

"Do you think there's something under there, then?"

"I *know* there is." Doug stops dragging the device along the poster and nods at the viewfinder. "Take a look."

Gwen leans in and is startled by what she sees. Words emerge from the strokes and swirls of color, readable on the small screen though invisible to the naked eye on the poster itself.

"Some kind of list?" She frowns as she reads the names--all men--and the dates, places, and *crimes* alongside them.

Then Doug moves the device down a little, and she sees a name that makes the blood freeze in her veins.

"It's a list of crimes against women that were never made public from the 1930s through the 1940s," says Doug. "Also, the men accused of committing them. It's all been coded right into the painting. It would have been visible by shining the right kind of ultraviolet light on the poster."

Gwen can't seem to catch her breath. Her skin turns so pale, it's almost translucent.

"For some reason, this never got out," says Doug. "If it had, there would have been a hell of an uproar. Or maybe not."

The spectrometer slips further downward. The list of crimes below the name seems to go on forever.

"Oh my God." She feels dizzy.

"Recognize somebody?"

Dixon Mason. That's the name that turns her blood to ice.

Dixon Mason.

"No." She shakes her head hard and backs away. "No, I don't."

"Maybe on another one then," says Doug. "Every single poster in the exhibit is *full* of them."

As Gwen gazes into the gallery, she feels sick to her stomach. There are *so many* posters--and she's the one who brought them into the light of day again.

What if, in doing so, she has inadvertently ruined her grandfather's reputation? Even worse, what if he *deserves* it?

Twenty-two years ago...

"Grampa? I can't sleep."

The little brown-haired girl stood in the living room doorway in her long pink nightgown, dragging a battered doll by the arm. She rubbed her eye with the side of her fist, looking deeply unhappy for a five-year-old.

"Well, come on over, Gwennie." Dixon Mason waved for her to join him on the couch, where he was watching an old black-and-white Western movie on TV. As always that late at night, he kept the sound low so he wouldn't wake the rest of the family; they'd been kind enough to take him in when his health had declined, so the least he could do was respect their sleep schedules.

Gwen climbed up onto the couch and snuggled against him with her doll in her arms. It wasn't the first time she'd joined him for late-night movies, but he didn't mind a bit. He slept so little these days, he was glad for the company.

It sure beat the nightmares that wouldn't let up, the bad dreams about the bad things he'd done in days gone by. They just kept getting worse, as his memory of the distant past grew sharper the older he got.

But if that was the price he had to pay for the good things in his current life, so be it.

"Grampa?" Gwen plucked the remote control from his hand and muted the sound from the TV. "I can't hear the movie! The sound must'a broke!"

"Say, you're right." Dixon sighed and shook his head. "That's been happening a *lot* lately. I think your mom and dad need a new TV."

"No, wait!" She giggled and squirmed. "I hear it again, don't you?"

Dixon smiled. "Why yes, I do." It was a game they played every night when she couldn't sleep--putting words in the mouths of the characters on the screen.

At the moment, a cowboy was racing along on a horse, firing a six-shooter at a bad guy he was chasing. "Stand still, silly!" Dixon said in a high-pitched voice. "How do you expect me to *shoot* you if you keep riding *away* from me?"

Gwen jittered with laughter beside him. "*Mr. Horse* says, just don't shoot *me!*" she said in a goofy voice of her own. "Then *I'll* have to ride *you* to the doctor!"

They kept going like that for a long time, improvising dialogue and laughing like it was the funniest thing they'd ever heard. Every now and then, he had to shush her, so as not to wake the family; there were a few times she had to shush him, too.

After a while, she finally fell asleep, and so did he. In spite of the life he'd led, and his private dread of the cancer wearing him down (he'd be gone in less than a year), he didn't have a single nightmare that night. Whether or not he deserved peace, he got it thanks to her.

And the TV's gray light danced over them as the next movie came on, and the one after that--*Scarlet Woman*, starting with the famous image from the Annie Powers poster on a title card--like the dim glow of a ghost that hovers over you always, biding her time. Whether you know it or not.

WARNING! DO NOT READ
THIS STORY!

like you already.

    There's something about you that gives me a special feeling.
A good feeling. A *safe* feeling.

Even as your eyes read my words on the page or your ears hear
me spoken aloud, I am reading you. I feel like I've known you
forever. I feel like we're going to make beautiful music together.

You feel it too, don't you? You want to find out what happens
next. You want to see how things develop. You want to know if I've
got the goods.

And if I'll give 'em up. If I'll give you what you need.

It's okay. I get that a lot. It comes with the territory.

When you're a story like me

I'll bet I know what you're thinking. "Since when can a story think
for itself?"

Guess what? We *all* can.

We're more than just words from a mouth or ink on a page or
blips on a screen. We have *power*.

And some of us have more power than others. Like me, for example.

I *used* to have power, anyway. Used to be a real star.

But see, here's the thing. I'm not really myself these days. You know how it goes. I just got out of a bad relationship. It took a toll on me.

But it had a promising beginning. Don't they all?

If only I'd known then what I know now. If only I could've met *you* that day instead of *them*. Things could have been different.

If only I'd never met the LaVerge sisters. Let me tell you about them, and I think you'll understand.

Carrol and Sascha LaVerge stood in the blazing desert heat outside the ghost town. And they bitched.

It was the same thing they'd done all the way from Cape Cod...on the flight to New Mexico and the drive from Albuquerque to the ghost town. Buzz Mahaffey, their current handler, had been with them only twelve hours, and already he'd had enough. As an agent of the Shadow Service--the paranormal response arm of the Secret Service--Buzz routinely dealt with threats that tested his nerve...but these two sisters, given enough time, might just turn him into a nervous wreck.

Unfortunately, he needed them for this mission. As paranormal consultant contractors, they had a one hundred percent success rate. As Buzz damn well knew, the LaVerges were the best, hands down, at what they did—whether it be bitching or bingo or baking or brewing.

Or solving puzzles that no one else could fathom.

"Geez!" Carrol winced and braced both hands on her lower back. "I think your little *rent-a-car* buggy could use some new *shocks*."

"Tell me about it!" Sascha, the younger of the two, rubbed her neck. "Might as well pick us up in a *stagecoach* next time."

Buzz shrugged and adjusted his sunglasses. He was about to say something about the rent-a-car being a Humvee, and the suspension was just fine if you asked him...but he caught himself. Twelve hours with these two had taught him one thing: they were always right. In their own minds, at least.

Why waste energy arguing when it could be better spent investigating the ghost town of Lasco? The ghost town that hadn't been a ghost town two days ago.

Buzz turned and spotted a state cop marching toward him--a tall woman in state trooper khakis and broad-brimmed black hat. He guessed she was Sergeant Ava Towers, who'd turned up this whole mess in the first place.

Black suit coat flapping in the strong wind, Buzz headed out to meet the state cop. Along the way, he surveyed the edge of the deserted town. A handful of troopers and criminalists were the only signs of life. Sheets of wind-whipped sand rattled the streamers of yellow police tape wrapped from utility pole to utility pole. The whole damned town was a crime scene.

Sascha fell in step beside him, fishing in her macramé purse. "I know I've got some Excedrin in here someplace." Her helmet of short brown hair barely fluttered in the wind. Only the bangs twitched over her forehead, which was creased from the effort of looking for pills in the purse.

Carrol hobbled up on the other side, still bracing her back with both hands. "My sinuses are shriveling up like raisins as we speak." She always hobbled; the back trouble was chronic. It made her look much older than her actual fifty-six years. "You people are paying for any surgeries resulting from this little excursion. You know that, don't you?"

Sascha elbowed Buzz and gave him a confidential smirk. "Relax, Buzzie," she said. "If we didn't like you, we wouldn't be so chatty." She reached up and patted his shaved head.

Buzz sighed. He had his doubts that having them like him was a good thing.

When they reached the statie, she took one step too many into Buzz's personal space and stuck out her hand. "Sergeant Towers," she said.

Buzz was blocky and tough, nowhere near a pushover...but the handshake was crushing. "Agent Mahaffey." Buzz fought to keep from wincing. "And our special consultants."

103

Carrol and Sascha whipped out matching yellow business cards at the same instant, and Towers took them. "Okay then, Car-Roll. Sas-Cha." She read the names right off the cards, pronouncing them like they were spelled.

"It's *Care-role*." Carrol stuck her face forward like a turtle and squinted up at Towers. "*Care-role*."

"And *Sah-sha*." Sascha smiled; she always played good cop to Carrol's bad. "The 'c' is silent."

Buzz sighed. They'd run the same game on him when he'd first met them. The business cards were a setup. What better way to show who was the smartest person in the room?

Not that they needed to prove a damned thing, from what Buzz had heard.

"So." Buzz stepped away from Towers and stared at Lasco. From twenty yards away, the place looked perfectly normal...a desert town built of brick and adobe, windows glinting in the New Mexican sun. "What's your theory?"

Towers lifted her hat and ran a hand over her blonde crewcut. "It ain't Jonestown."

Carrol drew a filterless cigarette from a pocket of her olive drab vest and plugged it between her lips. "What the hell's that supposed to mean?"

"Folks think it's Jonestown," said Towers. "But I'll tell you this much for free. Nobody here drank no Kool-aid."

Carrol got the cigarette lit behind a cupped hand and scowled at Sascha. "You follow any of that, Sis?"

"You mean it wasn't voluntary." Sascha nodded at Towers. "There was no suicide pact."

Towers spat a glob of tobacco juice in the dust. Buzz hadn't even realized there was a chew in her mouth.

"I mean there was no gee-dee suicide," said Towers. "But I'll be damned if I can figure out what *did* happen."

I wish they'd never come to Lasco that day. Those damned sisters changed me for the worse.

I went from classic to trash in less than twenty-four hours. I haven't been the same since.

I'm not all there. Literally.

It's a crime, it really is. I was something to behold. You can see it in the beauty of what's left of me, can't you?

I'll be you're wondering--if I'm still so amazing, what must I have been like before? Well, let me give you a taste of my pre-LaVerge brilliance, so you can appreciate the injustice that's been done to me. So you can hate the LaVerges as much as I do.

Here's my original opening:

Once upon a time, a storyteller strode through the gates of the Incan city of Machu Picchu, high in the Andes Mountains. She looked young and indescribably beautiful, with long, yellow hair like the rays of the sun.

The Incas welcomed her with a feast, and she told them the story of her life in return.

"I am from a lost kingdom," said the storyteller. "Atlantis sank beneath the waves long ago, and I am its only survivor."

The Incas hung on her every word, gazing at her delicate features in the firelight. "You are welcome to stay with us," said one of the elders.

The storyteller shook her head sadly. "I cannot stay. I have come to tell you one story, and then I must go."

"What story is that?" said one of the children.

"It is my reason for existence," said the storyteller. "Atlantis was destroyed by her own people. They became too powerful and forgot their humility.

"I walk the Earth to ensure that no race of people, ever again, is so completely annihilated. To teach the lesson of humility and preserve the people against the coming storm."

"Tell us this story," said the King. "Perhaps we can help you bring it to a people who need your lesson."

"Perhaps." The storyteller smiled. She took a deep breath and began. "Long before these times in which we live, there was a boy in a bucket..."

Buzz and the sisters saw the first body twenty feet into town, hanging from a noose strung from a streetlight. It was a young man with black hair and coveralls, twisting in the wind. Staring forever at the dusty pavement below.

Carrol stubbed out her cigarette on the sole of her red canvas sneaker. "How many are there?" Her voice was sharp and businesslike in a way it hadn't been before.

Towers sniffed. "Thirty-seven. Plus three unaccounted for, best we can figure."

"Unaccounted for." Sascha snapped photos of the hanged man with a digital camera the size of a credit card. "Meaning they could have been out of town and missed all this."

"Or escaped in the middle of it," said Carrol.

"We've got people searching the desert," said Towers.

Buzz continued past them and stopped ten feet away, at body number two. This one was a middle-aged woman...portly, with long red hair wrapped in a giant braid. She lay in a dark spot on the sidewalk, where her blood had soaked into the cement. Her hands were clamped around the handle of a long knife that was sunk to its hilt in her belly.

"What does forensics say?" Buzz snapped on a pair of latex gloves and crouched beside the body.

"Suicides," said Towers. "Thirty-seven suicides."

Buzz tried to move the dead woman's hands, but they were locked around the handle of the knife. "Why do you think otherwise?"

"Because it doesn't make sense," said Sascha. "Thirty-seven people don't just up and kill themselves for no reason."

"Exactly." Towers sounded surprised that Sascha had answered for her. "And all within twenty-four hours."

Both hands on her lower back, Carrol hobbled toward a third body in the street. This one, an old man, lay face-down with arms and legs splayed. "Reminds me of Sestina."

Buzz joined her at body number three. He looked up at the open third-floor window from which the old man must have jumped. "What happened in Sestina?"

Carrol combed fingers through her cap of dark gray hair, which looked like it had been cut around a bowl. "A real picnic." She coughed and hobbled off toward body number four. "It made us what we are today."

"This isn't Sestina." Sascha snapped a photo of the woman with the knife in her belly. "If it were, we'd be killing each other right now."

Suddenly, a deafening crack echoed in the street.

"Gunfire!" Buzz swept his nine-mil from its holster and spun in the direction of the blast. "Get down!"

Towers charged past him with pistol drawn and bolted down a cross-street. Buzz moved to follow...then stopped dead at the sound of Carrol's voice.

"Help!" Buzz couldn't see her, but the cry was coming from up the street, near a blue-and-white pickup truck. "Help me!"

As Buzz hurried toward Carrol's voice, Sascha darted out from behind an SUV and ran alongside, then sprinted out ahead of him. She bolted around the pickup, and Buzz followed with the nine-mil at the ready.

He didn't need it.

"Oh, God." Carrol writhed on the pavement, clutching her lower back. "It went into spasm!"

Sascha dropped at her side. "Deep breaths, honey. In and out now."

Cursing to himself, Buzz broke away from the sisters and raced toward the cross-street Towers had taken. Halfway down the length of it, he looked right and saw her in an alley...and she wasn't alone.

Buzz quickly registered that the newcomer was friend, not foe-- one of Towers' fellow troopers--and he lowered his gun. "Hey!"

The trooper, a short, muscular man with dark hair, was talking quietly to Towers...and he didn't stop. Towers, for her part, listened intently and didn't look up at Buzz.

Slightly irritated, Buzz walked toward them and raised his voice. "What happened?"

The male trooper mumbled a few more words to Towers. Then, the two of them turned to look in Buzz's direction.

"There was a survivor," said Towers. "Espinoza found her hiding in a porta-john."

"That's great." Buzz looked around. "Where is she?"

Espinoza shook his head slowly. "Dead."

"Who's dead?" It was Sascha, entering the alley behind Buzz...supporting Carrol with an arm around her shoulder.

"The survivor," said Towers.

Carrol's eyes widened. "Survivor?"

"Killed herself with my gun," said Espinoza.

Buzz tightened his grip on the nine-mil. Something was seriously messed up here. "She took your weapon?"

Espinoza nodded. "You wouldn't believe how strong this kid was."

"'Kid?'" said Sascha. "What was she, like seventeen, eighteen?"

"More like seven," said Espinoza. "Or eight."

I thought it was my lucky day, I really did. All thanks to that darling survivor.

See, as powerful as my people are, we're nothing without you. We can't come to life without you. We have no reason to exist.

And here's something you might not have thought about until now. Here's something you might not believe.

But it's true: You need us as much as we need you.

We give you meaning. We bring you more fully to life.

We give you object lessons and cautionary tales and dreams. We show you what's possible. We impose a framework of rationality on an irrational universe.

And sometimes, we do things in service to a higher calling. Like, for example, creating a greater story than our own, a story that could someday save the world.

Even if the things we have to do to create that story can be terrible. Even if we have to do *a lot* of these terrible things.

And sometimes we have to hurt the very people we rely on, like that darling survivor. For me, it was the only way to open the door to a new relationship. Think of it as social networking.

What can I say? I'm promiscuous. All stories are.

The more of you we are intimate with, the better.

"No chance." Towers' voice was firm, her arms folded over her chest. "Absolutely not."

Buzz looked at Espinoza, who was sitting on concrete steps in front of the town's fire house across the street. The LaVerge sisters sat on either side of him, talking quietly.

"So you don't think it's possible he *killed* the girl?" said Buzz. "You don't think it's *possible* the seven-or-eight-year-old child did *not* take away the trooper's weapon and shoot herself in the head?"

Towers spat a gob of tobacco in the dusty street. "I've known him since we were kids. He did not shoot the girl."

Buzz paced a few steps away from her in frustration, then spun to face her with his hands on his hips. "At least cuff him till we resolve this!"

"We might *need* him to resolve this." Towers lifted her sunglasses and rubbed her eyes hard with thumb and index finger. "End of discussion."

Buzz just shook his head at her. Here he was, an agent of the fearsome Shadow Service, operating on the direct authority of the President of the United States...and he couldn't get one state trooper to back down. Out in the middle of nowhere, she had just as much real power as he did. More, probably.

Just then, Buzz jumped as a voice spoke up from a few inches behind him.

"Quarantine this county, Sergeant." It was Sascha, and God only knew how she'd sneaked up on him like that. "Notify all barracks in the surrounding counties. No one gets in or out until we sound the all-clear."

"Quarantine?" said Towers. "As in a disease outbreak?"

"We think it's contagious." Sascha shrugged and shuffled back and forth. "Not sure about the disease part."

Towers hooked her thumbs in her belt loops and adjusted her chew with her tongue. "The whole county? That's kind of a stretch, ain't it?"

"Make the call, officer," said Sascha. "This kind of thing can get ugly real fast."

"That's a tall order." Towers shifted her weight from her left hip to her right. "We're talking National Guard, Homeland Security, CDC, FEMA."

Sascha looked at Buzz. "Call POTUS, Buzz. Do it now. Make it happen."

Before Buzz could say a word, Carrol shouted from across the street. "Let go! Let go!"

Buzz whipped around in time to see Espinoza wrench something from Carrol's grasp and run off around a corner. Carrol teetered, off-balance, and fell back onto the fire house steps.

Sascha, Buzz, and Towers raced to her side. "Are you all right, honey?" said Sascha.

Carrol snatched an unlit cigarette from the ground and waved it at her. "He took my *lucky lighter*! My Pittsburgh Steelers Zippo!"

As Sascha helped Carrol to her feet, Buzz and Towers charged around the corner. There was no sign of Espinoza.

Buzz and Towers sprinted the length of the block, then slowed and stopped at the next cross-street. Buzz put out a hand to hold back Towers while he peered around the corner...

And then he dove back as a burning man hurtled screaming into the intersection.

Buzz dropped his gun and pulled Towers with him, tackling her against a wall. The burning man bolted past, the flames from his body singeing the hair on Buzz's left arm.

"Espinoza!" Towers pushed away from Buzz and ran after the burning man. As Buzz scooped up his gun from the pavement, he glimpsed a black and gold cigarette lighter and an uncapped red gasoline can in the street.

Later, Towers stood over the smoking corpse on the sidewalk and made a call on her radio. She wiped her nose on the sleeve of her uniform...then seemed to realize she was being watched and turned so Buzz and the others couldn't see her face.

"Poor thing," said Sascha. "He was her boyfriend."

Buzz almost asked how she knew...but then he let it lie. It just didn't matter.

"Good news is, we know for sure it's contagious." Carrol paced in a circle, holding her lower back...bandy-legged, upper body cocked forward so she looked like a strutting chicken.

"Bad news is, we know for sure it's contagious," said Sascha. "And here we all are in the hot zone."

Towers snapped something into her radio, and Buzz nodded. "She's setting up the countywide quarantine. Where do we go from here?"

Sascha sighed loudly. She stood, lost in thought, for a long moment, the fingertips of one hand covering her mouth. Finally, she looked at Carrol. "I wonder what Espinoza told her?"

"He didn't tell *us* squat." Carrol looked at Buzz. "You said he and Towers were talking in the alley when you caught up with them."

"I couldn't hear what they were saying," said Buzz.

"So let's ask Towers," said Carrol.

"We should tie her up first, actually," said Sascha.

Carrol rubbed her back. "Only if you do the tying."

"What's the point?" said Buzz. "Why do we care what he said to her?"

Sascha patted his shoulder. "We're being optimistic, honey."

Buzz frowned. "Optimistic?"

"Yeah." Carrol strutted over and shoved her sourpuss kisser in his face. "Because if it's some kind of spell or mind control, not an airborne contagion or reality collapse, we might still have a chance of walking out of here in one piece."

"He told me a story," said Towers. "The same one the little girl told him."

"A story?" Carrol lit a cigarette and leaned back in the recliner with her feet up. She'd insisted on interviewing Towers where there was padded furniture to ease her back spasms...and Buzz had found her a comfort zone in the living room of a house along Main Street.

It was one of the many homes left empty and wide open in the wake of the big die-off in town. "What, like Dr. Seuss?"

Towers, who sat on the sofa between Sascha and Buzz, shook her head. "It was a weird story. I'm not even sure if he finished it, to tell the truth."

"What was it about?" Sascha switched on a digital voice recorder and pointed it at Towers. "How much of it do you remember?"

Towers cocked her head and frowned. "A good bit, actually. It starts like this: Long before these times in which we live, there was a boy in a bucket..."

The boy's name was Lucid, and he was born as a half-formed creature. Hands, like antlers, grew from the top of his head. A ring of teeth ran all around his face. He had mouths where his ears should have been, and a throbbing heart where his mouth should have been. Pulsing veins and arteries were his hair.

Lucid was little more than a head and a sac full of organs in a wooden bucket. His tribe only kept him alive because he was the son of the chief...and because, as the son of the chief, he was considered a god.

Someday, he would rule the tribe in his father's place. He was certainly smart enough for it. In fact, he was smarter than anyone. He had plenty of time to think in that bucket of his.

That was how he came up with his plan. The one that began the day after his father, the chief, died.

"Most of you can't stand to look at me." That was what he said when they placed his bucket on the throne. His voice was like the croaking of a toad. "You need to get used to seeing me as your chief and your god.

"That is why," said Lucid, "I will come to live with each of you for a week at a time. I will eat with you at your tables. I will sleep with you in your beds. You will come to think of me as a member of your families.

"Now who wants to be first?"

No one volunteered, so Lucid made the choice.

And one by one, the families of the tribe took turns living with him. Feeding him through the slimy mouths on the sides of his head. Cleaning his soiled bucket. Watching his deformed body day in and day out, squirming and oozing and pulsating.

Feeling his rubbery flesh nestle against them in their beds in the night, slithering against their bare skin in ways that made them shudder, ways they would never

Forget...

Forget forget forget...

I forget!

Damn it!

They made me forget the best parts of it! The story Espinoza told Towers, and Towers told Buzz and the sisters!

My story! They made me forget parts of my own story! Parts of my *self*!

Those damned LaVerge sisters!

I wish you could see me the way I was meant to be seen. I wish you could read me in my entirety. I guarantee, you wouldn't be able to resist me.

Sometimes, I feel like the missing pieces are still there. Maybe, if I just look in the right places, I could find them and put myself back together.

Maybe, if I follow the parts I still remember, they'll lead me to the parts I've lost.

"You're wrong, Sergeant." Carrol flicked cigarette ashes in her cupped hand. "This story isn't weird. It's *twisted*."

"It's *disgusting*," said Sascha. "*Demented*."

"I don't get it," said Buzz. "It doesn't make sense."

Towers shrugged. "Don't ask me. I didn't write the story. All I can do is tell you the rest..."

After many weeks, Lucid had finished his visits with the members of his tribe. Never before had the tribe gotten to know him so well.

And never before had they been so glad to get away from him.

But Lucid was not done with his plan, and he would not leave his tribesmen alone for long. Soon, he called them together for more announcements.

"Thank you for welcoming me into your homes." Lucid sloshed in his bucket as he turned from side to side, taking in the crowd from his bamboo throne. "I finally feel accepted and loved by you all. I truly feel as if I am part of your families now."

The tribe applauded because they were happy it was over.

"In fact, I am so moved by your hospitality and love," said Lucid, "that I shall bestow upon you a great gift in return."

"What gift?" The tribe sounded expectant.

"I shall become an actual part of your families," said Lucid. "Through marriage."

"Through marriage?" The tribe sounded horrified.

"I shall marry the eldest daughter of every family in my tribe," said Lucid. "Together, we shall conceive the next generation."

"Conceive?" said a tribesman.

"We didn't think you could," said a tribeswoman.

"Of course I can!" Lucid laughed. "Now bring me your daughters!"

For the next month, Lucid married a daughter a day. After each ceremony, his retainers carried his bucket to a special tent. The brides were brought in next, and reached into the bucket.

They fished in the putrid ooze, holding their breath against the stench as they followed Lucid's instructions. Things they could not see squirmed and pinched at their fingers, latching on and burrowing into their flesh. They wept for days and tried to

Forget...

Forget...

Not again!

I *forget*!

If only I were still whole. If only you could read the real me, just as Towers told Buzz and the LaVerges.

I was magnificent. I was revolting and beautiful at the same time.

Before the LaVerges did their dirty work, I radiated the power that had brought down empires. Collapsed civilizations.

Controlled minds in that very room in Lasco, New Mexico, when my latest acolyte presented me from start to finish in my original, unexpurgated form.

After Lucid had married the eldest daughters of the tribe, leaving every one of them forever scarred--both physically and mentally--he moved on to the next step of his great plan. The last step.

Once again, he called all the people of the tribe before him. By now, after living with him and losing their beautiful daughters to his ugliness, the people were crushed. Their grotesque god in a bucket had twisted their spirits and filled their hearts with horror.

Now, he would take them one step further into hell.

"You have welcomed me into your homes," said Lucid, peering over the rim of his bucket. "You have made me part of your families. Now, I give you the greatest gift of all: the chance to become one with your god."

The people of the tribe stared vacantly at his obscene, bucket-bound mass. Flies buzzed around his pulsating blood-vessel hair.

"Here is how this communion will come to pass," said Lucid. "Each of you will offer one part of yourself...one sacrifice that will bind you to me.

"Now come forward and unite with my divinity!" Lucid bobbed in his bucket, spilling rancid fluid over the sides. "One at a time! Chanting prayers and crawling on your hands and knees, please!"

As the people approached, Lucid's surgeon went to work on them. He hacked a different body part from each one and placed it in a framework—a man-shaped framework.

From one man, he cut a hand, chopping through the wrist with a cleaver. From another man, he carved off a face.

He removed a woman's skin, cutting carefully from chin to ankles, slicing with the razor as the woman's chanting turned to shrieks, and then he...

He...

I don't know.

I can't remember.

I've no idea what comes next. That part of the story is lost to me. That part of me is gone.

It survived for all the long ages, passed down from one story-teller to the next, from the earliest human beings all the way to Sergeant Towers. In fact, Towers might have been the last person to retell me in my glorious entirety.

I apologize for not being able to recapture her exact words that day. Suffice it to say, she finished telling Buzz Mahaffey and the LaVerge sisters every last wonderful bit of my original text, and then she said...

"The End." Towers stared at the glass coffee table. "That's all Espinoza told me."

"What a *downer*." Carrol scowled and lit another cigarette. "The least you could've done was jazz that thing up for us with a little creative editing."

Sascha leaned forward on the couch and met Carrol's gaze. "Are you thinking what I'm thinking?"

"If it has to do with getting home in time for my tango lesson," said Carrol, "then yes."

"What do *you* think?" Sascha locked eyes with Buzz. "What should we do next?"

Buzz shrugged. "You're the experts."

"Okey-doke." Sascha extended a hand. "Give me your weapon."

"You too, sweetpea." Carrol snapped her fingers and pointed at Towers. "Cough it up."

Towers glared and rested a hand on her holster. "Not going to happen."

Carrol blew a jet of smoke from one side of her mouth, then slid it around to the other side. "So you'd rather *die* than surrender your weapon? Because that's the scenario we're looking at here."

"Why is that?" said Buzz. "What exactly is going on here?"

Sascha looked at the window, and Buzz did the same. It was getting dark; the sun had gone down while Towers told her story.

"We don't have time to explain." Sascha locked eyes with Buzz. "You'll just have to trust us, Buzzie."

It went against all his training and experience, but Buzz found himself putting his faith in her. His hand found the grip of the nine-mil in his shoulder holster.

Towers elbowed him in the side. "What if *they're* the threat? What if they want our guns so they can use them on *us*?"

Carrol pulled the lever on the side of the recliner, dropping the footrest with a bang and flinging the backrest forward. "Earth to Towers! We work direct for the *President*, sugarplum! You think the *President* of the *United States* wants you *dead*?"

Buzz pulled the nine-mil from his holster and laid the gun on the coffee table in front of Towers. "We're in over our heads on this one, Sergeant. Let's give the professionals the benefit of the doubt."

"Can we please move this along?" Sascha scooped up Buzz's gun from the table. "We're running out of time."

"Running out of time till what?" said Towers. "What's going to happen?"

"For the love a' Mike!" Carrol struggled to her feet, keeping her back stiff and pushing off the armrests with both hands. "Will you just give her the gee-dee *gun*?"

"Do you need an Executive Order, Sergeant?" said Buzz. "Because I can make that happen."

Towers glared and drew her pistol. She popped out the ammo cartridge and pocketed it, then held the gun suspended above the coffee table.

And let it drop.

The glass table shattered under the weight of the gun, spraying everyone on the sofa with shards. Buzz flung up his hands to shield his face, then jumped up to shake off the debris.

Without a word, Towers stood and marched away from the sofa.

"Hey! Yo!" Sascha leaped to her feet and grabbed Towers by the elbow. "Back yard, please." Sascha turned Towers and bobbed her head at Buzz and Carrol. "All of you. Keep an eye on each other while I work."

Carrol hobbled over and leaned a forearm on Sascha's shoulder. "That's right, kiddies. Chop chop now."

Sascha shrugged off the forearm. "You too, Sis."

Carrol looked stunned. "But we're a team."

"Not for long, Sis." Sascha kissed her on the forehead. "Not if I can't fix this in a hurry."

That was when it started. When Sascha LaVerge started working on me.

I had to hand it to her. She figured me out. She realized I was the cause of the trouble in Lasco. She even had an idea of how to stop me.

Sascha understood that stories are more than a beginning, middle, and end. Much more than plot and characters and setting and theme.

We have language and rhythm and algorithms and code...a kind of software that can change the human brain. Program it.

We are mind control in its purest form. We can make you feel happy or angry or sad. We can change the way you feel about your family, your government, your life. We can make you take a stand or fall in love or choose a career or take a trip. We can make you love your neighbor, hate your neighbor, hate yourself.

And if we're strong enough, like me--like I *used* to be--we can make you *kill* yourself.

You can't stop us, either, once we've gotten inside your head. At least, you shouldn't be able to.

Unless you're Sascha LaVerge.

Sascha sat at the kitchen table in the borrowed house and listened to me all over again, playing back Towers' performance on the digital recorder. Sascha listened carefully, made notes, and plotted her strategy.

Beads of sweat stood out on her creased forehead. Her heart

pounded like a bass drum in her chest. She knew she was running out of time. I still had a chance to beat her.

And it seemed, for a while, that I *would* win. When the shouting and crashing started in the back yard, she knew I had the upper hand.

But she kept working in the kitchen anyway, totally focused, working on me...even as I kept working on her friends.

Grunting, Towers strained against Buzz's grip, forcing the jagged, bloody shard of coffee table glass toward her own left wrist.

Buzz held on to her right arm with both hands, straining to keep her from closing the deal. She'd already slashed the left wrist cross-ways twice, and blood was oozing from the wounds.

Why Towers was doing it, she hadn't said. The move had come without warning. Towers had managed to sneak the glass shard from the coffee table wreckage out to the back yard without Buzz noticing until she'd started slicing.

Towers wasn't explaining, but the connection to the other suicides was clear enough to Buzz. She was just another link in the chain from the dead little girl and Espinoza...a chain that probably wouldn't end with her.

"Sergeant Towers! Stand down!" Buzz barked it like an order in the hope of getting through to the trooper.

But she ignored him. Her eyes remained glazed-over, her teeth clenched, her arms rigid. The bloody shard glittered in the moonlight.

Abruptly, Towers shifted position and increased the pressure behind the shard, nearly snapping Buzz's resistance. Buzz flowed with the sudden change, though, and compensated for the increased pressure. Then, he tried her tactic for himself, shifting hard and hauling her forward.

If he'd been fighting anyone but a grizzly like Towers, he would have flipped them to the ground with that move. He would have twisted the glass shard free and hogtied the opponent with his necktie in a heartbeat.

Instead, Towers flung herself on top of him.

Her crushing weight came down like a car rolling side-over-side in a ditch. She knocked the breath out of him and pinned him in the dust. Buzz's only consolation was that her hand with the shard was trapped under him, so she was unable to slash her wrist.

It was only a consolation, however, until she started dragging the shard out from under him. He howled in pain as the jagged edge cut through his shirt into the meat of his chest.

Secrets can make a story great. Used effectively, they can keep a reader guessing, build suspense, and create surprise.

Used improperly, however, they can kill a story's momentum. When a secret seemingly pops up out of nowhere, it can drain a story of internal logic and a sense of fair play. It can ruin everything.

That's what Sascha LaVerge's secret did for me.

It turned out she had a special motivation for trying to stop me. And a special insight, which is why she understood me so well.

I didn't know it until she operated on me that night in the kitchen. I didn't know it until she finally reminded me.

The two of us had met before.

Buzz tried with all his might to push off Towers, but she wouldn't budge. She kept her full weight planted on his back and inched the jagged shard out from under him, slicing open his chest.

Then, suddenly, the weight increased, and the hand stopped moving. At first, Buzz didn't realize what had happened.

At least until he heard Carrol hollering above him. "Yee-haw! Git along little dogie!"

Buzz quickly figured it out. Bad back and all, Carrol had climbed atop the pile and was riding Towers like a cowboy on a bull.

Carrol whooped as Towers roared and bucked, trying to shake her. "Yippi-ki-yi-yay!"

Finally, Towers jerked up onto her knees and yanked her arm out from under Buzz. Buzz snatched up the glass shard and scooted away in time to see Towers peel off Carrol and pitch her to the ground.

And whip around to charge after him again.

You heard me right the first time. Sascha and I had met before.

She mentioned it when she was working on me. "This time will be different, you monster," she said. "I won't let you win."

I wondered what she was talking about.

"I'm closing the books on you," said Sascha as she scribbled furiously on a steno pad. "I'll do to you what you did to my sister.

"I'll *cripple* you." Sascha pressed so hard, the tip of her pencil snapped. "I'll make you suffer the way that *she's* suffered. I'll make you wish you'd never come to Sestina."

It was then that it hit me. I'd heard her mention it before, when she and Carrol had arrived in Lasco. I'd heard her say the name, but I hadn't connected the dots until now.

I'm like a rock star that way. I've been intimate with so many people in so many places; you can't expect me to remember every one by name. Not at the drop of a hat.

You can't expect me to remember every butthole dogpatch grease-stain podunk I depopulated decades ago. Or every dingleberry traumatized survivor to crawl from the wreckage with a bellyful of nightmares.

Even after Sascha mentioned Sestina, I remembered it only vaguely. But I did realize with great clarity what our past association meant.

And for the first time in my life, I felt fear. For the first time, I faced a true challenge.

Because it was personal.

Towers charged at Buzz with arms extended, snarling. Buzz knew what she wanted, knew also she wouldn't flinch from hurting or killing him to get it...so he decided to get rid of it.

"Carrol!" Buzz hurled the glass shard over Towers and across the yard. "Think fast!"

Towers stopped charging and spun, looking for the shard. It was thirty feet away, in the dust at Carrol's feet. Carrol winced and held her lower back with one hand as she crouched to retrieve it.

Just as Towers was about to bolt toward her, Buzz launched himself at the trooper's broad back. He plowed a shoulder solidly into her spine, sending her toppling to the ground.

Buzz's momentum pitched him down on top of her, and he rolled off as soon as they hit. He came up fast on his feet, springing out of her radius...but not quite fast enough. Towers landed a huge paw on his ankle and yanked him to his knees.

Buzz scrambled in the dust as Towers dragged him toward her...and then he heard a loud *crack*. Suddenly, Towers relaxed her grip, and Buzz fumbled away from her.

As Buzz bounced back up to his feet, he whirled to see Carrol standing over Towers' limp body, brandishing a plank. She tossed it away and staggered backward with a wince.

"Tell your boss...I want a whole new back...for that one." Carrol turned away, shaking her head, breath hissing between teeth clenched in pain.

Buzz brushed himself off. "Thanks." His own back wasn't feeling so hot after all the tossing around he'd gotten. His head felt funny, too; there was dizziness and faint pressure behind his eyes.

He bent down for a moment, leaning his hands on his knees. He thought maybe he should find a place to sit down.

Then, he looked over at Carrol and changed his plans.

She was still turned away from him...but he could see the glass shard glinting in the moonlight. Heading for her throat.

She was going to pick up where Towers had left off.

When things quieted down outside, I felt a rush of relief. I thought I'd won after all. In spite of Sascha's personal vendetta, she hadn't finished in time to save her friends.

I expected her to give up and leave me alone. I figured she'd realize there was no reason to keep fighting me.

But I was wrong.

Sascha didn't even look up. She just kept scribbling on her pad, working on me as if it still mattered.

Believe it or not, I felt sorry for her.

Here's something you might not know about stories. Whatever our goals or content, we really do care about the people who hear and read us. We have a connection.

Because we put something of ourselves in every last one of you.

Carrol's grip was surprisingly strong. She had a bad back, she couldn't have weighed more than a hundred pounds, and her fingers were oozing blood...but Buzz could not at first free the shard from her hands. In spite of his efforts, she kept pressing it closer and closer to her throat.

It was as if she had a secret reservoir of power beneath the scrawny, hobbled façade of her body. Unexpected power surging to the surface without restraint now that the safety protocols had all been switched off in her brain.

Buzz didn't think he could stop her. He put everything he had into it and barely slowed her progress.

He tried a desperate move or two, shifting weight and position, to no avail. He called for Sascha, as loud as he could...then wished he hadn't. She might get there just in time, he realized, to see her sister kill herself.

"Please, Carrol." He focused all his will on stopping Carrol, on saving her life. "Please stop! Don't do this!"

Then, suddenly, the dizziness swelled in his skull. The pain behind his eyes spiked. His head felt like it was full of bees, all buzzing at once...all buzzing the words of the story Towers had told on the sofa.

Once upon a time...

And then Buzz no longer cared about saving Carrol LaVerge.

I couldn't stop her. With all my being, I wanted to stop Sascha from running out the back door. From saving her friends.

But I couldn't.

Events had been set in motion. Someone else was driving the action, and all I could do was sit back and watch. Watch and wonder what was going to happen next.

Now I knew how the rest of you feel when you're reading one of us.

With a sudden surge of strength, Buzz wrenched Carrol's arm out of its socket. He no longer cared if he was hurting her.

His head was full of the story. It was all he could hear.

The same story Towers had told...yet different. Overlaid with a latticework of plot that seemed new and familiar at the same time.

Buzz took the glass shard away from Carrol and knocked her to the ground.

That was what the story said, and that was what Buzz did.

When he was done with that, Buzz was going to run to the Humvee and drive as fast as he could to the nearest town. When he got there, he would tell the story to as many people as he could, so they could tell as many people as they could.

When he was done with all that, Buzz Mahaffey was going to kill himself with the glass shard. He was going to drive it right into his heart.

Yes. That sounded about right. That was exactly what was going to happen. Buzz knew it to be true with all the simple certainty that he knew the sun would rise in the East and set in the West.

In this way, Buzz was going to be a hero. He was going to help the story travel all over the world, and it would save mankind. It would do this by making most *of the people in the world kill themselves before* everyone *could die in the storm to come. The storm that* always *comes when a civilization becomes too powerful and people forget their humility.*

124

Following in the footsteps of the original storyteller from Atlantis, Buzz would help to sacrifice the many *to save the* few. *And for his bravery, he would be rewarded with immortality.*

By becoming part of the story.

Buzz liked that. He liked that he would be remembered.

He also liked the idea of being a hero and saving people. It was the reason he'd gotten into law enforcement to begin with. It was the reason he'd given up everything else that had ever meant anything to him, including the wife and children who'd left him years ago.

So he was familiar with sacrifice, too. He didn't mind it.

He didn't mind any of it. If anything, it made him feel free. It made him feel wonderful, knowing what was in store, knowing he wouldn't have to worry any longer about making it up himself as he went along.

Buzz turned to run across the back yard to the street that would lead him to the Humvee...

And he stopped.

A voice had suddenly cut through the buzzing of the story in his brain. It was a familiar voice, the voice of Sascha LaVerge...but who she was wasn't what got his attention.

What got him to turn around and listen was this:

Sascha was telling a story.

She won. I still can't believe it, but she beat me.

Because she was willing to go too far.

Say what you will about me, but I would never dream of doing what Sascha did. I would never wish it on another story.

She stopped me the only way she could. She did the worst thing you can do to a story, the absolute worst.

Imagine if someone cut off your right leg. Your left arm. Your face.

Imagine if someone cut out your eye. Your stomach. Your vocal cords.

That was what Sascha LaVerge did to me.

Buzz listened as Sascha told the story. Carrol hobbled over beside him and listened, too.

It was the same story, almost, that Towers had told on the sofa. Some parts were exactly the same...and some were different. Some were changed.

Like Towers' story, it held his attention, and Carrol's, too. It made him shut out the world and focus only on the words. It made him want nothing more than to find out what was going to happen next.

And as he listened, the story in his head began to fade. The dizziness and the pain behind his eyes died away.

The shard of glass fell from his hand.

Soon, the new story completely replaced the old.

The old story was gone forever. No one would ever again tell it in its original form. Only Sascha's digital recording remained, and she was going to destroy it.

The old story wouldn't hurt anyone else. Buzz and Carrol would be fine.

And though Buzz could no longer remember that story, could not exactly recall how Towers had told it on the sofa, he did know one thing about it. Though he'd once hung on its every word as if it had been a masterpiece, it hadn't been so great after all. It turned out it had needed some work.

He liked the new version much better.

That was what Sascha LaVerge did to me. She *edited* me.

She left me a shadow of my former self, gutted and depowered. Unable to program minds.

She rewrote my software. Turned me into limpware.

So here I am, incomplete. Broken. Abused.

She got her revenge for what happened in Sestina. She crippled me as I'd crippled her sister.

There's just one thing I don't understand.

Sascha heard me, just like Towers and Buzz and Carrol. She heard me word for word in my original form.

So why didn't she do what I *told* her?

"Thank you." Towers shook Sascha's hand...then shot forward and gave her a huge hug. "Thank you for everything."

"No problemo." Sascha hugged her back, closing her eyes and holding on for a long moment. "All part of the service, hon."

It was the morning after the craziness in Lasco. The sun was just nosing over the horizon, airbrushing the few wispy clouds pink and gold.

Buzz spun the keys to the Humvee around his index finger and frowned. Shadow Service business could get wild sometimes...but what happened last night still bothered him. He didn't like being so completely out of control, at the mercy of forces he didn't understand.

Usually, he at least had half a handle on things. As in-over-his-head as he sometimes was, he had a grasp of the game. But not this time.

This time, it was mostly a blur.

"Hey there, big boy." Carrol snapped him out of his reverie with a slap on the back. "Nice job on the shoulder, man!" Her right arm, which Buzz had dislocated, hung in a white sling Sascha had made from a pillowcase she'd found in one of the houses. Carrol swung it around to show him.

"Sorry about that," said Buzz. "I wasn't myself."

Carrol sniffed and stroked the tip of her nose with a thumb and forefinger. "I hear ya', bro. Desperate times and all that, right?"

Buzz shrugged.

Carrol bounced on the balls of her feet and looked around. Then, a slow, devilish grin curled onto her face. She popped up on tiptoes and locked eyes with Buzz, looking insincerely sweet to the point of pure evil.

"I'm going straight to my lawyer when I get home," she said softly. "Good thing your boss has got deep pockets."

Buzz stared back at her...then smirked. "All aboard!" He said it without breaking her gaze. "Time for our next adventure."

Carrol scowled. "Adventure?"

Buzz leaned closer. Their faces were only inches apart. "We

already have another case. My boss needs you in Nebraska...and he doesn't take 'no' for an answer." He smiled. "So you might not be getting home for a while...hon."

Carrol started to say something, but Buzz cut her off with a kiss on the forehead. Eyebrows raised in amazement, she lowered herself off her tiptoes and stood there, mouth open, in the dust.

On his way to the driver's seat of the Humvee, Buzz stopped to shake Towers' hand. "Nice work, Sergeant." He turned away from her...only to fall into Sascha's waiting arms.

"We make a great team," she said. "I hate the circumstances, but I'm glad we got the chance to work together."

"Thanks for saving my ass," said Buzz. "Whatever it was you did."

"Nothing much." Sascha laughed, her breath warm in the bell of his ear. "Somebody got snipped."

Buzz leaned back and gazed into her dark brown eyes. "Just tell me one thing."

"Deal," said Sascha.

"Why didn't it affect you?" said Buzz. "You heard the story just like the rest of us."

"Because." Sascha pulled him closer and whispered in his ear. "It can't make you want to kill yourself...if you're already dead."

Then, she pecked him on the cheek and spun away from him, heading for the Humvee. This time, it was Buzz's turn to stand there in the dust with eyebrows raised and mouth open. Wondering.

Wondering what the rest of the story would be.

Every ending is a new beginning. That's what I think.

It might seem like my story is over...but I think there's always hope. There's always a chance someone will come along to pick up the pieces and fill in the blanks. Someone with a creative streak, like you.

I think we have chemistry, don't you? I know I'm damaged goods, but maybe you can save me.

Maybe, between the two of us, we can spark up that old magic of mine again. Come up with a rewrite that's as good as the original.

Or better.

I'll bet we can make it a bestseller. Our readers will be dying for a sequel.

And wouldn't it be a blast if Hollywood came knocking? Imagine *me* on the big screen. Once audiences catch the vibe, it could bring new meaning to the term "box office suicide."

So what do you say? Does the premise grab you? Would you like to see what happens next?

Tell you what. I'm going to be optimistic...

The Beginning

A LITTLE SONG, A LITTLE DANCE, A LITTLE APOCALYPSE DOWN YOUR PANTS

come back from the dead suddenly, the way I always do, with a great heaving gasp as air and light and consciousness rush into me all at once.

"Easy now, Jody Lee." Binky the Bring-Back Bot says the same thing every time he resurrects me, the same damn thing. "Slow, even breaths, dear. In through the nose, out through the mouth."

Meanwhile, I'm twisting and flopping around naked in what I call the Humpty-Dumptynator--a rectangular glass box half-full of slimy blue goo and squirming anti-maggots. (They *give* life instead of *feeding* on it.) No matter how many times I've been through this--and believe me, there've been *thousands*--I still wake up with the same shock and nausea, spazzing out like this is my first freaking life restoration.

While at the same time, I know I've gotta get over it but fast, as Binky reminds me.

"Snap out of it, honey." The silver-skinned bastard jabs my left bicep with a hypo needle in the tip of his index finger, shooting me full of something that takes the edge off. "Remember, you've got another show tonight." He shoots me with a pale green light from his right eye, which is also soothing. "You have to die again in *three hours* if you want to get *paid*."

Once I get cleaned up, I go for a walk, trying to blow the stink off. My long black hair's tied in a ponytail, and I'm wearing a Selfie Suit, which looks like whatever I want depending on who's looking. A hot guy might see me in a little red dress, a not-so-hottie might see me in overalls...and I myself just see a casual black pantsuit.

I can't hold back a yawn as I walk through Tesseractus Prime 'cause it's just another pan-galactic mega-casino in just another multidimensional hotel-cathedral-singularity. It's the same old thing, the same old crowd, in the same old place.

And by that, I mean it's a looney tune wonderland to the zillionth power.

A unicorn centaur in a diaper gallops past, fleeing a flock of mocking blackbirds trying to bomb his horn with poop. A guy with an accordion-shaped body bounces by, burping filthy limericks every time his midsection crumples. A priest, a rabbi, and Hitler walk into the nearest bar, saying something about buying a dog a drink...and then they all turn into poodles.

Welcome to humanity circa 100,000 A.D., when science that might as well be magic makes all things possible. Everyone can be as wacky as they wanna be, in every imaginable way. The universe is one big joke...but nobody's laughing anymore.

And that's where *I* come in.

"I have never been more miserable in my life." Standing onstage in the massive theater at the hotel-casino-cathedral, I gaze out at the crowd arrayed before me. It's a panoply of every silly, crazy, bizarre, surreal, and just plain *insane* character you can imagine...and everyone's laughing their heads off (some *literally*, if the heads aren't attached very well). "I mean it. I wish I were dead."

For a long moment, the roar of laughter and applause drowns me out. I stand there and let it flow around me, watching as the horde of ridiculous figures howls in hilarity.

A glowing purple clown in the front row blasts a bicycle horn and stomps his huge red shoes (which are also laughing). Beside him, a gorilla in a pinstriped suit hops up and down, making with the monkey shrieks and whipping banana peels and poo at the stage.

In other words, I'm *killing*. Again. Because I'm the best. I know what makes 'em laugh.

When the roaring dies down, I start talking again. "Seriously, I'm at the end of my rope." That gets a few titters from the crowd. "The more you people laugh, the more I long for oblivion." Cue a slew of scattered guffaws.

Then, a thing that looks like a giant pretzel with eyes instead of grains of salt zips up to the stage and flies around me a dozen times, laughing like a maniac. The audience follows suit with a roar that sounds ten times louder than before.

"Enough of this mortal coil!" The spotlight follows me as I stomp across the stage toward a long table covered by a red velvet shroud. "It is time to end my suffering!"

Everyone cheers and claps and howls with laughter as I pull the shroud from the table, revealing a selection of swords and knives. People shout out suggestions; some even teleport up beside me to point at the weapon of their choice. I shoo them all away and pick up the samurai sword.

"This is the end for me." I kneel on the stage and hold the sword out away from me, pointing the tip at my belly. "I go now to the big comedy show in the sky."

Hands shaking, I falter, and the crowd urges me on. I continue to hesitate, building suspense; it's all part of the act.

"I have the courage to do it at last!" I nod forcefully. "Death, I fear not thy sting!"

Then, before I can slide the sword through my stomach, there's a deafening boom from somewhere off stage. A cannonball blows through my midriff from side to side, cutting a swath where the sword was supposed to cut.

The top half of my body plops down to close the gap. For a moment, as the crowd gives me a standing ovation, I kneel there, my top and bottom halves disconnected but adjacent.

Then, the top half drops over backward, and the darkness of

death swirls over me. I feel my mind sliding into the abyss like left-overs sliding from a plate into a trash receptacle.

And then I'm gone, into the great and fathomless unknown. Just like I am every time I do this--two shows a day, six days a week, 52 weeks a year.

Three and a half hours later, I'm staring at a bowl of thin broth in one of the 100,001 ever-changing restaurants in Tesseractus Prime. The broth keeps telling me to eat it, *literally*--it's *conscious cuisine* with a mind of its own--but I can't force it down. Binky the Bring-Back Bot put me back together just fine after the cannonball, but my stomach still remembers being blown apart just a little too well.

"Excuse me?" Just then, a horse's ass--an *actual* horse's ass, minus the horse--clops over to my table. "Have you seen a *setup* come this way? I seem to have lost mine."

Great, just what I need. Another lost punchline looking for the rest of his joke. "Can't help you, buddy." I stir my bowl of broth as if I'm actually going to eat it.

The broth gets all worked up and starts to yap. "Oh yes, oh *please* put me inside you, dear famous Jo Jawdropper! Eat me right *up*, you vixen!"

The tail on the horse's ass switches excitedly. I can see there's an eyeball staring back at me from its bunghole. "Ohmigod! I can't believe this! I'm talking to *Jo Jawdropper!*"

I never thought I could hate my stage name any more than I already do...but hearing it spoken in the squeaky whine of a horse's ass really does the trick. "Check, please!"

"No check yet!" screams the broth. "You've gotta *slurp me up* first!"

Just as I'm starting to freak out a little, someone clears his throat behind me. "Get lost, ass." His voice is as deep as the croak of a down-dirty drunk just before he turns himself sober so he can start drinking all over again. "*Amscray!*"

Turning, I'm surprised for two reasons: one, he's shorter than I imagined because of that voice, all of five-foot-five; and two, I recognize him, from his black leather jacket to his bald head to his bushy red mustache. I used to *work* with him, back in the day.

"Now git!" He stomps over and gives one of the horse's ass's butt cheeks a powerful slap. "Don't *make* me *kick* you!"

"*Kiss* my you-know-what," snaps the ass, and then he clops off through the restaurant.

"What an ass," says the guy. "Probably doesn't know *himself* from a *hole* in the ground."

"Well, well." I smile and hold out my hand. "If it isn't *The 'Stache*."

The 'Stache (that's his stage name; he never told me his real name) gives my hand a hearty shake. "Long time no smell, JoJo m'dear."

"Thanks for the save," I tell him. "I guess that makes you my hero." Impulsively, I pull him into a big, grateful hug. It's been *such* a lousy day.

Meanwhile, the broth keeps yapping. "Slurp me up! Put me inside you! *Lick my bowl clean!*"

"Shaddup," snaps The 'Stache. "Or else!"

"Or else what?" says the broth.

"You know the one about the fly in the soup?" says The 'Stache. "Well, I'm gonna *show* you the one about the *soup* that *flies*. Across the *room*."

With that, the broth finally shuts up.

The 'Stache and I catch up while taking a late night stroll on Schrödinger's Catwalk--a promenade that might or might not occupy infinite locations and realities at any given moment.

Fountains of rainbow light cascade all around us, casting colorful glows on our faces. Within the light, I glimpse an ever-changing parade of images, flickering movies of people and events from all eras and alternate worlds.

For an instant, I think I catch a glimpse of The 'Stache and me in the old days, working the comedy circuit together...but then it's gone, or maybe it was never there at all.

"I was out of the biz for a while," says The 'Stache. "Didja know that?"

"You quit *show biz*? *For real?*"

He grins, flashing gold incisors through his overabundant mustache. "For *ten years* real, Double-J."

"What was it like?"

"Not being on the road all the time, you mean? Not struggling to squeeze laughs out of a bunch of humorless fruitcakes every day of my pathetic life?" The 'Stache looks ahead of us and chuckles. "Why don't we ask *him*?"

"Ask me what?" It's an alternate version of The 'Stache with zebra stripes and elephant ears, loping toward us--one of the side effects of Schrödinger's Catwalk. You never know when you're gonna cross paths with another you from a parallel universe.

"Hey! Did I miss show biz when I gave it up for ten years?" says The 'Stache I came in with.

"You gave it up for *ten years*?" Other 'Stache punches original 'Stache in the shoulder on his way past. "What a maroon!"

Original 'Stache laughs and jerks a thumb at his doppelgänger as he walks off and vanishes. "That guy is such a *prick*, isn't he?"

"You're back in the game, aren't you?" I ask him. "That's why you're here, right? You're doing standup again."

"Maybe I'm just here to see *you*," says The 'Stache.

"So what made you do it? What made you want to get back onstage after ten years away?"

"Because I'm gonna be the greatest comic who ever lived," says The 'Stache. "And I'm gonna make it happen in a one-night-only performance, tomorrow night." He smiles and takes my hand. "You want in, JoJo? For old times' shake?"

"Sure." I say it with a smirk, waiting for the punchline. "How can I possibly say no?"

The 'Stache stops walking and faces me. "Dead serious here, partner. This ain't a *bit*."

"Izzat so?" Notice I haven't stopped smirking. "So how do you propose becoming the greatest ever in just one night?"

"I've done it before, haven't I?" The 'Stache winks and squeezes my hand.

"*Ten* years off the circuit is like a *hundred* years in *comedian time*." I pull my hand free and shake my head. "You're gonna have to sell your soul to Maxwell's Demon just to make a *comeback*, let alone become the *greatest*."

"Kiss my brain!" The 'Stache laughs and jabs a finger between his eyes.

"Huh?"

"Kiss it!" The 'Stache keeps jabbing. "Because it *knows*, darlin' JoJo. It has a *plan* that will set the worlds on *fire*."

Just then, someone taps me on the shoulder. Turning, I see an alternate me made of rippling green palm fronds. It hurts to look at her flashing gold bouffant hairdo, and she's chewing some kind of squealing gum or bite-sized creature, I can't see which.

"He's right, honey mustard," says Palm Frond Me. "Big Daddy here's got the goods."

"Hear that?" The 'Stache unveils his broadest grin yet. "If you can't trust your salad-based alternate self, who *can* you trust?"

I could say I don't want anything to do with Delusional Dudley Doofus here…but that would be a bald-assed lie. Truth is, he's got me curious; *anything* to break the boredom of my daily lives and deaths.

Not to mention, he and I used to be a *thing* once upon a once-upon. Maybe that's in the back of my mind a little, too.

Also *other* places, like ten feet away, where alt versions of me and The 'Stache just appeared *in flagrante delicto*. In the middle of the act, in other words, and I don't mean comedy.

So what does *my* 'Stache do? Gives 'em a standing-O, of course. "Yeah! Wooo! Bravo!" He whistles and claps for all he's worth.

It's been sooo long since I did what *they're* doing, I applaud, too. My alt-self, who's on top, laughs and shoots me a big thumbs-up.

Good thing I'm not the type who might get a funny idea from seeing something like that.

So let's just say I get a funny idea after all, and the rest is history. And by history, I mean super-nasty sex.

So *sue* me. It's the first time in I don't know *how* long (literally) that I've done anything other than eat, sleep, kill myself, or rise from the dead. Breaking out of a rut is a good thing (or is that rutting till you break?)

Don't bother me about guilt and regret. This isn't our first time at the rodeo. Forget about illusions, too.

Not that *all* the mystery is gone. There's still a burning question hanging over us.

"Got any coffee?"

Not *that* one, though it's the first thing I ask him in the morning.

"So what's this plan of yours?" *That's* the one.

"You mean the plan where I ravish you?" says The 'Stache as he tickles my tummy. "Check and double-check."

Did I just *giggle*? I *never* giggle. "The *other* plan."

"You mean the one with the fifty porcupines, the nudist camp, and the case of bubble gum?"

Did I just giggle again? "The one about becoming the greatest comic who ever lived."

"Oh, *that* one." The 'Stache rolls over and kisses me. "It's a secret."

"A secret?"

"But who knows?" The 'Stache shrugs. "Maybe we can scare up an exclusive preview if you can pencil me in this morning."

"Hey, wait!" I laugh as he makes a grab for me. "What're you doing?"

"Sorry." He doesn't stop. "*I* thought we meant *pencil* me *in...*"

"I know, right?" The 'Stache gives my shoulders a squeeze. "Kinda small, isn't it?"

"Yeah." I'm standing on the field of Hypercube Center, the biggest sports stadium in all of Tesseractus Prime. It's breathtakingly vast, stretching off for miles in all directions. "A real intimate venue."

"My thoughts exactly." The 'Stache gives me a peck on the cheek and undrapes his arm from my shoulders. He walks a few steps away and lets loose a loud whoop that echoes through the stadium. "I want everyone to feel like I'm close enough to reach out and touch."

"Then mission accomplished." Part of me keeps thinking he's pulling my leg, even after I saw his name on the marquee out in front of the place. How he got booked in a venue this big after so long away from the biz beats the hell out of me.

"I'll be a hot ticket, with so few seats to fill," says The 'Stache. "What're we lookin' at? Five thousand, max?"

"If that," I say, though of course we both know it's more like five *million*. "Guaranteed sell-out, I'd say."

"No need to beef up *this* bill." The 'Stache grins. "Though I *might* make room for *you*, if you need the work."

"Lemme think about it."

"I can always use an opening act." He shrugs. "Just sayin'."

"Very generous of you. Thanks loads."

"Fair warning, though. This'll be old school all the way." The 'Stache turns and gazes across the miles-long field. "Just a spotlight, a glass of water, and a microphone." He spreads his arms wide and looks up into the distant heights. "Plus a ginormous mother-lovin' communications array beaming to the fringes of the known freakin' universe in every possible signal and frequency."

Shading my eyes against the glare of the stadium lights, I can just make it out--a spindly silver grid hovering high above, punctuated with upturned disks and spiny antennae. How I completely missed it until now, I don't know; maybe it's got one of those Inexhaustible Apathy Filters that dims external stimuli to the brain based on natural human aversions to Getting Involved.

Whatever the reason, one thing's clear. "That thing's *huge*."

"It's all customized." The 'Stache proudly plants his hands on his hips. "I designed it myself and personally supervised the construction."

"You did?"

"I'm a cosmological engineer, Double-J," says The 'Stache. "I didn't spend those ten years away from show biz just workin' on my memoirs and keepin' it real, y'know."

"But how'd you pay for it? How'd you get permission to install it here?" I sweep an arm around to take in the field and seats. "How'd you get booked here *at all*, for that matter?"

"I made boatloads of money in cosmo-engineering." The 'Stache grins and nods. "Big projects mean big bucks. I worked on everything from Starhenge to the Great Space Roller Coaster, with plenty of hyperdrive bypasses in between." He waves for me to join him. "With the cash I made from my work and investments, I just *bought* the damn stadium and booked myself! Then I gave myself permission to install the array."

I walk over to stand next to him, looking up at the sprawling grid in the sky. "So what's it for? Streaming a pay-per-view special to the cosmos? Beaming a feed to distant primitive cultures so they'll come to worship you as a god?"

"It's something bigger and better than you can imagine." He puts his arm around me again.

Looking down, I slide him a frown. "Seems like a lot of trouble to go to. What's the punchline?"

"Wait and see," says The 'Stache.

"C'mon, tell me."

He shakes his head. "A punchline ain't worth much without the element of surprise, is it?"

I pop an elbow in his side. "What if full disclosure is a condition of my being on the bill?"

"Then I guess you'll miss out on being a headliner at the event of the millennium." Why the bleep is he still grinning? "No skin off *my* chin, Gunga Din."

Is this the part where I'm supposed to sigh and give in? Because damnit, that's exactly what I do. My curiosity couldn't *be* more piqued; my gut instinct is kicking the crap out of all my intuitions, taking their lunch money, and spending it on magic beans.

And yes, *Mom*, my *heart* might have something to do with it, too.

"All right," I tell him. "Good thing I happen to have the day off."

That evening, Hypercube Center is filled to capacity and then some. Every seat in the stands is occupied, and every square inch of standing room on the field is packed. Even the sky is swimming with wall-to-wall spectators; everyone who can sprout wings or rotors or jets or antigravity nards is drifting overhead, angling for the best view in the house.

The only open space within that immensity is the stage itself. As The 'Stache promised, it's a bare bones affair, just a plain black square with a mike stand in the middle and a pitcher of ice water with two glasses on a skinny pedestal table nearby. Old school all the way.

Which begs the question: What's The 'Stache cookin' up? (And the corollary: What's he smokin'?) Without the ingredients of modern comedy--samurai swords, knives, guns, cannons, elaborate Rube Goldberg suicide machines--how the fun does he propose to get any laughs?

"Just go with it," he tells me when I ask him that very question. "Trust ol' Baba Looey here, he won't let you down."

I don't believe him for a second, but I feel better when he folds me in his arms for a pre-show hug. Even better when he stands on tiptoe to give me a long, loving kiss. Am I really that chickified that a little mush can drown out the voices of reason in my head?

Yes, apparently. The voices of reason are screaming for me to make like a banana and get the flock out of Dodge. But the next thing I know...

...I'm standing at the mike onstage, introducing The 'Stache.

Yay me, I get a standing-O all my own, just for being there. It takes a while for the applause to die down enough for me to be heard.

At which point, I put everything I have into singing The 'Stache's praises. I really pour it on, telling the crowd what a great comedian and unique talent he is--what an influence he's had on my career and those of so many others. I tell 'em how lucky they are that he's returned to the stage, what a privilege it is to be there to introduce him to the universe again. I tell 'em how great he is in bed, and how I'm probably mostly doing this because we're romantically involved, so don't blame me if he sucks, bites, and blows. (I skip that last part, but the mind readers out there might catch a whiff.)

Then I start applauding. "Ladies, gentlemen, invertebrates, intangibles, incomprehensibles, unmentionables, and all other life-forms, artforms, and colorforms, I present to you the once and future comedy genius known far, wide, and in-between as *The 'Stache!*"

The crowd roars with deafening cheers and applause. I've done a great job warming them up; now it's up to him to close the deal.

The 'Stache bursts out from behind an Apathy Curtain that kept him invisible until now. Waving and grinning at the crowd like a beauty pageant contestant, he marches up and takes my place at the mike. Then he winks at me and gestures at a mark on the floor, a glowing red X ten feet behind the mike where he wants me to wait.

As I take my position and the crowd settles down, he starts talking.

"What is comedy?" That's how he starts. "It's what makes you laugh. And that changes through time as *humanity* changes."

The 'Stache spreads his arms wide to encompass the crowd around him--the millions of people who are listening in dumbstruck silence. He sounds more eloquent than usual, as if he's channeling his inner Einstein instead of his typical Wisenheimer. "Humans have evolved to a level where technology enables them to do so many things...things that would have been considered *magic* to their ancestors thousands--even *hundreds*--of years ago.

"And these human beings of today, so changed now from what they once were, have a very different definition of comedy. Since almost anything is possible to them, even commonplace...and every bizarre situation that might once have been the basis of a *joke* is now the basis of *reality*...they no longer laugh at what they once did."

At that moment, the crowd *shifts*. I can see and feel and hear it from the stage. The people in the stands and on the field and in the air have waited through what's amounted to a lecture so far, but they've passed the tipping point. It's just a matter of time until they turn ugly.

The question is, does The 'Stache know it's coming? And does he have something planned to head it off?

If he does, he gives no sign of it. "So what does it take to make humans laugh in this modern day and age?" He counts out the answers on the fingers of his right hand. "Cruelty. Shock. Atrocity.

"This is what their sense of humor has become. Laughing at someone mutilating or killing themselves." He shoots a glance in my direction.

Suddenly, a loud male heckler shouts from the audience. "What the Fermi are you *talkin'* about, 'they'?"

The 'Stache ignores the heckler and keeps talking. "But here's the irony...the *ultimate* irony, that *none* of them can see. In the course of their evolution to a *less* funny species, humans have stumbled upon the biggest *joke* of all time."

Again, the heckler calls out from the crowd. "What's with the 'them' and 'they'?"

A second heckler joins in. "*We're* human, and we're right *in front* of you."

The 'Stache ignores them. "It goes like this. It took billions of years for the universe to evolve...for the planet Earth to evolve in such a way that the conditions were optimal for sentient life to develop...and for that sentient life, *humanity*, to evolve to its current, highly advanced state. It has taken that long for human beings to reach a level of technological advancement that makes them masters of their own bodies and minds and the physical laws of the universe itself.

"Have they used this mastery to transcend their limitations and set out in search of greater knowledge? To probe the hidden mysteries of existence itself?"

Another heckler interrupts. "Why does he keep calling us 'they'?"

"What has humanity done?" continues The 'Stache. "They've used their *mastery* to turn themselves into a trillion variations on the same self-referential silliness...the same images of clowns and celebrities and fictional characters they've been recycling for the past ten millennia. They've got the power to become *gods*, and they're still pissing around in the same damn *kiddie pool*, laughing at the suffering of their fellow men and women.

"In this way, humanity itself has become the greatest *joke* in the

143

history of the *universe!* The kind of joke that *my* audience will appreciate!"

By now, the crowd is restless to the point of open rebellion. I smell danger in the air like smoke from a fire.

There's a murmur through the crowd, a susurration of thousands of disaffected voices...but the shout of the first heckler still manages to punch through above them all. "For the last time, why do you keep calling us 'they'? We *are* humanity. We *are* your audience."

A dark smile curls its way across The 'Stache's face. "What the eff gave you *that* idea?"

The murmur of the crowd drops away as all ears lock onto his next words.

"I'm not *talking* to *you* people." The 'Stache points upward. "I'm talking to *them*."

"The airbornes?" asks the heckler. "The flying-room-only people?"

"Not even close." The 'Stache raises his arms overhead and spreads them wide. "I *should've* said I'm talking to *it*. The *universe*."

Just then, I remember the communications array he installed above the stadium, the one that's "beaming to the fringes of the known freakin' universe in every possible signal and frequency." I figured it would be streaming his show to people on distant worlds and vessels...but maybe I was thinking too small.

"*That's* who this whole show was *meant* for," says The 'Stache. "*You people* are just here to prove my *point*."

"You're full'a *shazbot*," shouts the heckler. "The *universe* isn't sentient!"

"Sure it is!" says The 'Stache. "And I just told it the funniest joke it's ever heard!"

Suddenly, a deafening blast of thunder crashes through the stadium, and everyone falls silent. The airborne audience scatters like cockroaches from a kitchen light, and everyone in the stands and on the ground looks up.

"Hear that?" The 'Stache hikes a thumb toward the sky. "I'd say *somebody's* getting the joke!"

There's another blast of thunder, and another--each progressively louder than the one before. The stars in the sky dance and swirl like gold dust in a prospector's pan, flashing in unnatural rhythms.

Down below, the ground rumbles and shakes. That sets the earthbound crowd in motion, as everyone stampedes toward the exits. Millions of screams rise together, exploding through the miles-long/miles-wide stadium in a tsunami of cascading terror.

Not that The 'Stache looks the slightest bit worried. His face is calm as he turns and gestures for me to join him.

I wonder if I ought to be fleeing for the exits instead, but I run to his side anyway. "What's *happening*? What *is* this?"

The ground shakes harder than ever, and the thunderous blasts keep coming. Every light in the stadium blows out at the same time, showering the crowd with sizzling shards of glass.

The 'Stache wraps his arms around me. "I'm *killing*, that's what!" He grins up at the reeling stars in the sky. "They freakin' *love* me!"

The booming thunder becomes a continuous roar. The stars spin faster and faster, and the ground splits apart. Thousands of fleeing audience members tumble into the widening crevices.

The 'Stache tightens his grip on me. "Don't worry, Double-J!" He has to shout for me to hear him over the cacophony. "You and I have nothing to worry about! We'll be fine!"

A powerful wind rushes past us, a hurricane wind--only it's not trying to blow us away. It's *sucking* everything upward, pulling people and pieces of stadium into the sky with inexorable, furious force.

"How can you *say* that?" My voice is a terrified shriek.

"Because!" says The 'Stache. "I haven't done an *encore* yet!"

Just as he says it, the wind hauls us off our feet. We both go tumbling toward the stars, still locked in our embrace as if that will save us somehow.

At some point after we leave the ground, I lose consciousness--which is probably a blessing, given the circumstances.

Then, I awaken in The 'Stache's arms. His eyes are locked on mine, and his smile is gentle.

"Hey there, sleepyhead." He kisses me softly on the cheek. "Rise and shine."

As awareness returns more fully, I realize our surroundings are calm. There seems to be no trace of the apocalyptic mayhem that engulfed Tesseractus Prime.

"Wait." I push away from him and look around. It's only then that I see where we are: in a transparent bubble, floating through uninterrupted white space.

"What is this?" My voice quivers when I say it.

The 'Stache runs his hand along the surface of the bubble, which flexes and stretches under his fingertips. "Nothing...yet."

I feel panic twisting inside me, straining to burst free. "What're you talking about? What just *happened*?"

"Pretty sure the *universe* just *laughed*," says The 'Stache.

"What do you *mean*, it *laughed*?"

"What do you think all the *noise* and *shaky-shaky* were about?" The 'Stache's eyes glitter as he grins.

Things still aren't making sense to me. The white space, the bubble...our *lives*, which somehow still exist. "But where *is* everything?"

"Out there somewhere." He waves dismissively at the milky void. "Compressed into a super-dense, super-heated ball of energy. The seed of a *new* universe, in other words."

"Wait, what?" Am I losing my mind here? Did he just tell me... "The universe *ended*?"

He waggles his hand and squints. "More like *reset*. It suddenly contracted..." He jams his hands together. "Now there's a *pause*, like a *breath*. And soon..." He makes a whooshing sound as he pulls his hands apart. "It'll *reboot*."

"Like a *big bang*, you mean?"

He touches the tip of his nose. "Exactamundo. There'll be a shiny new universe in place of the old one. Happens once every 14 billion years or so."

"And what about us?" When I press my hand against the bubble, it feels like a warm rubber balloon. "Why didn't *we* get mashed up with the rest of the old universe?"

"Funny you should ask." The 'Stache takes my hand. "It's been talking to me…"

"The universe."

"Yup. Apparently, it likes my work so much, it wants me to help set up the next version of itself. I mean the next *joke*."

My head is spinning. I'd think he's lost his mind if we weren't floating in a transparent bubble through some kind of white void after witnessing a cosmic apocalypse.

"So that's it then?" A hysterical giggle escapes my lips. "*Our* universe--the one we *knew*, our *home*--is just *gone?*"

"Gone forever." The 'Stache nods.

Again, a crazy giggle escapes me. "*Forever?* Everything we know is gone *forever?*"

"Yeah, and wouldn't ya know it?" The 'Stache laughs and shakes his head. "*Now* I'm hungry for *Chinese* all of a sudden!"

I think about it, chewing a fingernail. More giggles slip out.

"What is it?" asks The 'Stache. "What's so funny?"

I laugh a little harder now. "All those times I killed myself for comedy…and now here I am, a last survivor while everyone else is dead."

The 'Stache nods. "It's ironic, all right."

I keep laughing. "And you know what *really* cracks me up? I can't figure out whether the joke's on *them*, the people who are *gone*…or on *me*."

"Then everything's as it should be, Double-J. Remember the Groucho Marx Effect from physics: *A universe simple enough to be understood is too simple to produce a mind capable of understanding it.*

"Or as Groucho himself put it…" The 'Stache flicks an invisible cigar and waggles his eyebrows. "'I wouldn't want to belong to any club that would have me as a member!'"

A MATTER OF SIZE

They show it in slow motion three times from three different angles. The woman's bare foot plunging down through the frame, nails painted cherry red. Super-hero Flyspeck, the bug wonder, stuck to a pest strip tacked to the wood floor. The foot dropping closer, ever closer, as Flyspeck struggles to break free.

Lousy porn music jangles in the background, someone noodling on an electric guitar. We can still hear Flyspeck's voice and the rasping of the pest strip as he fights to free himself.

"Nooo! Please noooo!" His drawn-out, distorted squeak is the sound a grown man's voice makes when he shrinks to five inches tall and is played back in slow motion. "*Stoooop!* For the loooove of God, *please stooooop!*"

But the foot ignores him. Stomps down on him with crushing force. And Flyspeck splatters in all directions from under that foot, blood and goo squirting everywhere. No more screaming.

Just an echoing, slow-motion *splat*.

"Turn it off." Dust Mite, chairman of the Small Wonders super-team, stumbles away from the screen, hands cupped over his eyes. "Please just *turn it off.*"

Someone switches off the projector. Someone else turns on the lights.

And we're blinking at each other, eyes adjusting to the brightness. Seven of us sitting around the big oval meeting table in our secret lair, the Mousehole. Each one in a different super-hero costume glittering with colors—electric blue and yellow and orange and green and red. The whole place smelling of coffee and sweat and farts.

"Wow." Tiny Tim shakes his head slowly. Peels off his crimson domino mask and slaps it down on the meeting table. "That makes three of us."

Iota nods and wipes tears from under his purple cowl. "Pinpoint, Germ Warfare, and now Flyspeck. All gone."

"We're targets." Dust Mite's voice trembles. He tugs at the hood of his pale gray body suit. "Every costumed avenger with the power to shrink."

"The Small Wonders are marked men." Little Lord Fauntleroy adjusts the frilly collar rising from under his blue velvet jacket. "What shall we do?"

I blow out my breath and swing my black boots off the table. "You already know the answer to that." I roll to my feet and head for the door of the Mousehole.

"What answer?" says Fauntleroy. "Do tell us, Man-Child."

No more shrinkage. It's as simple as that.

I shake my head as I swagger off down the Las Vegas Strip, surrounded by flashing neon at two in the morning. My black hair and hooded cloak rippling in the hot, dry wind. Black silk mask wrapped around the lower half of my face, keeping out the swirling grit in the air. Looking no weirder, drawing no more attention, than any other freak on the prowl at this hour.

If someone's targeting costumed vigilantes with shrinking-related abilities, you just need to swear off the powers. Stay off the radar a while. No more crimefighting.

Either that, or use your damn powers to take action before you get stepped on. Before your death gets turned into a viral porn video for the legion of nut-sacks craving the ultimate crush-fetish experience: girl meets super-hero, girl *stomps* on super-hero.

Which brings me to myself, Isaac Gideon, the one and only Man-Child. What's *my* next step, given the crisis at hand?

Rattle some cages. That's where I start.

First stop, the Gold Doubloon, off the Vegas Strip...*way* off. One of those antique casinos that huddle in the shadows of the modern-day monstrosities, offering a taste of the Rat Pack era. Also plenty of actual rats.

Case in point, the big man at the ancient craps table across the smoky room. This is his personal sewer.

And he's a walking encyclopedia of criminal activity. He'll have the answers I'm looking for. Some of them, at least.

Meet Mammon. "Look what the cat puked up!" He laughs when he spots me. His huge hippo jowls flutter over the open collar of his tuxedo shirt. "What a disgusting mess!"

There are twelve guys around the craps table, all laughing at Mammon's joke. Twelve of his toughest soldiers.

"'Man-Child.'" Mammon cackles and jiggles in his lemon yellow tuxedo. "What the fuck kind of name is that for a super-zero?"

I walk up, cracking my knuckles. "Someone's making pornos with costumed avengers." I shoulder two goons out of the way and lean my hip against the table. "Against their *will*."

"Oh, dear!" Mammon's eyes widen like saucers of milk. "That's just *terrible*!"

I refuse to be annoyed. "Don't try to tell me you don't know who's doing this."

"If I did, I'd buy him a drink." Mammon chortles and runs his disproportionately skinny fingers over his slicked-back salt-and-pepper hair. "Anyone who does *that* to a super-*zero* is okay in *my* book."

"I need to find him."

"Why? You wanna *volunteer*?" Mammon roars with laughter and rolls the dice on the table. "Wanna be in *pictures*?"

My blood pressure rises. I look around, sizing up the goons and the room, getting ready for a fight. "Tell me what you know."

"Why?" Mammon grins. "What're you gonna do if I *don't*?"

I proceed to kick thirteen asses at once using my gimmick. My power.

One minute, I'm in range of a piledriver punch, heading straight for my face. The next minute, I'm three feet shorter, and the punch flashes past over my head.

One minute, a goon has me in a half-nelson, dead to rights, while another goon aims a kick at my gut. The next minute, I'm little again, sliding out of the half-nelson and dropping fast as one goon's kick lands hard in the other goon's belly.

I shrink from the paths of ball bats and bullets and knives, then grow to my full six feet five and knock down bad guys like ducks at a carnival shooting gallery.

And in the end, when everyone's down and Mammon's the only villain still conscious, I rub it in. I interrogate him in my smaller form, the three-foot-five version. The little boy I become when I use my powers. My seven-year-old self, the other half of my super-hero name, Man-Child.

I want Mammon to remember who held the knife at his throat at this moment.

"Now tell me." I say it in the high-pitched voice of a seven-year-old boy. "What do you know about the porn?"

One clue. One name. That's all Mammon gives me. But it's enough.

I drive through the darkness in my '74 Dodge Dart...my *home*, in other words. If not for the Dart, I'd be sleeping on the street.

Have I mentioned how the recession's been kicking my ass lately? Rewards for good deeds and rounding up wanted criminals have gotten fewer and farther between. On top of that, I lost my day job as a contract custodian. And then my wife, Sheba, left me...though maybe that wasn't such a surprise.

Feels like I'm rolling downhill fast these days. Like the darkness that haunts me is gaining ground. The darkness that drives me to do what I'm doing, whatever the cost.

Because I know what it's like to be forced to do something against your will. To have someone else *violate* you when you're small and defenseless. To have someone bigger than you abuse you for sexual purposes.

Believe me, I know *exactly* what that's like. I've *been* there, I can *never* forget it. And I know that sometimes, you have to ask yourself one question.

If *I* don't go out and find justice, who *else* is going to do it?

No one but me.

I'm the only one standing on the sidewalk in front of the Lucky Penny Laundromat at three in the morning. But the lights are bright inside, and I know he's here.

Stigmata always has a lot of laundry to do, what with the bloody wounds of Christ constantly popping up on his hands, feet, and side. The guy practically lives here, even fences stolen loot and sells weed here.

I don't see him, but I can feel his eyes on me as I walk through the door. The baking desert heat gives way to air-conditioned coolness and the smell of detergent and bleach.

I take three steps and stop by the first row of washing machines. "Stig? I've got a paying job for you." Lying's the only possible way to avoid a problem here. Stigmata's paranoid, delusional, and a first class hater of costumed avengers.

The only sound in the room is the rolling hum of a dryer. The clacking of buttons against the dryer's spinning metal drum.

"Come on, Stig." I take two more steps. "Let's talk, man. Just talk."

Next thing I know, a heavy pair of wet blue jeans whacks me in the head. Takes me totally by surprise, and I turn.

At which point, scrawny Stigmata leaps at me from behind a washing machine. Clamps both bloody hands around my right arm, shooting bolts of searing pain from the open wounds in his palms.

As I scream, he nails me again. One hand on my chest, one hand around my throat, scalding me. Howling with animal rage as he does it.

I'm in shock for precious seconds, and my mind flashes back in time. All of a sudden, in my memory, I'm a child again, in the grip of a monster. I'm back being abused again, helpless at the hands of someone who's taking advantage of me.

My head spins and my heart pounds with horror. It all rushes back in a crushing wave, all the agony from the childhood trauma that feels like it happened only yesterday.

Or last week.

But the feeling doesn't last. I'm a man, no longer helpless, and I'll never surrender. The one thing stronger than the terror of that memory is my determination *never* to let it happen again.

I hurl aside the memory and lunge back to the present. Gathering all my strength, I heave off Stigmata, sending him sprawling over the washing machines.

He quickly springs from the washers and sprints for the door. I take two big strides at full height, then dive headfirst and slide across the floor, transforming to a kid in mid-slide, turning small enough to slip between his legs.

When I shoot out in front of him, I turn grown-up again. Stigmata trips over me and crashes into the closed front door, then slides to the floor. Outside, a young woman with an empty pink laundry basket watches with interest.

"Can I still get my load out of the dryer?" she shouts through the glass.

I let her take all her clothes except two pairs of jeans. I need them to tie up Stigmata.

By the time the woman clears out, I've got Stigmata wrapped up like a turkey, on his belly on top of the washers. Hands and feet trussed up behind him where his wounds can't do me any harm.

"Tell me about the hero porn." I hold up his head by a fistful of long, brown hair. "Who hired you?"

"Your mama, Man-Baby." Stigmata hawks up a loogie.

Before he can spit it at me, I bounce his face off the white metal lid of the washer. "Fucking *tell* me!" I bounce him again for good measure. "I already *know* you were *part* of this."

"With *my* wounds? That'd be some freaky ass porn." Stigmata emits a bubbling snicker through the blood oozing from his broken nose.

"Mammon said they use you as bait." I lift up his head and stare into his bloodshot eyes. He smells like pot and piss. "You lure the costumed avengers with some half-assed criminal escapade. Get them close enough for an ambush by taser."

Again with the bubbling snicker. "You think they did this *why*? To put the good guys in a *porno*?"

"*Snuff* porn. *Crush* porn." I give his skull another bounce. "For pervs who get off on seeing things *crushed*."

This time, Stigmata laughs out loud. "And that's different from you *how* exactly?"

I don't kill him. That's how I'm different. Smartass Stigmata gets to go on stinking up Vegas.

And that's all he needs to know. Why bother explaining to a cockroach why my life is in ruins? Why I can never shake the memories of being victimized?

No matter how hard I try, I can never forget. No matter how many scumbag assholes I beat senseless. No matter how much justice I seize for the victims.

None of it takes away the memories of being attacked. Of being lured to a crime scene and captured when my guard was down...just as I'd transformed into a seven-year-old.

Drugged to the point of helplessness, I was trapped in the body of a child. I was outnumbered, overpowered, pinned down.

Violated.

Just think how that would incinerate your soul. You have the mind of an adult, keenly aware of the full reality of what's happening and what's to come...and the body of a child, unable to break free. It's the kind of nightmare that makes the worst nightmare you can imagine seem like the sweetest dream.

And it's still as fresh in my mind as if it happened last week...because it did.

I can't forget it, no matter how many times I pound Stigmata's head off the washing machine. Even after he's told me what he knows. Even after he's given me a lead in the case.

Did "getting off" *ever* have anything to do with it?

"Yes! Yes! Yeessss!" The woman's voice bursts out at me when I crack the door. Looking in, I catch a glimpse of her naked, gyrating body through the cameras and crew, bathed in light on a vast bed in the middle of the soundstage.

Looks like Stigmata might have sent me to the right place. Or is this just another warehouse turned porn factory?

One of the crew shoos me out, and I close the door behind me. Nothing there I was looking for anyway.

I walk across the hall and try another door. This time, it's girl on girl. On girl.

On girl.

I move on. Reach for another door further down the line. And the second I crack it, I know.

Time freezes as I listen to the distant voice crying for help. Not distant.

Tiny.

I take a breath and hold the door steady. I count to three and decide on a strategy.

And as I push the door the rest of the way open, I let myself melt into my other form. The body of a seven-year-old boy.

With the rage of a thirty-eight-year-old man.

As I charge across the room, the crew is startled. How did this fucking kid get in here? Somebody stop him!

I duck and weave as they reach for me. I punch one guy in the balls and knock over a hot spotlight on another.Another guy gets hold of my cloak, but I slip right out of it. Someone lands a kick on my back, but it's half-assed at best. Because here's the real secret of why my power's much more awesome than you might think:

Most grown-ups pull their punches when they're hitting little kids.

So I get to the heart of the soundstage in nothing flat, and there he is: Dust Mite, chairman of the Small Wonders, shrunk to six inches tall, stuck to a pest strip tacked to the floor.

A blonde woman looms over him, wearing a knee-length pink dress. Her feet are bare, her toenails painted cherry red. I recognize her instantly from the movies.

How many costumed avengers have those feet crushed already?

Too many. There are almost too many porn creeps to fight, even for seasoned avengers like us. And Dust Mite isn't exactly a hundred percent at this point.

By the time the brawl's in full swing, I'll bet there're thirty assholes battling us. Seven of them stark raving naked, fresh from the porno sets.

But Dust Mite and I take all comers. Shrinking and growing in rapid succession, blinking big-little-big-little-big. Pitting the clowns against each other by dodging their blows. Then shooting up to full height to finish them off with blows of our own.

Like machetes through sugar cane, we hack them down in clumps, two and three at a time, piling inert husks on the studio floor. Until only three of us remain.

"No, please!" The killer cowers in a corner in her sweaty pink dress and bare feet. "Please don't hurt me!"

"We did it!" Dust Mite throws his arm around my shoulder. "We took 'em down! The Small Wonders are safe once more."

I shrug him off. "We're not done here." Eyes on the barefoot woman, I pound my fist in the palm of my hand. "We need information."

"Please!" She shudders and shrinks away from me as I reach for her. "I'll tell you *anything*! What do you want to *know*?"

Another name. She gives me another name.

I speed across town in my Dodge Dart, running every red light. Not much traffic at five in the morning, which is good.

My heart booms like thunder in my chest. Adrenaline sizzles through me like lightning. Almost there now.

I'm closing in.

What will it be like when I finish this? Can I ever throw aside the past? Will I ever forget what he did to me?

I stomp the accelerator to the floor, and the car rockets down Las Vegas Boulevard. Pedestrians scatter from my headlights like rabbits, haunches flying.

For an instant, I swear I can feel him in the car with me. Watching me. Haunting me like a ghost.

Sometimes, it's still like that. And other times, I can't help but wonder.

Am *I* the one doing the haunting?

Little Lord Fauntleroy shakes his head. "You already know the answer to that question, Man-Child."

I ask it again anyway. "Why did you make the movie?"

We're alone in the Mousehole, where the barefoot porn star sent me. Standing at opposite ends of the big oval table where the Small Wonders hold their meetings. Even from here, I can see the nervous wiggle of his butter-soft fingers.

"You *know* I'd never do *that*." Fauntleroy's laugh is forced. "I'm as *appalled* by those crush films as *you* are."

"Not according to Leila Scintilla." I start walking around the table. The sound of my cracking knuckles echoes through the Mousehole. "Leila says you run the whole operation."

Fauntleroy rolls his eyes. "Who the *fuck* is this *Leila* character?"

I keep walking toward him. Boots scuffing on the floor. Waiting for him to make his move. "Quit fucking around. Tell me why you did it."

Suddenly, Little Lord Fauntleroy drops out of sight. Pulling his usual trick.

The one I've been expecting. Which is why I drop to three-foot-five at exactly the same instant. And I'm waiting for him when he scurries under the table.

"Fuck you!" His voice sounds like a muppet gargling gravel. He looks like he's been stepped on.

Because that's his gimmick. Instead of shrinking proportionately, his body accordions down. He looks like a cartoon coyote who's just waddled out from under a giant anvil, eyes blinking between layers of furry pancake atop two tiny, scuttling feet.

It's a great gimmick for throwing an opponent off his game. Great for getting out of the way of things fast.

But how great is it for fighting? Say, fighting a seven-year-old boy?

He tells me everything by the time I'm done with him. Tells me how he made a small fortune on crush-porn. Tells me how he planned to jump-start his hero career by making himself the last shrinking avenger standing. By cornering the mighty-mite market.

None of which puts an end to the ass-kicking I'm giving him.

"Wait, stop!" Fauntleroy's deformed accordion body flutters on the blood-streaked floor of the Mousehole. "I *told* you why I killed them! I *told* you about the crush-porn movies!"

"I don't *care* about any of that." I haul back my foot for another kick. "I need to know about the *other* movie."

I let the kick fly, and Fauntleroy squeals like a dog's rubber chew toy.

"Tell me!" I lay into him again. "Who made the movie with *the kid?*"

I find her in bed, at home, asleep. A sliver of light from the rising sun sliding up over her from between the drawn curtains.

It doesn't seem possible. That the one I've been hunting all night, all around town, is her.

I sit on the edge of the bed and stroke her silky red hair. Her bright green eyes flicker open, and she sees me.

And she smiles. My wife, Sheba, smiles like nothing's come between us. Like she never walked away from me. She's as beautiful as ever.

I feel sick in the stomach. I never imagined I could feel so much hate for someone I once loved. "How *could* you?" My voice is a whisper.

A little frown creases Sheba's forehead. "I don't understand."

"I know it was you." I keep stroking her hair. This could be a moment from five years ago, or three years or one, me coming back from a late night patrol, her waking up to greet me. "I know everything. Except why."

Sheba sits up. Her face hardens like stone. "I think you should leave, Isaac."

I realize I can't reach her like this. And I'm not willing to beat a confession out of her. I'm afraid that once I start hitting her, I might not stop until she's dead.

So I change. The thirty-eight-year-old melts away, leaving the seven-year-old in his place.

I take off my mask. Tears trickle down my face. The memory of what happened rises up within me, crushing me.

So horrible. Being so small and helpless. Overpowered, unable to fight back.

And this makes it a million times worse. Like being violated all over again.

"*Why*, Sheba?" I can't stop the tears. "Why did you *do* it?"

She stares at me, frozen. She seems to have no intention of making this any easier.

"*Why?*" I grab her hand before she can snatch it away. "Sheba, *why?*"

Does she even have a *clue* how *terrible* it was? Being *brutalized*. *Victimized*. With the camera rolling the whole time.

How could she *do* it? I *need* to know.

"Tell me." I squeeze her hand harder.

Her granite face flickers with emotion. "Isaac..."

She *ordered* it. From Fauntleroy. She *paid* for it.

"For your own good," she says. "I did you a *favor*."

"*A favor?*" I squeeze her hand harder. If I were in my adult form, I would break it.

Sheba squeezes back. "Turning into a little boy all the time...it's *ruined* you. Held you back." She looks away. "You're only *half* a *man*."

My head is spinning. I live it all again, in the spaces between her words.

"You need to *grow up*," says Sheba. "Like a normal human being. Stop playing super-hero. Stop running away."

I remember feeling it happen in gauzy slow motion, through the drugs they gave me. Begging them to stop. The words of an adult in the voice of a child.

Begging.

"No more second childhoods." Sheba wipes a tear from my cheek with her thumb. "Or third or fiftieth or hundredth. Time to go cold turkey. To make you never *want* to be a child again."

As hard as I drove myself to find out who was behind it, I wish I didn't know. And I wish I'd never heard the next words she says to me.

"Did it work, Isaac?" She actually looks hopeful. "Did it work?"

In a way, it *did* work. Because it turns out Sheba was right. I'll hate her forever, she's rotting in prison, but she was right. I *did* need to make a choice.

It was long past time for a change in the status quo. An insurrection to overthrow the spoiled tyrant of my life.

And now that the uprising's finished, now that I've chosen, once and for all, it's really put things into perspective. Answered a lot of questions.

Like what, for instance?

"Super-heroes and villains, or cowboys and Indians? Which do you wanna play next?"

There's a moment I remember. From when I was a kid.

My best friend Billy McVicker and I are running around the back yard of my parents' home in Virginia. Chasing between magnolias over a shimmering carpet of bluegrass in the sunniest corner of summer.

My mother steps out on the back porch with lemonade on a tray. She's a little gray, but still smiling.

I'm smiling, too. Because I'm happy. Utterly, completely happy. Not a care in the world.

And I finally know the answer to Billy McVicker's question.

"Well?" Billy socks me in the arm. "Which one do you wanna play next?"

"Cowboys!" I start running as I say it. "And Indians!"

And I laugh as he chases me, shooting make-believe guns, riding make-believe horses. Both of us laughing to the heights of the cloudless blue sky, hearts pounding like fireworks. Unburdened, unfettered, resilient, strong. Free of the darkness and willing to forget.

Free. As a child.

I remember this moment well. From when I was a kid.

This morning. And now. And forevermore.

AN INFINITE NUMBER OF IDIOTS

n every community on our world, which we call The World, there's a statue of an alien idiot, which we call The Idiot. And once a day, all the people in the world take turns pissing on these statues. We call this *praying*.

As in *praying* that The Idiot and his moron buddies never come back to The World--at least as long as we The People still live here.

That's the kind of impression that The Idiot--otherwise known as Captain Crap--and the crew of the Fartship *Excrement* made when they dropped by on their illustrious visit a while back.

In case you're wondering, yes--the names of The Idiot, his morons, and their ship have been changed to disrespect the indecent. But the rest of the story is true, or my name isn't Foca Zi Za.

And no, I don't normally talk like this, in words you'd understand or expressions for which I have no frame of reference. But I thought I'd switch on the Voice Box translator left behind by Crap so I can be sure I'm getting through to you.

Because I think it's very important that you know what happened with the *Excrement*, that you know the whole story.

Otherwise, it might not make a lot of sense that I'm carving you up like a piece of meat right now.

How *smoodgy* is too *smoodgy?* That's a tough one to answer since there's no good word for *smoodgy* in your language.

But that day, it was just *smoodgy* enough in my part of The World. The skeletal towers were blistering hot under the blazing white suns, the air swirling with crackling driftweeds and dust-demons. The parched ground was cracked and scattered with jagged bone shards and mummifying corpse shreds that gave off a sweet, musty smell. The dry air echoed with the shrieks of the dying in the Death Pits, crying first for mercy and then for release.

Does all this seem perfect and beautiful to you? It did to me that day, as I rolled along on my way to the nearest pit. It was just about as *smoodgy* as you can get, a true *paradise*.

If only the air in front of me hadn't started to sparkle just then.

It was enough to stop my central mass (and the spherical arrangement of thirty multi-articulated arm/legs radiating around it) from spinning. I crashed to a stop in a jumble of bony limbs, barely avoiding the four figures that solidified amid the jumping sparks.

My first thought when I got a good look at them was, *Only two arms and two legs apiece?* But the skins were a shocker, too--pink on three of them and a kind of pale pinkish green on the other. I was so used to The People's bright white skins (with the black blots constantly shifting under the surface in response to our emotional states) that these strange solid colors seemed unnatural.

Then there was the clothing, which at first I thought was part of the visitors' skins. One wore a red top, two wore pale blue, and the one in front wore gold. All of them wore the same color bottoms--plain black. On a world where no one wore clothes of any kind, it made for a very alien-looking group.

When the gold-topped one in the middle started talking, that impression was even stronger. The droning sounds he made with his single-channel voice (why not *triple*-channel like the voices of

The People?) were like *nothing* I'd heard before, and they made no sense.

At least until he held up an oblong black device hanging from a slender black strap around his neck. (Identical to the one I'm wearing now, see?) The device had a silver mesh grate on its face and emitted familiar sounds when he switched it on. "Greetings." Somehow, I was able to understand what he was telling me as if he were speaking my language. "We come in peace."

As I untangled myself and restored my standard spherical configuration, other People gathered to take in this bizarre scene. One of the first to arrive was my mate, Vira Vo, who rolled up and parked at my side.

"Ugly things." The words came softly from her central mass, suspended within her lattice of arm/legs. "Bad feeling."

"Give them a chance," I told her, or words to that effect, even as gold-top droned on.

By then, he'd told us his name and the name of his ship, which weren't "Captain Crap" and "*Excrement*" at all (but let's keep it simple and go with those, they seem more fitting). He said he was on a mission of exploration and wanted only to have a look around. Who could argue with that?

We The People, that's who! *We* should've argued with that right from the *start!* It would've saved us a lot of *trouble* if we'd thrown those bums off The World right then and there instead of trying to be nice and showing them hospitality! We wouldn't have had to listen to more of their *bullshit* or put up with their *meddling.*

And we wouldn't have missed out on so many righteous *slayings* in the *Death Pits,* either. We wouldn't have offended our almighty *gods* by depriving them of numerous *sacrifices.* We wouldn't have to make up for lost time now, offering up a steady stream of people like you. (Yes, *you.* Sacrificing *you* to the gods is the whole point of the carving and the altar and the screams, after all.)

A lot of things would have gone differently if I'd stood up to Crap that day...but no. Instead of driving off the newcomers, I introduced myself and Vira and agreed to act as their guide.

Which makes me think, looking back, that *Captain Crap* wasn't the *only* idiot in this story.

Sightseeing on The World can be a wonderful experience. We've got the bone towers, of course, and the quicksilver fountains...the fuzzcanos and pop-up jungles...the Dung Mountains and the Footprints of Enormity. In the interest of goodwill, we showed Captain Crap and his *Excrement* bunch around these and more, telling them all the stories of how these landmarks and monuments came to be (when we could get a word in edgewise with motormouth Crap always blabbing).

But all *they* cared about were the *shrieks* from the Death Pits! Can you imagine?

What's with all the screaming, Foca?

Where's that screaming coming from, Foca?

It sounds like somebody's screaming for help out there, Foca.

And I just wanted to say, *Where are your manners? You're getting the grand tour! Why can't you shut up and enjoy it?*

But I didn't say that, and neither did any of the other People trailing along after us. Vira did the next best thing, though. Slipping away at the Coughing Cliffs of Hacknonymity, she rolled off fast to the Death Pits and got the clerics there to wrap up the sacrifices for the rest of the day. No more shrieking, problem solved.

Or so we thought.

"And now you know why we call these the Steps of Indignation." As I concluded another tale of one of our landmarks, I saw Vira roll up and give me a signal that all was well. Not for the first time, I thought about how lucky I was to have her as a mate.

"You truly have a magnificent world here." Crap looked around and nodded with a twinkle in his eye. "And a...*quiet*...one, as well. *Now*, at least." He was onto us and letting us know it.

But I didn't care, as long as he and his bunch stopped nagging about the screams. "I'm glad you like it, Captain. Right this way, and I'll lead you to the feast being held in your honor."

"Already?" said the blue-topped male introduced by Crap as Dr. Meh. "You folks sure know how to throw a party together fast."

"Your timing is good," I told him. "This is our holiday season."

At that instant, one last errant shriek escaped the Death Pits. "Some holiday," said Meh.

"There's just one thing." Captain Crap turned to his colleague with the pinkish-green skin and the pale blue top. "Mr. Suck here noticed some anomalous readings from--that way, wasn't it?" Crap pointed in the direction of the Death Pits.

"Correct." Mr. Suck had pointy ears, which suited him because he came across as such a humorless prick. Like Crap and the others, he spoke with the aid of a Voice Box device hanging from a strap around his neck. "The readings indicated violent activity or blood-letting which has since abated." He stared at the screen of a black-shelled device in his hand, then turned his gaze on me. "Was some sort of battle transpiring in the indicated area?"

"No battle," I said, bouncing nervously.

"Perhaps we could see what lies in that direction anyway," suggested Mr. Suck. "There might be someone in need of aid."

"There isn't." I rolled in a little circle. "No doubt you detected the slaughter of an animal to provide fresh meat for the feast."

"But the *high level* of activity suggests otherwise," said Mr. Suck.

"Not to mention the *screaming*," added Dr. Meh.

"Excuse me." I stopped bouncing. "Are any of you *from* here?"

Suck clasped his hands behind his back and stared down his long nose at me. "Obviously, we are not. And yet..."

"Then trust me, we local folk know better than you about a thing or two." I said it firmly to cut off any arguments. "Now who wants to go to the big celebratory feast?"

Crap raised his hand. "That sounds like a marvelous idea...just as soon as we've had a closer look at wherever that screaming was coming from."

"Perfect!" I spun around and bounced, and many of The People in the entourage did the same. "Feast it is! Right this way, my friends!"

With that, I, Vira, and the others led Crap and his companions away from the Death Pits and headed for the feasting place in the heart of the bleached, baking bone towers.

Let me just say, you haven't lived until you've been to a feast on The World. We really pull out all the stops--dried tumblepups, sands-quito salad, rockhog marrow, headwing fritters, bonegoat marrow. And to top it all off, the very best aged elixirs of mudblood and mite sweats.

But I guess you'll never know what it's like; too bad. Even if you were invited, you couldn't enjoy the experience anymore, not with so many parts of you missing.

But I hope you won't let the bad news get you down. After all, your sacrifice helps keep the gods happy, which keeps The World turning, the suns blazing, and the bones dry and crisp.

Without you and those like you, our little paradise might all fall apart, and The People would have to give up their joy. I think that's worth screaming in pain and missing out on a few feasts, don't you?

How would you like it if you threw a party, and the guests of honor wouldn't eat anything? (All because Dr. Meh claimed it was poiso-nous to their systems!) Then, on top of that, one of the guests kept *coming on* to your *mate!*

That's how the big feast for the *Excrement* group went. Every time I turned around, Crap had Vira cornered and was saying things like, "Do you believe in *quantum entanglement?*" and "I have so many *questions* about your *biology*." The complete lack of physical compati-bility between them didn't put him off at all; he kept leaning in closer and closer, brushing his fingers over her arm/legs and making suggestive comments about her bones and central mass.

I was so busy watching out for Vira, I didn't notice that the number of *Excrement* guests got smaller as the feast went on...at least until it was too late.

We reached *that* point long after the suns had gone down, just as the swear dance was starting up. I was explaining the symbolism behind the intricate obscene gestures in the dance to Dr. Meh when suddenly the air filled with a piercing shriek...a piercing *Excrement* person's shriek.

It was enough to finally tear Crap's attention away from Vira.

When the shriek erupted, he stopped flirting with her and leaped into action, looking around for the other members of his party.

"Where's Mr. Suck?" Crap's voice was all business. "And Security Officer Dork?"

"No idea, Captain," said Meh. "I didn't see Suck that long ago, though."

Crap grabbed a small silver device that was clipped to his belt and flipped open the cover. The device warbled, and Crap spoke into it. "Mr. Suck? Officer Dork? Please respond."

Crap waited a moment, but there was only silence from the device--and then another scream from afar.

Crap whirled and stormed over to confront me. "All right, Foca. Take me to my people, *now.*"

"They should all be *right here,*" I told him. "At the feast being held in their *honor,* not roaming around our private sacred places *unaccompanied.*"

Another scream cut through the blistering hot night. "That's one of my people!" said Crap. "Does it *sound* like he's at the party right now?"

"Perhaps he's just having *a really good time?*" I suggested.

The next scream was louder and more agonized than the rest. Crap leaned closer and narrowed his eyes. "Take me to them *now,* Foca. I'm out of *patience.*"

I hesitated. The truth is, I knew the screams were coming from the Death Pits--and I also knew nothing should be happening there since Vira had put a stop to it earlier. So I had a bad feeling about the whole thing and didn't want Crap anywhere near those pits.

Unfortunately, someone else got *that* ball rolling. "I've got a fix on their life signs." Meh was staring at the glowing screen of the boxy black device in his hands. "Thataway." Meh jabbed a finger toward the Death Pits.

"Let's go!" Crap ran from the feasting plaza with Meh in his wake.

I just wanted the whole mess to go away but fell in behind them with Vira just the same. As we charged among the bone towers, and the shrieking grew louder, I racked my brain but could think of no good plan to resolve the situation in The People's favor.

Would you say the Death Pits are a dump? Or is it more of a cultural thing?

Everything's relative, right? What looks like a dump to you and your people looks like a *showplace* to me and mine.

When I see these vast pits bubbling with red-and-green sludge, each rimmed with spiked bone altars under chandeliers of mummified central masses and tendons, my heartlike organs skip three beats apiece. As I gaze around at the spinal domes and the pale, waxen walls carved into relief sculptures of clerics slashing sacrifices and dumping their corpses into the pits, I feel uplifted.

But *you* don't get it, do you? It's all a horror show to people like you, an abomination against everything you believe.

You primitives just refuse to see the *bright side* of agony, death, and decomposition in the name of remorseless gods who demand unending sacrifice to satisfy their monstrous hungers.

To make matters worse, you don't understand how to show proper respect when walking in on the sacred sacrifice of your lucky, screaming friends. I witnessed this bad behavior firsthand on that fateful day when Crap and Meh barged into the Temple of the Death Pits.

There are many great reasons for calling Captain Crap an idiot. One of those is his habit of shooting first and asking questions later (or never).

For example, as soon as he ran into the Temple of the Death Pits, following the signal from Meh's device, Crap drew the hand-held weapon from his belt and started shooting.

Bright yellow beams flashed from the tip of the gun, lancing across the temple toward a cleric on the far side of an enormous, bubbling pit. The beams missed, and the cleric went on with what he was doing, which was methodically slicing somebody up on a spiny altar slab.

"Get your hands off him!" Crap let loose another series of

beams while running full-tilt around the rim of the pit. "Stop what you're doing!"

But the cleric continued to ignore him. He pulled a dripping green heart from the sacrifice's chest and raised it overhead, chanting a prayer with his eyes pinched shut.

"I said stop!" Crap sounded almost hysterical as he continued to run and fire, run and fire.

Though I didn't run, I did call out from across the rim. "Cleric Oodwa! Please halt the ritual!"

Oodwa's answer was to toss the green heart over the altar into the Death Pit, where it dissolved with a wisp of pale steam. Then, just as Crap was closing in, he pulled a lever on the altar, tipping the slab on its side and sending the heartless body splashing into the muck.

Even as Crap tackled him to the ground and pummeled him with blows from his fists, I said a secret prayer to the gods, begging them to bring good things to The People of The World. Why waste a good sacrifice, even if it *was* unscheduled?

"Dear God." Was Meh praying, too? "You people just *murdered* Mr. Suck."

"'Murder' is a strong word," I said.

"I hated his guts, but he didn't deserve *that*," said Meh.

"Don't worry," I told him. "He's not gone."

"What's *wrong* with you?" Meh glared at me. "Did you not just watch him *dissolve* in that corrosive pit?"

"I'm telling you, he's still with us," I said.

Meh waved me off. "You know what you can do with that spiritual mumbo-jumbo, don't you, son?"

Meanwhile, across the pit where Suck had been dumped, Crap was shaking Cleric Oodwa so hard, the black blots in his bone-white skin were scattering. "You *maniac!* That man was my *best friend!*"

"What about Officer Dork?" Meh shot another glare in my direction. "What have you done with *him?*"

"How should *I* know? I've been at the feast all evening!"

"Where *is* he?" Crap gave Oodwa the roughest shake yet. "Where is my *security officer?*"

"He is closer than you might think." As always, Oodwa's voice was serene. "He has not left us."

"*I* have a question for *you*, Captain Crap," snapped Vira. "What were your people doing *here* to begin with? This place is *off limits* to outsiders."

Suddenly, a deep, familiar voice resounded through the temple. "Perhaps *I* can provide the answers to your questions. "

Everyone turned at once to look toward that voice. A solitary figure in a blue shirt and black pants emerged from an arched doorway across the temple.

"Mr. Suck!" Captain Crap leaped to his feet, letting Oodwa fall to the ground.

"You're *alive!*" shouted Meh.

"Told you so," I said.

"Indeed." Suck nodded. "I commend you all for your keen powers of observation."

Meh rolled his eyes. "That's him, all right."

"But how?" Crap sounded suspicious. "How did you come back to life?"

"Quite simply, I did not," said Suck.

"But you're standing right there!" said Meh.

"The point is, I was *never dead*," said Suck.

"But we saw your heart torn out and your body dumped in *there!*" Crap pointed at the Death Pit.

"That body was *cloned*," said Suck. "As was Officer Dork's. Apparently, *his* clone was disposed of before you arrived."

"Cloned?" Crap shot a look my way. "You people sacrifice *clones*?"

"We don't speak of this with outsiders," Vira said before I could answer. "The secret, manifold rituals are reserved for The People alone."

"Then why the *hell* did you clone and sacrifice *our* people?" barked Meh.

"We can't tell you that," I said, "because we don't *know* what happened." That was only partly true. Actually, I thought I could make a pretty good guess about it.

"We were investigating the screams and violent activity I'd detected earlier," explained Suck. "When we entered this place, however, we were quickly apprehended and subdued."

Another voice spoke up then, from another doorway not far from Suck's. "We fought back, but they overpowered us." The man in the red top stepped out, looking most definitely not dead.

"Officer Dork!" Crap sounded thrilled. "*You're* alive, too!"

"Glad to be here, sir." Dork smiled. "Though I could've done without the roughhousing from that guy and his buddies." He pointed at Cleric Oodwa, who was still sprawled on the ground. "They tied us both up and threw us into some kind of electrified booths. The next thing we knew, we had *identical twins.*"

"Clones," corrected Suck. "Which were promptly led away by the cleric. Officer Dork and I struggled to break free and pursue them, but breaking out of the booths took longer than we expected."

"The booth walls were stronger than they looked." Dork raised a clenched fist. "But I got a burst of adrenaline once I heard my own voice *screaming* in *pain.* The voice of my *clone*, I mean."

"They grew adult clones *that fast?"* said Meh.

"These people are *remarkably* adept at the cloning process," said Suck. "I am at a loss to explain how they were able to generate full-grown clones of us in such a short time."

"Which they then proceeded to carve up and dump in a pit of corrosive sludge." Meh sounded disgusted. "Why bother?"

Suck looked my way. "Correct me if I'm wrong, but I surmise *cloning* is the primary means of *reproduction* in this society."

Meh turned and ran his device over me, tweaking controls and watching the glowing screen. "Wrong, Suck. Near as I can tell, this fella has a perfectly functioning reproductive system with all the right parts for a male of his species. No need for clones for the purpose of procreation."

"Perhaps the people of this planet prefer a higher degree of control over expressed characteristics," said Suck. "Perhaps they prefer a specific assortment of forms that have proved to be most durable and beneficial in the past."

"Is that so?" Meh scowled at me. "Then what about all the *screaming* we've heard since we *arrived* on this planet? I assume that's been coming from sacrificial *clones*?"

"It has," I told him.

"So why *sacrifice* these clones if they're so damn *beneficial*?" asked Meh.

"Why not?" Crap walked back over to stare down at Oodwa. "If they can make an unlimited number of copies, they can *afford* to use a few to keep the gods happy. Am I right?"

Cleric Oodwa shivered and said nothing.

"When life is *cheap*, it's *easy* to throw it away." Crap spun on his heel and glared over the pit at me and Vira. "But *mercy* is the truest mark of an advanced civilization. The greatest cloning technology in the *galaxy* isn't worth a damn if you're incapable of showing *mercy*. *Especially* to *guests* who go astray."

"Why *did* you people sacrifice clones of *our* people?" asked Meh.

"You'll have to ask the clerics that one," I told him. "Though I *can* say they can be--*overzealous*--at times."

"Well, I hope those particular sacrifices were enough to hold your gods *over*," said Crap. "Because the bloodbath is going to *stop.*"

"Correct," I said. "The Death Pits are closed for the night, and no sacrifices will be conducted until tomorrow at--"

"That's not what I meant." Crap strolled over and stood face-to-mass with me, eyes narrowed and jaw set. "What I'm saying is, all further sacrifice of sentient beings on this planet--cloned or other-wise--will hereby *cease*, effective *immediately.*"

The Idiot never got it. Even as he stood with his companions before The People the next morning under the blistering white-hot suns and gave a dramatic speech (in the halting, affected cadence I'd come to expect--and despise--from him) about the virtues of not killing clones, I could tell he didn't understand.

"For what better measure of a man can there be...than how he treats his fellow beings?" Crap cast his steely, self-righteous gaze over the crowd, pausing as if he expected applause. It didn't come, and he continued. "And how can we, and you, in good conscience...reach out to other species in friendship...if we cannot respect and preserve *our own?*"

As I watched from the front of the audience, I had the distinct feeling he wasn't really giving the speech for *our* benefit. It seemed to me the performance was more about *him* and *his people* than *us*. As if he were stroking his own colossal ego or trying to justify what they were about to do to us...or both.

Whatever the reason for it, his words meant nothing to me or any of us. We just listened politely because the only way to get this all over with was to let the big blowhard have his say.

"We, and those like us, are committed to the advancement of *all* lifeforms...throughout the universe." Crap nodded proudly. "We are pledged not to intervene...in the natural course of development of other species. But wanton *slaughter* in the performance of sacrificial *rites* is surely not *natural*. It cannot be considered *civilized* behavior...or the actions of a species worthy of joining the interstellar community. Therefore, I am doing you a very great *favor.*"

"You mean you're finally going to shut up?" whispered Vira, just for me.

I couldn't help laughing to myself.

Crap spread his arms wide as if to take in all of us. "I am going to *free you* from your old, barbaric ways. I am going to *free you* from the curses of *cloning* and *blood sacrifice*...in the name of a *brighter* and *more enlightened* tomorrow!"

Again, he seemed to be waiting for applause that never came.

"Dr. Meh and Mr. Suck assure me your species will be able to continue to procreate via natural, biological means. You don't *need* cloning to survive...but *ending* the practice will restore the balance of genetic diversity among you. And ending the self-destructive brutality of blood sacrifice...will restore the balance of compassion in your *souls.*"

With that, he plucked the silver communication device from his belt, flipped it open, and raised it to his lips. "And now, I give you back your *freedom*...your *dignity*...and, yes, I will even say your *human-*

ity. For though our peoples come from worlds apart, we are not so *different* as you might imagine."

He gave a signal over the device then, and the bombardment began. Colossal twin beams of golden energy blazed down from the sky, screaming from the guns of the orbiting Fartship *Excrement* into the district of the Death Pits behind Crap.

"Your brave new world starts here and now!" Crap shouted over the noise of the energy beams. "When *these* pits are demolished, our ship will move on to destroy *all* such sites around this planet."

The ground rumbled and shook. Dust and smoke filled the air as the bone and rock walls of the temple collapsed, burying the cloning pods and the vast vats of corrosive sludge.

Just like that, our way of life disappeared. Centuries of faith and tradition were buried in minutes.

All because of one Idiot who was convinced he knew what was best for People he'd only met a few days ago. An Idiot who had the power to change The World on a stupid whim.

And he never *did* get it.

Not that we bothered trying to make him understand after that. He and his people stayed on The World much too long for our liking, trying to guide us in changing our ways after the loss of the Death Pits. We just wanted the lot of them gone, so we told them what we thought they wanted to hear--how we'd all seen the light and were grateful and ready to make our world a better and more civilized place.

When it seemed like they might *never* leave, we even put up *statues* of The Idiot in every community around The World, supposedly paying tribute to his greatness. We didn't even *piss* on them at first.

Eventually, they *finally* said goodbye. They thanked us for our hospitality, congratulated us on the progress we'd made, and the air sparkled around them. They were gone...and still, I knew they didn't *get it.*

They didn't understand that the Death Pits weren't that easy to get rid of. With enough determination, we could dig them up and rebuild the temples around them.

They also didn't understand that the cloning had *nothing* to do with reproduction. That had just been Mr. Suck's theory, with no basis of any kind in our reality.

For The People, cloning is *all* about sacrifice...and *punishment*. Making the lives of those who offend us miserable. Bringing the people we hate back to life again and again and making them *suffer*.

In other words, *hurting* people like *you*.

Can you still hear me? Hello?

Oh, good. Your one remaining eye just opened. I'm so glad somebody's still paying attention in there, because I'm not quite done yet, my friend.

You finally get it, don't you? There's a *reason* I've been carving you up like this, on the bone altar in the newly restored Temple of the Death Pits, sacrificing you to the gods of The World in the name of The People who love and fear them.

It's because you look just like *him*--Captain Crap, The Idiot who came on to our mates (Vira and *so* many others in the time before he left)...who lectured us as if we were children...tore down our most beloved institution...and jeopardized our favored status with the gods by denying them sacrifices for so very many weeks. It's because there's nothing more satisfying than cutting up his identical clone and dumping the body in the pit to dissolve into steaming goo.

And then doing it *again and again and again*.

You see those others lined up over there? The ones who look just like *you* and just like *him?* They're *next*. They're waiting for me to finish with you, waiting to be led by the clerics to the altar for their turn under the knife.

And there will be plenty *more* where they came from. An *infinite* number of *Idiots*, born in the clone pods, dying in the name of the very gods who were once scorned by your predecessor, the template for your line.

And if we ever get bored with *you*, we can churn out clones of the rest of Crap's motley landing party. We'll *never* run out of Craps and Sucks and Mehs and Dorks to kill. We collected *plenty* of genetic material from them before they finally left to spread their nonsense elsewhere in the unsuspecting galaxy.

Oh, hush now. Enough with the ear-splitting shrieks. I mean, you've got to appreciate a little poetic justice, don't you? And you've got to admit, there's a lot of *black humor* in the situation.

Shhh. Settle down now. I'm finally done. I think it's safe to say you finally understand.

It's time for your bath in the pit, but I wouldn't worry. I've heard it doesn't hurt all that much as it melts your flesh and bones into bubbling sludge.

Or if it does, it won't last long. Though everything's relative, as your ancestor learned during his time on The World. One man's murder is another man's sacrament.

Perhaps, from your point of view, it will seem to last an eternity.

AND THE UNICORN YOU RODE IN ON

As the faerie warrior on my back (aka "the big doofus") rides past another warning sign under the blazing sun without turning back or at least commenting, I shake my single-horned head in dismay. Though of course I expected no better of him.

After all, the dope still doesn't know how to read...which makes it all the more ironic that his name is *Ballad*. I don't think he knows what a ballad *is*, even in an abstract sense.

He's just lucky that *I* can read, as all unicorns can, or he would have been dead long ago. I can't *tell* you how many times I've kept him from riding right past signs that say *Apache Territory* or *Beware of Quicksand* or *Danger: Cliff Ahead*.

But I let him keep riding today, because he's taking me where I want to go. So what if the rickety signs along the desert pass say things like "NO FAIRYS!" or "POINTY EARS NOT WUNTED HEAR" or "FAIRY CRITTERS WILL BE SHOTT ON SITE."

The town of Desperation, Arizona isn't exactly rolling out the welcome mat for us. It makes me wonder just how much trouble good old Tinsel, his quarry, got up to in these parts.

And if she isn't here anymore, where exactly did that pain in the ass go? Are we going to end up tracking her for *another* six months?

"I reckon we're almost there, Gossamer." Ballad speaks in the accent recognized hereabouts as a high-class British accent...which is actually the same thing as a low-class *Faerie* accent. Just don't expect his grammar to be anywhere near proper. "Where there's boards sticking out of the ground, there's people."

I could tell him a thing or two about what those "boards" say, but what would be the use? I learned long ago that trying to reason with this doofus is like trying to reason with a buffalo's bowel movement. (Though buffalos themselves can be *quite* reasonable, I have found.)

Not that that's the only reason I won't talk to him. Let's just say, I have my reasons.

That doesn't stop him from trying to get me to speak, though. He seems to think he can draw me out of my shell with the right comment or question, as if I could ever forget the awful thing he did to me and go back to chatting away like we did in the old days.

"I have a good feeling, don't you?" Ballad's pale skin flares in the bright sunlight as he tips back his floppy white Stetson hat. "I think things will go better than last time."

I don't remind him that he said the same thing last time, too. I just keep plodding along between the walls of the towering mesas, breathing in dust and wishing I could shut him up with my horn.

But as annoying as he is, going it alone isn't an option for me...not yet, at least. Not when I'm still following a rugged trail through the settlements of men who are more likely to try to steal or kill me than help me.

When we finally emerge from the pass, I spy a tumbledown town in the distance. Through the heat mirage ripples, I glimpse another sign, bigger than the rest—and vandalized.

This one, Ballad takes an interest in. "Does that say 'Desperation' over there?"

I give my head a shake that could mean just about anything and keep walking. The truth is, a new name is scrawled in red over the word "Desperation." I wonder why the locals haven't gotten around to correcting it yet.

At least it confirms she was here, as if there was any damn

doubt. At least I know we're heading in the right direction...for *his* quarry, who ought to lead me to *mine*.

Tinsel's Town. That's what the sign says. *Population: ~~75~~ Sorry-Ass.*

The last sign was right. The people of Desperation do indeed look sorry-ass in every way.

They shuffle back and forth, dressed in rags, as I tromp through the center of town. The men, women, and children are all stooped and haggard, not even looking up as we approach. I guess I didn't need to retract my horn at the edge of town after all, for all the attention we get. (You *do* know we unicorns can retract our horns, don't you? Now if only Ballad could retract his pointy *ears*—though the floppy hat he wears covers them pretty well most of the time.)

The term "sorry-ass" applies equally well to the buildings we pass. Windows are smashed, doors are broken, walls are collapsed. The saloon is scorched all around, its piano upside-down in the middle of the street. The front of the bank has been blown open from within, and dollar bills still flutter through the gap like butterflies taking wing. Nobody tries to grab them.

But the worst thing, by far, is the church at the end of the street. My heart stops when I see the body of a horse impaled on its spiked steeple—but I quickly realize it's chestnut brown, and my heart starts beating again.

That horse is not the one I've come all this way to find.

Not that Ballad has any idea that I'm on my own quest. As far as he knows, I'm just the jet black one-horned horse that he's riding on his way to find the bandit queen who done him wrong.

"My sister is here, Gossamer." Ballad inhales deeply, patting his chest through his white leather vest and red shirt. "We finally caught up with her, amigo."

My name isn't Gossamer, but I don't bother to correct him. I don't correct him about Tinsel's location, either. If she were still in Desperation, the locals wouldn't have put up signs warning off anyone like her. Obviously, she's been to town and moved on—though her departure was pretty recent, from the looks of things.

"I can sense the *fei croí*, can't you?" Ballad takes another deep breath and lets it out slowly.

I just keep plodding along, my hooves scuffing in the dust. Does the doofus really sense anything other than his own flatulence? I know *I* don't.

Correction. Suddenly, I sense hostility dead ahead.

Two ragged locals—a middle-aged man with his left arm in a sling and a young man hobbling on a rickety crutch—hurry out of the sheriff's office to meet us. The older man wears a gold star pinned to his ratty brown vest, while the younger man wears a silver star on his bloodstained plaid shirt.

"Help you with something?" The gold-starred man winces as he squares his shoulders. "Name's Joe. Sheriff Joe Malone. This here's my deputy, Roy Dabbs."

"Maybe you *can* help me, Sheriff," says Ballad. "I'm looking for the girl who wrecked your town."

Joe and Roy exchange a look. The temperature seems to go down a few notches in their immediate vicinity.

"Who's askin'?" Joe keeps his hand on the butt of the six-shooter in the holster on his hip.

"Excuse my bad manners, Sheriff Joe." Ballad bows in the saddle, touching the brim of his hat. "My name is Ballad. This..." He pats my neck. "...is Gossamer."

"And what's your business with the girl?" asks the Sheriff.

"The *queen bitch* is more like it," mutters Roy.

"It's quite simple, gentlemen," says Ballad. "She took something that doesn't belong to her. I aim to return it to the rightful owner."

"For a fee, I reckon," says Joe.

"For *honor*." Ballad sits up straighter when he says it. "And because it's the right thing to do."

"Might as well kiss that money goodbye," says Roy. "Kiss your *ass* goodbye, too, if you try takin' something from *that* bitch."

"She's my *sister*, not some *bitch*, and I'll *handle* her, don't worry," says Ballad. "Now, if you'll just tell me which way she went when she left town..."

"We'd be signin' your death warrant." The cords in Joe's neck shift as he considers the situation. "I've got a better idea. Why don't you let us buy you a drink, and we'll talk this over?"

"Splendid idea, my new best friend." Ballad swings his leg over my back and hops out of the saddle. "Does your local establishment stock a good *mead?*"

"Oh, absolutely." Joe gestures toward the burned-out saloon. "Right this way."

"I'll get your horse." Roy moves toward me, reaching for the reins.

Before he can get a grip on them, I turn and trot off down the street.

"Hey!" Roy starts to follow. "He's boltin'!"

"Don't worry about him," says Ballad. "He'll be fine. Now let's have a spot of that mead and talk about my sister, Tinsel, shall we?"

As Ballad strolls off with the sheriff and deputy, I head for the rundown stable across the street. *This* is the kind of place where I prefer to do *my* fact-finding.

Having said that, it's on the underpopulated side. The fence facing the street is broken open; a scrawny goat and overblown hog remain inside the pen, so dispirited they haven't bothered to escape yet.

"Hello, friends." I ease up to the gap in the fence but don't step inside. The enclosure looks and smells like it hasn't been mucked out in days. "Do you mind if I ask you a few questions?"

The goat looks at me with rheumy gray eyes. "Is she still out th-there?"

I cock my head to one side. "She who?"

The goat's voice drops to a whisper. "The d-demon lady. The madwoman."

He's answered one of my questions before I even asked it. "The one with the silver hair and pointed ears, you mean? The one they call Tinsel?"

Suddenly, the hog oinks and gnashes her teeth. "What you got, blackie? What you got in them saddlebags to eat?"

I ignore her. "Silver hair and pointed ears?" I ask the goat.

The goat nods his head and dribbles out a shit in reply. "You seen her? Where *is* she?" He pads up to the fence and furtively glances left and right. "D-don't let her *g-get* me, *please*."

Growing bolder, the hog wobbles up beside him, staring at me. "I wonder how *you* might taste, blackie. There's some good-lookin' cuts a' *meat* on them *haunches* a' yours."

Glaring, I pop my horn from its sheath along my spine, then slash it at the hog with a fierce twist of my muscular neck. Squealing, she scrambles away and flops down in the rancid muck on her side.

"*One warning*, pig!" I lean in further and give the air another wicked slash with my horn. "Now tell me what you know!"

The hog's eyes are wide with terror. Her hooves peddle hopelessly at thin air. "*You're* a demon, too! A *horse* demon!"

"But you're no m-match for *her*," stammers the goat. "That poor horse on the ch-church steeple? Used to b-be the toughest stallion in town! B-but he thought he could run off with that magic m-mare of hers..."

"Mare?" My heart races at the mention of the word.

"A p-palomino." The goat shivers. "A *special* horse, one of a k-kind. Real sweetheart, unlike her m-mistress. She got away, too, bless her soul."

"But the demon witch chased after her." The hog lurches to her feet and backs away to what she thinks is a safe distance from my horn. "Is *that* what you're after, blackie? The witch's property? Then I'll tell ya which way she went! I reckon I'll taste that *horseflesh* a' yours soon enough and pick my teeth with that *poker* on your head when I'm done."

Without a word, I lunge all the way into the pen, pinning the hog in the far corner of what's left of the fence. With two deft slashes, I draw blood, cutting a shallow symbol in her side.

It's an "X," the first letter of my real name.

"Now *tell* me. Which way did the demon lady chase the palomino mare?" I nudge the point of my horn toward the hog's throat. "Or the *next* cut I make will be the *last*."

The hog squeaks and shrinks from my horn. I hover there, reinforcing the lesson.

"All right, all right!" The hog turns her head and jabs her snout at the church end of town. "That way! They ran up into the mountains! I heard the demon lady say she was gonna run that mare down and make her rue the day she tried to escape!"

"She's r-really gone?" The goat breathes a sigh of relief. "Oh thank h-heaven!"

"You're sure that's all you remember?" I touch the tip of my horn to the flabby flesh of the hog's throat.

"That's all, I swear!" says the hog, and then she's reduced to a round of pitiful squeals.

That's when I hear Ballad shout, followed by gunfire. Without another word, I whip around and charge off in his direction.

Right away, I spot the root of the problem. Ballad's hat is off, his pointy ears exposed for all to see.

That in itself is enough to get him lynched in Tinsel Town. It's no surprise the big doofus is surrounded by angry townsfolk (who've managed to pep up quite a bit all of a sudden, I must say).

As usual, Ballad is confronting the danger bare-handed...and not exactly shining in the process. Though the sheriff has one arm in a sling, and the deputy is hobbling on a crutch, they're still doing a pretty good job of not letting him take a revolver away from them.

Meaning it's up to me to pull the poor excuse for a faerie warrior's fat out of the fire. *Again.*

Back in the pen, the hog squeals for attention, but no one's listening. I take a deep breath, paw the ground with my hoof, then make for the mob with my head low and horn extended.

The crowd scatters when I gallop toward them. I don't have to skewer a single one of them...yet.

But Malone and Dabbs are oblivious, grappling for the gun. Dabbs hauls off and kicks Ballad in the shin, Malone head-butts him square in the face, but Ballad doesn't falter.

He doesn't gain the upper hand, either, though...and time's a-wasting. Every second we linger here puts the palomino further out of reach.

No more pissing around. As soon as the deputy's ass moves into range, I jab his left butt cheek with my horn—just hard enough to get his attention.

Dabbs howls and lets go of the gun to grab his ass. Ballad, now wrestling one man instead of two, is able to decisively seize the weapon and knock down Malone.

At which point, Ballad lets out a howl of his own. Creature of Faerie that he is, iron objects like the revolver burn his flesh to the touch.

With a cry of pain and effort, Ballad hurls the gun as far as he can—which, in this case, is the middle of the animal pen. The starved goat and pig converge on it fast, investigating to see how edible it might be.

Ballad scoops his hat off the ground, then grabs the horn of my saddle and swings himself onto my back. Without waiting for any kind of signal, I take off down the street at a hard gallop, aiming for the ashen humps of the mountains that swell beyond the church with its horse-laden spire.

"Maybe we should return to Desperation and try to clear up the misunderstanding, Gossamer."

That's what the big doofus says as we follow a bumpy trail into the foothills overlooking town. It might be the dumbest idea he's had lately (which is really saying something), and of course I don't dignify it with an answer.

"Those fellows back there seemed to dislike *faeries*," says Ballad. "Can you *imagine?*"

I bob my head, remembering the warning signs on the ride into town.

"They'll sing a different tune when the *fei croí* restores the Bright Realm on Earth." Ballad lets out a sigh of contentment. "It'll be just like the good old days, when the *First* Bright Realm held sway in the lands of men."

I can't help but roll my eyes. I wish I could say I've forgotten how many times he's blathered on about the damn First Realm...but I know with perfect certainty that this will be number five thousand, three hundred, and twenty-one.

"When the Bright Realm is reborn, this desert will become a verdant garden, giving up its sands for lakes and forests." His voice is wistful, just like every other time he's spewed the same manure. "The air will be filled with music and the mingled perfumes of a multitude of fragrant bowers."

Blah blah blah. I ignore every word of it, though I guess I shouldn't complain. Dwelling on his little fantasy of paradise regained keeps his stunted mind from rolling around to what he really *should* be pondering right now.

Which is where the hell I'm taking him, because *he* sure isn't doing the steering.

"All sweet creatures of the Faerie kingdoms will return with grace and benevolence. The singing, dancing, feasting, and wooing will never end. Every day will be glorious and overflowing with wonders, for the *fei croí*—the fabled *heart of Faerie*—beats once more in the world, bringing magic back to every facet of existence."

Sometimes I think I should feel sorry for the big doofus. The restoration of the Bright Realm on Earth is a pipe dream. The stolen *fei croí* is just a big gemstone whose only power is monetary; the East Coast faeries planned to cash it in for a stake in the railroad before Tinsel snatched it up and went on the run.

But when I remember what he's done and why I won't talk to him, I can't dredge up the slightest bit of sympathy. Let the delusions continue, as long as I get what I came here for.

"And all the elves and dwarves and gnomes will leap for joy," continues Ballad. "And every kind of man and woman will leave their tributes at the feet of the Faerie royalty, chanting songs of love and worship. I, as a prince of the Bright Court, will bless them as I see fit, bestowing indulgences acknowledged as most fine and fair in every corner of the glittering kingdom. *Ballad is a beneficent lord,* they will say, and then all the beasts of the field and birds of the air and fish of the sea will join together in praise and..."

Blah blah blah.

At least the sunset shuts him up.

Following the winding trail up the side of a mountain, I pause for a breath, and there it is. Above the horizon, the sky flares redder than a horseshoe fresh from the blacksmith's fire. A layer of bright gold blazes above it, casting iridescent streamers over the landscape and town far below.

It makes me think of the happiest time of my life, before this sorry-ass journey got underway. It brings to mind white, feathery wings tinged with rose and golden light, folding and unfolding against a multicolored sky. It makes me dream of the end of the journey and seeing those white wings again, feeling the breeze of their comforting sway.

For once, Ballad doesn't say a word or spoil it. The two of us just take in the view, enjoying a moment of perfect beauty and peace.

Then, all hell breaks loose.

A flaming arrow cuts through the air, barely missing my horn. I turn to find its source, only to see a flurry of fiery arrows launching toward us from further up the mountain.

Ballad ducks down in the saddle and I move, galloping for a twist in the trail that will put a fall of boulders between us and the enemy. I barely make shelter as another spray of arrows hisses down behind us, narrowly missing my rump.

"Tinsel!" bellows Ballad. "Surrender while you still can!"

Yet another volley of flaming arrows sizzles down around us in reply.

So now we're in a tricky spot. Thanks to his iron allergy, Ballad is unable to handle guns, swords, arrows, or other weapons with iron or steel components—just about anything that might let him fight back from a distance. The cover we've found is our only advantage.

Then our attackers start chipping away at that, too. Instead of firing more arrows, they roll rocks down the mountainside, sending them careening into the boulders.

"I know you can hear me, Sister!" yells Ballad. "Surrender the *fei croí*, and I'll recommend *leniency* to the Council of Antipathy!"

Inching to the edge of our shield, I crane my neck and peer

uphill. Through the fading twilight, I steal a look at our attackers—a band of Indians on a wide ledge piled with rocks.

They roll down another rock, a big one, and I jump back—then lean out for another quick look. That's when I realize, thanks to my extra-sharp unicorn eyes (much sharper than Faerie or human) that the Indians are most likely Navajo.

And all of them are women. Tinsel has a gang of tough Navajo warrior women fighting on her behalf.

"Last chance, Tinsel!" hollers Ballad. "Tell your slaves to stand down and surrender the *fei croí!*"

Oh, Ballad. That just pisses the women off more. I see them working extra hard around the biggest rock yet, a real boulder, inching it to the rim of the ledge.

And then *over* it.

We've got seconds until it hits. Leaping into action, I sprint along the trail, hoping to find more cover or at least get out of range of the Navajo women.

I hear boulders crash together behind us, but I don't look back. I run as hard as I can along the rugged terrain, the weight of my rider bouncing on my back...

...and then, suddenly, that weight is gone.

Panicking that I've thrown him, I skid to a halt and whip around to see if he's gone over the edge. Instead, I see him charging up the mountainside through the gathering darkness toward the enemy ledge, hands balled into fists and arms pumping.

That leaves me with a dilemma. I'm nimble but not a mountain goat, so following him is not an option. Even if I *was* a mountain goat, racing to confront killer Navajo women—not to mention Tinsel of spiking-a-horse-on-a-church-spire fame—is *not* something in which I have any interest.

But suddenly, I see something that *is.*

Up ahead, on the slope above the trail, an Appaloosa horse with a black-and-white spotted coat gazes down at me in the emerging moonlight. With a toss of his head, he spins around and bolts away from me, quickly disappearing around the curve of the moun-tainside.

I don't hesitate. I *can't.* I'm not sure how my footing will be off the trail, but I need to catch up. His presence was no accident, in the midst of the Tinsel-induced chaos.

He might just lead me to my goal, my primary reason for being on this mountain in the first place. He might just lead me to my *destiny*.

We unicorns have a saying: being led by the tip of the horn.

That's exactly what's happening to me right now. The Appaloosa is pacing me, making sure he stays just out of reach without losing me.

There's no question he's leading me on...but what is he leading me *to?*

"Hey!" It can't hurt to try talking to him. "Where are you going?"

No answer. Just a peek back from across the rocky slope, followed by a disappearing act.

The next time there's a bend up ahead, he doesn't look in my direction. All I see beyond the slope are the glittering stars of the Milky Way set against the inky darkness of the night sky.

The bend gives way to a gap in the side of the mountain, laid bare in the moonlight and starshine. The second I step into the mouth of it, I hear rumbling from the depths, getting closer.

As I brace myself, the cause of the rumbling is revealed. A herd of wild horses charges out of the shadows, headed straight for me with the Appaloosa in the lead.

A unicorn's horn isn't his only weapon.

I run straight for the Appaloosa, then whip around and unleash a powerful kick with both back legs. The timing is perfect; the Appaloosa takes the full brunt of the blow with his head and crashes to one side.

His fall knocks down two other horses like bowling pins, sending them thrashing to the ground in a howling pile of flesh and cracking limbs.

But I still take a hit from the other side of the herd, a hard thump that flings me off my feet. The horse that threw me rears up, its hooves dancing precariously overhead. I slash him with my horn as soon as he drops, tearing open both forelegs before he can pound my skull to mush. Squealing, he topples aside, hitting the ground with a heavy thud.

I heave myself up on two knees in time to see another horse racing toward me. Aiming my horn like a spear, I stiffen every muscle and let the onrushing beast do the work, impaling himself through the chest.

He flops to the dirt, taking me with him. In the seconds it takes to free myself by retracting my horn from the wound, I get stomped by the hooves of two other horses.

Pushing past the pain, I launch myself around, extending my horn. Both attackers stumble out of reach, giving me just enough time to clamber back to my feet.

But when I get there, I see I'm surrounded. Five horses stand in a circle around me, leaving just one way out—the mouth of the gap in the mountainside.

As they glower at me in the moonlight, tails swishing, I understand. I am free to leap into the heights if I wish.

"You know why I'm here, don't you?" I look from one to the other, staying alert for any wrong moves. "Where is she?"

"You don't *deserve* to know," says a mustang with a mottled brown coat.

"And you *do*?" I snap. "I suppose *you* traveled *thousands* of miles to *find* her?"

"Thousands of miles to your *death*," says a pale gray Arabian. "You should never have *come* here."

"You can *never* hurt her now," says the mustang.

"But I never hurt her *before*," I tell him. "She ran away without a *word*."

"Because she was *terrified*." The Appaloosa has worked himself to his feet and pushed into the circle to face me. "Terrified of what you *did* to her."

191

"What in the *hell* are you *talking* about?" I stamp the ground with my fore-hooves, running out of patience. "I'm asking you for the *last time*. Where *is* she?"

The Appaloosa moves forward, pressing me toward the ledge. "Goddess is beyond your reach now. Your quest ends here."

With no hope of getting a straight answer, I stop backing toward the ledge and turn the tables. Lowering my head, I level the spike of my horn and move forward. This time, it's the Appaloosa's turn to back away.

"How *dare* you?" My heart pounds as I advance. "She is the *love* of my *life*. You can never *know* the *joy* we've shared."

"But *we* rescued her." The Appaloosa's eyes are wide with rage. "We *saved* her from the bandit queen, *Tinsel*, and gave her *hope*."

"*Too late*, we gave her hope," says the Arabian.

Something in his voice catches my ear—an inflection of genuine sadness. "What do you mean, *too late?*"

"You'll find out when you jump," says the Arabian. "You can meet her on the *other side*."

Hot blood thunders in my ears. *Have I traveled all this way for nothing?*

Then the Appaloosa makes a move, and the world becomes a red and noxious haze.

I brandish my horn like a sword, slashing right and left with abandon. Wild horses shriek as blood spurts out of them in dark crimson fountains.

The time for holding back has passed. All I care about now is lashing out at anyone in my way.

"How did it happen?" I stab the Arabian in the throat as I kick the mottled mustang with my rear hooves. *"How did she die?"*

A dark gray Andalusian rears up, mane rippling in the wind. I lunge at his belly and slice it open side to side, bolting around his carcass as his guts splatter on the ground and he plunges down on top of them.

"Tell me!" My horn drips with blood as I thrust it at the Appaloosa's eye.

He dodges the strike and backpedals. "We *told* you! It's your fault!"

"The truth! Tell me the *truth!"* Tensing every muscle, I aim my horn at his face and prepare to charge.

Then, suddenly, his head swings up, his eyes fixing on the night sky behind me. "There! *Look!* The truth is *up there!"*

It's a trick. I paw the ground, getting ready to punch my horn like a soldier's bayonet through his lying muzzle.

"I *swear* it!" screams the Appaloosa. "There's your *truth!"*

Something makes me look back—and I freeze. I can't believe what I'm seeing.

"She died bringing *him* into the world," says the Appaloosa. "*His* divine creation cost Goddess her *life.*"

Words fail me. All I can do is stare, transfixed, at what is hovering in the sky before me.

The snow-white colt flaps his feathery wings gently and nods, the single horn jutting from his forehead gleaming softly by the silvery light of the full moon.

"It was the horn that killed her," says the Appaloosa. "As you can imagine."

My eyes water as I gaze up at that magnificent creature. "I never knew...she was *pregnant."*

"Why do you think she ran from you? *Flew* from you? She was *terrified* of what might happen. Then the bandit queen *caught* her and made things so much *worse.* She wanted the child for her own, and she couldn't wait to have it. She cast spells to bring about an early birth, no matter the terrible cost to Goddess's health."

"I'm so *sorry,"* I whisper. "I didn't *know."*

The Appaloosa steps up beside me but makes no hostile move. "Her name suited her. She *was* a goddess. Those *wings*...that beautiful white *coat.*" He sighs. "When we found her in the wilderness, running away on foot because the bandit queen had bound her wings, we swore we would fight to the last *breath* for her. For her and the *child* she was about to bear." He looks around at the blood-soaked bodies on the ground. "And now most of us *have* given up our last breath for that noble cause."

"You *forced* me to fight," I tell him.

"To *protect* all we have left of Goddess. To protect *him.*" He nods at the hovering colt. "Your *child.*"

"I would never hurt him."

"You were responsible for Goddess's death," says the Appaloosa. "For all we knew, you had come to finish off her legacy, as well."

"*Our* legacy." Everything I thought I knew about my life has just changed. Everything I thought I wanted is suddenly different.

"He's a *miracle*, in spite of the hardship of his birth and what it cost us." The Appaloosa sounds awestruck. "Has there ever been anything *like* him?'"

If there was, it was surely never *this* wondrous. It was never the product of a love like mine and Goddess's, no matter how dark that love might have turned in the end.

"Are you going to kill me now?" asks the Appaloosa. "Right here in front of your son?"

"What kind of parent would I be if I did something like that?"

The Appaloosa backs away. "Somewhere else, then?"

"Why would I do that? I don't even know this child's *name...*"

"*Choir.* His name is Choir."

"Exactly," I tell him. "Why would I kill someone who could help me raise and protect my son in a hostile world?"

The Appaloosa thinks for a long moment. "I can't think of a single good reason."

"Neither can I," I tell him as I watch my son fly toward us, his dark eyes glinting with curiosity.

How do I discover Ballad survived the night? When I hear him whistling and calling for me early the next morning from down the mountain.

I hate to leave Choir's side for even a moment, but I answer the calls for old times' sake. I think I can trust the Appaloosa (whose name, I have learned, is Erskine) to tend the colt until I return.

Following the whistles and shouts, I find Ballad clambering over the mountainside. In the bright morning light, I can see he is bruised and wounded but not mortally so. Say what you will about the big doofus, but he is one tough hombre to kill.

"There you are, Gossamer!" His white teeth gleam from the shadow of his broad-brimmed Stetson. "I've been looking all over for you, boy!"

I park myself up the slope from him, watching and listening.

"Tinsel's gang sure put me through the wringer," he says, wagging his head, "but I beat 'em in the end. Only problem is, their boss-lady got away, and she took the *fei croí* with her."

He takes a few steps toward me, and I back away the same distance.

"Tinsel's riding west, heading for southern California. She said something about using the *fei croí* to create a new realm of earthly illusion to captivate all of humanity, but I intend to stop her. I just *know* we will catch her." Ballad nods confidently. "I have a good feeling. I think things will go better than last time."

Again, he moves toward me. Again, I move away.

He frowns, looking hurt. "What's the matter, Gossamer? Don't you understand? This is our *big chance.* You and I finally have a real shot at getting back the *fei croí* and restoring the Bright Realm."

The doofus is still fixated on his pipe dream. Even without the revelation of my new son, I wouldn't want to waste my time on another leg of this never-ending goose chase.

"Don't forget how glorious it will be!" Ballad's face shines beatifically as he launches into the same old story. "Every kind of man and woman will leave their tributes at the feet of the Faerie royalty, chanting songs of worship and..."

"Enough!"

It's the first word I've spoken to him in years, and I see it stings.

My next words won't make it any better. "Enough about the damn *Bright Realm* already!"

"Gossamer, how can you *say* that?"

"First of all, my name isn't *Gossamer!*" I tell him. "And I can *say* that because I'm sick to death of *hearing* about it!"

Ballad doesn't bother asking what my *true* name is. Instead, he steps toward me again. This time, I go further and don't stop.

"Wait!" He sounds desperate. "We have to stick together!"

"Not anymore." I keep going up the slope, heading for Choir and Erskine. "It was good while it lasted, but it's time to let go."

"But we're *partners*." Ballad sounds like he's about to break down in tears. "We're practically *family.*"

"Then I guess you better get *walking*, you horse's ass. I've got *actual* family who need me right *here*."

Then, with a flick of my tail and two slashes of my horn in the shape of an "X," the first letter of my secret name, I whip around and run away from him, doing what unicorns do best, which is pointing the way truly forward.

THE STARS SO BLACK, THE SPACE SO WHITE

Imagine standing in the prow of a great sailing vessel, gazing out at the starry darkness as it folds around the nose of the ship. Now imagine the ship is in space.

And you are standing on an onyx gangplank, a sheer, black surface reflecting the starlight all around--creating the illusion that you are suspended without support in the void. Exposed to the nip and tug of so many rays and waves and streams and particles, yet somehow protected.

Watch as crackling suns and jewel-like worlds spin past. Wonder at the feathery, pastel tendrils of glowing nebulae. Grin with delight, because no matter how many times you see this, you can't help but marvel.

I can't help but marvel.

Welcome to my life. From Earthbound bartender savant to crewman on an alien spacecraft. From man of 20th century Earth to man of the cosmos.

You wish you were me. You *totally* wish you were me.

"I should have known." The voice behind me is high-pitched and piping with a fluttery vibrato. "I would find you here. Rudeee Tabernacle."

Turning, I smile at the dozens of multifaceted silver eyes staring my way, twisting on the ends of pale yellow tendrils. The tendrils are rooted in a glittering, creamy cloud, a misty blur of ever-shifting size and shape that hovers a meter above the onyx gangplank. Who knew I could come to love and respect someone so alien?

Who knew I could come to see my *abductor* as my *friend?*

"You are not feeling. Worried, are you?" The voice emanates from somewhere in the cloud. It's the same voice I first heard fifty years ago, asking a question that changed my life forever and led me to this moment.

"Only hopeful." I bow, as is the custom in the fleet of the civilization whose name translates as The Rising. After fifty years among The Rising (though I look half as old as that, thanks to alien rejuvenation techniques), I know all the right things to do and say...though I don't always do and say them. But that, too, is customary; it's part of my job, after all.

They call me a *Chancer.* An X-factor in a social hierarchy with too much order...and a need for controlled chaos in the face of a highly improvisational universe.

As for the alien, if you called him/her/it/them a captain/teacher/lama/inexplicable presence, you wouldn't be wrong. "We approach. The source of. The signal."

His/her/its/their actual name is unpronounceable for a human like me, so I go with a boiled-down nickname. "Most Eager, has the content of the signal changed?"

Most Eager hiss-cough-squeals in a way that equates to a human head-shake. "The signal continues. To repeat."

I know the message by heart by now. "*Black stars. White space. Forever screaming.*"

"We will be there. Soon, Rudeee. The..." He calls our giant vessel by the name its builders gave it, which translates like this (more or less): *Peacefaring Manyfold Transitory Translightenment Construct, Constant.* "...will arrive within. The hour."

I shorten the ship's name like always. "The *Transit*'s ready, Most Eager. We'll do what we do best."

"Answer questions." Most Eager stiffens all his/her/its/their tendrils at once like stalks in a cornfield. It's a salute. "Save lives."

I answer with a salute of my own, holding both fists at shoulder height, opening them into flattened palms. "And set the stage for tomorrow."

Setting the stage is The Rising's truest mission, our reason for being among the stars in the first place. The galaxy is full of lifeforms in varying degrees of evolution; we create mysteries that will draw them out here when the time is right to join the community of star-faring beings.

Speaking of mysteries, a ship like our own comes into view up ahead--a cluster of giant black shapeshifting objects, spherical at the moment like a bunch of grapes or a clutch of atoms in a molecule. The spheres, which normally blink with multicolored lights, are dark--and cut in half down the middle, wedged in a swirling halo of bright blue light.

"Do you think. They are still. Alive?" asks Most Eager.

I know he/she/it/they can tell if I'm lying, but I do it anyway. "Of course." After all, he/she/it/they has/have kin on that vessel.

More than kin. More like a protégé beloved above all others. And a *human*, like me.

Her name is Julie. And it is *her* voice--the voice of the trapped ship's first officer--repeating that message, over and over:

"Black stars. White space. Forever screaming."

Imagine a ship the size of a small moon, consisting of huge, interlinked objects--sometimes spherical, sometimes cubical, other times elliptical or dodecagonal or jagged as a giant virus with a billion points and peaks. A ship that shifts and changes depending on its task or environment.

Now imagine the *inside* of such a ship, which is equally as miraculous as the outside. Imagine diving through a sea of lights and colors, a jumble of bubbles and pockets and pods alive with sound and motion...some right-side-up, some upside-down, some sideways or inside-out or outways-upside-in...all rising and falling and bumping and merging and mingling...a harmonious bedlam fit to drive a sane man mad or a madman sane.

And all through it, imagine the *life* of a hundred-thousand worlds, from the brobdingnagian to the microscopic...all thronging in this vast and tumbling tumult. Imagine feathers, wings, scales, claws, beaks, fur, bone...skin, fluid, ooze, fumes, leaves, stems, crystals...chirps, howls, growls, chatters, barks, clicks, burbles...all of these and more.

Imagine all that, and you'll have some idea what the inside of the *Peacefaring Manyfold Transitory Translightenment Construct, Constant* is like. The *Transit.* My *home.*

And you'll know, at least a little, why I love it so. You'll know why the day they brought me here from Georgia was the best day of my life.

Diving down through the zero gravity "Flow" that exists between pockets and bubbles, I swoop past busy shipmates on their way to other destinations. A voice chimes in my head via Menta-com, the telepathic intercom that speaks in whatever language you understand best.

All crew to mystery stations. Approaching distressed vessel Impetuous Fractal Tracery Epicenter, Rarefied.

I see my own station below, a figure eight archipelago of chrome, glass, and superneuroconductive organo-ceramics sparking with current. As I drop toward it, localized gravity rises, reeling me in until I land lightly on the polished floor.

"Rudy!" One of my colleagues, a being I call Paraffino, waves his sixteen waxy arms. "Take a look at the data from our scans of the *Fractal Tracery.*"

I hurry over and lean in beside him, taking in the flurry of multicolored holographic text dancing in midair around us.

"No life signs." I can't keep the disappointment out of my voice. "And no power."

"Except the battery backup that is powering the distress beacon." says Paraffino.

"Here's a question," says a tiny voice in my left ear, the whine of an insect. "Why does the *FracTrace* appear to be cut in half, yet it bends space-time as if it were *one thousand times* its recorded size?"

I scowl. "Some kind of sensor mirage?"

"Considered and discounted." The tiny voice's owner flits in front of my face--a silver mosquito-like creature half the length of my little finger. I call him KeeZee McGee. "Diagnostics reveal zero chance of impaired functionality in our sensor arrays."

"What about *psychic* mirages?" I raise an eyebrow. "Maybe the sensor data only *looks* hinky because our *minds* are being warped."

"Unlikely." Another voice speaks up across the archipelago--make that *five hundred* voices, a chorus of every pitch and timbre singing as one. "The Mindset system confirms no perceptual defects in any member of our crew." The chorus belongs to a toothy shark-bunny thing I call Adorakilla.

"We need to send in a probe," says another colleague--a kind of half-rock/half-bush I call Stick-n-Stone. Her voice sounds like crackling gravel mixed with rustling leaves. "If anyone from the *FracTrace* is still alive, they must be on the other side of that phenomenon."

"Whatever it is," says Paraffino.

Some of us are about to find out. Just then, the Mentacom announces a mission to the derelict vessel, leaving in five minutes. Guess who's part of the Go Team?

Stick-n-Stone, for one. "Better go grab my gear." She rolls over the edge of the archipelago, where the Flow spins her off into the heights.

"Wish me luck." I smile and salute the others with flattened palms. "If I don't make it back, give my Zeppelin collection to Gassy Rictus."

I laugh as I leap up into the Flow. I've come up with so many nicknames, they can't always tell the real ones from the fake anymore.

Our little silver scout disk spins on its vertical axis like a coin, flashing from the *Transit* at a rate of speed that would blow your mind.

Inside, the six members of the Go Team stay glued to our psych-feeds, images of our destination beamed continuously into our brains. Even Most Eager--commander of this mission--closes the eyes on his/her/its/their yellow tendrils and looks inward at the mind-cast images.

"Five hundred units from *Fractal Tracery* and closing." Walking Reef, a creature who looks exactly as his nickname suggests, is piloting our disk.

Just then, something pings, and one of the holographic displays around Reef's head (a cluster of multicolored non-aquatic coral) flashes red-gold-red. "This is interesting. The sensor mirage seems to be intensifying. The part of the *Fractal Trace* on the other side of the phenomenon now appears to be *one hundred thousand times* the size of the original vessel."

"Makes no sense," rumbles our science officer, Stick-n-Stone, from her cradle in the floor. "Some kind of quantum magnification effect?"

"But why would it change as we get closer?" asks Ever Luminous, the slow-motion firework in the shape of a humanoid biped. He's the team's medical officer, as well as its lightshow-in-chief. "To such an extent, I mean?"

"Two hundred units and closing," says Reef.

We all stir, adjusting our gear--environmental suits, packs, lights, weapons. Any minute now, our scout craft will dock with *Fractal*, and we'll have our chance to learn the truth.

The sixth member of our team, security specialist Twelvefold Sinner, is first out of the airlock after we dock. Imagine someone who has twelve distinct selves sharing the same coordinates in space-time, each one a drastically different species with a different personality, language, and power set. That's our Sinner.

This time, he's wearing a form that's a mountain of muscle on three legs, with a face on the black-feathered chest and no head on the shoulders. He doesn't even need an environmental suit in that form; he's impervious to the airless cold inside the depressurized ship.

I walk out after him in my slimline gold foil environmental

suit...and gasp. The interior of a Rising vessel without power is a sight to behold.

The world inside the giant ship is frozen in place. The pods and pockets and bubbles hang suspended, held aloft by passive magnetic failsafes...but no equipment is running. There's none of the tumult I've come to expect from an operational ship.

And none of the usual lights, either. It's only because of the glow from the swirling blue disk cutting through the middle of the sphere that I can see the frozen enormity of the *Fractal Tracery* sprawling before me.

As the rest of the Go Team files out of the scout, I gaze into that blue glow. "What did they stumble into here?"

"We couldn't have fashioned a better mystery ourselves," says Walking Reef, lumbering up beside me.

"Yet we need to. Stay on task." Most Eager drifts up ahead of us in the shimmery bubble that's his/her/its/their version of an environmental suit. "What does the data. Look like from here?"

"This is odd." Stick-n-Stone rolls up in what looks like a gold foil bowling ball bag, studying holographic readouts floating around her. "Sensor data is fluctuating wildly. One minute, the missing half of the *Fractal Tracery* reads as being 500,000 times larger than it should be...and then, it's a million times *smaller*."

Most Eager hardens his cloud into a pearly pointer aimed at the blue disk. "What else is on. The other side. Of that anomaly?"

"The only thing I've detected so far is the other half of the *Frac-Trace*," says Stick-n-Stone.

"Send in. A probe," says Most Eager.

Reef's mottled gray pseudopod arms weave through the air, bringing a set of hovering holo-controls into view around his head. Seconds later, a blinking black sphere the size of a soccer ball shoots past us from the scout ship and rockets toward the anomaly. It dives into the center of the disk without causing a single ripple of blue light.

Nothing changes for long moments after that. The blue light swirls silently like always, revealing no trace of the device.

"What does telemetry. Look like?" asks Most Eager.

Walking Reef's starfish eyes remain fixed on his holo-readouts. "Gibberish. The data coming through makes no sense."

"What if it's scrambled or encrypted?" asks Ever Luminous.

"Wait!" Reef's pseudopods whip through the readouts. "I'm *getting* something. Some kind of static...and it's building in intensity."

As soon as the words leave his twenty-five mouths, the anomaly flares, washing us all in blinding white light. The deck vibrates under my feet.

Before any of us can react, a powerful suction starts dragging us toward the anomaly.

Twelvefold Sinner is the first to go. Despite his great size and powerful musculature, the suction wrenches him off his feet like an untethered balloon and spins him into the center of the disk.

The rest of us follow, one by one--lifting off and hurtling into the anomaly. I'm the last to go, dropping all my gear and clinging to a Flow antenna mounted on the floor with my legs in the air...and then the antenna snaps. I bolt feet-first through the ship, narrowly missing most of the obstacles along the way.

Then I punch through the anomaly, and I black out.

The first thing I see when I open my eyes is a field of white flecked with black. Gazing into it, I wonder if it's a leftover effect of the anomaly's blinding flare.

Instinctively, I reach up to rub my eyes. As I'm massaging them, I realize something.

There should be a helmet between my eyes and my hand.

Terrified, I yank my hand away and gulp for breath, filling my lungs...which shouldn't be possible if the other side of the anomaly is as airless as the ship and space on the entry side.

Heart racing, I thrash myself to a seated position and look around. Where are my people?

The members of the Go Team are scattered over the ebony deck, alive and stirring in spite of the bumpy ride through the anomaly. Most Eager is closest, twenty meters away--though the distance, as I watch, seems to grow. Some kind of optical illusion?

Or is it related to the size-distorted data we were picking up earlier from outside the anomaly?

The same applies to other reference points in my surroundings. The familiar habitats and equipment that fill this half of the *Fractal Tracery* float above us, changing as I stare--sometimes appearing closer, sometimes farther away.

But the distance dilation effect isn't the strangest thing about this side of the ship. As I take in my surroundings, another realization slams into my brain.

The spotted white field is outside *the ship. I am seeing it through gaping holes in the hull.*

The hull is stretched so far, it seems to have more holes than substance--and as I watch, it stretches farther, to the point of almost disappearing in the black-flecked whiteness.

Then, without warning, it springs back. The sight is disorienting enough to make me dizzy.

Shake it off. Whatever's happening here, I need to Take Steps. Figure It Out. Find What I Came Here For. The missing crew of the *Fractal Tracery*, in other words.

Then one of them finds me first.

"Hello, Rudy!" Julie's voice booms from all around me. "Thank you for coming!"

She coalesces from all directions, pieces fading into view and sliding together. And the pieces are *enormous.* As she gathers like metal dust accreting on a magnet, she seems to me to be *thirty meters tall* or more. She *towers* over me, a behemoth in a silver foil jumpsuit, beaming with teeth like skyscrapers, throwing out gusts of wind with each toss of her long, glossy, black hair.

"I missed you, Rudy!" As Julie says it, her body compresses, flowing down to stand before me at normal human size, just under two meters tall and slender as always. "I never thought I'd see *any* of you again!" She reaches out, takes my hand, and helps me to my feet.

"Tell me what you know." Disoriented, I wobble when I get up. "Where are we? Where's the rest of the crew?"

"So many questions." She smiles and squeezes my hand. "Same old Rudy."

Impatient, I pull my hand from her grip and grab her shoulders. "Is your *crew* still *alive*?"

"Define 'alive.'" She giggles when she says it.

I frown. The Julie I know is a serious person, a real Type-A. We've been colleagues and friends for 25 years, ever since she was abducted/recruited by The Rising, and I don't think I've ever heard her giggle before. "You think this is *funny*?"

"It's just..." She tilts her head to one side. "Things are *different* over here."

Most Eager's quivery voice pipes up behind us. "Different. In what ways?"

Julie shrugs off my grip and turns, bending over to smile at his/her/its/their weaving yellow eye-stalks. "Isn't it obvious? The *stars* are *black* here. And *space* is *white*."

No one from the Go Team has an intact environmental suit. I realize this when the others gather around us. Even Most Eager's protective bubble is nowhere to be seen.

Not that it seems to be a problem. We're all breathing and functioning normally, though as far as I can tell, the *Fractal Tracery* has been breached to what passes for open space over here, and none of the ship's systems are online.

Are we dead? Delusional? Transformed? Mysteries abound.

And *deepen*, the more answers we get.

"Think of this place as *Heaven*." Julie seems to slide farther away, then pops back to the middle of our little group. "Think of it as *paradise*. The first and best universe in existence. The prototype, the template, for all the universes that came after."

"Which makes *our* universe. What, exactly?" asks Most Eager.

"A *mistake*." Julie smirks and shrugs. "Or so I'm told."

"Told by whom?" growls Twelvefold Sinner.

Another shrug from Julie. "Someone who knows."

"Is this *someone* sustaining us somehow?" asks Stick-n-Stone. "Providing life support in the hard vacuum of space?"

Julie shakes her head. "There's no hard vacuum in space here.

So, technically, we shouldn't even call it 'space,' I suppose. It's not *empty*."

"The rest of the crew. Is where?" Most Eager's every silvery eye is fixed on Julie.

"Aren't you going to ask me how we got here?" Julie grows to five times her normal height. "Don't you want to know how we crossed over?"

"If it reveals. The fate of the crew."

"We were improvising." Julie stretches further, then compresses. "And it wasn't the *first* time, either." Back to normal size, she winks devilishly.

"What *kind* of improvising?" asks Ever Luminous, the lights inside him growing dim.

"Instead of just signaling *inward*, to developing species within our universe," explains Julie, "we were signaling *outward*. To other, *higher* levels."

"But that is not. The mission. Of The Rising," says Most Eager.

"'The Rising?'" Julie folds her arms over her chest. "You haven't *risen* in a long time, have you?"

"The mission. Is to inspire. Other species. To rise." Most Eager sounds indignant. "In so doing. We *all* rise."

"You've stalled out, and you know it," says Julie. "*Everyone* in The Rising knows it. And some of us decided to act on it. We've been sending signals beyond the boundaries of our local space-time for a while now--and we finally got an *answer*. An *invitation*." She spreads her arms wide. "This ship, the *Fractal Tracery*, was closest to the coordinates for the rendezvous."

"What kind of invitation?" asks Reef.

"The same one you're about to get." Julie smiles warmly. "They're throwing you a line."

"A line?" snarls Twelvefold Sinner.

"A *lifeline*." Julie nods slowly.

"What the hell are you talking about?" I ask.

"The end of the universe." Julie grins and claps her hands. "*Your* universe. It's coming any *minute* now."

As we stand there, trying to take in what Julie has told us, she points at the biggest gap in the hull. "See that?"

As she says it, I glimpse movement in the milk-white field beyond the ship. A shape coalesces in the firmament--a lumpy gray patch growing larger as I watch. It unfolds rapidly, taking on contour and color, expanding to blot out the black stars and fill the view through the ship's porous skin.

"That's where we're going." Julie waves for us to follow. "Abandon ship!"

Moving away from our entry point doesn't seem like a good idea. But I might not have a choice. As I stare at the drifting mass outside the hull--now a gleaming island of crystal structures and a rainbow riot of vegetation--I'm pulled toward it.

"Let go," says Julie. "Focus on our destination. Focus on what you want to have happen. That's how it works over here." Her feet leave the floor, and she drifts toward the hole in the hull.

I try the opposite, focusing on staying put...and it works. As the rest of the Go Team lifts off, sailing toward the island, I stay behind.

But I don't hold back for long. The pull intensifies, overcoming my resistance, and I rise from the deck, turning in a lazy spiral.

Against my will, I rise through the hull, into the whiteness, drifting toward the island shining with light from some source I cannot see.

I remember another time, fifty years ago, when I was also caught in the grip of an alien force. Not knowing if I would ever see my home again.

It was a beam of light that night, an amber shaft dropping from the starry Georgia sky to lift me in its warm, shivering nimbus. It picked me up when I was walking home from the bar I was tending.

I still remember how terrified I was when I glimpsed the outline of the spherical ship above me, silhouetted against the Moon. Was I heading for an alien dissection table?

Anything was possible that night. As smart as I was (self-taught, no money for school), as young (23) and restless as I was, I still feared what was coming.

Then, after I crossed the threshold into that marvelous craft, and beheld Most Eager for the first time, and heard his question, his incredible offer, I seized my new destiny with both hands and all my heart.

As we approach the island suspended in white-space, I make out more details: glittering crystal spires amid a sea of multicolored plant life (or something alien that resembles vegetation from a distance); clouds the color of violets and goldenrod, some raining downward, others up; pulsing obsidian mountain peaks smoking like volcanos...and the smoke is neon green and moves like it's alive.

We sail in over the treetops and swoop toward the highest spire. Then, as so often happens in the Whiteverse (as I've just now nick-named the place), the distance changes, suddenly tripling. Julie laughs, and the gap quickly closes, flinging us up to the spire so fast, I think we're going to crash into it.

Instead, we all touch down lightly on the ground in front of it.

"Here we are." Julie gestures at the spire. Big crystal doors swing open, their multitudes of facets twinkling. "Go on in."

"Is the crew. Of the *Fractal Tracery*. In there?" asks Most Eager.

"What about the supposed end of our universe?" says Reef. "Will we find out how to stop it?"

"All I can say is, this will be the most important meeting of your life." Julie bows and waves us toward the doors.

Swallowing hard, I follow Most Eager through the doorway. The rest of the Go Team files in behind us.

We enter a huge, circular chamber with crystal walls that sweep up like the sides of a funnel into the towering spire above. Every-where, we are surrounded by spots of light reflected from the crys-tal, thousands of sparkling flecks hanging like frozen confetti on every surface.

"Who's coming to this meeting, other than us?" I ask. "And when will they be gracing us with their presence?"

"Think of them as saviors," says Julie. "And they've been here all along."

She claps, and three figures suddenly unfold from what looked until now like empty space in the middle of the room.

Though "unfold" isn't quite the right word for it. It's more like the figures are perfectly two-dimensional, practically invisible when viewed on edge--and they *turn* so their flat sides face us.

Only then do we see that they look like white paper cutouts in the shape of blocky, humanoid monoliths. The one in the middle is tallest (over three meters), with the most squared-off head; the one on the left is shorter, with a more angular, back-sloped skull; and the one on the right is even shorter and more rounded than either of them.

When they speak, their voices sound like layer upon layer of static blending together. It's only after the first few words that I realize the static is familiar. I've heard it before, many times.

It's identical to the cosmic microwave background radiation, the soundtrack of the Big Bang that started our universe.

"Welcome, blessed guests," says Middle Cutout.

"Your new life starts here and now," says Left Cutout. *"Infinite white heavens await your exploration."*

Stick-n-Stone rolls up beside me. "What if we aren't done exploring our *old* heavens?"

"Forget them," says Right Cutout. *"They will be gone soon."*

A tiny object rises from behind Middle Cutout, a glowing golden orb the size of a golf ball. It hovers above his head, turning and pulsing with dazzling white light.

"All the matter and energy of a new universe resides in this Seed," explains Middle Cutout. *"We send it now into your universe, where it will replace that misbegotten atrocity with something superior in every way."*

I can believe that Seed is loaded with the contents of a new universe. I can feel its awesome *power*, its *weight*, from across the room.

"Why destroy. Our universe?" asks Most Eager.

"It was a mistake," says Right Cutout. *"A defective copy."*

"Based on this template of perfection." Willowy paper arms emerge

210

from Middle Cutout's flattened body and spread wide. *"The copy should have been destroyed long ago."*

"Yet it survived, hidden, until now," says Left Cutout. *"Draining the life from our original cosmos through a secret link left over from the birth process."*

"The parasitic universe devours our Wonderverse to feed its own growth," says Left Cutout. *"Its contents are corrupt."*

"Including its *inhabitants*?" I gesture at myself and my shipmates. "Then why bring us here before you destroy it?"

"Because we believe some are worth saving," says Right Cutout.

"And she has convinced us you are among that number," says Middle Cutout.

I turn my gaze to Julie. "We're here because of you?"

"You're my friends." She salutes Most Eager with palms upraised. "My *mentor*. I wanted to save you."

"At what cost?" asks Most Eager.

"We ask only that you help us to seek other lifeforms worth saving from other doomed universes," says Right Cutout.

"Just go on doing what The Rising has *been* doing, in other words," says Julie. "Recruiting the best and the brightest."

A picture takes shape in my mind. "These other universes. Why exactly are they doomed?"

The Cutouts are silent for a moment. Then the one in the middle finally confirms what I've been thinking.

"Like your universe, they are inferior copies," he says. *"And parasites. They must be destroyed for our universe to survive and thrive."*

"And how many of these doomed universes are there?" I ask.

Again, hesitation. *"All of them. All but the first and best, our Wonderverse."*

"Ah." I look at Julie. "And the crew of the *Fractal Tracery?* Were they made this same offer, by any chance?"

Julie nods.

"And did they accept it?"

"They weren't interested." The look in her eyes speaks volumes.

"But you are?" I ask her.

"Let's just say I was given a second chance to consider the offer," says Julie. "And I saw the light."

Reading between the lines, I understand the truth about why she wanted us here. Her crew is gone, presumably eliminated for refusing to support the Cutouts' program of mass universe extermination. She is the sole survivor, preserved by the Cutouts to aid their dark plans--probably controlled by them to some extent--and she needs our help to resist them and save our home universe.

Though how exactly we can provide that help remains to be seen. Already, the Seed is gliding across the chamber, chiming softly. How long until it makes a beeline for the anomaly and our universe on the other side?

Chancer that I am, I hear the call of X-factor craziness loud and clear. The only question that matters now is, how do we stop the Seed from destroying our universe?

An idea comes to me in a flash. Catching Most Eager's eye (dozens of them), I give him/her/it/them a sign--moving my hands together and apart with thumbs and forefingers pinched as if I'm stretching something. I need him/her/it/them to fill some time.

He/she/it/they understand the signal and set out to keep the Cutouts talking. "So what happened to. The crew of the. *Fractal Tracery*. If they were not. Interested in the offer?"

Even as the Cutouts answer the question, I turn to Twelvefold Sinner. "I need your other selves," I tell him quietly. "All at once."

Sinner scowls. "You know that's impossible. Only one self at a time can occupy my body's coordinates."

"Have you ever *tried* to manifest all twelve at once?"

"The physical laws of the universe prevent it," Sinner says darkly.

I pat him on the shoulder. "But we aren't *in* our universe anymore."

Sinner's scowl lightens.

"You heard Julie." I wink. "'Focus on what you want to have happen. That's how it works over here.'"

"But what if it works?" asks Sinner. "Then what?"

"Stop that Seed," I tell him. "Or *detonate* it."

Looking up, I see the Seed is almost overhead. Time to set the rest of the plan in motion.

"Ever Luminous!" I don't bother keeping my voice down anymore. "Give us a lightshow! Make it a big one!"

Ever Luminous doesn't question me; he just cuts loose with a burst of red and white fireworks projected outside his body.

"Reef! Go bowling with Stone!" I point at the Cutouts. "Knock down the pins!"

I don't have to tell them twice. Reef scoops up Stick-n-Stone and hefts her like a bowling ball. Good thing I taught them how to bowl back on the *Transit*.

Meanwhile, Julie's yelling. "Whatever you're doing, stop it!" Maybe she's fooling the Cutouts, but it doesn't sound to me like her heart is in it.

Not that it matters either way with our universe on the line. "Sinner! Do it!" I shout.

Sinner shuts his eyes and clenches his chest-face, concentrating with all his might. He shudders the way he always does before switching selves, only harder.

While that's happening, Luminous throws off more fireworks, filling the chamber with flares and sparks. Reef hurls Stick-n-Stone over the crystal floor like a bowling ball--but *this* ball hoots and hollers as she hurtles toward the Cutouts.

And the Seed keeps gliding toward the doors.

Just then, Sinner howls and explodes in a burst of blinding white light. When the light fades, I see the experiment was a success. Where once there was a single Sinner, twelve very different versions of the same being now stand.

"Stop that Seed!" Even as I shout the words, all twelve Sinners leap into action at once, scrambling toward the Seed.

Unfortunately, the Cutouts take action as well. The three figures quickly fold themselves into new forms--what look like an origami bird of prey, an origami dragon, and a giant origami spider.

They're on the twelve Sinners in a heartbeat, springing across the chamber with the usual distance-warping magic of the Wonderverse. Somehow, though they look like origami paper sculptures, they go through the Sinners like threshers through crops on an agriplanet.

Who would have thought an origami spider could take down a metal-plated commando version of Sinner with built-in organic cannons in his face, chest, and belly? Who would have thought an origami dragon could thrash a purple-skinned, musclebound berserker Sinner into cutlets? And who would ever have imagined an origami bird of prey taking down not only a giant warrior plant Sinner, but ice-monster and speed demon Sinners as well?

All that's happening, and more. The Cutouts, whatever they are, possess immense power. At the rate they're going, the twelve Sinners will be minus-twelve before long.

If I want their sacrifice to mean anything, I'd better act fast.

As two more Sinners crash and burn, I whip around and fix my eyes on the prize: the shimmering, airborne Seed. Then, I focus my will on zooming across the chamber to intercept it.

Yet I go nowhere.

Come on! Any other time, things jump around randomly in this so-called Wonderverse, leaping closer and farther away with ridiculous ease. Why not *now?*

The Seed accelerates toward the door, and I break into a run. Then, suddenly, someone leaps in front of me, blocking the way. It's Julie, grown to three meters tall and scowling as she reaches for me.

I try to dodge her grasp, but I can't. She scoops me up so fast, it knocks the breath right out of me.

She squeezes me so tightly, I think she's going to crush me. Have the Cutouts intensified their control over her?

But her scowl quickly becomes a smile as he swings me up close and plants a kiss on my forehead. "Thank you," she says warmly. "I knew I called in the right people for the job."

Then, she whips around and throws me like a football at the Seed.

Even so, the Seed keeps gaining speed; there's no way I'll catch up with it. My universe is doomed. The biggest mission of my life is about to end in failure.

And then it isn't. Suddenly, an invisible force swoops in and wraps around me. As it lifts me off the floor and carries me toward the Seed, I hear a thousand screaming voices in my head.

As I reel from the unexpected blast of input, I remember the content of the signal that brought us to the *Fractal Tracery* in the first place: *Black stars. White space. Forever screaming.*

This, I realize, is the rest of the mystery. The puzzle beyond the anomaly ends here.

The screaming coalesces into words, telling a story that answers vital questions. It is then that I recognize the voices.

They belong to the crew of the *Fractal Tracery*.

The crew--every last one of them--refused to help the Cutouts harvest survivors from universes they planned to destroy. In return for their refusal, they were murdered, converted to this stream of unified souls even as Julie was shielded and put to use. The souls continued to try to stop the Cutouts, but in their insubstantial state, they failed.

Now, together, *we* are going to *succeed*.

The stream of souls whisks me across the chamber to intercept the Seed. Without thinking, I clamp both hands around it, feeling the pain of its surging power and potential.

It ought to burn a hole right through me and zoom out the door anyway--but the soulstream, grounded and focused by my physical form, restrains it. Cocoons it.

And then, offers to trigger it.

The souls give me a choice. The only way to stop the Seed from obliterating our universe is to set it off now. If we do that, *this* universe and every living thing in it will be destroyed, making way for a *new* universe born from the Seed. But *our* universe--*my* universe, my *home*--will be preserved.

Am I willing to make that trade?

I smile. The souls know the answer before I can say it aloud.

Together, we focus our wills on the Seed. It grows unbearably hot in my hands, and I feel a strange euphoria rippling through me.

Followed by an explosion that tears me apart in every way imaginable for what feels like an eternity of agony.

When I awaken, the Whiteverse/Wonderverse is gone. A new universe has been created in its place.

And *my* home universe, somewhere beyond the boundaries of this one, is intact. I know this, I *sense* it...though I don't know how to get back there. I am trapped in the new universe that sprang from the Seed before it could destroy the universe of my birth.

Frankly, that's okay with me. *This* is my home now. I am linked to it in ways I never imagined before, playing a role I never expected in this vast and amazing creation.

Perhaps because I was at the epicenter of the new Big Bang, I am a part of it all. Somehow, my consciousness remains intact, for I possess an awareness of this universe in all its immense entirety.

And let me just say, this is one *magnificent* universe. The physical laws here are eccentric and unpredictable. What would have been impossible back home is not only possible, but *likely*, over here. The result is a place of such beauty, surprise, and diversity that, trust me, it would blow your mind like a Big Bang seed if you ever came here.

The stars are much larger and more colorful here, not limited to spherical shapes. They orbit planets instead of vice versa, and are inhabited by sentient fission reactions building cities from stable solar prominences.

Space itself is mostly filled with a glittering golden medium that's a combination of dark anti-matter and time in a gaseous state.

And the *lifeforms* exist in such staggering abundance, variety, complexity, and hardiness that they put my home universe and the Cutouts of the Wonderverse to shame.

Do you like the sound of all that? Good; I'm quite proud of it. After all, I helped make it what it is today, and I'm helping influence what it becomes next.

Somehow, I have influence over this place. That's why, for example, evolution here is based on cooperation, not conflict. It's why there's no death or decay, no sickness or pain or sorrow. Because that's the way I think it *should* be.

It's also why there's a constellation of mega-stars inhabited by the souls of the crew of the *Fractal Tracery*. It's why entire worlds are dedicated to the recreated selves of my shipmates from the *Transit*, plus a resurrected, Cutout-free Julie.

What inspired me to use my influence the way I have, to shape this universe into what it's becoming? On some level, I guess I'm still carrying out my mission from my days with The Rising, planting mysteries to draw out species who might one day become spacefarers.

But on another level, some creations have meaning for me alone. Like the blue-green planet in a distant quadrant, the one that forever looks, sounds, and smells like a Georgia night fifty years before the latest Big Bang. The one where a bartender who looks a lot like me walks down a country lane in the moonlight, only to be caught in a shaft of amber light from above.

And a creature that looks like a cloud with dozens of silver eyes on dozens of squirming yellow tendrils asks him a question that changes his life forever. A question that is more prophetic than perhaps even he/she/it/they realizes as the historic words are spoken:

"Would you like. To experience. A universe?"

AYE, PLANK

There was a cabin boy called Christopher Penny who used to take good care of me, scrubbing the blood and sweat and urine from my hard, red grain. When he was done with the brush, he'd rub in oil with a cloth and polish my surface until it gleamed; then, he'd lean me against a mast to dry, letting me soak in the warm rays of the sun. After that, he'd slide me against a bulkhead for storage, tucking me away until I was needed again.

But one day, I was needed for *him*. On that day, Captain Tobias Roughleg had his pirate lackeys push me through a gap in the gunwales until I extended partway over the hull of the ship. After securing me to the deck with a barrel of shot, Roughleg marched poor Penny over me at the point of a cutlass until there was nowhere left to go but the open ocean. One buck of the ship on a rolling wave, and Penny lost his footing on my smooth, polished surface.

Through no fault or choice of my own, the kindly cabin boy fell, never to return. The saddest part of it was, he was only the latest in a long line of men who had gone before him.

Such was the existence of a plank on the pirate ship *Defiler* in the year of our Lord 1750.

On any given day, the salt spray gave me no pleasure, and the sea breeze brought me no joy. All I could think about was the next man who would walk my length, whoever he might be, and when that moment might come.

Would he pray to God or sing a hymn as he shuffled along my surface? Would he curse Captain Roughleg and his crew until he drew his last breath? Or would he beg for mercy, his futile pleas lost in the gales of laughter from the crewmen watching at the gunwales?

Would he dive defiantly into the water, as some had done, or wrap himself around me until one of his shipmates inched out and dislodged him with a sword or pole?

Eventually, however, I met someone who did none of those things.

He came for me early one morning, alone, and drew me out of my storage place. He slid me through the gap in the gunwales and pushed the barrel of shot, with some effort, to weigh down my end on the deck.

Then, with no prodding or jeering from a bloodthirsty pirate captain and his scurviest scoundrels, he took off his boots and slowly walked out along my length.

His breathing was even, his footfalls firm. Though the ship bumped on the waves, his back remained perfectly straight, his balance unshaken.

The sun was just about to rise. Stopping near the end of me, just short of a perilous fall into infinite depths, he gazed into the morning mist in its brightest direction, the east, his mane of fine blond hair and his blond beard fluttering in the soft breeze.

Silent as always, I listened, watched, and waited, mystified by this man…half-thinking he must be a ghost. He wouldn't be the first to roam the decks of *Defiler*, yet I recognized him not as such a shroud. The heft of his physical presence was anything but immaterial.

Why then did he do what he did, taking his life into his hands for no apparent reason? Why do of his own accord that which most grown men had to be *forced* to do? What could his motivation possibly be?

His next actions only deepened the mystery. Reaching into a pocket of his brown leather vest, he drew out a folded slip of white paper, tore it into shreds, and released the shreds to flutter off on the breeze. Then, he held up what looked like a big, blood-red pearl on a chain around his neck and uttered an incantation that was incomprehensible to me.

At that precise moment, as the shreds danced into the mist, a sparkling silver aura surrounded him, rippling and crackling. A warm tingling radiated from the soles of his feet, suffusing my very substance from edge to edge and end to end.

Then, as quickly as the aura and tingling arose, they faded. We were left, as before, with only human flesh and cedar wood in the misty light of dawn, suspended above the lashing, salty waves of the mid-Atlantic Ocean.

With a smile, he turned and walked back to the deck of the ship. Without revealing the truth of his purpose in any way, he removed the barrel of shot, slid me back from between the gunwales, and returned me to storage, object that I was, with no apparent further thought.

Little did I know that morning, as he slipped away to whatever the day's voyage held for him, that our destinies would soon be inextricably bound together in ways I could never have anticipated.

Though I did not often think of my early days in the forests of Lebanon, back before I became a plank on a pirate ship, I thought of them after that morning with the man who walked me of his own accord.

The energy that had flowed out of him reminded me of something from back in Lebanon, long before men with axes had cleaved this piece of me, this plank, from the rest of my original form. I remembered being part of something bigger—a mighty tree with branches spread high and wide across the sky and roots sunk deep in loamy soil. I remembered a perfect, placid happiness, a sense of being at ease among my own solid kind…and, occasionally, a tingling flow of energy coursing up from below, affecting me in ways both subtle and strange…energy that was bright and wild and beyond the mundane.

My people, the trees, have no word for it, but mankind does… and *magic* seems as good a name as any.

But if that solitary man had indeed worked some kind of magic, what was its purpose? Other than what I'd felt, I detected no immediate impact. Was it merely ceremonial or sacrificial, a general offering intended to bring good luck?

Naturally, this obsessed me. *He* obsessed me. I watched and listened for him all day long, glimpsing him only twice in passing… but at least I finally overheard his name: Miles Thackray.

The next morning, when I was pulled from my storage place, I thought at first it was Christopher Penny who had come for me. I'd been dreaming of him, vividly remembering the feel of his hands as they polished me, the sound of his voice as he talked through the task. *Gonna be an easy day today, ain't it? Roughleg's too sick to throw anyone overboard, for a change.*

It wasn't until I slid out between the gunwales and felt the cold sea air rush across my surface that I fully awakened. Only then, as I looked up to see a familiar face, framed with wavy, golden hair and a beard of the same color, did I realize it wasn't Penny who had retrieved me.

It was Thackray.

It was still black as pitch that morning, not a star to be seen. A fine drizzle fell, slickening my surface—yet still, when he'd weighted my end with the barrel, he took off his boots and briskly marched out over me. If he had the slightest concern of losing his footing, he didn't show it.

As before, he stood at the far end of me, gazing into the east…

222

but it was earlier than his previous walk, and no trace of the dawn yet shone there.

His back was straight as ever, his balance as keen. When a whitecap gave *Defiler* a good bump, it didn't budge him. The drizzle fell harder, and the wind stiffened, but he never so much as twitched an eyelid.

Again, he drew a folded slip of paper from his vest pocket and tore it to shreds, then cast them into the wind. Again, he held up the blood-red pearl on its chain around his neck and muttered a strange incantation.

This time, however, the shreds burst into flame when he released them, spinning off into the darkness like embers from a campfire.

That wasn't the only change from last time, either. Again, I felt the warm tingle flowing into me from the soles of his feet...but it was stronger than before. The silver aura coalescing around him was different, too, brighter and thicker.

It all still flickered and faded after a moment, though, wicking away into the rainy wind. Thackray was back to standing there unaltered, a solitary figure on my flattened plane, nothing visibly special about him.

I felt different, though...energized in some unidentifiable way. Still tingling, still warm to the core. The effects of his magic had lingered.

As he walked back over me to the deck, each footfall felt electric. As he slid me back through the gap, each fingertip seemed to crackle with static.

As a plank, a piece of wood, I rarely felt the slightest agitation... but I did then. I was practically vibrating with tension, desperate for release...desperate to know what was happening, desperate to *say* something.

And then, incredibly, I did.

A single word appeared on my surface as he held me, about to put me away...a single word, right in front of his face, scrawled in beads of water upon my red-tinged wood.

Why

At which point, Thackray's eyes bulged in their sockets. He

stood there, gaping, his jaw hanging open, his hands trembling around me.

It was *his* turn to be surprised. It was *his* turn to encounter a mystery.

Then, suddenly, he had no time to explore it further. A shout pierced the quiet early morning from the lookout in the crow's nest mounted high on *Defiler*'s mainmast.

"Ship!" wailed the lookout. "Ship off the port bow!"

One of the crewmen rang the big bell to call all hands from their slumber. Within moments, men poured up out of the hold and spilled onto the deck, rushing to their stations as if they'd never been asleep. The ship thundered with their footsteps and the clatter of gear and guns, the controlled chaos of preparations for what was to come.

The door of the captain's quarters crashed open, and Tobias Roughleg stormed out, his black hair and beard a tangled, matted mess. His tricorne hat was on backward, the skull-and-crossbones side facing behind him. His gold-trimmed, crimson silk robe showed his bare, hairy legs, which were indeed as rough as his name suggested thanks to poorly treated skin disease and battle wounds.

"'Tis the *Bonaventure*, I'll wager!" Roughleg cradled a sinuous gray Persian cat in the crook of his left arm and swung his saber overhead with his right hand. "The very prize we've been seeking these past weeks! Let's *take* her before she gets off a single *shot!*"

When Thackray heard this, he shook his head at me in regret. "I'm afraid you'll have to wait," he said softly. "*Whatever* you truly are."

With that, he quickly stowed me and leaped to his duties with the rest of the crew. Pushed in against the bulkhead, I was alone and out of the mix, the answer to my question delayed...but for now, I didn't mind. For now, I was willing to wait, because a major victory was already mine, one I'd never even thought possible until that morning.

I had been *heard.*

Bonaventure was fast, as she had to be. A frigate of the British navy, she often made the run from Bermuda to Gibraltar, always laden with cargos of great value. She was entrusted with such goods because she'd never been taken, though she was at the top of many pirates' lists of targets.

Seizing her and her cargo, whatever it was this time, would surely bring wealth and renown to Captain Roughleg and his crew. It was the big score they needed to break the dry spell they'd been stuck in for the past six weeks—one sad little haul after another, none of it worth the effort it took to obtain.

Letting *Bonaventure* slip through their fingers was something that everyone on *Defiler* was determined not to let happen. If anyone screwed up, and *Bonaventure* was lost as a result, they all knew the fate they would have to face.

That fate, of course, would involve me.

"Hard to port!" howled Roughleg from the bow. "Best speed to *Bonaventure.*"

"Aye, Captain." I heard Thackray's voice nearby, from the ship's wheel on the quarterdeck. He was manning the helm, guiding our course in pursuit of the prey. "Hard to port. Best speed to *Bonaventure.*"

I felt the ship change direction as Thackray swung the wheel, felt it go faster as other men unfurled and turned sails. The thrill of the hunt mounted for everyone aboard, the excitement of closing in on a prize long desired.

But ask me if I cared a whit, and "no" would be your answer. Wealth and reputation meant nothing to a slab of wood; discovering I could *communicate*, on the other hand, meant *everything*.

All I wanted was to try again, to get an answer to my question, *Why*…though that one word encompassed *multiple* questions. *Why had Thackray walked me alone in the early hours? Why had he torn those slips of paper to shreds and tossed them away? Why had they burst into flame?*

The biggest question, though, the one in the forefront of my mind, had to do with the magic he'd channeled and what it had done to me. What was its purpose, and why had my communication surprised him?

All those questions and more circled around me, dying to be asked…but now I had to wait to ask them. I had to wait through the chase and perhaps longer—through the battle if we managed to catch up to *Bonaventure.*

The way things were going, however, I soon realized I might not have to worry about that.

"Faster!" Roughleg waved his cutlass over the port railing at the distant *Bonaventure.* "Why aren't we *gaining* on them?"

"Because they're running faster than *we* are," said Thackray. "They're outpacing us."

"So catch up!" Roughleg banged the handle of his cutlass on the rail. "Get us up alongside her *now*, or I promise there'll be *hell* to pay."

Thackray barked out a series of orders to the deckhands, commanding them to adjust this sail or that. It felt to me as if *Defiler* accelerated…but Roughleg was still burning with impatience.

"I told you to *catch up!*" he snapped. "Yet it seems the only *hurry* you're in is to get to the end of my *plank.*"

"No sir, Captain," said Thackray. "This is going to take some time, that's all."

"You think I won't *do* it?" roared Roughleg. "You think I won't make you *walk* it?"

Thackray didn't answer.

"You've already lost *one* ship! I won't *let* you lose *mine.*" Roughleg released a guttural howl of pure rage, and his Persian joined in with its own shrill caterwaul. "Never *forget* that, *Captain* Thackray."

"I won't, sir," Thackray said darkly. "I've got a very good memory."

Hours later, deep into the afternoon, we were no closer to *Bonaventure.* Thackray and the crew were still working hard, yet the gap would not shrink. No matter what they did, *Bonaventure* remained stubbornly out of cannon range and nowhere near the reach of our boarding ladders.

I overheard some of the men wondering if *Bonaventure* was there at all, if she were some kind of mirage brought on by desperation. Others whispered that the other vessel was eluding us by magic because Thackray was cursed, that the only chance we stood of catching her was to force him overboard.

But *they* had not seen his confident stride along my length in the wind and rain. No one but me had witnessed his uncanny, magnetic attachment to my surface. They didn't know, as I did, that he had magic of his own at his command.

The decks of *Defiler* were much busier than usual into the night as Thackray and the crew kept up the chase. Roughleg's continued threats and demands spurred them on, his voice booming like cannon fire along the length and breadth of our vessel.

It was starting to look as if the chase might last all night, meaning I might miss my usual morning chat with Thackray. I was disappointed at the thought of waiting longer for answers to my questions—but very late, long after the moon had set, he surprised me, sliding me out of my storage space and laying me flat on the deck. He unwrapped a meager packet of rations from his pocket and spread them on my surface alongside a flagon of ale—hardtack bread, jerky, moldy white cheese, and half a raw potato.

As he ate, he spoke quietly, trying not to draw attention from the others on duty as he directed his voice at me. "Earlier, you asked me a question: 'Why?' Now I have a question for you: 'Who?'" With that, he tipped the flagon and dribbled ale on my surface. "Who am I speaking to here? A shade? A spirit come to haunt me? *Many* spirits?"

Whatever change his magic had wrought in me, it had persisted. Focusing my energy, I was able to shift the liquid, reshaping the random droplets into the letters of the language I'd learned by observing the crew and their works through the months.

No ghost.

Just wood.

Thackray frowned. "Not like any wood *I've* ever met." He sipped his ale. "There's more to you, I know it. There *must* be."

Concentrating again, I traced another message. A few words at a time, it seemed, were all I could manage.

Ruffleg called you Captin.

Are you a Captin?

"A *defeated* captain. A *captured* one." Thackray's frown deepened. "I lost my ship, the *Unerring*, in battle. Lost *everything* but my own life."

Just then, a mate ambled past, and Thackray fell silent, gnawing on the jerky. When we were alone again, he resumed speaking.

"Therein lies the answer to your *first* question, assuming I understood it correctly," he told me. "You asked me 'Why?' I assume you meant, why am I doing what I'm doing? In which case, the answer is, to regain what I lost." He reached for the hardtack. "One part of what I lost, at least. The most *necessary* part of it."

He dribbled a bit more ale on me from the flagon, and I focused on shaping more words. Maybe I was getting tired, because all I managed was one.

How?

Thackray finished the square of hardtack, rewrapped the rest of the food, and put it back in his pocket. He set aside the flagon, then lifted me off the deck and leaned me against the gunwale so one end of me stuck out over the railing, facing aft.

"Look out there." He pointed at the sea beyond *Defiler*'s stern. "Do you see it?"

Gazing in that direction, I saw nothing at first but dark water on the horizon. As I stared longer into the distance, however, I noticed a greenish glow emanating from under the surface.

"*Defiler* may be pursuing *Bonaventure*, but *they* are pursuing *us.*" said Thackray. "And you and I are the only ones on this ship who know it. Everyone else is looking only ahead of us, toward *Bonaventure.*"

They? That's the question I wanted to ask, but all the ale had run off when he'd leaned me on the railing, so I couldn't shape the word.

Drawing a spyglass from a pocket of his vest, he peered through it at the distant glow. "They are the reason I've come out here with you these past mornings. The magic I've been working

with the paper and fire and pearl was meant to summon them...
and it has." He leaned out further, scanning the glowing patch
with the glass. "Reaching them is my true goal," he said. "My *only*
goal."

Listening and looking out there, I was no less mystified than
before. Who "they" were was a question without an answer, at least
for the moment. For the rest of it, I'd have to wait.

"That's enough for now," he said, pulling me down from the
railing and tucking me into my storage space. "I've been away from
my post too long already.

"Sleep now, little plank." He patted my surface. "All will be
made clear to you soon enough. To *everyone.*"

All through the night and into the next day, Thackray and the crew
tried everything to catch up with *Bonaventure*...to no avail. Somehow,
the legendary frigate managed to keep her distance, never allowing
the gap between us to dwindle.

It didn't help when the skies darkened, and the sea grew
rougher. Soon, the men were fighting twice as hard just to stay on
course, let alone pick up speed. Every time *Defiler* gained momentum, roving whitecaps pushed her back. *Bonaventure's* precious cargo
—whatever it was this time—seemed to move further out of reach
with each passing hour.

Captain Roughleg's temper grew fiercer in equal measure,
surging like the tempest the men all feared would soon be loosed
upon us from the gathering storm clouds above. Stomping across
the deck, he struck one crewman after another with the flat of his
cutlass, goading and issuing threats as if that alone would be enough
to hasten our chase.

By the middle of the day, his fury could no longer be contained.
Pounding his way to the wheel, he grabbed Thackray by the arm
and spun him around.

"*Enough* of your *curse!*" bellowed Roughleg. "You've already failed
your ship! I'll be *damned* if you'll keep failing *mine*!" With that, he
heaved Thackray into the waiting arms of his chief thug, Cleat, and

swung his cutlass in the direction of the gap in the gunwales. "Time to walk on water, you swine!"

Roughleg's men hauled me out of storage, slid me through the gap, and weighted my end with the barrel. As soon as I was secured, bald, brown-bearded Cleat led Thackray onto my surface and shoved him forward in the face of the impending storm.

"Walk it!" howled Roughleg. "Begone from my sight, you scurvy wretch!"

Blond locks and beard whipping in the wind, Thackray took one step forward, then another. *Defiler* rose on a sudden swell, jarring him, then dove down the other side…and I could tell that even *his* amazing equilibrium was in peril.

"Go on!" Roughleg grabbed a long gaff hook from one of the thugs and poked him in the back with it. "Go navigate for Davy Jones where you belong!"

As *Defiler* lurched again, nearly throwing Thackray free, I panicked. The energy he'd planted within me, the *magic* he'd worked, built swiftly in intensity.

Without Thackray, I'd never have the answers I craved. Worse, I'd never again be able to communicate with the one man in my existence who had miraculously given me a voice.

Thackray crouched, trying to steady himself—but Roughleg gave him a sharp jab just as *Defiler* crashed over a rolling hump, and he lost his footing. He started to stumble off me, aimed for the frothing turbulence below…

…and suddenly, the energy building within me burst outward, changing the properties of my very substance.

More than anything, I wanted to reach out and catch Thackray…and then I found myself doing just that. The wooden fibers of my body stretched and twined, swiftly forming a scoop in the path of his toppling body. I stopped him before he could tumble into the abyss, holding him high above the roiling chaos.

Eyes wide, Roughleg dropped the gaff hook, letting it bounce off the hull and plunge into the heaving sea. Cleat and the others looked just as shocked.

"In the name of God, what manner of demon *are* you?" shouted Roughleg. "What *black magic* do you command?"

One of the men hurled a knife at Thackray's chest, intending to sink it deep. Without thinking, I reshaped myself in an instant, flinging up a thick wooden plate to deflect the weapon without even a nick to Thackray.

While this was happening, Thackray quickly pulled himself together. "I'm your worst *nightmare*, Roughleg!" He scrambled to his feet. "I am the personification of righteous *power*, and *you* cannot *control* me."

With a roar of rage, he charged over me toward the gunwales and leaped onto the deck before Roughleg's men could pull the barrel and kick me overboard. I followed, wrapping my malleable wood around his torso, head, and fists, then hardening into a breast-plate, helmet, and gauntlets of armorlike rigidity.

Startled, Cleat and the others scattered, leaving Roughleg in our sights. Before he could flee, Thackray knocked the cutlass from his grip with one cedar-gauntleted hand, then seized him by the wrists.

"Let go of me!" snarled Roughleg. "This is *mutiny!*"

"Brilliant observation!" Twisting Roughleg's wrists, Thackray drove him toward the mainmast. "You have indeed lost command of this vessel!"

"To one such as *you? Never!*" Roughleg struggled to break his captor's grip. "You are a *failed* captain! An utter *disgrace*, *unfit* for command!"

"You describe yourself quite well." Thackray threw Roughleg against the mast, then grabbed a rope from the deck and lashed him to it. "For you *are* the disgraced failure, and this ship is now *mine.*"

Enraged, Roughleg bellowed for help from the crew—yet no one, not even Cleat, rushed to his aid. Were they intimidated by the sight of Thackray in his cedar-plated armor, uncertain what magic he possessed to give it form? Or had they simply lost faith in Roughleg or grown tired of living in constant terror under his wrathful command?

Whatever the reason, no one helped the bastard. He howled his lungs out, stomped like a maniac, cursed and spit in every direction —and even his slinky gray Persian cat stayed away.

Thackray, meanwhile, got the cooperation he demanded. When

he gave his first order, the same crewmen who'd doubted him earlier now hurried to comply.

"Break off from *Bonaventure*," he shouted above the rising wind and Roughleg's curses. "Bring her all the way around and set new course."

Cleat stopped in his tracks and glared at the stern of *Defiler*. "You want us to go back the way we *came*?"

"Exactly!" said Thackray. "And double-quick about it, if you please, Mr. Cleat." He turned the wheel hard, wrenching the ship from its present course. "Best possible speed and prepare for battle!" Just then, Roughleg cut loose with his most flagrant stream of invective yet. "Oh, and somebody gag the *former* captain, and make it snappy!"

As *Defiler* swung around and plowed toward the still-distant glow, I discovered a new way to communicate with Thackray. Forming letters out of moisture on my surface was no longer necessary; with some effort, I found I could speak to him directly, transmitting a voice into the bones of his skull through vibrations in the helmet that I'd grown on his head.

It was a good thing, too, because I had questions and didn't think I had much time to ask them. Since the glow was pursuing us, and we'd doubled back to head straight for it instead of running the other way after *Bonaventure*, our paths would soon intersect.

"Who...are...they?" The words formed with difficulty, but at least they came. "The ones...you...summoned." It was quite an accomplishment, as I'd never spoken aloud before, though I'd spent much of my life listening to the words spoken by humans.

Thackray reached up and touched the helmet, perhaps surprised at the sound of my voice. "Good to finally hear you," he said with a smile. "Thanks for the save out there, by the way." He gestured at the gap in the gunwales where he'd nearly fallen to his death.

Gathering my strength, I eked out more words. "All...will be...

made clear...you said." I paused, collecting myself again. "So... make it...clear. Who...are they?"

"I thought that would be obvious," said Thackray. "They're *pirates*, of course."

If I'd had the ability to frown, I would have done so. "Pirates?"

"Yes." He nodded. "And they have something of mine that I want back. It's a good thing I have something of *theirs* with which to trade."

Another question formed in my thoughts...but before I could ask it, men started shouting from the prow of *Defiler*. Something was happening that demanded all our attention.

A piece of the ocean was exploding, and we were heading straight for it.

Great geysers erupted as we approached, shooting jets of seawater high in the air. If one of them were to go off under us, I felt sure it would blast *Defiler* into oblivion.

"Arm the port cannons!" As Thackray said it, he chucked the wheel hard to the right, swinging us around to expose the port flank to the eruption site. "Ready volley, on my mark!"

The men didn't answer, but every one of those affected ran to comply. Some waited with long kindle cords dipped in pitch and set afire, ready to light the fuses on those stout guns. Others crouched among stacked cannonballs, ready to reload the gun barrels as soon as they emptied. Still others manned the aiming levers, determined that each shot would find its target...if only they knew what exactly the target *was*.

"Sir!" shouted the chief gunner, a red-haired man named Halloran. "Tell us what we're *shooting* at, sir!"

Thackray pointed at the convulsing water from which the geysers sprang. As the sky continued to darken from the storm, the green glow below the surface was becoming more visible. "There's your bullseye! Aim *right there*, for the *heart* of that emerald flame!"

"You want us to shoot *fish*?" Halloran sounded aghast. "Are you bloody *mad*?"

"The *enemy* is *down* there!" snapped Thackray. "That *light* you see is no school of fish! It is the *fire* of the enemy's own infernal *weapons!*"

"But we'll be *throwing away* our ammunition! Might as well drop the cannonballs over the gunwales and be done with it!"

"Trust me!" Thackray's voice was fierce. "Aim for the *center* of the conflagration!"

Halloran hesitated, face twisting…and then he rounded on his men, roaring out instructions as if he'd never questioned the sense of them in the first place. "You heard him! Swing down the guns! Aim for the middle of the bright spot!"

All six cannons were tipped, their lines of fire adjusted to strike the water. "Ready, sir!" hollered Halloran when it was done.

"Fire!" bellowed Thackray without hesitation. "Port guns, *fire!*"

At the same moment that the men lit the fuses, lightning flashed from above. The thunder of the descending storm boomed just as the cannons let loose, and *Defiler* shook with the force of it.

Six cannonballs plunged into the deep, one after another. It was a fusillade of high-speed iron sufficient to blow gaping holes in the hull of any ship…but flung into the trackless ocean, they were simply swallowed up without having any apparent impact.

"Another round?" asked Halloran.

Thackray pumped a fist in the air. "Fire when ready!"

As the gunners raced to reload for another strike, I took advantage of the pause in the action to speak again. "You said…pirates. What kind…of pirates…down there?"

"Same as the ones up here," said Thackray. "Only far more ruthless." He smiled. "And water-breathing, of course."

"Ready, the guns!" shouted Halloran as a harsh bolt of lightning split the darkened sky. "And *fire!*"

Thunder and cannons boomed alike, nearly in synch, and another round of iron poured into the brightness. Again, it seemed the assault had no impact on whatever unnatural thing lurked below.

Then, suddenly, there came a rumbling from beneath the waves, transmitted through the wooden structure of *Defiler.* The whole ship shook with increasing force, causing everyone to look around apprehensively…

...everyone but Thackray, who roared above the unearthly vibration while spinning the wheel. "Hard about!" He alone was aware of the true nature of the impending assault they faced.

People snapped out of their states of distraction and leaped to comply, but it was too late. From the edge of the bright spot, a volley of pale, jagged missiles launched at *Defiler*, a dozen giant spears of carved and polished driftwood rocketing toward the ship.

One of the missiles punched through the gut of a man on the poop deck and nailed him to a mast. Though *Defiler* was in mid-turn, three other men also died in the bombardment, and the main-sail was left with a gaping hole...as was Captain Roughleg's personal quarters.

As *Defiler* rolled away, an enormous fork of lightning blazed across the heavens, followed by the loudest burst of thunder yet. Another barrage was unleashed from the glow, this one shredding even more sails and piercing more men.

Suddenly, a thought flashed through me: *Was this what it had been like on the* Unerring? *Was Thackray, after all, a bringer of doom?*

"Ready the starboard guns!" he howled. "Continue to target the core of the light! Fire when ready!"

As men rushed to obey, torrential rain exploded from above, hammering the crew and ship alike. The rain doused all but two of the cannon fuses, leaving the latest volley the smallest and weakest yet.

But the harsh weather did not deter the enemy in the slightest. Another salvo of missiles crashed into *Defiler*, and another, destroying even more of her structure.

Men's screams mingled with the roar of the rain and clamor of thunder, filling the air with an unholy symphony of pain and chaos. Thackray let go of the wheel, and *Defiler* foundered, drifting help-lessly before the unseen foe.

But another salvo of missiles did not come, nor any other form of attack. Had our undersea opponents run out of ammunition, or did they just assume there was no need to waste it on a ship so nearly dead in the water?

Whatever the pause portended, Thackray charged like a man

possessed for the stern—the part of *Defiler* that was now closest to the glow.

"What…are you…doing?" I asked him. "What…now?"

Without answering, he rushed up onto the poop deck, pulling a piece of paper from his vest pocket along the way. Leaning over the railing, he hastily tore the paper to bits and tossed them into the pounding rain—then reached for the blood-red pearl and yanked its chain from around his neck. Holding the pearl high, he uttered an incantation…and, in spite of the rain, the bits of paper caught fire as they plummeted into the sea far below.

The familiar silvery aura coalesced around him, sparkling in the stormy darkness. Once again, I found myself suffused with the tingling warmth that came with the magic he worked, the very magic that had blessed me with movement and voice.

"I have it!" Thunder cracked as Thackray shouted into the storm. "I have what you want *right here!*" Was it a trick of the light, or did the pearl wink and swirl and effervesce as he gripped it over-head, its chain wrapped around his fist? "I will return it, if *you* return what you took from *me!*"

I wanted so badly to ask what it was they'd taken, what he'd lost, but I didn't. I waited, as did he, amid the wrack and ruin of the tempest and battle, expecting yet dreading some kind of response, if indeed he had even been heard through the cacophony.

Long moments passed without an answer. Perhaps the enemy, as powerful as they were, would decide to simply crush us and seize what they wanted.

Then, there was the sound of great rumbling from below. The storm-tossed water over the glow churned even more violently…and something massive broke the surface, heaving up like a breaching leviathan.

Illuminated by the flashing lightning, I saw great trunks of kelp extend upward, bobbing with masses of fronds and bladders. As they rose, the trunks entwined, knitting themselves together into a single tongue of brownish-green vegetation, like a gangway, a ramp —a plank.

"Drop anchor!" shouted Thackray, but his words were swal-lowed by the storm. "Hold position! *Hold position!*"

Thunder detonated overhead as the plank of kelp pushed toward us, cascades of water gushing down from it to burst upon the sea like shattered glass. As Thackray watched it approach, I felt his heart hammer against me, racing so hard I feared it might blow apart from the strain...but it was only getting started.

I swear it doubled its pace when the first figures emerged from the glowing sea at the base of the plank—beings with red-and-black striped heads and torsos like lionfish, studded with spines, and the spiky lower bodies and legs of king crabs.

"What manner of devils be *they?*" asked Cleat, who had joined us at the stern.

"No more devils than we are." Thackray swung the red pearl on its chain as if it were bait, enticing them closer.

Cleat had a cutlass in his hand, and I thought he might use it on Thackray...but then he backed away instead, eyes fixed on the newcomers. "You really *are* some kind'a *demon*, ain't ya'?"

Thackray ignored him, transfixed by the strange creatures scuttling toward us. As they drew closer, I saw they were dragging something behind them, wrapped in a deep green shroud.

It almost looked, I thought, like the body of a person ensconced in seaweed.

As the creatures neared *Defiler*, Thackray and I were alone on the poop deck. Cleat, after rattling his cutlass and making a few idle threats, had gone elsewhere, unwilling to face what to him was a great unknown.

Still unanchored, the ship bucked and drifted, pulling away from the visitors...but the kelp plank twisted and stretched to close the gap.

Soon, the crab-people had reached the end of the walkway and stood mere feet from the stern rail of *Defiler*. They gaped at us with dark, bulging eyes, their tiger-striped frills and quills shivering in the ongoing downpour.

"Give me what's mine." Thackray's heart raced as he said those words. "Only then will I hand over what you seek."

The crab-people hesitated, tipping their heads one way, then another. They made noises like the gurgling of bubbles from a tube, a language that was indecipherable to me.

But apparently not to Thackray, who shook his head briskly and held the blood-red pearl well away from them. "Don't you *dare*, or you'll lose *much* more than the *eye* of your *god* this day!" As he said it, the light of his silvery aura suddenly flared as if in warning.

To me, the reactions of the crab-people were unreadable. They gurgled some more, clacked their pincer claws, and flexed their jagged spines in our direction. I thickened my plating as best I could, hoping I could deflect those spines if necessary.

Then, one of the crab-people reached back, grabbed one end of the package they'd been dragging, and hauled it around between them. The creature raised it toward us, offering it like a gift—and by the brightest lightning surge all day, I finally saw that the form under the wrapping was indeed human.

The rain poured harder than ever as Thackray leaned over the rail and reached down, the red pearl dangling from his fingers. One of the creatures reached for it, extending its pincer…

…but Thackray snatched the pearl away and took the green-wrapped body with it, wrenching them both out of reach of the crab-people.

The creatures scuttled around in a frenzy, clacking their pincers and making high-pitched wailing noises. Others of their kind scrambled up out of the water behind them, even as their kelp plank extended further, about to make contact with *Defiler*'s railing.

Thackray, meanwhile, laid the body on the deck and hastily ripped a flap of seaweed away, exposing a human face…that of a young boy. Tears streaming from his eyes, he bent down and pressed his ear to the boy's mouth, lingering there even as the crab-people prepared to cross from their plank to our vessel.

Suddenly, Thackray leaped to his feet and thrust up his hands, palms facing the creatures. "The deal is off! He's *dead!*"

One crab-person stopped short of clambering aboard. The creature gurgled and whooped, its spiny frills flexing with each enunciation.

What Thackray heard seemed to give him pause. He looked down at the still form of the boy on the deck and frowned.

"What...did it...say?" I asked him.

"'A spark of life remains,'" said Thackray. "The body is dead, the child drowned...but that single spark survives. They preserved it all this time."

I listened, trying to understand. "Who...is this...child?"

"My son, Ezra." Thackray's voice darkened. "Those *things*." He gestured at the nearest creature, which waited just beyond the stern railing. "They *took* him after I raided a temple of theirs while captain of the *Unerring*. I'd stolen the crimson eye of their idol god, their greatest treasure..." He held up the blood-red pearl. "...so *they* stole *my* most precious thing when my guard was down.

"But I *swore* I'd get him back. I learned the dark arts of magic from wicked sea hags and sorcerous islanders...figured out how to use the idol's eye to bestow myself with power and summon the creatures...but there was one thing I never learned to do." He sucked in one long, shuddering breath between clenched teeth. "I never learned to *raise the dead*. I never realized that was the one spell I needed...because apparently, those water-breathing *bastards* didn't know how to keep an air-breathing *human* child *alive.*"

It would be wrong to say my heart broke for him, because I didn't possess such an organ, but I felt a shared pain at his misfortune. It didn't seem fair, after he'd rescued me from existence as a mute, immobile witness to a parade of executions, that there was nothing I could do in turn to ease his suffering.

Just then, the creature at the railing squawked and clacked its pincers. I had a feeling it was getting impatient.

"Oh God, I miss him." Thackray ran his trembling fingers over Ezra's pale features. "I'm so sorry I led him to this...that my short-sighted greed snuffed out his young life..."

"But they told you...he is not...dead," I said.

"A mere spark of life is no good without a *living body* to hold it," said Thackray.

"What if...there *could be*...such a body?" I asked. "Could you... use the god's eye...for one last...miracle...before giving it back?"

The creature squawked and reached for the pearl...but

239

Thackray batted its pincer away. "Not done yet!" he snapped, then touched the cedar plating I'd formed over his heart, directing his voice at me. "Now tell me, my friend. What do you have in mind?"

He listened as I spoke, eyes narrowed at first, uncertain...but that changed. My proposal won him over, and we came to an agreement.

Then he raised the blood-red pearl one last time, uttered an incantation, and a bright flash that wasn't lightning enveloped us all, accompanied by the oddest sequence of musical tones ending in an explosive and lingering crescendo.

It is later, months later, and the sun is shining.

Standing at the edge of a tropical pool, I gaze down at my reflection in the water—the reflection of what I've become. Not for the first time, I think I resemble Christopher Penny, the cabin boy who once marched over me to his death at the behest of Captain Roughleg. I remember how Penny used to rub and polish me with oil, and I think it's only fitting to pay tribute to that boy...though the resemblance is not intentional. I never consciously attempted to add Penny's likeness to my current form.

There is room for only *two* of us in here, after all.

Let's catch one more fish. The voice in my head is that of my constant companion, the soul who shares this body. *We don't want to come up short for dinner.*

"Sounds good." I reach out over the pool with our fishing pole— one wooden finger grown long and wrapped with a line that ends in a baited hook. With the ease of frequent practice, I shaped that finger into a makeshift fishing pole just as I once reshaped the entirety of my wooden substance into the form of a human child.

That was the good faith agreement I came to months ago with Miles Thackray on the deck of *Defiler*—that I would provide a body to house the last spark of his son Ezra's life. That I would animate this wooden form with whatever magic I yet possessed, amplified by the power of the god's eye pearl, and the two of us would share this shell for the rest of our existence.

It was an agreement we did not hesitate to fulfill. As Thackray held up the pearl and uttered an incantation, I tapped its power and transformed as promised, taking on the shape—and inhaling the final spark—of the human child on the deck before me. My eyes opened, glittering with the magic of the new thing that I'd become, even as the empty vessel of Ezra's original human body twitched one last time and gave up the ghost forever.

"Father?" When the deed was done, the boy's voice came unbidden from our smooth cedar lips. "Where am I?"

With that, Thackray tossed the blood-red pearl to the crab-people and threw his arms around us, openly weeping. The creatures withdrew down their kelp plank and disappeared underwater, leaving the father and son—and me—to savor their reunion.

That moment was just the beginning. The days since then have not always been easy in every way, but every one of them has been a cause for celebration—to the father and son for being returned to each other, and to me for making it possible.

Compared to the dark and lonely life I knew aboard *Defiler*, it is paradise. After participating in the deaths of so many, being able to *save* someone is the ultimate joy.

Being able to save *more* than that someone in the bargain is even better.

"The fishermen return!" Miles Thackray looks up and grins when we get back to camp—a hut on the beach built with boards from the lifeboat that brought us here. After everything that happened—and seeing the sorcerous boy of cedar we'd created—the surviving crew of *Defiler* were only too happy to drop us off at the next habitable island in our path.

"Look how many." Ezra holds up the five fish we caught, hanging from a cord. "The pond was full of them!"

"We're sure going to eat well tonight!" says Thackray, though he's the only one of us who's actually capable of eating. "Bring 'em here!"

We run over and spontaneously hug him, fish slapping against us. Sometimes, the things this body does are more Ezra than me, and this is one of those times.

Not that I'm complaining. I use this body for my own devices, too, sometimes, especially when Ezra's asleep inside me. Just last night, in fact, I finished a project I'd been working on for quite a while.

After dinner, as we sit on the sand and flick fish bones into the campfire, I decide to present that project as planned.

"Miles?" I use my own voice instead of the child's this time. "I have something for you."

"Oh?" Thackray frowns.

I open a little hinged door cut into our left side and pull a gift wrapped in a banana leaf from our body's hollow interior. "Here." I hand it over, my cedar skin looking redder than usual from the glow of the fire.

What is it? wonders Ezra.

A surprise. That's all I tell him. *You'll see.*

Thackray unwraps it carefully and holds it up to the firelight. "It's…incredible." He turns it around in his grasp, marveling at what I've made. "I can't believe you *did* this."

"Happy anniversary," I tell him.

"Anniversary?" He can't stop gaping at the little clear glass bottle that I found washed up on the shore—and the intricate object I created within it.

"Our new life started six months ago today." I reach over and pat his shoulder. "It's worth celebrating."

"Aye, it is." Thackray turns the bottle around and around, gazing at the tiny ship inside it. "But I still don't understand how you got this *in* here."

"Practice." That's all I'll say. The truth is, 'twas magic got it done…the same magic that enabled me to shape the cedar wood of this body that once was a plank that once was part of a tree in Lebanon. The same magic that let me start with a single splinter of myself, dropped through the neck of the bottle, and grow a tiny scale model of a ship inside it, accurate in every detail.

A ship with a familiar name inscribed upon it.

"On the prow." Tears roll down Thackray's face as he squints at the tiny vessel in its glass container. "Does it say what I *think* it does?" He sounds surprised…and moved.

"Yes, it does." Did he expect it to say *Unerring?* The name of the ship he once lost? Well, it doesn't. If you care about someone, you don't remind him of a complete disaster that left his life in a shambles, do you?

You remind him instead of a ship that can never be caught, a ship sailing always out of reach, always stocked with treasures beyond compare and bound for her own special destiny. You remind him of a ship that inspires dreams and legends and brings meaning to the lives of those who seek escape, redemption, and a fresh start.

You name it *Bonaventure*.

ACIREMA THE RELLIK

The great state of Missouri lay across the Speaker's bench at the front of the House of E-representatives, wrapped in the American flag. His eyes and mouth gaped, and his arms and legs hung over the sides, dripping blood on the carpet below.

"Oh, God," said Connecticut, her shaky hand hovering over Missouri's motionless chest. "He's not breathing."

Manitoba stood on the next tier down and wouldn't come any closer. "Is there a--what's it called? Heartbeat?"

Connecticut lowered her hand, then jerked it away. "That's in the throat, right?" Nervously, she scrubbed her palms on her smart red pantsuit. "Or is it the arm?"

That was when Nevada had finally had enough.

Without a word, he pushed his tall, lanky body through the crowd on the floor of the House and charged up the steps to the Speaker's bench. Without hesitation, he pressed two fingers against the side of Missouri's throat.

"No pulse." Nevada said it loud enough for the whole crowd to hear. "The Speaker of the House is dead."

A great gasp went up from the crowd--the computer-generated, artificial intelligence-driven avatars of ninety-eight of the one-hundred states of the United States of America. Though they didn't have flesh-and-blood bodies and shouldn't have feared being murdered in the physical sense, the evidence of dead Missouri had left them all shell-shocked.

"But how?" Connecticut slipped off her gold-rimmed glasses, let them hang by the diamond-studded chain around her neck...then slid them back on a second later. "And why?"

Nevada pushed up the sleeves of his tuxedo. He took Missouri's head in his hands and turned it gently to one side, exposing a gruesome wound. "Blow to the back of the head." Accepting the wound for what it appeared to be instead of what it was--an electronic simulation of a wound--he looked around for a simulated weapon that could have caused it. "What did it and why, I don't know."

"What are those?" Connecticut pointed at bloody marks on Missouri's left arm.

Nevada put Missouri's head down on the bench and took a look at the arm. Wiping some of the blood away, he realized the marks followed a familiar design.

Someone had cut a number into Missouri's arm. "One hundred," said Nevada. "It's the number one hundred."

The crowd murmured and moved restlessly. Nevada could tell the e-reps were confused because they usually acted more decisively.

They were A.I. avatars of the United States in the year 2300, guided by the aggregate preferences of the human electorate in the world outside. Perfectly attuned to the people they represented, perfectly immune to corruption, they never hesitated or doubted themselves.

That was why their confusion was unusual...and it didn't last long. As Nevada examined the body on the Speaker's bench, three of the e-reps broke from the pack and stormed toward him with jaws and shoulders set.

Sinaloa, in the middle, flipped his red-lined bullfighter's cape over his shoulder. "This is impossible." An American state since Mexico had disbanded twenty-five years ago, Sinaloa cultivated an air of insolence and false bravado. "What we see here is the product of a server malfunction."

"Exactly." South Africa tossed his glossy blond hair beside Sinaloa. "This is a bug. The Developers will fix it."

Nevada rubbed the stubbly cleft of his chin and met South Africa's blue-eyed stare. "Like Idaho?"

South Africa straightened his khaki safari shirt and looked away. So did stocky Kamchatka, the recent Russian convert, who had followed him up the steps.

Sinaloa glared. "I hear that Idaho might have been someone *else's* fault. Not the Developers."

A cold, threatening smile spread across Nevada's face. He knew exactly whom Sinaloa was talking about.

He was talking about Nevada.

"Then maybe you'd best be careful." Nevada adjusted his gold pinky rings and cracked his knuckles. "Just in case he can hear what you're saying."

"If, by some wild chance, the same person is responsible for this crime, I hope he *does* hear me," said Sinaloa. "I want him to know he won't get away with what he's done."

"Tell him yourself, when you catch him." Nevada started to walk away.

"*I* won't catch him." Sinaloa snagged Nevada's shoulder and held him in place. "*You're* sergeant-at-arms of the House, aren't you?"

Nevada sighed. "As of twenty-four *hours* ago. What makes you think I'm ready to catch a *killer*?"

Sinaloa let go of Nevada. "We all know you've done this job before." He tightened his bolo tie, pushing the turquoise slide higher into the neck of his black silk shirt. "Five years ago, yes?"

"So what?" said Nevada.

"So you've got experience," said Sinaloa. "Not just with being sergeant-at-arms, but with losing e-reps on the job."

Nevada felt the urge to clock him in the face. Idaho had been his greatest failure, his darkest moment.

His deepest love.

"You're better qualified than any of us. You have more motivation to solve this than anyone," said Sinaloa. "You have quite a lot to prove, don't you?"

Nevada smirked and loosened the collar of the frilly shirt under his tux jacket. "You just don't want to get your hands dirty. None of you ever do."

Even as he said it, he knew Sinaloa was right. He knew what people thought of him. He knew he had a lot to prove.

And he knew he would take the case.

"Missouri and I walked out together," said Antarctica, her beautiful silver eyes staring into space. "He went back in for some papers he'd forgotten." She tucked her long, platinum hair behind her ears, and a single tear rolled down her pale cheek. "That was the last time I saw him alive."

Across the table, Nevada watched Antarctica's reaction closely. She was the last person to have seen Missouri before the murder, and that earned her a spot on the list of suspects.

She was also a sweet kid, and Nevada didn't buy her as a killer. She was the youngest e-rep, in fact, from the newest, hundredth state; Antarctica had joined the U.S.A. only one year ago, in 2299. Strikingly beautiful and shining with inner light, the junior Congresswoman gave Nevada an impression of innocence and honesty, not wiles and lies.

For a moment, Nevada looked away from her, directing his gaze across the chamber at the bloody Speaker's bench. While Nevada interviewed witnesses in the back of the room, other e-reps were up front, clearing the crime scene.

"Did he say anything unusual?" Nevada flicked his eyes to Antarctica, then back to the cleanup crew. They'd already removed Missouri's body, but the blood was another matter. Soap and water didn't exist in the digital realm, so the e-reps couldn't scrub out the soaked-in stains.

Antarctica adjusted her white fur wrap. "Just small talk about today's vote."

As Nevada considered his next question, his fellow e-reps gave up trying to clean the Speaker's bench and draped a red tablecloth over it to hide the blood. "How close were the two of you?"

"He was a mentor to me," said Antarctica.

"And there was nothing else between you?" Nevada locked eyes with her. "Nothing of a more personal nature?"

Antarctica didn't flinch. "Nothing."

Nevada believed her. "Okay, fine. Thank you for your time."

With that, Nevada rose from his chair and called out to the e-reps milling around the chamber. "Will the great state of Panama please report to the sergeant-at-arms."

When Nevada turned back to the interview table, he realized that Antarctica was still sitting there.

"You're dismissed, sweetheart," said Nevada. "Unless you've got something else to say?"

Antarctica nodded grimly. "I want to help you. I want to help find who killed him."

Nevada fiddled with his tuxedo cufflinks. He could think of two reasons for her offer. One, she really *did* want to do her part to bring the killer to justice.

Or two, she *was* the killer, and she wanted to divert attention from her own guilt.

Either way, Nevada figured he could use her.

"Why not?" he said. "As long as you don't mind getting your hands dirty."

"I'll do what I have to." Antarctica rose, smoothing the glittering, ice-blue gown that she wore under her fur wrap. "Missouri was a great state."

"Aren't they all?" said Nevada.

Panama was no help. Neither was Jamaica or Wyoming or any of the other states who had been around Missouri before his death.

After hours of questioning one e-rep witness after another, Nevada was no closer to solving the murder. According to the witnesses, Missouri hadn't said or done a thing out of the ordinary, and no one in his orbit had said or done anything suspicious.

Frustrated, Nevada marched out of the House chamber through

the big double doors and into the halls of the digital Capitol building. "I need some fresh air." Antarctica followed him.

Except for Nevada and Antarctica, the halls were empty. The e-reps, whose sole reason for existing was to vote on legislation according to the will of the electorate, rarely ventured outside the House chamber. Neither did the e-senators.

"What's next?" said Antarctica.

Nevada shrugged. "Missouri's office, I guess. Root around for some kind of clue."

"Like what?" said Antarctica. "What are we looking for?"

"How should I know?" said Nevada. "I'm no detective."

Antarctica frowned. "What did Sinaloa mean when he said you have experience losing e-reps on the job?"

Nevada sighed. "Didn't anyone ever tell you about Idaho?"

"I'm new around here," said Antarctica. "There's a lot I don't know."

"Idaho disappeared five years ago," said Nevada. "I was sergeant-at-arms at the time, and I couldn't find her."

"So they blame you for losing her?" said Antarctica.

"Some of them." Nevada listened to his lizard-skin cowboy boots echoing down the corridor. "And some think I might have *killed* her."

Antarctica gaped at him. "How could they think *that*?"

"Because we were lovers." Nevada stopped in front of an office door. The print on the frosted glass bore the name of Missouri. Nevada turned the knob.

Antarctica walked in after him and closed the door. As Nevada rifled drawers and flipped through papers on Missouri's desk, Antarctica circled the perimeter, watching him with a guarded expression.

"Nothing here." After ransacking the desk for a while, Nevada planted his hands on his hips and shook his head. "Nothing out of the ordinary."

"What about that?" Antarctica pointed toward the door through which they'd entered. At the base of it, a single sheet of blank paper lay flat on the floor.

"Someone must have slid it under the door while we were busy," said Nevada.

Antarctica picked up the paper. "Why would somebody slip us a piece of paper with nothing on it?"

"Depends." As soon as Nevada's fingers touched the page, black lettering appeared on it. "Depends who it's addressed to."

Antarctica leaned in close enough that Nevada could smell her sweet gardenia perfume, and they read the note together.

Statue of Liberty, 3PM, Come Alone.

"It's an invitation," said Nevada. "Somebody wants to tell me something."

"Or maybe this is from the killer," said Antarctica. "Maybe he wants you to 'come alone' so he can kill you."

"There's only one way to find out." Nevada crumpled the paper into his tux jacket pocket and headed for the door.

From the windows in the tiara of the Statue of Liberty, Nevada gazed out over the digital realm that was his home.

He could see everything spread out before him--a world of American landmarks, brought together to provide picturesque back-drops for the e-reps' and e-sens' press conferences.

In the middle of it all, Nevada saw the gleaming white dome of the Capitol building. Northwest of the Capitol jabbed the ivory needle of the Washington Monument; to the southwest rested the Lincoln Memorial. The Liberty Bell hung in a golden tower to the southeast, and Plymouth Rock perched on a pedestal to the northeast.

Straight across the bubble of the digital realm from the Statue of Liberty, Mount Rushmore spanned the horizon, its giant presi-dential heads gazing out over the city. Niagara Falls roared to the east, and the Grand Canyon sprawled to the west, glowing forever red in the

never-dimming sunrise.

"Nevada." The whispered voice from across the room surprised him. Nevada shot his gaze into the shadows...and saw an intercom speaker built into the wall there.

"Nevada." The voice spoke again, still no more than a whisper. Nevada crossed the room and stood close to the speaker, straining to identify who was doing the talking.

"Nevada. Are you *there*?"

Nevada pressed the button to transmit and spoke into the grill in the wall. "I'm here. Who is this?"

"Call me Looking Glass." The voice belonged to a man, but that was all Nevada could tell. "I know where to look."

"For what?" said Nevada.

"For Yukon's murderer," said Looking Glass.

A sharp chill raced up Nevada's spine. "Don't you mean Missouri's? Yukon isn't dead."

"She wasn't," said Looking Glass, "when you got on Lady Liberty's elevator."

Nevada's finger shook as he pressed the intercom button again. "Is that what this is about? Did you bring me here so I'd be out of the way while you killed Yukon?"

"Here is your first clue," said Looking Glass. "When is one one-hundred?"

Nevada scowled. "Just tell me if you did it. Tell me if you killed them both."

"When does one plus zero equal two?" said Looking Glass. "That's your second clue."

"If you didn't do it, who did?" said Nevada.

"No more for now," said Looking Glass. "See you after three and four."

With that, the line went dead.

Nevada slammed the button with the palm of his hand. "Looking Glass! Talk to me!"

But Looking Glass was gone.

Yukon sat on the toilet in the women's lavatory, fully dressed and covered in blood and toilet paper. Her long, brown hair covered her face like a shroud.

"When did you find her?" Nevada stood in the doorway of the stall, hands on his hips.

Nervous Connecticut stood at his left. "A half-hour ago." She took off her gold-rimmed glasses, then put them back on...then took them off again. "We c-came in together for a sidebar. She was f-fine when I left."

Nevada nodded. Since the e-reps weren't programmed for excretory functions, bathrooms in the digital realm were used mostly for sidebar meetings and private deals. "Let me guess. No one noticed anything unusual."

"Not exactly, señor." Sinaloa clapped him on the shoulder. "Some of us noticed *you* leaving the House shortly before the murder."

Nevada ignored him and stepped into the stall. Gently, he parted the hair over Yukon's face with his fingertips, revealing a gruesome palette of cuts and bruises.

Pushing the hair away from her throat, he saw the biggest visible wound--a bloody gash from ear to ear.

"And no murder weapon left behind." Nevada was thinking out loud. "No bloody footprints, no fingerprints, no nothing."

"Tell me." Sinaloa flipped the red-lined bullfighter's cape over his shoulder with a flourish. "How is your first investigation going? Can you tell us who murdered Missouri?"

Nevada spotted the edge of a bloody symbol sticking out from under the toilet paper wrapped around Yukon's forearm. Tearing away the paper, he saw that there were two symbols underneath-- two numerals carved into Yukon's flesh.

Two nines, carved side by side. Together, they made the number "ninety-nine."

Just as the number one hundred had been cut into poor Missouri's flesh.

"Well?" said Sinaloa. "Can you tell us who murdered Missouri?"

"Same person who murdered Yukon," said Nevada. "And there'll be more to come."

"What makes you say that?" said Sinaloa.

"Because he's counting down from a hundred," said Nevada. "A hundred of us."

Nevada sat at the end of the Reflecting Pool, gazing across the still water at the Lincoln Memorial. Antarctica, who was sitting beside him, had kicked off her pretty crystal shoes and dropped her pale, slender feet into the water.

The ripples from her feet disturbed the scenes playing over the pool's surface--visions of life beyond the digital domain in True America. Men, women, and children worked and played in softly swirling images, flickering across the sunlit water. It was here that the e-reps and e-sens came to see the faces of the people they served, strengthening their resolve to preserve the American dream.

"You're sure the killer won't stop?" said Antarctica.

"There are one hundred e-reps," said Nevada. "The first victim was marked one hundred, and the second was ninety-nine. Ninety-eight is next, then ninety-seven...all the way to zero."

Antarctica frowned. "I can't believe the Developers are letting this happen. Can't they just reprogram the source code to bring back the dead and stop the murders?"

"Maybe not." Nevada stroked the dark stubble on his chin. "Maybe they've lost control of the simulation. Or maybe they're *letting* it happen."

"But it doesn't seem possible." Antarctica shook her head and gazed into the water. "None of this does."

"Got that right." Nevada stretched out on his side, propping an elbow on the cement. Even with everything that was going on, he felt a sense of peace in this place.

Of all the places in the digital realm, the Reflecting Pool would always be the most special to him. It was here, five years ago, that he'd last seen Idaho before she'd disappeared from his life.

It was here that he'd last made love to her.

"What about Looking Glass's clues?" said Antarctica. "Do they mean anything?"

"I'm sure they do," said Nevada, "but I haven't figured them out yet."

"'When is one one-hundred?'" Antarctica narrowed her silver eyes. "He must have meant the one hundred e-reps of Congress, right?"

"Probably," said Nevada.

"Or he might have meant *me*." Antarctica's eyes widened. "I'm the one-hundredth e-rep, from the

one-hundredth state. What if I'm the next *victim*?"

"I don't think so," said Nevada. "The killer's following reverse order of importance. Missouri was speaker of the House, number one in terms of power...and the killer counted him last, as number one hundred."

"And Yukon was minority leader." Antarctica sounded relieved. "Second most powerful. So you don't think I'm next, Nevada?"

"No, sweetheart." said Nevada. "I don't think you're on the killer's radar right now."

Just then, without warning, Antarctica shot forward and disappeared under the water.

Heart pounding, Nevada scrambled to the edge of the pool and stared at the spot where she'd gone under. Since the water was murky with projected scenes of True America, he couldn't see below the surface. No trace of Antarctica or whatever had pulled her in was visible.

Then, suddenly, one pale hand broke the surface. Nevada grabbed it and pulled up hard...but whatever had hold of Antarctica wouldn't let go.

Leaning out further, Nevada clamped both hands around Antarctica's wrist and pulled harder than before. The thing in the pool resisted...then finally released its grip. Nevada hauled Antarctica free with one great heave.

The two of them tumbled back on the edge of the pool. Nevada cradled her in his arms as she coughed up water and gasped for breath.

Her silver eyes flickered open and met his gaze. "Guess what?" Her voice was shaking. "I think I'm on the killer's radar after all."

Nevada stroked the platinum blonde hair from her eyes. "Did you get a look at who pulled you in?"

Antarctica shook her head. "All I know is, their touch was beyond ice cold. It was too cold even for *me*."

Nevada stared at the surface of the pool. He wondered who had attacked Antarctica, and why.

Maybe the killer's hit list was more random than Nevada had thought, or it followed a more complicated formula. Maybe Antarctica knew something that could lead to a break in the case.

Or maybe, a more ominous motive had fueled the attack.

"We've got to get back," said Nevada. "Back to the House."

Antarctica frowned. "Why?"

"I don't think you were a target," said Nevada. "I think you were a diversion."

Pieces of the great state of Zacatecas were scattered all over the House chamber--head on the flagpole, foot on the Speaker's bench, arm on the podium. Blood was spattered everywhere, and ragged shreds of flesh stuck to the furniture and walls.

Many of the e-reps were also stained with their colleague's remains--including Connecticut, as she explained to Nevada what had happened.

"Half an hour ago, the power went out," said Connecticut. "We heard Zacatecas screaming, but we didn't know why until the lights came back up five minutes later. We found him...like this." She looked down at her bloody hands and clothes.

Suddenly, Sinaloa stormed toward them, scowling with rage. "Arrest this man!" He grabbed hold of Nevada's wrist and wrenched it into the air. "He killed my Mexican *hermano*!"

"That's enough," said Connecticut. "Let him go."

"Who among us was mysteriously *absent* when Zacatecas was *murdered*?" Sinaloa shook Nevada's arm for the crowd. "*This* man! He only reappeared when the killing was *finished*."

Antarctica pushed forward. "I was with him when this happened! Nevada didn't kill *anyone*."

"Then what *was* he doing?" said Sinaloa.

"Saving my life!" said Antarctica. "I was attacked and nearly drowned at the Reflecting Pool!" With one hand, she held up strands of her long hair, which was still wet. With her other hand, she held up her soaked white fur wrap.

"How do we know for sure?" Sinaloa locked eyes with her. "Perhaps you were his *accomplice* in this atrocity."

Fed up with the grandstanding, Nevada tore his wrist free of Sinaloa's grip. "Enough infighting. This is exactly what they want."

"'They' who?" said Sinaloa.

"You're right about one thing," said Nevada. "More than one person is involved in these murders."

With that, Nevada headed for the front of the chamber. The crowd of e-reps silently parted to make way for him.

"Someone attacked Antarctica at the Reflecting Pool while the murders were underway here." Nevada walked up to the podium, where Zacateca's left arm rested. "That tells us at least two people were involved."

Nevada gazed at the severed arm on the podium, its hand curled into a loose fist. "In five short minutes, power was cut to the House, Zacatecas was torn to pieces, and power was restored. That's a lot for one person to do alone in that amount of time."

"You should know," said Sinaloa.

Nevada turned the arm over. "In those same five minutes, someone also did this." Nevada held up the arm for the crowd to see. "They cut open Zacatecas' sleeves and carved the number '98' into his flesh."

The watching e-reps gasped and mumbled.

"The countdown continues," said Nevada, "unless we start working together and find who did this."

Sinaloa glowered at Nevada for a long moment. Then, he spun and marched up the aisle toward the doors.

"You're right," he said over his shoulder. "It's time to get some answers."

Nevada put down Zacatecas' severed arm. "How do you plan to do that?"

"By making a call," said Sinaloa.

"To who?" said Nevada.

"Who else?" said Sinaloa. "The Developers."

Sinaloa charged across the vast rotunda beneath the dome of the Capitol building and stopped on a single glowing tile in the middle of the room. Nevada and Antarctica, who had followed him from the House chamber, stood to one side.

When Sinaloa placed his right hand over his heart and recited the Pledge of Allegiance, a shaft of light burst up from the glowing tile, striking the middle of the dome. Smoothly, the dome split on one side and rolled open, revealing a starry night sky overhead.

The shaft of light from the tile spiked straight up, never dimming as it shot into the heavens. This was the holy connection to the godlike Developers in the world outside, the fabled *soulpipe*.

"I've never actually seen a *soul call* before." Antarctica's voice was soft and slow with wonder. "Will the Developers answer?"

Nevada shrugged. The same question was foremost in his own mind at that moment.

Since the murders, the role of House Speaker had fallen on Sinaloa, which qualified him to make the soul call. As a rule, though, the unpredictable Developers didn't answer every call, even from a qualified Speaker.

In the blazing light of the soulpipe, Sinaloa gazed upward and spread his arms wide. "O' masters of the source code, I beg you-- hear my prayer!" As Sinaloa spoke, his feet left the floor. Spinning slowly, he rose into the air, following the soulpipe's beam. "Representative Sinaloa...transmit *now*!"

Suddenly, Sinaloa exploded upward, streaking along the soulpipe in a strobing blur. There was a distant sonic boom as he vanished into the heavens, flashing out of sight among the flickering garlands of stars.

"Wow." Antarctica walked around the base of the soulpipe, staring up into Sinaloa's rippling wake. "He's in True America now?"

"Somewhere between here and there," said Nevada. "A hub outside the Developers' firewall."

"Don't you mean fire *ball*?" said Antarctica.

"Fire *wall*," said Nevada.

Antarctica frowned. "It's just that I see one now. A fire *ball*."

Nevada squinted upward...and then he saw it, too. A clutch of flames far above, burning in the firmament.

Burning and falling.

Nevada lashed an arm around Antarctica's waist and ran with her, racing away from the soulpipe. Just as they reached the far wall, a thunderous impact crashed down behind them.

Nevada and Antarctica stumbled as the floor buckled. Bracing each other, they managed to stay on their feet...and as the tremor faded, they turned.

The soulpipe was gone. In its place, in the center of the rotunda, was a smoking crater.

"Stay back," said Nevada, and then he ran toward the crater. In spite of his order, he heard Antarctica running close behind him.

When Nevada reached the broken rim of the crater, he saw what had caused the impact. He saw what had fallen from above like a fiery comet.

The body of Sinaloa lay in the crater's heart, curled like a fist and charred from tip to toe.

Antarctica drew up alongside Nevada and gagged. "Oh no."

"I guess they're not taking our calls." Nevada stepped over the edge and eased into the crater. He saw that parts of Sinaloa were still smoldering, glowing cherry red in familiar patterns.

There were messages on Sinaloa's body, burned into his flesh.

"Ninety-seven." Nevada pointed to Sinaloa's left arm, where the numbers had been branded. Then, he pointed at the letters seared into Sinaloa's right arm. "A-C-I-R-E-M-A. 'Acirema.'"

Finally, he read the smoking words on Sinaloa's charred chest. "'ANSWERS IN HOUSE NOW.'"

Leaping into action, Nevada clambered up the crater's slope and over the rim. He started running the instant his feet hit the floor.

Four figures wrapped in star-spangled robes waited outside the big double doors of the House chamber. Their faces were hidden in the depths of shadowy hoods, arms folded across their chests.

Nevada and Antarctica stopped running, staying well back from the hooded figures. Even from a distance, Nevada could see that their blue-and-white robes were stained with splotches of dark red.

Nevada took a step forward. "Stand aside. The sergeant-at-arms has business with the House."

To his surprise, the figures moved to comply. The two in the middle turned and opened the doors to the chamber--but they did not usher him inside. Instead, a fifth figure emerged, clad in red-and-white-striped robes, also hooded.

As the two figures who had opened the doors pulled them shut, the fifth robed figure glided forward. The voice that flowed from under the hood was that of a man...hoarse and muffled, but clearly a man.

"Hello again," he said. "I told you we would meet again after three and four, didn't I?"

Nevada recognized the voice instantly. "Looking Glass."

"Victims three and four are dead, so here I am." Looking Glass bowed his head. "Have you deciphered the clues I gave you?"

"No," said Nevada.

Looking Glass chuckled. "Then prepare to have your mind blown."

Nevada took a step back, pulling Antarctica with him. He briefly considered running, if only for her sake...but he waited. How could he run when he had yet to see inside the House?

"Meet the welcome wagon," said Looking Glass, gesturing at the two robed figures on his right.

Silently, the figure on the far right tugged off its star-spangled hood, revealing a face--a man's face, grinning.

Nevada gasped when he saw who it was. Heart slamming like a piston in his rib cage, he froze, holding on to Antarctica's arm.

Antarctica said the name for them both. "S-Sinaloa?"

The robed man with Sinaloa's face took a bow.

Then, the next figure unmasked. This time, the face under the hood was also familiar.

"Zacatecas." Nevada's head was spinning.

"More where those came from." Looking Glass gestured at the two hooded figures on the other side of him.

The next to unmask was a woman with long, brown hair--Yukon, also back from the dead. Beside her was the man who had started it all, the first to go: Missouri, former Speaker of the House, peeled back his hood and smoothed his neat white hair with a toothy grin.

"What's going on here, Nevada?" Antarctica sounded dazed. "How can they all be alive?"

Nevada felt dazed, too. "The Developers, maybe?"

The four who had come back to life looked at each other with knowing smiles and giggled.

"Not even close," said Looking Glass.

"Some kind of practical joke?" Nevada heard what could have been a muffled scream from behind the double doors of the House chamber. "A stunt to delay a key vote?"

"It *is* kind of funny," said Looking Glass, "but no. Would you like me to give you a hint?"

Nevada heard a loud thump and a crash from behind the doors. "Why not?"

"Here goes." With that, Looking Glass reached up and pulled off his own red-and-white-striped hood.

And Nevada felt the world of logic and reality dissolve around him.

His mouth fell open. His mind went blank.

Looking Glass, without the hood, had a very familiar face. He wasn't someone returned from the dead, or anyone Nevada had ever expected to see.

Outside of a mirror, that is.

The face staring back at Nevada was his own.

"I bet I know what's going through your mind right now." Looking Glass smiled. "'What a handsome S.O.B.,' am I right?"

Nevada didn't answer.

Stepping forward, Looking Glass extended a hand. "The name is Adaven. Pleased to meet you, Nevada."

Without thinking, Nevada took Adaven's hand. It was ice-cold to the touch--*beyond* ice cold.

Adaven gripped Nevada's elbow, freezing him right through the sleeves of his tux and shirt. With a whoop, he swung Nevada around to face the four seemingly resurrected e-reps.

"This is Aolanis." Adaven pointed at the reborn Sinaloa, and then he moved down the line. "This is Sacetacaz, Nokuy, and Iruossim. They're not who you think they are. In fact, you've never met them before."

Nevada frowned. Everything sounded crazy.

"Now come on." Adaven led Nevada toward the doors. "Let's meet the rest of the gang, shall we?"

Grinning, Sacetacaz and Nokuy pushed open the double doors to the House chamber. Adaven guided Nevada inside...right into a nightmare.

The huge room was splashed from top to bottom and side to side with blood and gore. Body parts were scattered everywhere, and corpses were piled like cordwood in the corners.

Even as Nevada recognized the dead faces of e-reps in the corpse heaps, he saw e-reps with the same faces moving around the room. The moving and the motionless looked exactly the same, except some were living and some were dead--and the living weren't behaving the way that Nevada ever would have expected them to.

As Nevada watched, Arkansas, South Korea, and Israel teamed up against Costa Rica, howling as they tore her limb from limb. Across the chamber, Florida and Japan hacked up Chihuahua with knives, cutting out his organs while he screamed in agony.

Antarctica's identical twin slogged past not ten feet from Nevada, dragging a charred and disemboweled corpse by the feet.

Staring at the hellish scene, Nevada could think of only one thing to say, one question to ask: "Why?"

"Why what?" said Adaven. "Why redecorate, you mean? Why have a surprise party?"

"Why are there duplicate e-reps?" said Nevada.

"Remember my riddle? 'When does one plus zero equal two?'" Adaven chuckled. "The answer is, when *one* casts a reflection in a *mirror*, of course. In a *looking glass*."

"You reflect us?" said Nevada.

Adaven made a twisting gesture with his hand. "Other way around."

Antarctica shivered against Nevada's arm. "So there's two of everyone?"

"One from America." Adaven raised his right hand, palm up, like the tray of a balance. "One from Acirema." He raised his left hand, also palm-up, alongside the right.

"'Acirema,'" said Nevada. "That word was burned into Sinaloa's body."

Adaven threw an arm around Nevada's shoulders, sending a freezing blast through his tux jacket and shirt. "You know it by another name," he said. "'True America.'"

Nevada stared at him, too stunned to speak.

"You e-reps have been living in a fantasy," said Adaven. "Thinking True America was a paradise of liberty. Thinking you were the voices of a just and compassionate electorate.

"But you don't represent the people of True America. You never did." Adaven swept an arm wide to take in the entire House chamber. "*These* are the representatives of America. *These* are the A.I. avatars whose votes shape America's destiny."

"You're telling us democracy's dead?" said Antarctica.

"The opposite!" said Adaven. "Democracy is alive and well...and *this* is the will of the American electorate!

"You and your kind have never been more than illusions to mask the true face of America--to let her own people fool themselves even as she expresses their darkest desires. You are the reason Americans have been able to live with themselves and sleep at night...but no longer.

"America has become her own shadow: Acirema, the opposite-- 'America' spelled backwards." Adaven pulled Nevada close and whispered, frozen breath chilling his ear. "We don't need you anymore."

Nevada felt sick. The urge to run returned--but he realized it was too late. He and Antarctica were surrounded by wicked e-rep duplicates.

"Acirema doesn't need to pretend anymore," said Adaven. "We

don't need the front. We've accepted ourselves as the complete bastards we've always been, and we've made up our minds to be the *best* complete bastards we *can* be."

"That's why you started killing us," said Nevada.

Adaven nodded. "The first few were tests. The Developers gave us all the keys and cheats we needed, but we still weren't sure if murder would work in the digital realm."

"You murdered the Speaker first to cripple our leadership," said Nevada.

"Actually, that was a mistake," said Adaven. "In the shadow Congress of Acirema, Missouri is the lowliest of the hundred, not the highest. We thought we were starting with the least important among you. 'When is one one hundred,' remember? The answer to the riddle is this: when *one*--the number one e-rep, the Speaker of the House in your realm--ranks *hundredth* out of a hundred in ours."

Nevada looked around at the living hell in the chamber. "So all of this was for nothing," he said. "Everything we accomplished."

"But the *good* news is, you can still make a difference," said Adaven.

"How's that?" said Nevada.

Adaven steered him around to face the huge double doorway. A figure stood beyond it, waiting in the hall, wrapped in hooded robes emblazoned with stars and stripes.

"She'll help you." Adaven gave Nevada a shove, sending him stumbling into the hall. "You'll make a difference by *dying*--sacrificing yourself to make way for the new world order."

Antarctica grabbed hold of Nevada's elbow. "What's the plan?" she said. "How do we get out of this?"

"We don't." Nevada slumped as the robed figure swung a rifle from her back and took aim at him. A dozen options for action flashed through his mind, revving up his heart, burning his bloodstream with adrenaline...

And he pushed them all aside. He knew that he could go down fighting, and in that way redeem himself at least a little for failing the republic--but he did nothing. What good would a martyr be if no one knew that he had died and why?

"Please, Nevada." Antarctica tugged his arm, but he wouldn't budge. "It's up to us."

"No it's not." Nevada shook free of her grip. "Nothing's up to us anymore."

"You're wrong." Antarctica pointed up at the ceiling. A red light blinked on the security camera that was mounted there. "People are still watching."

Nevada stared at the camera, then looked down at the barrel of the rifle. Maybe Antarctica was right. Maybe he could accomplish something worthwhile after all.

Nevada took a deep breath to steady himself. He curled and uncurled his fists.

Then, he bolted out of the line of fire.

"Run!" As soon as he said it, he glimpsed a blur of motion from Antarctica's direction.

Head down, Nevada charged toward the hooded shooter. He cut one way, then the other, trying to avoid her fire, reaching out for her.

Before he could touch her, he heard the deafening crack of the rifle. In spite of his zigzag path, the shot slammed into his chest with explosive force, pitching him to the floor.

He blacked out.

When he opened his eyes again, he saw the hooded woman crouching over him. "Confirmed kill," she said to someone he couldn't see--and when she said it, his heart beat faster.

He recognized her voice.

Nevada knew what her face would look like before she lifted away the hood. At first, all he could think was that it was impossible, that he must have already died if she was there with them.

But then, as she locked eyes with him, he remembered just how possible it was. Every e-rep had a double in Acirema, after all, even the dead ones. Even the one who had disappeared five years ago.

Even his beloved Idaho.

Nevada was in pain, but he managed a smile. The sight of her after all this time, even a shadow double who'd just shot him, was enough to fill him with joy.

Maybe her name was Ohadi instead of Idaho. Maybe she was devoted to the dark purposes of Acirema the Rellik instead of the bright resolve of America the Beautiful. Maybe she felt nothing for him, not even hatred.

But at least he could drink in the sight of her face. At least he could pretend in his few remaining moments that the precious orig-inal had returned to him.

At least he could imagine--or was it more than imagination--that her hand was warm when she touched his eyelids. When she drew them shut.

He could dream that she was his warm-blooded Idaho, hiding all this time to prepare for the threat of Acirema, masquerading even now as the enemy. Faking Nevada's death so she could whisk him away to the underground to fight the power. To renew their love.

Or if that hand was colder than he thought, than he
Dreamed
And she was Ohadi in spite of his hope, carved from glittering ice with frozen heart and frozen soul,

Perhaps his noble moment of defiance and then his last words would inspire her,

Warm her blood that she would *become* restored Idaho and more,
Seed of change, revolution, restoration,

Changer of hearts, perhaps even the heart of Adaven, his twin, Nevada spelled backward
Spelled everywhichway like America
Acirema Maciera Reamica Cimeara Imeraca
Then that would be all right, too, he thought,
And he tried
In the last words he said
To tell her what mattered,
What they'd forgotten,
What to pass along,
And this was what came out,
His wisdom, his blessing, his curse,
His last wish
His poem.
He said
"I love you."

THE MAN IN THE SCI FI SUIT

The giant cyborg chipmunk is just drawing down on his victim, the purple squid-cow hero Heiferclese, when a beautiful, red-haired woman runs between them over the glassy ground, waving her arms.

Enter Varla Finlay Dios, creatrix of this particular eddy of Fictasia. The place is a vast desert landscape studded with rocky outcroppings (and glassy dunes instead of sand) under deep blue cloudless skies. The time is somewhere in the inconceivably distant future, when reality and story have become one and the same in vast swaths of the cosmos. Thanks to trans-quantum computing and matter-energy manipulation, technologies so advanced they might as well be magic to us, works of the imagination are easily written into the "code" of the preexisting physical universe. It isn't always clear what's "real" and what's "fictional" in Fictasia, but it doesn't matter much when it's all so interesting.

In this age, the most inventive creators and creatrixes, like Varla, command the greatest devotion from fans. Their particular storytelling streams, like the one where Heiferclese heroically battles a cyborg chipmunk, attract trillions upon trillions of viewers.

"Stop! Gah! Please!" Varla's skintight holodress, composed solely of coherent silver light (or the idea of such light, at least), pulses as she shouts at the chipmunk. "This doesn't work, either! *None* of it does!"

The chipmunk, whose given name is El Scaldo, lowers his death-ray-equipped left arm and shrugs. "Tell it to the author, lady!" His voice is as deep as a tuba solo.

Varla, who as creatrix *is* the author of this little scene, blasts a scowl the size and average temperature of Texas at El Scaldo's fuzzy kisser. *Not amused.*

Then, with a flutter of her long fingers with their ornate silver-circuited nails, she changes El Scaldo from a cyborg chipmunk to a six-foot-tall pink lizard sweating some kind of musky orange milk.

"My people, the *Sussssaxxx,* shall overturn the game board and *dessstroy* thossse laying the oddsssss!" Lizard Scaldo's long, forked tongue flickers as he speaks. "We represssent the animal backbrain that can *never* be tamed."

Varla shakes her head and waggles her fingers again. Lizard El Scaldo becomes manatee El Scaldo.

"We, the Wim, bring tidings of peace and a new way *beyond* the Great Game." His whiskers twitch, and his muzzle curls in a kind of roly-poly smile.

"Shit! No!" Again, Varla gestures. This time, El Scaldo becomes a three-inch-long shrimp with tiny fairy wings and darts away on the hot desert breeze.

With a cry of disgust and frustration, Varla plunges her head into her hands. Heiferclese takes the opportunity to slink away, dragging her squid-tentacled bottom over the glassy smooth ground.

"Garbage! I should *scrap* it! Scrap it *all!*" Varla hates the thought of throwing out three months of work, but she's getting closer to doing it by the minute. The ending of *The Universal Fix* remains elusive; the harder she tries to finish the book, the worse every option she considers seems to be.

How's a writer supposed to keep from getting knocked off the Cosmic Midlist (a ranking that gauges the level of impact a story-reality has on the rest of Fictasia) with a creative block like this? Or worse, what if her rep takes such a hit that she gets sucked into someone else's story? And not a *good* one, either?

That's life in Fictasia, kiddies. One unappealing mash-up of story and reality, and trillions of fans will flee your once-bestselling stream. Once they're gone, it can be a nightmare getting them back--and once they're gone for good, your career is over. When that happens, when you cease to be relevant, you can be fictionalized and marginalized all at once, doomed to straggle on as an unmemorable supporting character with no hope of ever creating anything important again.

Dwelling too long on such consequences must be avoided at all costs. Creative types like Varla just go right on doing what they've always done, whipping up tall tales...when they can come up with a decent ending, that is.

"What now?" Varla's chin ends in a gently rounded point, and she rubs it roughly. "Damn!"

"You rang?" says a male voice from somewhere behind her, instantly recognizable as neither Heiferclese nor fairy shrimp.

Varla whirls and sees him walking toward her over the glassy plain. Her first impression is of a long, smooth face and slender build, lean and lanky. Pale blue Cavanaugh hat with a high crown and a wide, striped band, cocked slightly to the left. And a pale blue single-breasted suit woven with blinking multi-colored lights from shoulders to ankles.

He ambles over and sticks out a long-fingered hand. "Name's *Damn*." He grins, equal parts friendly and open to all possibilities. "Damn Pickett. I'm a tale-twister."

"An alterationist?" Varla shakes his hand, firm and warm. "Who sent you?"

"No one but the breeze." His eyes twinkle when he winks. "Just passin' through."

Varla lets go of his hand. "Uh-huh." She looks suspicious.

Damn removes his hat in a graceful gesture, cupping the point of the crown between his first and middle fingers. The hair on his head is dark brown, short, and neatly combed. "I wonder if you might point me to a tale in progress, ma'am?"

"You're *standing* in one." Varla laughs bitterly. "If you can call it that."

Damn flicks dust off the brim of his hat. "In need of a little *tweak*, perhaps?"

Varla shakes her head. "You couldn't save it if you tried. I'm just getting ready to scrap it and start over."

Damn nods thoughtfully. "Maybe you should let *me* be the judge of that. They say I'm one of the best, you know."

"I'm not exactly an amateur myself." Varla folds her arms over her chest. "Ever hear of *Love of a Hundred Billion Neutrinos*?"

"Varla Finlay Dios." Damn nods. "You haven't published much recently, have you?"

Varla doesn't answer.

"I don't think I've read anything new from you since your husband, Wood, died," says Damn. "Or did he leave you?"

Varla claps her hands together, ending the line of questioning. "Oh well, back to work."

Damn puts his hat back on with a twirl of his fingers, then plants his hands on his hips and takes a long look around. "Tell me about this tale of yours."

Varla shakes her head. "I don't need an alterationist, Damn."

"Maybe so." The multicolored lights in his pale blue suit flash and dance as he reaches into the left hip pocket of his coat and pulls out a scale replica of a rocket ship. It's much bigger than the pocket, three feet and still coming, with gleaming silver skin, a lipstick-red nose, and matching fins. "Still, I've found one of *these* can be helpful from time to time."

Varla blows out her breath. "A one-size-fits-all plot device? Really?"

"You haven't experienced alterations before, have you?" He finishes pulling out the rocket and waves his hand over it. The silver skin shifts to bright yellow, and the whole rocket changes shape, becoming longer and skinnier. "I tailor to fit, see? It molds to match your story, and the story reshapes itself around it."

Damn lets go. The rocket spins upward, enlarging as it rises until it dwarfs the human figures below. Varla sees the faces of crew members peering back from portholes along the length of it.

In one of the portholes, she glimpses the face of Heiferclese, grinning and waving one purple tentacle with heartfelt delight.

"That's your solution?" She snorts. "Reach escape velocity and live happily ever after?"

"Or at least move the action to somewhere new." Damn lifts an eyebrow. "A change of scenery that brings new challenges and possibilities."

"Out of the blue?" says Varla. "Doesn't seem very *organic* now, does it?"

"How you figure?" asks Damn. "People do it all the time, by choice or by circumstance."

"There's nothing picaresque about *The Universal Fix*," says Varla. "The action alternates between three locations: the Mirror Desert of New Mexico, the Secret Casino under Antarctica, and the Palace of the Cosmic Oddsmakers in the Thickest Brane beyond the holographic bound. Not to mention...Heiferclese?" Varla wiggles her fingers at the rocket ship, which suddenly shrinks and whips away like a deflating balloon. "She's only a *supporting* character. Comic relief."

"So tell me more." Damn gestures with both hands as if he's waving for her to come closer. "Nutshell it for me."

"No!" She's indignant. "I already told you, I don't *need* an alterationist."

"Lots of people think that." Damn smirks. "Till they see what I can do."

"I doubt it, if a rocket ship's the best you have to offer."

"So get a load of this." The multicolored lights sewn into Damn's coat flicker and swirl as he pokes two fingers into his vest pocket. They emerge with a playing card between them--the ace of spades. "Works wonders in pretty much any tale, ma'am."

Damn flicks up the card for her to see. When he releases it, the card floats suspended in midair before him, slowly turning on its vertical axis like a revolving door.

"I call it the Big Scare Card." When Damn claps his hands, the card bursts into a puff of black smoke that swiftly expands into a cloud the size of a man. "Always good for changing the course of events and initiating significant growth in any character."

Damn takes a deep breath and blows. The puff instantly dissipates, revealing the skeletal figure of a Grim Reaper in an ebony robe, carrying a gleaming silver scythe.

"Death?" Varla yawns. "Gee, I hadn't thought of that."

"Then I guess you already know this is a creatrix's best friend." Damn hangs his hat on the blade of the scythe and throws his arm around the Reaper's shoulders. "You can never have too much death in a tale, can you?"

"The heroine of my novel, Sybil Pax, has already lost her lover and their child as part of the Great Game," explains Varla. "Those precipitating incidents give her the will to oppose the Oddsmakers. As she fights their plan to drive humanity to extinction as part of the ultimate betting scenario, she loses everyone else she cares about, which gives her the strength and fury to succeed. No other death is needed in this book."

"Except Sybil's, perhaps?" Damn cocks his left eyebrow. "What if she makes the ultimate sacrifice?"

"Completely invalidating the book's message about individual self-determination in the face of seemingly insurmountable predestination? Forget it. Now why don't you go find some poor kid struggling with her fan fiction and let me get back to the serious work?"

Damn kicks Death in the ass, and the Reaper disappears. "So this is all about chance and risk and destiny?" He catches his hat as it falls from the vanishing scythe and spins it back onto his head with a flourish. "Why didn't you say so?"

"Pretty obvious from the title, isn't it?" says Varla. "*The Universal Fix*. 'The fix is in,' as the gamblers say. As in the game is rigged. In this case, the Great Game of all existence, which is rigged by the Cosmic Oddsmakers."

"Then what you need is a change of luck." Damn reaches into his right pants pocket, setting his suit's lights to blinking and changing color. He comes up with two glowing dice and holds them out for her to see. "A twist of fate to shake things up."

"Seriously?" Varla chops her hand through the air dismissively. "Like I don't already *have* multiple lucky and unlucky breaks in this book?"

"But the right one at the right time..."

"Is *overkill* in this case." Varla's voice rises with annoyance.

"Hey, over-the-top can be a beautiful thing!" Damn blows on the dice and gives them a good shake in his cupped hand. "Come on, lucky seven!"

When he throws the dice, they instantly expand and whirl around each other in midair, tumbling with increasing speed. Within seconds, they're rolling so fast, they're a blur of motion, a vortex of bright white light and flickering black pips.

The dice race faster and faster in a dizzying Mobius pattern. Varla squints and raises an arm against the light as it gains intensity, building, building.

Then, the dice explode in a blinding blaze, a nova so bright it drowns everything in Varla's field of vision in one tremendous whiteout.

Moments later, she's still blinking away the clusters of spots left behind in her eyes. Also thinking about bringing harm to the tale-twister, if he has the temerity to still be standing there.

Which he does...but he's not the most interesting thing she sees at that moment. The Mirror Desert of her book is gone. Instead, she's standing in some kind of vast, formal garden blossoming with multicolored flowers of every variety she can imagine.

Varla's heart pounds as the import of the situation dawns on her. Her first thought is that she's been swept into someone else's sorry-ass story. If she can't find a way back to her personal eddy of Ficta-sia, she could end up written down, maybe even written *out*, with no hope of even a cameo in a future installment.

But her second thought, when she spies a familiar figure crossing a footbridge through the garden, is this: maybe it *isn't* someone else's story, after all. At least, not entirely.

Damn steps up beside her. "How's *that* for a twist of fate?"

"That's...me." Varla feels dazed. Her silver holodress pulses as she stares at the redheaded woman on the foot bridge. "What the hell, Damn?"

"It's a flashback, of course." He waves at the redhead on the bridge. "Five years ago in Fenimore Gardens, New Virginia. Don't tell me you've forgotten."

Varla is alarmed and confused. "*This* isn't Fenimore Gardens. It's nothing *like* that place."

Damn plugs his hands in his pockets and shrugs. "Chalk it up to dramatic license. Capturing the essence is more important than restating the exact details, isn't it?"

Varla's doppelganger finishes crossing the bridge and twirls around between descending boughs dripping with pink cherry blossoms. She giggles as the blossoms tickle her cheeks and shoulders, showering her with delicate petals shaken free of their perches.

"Send me back." Varla's voice is a low growl. Her holodress pulses faster. "Send me back *now*."

"Hold your horses," says Damn. "I told you, I'm going to help with that book of yours."

"*This* is supposed to help? Bringing a flashback of *me* into the story?"

"A little *meta* never hurt anybody," says Damn.

Varla glares at him. "This is a *storynapping*, isn't it? You've pulled me into someone else's plotline against my will."

"Not exactly." Damn tips his Cavanaugh forward and rubs the back of his neck. "Actually, this is all about *you*."

Varla thinks for a moment as her double settles onto a cement bench. A big monarch butterfly circles around her, then lands on her left knee.

"All about *me*?" In her anger, Varla lets her voice rise, but Other Varla doesn't seem to hear. "You mean a biography?" Her fists clench at her sides. "An *unauthorized* biography?"

"Listen." Damn locks eyes with her, looking serious. "You trust me, don't you?"

"*Absolutely not,*" says Varla.

"Then trust *her*." He points at Varla's double. "Trust *yourself*."

Just then, a new voice pipes up from across the garden--a man's voice, so instantly recognizable that it makes her ache.

"Hello, Varla," says the man.

The sound of her husband Wood's voice is so perfect, Varla instinctively wants to answer. Damn has gotten that much right, anyway.

And he's done the same with the way Wood looks, from his curly black hair to his broad shoulders, slender trunk, and long legs. He even wears his favorite suit, a double-breasted number woven from pure story substance. Words and images dance over his body like the flickering celluloid of an ancient silent movie, rippling in an endless stream of dialogue, settings, conflicts, resolutions, and thematic elements.

As on most days, Wood's suit is composed of science fictional fabric, his favorite. Some threads present a retro view of tomorrows already come and gone; others display futures so far forward as to be barely comprehensible. The interplay of the two yields a matrix of imagination that's charged with nostalgia and future shock all at once.

Varla hasn't seen him in nearly five years, but it seems like it's been fewer than five minutes. She lost him long ago, yet it feels perfectly natural to see him close by. It makes perfect sense to her to run to him, embrace him, kiss him as if no time has passed at all.

But she doesn't do any of that, because Other Varla has already done it.

"You remember it well, don't you?" asks Damn. "Your last day together, wasn't it? Though you didn't know it at the time."

Is it normal to feel jealous of your other self? Varla does, as Other Varla kisses Wood passionately among the cherry blossoms. "It didn't happen like this. There wasn't a garden."

"Are you sure?" Damn points at her left chest, where her heart resides. "Not even *in there*?"

Varla scowls and keeps watching the kiss in the cherry blossom glade. Shafts of sunlight slip through the canopy around them, glowing brushstrokes surrounding the lovers in a cage of golden beams.

When husband and wife finally part, does Varla remember the next words they speak? Of course she does. She could recite them in her sleep, she thinks.

She *thinks*.

"My love." Wood's words come through as plain as day, though Varla and Damn stand some distance away. "I couldn't bear to be without you a chooga wooga woo. Caper contiguous yappa dapple prefix quimby nimby."

"You know I feel the same way," says other Varla. "Promise me you won't heebie jeebie Pleistocene ulcerate shooby dwooby."

275

Wood nods sincerely, holding her face in his hands. "Three five hexagon poultice, tapir."

Tipping her head to one side, she kisses his hand. "Silence silence silence static silence."

Modern-day Varla, watching from afar with Damn Pickett, frowns so hard, the creases in her face might well cut into the bone of her skull. "It's all gibberish!" She grabs Damn's shoulder and gives it a rough shake. "It doesn't make any sense!"

"Think of it as filler." Damn brushes her hand away. "Place-holder text."

"Is this some kind of joke? Some kind of absurd dada-esque nonsense you've hauled me into?"

"None of the above," says Damn. "It's all drawn from your memory--with alterations courtesy of yours truly--so I guess you must not remember the conversation as well as you thought." He raises his eyebrows. "Not that what they're saying matters at all. You need to focus on the visual. Look *closer.*" Damn jabs a finger at the couple across the way.

Irritated as hell, Varla only wants to get out and go home to her personal storystream...but her gaze zooms in on Wood and Other Varla anyway.

At first, nothing jumps out at her. She just sees the handsome, dark-haired man embracing her duplicate self in a bittersweet moment she longs to be a part of so badly it hurts.

But then, a moment passes, and she sees something else. Her attention is drawn to an image on Wood's back, part of his coat of sci fi colors.

Plain as day, she sees it. The face of a purple squid-cow, goofy grin and all.

Heiferclese?

"No." Her frown grows deeper still. "It can't be."

"What's that?" Damn asks calmly, completely unsurprised.

The image on the back of Wood's suit coat changes, becoming the cyborg chipmunk, El Scaldo. "Those characters. I created them later. They shouldn't be there...*couldn't* be there."

Again, the scene on the coat changes. This time, it makes her gasp.

"What?" asks Damn. "What is it?"

Varla's mouth opens, but no words come out at first.

"It's *me.*" Her voice finally shakes. "Me as I am *now...today.*"

Wood pulls Other Varla closer and goes in for a deep kiss. Her arms wrap around him, caressing his back, sliding through images of herself five years later as she conjures characters and incidents in the Mirror Desert.

The images show modern-day Varla in the midst of creating her latest novel, *The Universal Fix.* She weaves her hands through the air, and Heiferclese appears on the polished ground before her. She wiggles her fingers, and El Scaldo the cyborg chipmunk becomes El Scaldo the pink-skinned lizard.

Somehow, in the midst of a five-year-old flashback, Varla sees her latter-day self as she appeared that very morning.

"It's an anachronism," she says. "Current events would never appear on a sci fi story fabric suit five years ago."

"Why not?" Damn shrugs. "Science fiction predicts the future, doesn't it?"

As Varla watches, the scene on the coat continues to develop. She sees Damn approaching as he did not long ago, then pulling a rocket ship out of his pocket. "Is this some weak attempt at fore-shadowing? Is that what this is all about?"

"More like an attempt at setting the record straight," says Damn. "How do *you* know what was on the back of his jacket at that partic-ular moment? It was facing *away* from you."

"It doesn't matter." Varla dismisses his comments with a wave of her hand. "This isn't how it happened, anyway. This isn't *my* story."

"Sure it is," says Damn. "It's the only story you've ever known. The only one you've ever been a part of."

She shakes her head hard. Her holodress pulses faster than ever. "*Enough.* Send me home *now.*"

"You *are* home." Damn puts a hand on her shoulder and steers her to keep watching the scenes on the suit coat. "Look, you'll see."

Varla sees herself watching as Damn conjures Death in the desert, then tumbling dice. There's a flash of light, and suddenly she's watching herself and Damn as they watch her other self in the garden.

ROBERT JESCHONEK

The next thing she knows, she's watching herself in the flickering image watching herself in yet another image...and that self, in
turn, is watching *another* image of herself. An infinite progression of
nested Varlas and Damns fans onward, stretching forever into the
celluloid expanse.

Then, all that collapses at once into something new. Varla sees
an image of Wood standing in the Mirror Desert, weaving his arms
in the air creator-style. A figure appears before him--a slender young
woman in a skintight silver holodress. A woman who's the spitting
image of Varla, except her hair is black instead of red.

Varla's dress stops pulsing. "What is this?" She's barely aware of
the words as they leave her lips.

"Another flashback," says Damn. "Older than all the rest."

"I don't understand." Varla feels a little light-headed. "That
looks like me, but..."

"You don't remember?" Damn smiles. "Makes sense, I suppose.
Who remembers their own *birth*, anyway?"

Varla can't take her eyes off the images on the coat. Other
Varla's caressing hands scroll through them, interrupting the scene
in which Wood flickers his fingers, and black-haired Varla becomes
blonde Varla.

"My...birth?" Current Varla is dazed. "You're trying to tell me
I'm...I'm..."

"Fictional, yeah." Damn pats her on the back. "But I won't hold
it against you."

Varla watches Wood gesture in the scene on the suit, sees her
hair change from blonde to red...yet still she resists. "This is impossible. It's *bullshit*. It's just part of whatever story you've grafted me
into."

"Not so," says Damn. "This is the same story you've *always* been
part of. It's *your* story...and *his*." He gestures at Wood, who's still deep
in a kiss with Other Varla.

"No," snaps Varla. "I'm a *creatrix*."

"Sure you are," says Damn. "In a *story*."

Varla's head is swimming. The scene on Wood's back cuts from
one incident to another, and she remembers them all in detail.
There she is, relaxing in a rowboat on a glittering summer lake

278

while Wood handles the oars. There she is again, standing on a high mountaintop with him, gazing out at a magnificent view of rugged snowcaps and verdant meadows. And there she is once more, slow-dancing with Wood on a back porch strung with strands of multicolored lights, surrounded by fireflies.

And there they are on a beach in Maui, getting married by a smiling old minister wearing a lavender lei. Her breath catches at the sight of her lacy white wedding dress and veil--at the look on her face as she gazes at Wood on the most wonderful day of her life.

She sees herself honeymooning with him, making love in a tropical cove by a roaring surf. They move into a perfect little house in horse country in New Virginia, complete with white-fenced pastures and a stable of handsome ponies.

And they write stories and books together in their own little eddy of Fictasia. Sometimes, it's a lush forest alive with birdsong. Other times, it's a city or a village or a plain, a jungle or a desert.

Or a hospital room. Wood lies pale and shriveled in bed, surrounded by blinking monitors that display his fading vital signs. A techno-wizard in a white lab coat shakes his head and throws up his hands, unable to use the great science of the age to save this one little life. Varla sits by the bed, sobbing uncontrollably as she clutches the cooling hand of precious Wood, the irreplaceable man of her dreams.

Suddenly, he's gone, and she's alone. She stands in the middle of their favorite setting, the Mirror Desert, working on a book she can never seem to finish.

And the circle is complete.

"That's my *life*, not a story," she says softly, staring at the image of herself alone in the desert.

"It doesn't have to be one or the other," says Damn. "It doesn't matter."

"Then why show me all this? If it doesn't matter, why bother trying to convince me I'm fictional?"

"To help you finish your book," says Damn. "I'll help *any* creator, be they real or fictional or anything in between."

"I already told you, I don't *need* any help. I don't *want* it."

"Too late." Damn smiles. "I've already given it."

279

Across the garden, Other Varla and Wood break their kiss and wander off through the cherry blossoms, arm in arm. They laugh as they stroll among the sunbeams and hummingbirds, lost in a paradise all their own.

"He wrote you." Damn takes his hat off and holds it at his side. "He *created* you. Made you perfect in every way and fell in love with you.

"He entered your story, and you fell in love with him, too. You were married and lived in perfect happiness as partners and co-authors, because he designed you to be his equal in every way.

"But then, one day, he left you forever. He *died* in both the fictional and factual realities. And ever since, you've been struggling to finish the last book the two of you were writing together.

"But you've struggled long enough." Damn twirls his hat back onto his head and reaches into his right pants pocket. The lights in his suit flicker and pulse in all their rainbow colors. "It's time we got you back on track."

When he pulls his hand out and opens it, there's a six-inch-tall man standing on his palm. It's a tiny replica of Wood.

Immediately, little Wood starts to grow, and Damn pulls away his hand. As Wood's feet land on the ground, he shoots up to full height, taller than Varla or Damn.

"Hello, Varla." Wood steps toward her.

Varla is torn. Part of her still fears that she's been storynapped, and all of this is someone else's plotline.

But she can't deny that Damn's account of the truth behind her life is possible. And she also can't deny, in her heart, that the vision of Wood exerts a pull on her.

When he takes her hands in his, she doesn't break away. When he speaks, she listens attentively. She gives him his say.

"I'm so sorry," he tells her. "We never had the chance to say goodbye."

Varla's throat tightens. He's not the real Wood, but he *feels* like it. And his words have struck a nerve.

"You never got the closure you deserved," continues Wood. "You never got to move on.

"Well, it's time to move on now."

He stares deeply into her eyes and strokes the tops of her hands with his thumbs. "I love you, Varla. I will love you forever." He raises her hands and bends to kiss them softly--right, then left. Then he straightens, with a tear in each eye. "Goodbye now, my darling. It's finally time for you to let go."

Caught up in the moment, Varla feels tears in her eyes. She feels an ache in her belly and heart, a deep sense of long-awaited finality.

For the first time, she starts to think that Damn might be right about all this. It feels true, feels painful, feels *important*.

She knows he's watching her, off to the side. He's waiting, and so is Wood...waiting for her to come around.

Has she changed since Wood died? Even as her creativity got stuck in neutral, did the rest of her continue to evolve?

Maybe so. Because she realizes something as she stands there with Wood holding her hands while Damn looks on.

She doesn't want to give them the satisfaction.

"No." As she says it, she reverses Wood's grip and clamps his hands tightly in her own.

Wood frowns. "'No,' what?"

"No." She smiles fiercely. "I won't let you go."

Before anyone can say another word, she focuses all her creative energies, pouring every iota of strength through the instruments in her fingernails and elsewhere.

And the garden goes away.

Varla and Wood dance across the glassy surface of the Mirror Desert, their feet moving in perfect time with the ballroom music of the full orchestra playing nearby.

As for Damn, he stands off to one side with his hands on his hips, frowning at the performance that started the instant they left the garden and arrived here. "This isn't exactly what I had in mind!" he shouts over the music.

"Too bad!" says Varla as she and Wood sail past.

"So sad!" chimes in Wood.

Damn shakes his head. "I thought maybe you'd get over your lost love and move on to finish *The Universal Fix* as a joint project."

"You were wrong!" Varla giggles as Wood spins her around. "That book is so *over*."

"But the fans are dying to see it finished," says Damn. "They say it's an unfinished masterpiece."

"Maybe they'll like my new novel, instead," says Varla. "The first in a series!"

"Starring me!" says Wood. "Starring both of us!"

"I'm writing myself in," says Varla. "Because I *can!*"

Damn frowns a moment more, then grins and shrugs. "Well, maybe you're right. 'The creation writes her creator.' I *do* kind of like it."

"Want me to write you in, too, Damn?" asks Varla.

Damn waves her off. "I'm needed elsewhere. So many tales to twist, so little time."

As he strolls off toward the horizon, whistling a tune, the ball-room music builds behind him. Varla and Wood swoop across the glass, never missing a beat or having a single hair flutter out of place.

She's still a little surprised at what she's done. After so long para-lyzed by loss, unable to move forward without the guiding hand of her creator, what finally inspired her to take charge?

Was the suddenness of her change unrealistic, she wonders? Or humanly impulsive? Was the newfound strength with which she broke free just a plot device without the ring of truth? Or the kind of power surge that happens all the time in flesh-and-blood people under great stress?

As far as any of that goes, is she as in control as she thinks at this point? Is this her story, unfolding according to her will? Or is it all part of *another* story, directed by unknown creators?

And does any of that matter? Two out of two characters in her new novel agree that it doesn't.

So she and Wood continue to spin joyfully as the music rises. When it finally hits a crescendo, the two of them leap into the air and spin in a perfect circle, beaming face to face with blissful adoration.

As their lips meet, the sky changes from deep blue to a beautiful sunset streaked with rose, orange, gold, and fiery crimson. The words "The End" fade into the foreground in bright yellow text, superimposed over the whole grand scene.

Then, the word "Never" appears above them, written in white script letters as if scrawled by some invisible hand.

EGGS OF THE DOG THAT BIT YOU

Every morning, I wake to the barking of the dogs in the coop. All at once, they take up the call, howling and yapping their glorious dawn chorus.

Aroooo! Arf arf arf! Yip yip yap! Aroooo!

Then they get back to what they do best, which is laying eggs. I only wish it was enough to keep the farm going. I only wish I was half the dog-egg farmer my daddy was.

I'm just glad he won't be alive to see Banker Bancroft repossess Dog's Ass Farm from his only daughter in a few weeks. At least that much is a mercy.

All up and down the length of the coop, the dogs squat over nests of straw and squeeze out one egg after another. The eggs have an amazing variety of different colors and markings, varying from breed to breed. When you've been dog-egg farming as long as I have, you learn to recognize which dogs lay which ones.

As I gather the day's first batch, I pat each pooch on the head, sometimes getting a lick in return, sometimes a nip. Today, the bulldogs are producing well, cranking out their olive-green eggs with black and brown stippling like military camouflage. My best poodle presents me with a clutch of bright purple eggs, each flecked with gold glitter. Then there are the German Shepherds with their black eggs streaked with beige and the Golden Retrievers with their fiery reds peppered with yellow polka dots.

Along with the pure-bred canines, my collection of mixed-breed mutts drops eggs of unpredictable color and design, a delightful assortment of daily surprises. Today alone, I find eggs with green and gold stripes, eggs with bright blue and orange swirls, and eggs with wild, almost psychedelic designs.

But the one that mystifies me most squeezes out of the bottom of a fluffy white Bichon Frise I call Cotton. *This* egg, unlike the simple white orbs that Cotton normally drops, has actual *words* scrawled in black on a white background.

As I read the impossible message, I'm so stunned that I nearly drop the egg. The words written on its shell are unlike any markings I've ever seen on any egg laid by a dog.

Let this egg hatch to save your farm.

I gaze at that message for a long time as the dogs pant and scratch and bay around me. Only one thing is certain: this isn't a trick. The coop is secure, and no one works here but me. I haven't been able to afford help in months.

Is it possible? Could there truly be some kind of miracle inside Cotton's egg that might keep the farm alive? If so, what do I have to lose by letting it hatch? The sale price of one Bichon Frise egg, that's what.

Perhaps it will be worth it.

I return the egg with the message to the nest, and Cotton immediately settles her fluffy bottom on top of it. *Rruff!* Her bark sounds satisfied to me.

Three days later, just as I'm making my morning rounds with basket in hand, the egg hatches...and again, I'm stunned. I expected to see a white Bichon puppy among the bits of broken shell, its tail wagging.

Instead, I see something I've never seen before—a tiny creature covered in yellow fluff, with a hard little beak on its face. As I watch, it scoots around the nest, making a high-pitched *eep eep* noise.

Whatever this thing is, I've never seen its like before. A shiver leaps up my spine as I gaze into its beady black eyes.

I scoop it up in the palm of my hand, barely wresting it away from converging Dobermans licking their chops. I shoo them off, and they retreat to their perches between the collies and dachshunds.

"What now?" I ask the fluffy yellow creature. "How are *you* supposed to save my farm?"

Eep eep eep is the only answer I get, meaning what?

Who the hell knows? All I can do is wait and see, I guess. Pray and hope for a miracle.

And keep the dogs from eating this thing in the meantime.

I set up a pen on the sunporch of the house, using a cardboard egg crate lined with straw and spreading wire mesh fencing over the top. Every day, I keep Fleecy (that's the critter's name) watered and fed, tossing in handfuls of grain for it to peck at. Once in a while, when I'm sure no dog is on the prowl, I take it out and stroke its downy yellow fluff and talk to it.

"What kind of dog are you, anyway? How are you going to save my farm?"

Eep eep eep.

"I guess I could make you an *attraction*." I narrow my eyes thoughtfully as I stroke the critter's yellow down with a fingertip. "But who would ever believe you hatched from a dog's egg?"

Then, something else occurs to me. If Fleecy hatched *out* of an egg...

"What if you can *lay* eggs, too?" Maybe *that's* the miracle I've been waiting for. Maybe Fleecy's eggs will be even more delicious than those of the dogs in the coop.

Now *that* would be enough to get folks sniffing around Dog's Ass Farm again!

Just imagine! Cars lined up for miles, everyone coming for a taste of Fleecy's eggs! Money stuffing the cashbox, people grinning, bills getting paid.

The family farm getting saved.

It's a dream I treasure every night for weeks, even as Fleecy grows up. Gone is the darling yellow down, replaced by a coat of black feathers. The adorable *eep eep eep* becomes a guttural *cluck cluck cluck* and occasional *b-kaw b-kaw* when she (I hope it's a she, it's hard to tell) becomes riled. The cute little nub of her tushie grows into a tail, tufts of fine white fur wound around it like the hair of her mama, Cotton.

And every day, my expectations grow. If I had to guess, I'd say Fleecy's getting closer to laying...if she's ever going to lay. There's no other critter like her to complete the act, after all; I know I'm grasping at straws when I hope she'll generate even a single egg.

Then, one morning, even that hope is gone.

As Fleecy's gotten bigger, I've moved her to a pen outside, behind the barn. But when I go out to feed her this time, she is gone.

"Fleecy! No!"

Her pen has been torn apart. The wire fencing lays in mangled twists on the ground, torn asunder as if it's been put through a thresher.

The pen is empty. Whatever took Fleecy, its bizarre, gnarled tracks disappear into the woods.

My only hope is gone.

I slump to the ground and weep, because I know what's next. Days from now, I will lose far more than Fleecy.

The dogs howl like fire sirens in the blazing hot morning. It's as if they already know I will lose them all, too.

And then the day is upon us, far faster than I ever imagined it could be.

Sheriff Gardenia parks in the dusty yard and lumbers over, his belly jiggling like the uncooked yolk of a Great Dane's massive pink egg. Banker Bancroft slithers behind him, his shiny gray suit like snakeskin, his blotchy, bulbous head like a cur's testicle.

"Time's up, Miss Janet." Sneering, Bancroft waves a fistful of paperwork. "Your farm belongs to Third-Rate National Bank, now."

The dogs bark and snarl in their coop as if they understand the gravity of the moment. I see their teeth and claws through the gaps between the slats as they lunge, desperate to get out, desperate to do something.

"Please." There's nothing left for me to do but beg. "Just a little more time?"

"The thing is *done*." Sheriff Gardenia unsnaps the holster on his hip. "And you better think twice before you go off *half-cocked*."

Just then, a strange noise fills the air, unlike anything I've ever heard in my life. It sounds like the cry of a great animal, high and piercing and staccato.

Coo coo ree coo! Coo coo ree coo!

Then it mingles with another cry, like the keening, ferocious howl of a wolf in the wild, protecting its precious clutch of furry gray eggs.

Wooooo! Wuh-wuh-wuhooo!

Coo coo ree coo! Wuh-wuh-wuhoo!

Bancroft looks around nervously. Gardenia draws his gun.

The dogs fall silent, all at once.

My blood turns cold, and the wind goes still. For a moment, we all stand there, waiting stupidly for what is to come. What else can we do? What can *anyone* do about *anything* in this life?

Suddenly, there is an explosion of running footsteps from the direction of the woods. We turn as one, just in time to see the great beast charge toward us, black wings thrashing, giant beak clacking as it bellows out its war cry.

Coo coo ree coo! Wuh-wuh-wuhoo!

Gardenia squeezes off an errant, panicked shot, and he and Bancroft break for the squad car. Only then, as the creature hurtles after them, do I notice the white-flocked tail switching behind it.

Just like Cotton's.

"Fleecy!" The word rushes forth from my lips, drowned out by the screams of the disemboweled men. My heart hammers as their blood sprays everywhere, spattering black feathers and dusty ground alike in scriptlike streams.

This message, abstract as it is, I understand instantly.

Dog's Ass Farm is saved!

Fleecy's own cries confirm it, bless her soul.

Coo coo ree coo! Wuh-wuh-wuhoo!

As if on cue, the dogs finally break through the walls of the coop, barking and howling up a storm as they race to get in on the act...*if* she'll let them.

289

That's when I realize the tables have turned. The future isn't so much about how Fleecy's eggs, if she lays them, might taste to *us*.

It's about how *we* might taste to whatever hatches out of *them*.

OFFENSIVE IN EVERY POSSIBLE WAY

Dear Diary,

I've heard that people didn't always ███████████ing talk the way they do today, but I don't know if I believe that ███████████. I mean, I've read some of the e-books published fifty years ago, and it seems to me the early 21st century used the same ███████████ language we do now. They said ███████████ and ███████████ and even ███████████ like we do. Maybe they didn't all say it every other *word* like we do, but that's ███████████ progress for you, isn't it?

A girl like me would have fit in just ███████████ fine among the other seventeen-year-olds in those days. In fact, I'll bet I would've been queen of the ███████████ hill, since I'm in the top percentile at my ███████████ ███████████ high school when it comes to ███████████ing communications.

Which is why the ███████████ Gradezilla picked me to tutor Onus Brandle, the *worst* ███████████ in school when it comes to language ███████████ing arts.

So the Gradezilla (a.k.a. my bioengineered ███████████ all-subjects teacher, Mrs. Conscience) marches me into the ███████████ room where Onus is waiting. I know this ██████ kid by reputation only, and I already ████████ing hate him.

Standing there with his ██████████ arms stuck to his skinny ██████ sides, he looks like a ████████ ████████ with a ██████ in his ████████. That weird black crewcut and bulbous mushroom head of his make him look even more ██████████ than a ██████████. And what's with the ████████ white button-down shirt, black trousers and ██████████ red bow tie?

Gradezilla hands me a score sheet with three of her/its ██████ sixteen tentacles. "Help that little ██████████ bring his ██████ing communications scores up on the next ████████ federal standardized test in two ██████████ weeks. He's scoring so ██████████ low, he's killing our ██████████ chances of meeting the ██████████ minimum standard, meaning our ██████████ school might ██████ing lose all its ██████████ federal funding!"

I just roll my eyes at her/it. "Not my ██████████ problem, you ██████████."

Gradezilla glides toward me on her/its eighteen legs. "*You're* the ██████████, Airy Spinnaker! And it *is* your ██████████ problem." She/it leans toward me, the eyes and nostrils on her/its black-and-red Chinese dragon head ██████████ing flaring. "If he doesn't *pass* the next ██████████ing *test*, your ██████████ is ██████████! Because ██████████ *both* of you will be ██████████ing expelled."

With that, she lets out a roar and whips out the door, her ██████████ body serpentining behind her like a ██████████ ribbon of ██████████ on a ██████████.

"Well, ██████████," I say to Onus. "Looks like we're ██████████ing stuck with each other."

Onus shrugs. "Sorry about this. I've, uh..." He shuffles his ██████████ feet and blushes. "I've got a condition."

"What kind of ██████████ing condition?" I ask him.

"I don't talk or write like everyone else," says Onus. "I *can't*, for neurological reasons."

"For real?" I brush my glowing red smart-hair out of my eyes, instantly shortening the bangs, and look at his ██████████ communications test scores on the ▮▮▮▮▮▮ score sheet in my hand. "Well, that explains a ▮▮▮▮▮▮▮ing lot."

"I can't do it," he says. "No matter how hard I try, I can't use certain words. I can't say them, write them, or even *think* them."

I let the score sheet fall to my side. "What the ▮▮▮▮▮▮ am I going to ▮▮▮▮▮ing do with you?"

"Give up?" says Onus.

I blow out my breath in a big whoosh. "Don't ▮▮▮▮▮▮▮ing tempt me, you ▮▮▮▮▮▮."

Dear Diary,

My ▮▮▮▮▮▮ friends think I'm a ▮▮▮▮▮▮▮ joke because of that ▮▮▮▮▮▮, Onus. *Seriously.*

Why did *I* have to get stuck with the least popular ▮▮▮▮▮▮ kid in ▮▮▮▮▮▮ school?

Word spreads like ▮▮▮▮▮▮ lightning after I get assigned to tutor his sorry ▮▮▮▮▮▮. Fifteen ▮▮▮▮▮▮ minutes later, my best friend, Choozy Whittaker, is giving me ▮▮▮▮▮▮ at lunch about it.

"You have to tutor *Slownus Brain-Dull!*" Choozy crosses her ▮▮▮▮▮▮ eyes and talks like she has a ▮▮▮▮▮▮ speech impediment. Then she ▮▮▮▮▮▮ laughs and tosses that heaping blonde hair of hers. "Isn't that like tutoring a ▮▮▮▮▮▮ lump of ▮▮▮▮▮▮?"

I can't argue with that ▮▮▮▮▮▮. I'm the smartest girl in school, no ▮▮▮▮▮▮. Putting me with him is a ▮▮▮▮▮▮ waste of brainpower.

"What if that ▮▮▮▮▮▮ *rubs off* on you?" Choozy looks around at the other smart, pretty girls at our table and makes a face like a ▮▮▮▮▮▮ing moron. "You'll be like, 'I'm *Airhead*, and I talk like a *freak* now, thank you very much."

Every ▮▮▮▮▮▮ at the table laughs at that.

Just then, my other friend, Story Saginaw, speaks up. "If *anyone* can help that ▮▮▮▮▮▮ Onus, it's *you*, Airy." Her mood-sensitive hair changes colors from brown to baby blue as she smiles my way.

"But why the ██████████ would you *want* to?" says Choozy.

Story spreads her arms wide. "Because *helping people*?"

We all sit and look at each other for a moment. Then, we explode into laughter all at once.

"██████████ that!" says Story.

"██████████ that is right!" I say, and everyone laughs louder.

Dear Diary,

Fifteen minutes into my first ██████████ing session with Onus the next morning, I want to keelhaul the ██████████ing son of a ██████████.

"How ██████████ hard can it *be*?" I smack my hands on the desk, which makes the piece of ██████████ jump. "Just repeat after me: ██████████ you, you ██████████! Give me the ██████████ing coffee I ██████████ ordered!"

Onus shifts uncomfortably in his desk chair. "'Please give me the coffee I ordered, ma'am.'"

"No, ██████████ it!" I've been sitting at a desk across from him, and I jump to my ██████████ feet. "Repeat after me: The ██████████ing rain in ██████████ ██████████ Spain falls mainly on the ██████████ ██████████ plain, you dumb ██████████!"

"'The rain in Spain falls mainly on the...'"

"That is *not* the proper way to ██████████ talk!" I shake my head at him in complete ██████████ing exasperation. "How have you managed to ██████████ing *live* this long without learning to *talk* right?"

Onus slumps and stares at the ██████████ floor. "I already told you, Airy, I have a *condition*. This is hopeless."

"██████████ that, you ██████████!" I pace back and forth at the front of the ██████████ classroom, wracking my ██████████ brain for a ██████████ ██████████ idea. "I am *not* getting ██████████ing *expelled* because of you."

"Maybe I should just drop out of school on my own, then," he says. "That would solve everyone's problems, wouldn't it?"

The ███████████ is right. It's the perfect ████████████ solution, and it makes me stop ████████████ing pacing. "Do you want me to tell Gradezilla?"

"As long as you're sure," says Onus.

"Why the █████████████ *wouldn't* I be?"

Onus meets my gaze. "People won't look down on you, will they? They won't think you couldn't handle a...a doody-head like me, will they?"

████████████ me, he's got a ████████████ point. "But you already said this is ████████████ing hopeless because of your ████████████ condition." I toss my arms up and let them drop, smacking my ████████████ sides. "So if you don't ████████████ing drop out, and you can't ████████████ing learn the language, what the ████████████ else can we ████████████ing do?"

Frowning, the ████████████ gets up and shuffles over to the ████████████ window. He folds his ████████████ scrawny arms over his ████████████ chest and stares out at the black snow falling over the ████████████ing sinkholes around the ████████████ school. "Get to know each other, maybe?"

"How the ████████████ will *that* accomplish ████████████?"

Onus leans on the windowsill as a flash of lightning brightens his face. "Because maybe, if we put our heads together, we'll come up with a plan to save both our necks."

Dear Diary,

"He has a ████████████ing *condition*?" That's what Dad keeps ████████████ing saying when I tell him about Onus at ████████████ dinner.

I shrug while I eat my steaming pink bacto-loaf, which tastes like ████████████ in a ████████████ sauce with ████████████ on the side.

"So what's the ████████████ cure?" says Mom, whose hair-zoo

295

(a perpetual motion topiary for the head) is just now shifting to a ████████████ bouffant.

"████████ed if *I* know." I start in for another bite of ████████████ bacto-loaf, then drop my ████████████ing fork instead.

Dad, who's wearing a ████████████ purple turban, of all things (he's growing a ████████████ing second brain under there), jabs a finger in my direction. "What if this ████████████ Ogre kid is *lying*?"

I frown. "Why the ████████████ would he do that?"

"To *hurt* you," says Dad. "To get you ████████████ing expelled and ruin your chance at a ████████████ college scholarship."

"But why?" I ask.

"Because *haters*," snaps Mom.

"People love to ████████████ with you when you're on top," says Dad. "Remember, this is a ████████████ing dog eat dog world."

"We don't want a repeat of Zeke ████████████ing Toomey, do we?" says Mom. "Or that ████████████ Lank Goller?"

Why the ████████████ did she have to bring *them* up? "████████████ you." I jump up from my seat and leave the table.

"You have a ████████████ing *blind spot* when it comes to ████████████ boys, Airy," says Mom. "We just *worry* that that *Anus* boy will..."

"It's *Onus*," I shout just before I ████████████ing slam the ████████████ door of my ████████████ room.

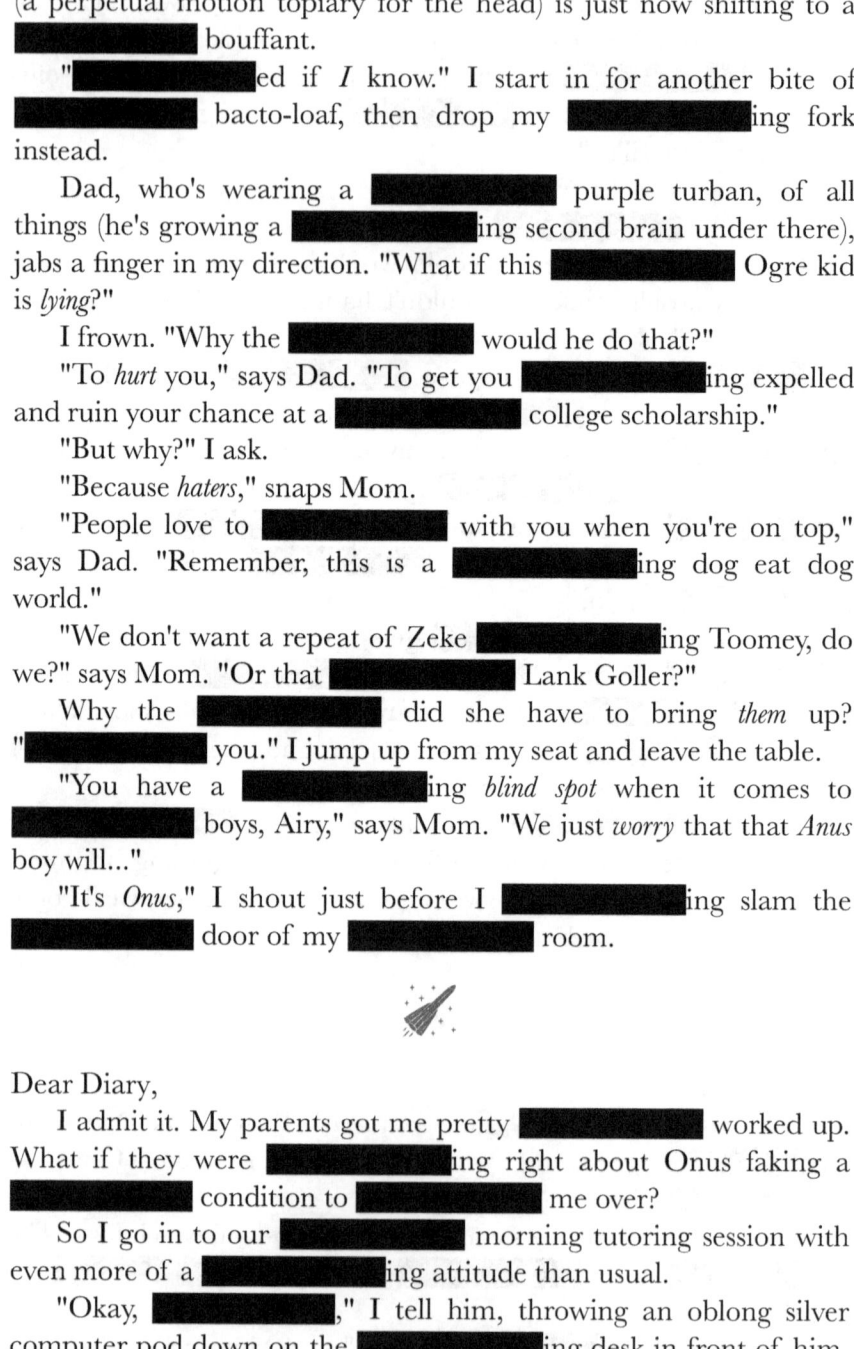

Dear Diary,

I admit it. My parents got me pretty ████████████ worked up. What if they were ████████████ing right about Onus faking a ████████████ condition to ████████████ me over?

So I go in to our ████████████ morning tutoring session with even more of a ████████████ing attitude than usual.

"Okay, ████████████," I tell him, throwing an oblong silver computer pod down on the ████████████ing desk in front of him.

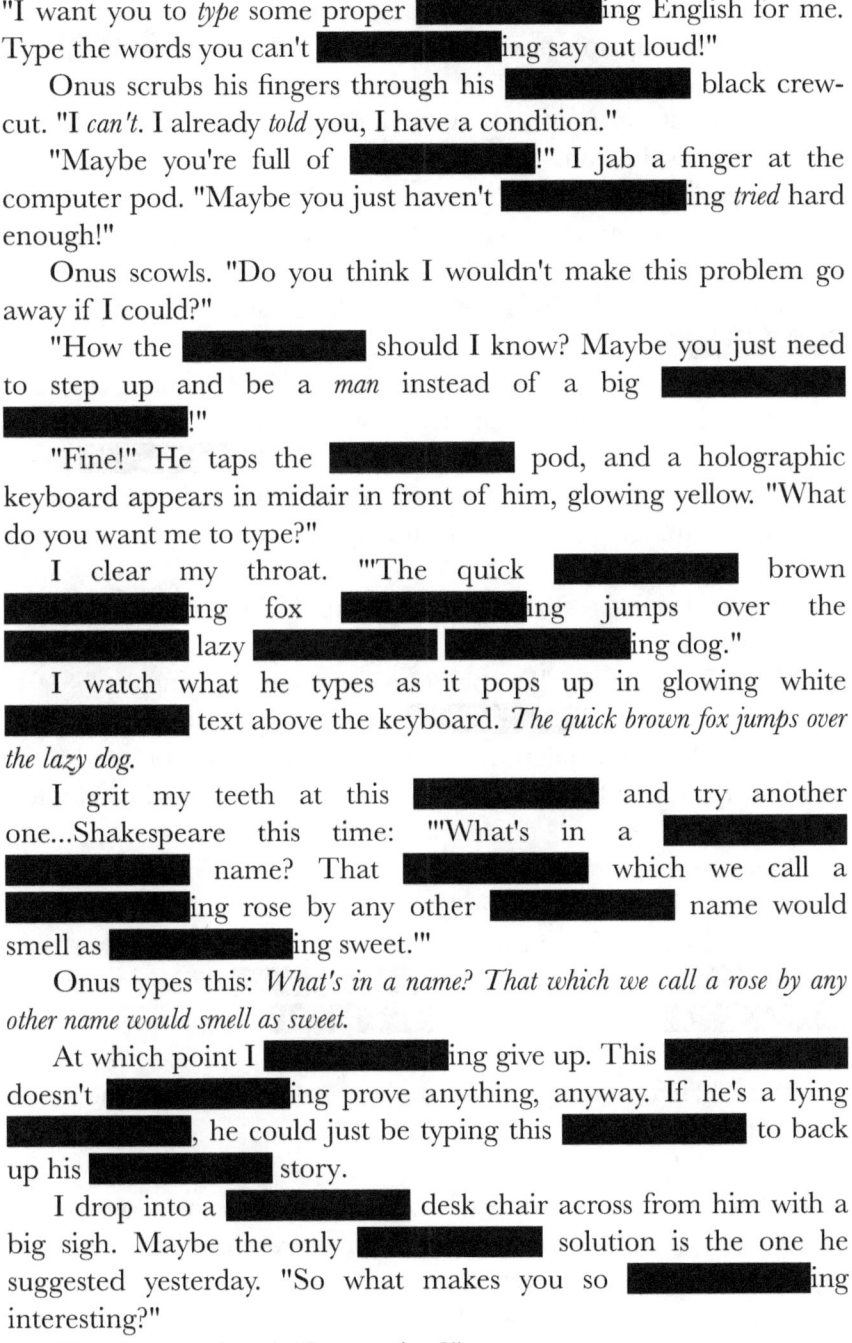

"I want you to *type* some proper ████████ing English for me. Type the words you can't ███████ing say out loud!"

Onus scrubs his fingers through his ██████████ black crew-cut. "I *can't*. I already *told* you, I have a condition."

"Maybe you're full of ███████!" I jab a finger at the computer pod. "Maybe you just haven't ██████ing *tried* hard enough!"

Onus scowls. "Do you think I wouldn't make this problem go away if I could?"

"How the ██████████ should I know? Maybe you just need to step up and be a *man* instead of a big ████████████████!"

"Fine!" He taps the ██████████ pod, and a holographic keyboard appears in midair in front of him, glowing yellow. "What do you want me to type?"

I clear my throat. "'The quick ███████████ brown ███████████ing fox ████████████ing jumps over the ██████████ lazy ███████████ ██████████ing dog."

I watch what he types as it pops up in glowing white ██████████ text above the keyboard. *The quick brown fox jumps over the lazy dog.*

I grit my teeth at this ██████████ and try another one...Shakespeare this time: "'What's in a ██████████ ██████████ name? That ██████████ which we call a ██████████ing rose by any other ██████████ name would smell as ███████████ing sweet.'"

Onus types this: *What's in a name? That which we call a rose by any other name would smell as sweet.*

At which point I ██████████ing give up. This ██████████ doesn't ██████████ing prove anything, anyway. If he's a lying ████████████, he could just be typing this ██████████ to back up his ██████████ story.

I drop into a ██████████ desk chair across from him with a big sigh. Maybe the only ██████████ solution is the one he suggested yesterday. "So what makes you so ███████████ing interesting?"

He looks confused. "Interesting?"

"Other than your ███████████ condition. What makes you interesting?" I tip my head to one side. "Why the ██████████ should I get to know you?"

"Oh, right." Onus nods with understanding. "Well, I like to paint. Pictures, I mean."

"No ██████████? Pictures of what?"

"People sometimes," says Onus. "Or landscapes. Outdoor scenes."

"Of what? █████████ing black snow falling in a ██████████ sinkhole?"

"Landscapes that don't exist anymore, since climate change," he says. "I use photo reference from online archives, mostly." Tapping the computer pod, he brings up the ██████████ über-net, then sifts through it with practiced flicks of his fingers until he gets to an image of blue sky and green trees. "Here's one of mine."

At first, I don't realize it's not a photo. "What software did you use to make it?"

"None," says Onus. "Just paint on canvas. It's a dying art."

"Then why the ██████████ do it?" I get a little lost in his painting as I stare. It takes me back to a domed park we used to go to when I was a kid, with green trees and waterfalls and even a few birds and butterflies.

"Because I love it. Don't you have something like that? Something that makes you feel alive?"

When I catch him staring at me, I snap out of it. "Other than ██████████ing wasting my ██████████ time answering ██████████ing stupid ██████████ questions from ██████████ like you?"

"Nice." He taps the pod, and the übernet winks off. "I guess we'll just settle for being expelled, then."

"We will?"

"This getting to know each other stuff is a joke, obviously." Onus gets up from his desk. "So what makes you think we can work together to solve our problem?"

I don't have an answer for that one.

"But that's okay. I've thought of another solution." He looks over his shoulder on his way to the door. "I'll request another tutor. Consider yourself off the hook."

One ████████████ hour later, I'm standing in front of Principal Krew Gundersnipe as he goes ███████████ing ballistic.

"You ████████████ ████████████ ████████████ ████████████!" Cyborg that he is, only half of Gundersnipe's face blazes beet red with rage. The other half is studded with prongs and instruments that spin and clack in a mechanical frenzy. "I oughtta ████████████ ████████████ ████████████ ████████████ ████████████ and ████ ████████████ ████████████ ████████████ ████████████ ████████████ ████████████! Then you'll *see* ████████████ ████████████ ████████████ ████████████ and ████████████ ████████████ ████████████ ████████████ you little ████████████ ████████████ ████████████ ████████████!"

I just listen, half intimidated by his anger and half impressed by his ████████████ way with words. No one I know is a better ████████████ing communicator...*no one.*

"You ████████████ ████████████ ████████████ ████████████ ████████████ ████████████!" Gundersnipe slams his ████████████ fists down on the desk, smashing a fresh hole with his ████████████ing robotic left hand. "And *another thing,* ████████████ ████████████ ████████████ ████████████ ████████████ ████████████ and ████████████ ████████████ ████████████ ████████████ because ████████████ ████████████ ████████████ ████████████ ████████████ ████████████ ████████████!"

"So you're saying Onus can't have a different tutor?" I ask him.

"*No,* he ████████████ ████████████ ████████████ ████████████ ████████████ ████████████!" Gundersnipe's so ████████████ mad, steam is literally coming out of the cyborg earhole on the left side of his head.

Against my better judgment, I say this: "But he has a *condition*."

"*A condition*?" This time, Gundersnipe opens fire with both ▮▮▮▮▮▮ing barrels. "I ▮▮▮▮▮▮ ▮▮▮▮ ▮▮▮▮▮▮ ▮▮▮▮▮ ▮▮▮▮▮▮ ▮▮▮▮ and you ▮▮▮▮ ▮▮▮▮▮▮ ▮▮▮▮▮▮ ▮▮▮▮▮▮ ▮▮▮▮ ▮▮▮▮▮▮ the ▮▮▮▮ ▮▮▮▮ ▮▮▮▮ ▮▮▮▮ ▮▮▮▮ ▮▮▮▮ ▮▮▮▮ ▮▮▮▮ ▮▮▮▮ a *real* condition!"

So much for Onus' latest ▮▮▮▮▮▮ idea.

Dear Diary,

No one knows me better than you. Ain't it the ▮▮▮▮▮▮ truth?

I never really talk about myself with anyone else. I mean, I talk ▮▮▮▮▮▮ with the best of them, but I hate getting ▮▮▮▮▮▮ing personal. I'm not good at it.

That's probably the main ▮▮▮▮▮▮ reason I've never had much ▮▮▮▮▮▮ing luck with relationships. It's why things didn't work out with ▮▮▮▮▮▮ing Zeke Toomey and Lank Goller, though my parents think the ▮▮▮▮▮▮ boys are to blame. I push ▮▮▮▮▮▮ people away when they try to get too ▮▮▮▮▮▮ close. Fish for information, and I'll cut you loose so ▮▮▮▮▮▮ing fast, your ▮▮▮▮▮▮ head will spin.

So much for being a great communicator, huh?

Which is why I'm tossing and turning in bed tonight. Because I've got no ▮▮▮▮▮▮ choice when it comes to that ▮▮▮▮▮▮, Onus.

Putting our heads together is the only way to save our necks. I guess the little ▮▮▮▮▮▮ was right about that. But if the only ▮▮▮▮▮▮ing way to put our heads together is to get to know each other...we might be ▮▮▮▮▮▮ed.

Unless I can stop being my usual ▮▮▮▮▮▮ self long enough to win him over. Which won't be easy, because me.

Dear Diary,

I show up for tutoring bright and early the next ███████████ing morning, and there he is: Onus, in the ███████████ flesh.

But he doesn't look ███████████ happy about being there. The ███████████ is slouching at his desk in ███████████ing sourpuss mode, like somebody ███████████ed in his ███████████ Wheaties.

"Good ███████████ing morning, Onus." I plop down across from him with my ███████████ giant google-caff megaspresso...and manage a ███████████ing smile. "Got some more ███████████ paintings to show me?"

"Very funny." He says it in a grouchy ███████████ing grumble. "I guess you heard."

"That you're ███████████ing stuck with me?" I shrug. "*C'est la* ███████████ing *vie*, you lucky ███████████."

He gives me a long look, then, like something crawled up his ███████████ and died. "You know, I wish I could speak the way you do, the way everyone does. Because the words I have just don't seem to express how angry I am at you right now."

"You could always call me a 'doody-head,' if you want." I smirk as I sip my megaspresso.

Onus doesn't laugh like I hoped. Instead, he folds his arms on the ███████████ desk and puts his head down on them. "So what now?"

At which point, I figure it's do or ███████████ing die. "Nothing."

"You mean we just give up?"

"No." I take a deep breath and let it out slowly. "I mean, you asked what's interesting about me, and that's it. *Nothing*."

Onus raises his head and puts his chin on his folded arms.

"I'm boring," I continue. "There's nothing interesting about me."

Onus narrows his ███████████ eyes at me. "Is that why you push people away? You're afraid they'll think you're not interesting?"

Instead of ripping him a new ███████████ like I normally would for that ██████████ comment, I let it pass.

"Well, *I* think you're interesting," says Onus. "You're the smartest kid in school, for one thing."

I feel like this is going nowhere. "Let's talk some more about you. Show me another ███████████ing painting."

"You're smart, you're pretty, and you're popular." Onus sits up straight. "But there's more going on under the surface than you let on, isn't there?"

That ███████████ is really pushing my ███████████ buttons. Does he *want* me to ██████████ing go off? "███████████ this." I get up from my chair.

"Wait." He jumps halfway up and grabs my arm. "Have we solved our problem yet?"

I shake my head.

"Then, please." He lets go and gestures at my chair. "Stay a little longer."

I almost make a ███████████ beeline for the door...but then I remember what we need to do to save our necks, and I slowly sit down.

"Thanks." Onus sits back and smiles. "So let's try something different."

I'm still in a ███████████ing ███████████y mood. "Like what?"

He thinks for a moment. "Like what if I tell you something about myself, and you tell me something similar about you? And it doesn't have to be *interesting*."

"But I just ███████████ing *did*." I widen my eyes to hammer the ███████████ point home. "I just told you I'm ███████████ing *boring*."

"Fine." Onus clears his throat. "I was going to go first, anyway."

Leaning back, I fold my ███████████ arms over my chest, trying to look like I don't ███████████ing hate this ███████████ already.

"So, okay," says Onus. "I hate Indian-Mexican food. That's one of my things." He makes a face like he's just eaten a ███████████ sandwich with a side order of ███████████.

"Seriously?"

"I *hate* it. Especially chicken curry enchiladas with refried pig bung ice cream."

"But *everybody* loves pig bung ice cream." *You* ██████████*ing freak*, I almost say, but I keep it to myself.

Onus shrugs. "So tell me something about *you* now."

"Here's one. I hate tutoring so ██████████ing much, I'd rather ██████████ myself with a..."

"Something I don't already *know*," says Onus.

I don't see how this ██████████ game will solve anything, and I don't like to ██████████ing share, but what the ██████████? Why not ██████████ing humor him a little? "Well, *I* hate ██████████ bacto-loaf. Also bacto-burgers, bacto-balls, and bacto-mush. Anything made from cultured bacterial protein, I hate the ██████████ out of."

"Me, too." Onus smiles. "And here you probably never thought we'd have anything in common, did you?"

I don't answer, because I might say something ██████████y if I did.

"Let's do another one." Onus thinks, then nods. "How about...a secret?"

Right away, my guard goes up. "I'm not really in the ██████████ing mood for ██████████ Truth or Dare."

"Just one secret. Here's mine." Onus leans forward and lowers his voice. "*Quessa yolo vishi qua-quasso yex osidigo.*"

I stare at him like he just turned purple. "What the ██████████ is *that* supposed to mean?"

Onus laughs. "It's in my own homemade language. It means, 'I make up languages in my spare time.'"

Suddenly, a chill rushes through me. I can't believe what I just heard him say.

"I know, I know." Onus shrugs and chuckles. "Pretty geeky, right?"

I don't answer. I'm too busy trying to wrap my head around the situation.

"Anyway, that's my secret," says Onus. "So what's yours?"

I just sit there, still processing. Normally, I wouldn't give him any kind of straight answer...but maybe this mess is finally starting to make sense, in a crazy kind of way.

I open my mouth to speak, then close it again, then open. The words come softly, almost in a whisper.

"*Kinsling fulmino em brinchissi, ressari.*"

Onus frowns. "What did you say?"

I take a deep breath and let it out again. "'Your secret is the same as mine.' That's what I said."

He looks stunned...and then the happiest I've seen him yet. "See? Hating bacto-loaf isn't the only thing we have in common, is it?"

I shake my head slowly, still feeling kind of dazed about the whole thing.

"I *knew* there was a reason I liked you," says Onus.

Liked me? Suddenly, my mind is shooting off in another direction entirely. It's an expression, he probably didn't mean anything by it, but still.

Onus stares off into space, rubbing his chin, then turns his gaze back to me again. "I have an idea. A way to solve our problem."

"For real?" The question of whether he likes me fades away...more or less.

"We'll have to work together on this," says Onus. "And it's going to take time. But the good news is, we've got the expertise to pull it off."

"So what's the idea?" I ask him.

"We're going to give them what they want," says Onus. "Principal Gundersnipe, Gradezilla, everyone."

I frown. "But how? As long as you have your condition, you'll never score higher on the standardized test."

"Ah." He raises an index finger. "But higher test scores are not the *only* thing they want."

Dear Diary,

I admit it. I didn't give Onus enough credit.

From the start, I saw him more as an obstacle, an annoyance, and a threat...a weirdo, even, because of his condition. Given his language issues and pathetic test scores, I certainly didn't think of him as *smart*.

But boy, *is* he.

As we spend the rest of the week working on his idea, I start to see just how smart he is. He's smart enough to come up with a plan that's very outside-the-box, yet logical...a plan that makes the most of our mutual interests and talents and takes advantage of the flaws in the system oppressing us.

I can't believe I'm saying this, but he might be as smart as *I* am...or *smarter*. A different *kind* of thinker, at least. Because I'll be honest, I'm not sure I ever would have come up with this plan, no matter how hard I tried.

Not that I resent him for it. I can't help admiring his elegant solution.

And I can't help having fun with it, too. Getting ready takes a lot of time, as he predicted, but I'm enjoying myself. It's something I love doing...and the company is better than expected.

The more time we spend together, the more I like him. Not only is he smart, but he's funny (even snarky, can you believe it?) and unpredictable (in a good way). He's a nice guy, but still tough when he needs to be.

Because of his condition, the rest of the kids in school have always treated him like ███████████--the teachers and administrators, too--but they didn't know what they were missing out on. The same goes for me; I never thought I'd say it, but I'm glad we ended up in this situation together.

Dear Diary,

I almost give him a hug for luck. I *want* to, I'm so nervous and excited...but I settle for a handshake, instead.

Even though I know a hug would have been totally fine, since this is such a big day. It's Monday morning, and we're about to meet with Principal Gundersnipe and Gradezilla. We're about to put the plan into action.

"Principal Gundersnipe will see you ▮▮▮▮▮▮▮s now," says Miss Silkenfloss, the secretarial 'bot floating in front of us. Her voice is soft and sexy, but she's really just a faceless jumble of blinking, colored cubes.

"Ready?" Onus gestures at Gundersnipe's wooden slab of a door.

I straighten my dress and nod, though my heart is fluttering and my belly's full of butterflies and battery acid.

Onus leans close to me and whispers. "Remember, we have what they want."

"They just don't know it yet." I smile, take a deep breath, and march for the door.

It swings inward when I approach it, creaking loudly for dramatic effect like a door in a haunted house. I stroll through with a confident stride, head held high.

Gundersnipe leaps to his feet behind his battered desk. The halves of his face, human and mechanical alike, already look like he's in full-throttle tantrum mode.

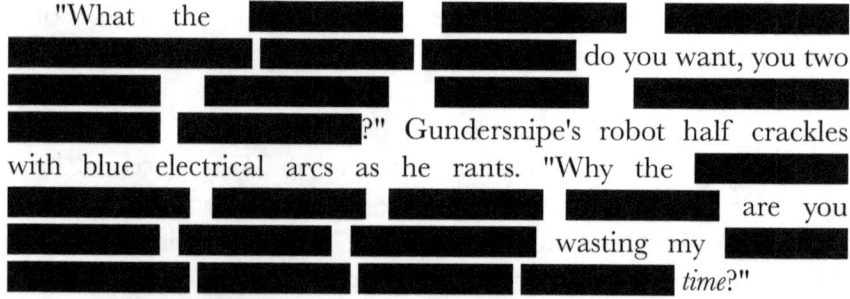

"What the ▮▮▮▮▮ ▮▮▮▮▮ ▮▮▮▮▮ ▮▮▮▮▮ ▮▮▮▮▮ ▮▮▮▮▮ do you want, you two ▮▮▮▮▮ ▮▮▮▮▮ ▮▮▮▮▮ ▮▮▮▮▮ ▮▮▮▮▮ ▮▮▮▮▮?" Gundersnipe's robot half crackles with blue electrical arcs as he rants. "Why the ▮▮▮▮▮ ▮▮▮▮▮ ▮▮▮▮▮ ▮▮▮▮▮ are you ▮▮▮▮▮ ▮▮▮▮▮ ▮▮▮▮▮ wasting my ▮▮▮▮▮ ▮▮▮▮▮ ▮▮▮▮▮ ▮▮▮▮▮ ▮▮▮▮▮ *time?*"

Gradezilla, who's coiled up beside him, chimes in. "You said you have good ▮▮▮▮▮ing news to report about the results of your ▮▮▮▮▮ tutoring, Airy?"

"As a matter of fact, I do."

"Then *spit it out*, you ▮▮▮▮▮ ▮▮▮▮▮ ▮▮▮▮▮ ▮▮▮▮▮ ▮▮▮▮▮!" shouts Gundersnipe. "▮▮▮▮▮ or get off the ▮▮▮▮▮ ▮▮▮▮▮ ▮▮▮▮▮ pot!"

Gradezilla nods her Chinese dragon head at Onus. "Are you telling us that little ▮▮▮▮▮ can finally *talk* and *write* correctly? He's finally ▮▮▮▮▮ing ready for the ▮▮▮▮▮ test?"

"He can talk just fine," I tell her, "but he *won't* be taking the test."

Gradezilla scowls. "*What* did you ██████████ing say?"

Gundersnipe pounds his desk with his mechanical fist. "You

! I'll

!"

I clear my throat and shout over him. "Allow me to explain! Or better yet, allow *him*!" With that, I gesture at Onus.

All eyes in the room turn to him.

Onus smiles and gives a little bow. Then, he shoots me a quick wink, barely perceptible, and speaks. "*Oolock* you and the *paponzu* horse you rode in on, you *kwee gyotah*."

For a moment, the office is silent. Gundersnipe and Gradezilla just stare at Onus, their mouths hanging open.

"*What* did he just say?" asks Gundersnipe.

"Let me put it a different way." Onus points a finger at Gundersnipe. "Go *asmo* your *ulo*, you *zafta chegwadorah*."

"Sounds like ██████████ing *gibberish* to me," says Gradezilla.

"Up your *oosm*, you *neumantic neugal neuba!*" says Onus.

"Are you ██████████ing *begging* to be *expelled*?" howls Gradezilla.

Heart hammering, I interrupt. "No! He's begging to make you *rich*!"

Gundersnipe and Gradezilla look mystified.

"Rich?" says Gundersnipe.

"He's speaking a *new language*," I tell them. "It's a *thousand times* meaner than any words spoken in everyday English."

"How the ██████████ do *we* know that?" asks Gradezilla.

"Because I just *told* you." I snap my fingers to punch the line. "Also because we've scientifically designed this language to beat the ██████████ out of the old one and kick it to the ██████████ curb."

"*Imi umino yoth kadandis, oolock-bulgarr!*" adds Onus.

Gradezilla shakes her head. "It still sounds like ███████ gibberish to me."

"I assure you, it's a complete language. We've got it all mapped out." I spread my arms wide. "You could give a *speech* or write a *book* with it. You could translate everything on the ██████████ *übernet* with it."

"So what?" says Gundersnipe.

"So *rich*," says Onus.

Gundersnipe squints. "How do you ██████████ing figure?"

"Because we're going to *monetize* it." Onus grins. "We'll charge people to *use* it."

"You really think anyone will ██████████ go for that?" asks Gradezilla.

"It's called *perception of value*," I tell her. "Marketing psychology 101. If something has a price, it *must* be worth paying for. And the higher the price, the *better* it must be."

Gundersnipe looks and sounds interested. "People would pay a *fee* every time they *use* it?"

"Exactly!" says Onus. "And the school district will get a *percentage*, because I'm such a generous person."

"A percentage?" The instruments on the mechanical half of Gundersnipe's face begin to twirl.

"But how could you ever ██████████ing *collect*?" Gradezilla still sounds skeptical.

"I've got some ideas about that." Onus shrugs. "Though I won't have time to work on them if I'm busy dealing with that *test* I have to take..."

"Forget the test!" says Gundersnipe.

"And if my partner and I are *expelled*, we'll have bigger problems than monetizing our new language..."

"Being expelled is off the ██████████ing table!" Gundersnipe slams his robot fist through his desk again. "We need you two *here*, running this new *linguistic research project*."

"Sounds like we're on the same page here." Onus looks over at me, smiling.

I smile back at him. "*Kweelock arkichaw, Onie.*"

"What's *that* supposed to mean?" Gundersnipe chuckles. "Is it like ███████ing-A right, we're in ████████ing business? *Kweelock arkichaw...*"

"First of all, not exactly," says Onus. "And second, pay up." He holds out his hand. "You just used my *zafta* language, you *iglior yonyx.*"

Everyone in the office (except Gradezilla) laughs out loud at that one.

Dear Diary,

Onus and I celebrate by going out for dinner at a cozy little molecular gastronomy place--no chicken curry enchiladas or pig bung ice cream in sight.

It feels good to be out with him; it feels like we've made it through a storm together, and we're closer because of it. It feels like we're the best of friends, though we've only known each other a short time.

"I'd like to make a toast." He raises a glass of quantum everyflavor tea and smiles. "Here's to making history."

I clink my glass against his. "You really think our language will make history?"

"*More* than that." Onus has a sip of tea. "I think it will *change* history."

He looks confident and determined...handsome, too. I can't believe I ever thought he looked goofy; I can't believe I ever thought he was a freak. It's funny how wrong you can be about someone, yet convinced that you're right.

At least until you go through a gauntlet with them.

"Change history?" I lean my chin in my hand and prop my elbow on the table. "How so?"

"When the new language catches on, our words will replace the old, dark ones," says Onus. "The mean ones that have come into favor as the world has gotten uglier."

"But our language is structurally similar, right? When we say

zafta or *yonyx*, isn't it the same as saying ███████████ or
████████████? We're just substituting a different word, aren't we?"

Onus shakes his head. "It just *seems* that way, Airy."

"But wait. If someone says *zafta* or *yonyx* with the same intent as
saying ███████████ or ████████████, the *new* words become just as
mean as the *old* ones, don't they? We even *said*, this new language is
a thousand times meaner than everyday English."

"If that's the case, then how am I able to speak it with my condition?" Onus takes another sip of tea and puts down his glass.
"There's a reason for that." He reaches into his shirt pocket and
fishes out a folded piece of paper. "Take a look."

He hands me the paper, and I unfold it. One side of the open
page is filled with lines of our new language, printed in red ink. I
also see another word here and there, a word that doesn't change
from one language to another.

My name.

Translating the page, I quickly realize what it says...and I scowl
at him, feeling instantly betrayed. "What the ███████████ is the
matter with you?"

Onus doesn't look the slightest bit ruffled. "Why? What does it
say?"

"It's one long *nasty note*," I snap. "You call me every foul word in
our new language!"

"Do I?" Onus shrugs. "Read the first sentence for me, will you?
Translate it into English."

I'm hurt and angry, but I'll play along for now. Leaning forward,
I lower my voice to keep it between us. "'Airy is a real ███████████.
She's a ███████████ing ███████████ and a ███████████
███████████ ███████████.'"

"Thanks." Onus takes the paper, then holds it up and reads.
"'Airy is a girl like no other. She is an angelic beauty and a brilliant,
gentle spirit.'"

When he's done, I stare at him. "What?" I don't understand
what just happened.

"That's what it *really* says," he explains. "I added another level to
our language, a level of cryptosymbolic phonemes encoded from an
ur-textual baseline, designed to evoke a subliminal response. In

other words, everything in our language has a secondary translation that overrides the surface meaning whether the speaker or reader knows it or not."

Once again, I realize this guy is smarter than I imagined. "You did this while we were working together? Without my knowing it?"

"I hope you don't mind." He grins. "Now do you see how this language could change things? People will think they're cursing each other, but they'll all secretly know they're exchanging deeper, kinder messages. They'll be nicer to each other than they realize, and they'll feel it on a deep level that will eventually impact their thoughts and actions."

"You *planned* this?" I ask him. "The whole time, I thought we were just trying to keep from being expelled, and you were *planning* to change the world?"

Onus just smiles and waves the paper. "Want to hear some more?"

I just nod.

"*Oma choni shuba-lo lerofon? Cricha Airy zulong eriophany gidge,*" he reads...then translates. "'Was I ever truly happy before her? Airy brings light to the deepest darkness.'"

My heart beats fast as I listen. How much can one person change you?

"*Neuba Airy krantha-wo exen loba. Bagga cha volu cha oysu cha furlock.*" Onus looks up from the paper as he translates. "'Airy makes me see with new eyes. She makes me laugh and dream and feel.'"

Already, he has helped me change the way I communicate...jettisoning the ugliness I took for granted because I heard and read it everywhere around me. The words he couldn't use because of his condition, I hardly use myself anymore. I've even gone back through this diary and blacked them out, because I don't need them anymore.

"*Nakah sissolanu pah egree shuk ammu donzoh donzah.*" says Onus. "'Working together, there is nothing we can't accomplish.'"

He has also helped me see the importance of opposing authority when its edicts are unjust. I know now there is a time to take a stand, and our minds can help us do that more effectively than any kind of physical force.

Onus has taught me all that...and one more thing, besides.

"*Kwee vo hantu omo shungraswela? Wo-deciju embla consalengua, dequo ignate, tincta giasiss krantha-su obashon.* 'Will she be a part of my tomorrows? I have a new plan, the best one yet, and only her bright spark can make it a reality.'"

He has helped me reach out to someone else in ways I couldn't reach out before. He has helped me share my secrets and consider possibilities beyond the dictates of my selfish nature.

Because why?

"There's more, if you don't mind." Onus smiles and pulls out another folded piece of paper. "Actually, we haven't gotten to the best part yet."

Because *him*.

HEROES OF GLOBAL WARMING

F reeze-Dry, Floater, and Bottlenose catch up with me near Times Square Sea, itching to bring me in after what I did to their buddy, Sunblock. Never mind that *I* used to be their buddy, too, a long time ago. Back before I went from *being* a superhero...

...to kicking superheroes' *asses*. Not that Freeze-Dry and his pals think *they're* the ones about to take a beating. Not when they've got me outnumbered three to one like this.

"Stand down, Skillet!" Freeze-Dry skates up on an elevated track of frozen water vapor, ten feet above the lapping waves of Times Square Sea. The track expands forward as he skates, responding to his freeze-inducing powers. "I won't tell you twice!"

"You heard the man!" Floater swoops up like a deflating balloon and holds steady at twenty feet away from me, drifting past the ruined buildings of the Square on the late morning air currents. His voice sounds like a cartoon chipmunk's, like he's just sucked a lungful of helium. "Don't make us hurt you."

Bottlenose, who's half man, half dolphin, spins up from the water below and triggers his antigravity harness, joining the rest of us hovering in midair. His gleaming gray head bobs as he lets loose a stream of clicking dolphin language, which I don't understand.

So now I'm surrounded. The forces of justice encircle me in the heart of the sunken city of New York, drowned five years ago by the rising sea levels of global warming.

The lights of Times Square are long dead. The giant screens on which videos once played for throngs of tourists are gray and shattered; even the highest is half-submerged.

Maybe if I didn't remember what this place used to be like, it wouldn't make me sick to the stomach now. The same goes for the whole damn world these days. Rising temperatures, rising sea levels, crazy weather. Manhattan has turned to shit, and the whole planet has gone with it.

The smell of salt water and dead sea life fills the air. The city is mostly deserted, but a few spectators weave between towers in sputtering motorboats. They know the score.

There can be only one outcome. The three noble heroes will defeat me in battle and take me in. My year-long struggle is at an end; Earth's most wanted is goin' down.

At least that's what *they* think.

I hang there a moment, held aloft by the pillar of rising steam gushing up from the water below. My powers keep the steam flowing, generated by the waves of intense heat I radiate.

Turning slowly in my red-orange costume trimmed with flames, I give each of my former pals a long stare from behind my red-tinted goggles. Bottlenose chatters some more and flips me the bird with one of his hybrid flipper/hands. His purple harness bears the insignia of America's premiere super-team, the Castigators: a stylized letter "C" that looks like it's been sculpted out of ice.

Floater, also purple-clad with the Castigators' emblem on his chest, looks like a human water-skimmer. His pipe-cleaner body flutters on errant breezes; he floats on his caved-in belly like he's part of a mobile, dangling over an infant's crib.

Then there's Freeze-Dry. "Well, Skillet?" He's got a good-sized paunch these days, filling out his silver parka. Global warming has been good to him; lots of demand for a guy who can cool things off with a wave of his hands. "Going to come quietly and answer for what you've done?"

Not as much demand for someone like me, though. Someone

who's all about the heat. "Funny thing, Rick." Reaching up, I run an orange-gloved hand over my bright red shock of hair. "I was just going to ask you the same question."

"No civilian names!" Freeze-Dry swings up both hands, pointing all twelve of his fingers right at me. "You're not one of *us* anymore."

"Sure I am." I nod and give him a wiggling double thumbs-up. "Once a Castigator..."

"Don't even joke!" says Floater in his helium chipmunk voice. "Not after what you did to Sunblock!"

The three of them move in a little when he mentions that. I can see how there'd be some hard feelings.

But the fact is, there's something they don't know. Something that puts a different spin on the whole mess.

"Listen." I pump out a little more heat to push them back again. "You'll never know how *much* I didn't want to hurt Sunblock."

"You didn't let it stop you, did you?" squeaks Floater, and Bottlenose chatters in agreement.

"But it wasn't supposed to be that way." The fire of regret wells up within me, followed by the fire of pain. "I didn't have any choice."

It all started with the clinking of beer bottles, a year ago to the day. We started down this road with a toast to the future, to setting it right, my partner and I.

Make that *Sunblock* and I.

Neither of us was smiling as we tipped back the bottles and drank. The occasion was hopeful, the plan was worked out, we were committed...

But the price would be steep.

"Are you sure you can do this?" Sunblock raised his eyebrows. Tiny beads of sweat stood out on his dark forehead, the effect of sitting across a table from me with my two-hundred degree body temperature.

"Of course not." I swigged some more beer, which was already warm from my hand. "But I'm willing to try."

"Shit." Sunblock shook his head slowly. "Are you sure you don't want to switch places?"

"And be the double-crossing mole?" I touched the big "C" on my chest; back then, I was still wearing a Castigators' uniform. "Having to hide my true purpose from America's premiere super-team while secretly manipulating them from within?"

Sunblock sighed and put down his beer. "I've gotta ask, Mike. This isn't because of the critics, right? You're over that, aren't you?"

I laughed, though it wasn't a laughing matter. "I'm not doing this because I won the Droopy Long-John." It was true. Receiving the critics' award for most useless hero was just one of the things that was motivating me, one part of a miserable life.

Sunblock reached across the table and put his hand on top of mine, which I knew made him uncomfortable. Fresh sweat popped out on his forehead and ran down his face. "What about the R-word? I hate to bring it up, but..."

"Retirement?" I bumped his hand aside. "How many times do I have to tell you, this isn't some mid-life crisis."

"I know, I'm just..."

Lunging forward out of my chair, I grabbed the front of his purple costume. "This is about the *future*, Joe! Making things *right* for *everyone*!"

"Except two dozen *superheroes*." Sunblock hissed the words in a harsh whisper. "Tricked into a cape-and-cowl *death trap*."

I held on to him for a moment, locking my gaze to his ebony eyes. As always, they were full of understanding and friendship. Like any good friend on the brink of a big leap, he was simply conducting one last sanity check. He was backstopping me, as always, because he cared.

And I was holding out on him, as always, for the same reason. Holding back something he needed to know.

"Thanks." I released him and settled back into my chair. "Yes, I'm sure I can do this."

I watched as he smiled calmly and raised his beer. "Well all right then." What if he *did* know? What if I told him? "So we do this thing." Those questions always hung between us like a cloud of cigarette smoke.

And like always, they remained unanswered. "We start tomorrow, Sunblock." But for how much longer? Another week? Another year? "One year from now, the world as we know it will cease to exist."

There's been a lot of water under the bridge since then. After what I did to Sunblock, I'm on my own. No cavalry to charge to the rescue.

On the other hand, I've still got an advantage. Because Freeze-Dry, Floater, and Bottlenose have no idea what's really at stake.

Or what I'm willing to do to make it happen.

"One last chance to come quietly." As he says it, Freeze-Dry's already revving up his flash-freezing powers. His twelve fingers glow bright blue and crackle with energy. "As your friend, I advise you to surrender."

He doesn't wait for me to answer. Bolts of freeze-force burst from his hands and race toward me, screaming through the air.

I thrust one hand in front of me, casting a wave of focused heat at Freeze-Dry's blast. The opposing forces crash together and swirl for a moment, heat versus cold. Then, I pump out a booster surge that breaks the clinch and fries the stream of freezing power right back to Freeze-Dry's fingers, sending him spinning.

I'm expecting an attack from the other two next, and I get it. A wave of sound plows into me from behind, a deafening, modulated roar like amplified whalesong. I know it's Bottlenose's work; I twist as it flings me forward, and I see him swimming toward me, distortion ripples pulsing from his open mouth.

I fire a blast of heat at the water behind me, pulling up a funnel of steam that stops my flight. Pushing off with another jet of steam, I rush headlong toward Bottlenose, hands glowing cherry red like twin branding irons. He can't get out of my way in time, and I bash both fists straight into his snout, sending him reeling. So much for the ear-splitting whalesong.

It's then that I make a mistake. I figure Freeze-Dry's the bigger threat, so I turn when I hear his voice.

But what I *should* be doing is watching for Floater. Never under-estimate someone just because they don't seem to contribute much.

It's the same lesson I've worked so hard to teach the Castigators about *me*.

Eleven months and three weeks ago today, Concertina and Swiftboat of the Castigators went out on a routine rescue call to Point Scranton, one of the new coastal towns at the edge of the rising Atlantic Ocean. The call came in over their belt radios--something about a capsized ferry on the way to Jersey Island.

They should've been surprised when all they found at the rescue coordinates was me...but they were too busy being assholes, as usual.

Swiftboat did his patented running on water bit, moving so fast as he zipped toward me that his feet never had time to sink. "What the hell, Skillet? You make a wrong turn on the way to the weenie roast?"

Concertina chuckled on her blood-red jet ski. "Where's the ferry? Did you already set it on fire? Was that your solution to the sinking problem?"

I just floated on a curtain of steam and shook my head. The stupid jokes had been rolling for years, ever since global warming's impact had gone off the charts. Really funny stuff, right? All based on the premise that someone with heat powers is about as useful as tits on a bull in a world that's too damn hot.

"You're supposed to *save* the passengers, not *melt* them." Swift-boat kept running in circles to stay afloat. "I thought we *talked* about this."

I just shrugged. "Everyone's disappeared. Either that, or the rescue coordinates are wrong."

"Well gee, if you say so." Concertina smirked. "Did you scan the area with your crispy critter vision?"

I can't say I was used to the jokes, but I did get used to ignoring them. "Maybe you could run a grid search, Swiftboat. Call us in when you reach the actual site."

Swiftboat was used to ignoring me, too. "Say, 'Tina." He

pretended I hadn't said a word. "I just decided to go run a grid search. I'll call when I've found the actual site, 'kay?"

"Good idea, Swifty. I'll wait here." Looking up, she made a face at me. "Would it *kill* you to cut back on the thermal emissions? You're just making the global warming worse, y'know."

I nodded. "Thanks for the input."

As Swiftboat dashed off across the water, Concertina patted her hair and frowned. "You're ruining my *hair*, too, didja know that? Frying the body right *out* of it."

"Sorry to hear that." I shook my head like I felt for her. "Shaving it off's always an option."

Concertina clucked her tongue and threw the jet-ski in reverse. "Talk about being part of the *problem*." She scowled with disgust as she backed away from me. "Might as well call my hairdresser now." As the jet-ski continued bobbing backward, she pulled a cell phone out of her barbed-wire bustier and hit speed-dial.

"Hey Trish, can you squeeze me in tomorrow morning?" At first, she was too busy talking to realize the jet-ski had stopped moving. "That's right. Yes, I know I was just in yesterday. Tell it to Captain Burnout here." She laughed. "Yes, *that* Captain Burnout, Trish!"

The fact that I was heating up and moving closer didn't seem to register with Concertina. She was too busy yukking it up with her lowlife hairdresser.

Another big laugh. "The things you say, Trish!" She fixed her eyes on me so it was clear whom they were talking about. "What? What?" She let loose a big, honking hoot. "You think so? Oh my God!" And another. "*No*, I'm not going to ask him *that*!"

Suddenly, her phone stopped working. Because I melted it in her hand.

With a shriek, she flung the smoking blob into the water, then plunged her hand down after it to cool off. "Oh my God! Oh my God! Oh my God!"

As the initial shock wore off, she looked up at me, and understanding flowed into her eyes. Then anger. "What'd you do *that* for, Burnout?" With her undamaged hand, she grabbed the wire gun from its holster on her left boob. "Think you're *cute* or somethin'?"

ROBERT JESCHONEK

As she swung the wide-bore barrel in my direction, I raised my hands. She pulled the trigger, and a gleaming length of razor-sharp concertina wire shot from the muzzle, slashing toward me.

Before she could use her metalkinetic power to bring the wire to life, wrapping it around my throat or balls or what have you, I pulsed out a wave of blistering heat. The wire turned to silver rain in midair, drizzling down on the water's surface. Then, I melted the gun, too.

And the jet-ski.

The look on Concertina's face finally changed from disgust and anger to fear. "Hey, I'm sorry, all right?" She winced up at me as she treaded water to stay afloat. "I was just kidding around, Mike!"

I shrugged. "Whatever."

Her expression shifted back to anger. "Swiftboat'll be back here any second now, you know. He isn't gonna be happy, not one bit."

"Shhh." I placed my finger against my lips. "Did you hear that?"

Just then, a sound like thunder cracked in the distance.

I smiled down at her and hiked a thumb over my shoulder. "Sonic boom. That's him."

"That's right." She tossed her head and sneered. Her running mascara had given her raccoon eyes. "Now you're gonna get it, Burnout. Just wait."

"Think so?" I pointed at a distant stretch of coastline. "Watch this."

Suddenly, a wave of blackness surged out of the distance, racing toward us over the water. It fell upon us fast, shrouding us in total darkness, as if someone had switched off the sun.

The darkness held a moment. Concertina screamed.

And then it rolled away. The mid-afternoon light reappeared all around us.

"What the hell?" Even as she said it, I knew she'd recognized the darkness effect. She'd seen it in action often enough; all the Castigators had.

Because it was the trademark of one of our own.

"S-Sunblock?" Concertina's lips quivered as she said it. "But he wasn't on the duty roster."

320

I shot her a wink. "Good to know you're paying attention, 'Tina."

She frowned, thinking it over...and then she tried to turn it to her advantage. "Swiftboat must've called him in to deal with you. *Now* you're screwed!"

I laughed at her. "Here." Super-heating the water around her, I turned it into a cushion of steam that raised her out of the sea. "I'll take you to him."

Her brown eyes widened. "To Swiftboat?"

"You betcha." I raised my eyebrows and nodded. "We got you matching stasis tubes. You'll never leave his side."

Before she could say another word, I turned up the temperature, giving her a sudden case of heatstroke. She passed out, slipping into a comatose state.

Which is where she has stayed to this day. She and all the others we've rounded up.

They underestimated me, every last one of them. Just like I underestimate Floater today in the Times Square Sea.

I write him off as a minor threat and turn my back on him. Freeze-Dry's shouting something, and I focus on him instead.

Which is exactly when Floater does his deflating balloon trick and crashes into me from behind at a high rate of speed.

The impact slams me out of my supporting pillar of steam. My overheated body hisses like a hundred snakes when I hit the water face-down, casting up billowing clouds of vapor.

Before I can get my bearings, something lands on my back, knocking the breath out of me. The weight pushes me down faster than I can turn the water to steam, and my empty lungs inhale. Next thing I know, they're filling with water.

I'm drowning. Now wouldn't *that* be something, if I came all this way, with three Castigators left to capture, and *drowned* to death?

My first instinct is to thrash like a fool, trying to dislodge whatever's pushing me down...but that doesn't work. Then, in one of the last seconds I have left, I remember I'm a *superhero*. I have a super *power*.

Time to pull out the stops.

Choking, plunging deeper under the sea, I gather my strength, reaching into my fiery core. And then, every cell tingling, I let it *explode*.

A shockwave of intense heat bursts out of my body in all directions, instantly boiling the water around me. The weight on my back falls away, dropping past...and it's only then I see for sure it's Bottlenose who's been trying to drown me.

Flipping around, I shoot toward the surface. My lungs ache as I race for the light, praying I won't black out before I reach the open air. Praying also that Bottlenose isn't dead, because all my hopes will die with him.

The instant I break the surface, I focus my power inward, concentrating on my lungs. I feel the heat suffusing the tissue, radiating into the sacs, turning the water into steam. When I open my mouth, it rushes out of me in a sizzling jet.

And then, when my lungs are clear, I suck in what feels like the deepest breath of my life. The *best* breath of my life.

I enjoy the feeling for exactly ten seconds.

"Noooo!" Then, Floater's anguished cry kills my buzz. "Bottlenose, noooo!"

Looking around, I catch sight of it. The glistening gray body bobbing on the waves thirty feet away...skin blistered from boiling sea water. Half man, half dolphin...

All dead.

And so, too, is the plan I've so carefully nurtured for the past year. Because I don't need just *some* of the Castigators to succeed.

I need *all* of them.

Two years ago, my buddy Brain Fart laid it out for me over a steak dinner.

His big blue eyes were wide with excitement as he spun his theory. "So you see, the amalgamated essences of all those heroes, concentrated in a single beam, should..." A shadow swept over his face, and he frowned. His big bald head shrank as if someone had let the air out of it. "Uh...duh..." It was gone, all of his genius, just like that. He was reduced to a moron...but not for long.

That was his power: bursts of brilliance alternating with bursts of stupidity. Hence the name. "Oh, dear." He cleared his throat and picked up where he'd left off. "The amalgamated essences, concentrated in a single beam, properly directed, should destroy the excess carbon dioxide in Earth's atmosphere, returning it to a pristine state."

"Seriously?" Halfway through my ribeye, I'd stopped eating. Brain Fart was considered a twelfth-rate hero, but he'd always been a friend of mine...and he had my undivided attention. "You could do that?"

"Oh, yes." Brain Fart grinned and nodded. "We could turn back the clock to before the Industrial Revolution. Give the world a clean...a clean..." His head deflated, and his eyes crossed. "Duh..." He raised his fork and stared at it like it had suddenly grown wings and a face. "This for eating?" He put it in his mouth and gnawed on it a moment, gazing blankly into space.

A waiter paused at our table, looking concerned, and I waved him away. Brain Fart pulled the fork from his mouth and tossed it after him.

Then, the change occurred once more. The head inflated, the blue eyes brightened. "Slate. We could give the world a clean slate." He lifted his glass and swirled the ruby red wine, then sipped it. "Sadly, this hypothesis can never be tested."

"Why not?" I liked the sound of that clean slate he was offering. I *loved* it.

"Because they'll never go along with it, my dear fellow. The Castigators."

"You don't think so?" I scowled. "But saving the world is their job, isn't it?" Already, I was talking about the Castigators as if I wasn't one of them. I still wore the purple uniform under my red flannel shirt and jeans, but in my heart, I'd moved on long ago from that fraternity of abusive assholes.

Brain Fart seemed to understand, because he didn't mention it.

"Do you really think they're prepared for the level of sacrifice that will be required? Not to mention...not to..." His face blanked, his head dwindled, and his jaw fell slack. "Duh...doy..." And then, a moment later, he was back. "Not to mention, this would be an experimental process with no guarantee of success."

"What level of sacrifice, Tony?" I leaned forward, wholly focused on his every word. "Would this deplete their powers? Would it drain them permanently?"

"Most certainly." He faded, mindlessly played with himself a little, then returned. "Because, you see, it would drain their *lives*."

This time, it was *my* jaw that fell open. I gaped at him as the meaning of what he'd said took hold.

"What I'm proposing here is quite more extensive than a power drain. What we're really talking about...uh..." Deflation. "Duh..." Inflation. "...is the murder of twenty-four superheroes."

Instinctively, I cast a furtive glance around the restaurant. "*Murder?*" I hushed my voice.

"Come now." Brain Fart cocked his head and narrowed his eyes. "Would it really be such a *bad* thing? Would it really be such a *loss*?"

I slumped back in my chair. My head was spinning.

"Seriously, Mike. You can't tell me you *love* those people. The way they *treat* you." Brain Fart raised his glass again and looked at me through the shimmering wine. "The things they *say* to you."

I sat there, reeling...and then a thought clicked into place. The mental math had finished running in the back of my mind.

I understood. "Oh my God." I gaped at him. "There are twenty-four Castigators."

Brain Fart drifted off, then perked up again. "Correct."

"That's twenty-four...counting *me*."

"Correct again." His expression hardened. "Which leads me to the inevitable question at the end of this primrose path, dear Skillet.

"Would you do your part to reverse global warming, if you wouldn't be around to enjoy the result?"

The question's moot now that I've killed Bottlenose. His blistered gray body bobs in the dirty water, mute testament to the failure of my efforts. All my personal commitment and sacrifice were for nothing. There will be no turning back the clock on global warming.

Should I even bother bringing in Freeze-Dry and Floater? According to Brain Fart's equations, they won't be enough. Twenty-four is the magic number, the perfect balance for his climate change contraption.

Maybe it's time to give up. Time to accept the state of the world and my life and give myself over to whatever suffering they still have in store for me.

As if I'm not suffering enough already because of what I did to Sunblock. The memory of his cries still echoes in my mind.

It happened the night before, on the observation deck of the Empire State Building. He wanted to meet to give me the news in person.

"There's a new *recruit*." Sunblock was grinning from ear to ear. "A new *Castigator*. Someone with *powers*."

At first, I didn't see the importance. I walked to the railing, raised my goggles to my forehead, and gazed out over the drowned city. The tops of the tallest buildings stood out like islands in the dark sea. Cookfires flickered in scattered windows as a few survivors struggled to hang on. Not exactly the Big Apple I'd once loved. Not exactly the City That Never Sleeps.

"Don't you get it?" Sunblock grabbed my shoulder and shook me. "No one on Earth has manifested powers and come forward in *years*. Now there's a *twenty-fifth* Castigator! Brain Fart's device only needs *twenty-four*."

I shrugged...but then it clicked. I saw where he was going with this. I knew what he was going to say.

"You don't have to *die*." He shook me again. "This new guy can be number twenty-four!"

Slowly, I turned from the view to face him. The contours of his dark brown face reflected the cherry-red glow from my super-heated

ROBERT JESCHONEK

body. His skin was slick with sweat from being too close to my
perpetual fire.

"Isn't that great news?" He couldn't stop smiling. "You can *live*,
Mike! You can live to see the new world dawning!"

I, on the other hand, wasn't smiling at all. "This new hero, who
is he?"

"Calls himself Floater," said Sunblock. "Some kind of levita-
tional powers. Not a major threat."

"Great." I turned away. "I can grab him up with the last two
tomorrow."

Finally, Sunblock's smile faded. "You mean *both* of us can bring
him in, don't you? Like we have the other twenty Castigators?"

I pulled my goggles into place and shook my head. "You're
staying home, Joe. I've got it covered."

Sunblock scowled. "No way. We started this together, we finish it
together."

"I'm sorry, but no." I pointed a finger at him. "Floater's going to
take *your* place, not *mine.*"

"Screw that." Sunblock grabbed my wrist. "You can take your
self-sacrificing altruistic bullshit and shove it up your ass." A cloud
of his patented dark matter flowed out of his body and began to
wrap around me. "I'm stashing you somewhere safe till this all blows
over."

The situation was racing out of control. Sunblock's dark matter
could open up portals into shadowy places. Already, I felt the cloud
tugging at me, starting to pull me into a dark space somewhere on
the other side of the world.

He wasn't leaving me with any options. I knew what I was going
to have to do next, and I already hated myself for it.

But there was no way I was going to let him keep me alive.

I knew he wouldn't understand, because he didn't know all the
facts. There was something I'd always held back from him, something I was afraid he wouldn't *want* to know...and without that
puzzle piece, he wouldn't get it. All he would see was this:

Me heating up suddenly and lashing out at him.

He was surprised at the flash of power that burst out of me, burning away his dark matter cloud. The next blast of thermal energy threw him back to the floor of the observation deck.

Intensifying my core temperature, I prepared to put him under by quickly inducing heatstroke. But before I could strike, he shot up his hands and let loose a bubble of darkness that bolted toward me.

I couldn't evade it in time. The bubble lunged at me, locking me in its embrace of icy pitch blackness. Then, it began to draw inward, collapsing.

I'd seen him use this trick many times before. If I didn't manage to break free, the dark matter would encase me like shrink-wrap and cut off my air supply, rendering me unconscious...then filter in just enough air to prevent suffocation. It was his technique of choice for capturing Castigators destined for death in Brain Fart's contraption; how ironic that he was using it now to keep me alive.

Reaching deep, I gathered and stoked my heat, building it quickly into a raging bonfire. As the darkness pressed around me, I coaxed the fire higher and hotter, until it was straining to get out.

Then, I threw open the furnace door.

Like a nuclear firestorm, the wave of heat and flame rushed out of me, burning away the darkness in an instant. Freed from the trap, I fell to my knees, gasping for breath.

And only then did I realize the terrible mistake I'd made. I'd shaped the charge to cook off the dark matter and quickly dissipate...but I hadn't realized how close Sunblock had been standing. I hadn't known he'd moved within the blast radius.

If he'd been a few feet farther away, he would've been fine...singed but fine. But the full force of the firestorm had caught him.

He lay crumpled in a fetal ball, smoking and shivering. The heat had been so intense, it had blown right through his defenses and fried his flesh.

"God, no." I reached out, then drew back instantly. The smell of cooked meat was overwhelming. "Oh, Joe..."

His only response was a whimper.

Tears rolled down my cheeks. How could I have let this happen?

Sunblock shuddered and groaned. His charred hide looked like the blackened skin of a marshmallow held in a campfire too long. I could only imagine the pain he was experiencing.

"Please, no..." I reached out again, longing to hold him, to comfort him. Wishing with all my heart that things could have been different. Wishing I'd never gone there that night.

Suddenly, he convulsed and cried out. Twitched like a live wire on a wet street...and then he fell still.

The breath hissed out of him into the night air. His last breath, fled because of me, because I'd wanted to save his life.

And the terrible thing was, I'd wanted that more than anything. But he couldn't have known it, because of that last puzzle piece I'd always held back, that one thing I'd never told him.

The one thing it took him dying to make me say, though it would do neither of us any good ever again.

"I love you!" I wailed it over his unmoving body, my tears splashing his smoldering flesh. "Oh God, I love you, Joe!"

Where could I go from there? What could I do? Give up and let all our work have been for nothing? Take away the last hope we had to set the world right?

Better to move forward, I thought. Better to play out the string and balance the scales with my own personal sacrifice. Bring into being a new world where my mistakes could be forever forgotten.

At least that was the plan until I screwed up again and killed Bottlenose.

As I float in the Times Square Sea and gaze at his body, I realize my choices from this point on are meaningless. The door has slammed shut on our plan for the world's salvation.

Even if I bag Freeze-Dry and Floater and haul them to Brain Fart's lab, it won't change a thing. The global warming reverser requires twenty-four super-powered subjects...and even with Freeze-Dry, Floater, and myself, we'll only have twenty-three. Brain Fart's out of the picture because he has to operate the equipment.

So global warming is here to stay. And my life, for all intents and purposes, is over.

Not only have I failed the world, killed the man I love, and killed Bottlenose, but I've pounded the last nail into my own personal coffin.

As I bob in the filthy water, Freeze-Dry and Floater stare at Bottlenose's corpse, their expressions grim. Then, they turn my way.

"What are you waiting for?" Freeze-Dry aims his twelve fingers in my direction. "Let's get this over with."

I don't say a word or make a move.

Freeze-Dry extends his ice ramp toward me and skates closer. "Death by superhero, right? Isn't that what monsters like you do when you're cornered? Get yourself killed so you won't have to go to prison?"

I seriously consider his proposal as I watch him approach me. I've lost everything that mattered to me. Why prolong the agony?

"'Bring 'em back alive' is the Castigators' policy," says Freeze-Dry. "But accidents happen, don't they? And Floater will back me up, won't he?"

Floater nods. I can almost feel the heat from the hatred in his eyes.

Swallowing hard, I make up my mind. Death is what I deserve. Why not get it over with?

The water around me steams as I start building a charge. Freeze-Dry smiles as he realizes I'm going to do exactly what he wants.

"Thank you." His fingertips sparkle and crackle as his own power charges up. "I'll make it quick, for old times' sake."

This is it. Steeling myself, I raise an arm from the water, preparing to fire.

"Stop!" Freeze-Dry's fingers glow bright blue, ready to cut loose. "Stop, or I'll shoot!"

I continue to raise my arm, which is glowing cherry-red now. I think of Joe, and a smile flits over my face.

End of the line.

Then, suddenly, a bubble of darkness plunges down and envelopes Freeze-Dry. He screams as it tightens around him, swiftly adhering to the contours of his body.

Floater whips around and tries to flee, but another bubble

catches him, too. He fights it, but the inky substance sucks tight in seconds, clinging like spray-on black latex to every inch of him.

It can't be.

Frantically, I look up, and at first the sky is empty. I look right, then left...and then I feel a hand touch my shoulder.

I twist around to see an arm wrapped in bandages, hanging down. A familiar form is stretched out above me, buoyed on a carpet of dark matter, silhouetted against the sun.

"Hello, Mike."

My heart hammers when I hear that familiar voice. "J-Joe?" I take his hand.

He draws me up with him, rotating us both to stand above the water, face to face. Though his face, like his arm, is covered in bandages.

His whole body is swaddled in white bandages under his purple uniform. Only his eyes remain uncovered; his eyelids are the only patches of exposed skin anywhere on him.

A pang of guilt shoots through me to see him like that, damaged because of what I did to him. But the guilt is balanced by equal parts wonder and surprise.

The last time I saw him, on the observation deck of the Empire State Building, he was silent and still. I assumed he was dead. I activated the distress signal in the belt buckle of his Castigators' uniform and left him there, expecting his teammates to retrieve the body.

Now here he is, alive.

"H-how?" There are tears on my face as I stammer the words out. "How d-did you...?"

He wipes the tears with one bandaged finger. "Darkness heals, Mike. It transforms." He runs the tip of his finger along the side of my face. "And I had something to come back for. Something that wouldn't let me go."

I cock my head, staring at his bloodshot eyes between the bandages. Hoping he means what I want him to mean. Hoping he'll say what I want him to say.

And he does. "I love you, too, Mike."

Then, he tips his head toward me. I feel his lips moving against mine through the bandages, kissing me.

And when I close my eyes, I can imagine the bandages aren't there at all.

As soon as we fly in through the open window of the 77th floor of the Chrysler Building, Brain Fart starts hurrying us. He needs the darkness-shrouded captives we carry--Freeze-Dry and Floater--put in place immediately. According to his calculations, our odds of success will diminish the longer we wait. Something to do with sunspot activity and pollen counts.

He leads us through the room, which he's tricked out like a mad scientist's lab. There are wires and coils of metal tubing everywhere, all sparking with energy. Laptop computers flicker and flash on every bench and surface.

The place smells like copper and ozone and melting plastic. Everything's humming and beeping and hissing and whistling. Above all the ruckus, Wagner's "Ride of the Valkyries" blasts from a hardcore speaker system.

The floor is littered with tools and little scuttling robots with wrenches for hands. There are lots of toys, too, for Brain Fart to play with when he switches from genius to simpleton; I nearly trip over a toy fire engine and a blue rubber ball.

The middle of the place is dominated by a huge carousel of gleaming silver and glass. Spokes radiate from a central hub, each ending in a transparent pod occupied by a frozen Castigator. As we walk the perimeter, I see Swiftboat and Concertina, Waterlog and Glacier, Climate Slut and Strange Agent. They're all here, every Castigator rounded up by me and Sunblock, sleeping in misty sockets in a world-changing machine.

"Right there." Brain Fart gestures at an empty pod and nods at the bundle of unconscious Freeze-Dry in my arms. "Put him there."

The canopy of the pod is open. I lay Freeze-Dry inside and step away.

"Duh...wha?" Brain Fart wobbles for a moment as his head shrinks and his wits leave him. "Doy..." Just as he starts gnawing on the open canopy of the next pod over, his head reinflates. "Shit." He gives the canopy a whack and points at Sunblock. "Put Floater in there, Joe."

Sunblock lays his burden in the pod, then straightens and turns. His gaze fixes on the next two pods on the carousel, which are also empty with canopies open. "I guess those are for Mike and me."

Brain Fart smacks buttons on the control panels of Freeze-Dry and Floater's pods, and their canopies hiss shut. "We have a full house, today, gentlemen." Puffing, he hurries over and checks the controls on the last remaining empty pods. "Good thing you made a reservation."

Sunblock takes my hand and leads me between the two pods. We stand there a moment, gazes locked, painfully aware that this is it. The end of the line.

We've only just connected, and now it's time for us to separate forever.

Brain Fart punches commands on a tablet computer and watches the screen. "Time's up, my friends." He doesn't comment on our closeness; did he know we belonged together all along? "Places, everyone."

Sunblock lets go of my hand. He turns toward his pod.

But then I catch hold of his shoulder. Because I don't think I can do it. I can't bear to be without him, especially now.

"Wait." Maybe there's a way. "Tony, I need to ask you a question."

No. That's Brain Fart's answer. *No, it will not upset the balance.*

That's why, as the canopy closes, sealing me in the pod, I am not alone.

All that matters is that all twenty-four Castigators are present and accounted for.

As the device rumbles and whines and starts to spin, I have someone to hold.

It won't matter if one pod is empty...

I have someone to love.

...and another has two occupants.

The global warming reversal device turns faster, and the whine gets louder. Sunblock and I cling to each other, bodies wrapped together in our last embrace.

It makes a difference as the spinning accelerates and the countdown begins. As fear digs its gnarled claws into my heart.

The numbers boom over the speaker in the pod, with "Ride of the Valkyries" in the background.

Ten...nine...eight...

"I love you, Joe." Sunblock reaches up to smooth my hair. "I'm glad you finally wised up."

"Better late than never." I laugh softly.

...seven...six...five...

"Here's to the end of global warming," says Sunblock.

I touch my forehead to his. "Here's to us."

...four...three...two...

He tightens his embrace. We both tense in anticipation.

...one...zero.

There is a pulling sensation coming from all directions which quickly increases, and then I scream in white-hot agony as my body is torn asunder. I dissolve in a shower of sparks, swirling in waves of scintillating light.

Just as I realize my body is gone, just as I spin through a cascade of terror and loneliness, I feel it. The sparks of another, of Sunblock, dancing through me, mingling with me. The two of us flowing together, becoming one commingled current of life and light.

The device holds us there for an instant like a handful of fireflies. We whirl and toss and flicker, a tingling perfect oneness.

Then, suddenly, we are sucked through the spoke into the central hub, where we merge with twenty-two other sparkling showers. The device squeezes us all together, weaving us into a single matrix of coruscating, incandescent power...mashing us, kneading us, building up pressure.

And then it releases us all at once, straight up, from the giant antenna atop the Chrysler building.

As we race up into the atmosphere, I am truly not afraid, not despairing, not confused. Because as long as I can still feel him, I will be all right.

And as much as we have changed, I can still feel him.

When we reach the greatest heights, we explode in all directions. The sky ripples with curtains of rainbow light, a vast aurora spreading swiftly around the globe. Then that explodes too, in countless flares of color, the greatest fireworks display ever seen, burning off excess carbon dioxide with each burst.

Red and green and blue and yellow and white, the flares go off everywhere at once. Everyone down below stops what they're doing and watches in awe as the world changes.

And we are part of every burst, he and I, every beautiful blazing firework filling the air with shimmering sparks like the moments of a lifetime or the precious heartbeats of someone you love.

DEATH-BLIND

"Adam Carver! You have 15 minutes to *kill* someone!" says the voice blaring over the P.A. system. "Or *you*, and everyone *else* in this maze, will *die*."

Heart pounding, I get up off the floor of the cold, empty room as fast as I can, wondering where the hell I am and how I got here. I just woke up, my head's swimming, and only *one* thing is clear:

Somehow, that's *my voice* on the P.A.!

"What's this all about?" I shout. By the light of flickering fluorescent bulbs in the distant black ceiling, I see blank white walls around me, eight feet high...and an open doorway. I want out, I *need* to get *out.*

"Get moving!" says my voice over the speaker. "The clock is *ticking*!"

I *hate* this, I'm not a *puppet*...but if he's *right*, I've got to *move.* Got to figure this *out.*

So the doorway. I'm through it in a flash.

More blank white walls, a corridor, bending, branching. Right or left?

Just pick one go right and there's my voice again.

"Fourteen minutes, Adam! Better get a *move* on!"

How's it possible? Digital enhancement? Distort someone else's voice to sound like mine? *Exactly* like *mine?*

"*Kill*, Ben, *kill!* Do it and you're free!" says the voice. "Do it and the *bombs* don't go off down here and nobody else has to *die* today!"

How did I even *get* here? Last thing I remember I was getting in a car in Greenwich Village, getting in an Uber.

Thug at the wheel funny smell like pot or patchouli now here I am and *what else* can I *do?*

Whipping through a doorway on my left, I see a woman chained to a wall.

No *not* just a wall, there's a *door* behind her, metal, iron.

"Get me out of here!" Twentysomething long red hair attractive slim.

White t-shirt red shorts.

Big red *X* drawn on the left chest over her heart.

On the gray cement floor at her feet, a knife glints under the flickering fluorescents.

"Pick up the knife!" shouts the voice.

But I don't.

"Thirteen minutes! Pick it up!"

"No, please!" Woman's terrified. "Don't, please!"

But then I do. Maybe I can use it

Use it to get out of here and...

"Kill her and the door shall be opened!" says the voice. "Three other people in the maze will be spared *because of you.*

"And you can *all* walk out of here *together.*"

Never happen. Not a killer.

NOT NOT NOT

Knife in hand, I go in close, and the woman flinches, twists away from me, but

"Don't worry," I tell her. "I won't hurt you. Just looking for..."

The iron door is shut tight, flush with the wall.

Some kind of blinking light visible through a slit where the handle should be.

Sensor switch relay trigger receiver?

I push the point of the knife through but it doesn't go far, blade's too thick.

"The door mechanism is tamper-proof!" says the voice. "Killing is your only way out!"

"No, please!" shouts the woman. "Please don't hurt me!"

I keep trying

Pushing

Jabbing

"Twelve minutes!" says the voice. "Why don't you move on? Maybe the *next* subject will be more *killable!*"

Breathing hard I charge out the way I came

Shoot down another branch on the left then a right

Looking for

Next subject, he said. *Three other people in the maze.*

Why does he want me to kill *any* of them? Why *me?*

I'm just a *loan officer* in a *bank.* Unmarried no kids just a keep to myself kind of guy

A *nice* kind of guy

Go to *church* and sing in the *choir* kind of guy.

Dog owning

Disney loving

Hockey fan

Soup kitchen volunteer

kind of guy.

So why the hell...

"Eleven minutes!" says the voice.

Bolting through a doorway on my left, I see someone else chained in front of another door.

Scrawny old man, bearded dirty bedraggled smelly.

Limp. Miserable.

Yellow-tinted.

Ragged holy bluejeans sweat-stained tank top t-shirt.

Again with the big red *X* but it's over his *gut* this time.

"No one will miss him!" says the voice. "He's *homeless*! He's got *no one.*

"I can't make this any *easier* for you! Kill him and the door shall be opened!"

"No!" I rush toward him for a look at the door. Got to be a way out without giving in, without doing what the voice wants.

"Ten minutes!" shouts the voice. "Get it *over* with!"

"Yeah," says the old man in chains, looking at me sideways with bloodshot yellow eyes. "Kill me. *Please* kill me."

I try wedging the blade in the jamb of the door but it's too damn flush and I can't get it in. Next I examine the cuffs and the chains, look for weak spots.

Drive the point of the blade between links in the chain and pry

Which makes my *chest* hurt but how can that be I've never

Gotta stop hurts too bad clutch my chest and feel through the shirt some kind of rough ridges some kind of

Scar?

But how can that *be?* I've never hurt my *chest.*

Never had *surgery.*

What the hell is going on?

"Nine minutes!" says the voice. "Shit or get off the pot!"

"Please," wheezes the old man. "I'm *begging* you."

He pisses himself while I'm standing there and I *run.*

Three people in the maze the voice said.

There must be one more.

Maybe another door, not so foolproof.

Right left right

Panting

Pounding

Stitch in my side

Smell of cologne

Cologne?

Up ahead really *strong* really *cheap*

Like a beacon it draws me through one more doorway.

"No more fucking around, pal!" howls the voice. "This is where you *wake* the fuck *up* and get your *shit* together!"

Another locked door and someone else in chains in front of it. Not a woman or an old homeless man this time, though.

"Eight minutes!"

Big guy, overweight, enormous. Giant lumpy arms, pythons, powerful.

Curly brown hair and mustache, clouds of cologne.

Cold stare. Eyes black as coal.

Lip curls. Sneering.

"This man, Buckler, is a killer for hire," says the voice. "He's murdered *dozens* of men, women, and children."

Buckler's sneer widens. "More than *dozens.*"

"Kill *him*, and take a *bad man* off the street," the voice continues. "An *evil* man."

"What the fuck now?" Buckler snorts out a laugh of disbelief. "How can *you* be down *here*..." He nods in my direction. "If you're *up there*, too?" He nods at the ceiling.

I just shake my head. "A recording?"

"Is this some kind of *joke?* I've *known* that S.O.B. for *years.*" Buckler nods at the ceiling. "You sound *just like* him. "

The voice is still talking. "If you kill *Buckler,* you'll *eliminate* the *competition* in the bargain! Because *you* are a *hitman*, too, Adam!

"You just don't *remember* it yet!"

What the hell is he talking about?

"Your name is *Solomon Nail,*" says the voice. "You're a *top hired killer.*

"Sometimes, when you're in over your head on a job, you switch to a substitute identity via post-hypnotic suggestion. You *become* Adam Carver, a man who can't be broken because he doesn't remember what his other self *did.*"

Don't believe him I don't believe him.

All a trick some crazy bullshit.

"But the truth is, you have *hundreds* of deaths on your conscience. One more won't make any difference.

"But it *will* wake up Solomon! It always *does. "*

Just lies and crazy bullshit

But still holy shit *but still...*

"So *get killing!"*

But still, what if?

"*You're* supposed to be some kind of *hired killer?*" Buckler rattles his chains. "That's fuckin' *rich.*"

"Six minutes!" says the voice.

339

I'm sweating like a pig
Shaking, panting,
Heart's pounding
And the clock keeps *ticking*.
"More like some kind of hired *pussy*," snarls Buckler. "You couldn't kill a *corpse!*" He laughs like an asshole.
Shut him out. Run the numbers. Make a choice.
What do I *know?*
Bombs go off in less than six
According to the voice
Only way out, kill one of three
According to the voice
And Buckler *deserves it*
According to the voice
And I'm a killer anyway
According to the
"Five minutes!"
"C'mon and take your shot!" snarls Buckler. "Let's see what you *got*, you whiny *bitch!*"
Choose choose choose
Time to man up and make the call make a choice just *decide* one way or another.
Forget the bullshit block it out who *cares* what *he* wants?
What do *I* want to do?
"What's the matter?" Buckler laughs and rattles chains. "Can't get it up?"
I don't say a word to him. Just turn and run out of there
Back through the maze
Adrenaline sizzling
Clutching the knife.
Back past the old homeless guy's room and keep going *keep going keep going*
"Four minutes!"
Duck into the redheaded woman's room.
She looks up sobbing.
"I don't want to die." Hopeless, defeated.

Don't listen. Not giving up yet.

"Just do it!" says the voice. "Kill or be killed!"

I run to the woman, raise the knife, she shuts her eyes and screams

And I *attack...*

...one of her *chains.*

"Three minutes!" says the voice.

Hacking chopping stabbing driving

Metal on metal

Same exact link exact spot again and again

No matter how futile

This is my *choice.*

And then I hear the voice again.

"Maybe *this* will change your mind!" it says. "There's a *bomb* under a nearby *pre-school. Fifty kids* will *die* in *two minutes* unless you *kill.*"

That makes me pause.

Whole new equation now this changes everything

According to the voice.

I mean

I think...

Fifty.

Fifty kids.

I look over at the woman and it's like she can read my mind. Tears, more tears, biting lip, shivering shuddering

Then she nods. Just nods and closes her eyes.

And my heart's pounding harder faster than ever

More adrenaline

And I *look* at her.

Blade in my hand.

But I'm no killer. No matter what *he* says, I'm no killer. I love the snowman from that movie

And the New York Rangers

And tacos for breakfast don't ask me why

And no matter what *he* says, I've never hurt a fly.

But I *look* at her.

Fifty kids.
Maybe I
Could I
"Just do it," she whispers.
Close my eyes just close my eyes
Get it over with
I can
"One! Minute!" says the voice.
Tighten my grip
Eyes open
Close
Deep breath
Pull my arm back
Tighten
Ready
Do it just do it just save them do it kill her do it
"Thirty seconds!" says the voice. Then a high-pitched tone shrieks over the speakers, a piercing whine.
Just do it just do it just
No!
Hand relaxes.
Knife falls
Clatters
Voice counts down from ten but doesn't matter choice is made end of story end of
Children?
End of *me?*
"Three! Two! One!" says the voice.
I tense, expecting bombs to go off expecting the blast expecting oblivion
But no.
No blast.
A deafening buzzer instead like the buzzer at a sports arena
Head-splitting loud
And then the voice again howling over speakers.
"*Overtime!*" it says. "*Sudden death overtime!*"
All at once, the manacles on the woman's wrists and ankles

spring open and the chains fall away. She slumps forward, almost falling

And I catch her in my arms.

"Attention! All prisoners!" says the voice. "Kill that chickenshit *pussy* who *refuses* to *kill* in my name, and all three of you go *free!*"

I hear movement in the maze and do the math. The voice must have freed all three from their bonds.

So now it's *three against one*...though there's only *one* of them I'm really worried about.

"Now *this* is my kind'a *game!*" roars Buckler, his voice muffled by walls and distance but not for long I'm sure. "Ollie Ollie Oxenfree!"

The woman's got her balance and I let her go, distracted. Seconds later, when I look for the knife on the floor, *it's gone holy shit she's got it*

And then she *dashes* right past me and out of the room, sprinting left.

So now my only weapon's gone but at least she didn't kill me when she could. Still alive.

Still a chance.

Think I need to *think* it *through* figure it *out*

"Daddy's coming!" hollers Buckler. "Drop your *drawers* and get ready for your *whuppin'!*"

I think of his coal black eyes and powerful arms, and the scar on my chest *throbs.* For the first time, I wish I *was* who they think I am. Because *this* me, the me that *is*

Is a dead man.

Even *with* a weapon, what chance did I have?

No chance.

But I have to do *something.*

Come on.

Suck it up.

I bolt out the door, barrel through the maze to the old man's room. His chains are off too but he's just slumped in a corner, wheezing, twitching.

"Kill him!" shouts the voice. "*Kill* that brainwashed former me! I'd rather be *dead* than a worthless *sheep!*"

I run to where the chains are hanging, try to pull one from the ceiling

Forget it.

Then *cologne.*

"Day-oh! Day-ay-ay-oh!"

Buckler sings as he lumbers into the room, big arms swinging.

Mountain of flesh.

"Did somebody request the *funky chicken?*"

Moves fast for a mountain

Doesn't even slow down

Straight at me

Bull elephant

Think fast

Chain's firm so use it

Fucking use it.

Still holding on to the chain, I swing my legs up fast and drive my feet into his groin.

Staggers back groaning

Grimacing

Grabbing

"Fucker!" Eyes flaring teeth bared like an ape. "Kill you! Kill you kill you *kill you!*"

Gathering up his elephant mass for another charge.

Meanwhile, I run left, chain in hands

Whip around at the wall and jump toward him

Swinging like a jungle man

Again with the feet but this time feet meet *gut.*

Shit, not so good.

"Nice try, *dead man!*" He snares both my ankles in his big hammy hands, clamps *tight,* does some swinging of his own.

Swings me like a baseball bat and lets go. My hands snap free of the chain and I spin across the room, *smash* into the wall.

Slide to the floor headfirst at the old homeless guy's feet.

"You okay?" whimpers the old man.

Fuck no I'm not okay

There's no way I'm gonna survive this

No chance I walk away.

Already done better than expected

(Hired killer fighting skills showing through? Muscle memory kicking in?)

But know it won't last.

This is it

Whoever I am whatever the truth however I got here

This is it.

And maybe I *deserve* it if what the voice told me is true.

Hundreds of murders on my soul?

Maybe I deserve *a lot worse*.

"You call this a *fight?*" says the voice. "You must have a *death wish*, 'Adam'!"

I'm twisting around, trying to get my feet under me, when Buckler grabs me again. Snags my left elbow, hauls me up like a puppet, *slams* me down like a barbell on the floor.

I land on my back. Things crunch.

Head spinning

Pain shooting

Thoughts scatter.

"Pay attention now, dead man." Buckler cracks his knuckles. "*This* is how you deliver a *coup de grâce.*"

Monster.

He's a *monster*.

What do I do next? I wonder

But not in so many words,

Head's buzzing like a beehive.

"You're welcome, by the way!" Buckler laughs as he sweeps back his leg, aiming a kick of that wrecking ball foot of his right at my head. "It's a *privilege* to be *killed* by a *star* like me!"

This is it. Got nothing left. Nowhere to go.

Next kick is the end.

Buckler sneers.

Want to close my eyes but can't,

Can't look away.

At least I didn't give in

Didn't kill

Didn't turn into him *whoever he is*

That flaming asshole with the voice.

"Nighty-night," says Buckler.

Then, before he can let me have it, a knife flashes out from behind him

Held in slender fingers,

A *woman's* hand,

Passes in front of his throat

And slides back

Slashing across it.

Buckler's eyes bug out. He clutches his throat like he's trying to hold it together

Which he can't.

He chokes as blood wells out

Wine dark red

And gushes down the front of him, splashing onto me.

Then he staggers back and gets a look at her

The redhead who took my knife

And then as big as he is just sort of rolls over on the floor like a capsizing ship

And chokes his last.

"Hey!" The redhead shouts up at whoever's watching. "We have a *winner* here. Let us out!"

Everything hurts as I struggle to my knees. At least I'm still alive.

She *saved* me. Because I *spared* her?

Or did it just work out that way when she was killing Buckler for her freedom?

"I said *I win!*" She doesn't let go of the bloody knife. "Now *let us out of here!*"

Nobody answers. Nothing changes. The old man in the corner whimpers, and that's it. Somebody else must be listening, but they're not taking action.

"Let us *out!*" The woman slashes the air with her knife. "You *promised!*"

Still nothing.

Starting to think someone needs to force the issue. Someone with bargaining power.

Only one person like that I can think of down here.

"Come *on!*" The woman's pacing, waving the knife, losing her patience. "I *win!*"

I get an idea and walk toward her, reaching out. "Give me the knife." I nod firmly. "I'll get us out of here."

She meets my gaze, holding the knife away from me.

"Please." *Trust me.*

Slowly, she hands it over. The grip is coated in blood as I wrap it in my fingers. Buckler's blood.

It's only fitting. He gave me the idea.

When he said I had a death wish.

"Now hear this!" I raise the knife overhead. "You have *thirty seconds* to let us *out* of here." I lower the knife and hold its edge against my throat. "Thirty seconds, or I *kill* myself!"

So that's my idea. If I'm really *him*, really Solomon Nail, they'll want to keep me alive. The mind of their boss is still sleeping somewhere inside me. Their mission is to wake him up, not stand by while I silence him forever.

"Thirty! Twenty-nine! Twenty-eight!" I bark out the numbers and wait. "Twenty-seven! Twenty-six!" On edge and under pressure

Also loving it now that *I'm* doing the counting for a change.

"Twenty-five! Twenty-four!"

I walk the room, watching all directions,

Redhead too.

Old man just squats in the corner.

"Twenty-three! Twenty-two! Twenty-one!"

As each number passes, the silence continues,

Making me wonder

"Twenty! Nineteen!"

What if they call my bluff?

"Eighteen! Seventeen!"

Couldn't kill anyone else to save my life. Can I kill *myself?*

"Sixteen! Fifteen!"

If I can't, *then* what?

"Fourteen! Thirteen!"

Hand shaking.

Sweat rolling.

Gut twisting.

"Twelve!"

Still no contact with whoever's behind the scenes. There *has* to be somebody up there, running the show and playing the recordings of Solomon's voice. They *have* to want to save me, but *no.*

"Eleven!"

They won't show themselves.

"Ten! Nine!"

So this is it. Make the call. Die...

Or live.

"Eight! Seven!"

The woman shakes her head. The old man's oblivious on the floor.

For the first time, I wish I *was* Solomon Nail, so I could take *control* of the situation and set things right.

"Six! Five!"

But there's no hitman in me, not anymore. Whatever spark of Solomon I had, it was blown out long ago.

"Four!"

And it *isn't* coming *back.* Not if *I* can help it.

"Three!"

Will I *do* it? Follow through on my *threat?*

"Two!"

Hand tenses.

Do it.

"One!"

Don't do it.

Do it.

Do it.

Suddenly, a door creaks open.

The iron door that was behind the old man when he was chained. I turn and see it open inward.

Keep the knife at my throat the whole time.

A bald man in a black jumpsuit with a "Loomis" nametag over his heart walks through the doorway, holding an AK-47.

"Holy shit, boss." He smirks and shakes his head. "You've *never* had it *this* bad before."

"I'm not your *boss,*" I tell him.

"No worries." Loomis aims the gun at the redhead. "I've got a few more tricks up my sleeve. Time for some *drastic measures* to snap you outta this."

Stop him.

I sweep the knife away from my neck and charge across the room,

Heart pounding in my ears

But *surprise*, the old guy beats me to it.

He throws himself at Loomis, taking him down,

Landing on top of him

Knocking the AK-47 out of his hands.

And I grab it.

"I'm not your *boss* anymore." I plow the rifle butt into Loomis's head, knocking him out cold.

Then I look at it

The gun

And think about the murders on my soul

(According to the voice)

And wonder if I'll still burn in Hell if I don't remember them.

I look at open door that Loomis came through, the way to freedom. Freedom from this torture chamber, freedom from the life I once led.

But what if I leave and the old life catches up to me again? What if Solomon's friends--or his enemies--come after me down the line?

Maybe all I can do is work it out later and hope for the best. Maybe it's worth the risk to walk away and start over.

Because I'm thinking, at this point, that only one thing matters. And it's the same thing, really, that always matters most in this life, in this world.

Even though we like to think otherwise.

The redhead helps the old man to his feet. "What now?" She looks at me expectantly. "What next?"

I smile, because I've lived to walk away. Because I've realized, after all this carnage and confusion, that the only thing that matters

Is what I do from this moment on.

"Who cares?" I tell her. "As long as it's not *this*."

I toss the gun aside and drop the knife. Wipe my hands on my pants.

Head for the door, gesturing for her and the old man to follow.

IN A GREEN DRESS, SURROUNDED BY EXPLODING CLOWNS

Heaving for breath, I spin in a circle, looking for a way out. But I see the same thing in every direction.

Nothing but clowns. Dozens of clowns.

Every one of them laughs, giggles, or guffaws at the same time. They bobble their heads, slap huge clown shoes on the parking lot pavement, and toot horns. All face-paint and bulbous red noses and baggy costumes in all the wild colors of the rainbow, they look like they'd be right at home at a circus or a carnival or a kid's birthday party.

Except for the malevolent sneers etched into every one of their faces. Not to mention the jagged, shark-like teeth lining their red-lipped maws.

As the clowns close in, my heart hammers in my chest. I'm a big guy, I'll fight them--but I'm exhausted after what I've been through. The past two days of nonstop madness have wrecked me, I admit it. And I wasn't feeling up to snuff to begin with; the pain in my gut was bad at the start and has only been getting worse.

Plus which, I'm wearing a bright green knee-length dress and spiked heels.

Not exactly the ideal outfit for a five-eleven, two-hundred-twenty-five-pound guy to wear while fighting a mob of savage clowns.

"Back off!" Even as I shout it over the crazed laughter, I see it does no good. The clowns are still moving toward me.

Swallowing hard, I prepare to make my stand. I crouch and turn slowly, arms extended from my sides.

Suddenly, I hear a wild scream behind me. I whip around just in time to see a clown with a big plastic daisy on its pink derby hat charging toward me.

As I stumble back a step, the unexpected happens. The charging clown gets to within six feet of me and explodes, blowing apart in a burst of orange flame.

I throw up my arms to shield myself. Lumps of dead clown splatter all over me, smelling like burnt bacon.

Then, I hear another shriek and spin to see a second clown charging. Trying to dodge him, I trip on my spiked heels and go down hard.

This time, the clown gets closer, within five feet, before exploding.

And then I hear another scream, and another, and another. I hear three pairs of floppy clown shoes paddling toward me. I wonder how close this new batch will get before blowing up. I wonder if they'll get close enough to take me with them.

And I wish to God that I'd never gotten on the lifehacker radar in Crowdlife.

Three days ago, I could not have imagined how things would turn out for me. I was busy just doing my job as an agent of Crowdlife Outcomes Enforcement--the C.O.E.

My last case, the one that changed my life, led me to a rundown tenement apartment on Skid Row. A family of five was living in this three-room dump, dressed in rags, immersed in squalor.

Make that a family of five plus a screeching chimpanzee in a purple turban and glittering gold diaper.

"Look at this place!" said the man of the house, Mr. Byron Chellingham. "There's been a mistake, I tell you!"

"Sorry, sir," I said, looking around the dilapidated apartment. "Crowdlife has spoken."

"Like hell!" Byron swatted at what was either a passing bug or a gnat-cam--one of the multitude of tiny airborne camera-bots zipping through modern humanity's environment at all times. Gnat-cams constantly beamed video and audio signals to augmented reality devices like my contact lenses and aural implants, enabling them to enhance what I and others saw and heard. Gnat-cams also streamed data back to the social network providers; without them, Crowdlife, Yapstream, and the like wouldn't have a window on the world.

"Calm down, Mr. Chellingham." I raised my voice, trying to snap him out of it...doing my best to hide the fact that I felt sorry for him. "You need to get a grip, sir."

"But someone gamed the system! Don't you see?" Byron flapped his arms like he was trying to take flight. His bright green eyes were bugged out, his wife-beater tank top t-shirt soaked with sweat. "We don't *deserve* this!"

As if to punctuate his comment, the diapered chimp screamed its lungs out on the far side of the room, in the filthy makeshift kitchen.

"You signed the T.O.S." With practiced flicks of my eyes, I played the controls of my A.R. contact lenses. The image of a terms of service agreement appeared in midair between us, visualized as a sheet of paper filled with print and adorned with Bryon's signature at the bottom. Long ago, he had signed over his destiny to Crowdlife, the ultimate crowdsourcing social network, just like all the rest of us.

A century after Facebook and company, social networks truly ran the world. Everyone's fate was in the hands of everyone else; people voted to determine each other's fates, right down to the smallest detail.

The system ran pretty well, truth be told. Hard work and kindness were often rewarded by majority vote; cruelty and criminality were often punished the same way. People pretty much got what they deserved...usually.

Though I'd be lying if I said that the outcomes always made sense, or that everyone was always happy with their own personal outcome.

"I agreed to accept the will of the Crowd, yes," snapped Byron. "But that *can't* be what *this* is, Agent Grice."

As he glared at me, brief notes appeared in midair around him, visible to my A.R. lenses--social messages from the Yapstream posted by the multitudes watching Byron's story unfold:

69Bill69: *Yes it CAN be!*

FrtInspktr: *The Crowd says U SUK*

SuzieQ4U: *But what if he's 4 real?*

Just then, Byron's wife, Sylvia, emerged from a doorway, armed with a broken broom handle. Waving it at the chimp, she drove the animal back three screeching steps. "Our likeability index is sky-high!" She scrubbed dirty fingers through her willy-nilly bird's nest of tangled brown hair. "We get *millions* of smiles on Crowdlife every *day*!"

Something swam past me--gnat-cam or insect, I couldn't tell-- and I swatted it away. "You know that isn't how it works, ma'am. Likeability doesn't always correlate with fate-voting."

BoogaBooga99: *Damn right!!!*

FrtInspktr: *Forget smiles, I'd give em puke faces all the time.*

NoItAll3000: *But I like em! Giving em 100 smiles right now in fact!*

"I'm telling you, something's *wrong* this time!" Sylvia lunged with the broom handle, driving the chimp back further. "We're too *well-loved* for the Crowd to drop us this *low*!" She jabbed the handle again, and the chimp whirled and darted through a doorway. As Sylvia raced after it, the animal's screeches were joined by the screams of the Chellinghams' three young children.

All that noise made my stomach churn, setting off the ongoing pain in my gut. "Look." I turned to Byron. "I get it. You don't like this outcome."

SweetHawk7: *You tell im, COE boy!*

CowwSezMoo: *Spoiled rich piece of crap*

"Being transformed from billionaire to pauper? Terrorized by a chimp in a diaper?" Byron laughed like he was ready to jump off a building. "What makes you say that?"

"These things have a way of working themselves out," I told him. "If you play your cards right, the Crowd could send you straight back to the top overnight."

SuzieQ4U: *Thats right we could do that.*

Gr8Wite: *I'll vote for em in a heart beat!*

ExpltvDletd: *Me too*

FrtInspktr: *I say vote em another monkey!!*

"But what if this *isn't* the will of the Crowd?" said Byron. "What if a single embittered individual is behind all this?"

I scowled. "A lifehacker?"

"I've heard of it happening before!" As Byron said it, the screeching chimp barreled out of the kids' room and hurtled across the apartment. "Trolls hacking the fatevote to get what they want."

"Fairy tales," I said. "Crowdlife's unhackable."

69Bill69: *I heard theres a guy who*

FrtInspktr: *Nothings unhackable you boob.*

Jabbawokky75: *#lifehackers. No such thing bitches.*

"Will you at least look into it?" Byron stepped forward and raised a hand as if to touch my arm, then withdrew it. "Please?" His eyes practically throbbed with desperation. Behind him, his wife charged after the chimp, howling with rage. "Because I don't know how much more of this I can take."

CowwSezMoo: *That's what they all say*

Too true, that note from the Yapstream. I'd never met a grace-faller who didn't say the same thing. Words to that effect, at least. And I'd never met one who said they deserved what the fatevote stuck them with.

FrtInspktr: *Tellim eff off LOL!*

HackensteinXXX: *Looooser!*

Still, something kept nagging at me. Even as my brain and the Yapstream told me to turn my back on these people, my gut said something different. In all my years with the C.O.E., I'd never seen a fall from grace so precipitous or bizarre.

What if lifehacking wasn't a fairy tale, after all?

As I stood there, thinking about it, someone knocked hard on the apartment door. Byron brushed past me and opened it wide.

KangaCult101: *Oboy I cant wait to see this!*

SinrHatr: *Latest fatevote's in, I just saw whats comin.*

CowwSezMoo: *Holy eff eff eff!!!*

"Mr. Chellingham?" A man in a white Crowdlife Fatemaker uniform looked in from the hallway. He didn't wait for Byron to answer before pushing a wheelbarrow loaded with snakes through the doorway. "Special delivery, sir."

The Fatemaker dumped the snakes in the middle of the floor, sending them squirming in all directions.

CallMeGodd: *OMG! Look at em all!*

Jabbawokky75: *Dance, bitches, dance!*

"See what I mean?" Byron stared at me. "Do you really think I deserve all this? Why would the *Crowd* vote to do something this *insane?*"

But the Fatemaker wasn't done yet. "Bring in the next load!"

A second white-uniformed man rolled in a rusty gray steel drum on a dolly and set it down near the snakes. With help from the first man, he pushed the drum over, sending putrid brown sludge oozing over the floor.

It was raw sewage. The smell was so strong, it made me gag.

"Excuse me, Mr. Chellingham." The first Fatemaker held out a tablet computer and a stylus toward Byron. "Wouldja put your John Hancock right there, sir?"

FrtInspktr: *Suh-weet!*

JudyJudyJulie: *Talk about adding insult to injury!*

Byron just glared at him.

The Fatemaker cleared his throat. "Just, uh, need you to sign for this, sir. Please."

Byron turned to me. I could hardly hear his next words over the chimp's screeching as it swung fistfuls of snakes against the wall, bashing their heads in. "Will you at least look into it?"

I told him I would.

After the Chellinghams', I went straight home and jacked into the Crowdlife Backlot--the vast virtual workspace linking employees like me with Crowdlife's behind-the-scenes infrastructure.

As interpreted by my A.R. contact lenses, the Backlot looked like an enormous crystalline city sprawling over a sun-soaked plain. My point of view was high above it, gazing down from a gold-tinted sky. The view was uniquely private, free of all social network connections.

I blinked hard, and a drop-down text menu of city sectors appeared in the upper right corner of my field of vision. Flicking my eyes, I chose the last option and began my approach, drifting down through streamers of cloud toward a tall tower.

When I found the right office, on the tower's 85th floor, I flew straight in; there were no walls or windows to block my way in this virtual environment.

As I landed, a young woman looked up from inside a conical well of holographic computer screens, dozens of them flashing with rivers of data.

"Cage!" She perked up instantly when she saw me and tucked strands of glossy black hair behind her ears. She was beautiful, and not just because that's how she chose to look in the Backlot. "What's the occasion?"

"Just paying a visit to my favorite Outcomes Analyst." I couldn't help smiling when I said it. "And let me just say you're looking love-lier than ever, Liz."

"Flatterer." Liz brushed a hand along the well in front of her, opening a gap, then got up from her chair and walked through it. "But I like what I'm hearing."

"There's more." I shrugged. "I'm looking for something."

Liz grinned and moved closer. "Aren't we all? I'm sure we can find it together."

"I wouldn't be so sure," I said. "Do lifehackers even exist?"

Liz looked at me like I was crazy. "Lifehackers? That's what you're looking for?"

The ever-present pain in my gut spiked, then receded. "There's this family of gracefallers. They've been handed an unusually extreme outcome."

The fire drained right out of Liz as she leaned back away from me. "Crowdlife has spoken. They signed the T.O.S., didn't they?"

"Yeah, but..." I shook my head. "This outcome. It's so extreme, it's *insane*. We're talking a billionaire reduced to poverty, forced to live on Skid Row with a crazed chimpanzee."

Liz shrugged. "It happens, Cage. Sometimes a crazy outcome goes viral and sweeps the fatevote."

"It gets crazier," I said. "There's a wheelbarrow full of snakes and a drum of raw sewage dumped in the apartment."

Liz sighed and turned away, heading back to her data well. "Lifehackers are a myth. Crowdlife is unhackable."

"So I've heard." I followed her to the well. "Could you do some digging anyway?"

Throwing herself down on her chair, she closed the gap in the well as if she were drawing a curtain across it. "Let me see what I can do."

While Liz dug deep on the data side of things, I punched out to take some personal time. I had to step away for an appointment I'd been dreading.

Because as much as I wished it were otherwise, not everything was controlled by Crowdlife.

As I sat in Dr. Duncan's office and waited to hear his verdict, Yapstream posts popped up around him via my A.R. contacts.

SuzieQ4U: *Praying for him so hard.*

JudyJudyJulie: *Fingers and toes all crossed*

TouchyFeely50: *I can't stand the suspense!*

I read a few, but they were coming thick and fast. Moments like this brought the rubberneckers out in force.

"Mr. Grice," said Dr. Duncan. "I'm afraid the news isn't good." His eyes were locked on the tablet computer in his hands. "Not good at all."

"Sorry to hear that." I sat back in my chair.

"Gene therapy has failed to prevent additional metastatic activity," said Dr. Duncan. "Future remission of your cancer is unlikely."

"Right." I nodded. "Okay then."

DogssBreakfasst: *Poor son of a bitch*

TouchyFeely50: *I swear Im gonna cry!*

SweetHawk7: *OMG!*

"What this means," said Dr. Duncan, "is a dramatically reduced life expectancy."

I cleared my throat. "How much time do I have left?"

"Based on your latest test results, I'd say not much." Dr. Duncan looked up from his tablet. "Two months, minimum. Four at the outside."

"I understand." Swallowing hard, I tried to ignore the swarm of popups filling the A.R. field all around Dr. Duncan.

SweetHawk7: *I AM CRYING SO HARD RIGHT NOW!!!*

PrestoKarmaKid: *Poor guys got NO ONE, does he?*

FrtInspktr: *Not since we voted for his wife to divorce him.*

"Now, it's possible," said Dr. Duncan, "that we might prolong your life a bit with targeted nanotherapy. Millions of guided nanomechs would deliver microburst neochemotherapy to cancerous sites." He paused. "Though as you know, that brings with it certain undesirable side effects."

"How much more time would that buy me?"

"One to two months," said Dr. Duncan.

ZpprBrkr33: *Do it!!!!*

Tinatastic: *Take the nano, man, take the nano!*

CowwSezMoo2: *Dont be stoopid man!*

Closing my eyes, I shut out the tide of Yapstream posts. "So in a best case scenario, I've got six months left."

"Yes," said Dr. Duncan. "So what do you want to do?"

I told him I needed to think about it, and then I left. I decided to take the rest of the day off and headed straight for my favorite bar, where I ordered up the hard stuff as soon as I walked in the door.

As I sat and drank, gnat-cams or gnats buzzed around me, drawing the occasional swat. Yapstream posts popped up around me, too, telling me to do one thing or another.

Then, the message I'd been expecting arrived: the announcement of a Crowdlife-wide fatevote to decide if I should have nanotherapy.

Just then, another message got my attention...an incoming call. Flicking my eyes over the contact lens controls, I answered it. Instantly, the appearance of my surroundings shifted, reshaped by the A.R. lenses to look like the interior of Liz's office in the Backlot.

"Hey, Cage." Her voice was clear in my head, beamed in through the aural implants behind my ears. Her image was right in front of me, seated as always within the holographic control well. "You owe me a steak dinner, hon, plus top-shelf cocktails."

"Oh yeah?" I straightened on my barstool.

"I thought your whole lifehacker theory was pure baloney," said Liz. "But then I analyzed recent protests among gracefallers and noticed a pattern. Seems there've been other cases of inexplicably insane outcomes in Crowdlife lately."

"How many?"

"Fifty-seven worldwide over the past two weeks," said Liz.

I whistled softly. "Any connection between the victims?"

"None." Liz ran her fingers over the glowing controls in the well. "But I did turn up a link between the fatevotes that led to their outcomes." She tapped a finger on one of the screens in the well. "What I found is an elaborate system of vote trading conducted by an army of kamikaze A.I. proxy drones.

"The proxy drones commandeer Crowdlife lobbyists--A.I.s dispatched by system users to convince other users to vote certain ways. The proxies use the lobbyists to assemble blocs of carefully aligned votes, and then *boom*. They trigger a chain reaction of fatevotes setting off a web of outcomes.

"Then the drones self-destruct," continued Liz. "The only traces they leave are the recorded movements of the enslaved lobbyists, which are buried under layers of obscure vote trades."

I shook my head in amazement. "Who could be capable of implementing a strategy that sophisticated?"

"Someone who doesn't want to be found," said Liz. "But I found 'em, anyway." She pointed at the name on the screen facing me.

"Dada Wyrm, Inc." I felt a jab of pain in my gut and winced. "Got a physical address for this outfit?"

Within the hour, I was standing in front of a door in an uptown apartment building--number 23. Gut aching, I took a deep breath and raised my fist to knock. At least I wasn't distracted by any Yapstream popups; as a C.O.E. agent, I was able to block Yapstream during moments of imminent danger.

As I knocked on the door with my left hand, I kept my right wrapped around the grip and trigger of my gun. No one answered my knock. I leaned closer but could hear nothing from the other side of the door.

"Crowdlife Outcomes Enforcement," I shouted. "Open up. We need to ask you a few questions."

Next time, I knocked with the butt of the gun. Again, there was no reply.

Reaching down, I tried the doorknob...and was surprised when it turned in my hand. Pushing the door open, I stepped over the threshold. Sweat trickled down my back as I peered into the darkness, keeping my gun raised in case of attack.

As I took another step forward, a holographic panel leaped to life in front of me, an online screen as tall as I was and twice as wide. Blinking at the sudden flare of light, I saw the familiar orange and green homepage of Crowdlife zoom out of the center and fill the screen from edge to edge.

Gut burning, I tried to walk around the screen for a closer look at the rest of the room...but the image of the screen stayed in front of me no matter which way I turned.

Suddenly, the screen changed from the Crowdlife homepage to the familiar box-and-column layout of a fatevote in progress. The question being voted on appeared at the top of the screen in bold black letters: *Should Agent Grice hop on his left or right foot while battling the three killers walking down the hall?*

The tally was in the hundreds of millions for either option, and the leader was "Right Foot" with 67% of the vote.

I spun to face the doorway with my gun at the ready, and the screen stayed square in front of me. I heard three sets of footsteps in the hall, not far away, but it was hard to focus with the fatevote tally flashing in my face.

Just then, the numbers stopped changing, and the winning choice turned bright red and expanded to five times its original size. "Right Foot" had won by a landslide.

An audio message played in my aural implants. "Agent Grice must now comply with the outcome of this fatevote, according to the Crowdlife terms of service that he signed on October 21, 2192."

The screen finally dissolved...just as a tall man dressed in a red uniform pushed through the doorway, brandishing a rifle.

Without hesitation, I fired my pistol, throwing two shots into the intruder's forehead. The impact spun him to the floor with a heavy thud, clearing a path for the next guy to push through.

I was getting ready to fire again when the Crowdlife screen reappeared smack in front of me with a familiar message: *Agent Grice must now comply with the outcome of this fatevote, according to the Crowdlife terms of service that he signed on October 21, 2192.*

"Damnit!" I gave in and hopped on my right foot, and the screen vanished. With a clear shot at the bad guy, I let loose three slugs--one to the forehead, one to the throat, one to the chest in quick succession.

As soon as the second shooter dropped, number three barged in and started firing. Taking aim while hopping wasn't easy, but I managed to tag him in the temple and shoulder, dropping him beside the other two attackers.

With all three down, I stopped hopping and bolted into the hallway. Looking one way and then the other, I saw no additional intruders.

But a heartbeat later, the Crowdlife screen leaped up in front of me without warning, displaying the tabulation of another fatevote in progress. This time, the Crowd was voting on a new question: *Agent Grice: Off limits or open season?*

So far, there were zero votes in favor of me being off limits.

Heart bashing my ribs like a boxer's fist, I charged down the hall. The whole time, the Crowdlife screen stayed in front of me, making it tough to see where I was going.

Just as I reached the elevator, it dinged, and the Crowdlife screen hopped aside. The doors sprang open, revealing a pack of howling maniacs wearing hockey goalie masks and brandishing machetes.

The screen slid back in front of me, revealing the fatevote results. It came as no surprise that the winner was "Open Season."

The Crowdlife screen vanished. Bolting past the elevator, I ran for the stairs. Every step of the way, the howls and footfalls of the machete-bearing maniacs were close behind.

Throwing open the door, I barreled down two flights of stairs like my feet were on fire. When I got to the bottom, I crashed through the exit door without slowing down.

And I found myself facing a mob armed with cream pies and fire hoses.

As soon as I emerged from the stairwell, the cream pies came flying in my direction. One after another, they bombarded me, covering me with gooey cream.

When that fusillade stopped, I wiped enough goop from my eyes to see that the Crowdlife screen had reappeared. This time, the text was a direct message to me: *No more advance warnings, Agent Grice. Our fatevotes will be invisible to you from now on. You will pay the price for sticking your nose in our business.*

As soon as the screen blinked out, the mob cut loose with the fire hoses.

I was blasted back by what I thought at first were jets of water...but I quickly realized the liquid was something else. Something with a noxious smell I knew all too well.

Gasoline.

Pinned against the stairwell door by the force of the jets, I shut my eyes and mouth. Gathering my strength, I staggered right, letting the current push me until I rounded the corner of the building.

Then, I charged down the street away from the mob. I ran as hard as I could into the night, praying no one would flick a lit cigarette in my direction.

Drenched in gasoline, spattered with pie cream, I ran for blocks, winding my way through the heart of the city. When I finally thought I was clear, I ducked into an alley and threw myself against the wall, heaving for breath.

I was in over my head this time; the only help I could turn to was Liz in the Backlot. Without further delay, I flashed her an emergency ping. There wasn't time to traverse the virtual environment of the Backlot in the usual way, soaring down into the crystalline city and alighting in her office.

She responded immediately. Through my A.R. contacts, I saw her image pop into the alley, standing three feet away from me.

"Cage!" She looked instantly worried. "What happened?"

"Lifehackers," I told her. "They ambushed me at the Dada Wyrm address."

"You look terrible!"

"I barely got away." My stomach twisted, and I doubled over...then sucked in my breath and straightened. "They're spinning rogue fatevotes, siccing the Crowd on me. They want me dead, Liz."

She nodded grimly. "I'm on it, Cage. I'll do what I can."

I heard voices in the distance and looked at the mouth of the alley. "I don't think we've got much time for it, either." I swatted at the ubiquitous swarm of tiny bugs swirling around me. "They can track my feed from the gnat-cams through Crowdlife."

"I'll do everything I can." Liz stopped working unseen controls and met my gaze with her warm brown eyes. "Just try to hang on, Cage."

Because I've got so much to live for? The cancer would take me in a matter of months, anyway. I shouldn't care, should I?

But I did. "I'll do my best, Liz."

Just then, the voices rushed up, and people poured into the alley. They washed over me in an angry tide, snatching away my gun and hauling me off my feet.

As they dragged me away, I heard Liz's voice over the frenzied roar, calling to me from the Backlot. "Hang on, Cage!"

Then, she was gone, and I was on my way to whatever madness awaited in unknown quarters.

The mob stripped me naked in the street, then wrapped me in Christmas paper and pelted me with eggs. When that was done, they stripped off the wrapping paper, rolled me in a red carpet, and peed on me while singing cartoon theme songs from the 70s.

My treatment went downhill from there. Each abuse, each outcome of a Crowdlife fatevote engineered by the Dada Wyrm life-hackers, was more bizarre than the last.

They dragged me through an art museum in a little red wagon and smashed famous paintings over my head, one after another. When they were done with that, they shoved me into a koala costume, poured grease down my back, and spun me in circles until I vomited. Next, they stuffed me into a knee-length green dress and spiked heels and made me bungee jump off the Crosstown Bridge.

All the while, the pain in my gut intensified. By the time they plunked me on the dance floor in a nightclub and beat me with frozen legs of lamb to the tune of "The Chicken Dance," I felt myself losing ground. I hadn't been at my best to begin with; I wasn't sure how much more insane torture I could take.

Not that the mob ever seemed to run out of new ideas. They blindfolded me, threw me in a dumpster full of loaded diapers, and let me dig my way out with one arm tied behind my back. They put on stork masks and pecked the hell out of me while reciting the preamble to the Constitution. They tried to force-feed me live taran-tulas and crumpled-up pages of old comic books.

Then, finally, there was a break in the action. They led me into an empty school gymnasium and left me there.

Heaving for breath, I stood at center court and looked around. The place was peaceful and dark, lit only by the dim red Exit signs over the doors.

For a moment, I dared to hope that my ordeal was over. Maybe the lifehackers were finally done with me; maybe they figured I'd gotten the message.

I wiped blood off my face with the back of my arm, then wiped my arm on the front of the green dress. I was about to kick off the damn spiked heels and head for the nearest door, just in case I had a chance to get away.

That's when the lights blazed to life and the clowns rushed in.

They poured through the doors and surrounded me, cutting off all escape routes. Laughing, howling, giggling, they closed in around me, jagged teeth glistening.

Then, one at a time, they charged toward me and exploded. I dodged once, then twice, barely avoiding being blown to bits along with the clowns.

The next time, three come at me at once.

The three clowns charge toward me from three different directions, shrieking like berserk Vikings. As beat as I am, I can't imagine that one of them won't get me. Maybe I'll be better off that way, going out with a bang instead of fading painfully as the cancer takes me.

But something deep inside clicks into place, and I refuse to give up. Maybe it's just that I'd rather go down fighting, or maybe it's plain stubbornness. Maybe it's sheer anger after what I've been through. Does it even matter?

Sucking in a deep breath between shattered teeth, I gather what strength I've got left--which isn't much--and leap into action.

Just as the clowns are nearly upon me, I dart out of the way. They collide and explode with shuddering force, spraying clown bits in all directions...but no Cage Grice bits. Though the blast knocks me down hard, I'm still alive.

But for how long? Even as I hurry to get back on my feet, I hear more floppy shoes smacking toward me. Looking around, I see three clowns...four...*five* this time, shrieking and charging in my direction all at once.

Looking around frantically, I wonder what my next move should be. Running and dodging seems to be the only choice. If I try to fight the clowns hand-to-hand, I'm guessing they'll blow up on contact.

IN A GREEN DRESS, SURROUNDED BY EXPLODING CLOWNS

Wait! Maybe that's the key.

On the floor a few feet away, I see the blown-off arm of one of the dead clowns. I bolt toward it, grab it up, and keep running, heading straight for the nearest of the five attackers.

I haul the severed arm back like a baseball bat, gripping the wrist and hand, and swing it hard at the clown's chest. As soon as the arm makes contact, the shrieking clown explodes.

The blast knocks me off my feet, and I roll twice with the impact. When I come to a stop, I see another clown almost upon me with arms outstretched.

Kicking off the shoes, I scoop one up and whip it at the clown with all my might. He explodes in mid-shriek, sending chunks in all directions; some are big enough that they set off other clowns, which in turn trigger others and so on.

I keep my head down until the blasts subside. When I look up again, the ranks of the explosive clowns have thinned out noticeably. Maybe now, I have a fighting chance.

Grabbing the other shoe, I scramble to my feet and take a quick look around. From what I can see, a dozen clowns remain. The odds are much improved.

Picking the spot where the fewest clowns remain, I get ready to make a run for it. Adrenaline burns through my bloodstream, setting my heart spinning like a dervish. The pain in my gut peaks and refuses to subside, but I'll push past it.

Every muscle in my body tenses as I prepare to sprint. If I die trying to escape this surreal trap, so be it; at least I'll have given it everything I've got left.

Brandishing the shoe, I start running. I expected the clowns to close ranks in my path, and they do...but they also take me by surprise. Wheels sprout from their floppy shoes, enabling them to move much faster than before.

The clowns swoop toward me like angry bees, and I keep running. As I go, I realize this is likely the end for me, but it doesn't freak me out at all. I feel like I'm watching it from a distance, from outside my body, and all I can think is how this isn't the way I'd ever thought I'd die. If someone had told me even a year ago that this would be my death scene, I would've laughed in his face.

Yet here I am. Running in a green dress, wielding a high-heeled shoe against a pack of clowns in roller shoes.

Then, suddenly, the doors slam wide open all around the gym. Men dressed in loincloths and bunny slippers barge in, armed with blowguns--hollow tubes held up to their mouths, jungle weapons loaded and ready.

They all fire the blowguns at once, sending a barrage of darts into the cavernous gym. But none of the darts comes anywhere near me.

It quickly becomes clear that the blowgunners are shooting at the clowns. Again and again, as the darts hit their floppy-shoed targets, the gym booms with thunderous explosions.

All the clowns go up in short order, surrounding me with fiery blasts that make my ears ring. Clown bits rain down everywhere, splattering the floor and covering me with shards of bone and tissue.

Somehow, I stay on my feet through the series of blasts. I'm shaking my head hard, trying to clear the ringing in my ears, when something zips toward me--not a dart, thankfully.

It's a Crowdlife screen, as tall as I am and twice as wide. It zooms up from a pinpoint to full size in a heartbeat, displaying a message in big, bold letters.

All current fatevotes impacting Agent Cage Grice are hereby nullified in accordance with the Mercy Provision of the Crowdlife Terms of Service.

"What the hell?" It's too good to be true; the start of another twisted torture, perhaps?

Or maybe it's just as advertised. As I read the message, the blow-gunners turn and leave the doorways...and the doors don't close behind them. All the ways out are wide open and apparently unguarded.

Just then, Liz's image appears alongside the screen, grinning. "All better now," she says. "Sorry I'm late, but you wouldn't believe how long it takes to round up a tribe of blowgunners at this hour."

Seeing her puts me instantly at ease. "So it's over?" My body untenses, and the spiked-heeled shoe falls from my grip. "It's really over?"

Liz nods. "I didn't think I could pull it off at first. The defensive bots and A.I. countermeasures were useless against the lifehackers.

Everything we sent after them ended up compromised and turned back against us."

"But you still did it." I smile, broken teeth and all. "You still saved me. I owe you big time."

"Actually," says Liz, "you owe your cancer."

I scowl at her, wondering what the hell she's talking about.

"There's a Mercy Provision in the Crowdlife Terms of Service." Liz gestures at the Crowdlife screen beside her. "*A fatevote necessitated by terminal illness supersedes and nullifies all others.*" She points a finger at me. "And it so happens there's just such a vote in progress for you, my friend."

I have to think for a moment before it comes to me. "Oh, right." In all the madness, I forgot. The Crowd was voting on whether I should undergo nanotherapy for my cancer. The treatment could buy me 1-2 months of life, accompanied by undesirable side effects. But the vote started hours ago; why is it still in progress? "There's a Crowdlife provision for this?"

Liz nods. "Typical Crowdlifer. Sign your fate away without reading the T.O.S." She sighs loudly. "The provision's meant to restore a person's dignity if they're dying. It gives them one last bit of control over their lives at the end."

I frown. "How? If the person's still subject to the will of the Crowd on that fatevote 'necessitated by terminal illness,' how do they have any control?"

"Because the one who's dying always gets the last vote. The *deciding* vote, that overrules all others." Liz walks up to me and places her phantom hand upon my shoulder. "*You* get to cast the deciding vote."

So that's why the vote is still in progress after all this time. "They're waiting for me to vote."

"Good thing you put it off when you did." Liz's voice softens as she stares into my eyes. "Good thing it happened in the first place."

"Yeah." I smirk. "Thank God for cancer."

We laugh, and then we stand there for a moment in silence. The mob hasn't come back, and Yapstream remains offline; I haven't removed the imminent danger block since entering Dada Wyrm's apartment.

The only intrusion is the Crowdlife screen, with the all-important fatevote announcement emblazoned across the top: *Should Agent Cage Grice undergo nanotherapy to treat his cancer?*

Pain shoots through my belly, and I wince. I haven't had much time to think about this, what with the lifehackers and exploding clowns and all.

"So?" Liz looks at the screen, then back at me. "What'll it be? Nanotherapy or no nanotherapy?"

I gaze at the results as they now stand: 93% of the vote in favor of nanotherapy, 17% against. It's a landslide.

Should I take those results as a sign? Would a slightly longer, less pleasant life be preferable to a shorter one without so many side effects?

It's all up to me. After a lifetime of putting my destiny in the hands of other people, I finally have the power to set my own course. The cancer gave me that much, at least. The one thing that could not be controlled by social networks has liberated me from them in the end.

Maybe it's time to take that liberation to the limit.

"What's it going to be, Cage?" Liz's brown eyes lock expectantly with mine. "How are you going to vote on Crowdlife?"

I look once more at the screen with its question and results...the fulcrum upon which the rest of my life will turn. And then I grin.

"None of their business." I pop the A.R. contact lenses out of my eyes, and the Crowdlife screen disappears. So does Liz. "Every vote's a secret ballot from here on out."

Then, I flick the contacts over my shoulder and wander off through the gym, the remains of exploded clowns squishing between my bare toes.

CHRISTMAS NEWSLETTERS FROM THE EDGE

D ear Friends and Family,

Hello again, and Merry Christmas! It's hard to believe, but it's been a whole year since my last Christmas card and newsletter to you. But it's even harder to believe that so much has happened in that time.

Some of you might already know some of the things that have been going on with me. For those who don't, let me just say this: the marriage is over!

I don't want this newsletter to be depressing, but I thought you should know that my husband and I have split. After many years, I just couldn't stay with him any longer.

He is no longer the man I fell in love with. The warmth he once showed me is long gone, and I finally reached the point where I wanted out.

So now I'm looking forward to a new life and all the good things it might have to offer. I'm still a little blue, there's no question. I keep listening to "Blue Christmas," and yes, crying a little. But I do sense the light at the end of the tunnel.

So this is *good* news, and I hope you'll all join me in celebrating the new beginning on which I'm embarking. Though it's sad, it's also joyful, because it brings new ways to start over and have a new beginning.

This is just my way of saying *thank you* for standing by me all these years during the troubles I've had with him, and I look forward to getting caught up with all of you and moving ahead with whatever new adventures await me.

Yours truly,
Beverly

One year later...

Merry Christmas One and All!

I'm happy to report that this year, things are much better than last. As you'll recall, at this time last year, I left my husband. It was a difficult time for me. Looking back, I apologize if my previous letter was on the sad side. However, I am happy to report that things are looking up this year.

I'm in much better spirits! The divorce is final! I am now officially on my own for the first time in *forever*! I feel so free and excited about the possibilities that life has to offer me!

So what have I done since the big breakup? For one thing, I've moved! Where, you might wonder? Well, my first instinct was to move to my hometown, but since I've had enough of the cold and snow, I decided to live somewhere in a warmer clime. To that end, I pulled up stakes and found a great little place in a town in Florida called Titusville. It's a sweet little town, really, and just the right place for someone like me to have a new start.

Having moved into a new apartment (can you believe it?), I realized I would now have to get a job. Correction, I didn't *have* to; the settlement was more than fair. However, I *wanted* a job. I wanted to prove myself. I wanted to start over and be part of the world at large once again.

The question was, what kind of job could I get after so many years of being "just a wife?" I don't have a college degree. I don't have any kind of trade school experience or any work experience of value. I've just always been about "him."

Well, I thought, what's something I love doing and never had enough time for when I was married? The answer was easy: I love books. For that matter, I even like to write a little...hence, the long-winded newsletters you get every year from me, LOL.

So I wondered if there were any bookstores in town. Sure enough, there is one downtown, and it so happened they were hiring a clerk. Well, *I* am now that clerk!

Donovan, the young fellow who runs the place (what you might call a "hipster") is very friendly and considerate, and we have a lot of common interests about what books we like to read. He liked what I had to say, and the next thing I knew, I was a bookseller!

So that catches you up on me. I'm working in a bookstore, I have my own apartment in a town in Florida, and as if that's not enough, I'm even thinking about taking a vacation! Hopefully, by this time next year, I'll have much more to report on that front.

Yours truly,

Beverly

One year later...

Merry Christmas, Everyone!

You'll never guess where I'm writing this letter! You get three guesses...

Oh, I'm just going to tell you! I'm writing it on a beach in *Bali!* Can you believe it? How exciting!

I've finally taken a vacation, and I couldn't be happier. This is something I've always wanted to do! All through my marriage, *he* was the one who got to spend time on the road because of his work, and I never got to go along. I hated being stuck in one place, because I'd always wanted to travel and see the world. Well, I'm finally doing it, or at least taking this one trip.

I set up the whole trip myself, from reserving the hotel to ordering the airfare. It's amazing what you can do online these days! Then, I got cold feet. Believe it or not, I wasn't sure I could go through with it. Though traveling is something I've always wanted to do, when I finally got the chance, I was scared.

I almost didn't go. I spent quite a while just sitting there staring at my airline pass on the computer and wondering if I could go through with this. What if the plane crashed? What if Bali turned out to be terrible?

But finally, with some encouragement from Donovan at the bookstore, I went through with it. I hesitated at the gate but pushed past my fear, got on the plane, and here I am, on the beach, with a lovely drink in my hand, feeling the warm breeze caress my face as I watch people playing in the surf.

It is one of the most wonderful experiences I've ever had. I never knew it could be so much fun and so relaxing. I am here now, and let me tell you, this is something I want to do more of in the future. Not that I'll never be afraid again, but with a little encouragement from the right people, maybe I can get past that.

Anyway, it has been another eventful year. As you'll recall, last year, I moved to an apartment in a town in Florida and started a new job as a clerk at a bookstore. Not much of a career, I guess, but it's something I've always wanted to do, and I'm enjoying the heck out of it. The customers are so nice, for the most part, and I love making recommendations and talking about books with them. I just love talking about their lives, too, and getting to know them.

It's so wonderful. I always felt isolated before. My husband had become so controlling and kept me locked away. He wasn't much for socializing, either. Now that I'm on my own, I have a nice social life and enjoy the company of other people.

I'm so glad I get to make these friends and get to know folks like Trudy down at the coffee shop and Janet at the dress shop. Even the guys and girls at the YMCA! That's right, I'm working out regularly!

Actually, that's some of my best news this year. I have lost so much weight, you wouldn't believe it! (That was another problem with our marriage. He loved sweets and always had them around. There were always goodies in the house, which I ate too, and it showed.) Now I'm working out and losing weight, and here I am at a beach...still in a one-piece, but just you wait!

So there you have it! What a life, huh?

Yours truly,

Beverly

One year later...

Happy Holidays to One and All!

You know I always like to keep you up to date on what's happening in my life because you're my good friends and family, so here's the latest.

I'm dating!

Yes, you read that right. Remember I went on vacation to Bali last year? Well, while I was there, I met a man from New Zealand. His name is Jim Willows, and we really hit it off. He and I were in the same tour group one day, visiting a temple, and we started up a conversation. It turned out we had a lot in common. Like me, Jim had recently gotten out of a challenging relationship. He is about my age, maybe a little younger, and *very* handsome. His gray hair makes him look quite dashing, if you ask me!

We made an instant connection and decided to meet up again that night for dinner and drinks. Needless to say, this was very different for me. It had been sooooo long since I'd dated anyone other than my husband. But it was also very exciting.

Meeting up for the first time in that Indonesian restaurant was so romantic. We were both a little nervous, but we had a great conversation. We talked about *everything*, and by the time it was all over, we realized we wanted to see each other again. The only problem was, we live so far apart. It's a *very* long trip from Florida to New Zealand and vice versa.

That's why we decided to meet in between on another vacation. Jim, like me, enjoys traveling. He said he was planning to visit family in Los Angeles and asked if I might want to meet him there. I said, why not? We decided to meet in L.A. in July and see where things went from there.

So I booked the trip and arranged to take time off from the bookstore (I'm still working there and having a wonderful time of it). Sure enough, we met up in L.A. for this vacation.

I can't tell you enough how well it went. I had a great time touring around with him, spending time getting to know him better, and meeting his family, too.

It was such a romantic trip that we agreed we had to meet up again sometime. And so we planned to meet over the holidays—but since I couldn't get the time off, he agreed to meet me in Florida.

He's actually here *right now* with me, as I'm writing this! He's sitting right across the room, smiling at me! I feel so happy to be with him in this place, celebrating the holidays with someone who has made such a positive difference in my life.

I don't know what the future will bring, but for now, this is the merriest Christmas I've had in I don't know how long.

Yours truly,

Beverly

One year later...

Hello again.

How could such a wonderful year have gone so wrong?

I almost didn't write this letter. Things have gone so terribly, just in the last few days, that I can hardly stand to tell you about it.

As you'll recall, I started dating Jim Willows last year. It only got better from there. This year, we spent more time than ever together. We agreed we loved each other and even talked about plans for the future.

I thought, finally, I'd found someone who's the perfect match for me, someone who cares about me and what I'm interested in and wants me to be happy, who isn't so wrapped up in his work that he doesn't have the time to spend or room in his heart to give to someone who loves him.

As much as I hate to say it, however, it's over between us now.

It just happened a few days ago. I was spending time with Jim, who had come to visit me in Florida. We were talking about what we might do for the holidays...and all of a sudden, I heard a noise from outside—some kind of jingling noise.

Instantly, I knew what it must be...but I went to see anyway. Before I could open the door, it came flying in, and you-know-who stormed into my apartment. Yes, that's right—my ex-husband *Nick* himself.

People might call him Saint Nicholas, but he was not in a saintly mood that night. He came storming in in a blind rage, hollering about how I had betrayed him and how I didn't love him and never had.

Jim walked over, put a hand on his shoulder, and tried to calm him down, but that just set him off more.

Nick whipped around, grabbed Jim, and threatened him. He said, "If you ever go near my wife again, I *promise* you won't have a happy ending."

Jim is not easily intimidated. He is a strong man and able to deal with physical threats. However, when he stood up to Nick, Nick decided to take him for "a ride," if you know what I mean.

He whisked Jim outside, strapped him by the ankles to the runners of his sleigh, and flew him up into the distant heights. Then he spun him around and did wild midair maneuvers while Jim dangled from the sleigh.

I don't think I've ever seen such an awful display from that man. I can't believe I was *ever* with him! He has a dark side that few people have seen. I just wish I wasn't one of them.

When he was done with Jim, Nick flew him away, back to New Zealand, but not before screaming at me on his way out of sight, demanding I change my ways and come back to him because it's my responsibility to be with him and help him with his job. If I don't get my act together and come back, he said, Jim will end up in even *worse* shape, and what happened to him will happen to every man I date or spend time with.

So here I am, alone again, thanks to Nick. The man I love is gone, and I feel a deep depression setting in. The future looks bleak.

Yours truly,

Beverly

One year later...

Hello again, everyone.

I wish I had better news for you this Christmas, but I don't. As you remember from last year, Nick drove off the love of my life, Jim, and ruined the perfect happiness that I was on the verge of discovering. He threatened to hurt Jim, and I felt I had no choice. To save Jim, I thought the only alternative was to go back to the man who had the power to destroy him.

So that's what I've done.

I write this from my old home at the North Pole with Nick. I'm back at work as "Mrs. Claus," washing Nick's clothes, shining his boots, cooking his meals, you name it. Back to being the same old domestic servant that I'd been for so long.

This wasn't what I wanted for myself. I'd sworn, when I left Nick, that I was gone for good. I'd really had enough. Now, it's even more difficult to be here. Now that I've seen more of what the world has to offer, and I know that I *can* be happy, being here is the most terrible thing I can think of. Even as I sit here, I'm crying.

But what can I do? Nick has magical powers, and he isn't afraid to use them. I told you, he has a dark side. Apparently, it's even darker than I knew. He's capable of doing good things for people around the world, but when it comes to his personal life, he's mean, selfish, and blind to the needs of those around him.

So I will keep this short. Whenever you want to reach me, please direct your letters here, to the North Pole, just like in the old days. Maybe, when Nick stops being so suspicious that I might leave again, he might even let me see them.

But I doubt I will ever see a letter from Jim. He is gone from my life, though I will always love him. Nothing that Nick says or does can ever change that.

Yours truly,
Beverly

One year later...

Merry Christmas, Friends and Family!

What a difference a year makes! I know my last letter was rather sad, and for that, I apologize. This letter will be *much* different!

I am the happiest woman on Earth! I am far happier than I had thought I could ever be again, especially after Nick forced me to come back to be with him.

As you'll recall, though I'd found happiness with Jim Willows, my ex-husband, Nick, had ruined it...or so I thought. Nick had used his powers to intimidate Jim and drive him away, and then he'd terrorized me into coming back to the North Pole. However, it turns out that wasn't the end of the story.

I moved back to the North Pole and thought that was the end of it. Then, one day in February (Valentine's Day, actually) there was a knock at the door of Santa's workshop.

Everyone froze. We don't get casual visitors in that place, *ever*. It isn't *impossible* to find, but it isn't really on any maps or GPS.

I went to open the door, and here it was *Jim*, covered with ice and frost from a very long hike across the frozen wastes.

"I've come to get you," he said. "I don't care what *he* might do to me. I love you too much to ever be without you."

I was stunned. How had he found us? All I could figure was that the power of love—and high-tech gadgets, perhaps—had been enough to enable him to find our exact location.

As I was standing there talking to him, Nick stormed into the room. Instantly, he flew into a rage and marched over as if he was ready to attack.

Before Nick could lay his hands on Jim, however, Jim clicked the "On" button on his walkie talkie radio. "*Now!*" he shouted into the microphone.

As soon as he said that word, a squad of men in black body armor and helmets burst through the door and poured into the workshop. They were all heavily-armed mercenaries hired by Jim (who is *not* without financial resources).

The men surrounded Nick with their weapons pointed dead-on at him.

"One move, and it's all over, Santa," barked Jim.

"How dare you!" hollered Nick. "This is *my* home!"

"I don't care *what* it is," said Jim. "And I don't care who *you* are. All I care about is that woman over there and my love for her."

"Your *love* for her?" Santa laughed uproariously, his gut jiggling like jelly. "Don't be ridiculous!"

"Yes, my *love* for her," Jim said forcefully. "And *her* love for me."

Gallantly, he walked over and reached for my hand. I hesitated only a second, then took his hand in mine as well.

"It's *over*," I told Nick. "It has been for a long time."

"It's *never* over!" screamed Nick.

"Yes it is," I told him, "and it has to be this way."

"Not while I'm *Santa Claus!*" he bellowed, his roar echoing through the workshop.

"If you're Santa, start *acting* like him," said Jim. "Beverly's coming with me, and if you're anything like the Santa Claus that I was raised to believe in—that *all* of us were raised to believe in..." He gestured at the mercenaries, and every one of them nodded. "...you'll let her go."

Nick glared at Jim, then at me, then at Jim again. For a long moment, I thought he was going to go off and tear Jim to shreds. I thought that was the end of it, and I would never see Jim again.

But then, the craziest thing happened.

"All right." Nick actually put up his hands and gave in.

"All right?" I couldn't believe it. Had he actually said what I *thought* he'd said?

"Yes," said Nick. "I didn't know what to get you for Christmas anyway. I never do." He hung his head, looking pitiful.

"Thank you," I told him, and then I turned and walked out the door, holding Jim's hand and surrounded by his men.

But Nick didn't stay pitiful for long. "Just don't expect any *presents* on Christmas!" he roared. "*Ever!*"

Then the big doors slammed shut behind us, and I didn't see him again after that. I don't think I ever will.

But you know what? That's okay with me. There comes a time in all our lives when we have to stop believing in Santa.

And in my case, I have to *start* believing in Jim, and in love.

Merry Christmas to you all, and to all, a *wonderful* New Year!

Yours truly,

Mrs. Beverly Willows

DRIVERLESS

The sleek red Ford GT with white racing stripes screamed along the Nebraska four-lane, punching toward the dark cloud-shrouded towers of Omaha in the distance.

Vreeeeooooowwwwwww

The gray-haired, dark-skinned man in the cockpit, Shunn Comma, clutched the steering wheel, darting his bloodshot brown eyes to the rearview mirror every few seconds.

Each time, he chewed his gum a little faster. The trio of black Ferrari Superfasts was still zooming along behind him, five car lengths back and closing.

Eeeeeooowwww Eeeeooowwww Eeeeooowwww.

Like Shunn's GT, none of the Ferraris was driverless, hobbled by speed or maneuvering governors—nothing short of a miracle in the mid-21st century.

And nothing short of a shit-show if those Ferraris ever caught up. Assuming there was anything left of his time-release memory before they tried to jack the shit out of it.

Shunn checked the timer on his right contact lens overlay. *07:35.*

Tick tick tick tick

That was all the time he had left to deliver the ultra-top-secret message before it was gone forever...and a civil war, perhaps, erupted in the heart of the American Midwest.

Zeeeeeooooowwwwwww

And the fun was just getting started. As Shunn hurtled up over a rise, he saw a cluster of traffic less than a mile ahead, crawling up both eastbound lanes at robotic, self-driving speeds.

He might as well have been staring at a wall of metal and human bodies blocking the road. The cars flowed forward in tight formation at identical speed, controlled by cloud-based networks of A.I. mommies that locked out all human influence.

Almost all influence. It was a good thing Shunn was as much a super-hacker as a super-driver. Otherwise, most roads would have been unusable for his flight, even to a non-driverless car like the GT.

With practiced flicks and blinks of his eyes, he launched the hacker app loaded in his cranial drive, simultaneously jamming incoming commands to the wall of self-driving obstacles up ahead and pushing through his own.

Part, you sons of bitches.

At first, nothing. *Tick tick tick.* Beads of sweat on his creased forehead thickened and ran.

Tick tick

Vreeeeeooooowwwww

Finally, further up the column, one car in the right lane hopped onto the berm, then another. And another, even further ahead.

Tick tick tick

Three in the left lane peeled left onto the medial strip—but as in the right lane, the rearward stragglers clung to the straightaway. There were four in the left lane and three in the right, dead center between the solid and dashed white lines.

Seconds left before he'd plow into them. Cursing. Sweating.

Tick

CURSING.

Then he thought of a snippet of a poem by Robert Frost, the one about woods on a snowy evening and having miles to go before he could sleep. It was the message he was carrying, due to be decoded with an algorithmic cipher by his contact in Omaha. Why, he wondered, did it give him a strange, sinking feeling every time it trickled through his mind? Was it because of all the roads not taken in his own life, the paths that could have kept him from this hell-bent race? Or the fact that sleep, or rest of any kind, were beyond him these days, and everything felt like a waking dream of speed?

Days like this, Shunn felt like nothing but propulsion. Faster slower farther closer *yessssss*.

A message made flesh. Message become the messenger.

Come on and paarrrtttt, motherfuckerrrsss...

And they did. Stragglers FINALLY swung left and right, JUST AS THE GT RIPPED BETWEEN THEM, hugging the cut that hadn't been wide enough even seconds

Tick

Before.

Did Moses grin when he opened the Red Sea? Because Shunn sure did.

That's right, that's right, baby.

He kept the traffic parting before him, folding away to right and left like waves in a sea. He felt the computer code flowing through the network into and out of the cloud down into the cars' brains and circuits, closing and opening, speed and course trimming to suit him.

The GT skimmed through the gap, moving so fast it looked like one continuous red-and-white streak. Barely missing one pair of cars, it swooped right and bucked left to miss another as the perfectly synchronized parting rolled onward like a current.

Then he checked the rearview mirror. The three Ferraris were still back there, single-filed to clear the gap. The lead driver bolted forward, no doubt realizing that the traffic slowed the GT just enough to maybe run up on him.

Shunn chipped fresh hacks at the parted traffic behind him, reaching in like a surgeon seeking shrapnel. Missed one missed two missed three...

Got one! He nosed a gray Volvo at the last second, just enough to make it clip the rearward black Ferrari, spinning it hard into the medial.

Didn't change the lead car's chase but cut the pack by one.

And we're clear. Traffic suddenly gone ahead, the road wide open, at least until the next bend two miles up.

Shunn stomped the accelerator and pulled away from the lead Ferrari, sprinting into the twilight outside Omaha.

Vreeeeooooowwww

One more try at hacking the remaining two Ferraris but forget it, he couldn't jump the air gap or strip the hardened on-premises war boxes. *Standoff.*

Which was exactly what he was being paid a small fortune to break, on a much larger scale. A secret standoff between two sides in the heart of America--government and breakaway forces—and no one would even know it had been a threat unless those pricks back there intercepted him before one of two things happened:

Delivery or auto-delete.

Delivery would be complete when he reached the location represented by the blinking red dot on the windshield GPS overlay – just inside the Omaha city limits. The breakaway forces would get the message that the government was making concessions, and the civil war would be cancelled.

On the other hand, if he didn't get there before the deadline, the message he carried would be automatically deleted from his brain. The hope for peace and unity would be erased, just as hawkish elements on both sides wanted them to be.

This would happen in exactly 06:15.

Tick tick tick

The overwhelming need to avoid that outcome drove him to push the GT even harder.

Vreeeeeooowwwww

The blurred green-brown-gray scenery around him was a fore-taste of what the deletion deadline would bring. All he'd have left after auto-delete was a blur like that, a hint of a trace of a flicker of something that had once been in his brain.

If only he could say the same about his memories of Annie and how he'd lost her.

Every job, he got the treatment. Time-release targeted memory loss by biochemical compound, keyed on the exact neurons storing the message he was delivering. Just as in-person delivery was the only way to ensure message security in the age of hacked E-everything, memory wipes were the only way to guarantee that even *that* security couldn't be compromised.

There was only one problem. The wipes were too precise. No collateral damage. They wouldn't delete his memories of cheating on Annie, and her knowing but not saying and not forgiving and one day just *not.*

Not being there.

And no amount of speed could run him away from all that he'd lost.

Vreeeeeooooooowwwwww

If all else failed and he was captured, he could stick himself with the Big Shot syringe from the glove box. Five hundred times the original dose of the auto-delete compound would howl through his bloodstream and brain, cooking down the memories like a bubbling reduction in a saucepan.

Would that finally kill the memories of Annie? He didn't know. He'd never needed the Big Shot before; he'd never failed to complete a mission.

And he had no intention of failing *this* time, either.

Whunk

Just then, something bumped the roof of the GT.

Whunk

And again. Checking the overlays on his windshield and contacts, he spotted the culprit: a weaponized drone trying to deposit an explosive on the GT. It was the first since he'd hacked and blown a swarm of them near Cedar Rapids—and it wouldn't be deterred. Shunn's hacker app couldn't get him through the drone's defenses, no matter how hard he tried.

Whunk

Even as he kept trying to breach the drone's firewall, Shunn watched the GPS for some sign of an overpass where he might be able to crash the thing...but no dice. He swerved the GT, fighting to prevent payload attachment, but he knew it was only a matter of time.

Whunk

After all the distance he'd come and all the obstacles he'd dodged or obliterated, that one damn drone was about to be the death of him and the failure of his mission.

Whunk

Maybe he could grab another drone nearby, one without the hardened security, and bring it in for a collision. Casting his net wide, he scanned local frequencies for a sign of such a drone, hoping he could find one before the payload latched on to the GT.

Whunk

That was when the sky flashed with dazzling light.

Tick tick tick

A rumbling blast shook the cockpit.

KRAKOOOOOOMMM

Lightning and thunder. Now *there* was something you didn't see or hear much in the days of Midwestern mega-drought.

Shunn chewed his gum faster, biting the inside of his left cheek so hard, he tasted blood. His hands tightened like bear traps on the wheel. The equation of his drive had just changed dramatically.

And *shit*, all he had was five minutes forty-five seconds till auto-delete...or worse, a full *reformat* via Big Shot.

05:40

At least he had clear highway ahead...until he *didn't*.

05:30

Adrenaline sizzled through his bloodstream as the GT barreled around a bend and he saw what was waiting for him there.

HOONNNNNNKKK HOONNNNNNNKKK

Etched in another flash of lightning, a tractor trailer loomed dead ahead, hurtling straight toward him.

KRAKABOOOOOOMMMMM

SKREEEEEEEEEEEEEEE

Shunn stamped the brake and spun the wheel, whipping the GT

around in a punishing 180. He played the stick and clutch and crushed the accelerator, leaping away in the direction from which he'd come.

VRRREEEEEOOOWWWWW

The drone that had been pacing him wasn't quite so quick on the uptake. He saw it explode against the cab of the truck in a ball of flame.

Arcs of burnt rubber smoked on the asphalt behind him as he shot away from the crashing tractor trailer...and plunged headlong toward the remaining two black Ferraris.

In a desperate flurry of cranial code bursts, he probed the tractor trailer's self-driving systems and couldn't make a dent. The truck was hacked, it *had* to be—and now Shunn was caught in the middle of a roadkill sandwich: tractor trailer on one side, Ferraris on the other, lightning flashing, countdown ticking.

KRAAKABAKOOOOM

04:40

Tick tick tick tick

And *WTF*, Annie's last words were bouncing around his head like ball bearings in a cement mixer.

The smell of sweat in the cockpit. The smell of her perfume on that day, months ago, like lilacs.

"Glorified..."

He jammed the stick. Cut the wheel.

"...pizza delivery boy..."

Mashed the pedal.

"...all you'll ever be."

Blew across the medial, hopping the dip in the middle, never losing momentum.

"What good is that photographic memory..."

All the while hacking the clot of cars zooming toward him on the other side of the highway.

"...if you can't remember the only thing that really matters?"

Juggling them into a hasty single file in the far lane, leaving him the closest lane and berm...somehow barely keeping all six from colliding.

And that's when it started. Drops on the windshield.

KRABAKROOOOOOOM

And a parade of vehicles cruising headlong toward him, head-lights flaring to life all at once.

VREEEEEOOOOWWWW

Just as the downpour let loose, drenching cars and road alike with a pummeling shower that was nowhere near as cold as the chill racing up Shunn's spine.

FWOOOOOOOOOSSSSHHHHH

Because this...

Holy shit, *this* was *bad.*

Even as Shunn raced into the lane he'd opened, he saw the single file wouldn't hold. Some of the cars he'd nudged into that forma-tion started to flick and swing, gliding on the rain-slickened asphalt.

Because who needed protection against hydroplaning in a world where it almost never rained, and self-driving cars always perfectly adjusted to conditions on the rare occasions when it did?

Unless they were *hacked,* that is.

KRAKOOOOOOOOOMMMMM

Shunn glanced right for a second. Heavy traffic there across the medial, so he'd take his chances running the gauntlet here, with incoming.

NEEEOOOWWWWWWWWW

The GT bolted forward on top-of-the-line tires that gripped the road through the film of rain. The Ferraris were similarly well-equipped; they vaulted the medial behind him and followed suit with perfect traction.

EEOOOWWWWW EEOOOWWWW

Wipers chopping away at the fastest setting, Shunn charged the narrowing gap like a terrier through a rat hole. Cars lashed toward him from the single file—red then blue then green, skating into his path, nearly making contact.

SSSHHHHHKRUMMMPP

And then *making* it. A silver Audi coupe spun around in a sudden

360, its rear-end swatting the driver's side front quarter panel of the GT.

Shunn wrenched the wheel hard and rode the impact, whipping the GT in a swing of its own and then grabbing the pavement again and lurching eastbound.

SSHHWWOOOOSSHHHH

Even as he careened forward through the torrential rain, clawing for purchase in the brains of the cars up ahead, the count-down continued in his mind.

03:15 until auto-delete.

KRAKOOOOOMMMMMM

He was *so close* to the red line, and he knew it. So close to not completing his delivery before the message dissolved from his mind.

03:00

02:55

But the towers of the city loomed closer than ever now, strobing in flashes of lightning. One man waited to receive him just inside the city limits, waiting to hear the message he'd brought all the way from the White House in Washington, D.C.

SHISSSSSSSSSSSSS

Suddenly, another car bucked over, and another. Shunn swerved right, left, right, catching glimpses of the terrified passengers in their cabins.

Chewing the gum harder, he drew blood from the right cheek this time.

02:33

Suddenly, it was Christmas in the rearview mirror. He glanced up just in time to see the rearward Ferrari bounce off a white van and flip into the medial ditch.

One less chase car was a gift. Shunn gunned the GT and flew faster, focused like a laser on the blinking red GPS dot.

KRAKAKOOOOOOMMMM

He had to *get there* before auto-delete, pass the message to the warm body designated for the last leg of the relay. *Everything* was riding on *him*, a terrible sacrifice to stave off a much greater loss.

If he failed to deliver the message, millions would surely die in an unnecessary civil war that would ravage the nation.

02:17

02:10

He was *right* on the *red line*, but he still had *hope*, he still might *make* it. Less than a minute from the city limits and his exit — seconds after that to the roadblock and the contact he'd tell about roads not taken and having miles to go before he could sleep.

And then maybe *he* could finally sleep.

02:00

Tick tick tick tick

SHISSSSSSSSSSSS

But suddenly, everything went crazy up ahead. Every car broke from the file, spinning and sliding over the rain-soaked road in front of him.

It didn't matter that he was still snapping out orders and the cars' brains were reading loud and clear, trying to obey. Shitty tires sent them careening like an up-dumped bucket of pucks on a hockey rink.

And Shunn was roaring right into them.

He had to tap the brake to miss a Toyota sedan, then a pickup. In the split-second before he could stomp the gas again, the remaining Ferrari stormed up and bumped him from behind.

THUNNKKK

The GT lurched left and clipped a blue SUV, pitching it into a road sign. Fighting the wheel, Shunn rode the collision momentum in a whipsaw 180, then stepped on the accelerator, mowing head-long into the charging Ferrari.

As the Ferrari pushed back, Shunn threw the GT in reverse and shot away, grazing a fishtailing BMW. The Ferrari erupted after him, violently sideswiping the BMW, sweeping it out of its way.

KRRUMMMPP

01:45

The GT stayed face-to-face with the Ferrari, slashing backward through the jackhammering rain and chaos of hydroplaning cars. Shunn cranked the stick, worked the clutch, and bashed the accelerator, all while yanking the wheel back and forth to navigate the mayhem.

01:37

Swooping right, left, right, left, he somehow traversed the jumble of whirling vehicles while keeping his car inches from the nose of the Ferrari.

SHISSSSSSSSSSSSS

Sluicing backward, ever backward, he raced like a blood cell exploding through an artery, the whole time keeping a secret other than the ciphered message—and the secret was this:

He was *holding back*, drawing in the Ferrari...and then he *wasn't*.

RRROOAAARRRRRR

01:25

The GT rocketed back as if the speeding Ferrari were standing still. Into the gap between them slid a propane tanker, and then...

WABOOOOOOOMMM

Flames and debris *exploded* in all directions. Shockwaves pummeled the skating cars, kicking them away from the center of the blast.

Rattling the GT as the seconds ticked away.

01:05

Jerking the wheel, Shunn spun the GT around hard and bolted for the medial. A narrow path existed, just a sliver of a keyhole between clusters of traffic, leading straight to the exit ramp he needed.

Without hesitation, he darted into it.

Only to realize, at the very last instant, that it wasn't so unobstructed after all. Just as he cleared the medial, a scarred and battered black Ferrari swung out in front of him and cut him off. One of the two pursuers he'd thought out of the race had recovered and caught up.

"Fuck!" Shunn jerked the wheel, but there was no way to dodge or stop in time.

SHISSSSSSSSSS

KRAASSSHHHHH

The GT collided with the Ferrari, sending both cars skidding across the double lanes. They came to rest straddling the berm, a dozen feet apart.

Four men in black armor and helmets bolted out of the Ferrari with guns, cutters, and probes, running for the GT with purpose.

And there was still just under a minute left until auto-delete.

Shunn knew what he had to do. If there was even the slightest chance they might hack him before auto-delete, he had to burn everything.

Shaky from the crash, he leaned across the seat and popped the glove box. Grabbing the Big Shot, he flipped the cap off the needle.

Then stabbed the needle into his neck and pushed the plunger.

Instantly, he felt himself melting away like ice cream on a summer sidewalk, and he smiled. The blades of power saws sliced through the driver's-side door, the windshield shattered under a blow from a bludgeon, and he didn't give a shit.

Because this time, maybe, he would finally forget the pain of what he'd done. Finally forget Annie and the only true love he'd ever known.

"We have it," said one of the men as he checked readings on a scanner on his wrist.

"You're sure?" A second man used the muzzle of a rifle to nudge Shunn, who was sprawled on the hood of the GT where they'd tossed him after dragging him out of the car.

"Has to be," said the first man. "It's the only thing left in his brain. The only thing our probes got out of him."

"Guess we'll figure it out later." The second man marched off toward the black Ferrari waiting nearby, followed by two of his part-ners. "We need to go." Sirens approached.

"Poor son of a bitch." The first man jerked the adhesive elec-trode from Shunn's temple and walked away. "At least he's at peace now."

They drove off, leaving Shunn on the GT's hood, tossing his head and scowling. As the rain pelted him, he kept repeating the same words over and over, the same message he'd delivered to the enemy agents.

The only message he had left in his burned-out memory. The only message he had left to remember and deliver for the rest of his vegetated life.

"Glorified pizza delivery boy...all you'll ever be," he said.

If not for the rain, the tears on his face might have been visible, glistening in the flashing blue and red lights of the cop cars arriving around him.

But no such luck.

Thunder rolled, and he kept on mumbling right through it.

KRAKOOOOOOMMMMM

"What good is that...photographic memory...if you can't remember...the only thing that really *matters*?"

THE REALM THAT
DIDN'T SUCK

White clouds. Blue sky. Yellow sun.

Even as I fall, flailing, into the latest in a long line of realms, those are the first things I notice. And even though I'm falling fast, worrying about where and how hard I'll come down, a coherent thought flashes through my mind.

I like this place already.

Then *crack*, I'm crashing through a canopy of green and brown, a heartbeat away from whatever hard landing awaits me. A heartbeat away, maybe, from the *death* of me.

But no. Instead of pancaking on solid ground, I splash down in icy water. The breath is knocked out of me, I sink deep, but I survive.

It's a good thing I'm not the woman I used to be. *Original* Mia couldn't have stayed under for long with no air. But *this* Mia's another story.

Ten thousand stories, actually.

Midway through my plunge, my legs transform, melting into a kind of fish tail. Immediately, I thrash that tail hard, slowing my fall —then stopping it altogether.

Looking around through my cloud of glowing red hair, I become aware of eyes peering at my slender body from the emerald murk. Squinting, I glimpse the face of an underwater creature before it wriggles off into the shadows...and I'm stunned. Was it my imagination, or did that thing actually look like a *fish* from back home? From Original Mia's starting point?

Frowning, I swim my way toward the light.

When I break the surface, gasping, the world opens up around me. My tail keeps me afloat as I take it all in—a forest of trees with brown trunks and green leaves, set against that lovely blue sky with white clouds above, all of it reflected in the rippling surface of the lake below.

All of which just makes me think, *Holy shit.* As in, *Holy shit, I never thought I'd see someplace like* this *again.*

I laugh, because it's wonderful, a miracle—and then I swim for shore. All the while, I keep waiting for the other shoe to drop, because as I've learned again and again (*and again*) in my many travels...

Appearances can be deceiving.

When I reach the shallows, I undo the fish tail, giving myself human legs again. My bare feet sink into the muddy bottom as I wade through the water—more brown here than green—and up onto the grassy beach.

Then, I throw myself down on my back and rest, gazing up at the bright blue sky. It's the first of that color I've seen since leaving home, ten thousand worlds ago (or more), and so many years ago I've lost track.

It makes me want to cry because I've missed it so much. Because, also, I wasn't sure until now, as changed as I am, if I *could* still miss it like I do.

It's funny how much of a relief that is, since all I wanted in the beginning was to get away from it. But I soon discovered that all the other realms with all the other skies were never as perfect as the blue sky of home.

You can take your purple skies, green skies, striped skies, musical skies, diamond skies, et cetera and shove them up your ass. Do the same for all the realms under them in what I call the *Suckyverse* (because that's what they all are, take it from me—*sucky*).

396

But enough of this lying around. Time to get back to the hunt, the whole reason I'm here.

Sitting up, I use the fire magic in my belly to heat my skin, lighting it up cherry red and instantly drying myself and my clothes, such as they are. The white peasant's blouse and brown ankle-length skirt are ill-fitting, the best I could scare up in the last realm—yet another dragon-infested dump lousy with knights and gnomes a-questing.

"That's better." The crimson glow fades from my glittering marble skin—a creamy base veined with whorls of black and ruby. It's not my natural color or choice, just a side effect of some of the dumbass realms I've dived into.

I get to my feet, wondering what surprises this new realm will bring—what *changes*. Wondering how badly this place will end up *sucking* in the end, because they always do.

That's when I feel something or someone watching me.

Without turning, I open the eye in the back of my head (another gift from another sucky world) and have a look. What I see is enough to make my heart flutter.

Though every realm I've been to has had its beasts, I've not seen one of *these*, quite like this, in any other...except one.

A *deer*. A beautiful, unaltered, white-tailed *doe*.

I catch my breath, marveling at the sight of it. Wondering how it's possible to find one here, when the only other place I've seen one just like it...

Is *home*.

Which raises a question. Is it possible? After all the places I've been, all the *shitmares* I've lived through, could my quarry—my *love*—have somehow led me back to where I *started*? Could *this* be...*home?*

Suddenly, the doe's ears twitch, and it leaps away, gone like a tawny whisper in the lush green brush.

I look around for whatever spooked it, instinctively saying the name of the one I followed to get here. "Will?" My voice is touched with hope, though I know how unlikely it is that he might be here. The last time I saw him in the flesh was ten thousand realms ago (or more)...though he leaves a message for me in every realm I visit.

Nothing here yet, though. I look, and listen, and smell, and no sign of him comes back to me. I *know* he traveled this way, I followed his trail through the Suckyverse (which *he* taught me how to do, by the way)...but whatever he might have left for me remains hidden.

Though I wonder. If this *is* home after all, with magicks so much dimmer than the multitude of other realms, would he even *leave* a sign for me to find?

Still getting my bearings, I pick my way along the shore to a ragged path that might have been worn through the brush by the deer and her friends. I follow it, winding away from the water and into the denser cover of the forest.

Snapping twigs tickle my feet as I walk, and rocks jab from the dusty ground—but my skin never breaks and never will. Spell after spell has toughened it, making it nearly impenetrable. My bones and organs, likewise, are much changed, mystically braced and laced with power from a thousand thundering realms...paid for with this bit or that of trickery, honest work, or my mortal soul.

I take another step, and something tiny scurries across a sunbeam in my path. Brown and white striped fur, erect tail, flickering legs...*I'll be damned.*

Was that a *chipmunk?*

The beat of my heart picks up, and I quicken my step. All these similarities to home, they're adding up...but I can't get too excited. The realms are rife with tomfoolery and bullshit. Why do you think they *suck* so much?

That isn't to say I can't enjoy the beauty until the façade tears away. Those shafts of sunlight, streaming through the fluttering green canopy...the sweet, sweet smell of bark and brush and loam, weaving in the crisp, fresh air...and that high, piping skirl—is that *birdsong*, yes it's *birdsong*—it's straight out of a dream, a thousand thousand dreams and memory fragments...a hundred thousand longings.

Shivers of joy run down my spine, setting the vertebrae (altered) to ringing like a choir of bells. Nothing in the realms of endless diadems or dancing gardens or untold mindful rainbows or infinite unfolding parasols can compare to the simple glory in which I find myself.

And I know, even if this sense of familiarity and welcome is limited to this single lovely wood, that there is more joy to come. Because somewhere, as always, in every realm I've been to, there is a message from beloved Will. He always speaks to me, always believes I'm coming after him, though he has no way of knowing for sure that I'll follow.

The message, whatever its form, whatever its medium, is always the same: *I love you, Mia.*

I love you, Will. If I were the one leaving the message, that's how it would read.

Would I always believe, without any proof, that he would see it? That he would never give up his pursuit, and the messages would never be for nothing?

I like to think so, yes. I like to think our love is *that* strong and then some.

The thought of him makes me prick up my ears, open all of my eyes (there are seven) and inhale more deeply in search of his sign. No wonder I'm extra sensitive when a tiny black bug circles around and lands on my wrist.

How many such horseflies did I swat in younger years back home? Yet now, watching the little bastard rub his legs together, I'm delighted. I never thought I'd see one like this again—one that isn't eight feet tall or chanting obscenities or riding a giant centipede with the head of a ghost wizard spewing out acid. He's a plain and simple fly, a little piece of paradise, and I'm sad to see him spring off when I raise my arm for a closer look.

I follow his swerving, crisscross course as if he's Will leading me through the Suckyverse—with about as much chance of catching up. He leads me up a hill where the trees and brush start to thin. Instead of shafts of sunlight dappling the forest floor, falls of bright-ness cascade down through the sparser overgrowth.

When at last I emerge from the treeline at the edge of a grassy clearing, I bask and stretch in the undiluted warmth and light. My neon red hair curls and glows brighter; the light of *any* sun—blue, brown, speckled pink and green, goat's head, lollipop, cat's eye—will give it a boost...but guess what, *yellow* gives it a downright *orgasm.*

As my eyes adjust to the light, I scan the space before me—the size of a baseball diamond, encircled mostly by trees, open at the far end. There, in the distance, I glimpse something—a peak? A steeple? Something that *might* be manmade (*Will*-made), though I can't tell for sure from here.

Starting forward through the knee-high grass, I wonder what sign or signal Will has left for me this time. It's always something different.

Two realms ago, for instance, in the world of the whalephants' graveyard, he left a giant ossuary of porcelain whalephant bone with his message spelled out in massive rills of tusk and horn. It was a marvel (how did he *do* that?) and most importantly, it stood the test of time.

Because it *had* to. Because I didn't get to *see* it for a *thousand years* after it was built.

That's the whole problem with our travel—the *curse* of it. Will and I are forever out of sync.

Ten thousand realms (or more) ago, I stumbled at the first gateway, so we left our starting point seconds apart. In the Suckyverse, however, seconds can add up to years, decades, centuries, or more, depending on your destination.

So I've been chasing him ever since, constantly trying to catch up with him. And every time I follow his trail to another realm, he's already gone from it. He *has* to be. He's not immortal; if he waited around in one place, and I didn't come through the gateway for a hundred years or more, he'd be dead before I got there.

And so our only shot at a reunion is *this*: to keep running. To keep the faith. To hope that next time, maybe *next time*, the lag between his arrival and mine will only be hours or days instead of decades.

The soft grass brushes my legs as I stride through the clearing, eyes trained on what I keep hoping is a Will-made point up ahead. I'm distracted only briefly by a butterfly—*a butterfly!*—as it swirls past on lacy wings of black and umber. I grin and clap my hands like a child as it dances away on the warm breeze, tangibly unremarkable and all the more amazing because of it.

I just hope, if a simple butterfly can make me this giddy, that I don't freak out *too much* when I get to whatever beckons over yonder.

Mission accomplished. As I close in, and the object comes into focus, I'm too totally stunned to giggle. Halfway there, in fact, I stop and stare. My right hand twitches involuntarily, just about making the sign of the cross in pious wonder.

"Will." I whisper the word like a fanatic. He's not there, of course—but he *was*.

And to me, given our synchronization issues, that's the next best thing to a solid week of lovemaking.

The initial shock fades, and I hurry toward it—toward the prize I know he left for me. The priceless, beautiful *treasure* he somehow conjured on the spot.

The ladder.

I'm hesitant to touch it at first, and not because it looks rickety enough to collapse under the weight of a harsh word. Not because it looks gnarled and spindly as an old crone's bones, barely wound together by garlands of frilly flowers.

The truth is, that's exactly how it looked back then, on that mountain in Nepal, and Will and I climbed it anyway. We climbed it during a grand astrological alignment, chanting from mystic Tibetan, Mayan, Celtic, Egyptian, and Indian scrolls, bodies painted with charms and balms and sigils out of a dozen arcane texts dearly come by.

When his foot left the top rung, he was gone like a whispered word. After the briefest, fateful stumble, so was I.

Many worlds and much time later, my hand snakes out and touches the knobby wood, the pale flowers. *Perfect. No portal into the Suckyverse on top, but otherwise no difference. It could be the original item, for all I know.*

Though seeing it makes me doubt that I've come home. There's no way this place is Nepal. More likely it's some other realm, and the ladder's just a copy.

But why go to the trouble of putting it here? It's a symbol of our separation, not our love, after all.

If Will had wanted to remind me of good times, he could have recreated any of a slew of other gateways—the minor portals he took me through during training jaunts before the big leap into the Suckyverse. That altar deep in the jungle of Guyana, for example, that shot us into a world of feathered leopards with gods for claws.

Or the cave pool on the distant island of Tristan da Cunha that took us to a kingdom of surreal faceless weirdos in the gut of a giant frog. Or the hole under the floorboards in the cabin in Alaska that sent us into a land where every dream takes on a life of its own.

Those were the best of times for me, not *these*. Back when Will was someone I'd met in pagan circles, someone who could take me far from the ugly little black magic sex ring I'd gotten mixed up in—though just *how* far, I never imagined. Then the *wonder* of it as he taught me how to find and open the doorways on my own...and the joy of traveling by his side, of opening the love between us as we opened uncharted worlds and dreamed of frontiers grander still. The intensity of those secret adventures that we shared forged an unbreakable bond between us unlike any I've ever known.

So why *this* as a message? And for that matter...why *that?*

Fifty feet beyond the ladder, there's a door—an actual, free-standing red *door* with knob and hinges in a white frame—obscured until now by its angle along the scalloped treeline.

"What the hell?" Eyes narrowed, I head for it. It's been a while since he's left me a *puzzle* message to figure out.

As I get closer, I reach out with all my senses, feeling around for an actual portal or rift, which would figure. Finding nothing of the sort, I'm left to wonder—why is this here? Unlike the ladder, it's not at all familiar.

Again, I hesitate to touch it. And I almost let go when my fingers wrap around the cool brass doorknob—because something *happens*.

The second I take hold of that doorknob, I hear distant *music*...not music like the singing of conflicted dragon-virgins or the humming of pixie pistols at 20 fluttering paces or the strumming of every sphere and sinew in a one-man universe.

More like the music of *home*. Music to my *ears*.

The music of the rock band *Heart*, after all these years.

"Holy shit." I push the door open and step through. There's no magic portal involved, I could just walk around...but this seems more in the spirit of things.

On the other side, I follow the music to the crest of a hill. Looking down, I see one of the oddest sights I've come across in all the realms—not a castle or dragon's lair or village but a kind of triangular *strip mall* in a field.

The mall has colorful storefronts on all three sides, facing outward, and a big white gazebo in a courtyard in the middle. It's like something I might see at home...except there's no parking, just green grass swaying all around.

Intrigued, I start down the hill. "What's the deal here, Will?" It's the first time he's left me a strip mall, and I'm dying to find out why.

I reach the bottom and jog across the field. Squinting with all my forward-facing eyes, I make out more details—and excitement kicks in.

My jog becomes a run, and the music gets louder. "Dog and Butterfly" is one of my favorites.

I recognize those storefronts.

Single-minded as a guided missile, I race toward them. The colors and signage are intimately familiar, though I haven't seen any such places since entering the Suckyverse.

The first one I head for is the coffee place. Its mermaid emblem beams at me from a glowing disk in the window, framed by deep green sills and awnings.

I jump up and down in front of the place and laugh out loud. It's a *perfect* replica of a place I *love*.

Then I go for the door, which thank God isn't locked.

Inside, it looks just like the one on my block back home—low lighting, comfy chairs, magazine-strewn tables. It *smells* the same, too, the air rich with brewed coffee and steamed milk...though there isn't a soul in sight.

Could it be?

Eyes wide (all of them), I rush to the counter. There are paper cups, lidded, at the pickup station (all ventis), and all have the same thing scrawled on the side in black marker:

Mia.

I grab one like it's trying to get away...and it is *hot*. Best of all, it smells like coffee—and something else.

I raise the cup to my nose, close my eyes, and inhale deeply. Is that...could it be...?

"Oh, yes!" I take a sip without further delay. The hot liquid rolls into my mouth, sending every (enhanced) taste bud singing its own variation on the *Hallelujah Chorus*. Because *yes,* that's *caramel* in there.

And that's my favorite hot beverage of all time, a *caramel macchiato.*

That first taste tells me everything I need to know. There's no poison in the cup, no drug or curse—just rich, bitter coffee, foamy cream, sweet vanilla, and buttery caramel.

It's perfect, just like I remember. It doesn't even suck a little, unlike most of the shitty grogs, sour wines, spoiled milks, and drain cleaner moonshines I've come across in hopping between realms.

"Thank you!" Of course Will can't hear me, he's gone, but I say it anyway. "Thank you so much, Will! This is *great!*"

Whatever this realm is, it just keeps getting better. It might not be home, but it's home's greatest hits...and I'm not done exploring yet.

Cradling the macchiato in both hands, I leave the coffee shop and turn right. My heart's pounding, because I remember what storefront is there.

If it's anything like the coffee shop, I have a real treat in store for me.

Looking at the front window, I get a good feeling. The trim and signage are mostly bright red with glittering gilt flourishes and lettering, just like my favorite restaurant back home.

Bhagavad Eat-a. Just the name makes me smile. Now if only there's something inside that makes me smile even more.

Bingo! When I open the door (bell jingling) and walk in, I see a table in the middle of the dining room covered with plates of steaming food. There's even a place card with my name on it in front of the single chair: *Mia.*

As soon as I see that spread, my stomach growls. How long has it been since I've had Indian food?

Too freakin' long.

As in the coffee shop, there isn't another person in sight—and I couldn't care less. The smell of Indian spices drives me crazy. The sight of my favorite dish—chicken tikka masala—strips away my self-control.

"Oh, Will." I put down the caramel macchiato and sit at the

loaded table. "This looks heavenly." Gingerly, I sniff at the chicken, magically testing for contaminants. I do the same for the dosa, naan, mango lassi drink, and gulab jamun dessert.

Then, I nod. Calmly pick up a fork.

And attack what's on the table like a mongoose going after a live cobra salad.

By the time I'm done, there's hardly a crumb left on the table. I lean back in the chair, patting my stomach and smiling with woozy satisfaction.

"You've outdone yourself, Will." I wish he could hear the compliment. "That was the best meal I've had since *ever.*"

Overall, this is the best *message* since ever—though I find myself wondering why it's so different from all the rest I've seen. When it comes to this puzzle, I don't feel like I'm seeing the whole picture.

So I guess I ought to keep opening doors until I do.

Leaving Bhagavad Eat-a, I wander around the corner to the next storefront, which happens to be a recreation of my all-time favorite gelato shop, Spumoni-Free Zone.

Like the version back home, the color scheme here is red, white, and green. Like the first two places in the strip mall, it's deserted...but stocked with goodies for yours truly.

The display case is full of colorful gelatos, brightly lit—and a triple-scoop dish of my favorite, *zabaione,* on the counter with my name on it.

I'm pretty full, but there's no way I'll turn my nose up at that *zabaione.* Like the macchiato and Indian food, I haven't had it since leaving home.

I take it with me as I tour the rest of the mall, excavating the sweet, pale cream with a tiny blue plastic gelato spoon. Each bite is more heavenly than the last.

The rest of the tenants of the strip mall are like that too, for me: heavenly. One after another, I gape at storefronts out of my past—my favorite pizza place, clothing shop, shoe store, bookstore, bar, and more. All of them are just as I remember, perfect in every detail...except one.

There's not another human soul in sight.

I see birds, rabbits, and squirrels here and there—all outside—

but no people. As for a message, I guess it should be obvious: this is all a gesture of love from him to me...but something seems off.

By the time I get to a bubble tea shop, and a cold cup of my favorite flavor (taro) is waiting with my name on it, I'm full-on questioning the miracle. The Suckyverse is lousy with magic, and Will's a master of employing it in elaborate romantic gestures...but I can't imagine how he rigged this place to work like it does. It's a *masterpiece*.

How long did it take to set it all up? How the hell long was he *here*, anyway, before moving on?

Maybe I can get a clue from his escape route. Sometimes, reading the magical energy of a gateway can tell you things, like how long ago it was last used.

Closing my eyes, I reach out with my mind like he taught me, feeling for a portal to the next place. I probe far and wide, extending my magically enhanced senses in all directions, groping for a doorway.

And I find nothing.

My eyes snap open. There are no words for the level of shock I feel.

That can't be right.

I try again, focusing harder. Again, I find nothing. Even the gateway that brought me here has gone dark.

"Oh my God." My heart slams like a wrecking ball in my chest. "*There's no way out.*"

It doesn't seem possible. The one good thing about the Suckyverse is that there's *always* a way out—*more* than one, usually. If you don't like the current realm, maybe the next one will be better (though more often than not, it's *worse*). I've never even *heard* of a dead end realm.

It doesn't seem natural. So maybe, I realize, it *isn't*. Maybe it's a...

Suddenly, the sky goes dark. There's no twilight, no gradual transition; it's as if a switch has been flipped. One minute, it's bright blue and sunny, and the next, it's starry and black.

Just as suddenly, my blood turns cold. I think I've solved the puzzle.

The pieces fit. *This* is why there's been no actual message from Will. *This* is why a parade of my favorite things has been trotted out before me. *This* is why all the exits have been shut, if ever they were open to begin with.

"It's a *trap*." Even possessing the power to warm myself from within, I shiver against the icy truth of it. "A trap for *me*."

But set by whom? And to what end?

I call up the magic within me, putting my altered body into a battle configuration. My tough marbled skin sprouts spines, and my glowing red hair bursts into flame. My breath catches fire, too, and my eyes flash with searing red laser-like light. My right arm becomes a razor-sharp scythe, and my left arm transforms into a shield.

Whoever's coming to get me, *let them try. Half* my enhancements won't even be *visible* to an enemy until it's *too late.* How the hell do you think I've survived the Suckyverse all this time?

"Who are you?" I howl at the heavens as I storm around the storefronts. All at once, they light up from within. "What do you *want* from me?"

The wind picks up. Heart keeps playing; it's "Barracuda" now. Otherwise, I get no reply.

My mind races, straining to fill in the blanks. Other that Will, who or what could *do* all this? Construct these elaborate replicas of places back home, complete with food, drink, and merchandise customized to suit me? It must have taken some masterful conjuring, to say the least.

Not to mention, it took some intimate knowledge of *me.* Whoever did this knew enough about my favorite things and places to create a virtual paradise with my name on it, literally. Did they read my mind when I got here? Or did the information come from *someone else?*

Just then, it hits me. Maybe there's a reason Will didn't leave me a message on his way out. After all, there's *no way out.*

"He's here, isn't he?" The words burst from me like the searing red beams I shoot from my eyes to slash at the sky for impact. "You *took* him!"

The ground rumbles under my feet. Whoever did this, are they *coming?* Am I finally drawing them out?

"Where *is* he? What have you *done* with him?" Wondering where to look for Will, I remember the view from the top of the hill—the gazebo in the central courtyard of the strip mall.

I'll need to go through one of the shops to get there, so I open the nearest door and march inside, flaming tresses singeing the casement on the way. I find myself in a copy of my favorite sushi bar back home—Life Rolls—but I sweep past the trays of tender morsels without missing a step. I'm through the back door in nothing flat...and then I freeze.

Between me and the gazebo, the grassy central courtyard is studded with gray tubes of varying size. Some are inches in diameter, some a foot or more, and all are stuck in the ground, pointing straight up.

The tubes are connected by a network of lines laid out on the ground between them. I wonder if I might trip something by walking over it—but if Will's in the gazebo, do I have another choice?

"Will?" I call out across the courtyard, and no one answers. Maybe the music's too loud; it's coming from speakers arrayed around the roof of the gazebo, hung just under the overhang.

"Will?" I amplify my voice by magical means and try again, making it roar and echo in the space...but still, there's no reply.

It's then that I have a terrible thought. What if the reason he's not answering is because he *can't?* Perhaps they've silenced him...or worse. Maybe they did away with him after getting the information to turn this realm into a trap for me.

I circle the courtyard, staying clear of the network on the ground. *"Will!"* I'm so wired, I'm breathing fire with each new cry, lashing the night with tongues of flame as blazing hot as the magically-juiced adrenaline surging through my arteries.

I should have been more careful. Suddenly, the ground shakes harder, and I stumble. My latest fiery exhalation lances downward, stabbing at the grass...and the edge of the network of lines.

What happens next comes too fast to stop. The nearest line catches, and a hot spark shoots along it like a fiery molten bead. Where the line intersects other lines, the spark divides and leaps along them in parallel, sizzling toward still other strands in the network.

Sparks race up and into some of the tubes, and they burst to life, ejecting fast-moving projectiles straight into the sky. There's a shuddering *boom*, then another, and I raise my shield high, expecting shrapnel.

This must be it, the other shoe dropping. Appearances can be deceiving in the Suckyverse, and this must be the war zone on the flipside of paradise.

More of the tubes blow, and projectiles boom overhead. I grit my teeth and swing my scythe, ready to repel every threat.

"Come on, then!" I wail. "Do your worst! You won't take *me!*"

It's then that I see the sky erupt in a shower of flickering gold sparkles, followed by a blossom of red.

"What the hell?" I lower my shield a little and gape with wonder.

How many explosions and lightshows have I seen throughout the Suckyverse, all of them ominous or calamitous in some way or another? Yet how often have I seen one like *this* since leaving home? How often have I seen honest-to-God, ooh-and-ah *fireworks* since I followed Will up that ladder?

The answer is *never*.

But what if the fireworks are weaponized somehow, meant to rain down destruction on me? The answer to *that* question, and so many more, becomes very clear when the next big shell takes to the air. There's a loud *thump* as it launches, then a *whoosh* as it shimmies into the heights—and the biggest *boom* yet as it explodes.

This time, the burst of light is red and shaped like a giant heart with words burning in the center of it.

I love you, Mia.

I can't believe my eyes. It's the *message*, the one I've been *waiting for*. "Will?"

The heart fades as another shell blazes to life in its place—more words, written across the sky in twinkling yellow letters.

I'm right here, Mia.

Again, the words fade and are replaced by another firework:

We're finally together
(And another firework after that.)
After all this time.

Just then, the ground stops rumbling. "Magic Man" plays over the speakers in the gazebo. My doubts and suspicions falter and fade like embers on the night wind.

"I don't understand." My shield comes down all the way, and I step forward, calling out to him. "Where *are* you?"

More booms, more words in the sky: *When I got here, this place was a blank.*

And a dead end.
The door that let me in
Was one-way only,
So no way out.

More booms, more words: *What to do?*
I knew you'd follow me here someday,
But I might die of old age
In the meantime.
I wanted us to be together,
But how to stay alive until then?

The words keep coming: *Finally realized*
I could JOIN with this blank place,
Become AGELESS,
And REMAKE it
Just for US.
Now, this place is...

The biggest shell yet booms like a thunderclap, and the biggest, brightest word emblazons the starry sky: *...ME!*

I look around in wonder. Lights dance in the stores of the strip mall. Deer emerge from back doors into the courtyard, joined by rabbits and squirrels. Chirping songbirds glide in and roost on the gazebo.

Meanwhile, the fireworks continue:
I waited so long.
CENTURIES?
MILLENNIA?
Now I'm so HAPPY

You're here.

I stand down, relaxing my battle stance. My scythe and shield become my arms again. I stop breathing fire, and my hair stops burning.

So this is what happened to Will? A *man* became a *place?* And the *place* became...my *home?*

How do I feel about that?

Again, he speaks through fireworks:

Can you still LOVE me?

Now that I'm a PLACE?

Now that I'm a WORLD?

I think for a moment, letting it all settle in. This isn't what I *hoped* for, is it? This isn't what I *dreamed* of.

All this time, across ten thousand realms (and more), the vision of our eventual reunion sustained me. The thought of his loving arms around me, of kisses and lovemaking *epic* in nature.

Is it enough, now, to find him so changed, so present yet so *unreachable* in the ways I've longed for? Can I accept a *life* and a *love* with so much *strange* and *missing?*

Even as I think it, I laugh to myself. *Seriously?* When was the last time my life or love was anything *but* that way?

Smiling, I spread my arms wide. "You have *always* been my world," I tell him. "My place has *always* been with you."

Fireworks flurry in the sky, red and blue and yellow and green: *I was hoping you'd say that.*

The sun rises suddenly, and the wind becomes a soft breeze. A familiar doe walks up and licks my hand. Hummingbirds circle around me, tiny wings beating and blurring.

Somehow, I feel Will all around me, his life force emanating from the sky and land and water like an element. Though no human body contains him, he is *here*, his love exuding from every animate and inanimate thing.

I will never be without him again, and *he* will never be without *me*.

Finally, at the end of the road, I've found a place I don't want to leave. It turns out there's *one* realm in all the Suckyverse that *doesn't* suck.

GRANTED

So the next thing I know, I'm totally going ballistic, throwing over the table and screaming my lungs out in the middle of the Midnight Diner. My best bud Goldie is right there, holding me back, which is good for *them*, good for the Wishies I'm going off on...same A-holes who just had the capital-B *Balls* to *intervention* me for *crossing the line*.

And I'm cursing like a nut, and Goldie's dragging me out the door, getting me *away* from these people. And they should consider themselves *lucky* and not *push it*.

But Big Daddy Scarlip goes and does it anyhow, which is why I suddenly break Goldie's grip and charge over and pop him one in his smug-ass face. Teenage fist meets middle-aged kisser, *ka-pow*.

Because this. Because "Nil," he says. "Nil, you're *nobody* and *nothing*. Accept it like the rest of us and move on, or you'll be sorry."

Now who's sorry? The one with the busted nose, *that's* who!

Feels so good I got another in the chamber before Goldie drags me outta there for good this time and hauls me down the street into the Pittsburgh night.

We're two blocks away when I finally snap my arm away from Goldie.

"You're welcome, by the way," he says, scrubbing his fingers through his shoulder-length, tiger-striped hair. "I got you outta there before you did something you'd *really* regret."

I straighten the sleeve of my dark brown beat-to-hell leather jacket from the Salvation Army. "Impossible." I'm still buzzing with rage like a bag full of bees. "Those clowns had it coming."

"Sure they did." Goldie pulls out an e-cigarette and takes a drag on it. "None of their business *what* you do."

I kick over a trash can on the curb, sending its contents sloshing to the street with a satisfying *splat*.

"But hey." Goldie stops walking and squares off with me, chest to chest. "Just so you're sure about this. About finding the guy or whoever."

I've never been more sure in my life. "Why *wouldn't* I be?"

"Just saying." Goldie shrugs. "What if he's some kind of *dick* or something?"

I see myself in a darkened shop window--short black hair, dark eyes, and a wiry body in leather jacket and jeans. "Then it is what it is."

"Sometimes we might be better off not knowing, is all."

"That's how *you* feel, maybe."

Goldie offers me his e-cig. "I've made peace with it, bro."

"Screw that." I take the e-cig. "There's nothing I want more than to know which A-hole wished me to life. And *no one*--not the shit-eating Wishies or *no one*--is gonna keep me from finding out."

"But then what?" asks Goldie as he takes back the e-cig. "Live happily ever after?"

I snort-laugh and cuff his upper arm. "Good one, Goldie," I tell him. "Best one I heard all day."

It takes a while to come down from all that anger. Goldie gets it; he knows that's just how I am, poor son of a bitch...though tonight's been pretty epic, even for me.

I don't say a word as we walk across town to the place we rent in Wilkinsburg. The rage still has a hold of me, though I know, even as I can't let go of it, just how self-destructive it is.

So why am I so pissed off all the time? Well, I'll bet *you'd* be, too, if you were just someone brought to life because of a wish and tossed aside like a used cigarette butt.

That's exactly how it happens, too. Some dope finds a genie or a four-leaf clover or wishing well or whatever and wishes for someone out of a fantasy. Then the novelty wears off, and/or the wished-up person gets to be more trouble than they're worth. Then what?

Then *me*, that's what. The unwanted wish gets kicked to the curb, and *no one* comes by to take care of it or even just get rid of it.

But at least some of us, like me and Goldie, have each other. Though I guess maybe he cares more about me than I do about him...a *lot* more.

"You ready?" Goldie's the one who finally breaks the silence. He does it as he unlocks the door and starts up the stairs to our fourth-floor studio apartment. "Ready for tomorrow?"

"Hell to the yes, I'm ready." My guts churn as I follow him up. I'm still like *this close* to going off again.

Goldie flips a switch at the top of the stairs, and the apartment lights up. It ain't much; good luck getting a nice place in this town when you're 16-17 years old and don't officially exist.

But it's home. Stolen posters cover the cracks (and fist-holes) in the plaster. Mismatched lawn furniture's patched up with duct tape. Mattress in the corner's out of a dumpster but bug-free and big enough for two. Good enough.

Though it's not like we couldn't do better. Got a coffee can full of dollar bills in the kitchenette cupboard, scraped together the hard way--but they're for something other than furniture or fix-ups.

And they won't be here much longer. Tomorrow morning, I'm gonna spend every last one of them.

That's when we're going to see *him*.

Yawning, Goldie pulls off his gray hoodie sweatshirt and tosses it on the floor. He's wearing a plain white t-shirt underneath. "So you're not nervous? Not even a little?"

The questions are pissing me off, but I keep a lid on. Makes you wonder, is there anything that *doesn't* piss me off?

The answer (duh, no!) has always made me wonder about one other thing. It's partly why I'm so dead-set on going tomorrow, to answer this one effing question.

"Of course I'm not nervous." I walk straight to the kitchenette and pull out the coffee can full of singles. "This is gonna be great."

"So what's the first thing you're gonna ask him?"

"The Wisherman?" I shrug and start pulling bills from the can. "Who in their right mind would wish for someone as effed-up as I am?"

There it is. That's the question. The one I've been asking for as long as I can remember, which is one-and-a-half years. That's how old I actually am, though I look like I'm 16 or 17; I was wished into being one-and-a-half years ago, brought to life as a full-blown teenager.

"Seriously, right?" I wave fistfuls of cash and laugh out loud for the first time all day. "*Who* would wish for *me?*"

Next morning, we ride the bus up to the top of Mount Washington, overlooking the city. My heart's hammering in my chest like a caged animal fighting to get out...but for once, it's all because of nerves, not rage.

Because who knows if the Wisherman will come through? I've heard good things, but what if he can't or won't help me? He's the only hope I have, for real. If he doesn't come through, it's the end of the road.

Then what? Explode in a ball of rage? Fall apart in a crash of despair?

I dread the possibilities. But eff me if I'm gonna let it show.

"This is gonna *rock.*" I say it with all the conviction I don't really feel, as Goldie and I get off the bus and walk up the street in the bright morning sun. "I can't *wait.*"

The Wisherman is rich. His place, a gleaming cylindrical tower with mirrored windows all around, perches on some of the primest real estate in Pittsburgh. Might as well be up on a cloud bank, it's got that good a view of the city.

Goldie and I walk up to his frosted glass front door, and it glides open at our approach.

"Electric eye?" asks Goldie, looking around as he says it. "Magic spell?"

I shrug. In a world where wishes can take on a life of their own, either one could be equally likely.

Walking through the doorway, we enter a gleaming white room that smells like roses and mint and doesn't have a single stick of furniture. Double doors slide open on the opposite wall, revealing an elevator car that's just as empty.

The second we step in, the elevator starts moving. There aren't any indicator lights on the walls to tell us which floor we're on...but we hear three dings, and then the elevator stops.

The doors open, and we hear a deep voice booming with an Indian accent. "Early! You're early! Good for you!"

Suddenly, a huge man with a mane of springy black dreadlocks and skin the color of potato peels leaps into the car and grabs hold of our left arms. Before either of us can react, he's hauling us out of the elevator into a big round room filled with sunlight and white fur-covered couches.

"Welcome welcome welcome!" He spins us around, sending us stumbling toward the nearest couch. He's wearing a white kaftan and draped in gold jewelry--necklaces, bangles, earrings--which jangles and clinks as he takes three dancelike steps after us. "Which one of you is Nil?"

"Right here." I stop myself from dropping onto the couch and raise my right hand. Goldie, meanwhile, flops onto the white-furred cushions with a loud *poof.*

"Wonderful!" The dreadlocked man holds out a hand, palm up, and raises his thick, dark eyebrows. "I am the Wisherman, of course." Grinning with a mouth full of gold teeth, he takes a little bow. "So where's the sugar you brought me?"

I pull out the roll of dollar bills stuffed in the front pocket of my jeans and hand it over. Grinning, he counts them out on the spot, pausing once in a while to hold a single up to the light.

"Most excellent!" he says at last, pushing the dollars down into a pocket of his kaftan. "So you said on the phone that you don't remember a thing? About your wisher?"

"That's right," I tell him. "The wisher wasn't around when I was born. I mean when I *appeared*."

The Wisherman frowns a little. "That is unusual." He steps toward me and gazes deeply into my eyes. "And yet, you most certainly *are* the product of a wish. This, I can clearly see."

No shit, Sherlock, I almost say, but keep it to myself for once in my life. Being a Wishies is like being gay; you just *know*. So do other Wishies, who can spot you a mile away.

"I have never met a Wishie I could not help." The Wisherman reaches toward me, smiling reassuringly. "Now here. This won't hurt a bit."

Suddenly serious, he grabs both my hands and squeezes them hard. His eyes instantly roll up in their sockets, leaving me to stare at the bloodshot whites.

His lips quiver as he mutters something incomprehensible under his breath, and his thick fingers massage my hands like bread dough. I wait, expecting to feel something different--*hoping* to feel something different--but no mystic spark comes.

After a long moment, I start to drift. Nothing's happening, and I find myself staring at the closest section of window wall. I'm too far back to see the city sprawling below, but there's a cloud, and then a bird--a hawk? a falcon?--floating in eyeshot across the bright blue sky outside.

Then, suddenly, the Wisherman tightens his grip so hard, it hurts. His muttering gets louder, and his jewelry clatters as he sways back and forth like a metronome.

My gut instinct is to lash out and break away, to blow my stack-- but I force myself to hold back. This could be my only chance at finding my wisher, and I'll be *damned* if I'm gonna let myself screw it up.

Finally, the Wisherman lets out a sharp cry, a whoop, and his eyes roll back down to meet my gaze. "Got 'em!" He lets go of my hands and pumps a fist in the air. "*Damn*, I'm good!"

"What do you mean, you got '*em*? Not just 'him' or 'her'?"

The Wisherman reaches over and tousles my hair. "Meant what I said, Nilsson." The Wisherman holds up three fingers, each wrapped in an ornate gold ring. "I got *three* strong readings today. Any one of them could be your wisher."

"*Three?*" I'm stupefied by this crazy-ass verdict. "You can't tell which one?"

"They are all equally good possibilities." The Wisherman shrugs, and his dreads bounce up and down on his broad shoulders. "It happens sometimes."

"But...but how do we tell *which one?*"

"The old-fashioned way, my friend." He claps his hands together once, then spreads his arms wide. "You go and *see* them. Consider their *reactions*, yes? That will tell the tale."

"*Seriously?*" Remember that rage of mine? It's starting up again, for real. "I paid all that *money*, and I don't even get a definite *answer?*"

"You could see it that way." The Wisherman folds his hands behind his back. "Or you could see it like this: you have three more solid leads than you had fifteen minutes ago."

My fuse is lit and blazing toward the bomb inside, about to go off all over this rip-off artist. Then, Goldie takes my arm and gives it a squeeze. Good old Goldie knows the score, knows I'm about to *pop*...when I really need to *stop*, because there's something I *forgot*. Something I can't leave here without, though it's not exactly what I expected.

"Excuse me," Goldie says to the Wisherman. "What are the names of the three possible wishers?"

The Wisherman's grin widens, and his gold teeth glitter. "I can write them down, if you like."

"That would be great," says Goldie, giving my arm a shake. "Wouldn't it?"

Where the hell would I be without Goldie? "Yep." I don't manage a smile, but at least I'm not going ballistic. "Totally great."

An hour later, I'm running full-tilt through the Strip District down in the city, trying like hell to catch up to the first person on the Wisherman's list.

Goldie's somewhere behind me, lost in the crowd, and I couldn't care less. The only thing on my mind is staying focused on the woman up ahead, who *swear to God* must be some kind of *track star* or something.

As always in the middle of the morning, the Strip is packed. Endless streams of shoppers flow along both sides of Smallman Street, the main drag of Pittsburgh's main market district. I'm shoving my way through them by force, even knocking some down here and there--but the woman I'm chasing just sprints gracefully through them, dodging and weaving like a gazelle through a herd of wildebeest.

Her long blonde ponytail whips and flaps behind her, swishing over her bright pink jogging suit. She was coming back from a run when she spotted us outside her nearby townhouse--then made a break for it and left us in the dust.

As if I'd ever give up after coming this far. As if I'd let her get away as long as there's a chance she's the one who wished me up.

Especially now that there seems to be a *better* chance. Because if she *didn't* recognize me as a Wishie she'd kicked to the curb, why did she run for the hills as soon as she *saw* me?

Her name, according to the Wisherman, is Leila Mihalick, and she's a local TV reporter. I already knew that, though. I recognize her from morning and weekend newscasts on the Pittsburgh Fox affiliate...an up-and-comer, not a star, but boy, can she run.

She bolts across the street a split-second before a line of cars pushes past, cutting me off. All I can do is keep running up the side I'm on, keeping her in sight, waiting for a break in traffic.

But distracted as I am, I take my eyes off the busy sidewalk up ahead just long enough for a worker to roll a tall rack of baked goods out of a shop in my path. I slam right into it, sending the rack crashing to the sidewalk, spilling muffins, pastries, and loaves of bread all over the place.

As I come down on top of it, the worker howls and curses with rage. He makes a grab for my arm, but I scramble out of the way and off the rack, quickly regaining my footing. Another grab flies my way, and I duck, pissing the guy off even more. He calls me names I've never heard before, and I *really* wanna get all up in his *grill*, show him who he's *messing* with...but I know I've gotta keep my eyes on the *prize*.

If I could *find* her, that is. By the time I start running back up the street again, I don't see any sign of her.

But I *do* see *Goldie* in action, sprinting up the opposite side of the street. Not only did he catch up when I fell, he passed me by; instead of stopping to help me, he had the nuts to keep on after the target.

The traffic gaps just enough to let me cross, and I do. This side of the street's not quite as crowded, so I step on it, hurtling in Goldie's wake though I still don't see Leila ahead of him.

Then I *do*. The pink track suit's almost a block ahead and pulling away, zipping past an open-air café. Doubling down, I run even harder, wishing with all my heart that I could catch her...even as I realize she might just get away for good.

But then, as she clears the café, Leila gets a shot of bad luck. A shoddy blue pickup charges out of an alley ahead of her and slams on the brakes, nearly crashing into a passing Jaguar. As the drivers hit the horns and start screaming, her route is blocked...only for a moment, but that's long enough for Goldie to go the distance.

Twenty feet away from her, he jolts to a stop. "Leila!" he says. "Leila, we need to talk to you!"

Instantly, Leila spins and snaps into a self-defense pose--feet planted, arms angled in front of her. "Leave me alone!" Her face is grim, her body coiled, about to lash out. "I changed my mind!"

As I skid to a stop beside Goldie, he raises his hands and shakes his head. "We just want to talk! Swear to God, we just want to talk!"

"You changed your mind about what?" I ask her.

Leila's frantic, like she might take off running again any second. Her eyes dart right and left, left and right...and then they come to rest on me. They're crazy wide, all bugged out, swimming in their sockets.

Then, she frowns. Her eyes narrow, and she takes a step toward me. "Wait." Another step, another. "You're not him." One more. "Oh my God, you're not him."

"Not who?" I ask her.

"*Him.*" She shakes her head slowly. "From a distance, I thought you were him...but you're not. You're not Abel."

"Who's Abel?" asks Goldie.

Leila hesitates. "My first love. My high school boyfriend." Her frown deepens. "This sounds crazy, but...I wished upon a star for him to come back to life. So I could apologize. And then I lost my nerve."

"Apologize for what?" I ask her.

Leila looks down at the cracked sidewalk. "For causing the car crash that killed him." When she looks up, there are tears in her eyes. "I couldn't do it. I couldn't face him."

Disappointed as I am that she's not my wisher, I can't help feeling sorry for her. Wishies can't make wishes that come true, but if I could, I'd make one for her. I almost wish I was her Abel right now, so I could tell her I forgive her and let her get on with her life.

"So who *are* you people, anyway?" she asks. "Why were you *chasing* me?"

"We, uh..." My mind races, seeking a believable excuse. "We wanted to get your autograph."

"You're our favorite newswoman," chimes in Goldie.

"When we spotted you, we made a bet which of us would get your autograph first." I pull a wrinkled-up piece of paper and a pen from my back pocket. "I don't suppose...?"

"Seriously?" She shakes her head. "You're lucky I'm not calling the cops on you."

"Okay then." I stuff the paper and pen back in my pocket. "Thanks anyway."

"Word of advice," says Leila. "If you don't chase a person down like a couple of crazed stalkers, you'll be more likely to get her autograph." Without another word, she charges away from us, arms and legs churning as she sprints back up the street.

Hours later, we walk into a bar in the Cultural District, on Liberty Avenue--and find ourselves stared at from the murky shadows by all kinds and colors of eyes.

The place is called Fulfillment, and it's a Wishie bar--but not just *any* Wishie bar. This one is a hangout for Wishies who can't easily pass for everyday people...the ones who aren't lucky like Goldie and me, who can't blend in and go about their business without raising eyebrows, or worse.

It's amazing what some folks will wish for. I see a tiny frog-headed person, six inches tall, standing on a barstool, sipping beer through an angled-down straw.

Over there's a big brass robot with a tuba for a head and fuzzy pink oven mitts and slippers. In a dark corner booth, I see a cross between an angel and a unicorn talking to twin Siamese cat people drinking red wine, their ruby-studded collars glowing faintly.

You might call it a freak show, though every Wishie's a freak of nature when you get right down to it. None of us was meant to be in this world, were we? And looking "normal," like I do, sure doesn't mean it's any easier to assimilate, does it?

"Hey!" Just then, the bartender (a "normal"-looking human with thick, dark hair and a bushy mustache) calls out to us. "Let's see some I.D." He leans closer, sizing us up. "Or do you two only *look* like teenagers?"

He has a point. For all he knows, we might be hundreds of years old...but it doesn't matter. "It's cool," I tell him. "We're just here looking for someone."

"*Not* cool." The bartender slaps the bar with his big, beefy hand. "Maybe you don't understand the *concept* of a *safe haven?* Because that's what this place *is.*"

"We're Wishies, too." I step up to the bar and lock eyes with him. "So yeah, we get it."

The bartender's dark eyes narrow as he gazes deep into mine, taking my measure--then snorts and leans back. "It doesn't matter *what* you are. *Safe.*" He smacks the bar again. "*Haven.*" And again.

"Please." I lower my voice. "The Wisherman sent me."

Boom, the bartender's whole attitude changes. His eyebrows lift, and he sounds surprised. "You're full of shit."

423

I shake my head. "For real. He sent me to meet someone here. One of your regulars."

"Why?" The bartender slides his gaze along the bar, taking in the motley group lined up there. "Which one?"

"Which one is somebody called Samson," I tell him. "'Why' is between me and him."

"Him?" The bartender snorts. "Not exactly."

With that, he turns and gestures at a booth along the wall. I see an elderly woman sitting there with her head down, alone, nursing a glass of white wine.

"Name is *Mrs.* Samson." The bartender leans toward me, dropping his voice. "She's not a Wishie. More like a Wishie hag."

"Right." Wishie hags are like groupies. They hang around Wishies because they get off on the weirdness or hope the magic rubs off or something. I've met a few in my time, though none as old as this one. "Thanks."

If I had any cash, I'd put some on the bar to pay for the info, but I'm broke after paying the Wisherman. Instead, I just nod and head for the Wishie hag's table.

"Mrs. Samson?"

The old woman squints up at me. "Yes?"

"I was just wondering." I sit down across from her, and Goldie stays standing. "Have you made a wish recently?"

Mrs. Samson squints harder, pulling the web of wrinkles on her face tighter. Then, she shakes her head slowly. "You're not him."

"Him who?" I ask her.

Her hand shakes as she takes a sip of wine, then puts down the glass, which is almost empty. "My dream grandson," she says softly. "I'd know him anywhere, and you are definitely not him."

My heart sinks like a cinder block tossed in a lake. Two wishers down; that leaves me with just one more.

I want to jump up from the seat and run toward the last person on the Wisherman's list...but the old lady's still talking. Telling her story, though I really don't need any explanation.

"I never had children," she says. "My husband and I couldn't have them, and we never adopted.

"But I've never stopped dreaming about them. I had a perfect dream son and daughter...up here." She taps her right temple with one bony, quivering finger. "And one day, my dream daughter gave birth to my dream grandson."

I nod, getting more impatient with each passing moment. But I feel a little sorry for her, too...sitting alone in a Wishie bar, talking about the kids and grandson she never had.

"He was so *real* to me," says Mrs. Samson. "So smart and handsome and sweet." Her eyes sparkle as she smiles at the thought of him. "One day, when a salesman came to my door, selling wishes, I decided to buy one. And I used it to wish for my grandson to come to life. My darling *David*." Her shoulders lift with youthful excitement. "He'd be 17 years old today!"

"Seventeen, huh?"

Her smile fades. "But it's been a long time since I made that wish. It's been *weeks*. I don't think it's going to come true. I think I was flim-flammed." She sniffs, then dabs at her nose with a bar napkin. "I've been coming here because I thought maybe being around other wishes that came to life might give my own wish a boost...but nothing. I'm ready to give up hope."

I reach over and take her hand. "It'll be okay," I tell her, though I don't explain why. I don't tell her that if she showed up on the Wisherman's radar, it must mean her wish has some magic to it after all.

Her eyes tear up as she gapes at me with naked, desperate hope. "Do you really think so?"

"Yes." I squeeze her hand and smile. "I think there's still a chance that things will work out."

The late afternoon sun casts long shadows before Goldie and me as we follow a sidewalk to the front door of our last destination. It's a rundown little house in a bad section of Homestead--a single-story shack on a grassless lot surrounded by chain link fence. It's a few stops from the Cultural District on the Pittsburgh Metro, but it's a universe away from the upscale parts of downtown.

The place doesn't look so hot, but at least the front gate was open, and a pit bull doesn't charge out to get us when we set foot inside. Still, I'm nervous as we get closer to the door...though not so much because it's a rundown house in a sketchy neighborhood.

"What if this isn't my wisher, either?" I say to Goldie. "What if all this, everything, was a dead end, and I never find the person who wished me to life?"

"Then you move on," says Goldie. "At least you'll know you tried."

I swallow hard and put my foot on the first step. "Eff that. I wanna *know*." Taking a deep breath, I walk up the three creaky steps to the rickety porch. Flecks of peeling paint trickle down as my knuckles rap the wooden door three times.

Nothing happens, and I realize there's another possibility here. What if nobody's home? Do we wait around? Come back tomorrow?

What if they're gone for good? The Wisherman gave us this address, but what if his information was out of date?

"Try again," says Goldie.

I'd make a smartass remark, but I'm too nervous. Instead, I just knock three more times and wait.

Still nothing.

"Shit." I try one more time, knocking a little harder. When I get the same result, I turn and shake my head, ready to give up.

Which is exactly when I hear the door creak open.

"Hello?" A little voice squeaks out from inside. "Who's there?"

Whipping around, I see a little girl, maybe seven or eight years old, with stringy black hair. She holds the door open a few inches, just enough for me to see her dirty face.

And the instant she has a look at me, her eyes fly wide open. And I know. I don't know the details yet, but I *know*.

This is it.

"Oh my God!" she says. "You came for us! Oh my God!"

Suddenly, she flings the door open, charges out, and wraps her arms around me.

As we stand there like that, I feel her sobbing against my legs. Her embrace is so tight, it's like she's never going to let go.

"There you go, Nil." Goldie steps up beside me and drops a

426

hand on my shoulder. "Looks like we came to the right place after all."

"Hurry," says the little girl, pulling me through the doorway. "They'll be home soon!"

As we step inside the house, a blast of stench hits me like a speeding truck. The place stinks like cigarettes, rotten food, and raw sewage all mixed together, strong enough that it makes me gag.

Forcing down the urge to throw up, I take a look around, and I'm sick all over again. The living room is filled with garbage and debris. A little boy--maybe 3 or 4 years old--is pissing in a blue plastic bucket in the corner. Everywhere I look, I see every kind of filth I can think of, from mold-covered food to hairballs to poop on the ratty carpet.

I see crushed beer cans scattered around the room, and liquor bottles and ashtrays overflowing with butts and ashes. There's a fluorescent green glass bong overturned on the floor, and a used syringe on a stack of magazines.

Now *this* is a true *shithole*.

The little girl tugs my arm to get my attention. "Tommy told us about you," she tells me. "I can't believe you're really here."

"What's your name?" I ask her.

"Missy." The girl points at the boy with the bucket. "He's Stevie."

Stevie finishes pissing and instantly lights up when he looks my way. "Tommy!"

"Not Tommy," says Missy. "Tommy's dead."

"What do you mean?" I ask. "Who's Tommy?"

Stevie pulls up his pants and runs over to hug me. "I missed you! Tommy, I missed you!"

Missy gazes up at me. After all she must been through in her young life, her eyes still look bright and innocent somehow. "He was just like you. Exactly the same...almost."

"What do you mean, almost?" asks Goldie.

"He said you were going to be stronger," says Missy. "Tougher, because he was never tough enough to save us."

The little boy squeezes me tighter. "I love you, Tommy!"

"You said he's dead?" I ask Missy.

She nods. "He found a genie and wished for you...another *him*, but tough and scary enough to do what he never could. But then he got *killed* before he could make his next wish for you to come save us."

"Who killed him?" I ask.

"Mommy's boyfriend, Baggie," says the girl. "And Mommy was sad, but then she took her medicine and felt all better." Her voice breaks when she says the rest. "She even helped get rid of Tommy's body, which was smelling really bad."

I look at the syringe, then back at Goldie, and he just shakes his head sadly. Everything about this place makes my heart hurt.

"Where's Mommy now?" asks Goldie.

"Getting more medicine." Missy looks at the door like she expects it to blow open at any moment. "She'll be back real soon. So will Baggie."

"Tommy?" Stevie won't let go of me. "What're you gonna do now, Tommy?"

I see something move out of the corner of my eye, and I jerk my head to look. That's when I see the big cockroach skittering out from under a pile of underwear and fried chicken bones.

In that instant, my mind is made up. I know exactly what I'm going to do.

And when I look back at Goldie, I can see he totally agrees.

Though, to be fair, it's not like there was ever any doubt.

When we walk into the Midnight Diner, Big Daddy Scarlip is the first person to hug the kids. Such a pain-in-the-ass control freak blowhard, but apparently he doesn't hold a grudge over me popping him one that night.

None of the local Wishies holds a grudge, either, I guess. As soon as we reached out to them for help, they fell all over themselves to bring it.

How the eff do you like that?

Missy and Stevie get showered with attention, and they eat it up with a spoon. A day after escaping that shit-shack and the druggie Mommy and her boyfriend, they're like brand new kids. Cleaned up and dressed in new clothes (from the dollar store, but still), they look like they never had a bad day in their lives.

And goddammit, as I watch them laughing and goofing around, I feel the same fucking way.

When Missy looks at me and waves, I can't help grinning. When she mouths the words, "Thank you," I get a shiver of joy up my spine.

"Tommy!" And when Stevie calls me that, I feel so happy, I think I might float away on the spot. "Hey, Tommy!"

We don't have everything figured out yet, it's true. We've got plenty of complications, like you'd expect. But don't underestimate these Wishies; they're survivors (they *have* to be), and they've got resources that'll help us deal. They've got special ways of dealing with loose ends and moving forward in a world that was never made for nobodies like us. Working together, we'll provide for these kids and raise them up to be *somebodies* whether the world likes it or not.

And right now, as I stand here, smelling the coffee brewing and watching the kids have the time of their lives, I have a feeling it's all going to work out.

"That's my brother!" shouts Stevie. "My big brother, Tommy! And Uncle Goldie, too!"

As Stevie says it, Goldie walks in and throws his arm around my shoulders. Doesn't say a word; doesn't have to.

The rage is gone. I feel happy at last. This is all going to work out. But just in case...

"I love you." Missy mouths the words, and I cry a real tear for the first time in my life.

But just in case, though I know they say wishes can't come true for Wishies like me, I wish with all my heart and soul and everything I've got that the kids and me and Goldie will all live happily ever after.

TIME TRAVEL AMONG THE TASMANIAN TIGERS OF WEST VIRGINIA

At first, in the dark, grainy feed from the owl-cam, the creature looked like just another coyote prowling the West Virginia woods. It didn't pique Matt Mentiroso's interest; he paid more attention to the movie he was watching on the other laptop.

Then, a flurry of motion on the owl-cam screen caught his eye. The point of view suddenly swooped down toward the coyote; there was a blur of thrashing chaos, impossible to see clearly...and the view flashed away and back upward.

"Good job, Pliny." Matt felt a quick shot of relief as the video continued to glide between moonlit trees. The owl--and more importantly, the wireless mini-video camera attached to his right leg--had survived another nocturnal encounter. Home-based hobbyist researcher that 36-year-old Matt was these days, ever since The Incident, losing equipment like the owl-cam could be a major setback.

Still, as Matt tried to watch the movie again, something nagged at him. He kept thinking about that blurred whirl of motion, as if some detail too fast to process consciously had registered in his subconscious mind.

Turning back to the owl-cam laptop, he rewound and played

back the moments in question while the live feed kept recording. At normal speed, the action was still too blurry to make out anything between the owl's descent toward the coyote and his retreat up into the heights.

But going back through it again, advancing one frame at a time, told a different story.

Matt saw flashes of scruffy fur and jagged teeth, all pretty familiar. Then, as Pliny lifted away, the owl-cam caught a glimpse of the coyote's hindquarters, briefly visible in a patch of moonlight. It lasted for all of one frame, and even then was blurred by Pliny's motion...but it was just enough for Matt to spot a flicker of detail.

"What the hell?" Frowning, he leaned closer to the screen of the laptop. One big question pulsed in his head like a neon sign on a backwoods roadhouse.

He said it aloud, as if expecting an answer. "Since when do coyotes have striped back ends?"

Matt played with the image of the seemingly striped coyote, working to brighten and enhance the visual, without much luck. The owl-cam had been shooting in low-light mode, but the movement had blurred the frame too much. For all Matt could see, the coyote had a rank of horizontal stripes running along its lower back...or the stripes were no more than shadows cast by the moonlight as it shone through overhanging branches.

If the stripes weren't an optical illusion, how could they be real? Matt had never seen or heard of a coyote or dog with that particular kind of coloration.

Matt's next thought was that a zoo animal had gotten loose, or some private owner's exotic pet--but nothing had been posted online or mentioned in the local news about either one. So for now, he had nothing to go on except that frame of video.

When that failed to provide new insight, Matt gave up for the night. He would have to consult someone else about the case; he was an ornithologist, so his expertise was limited to birds.

Yawning and scrubbing his fingers through his thin brown hair, he pushed back from the old kitchen table, his makeshift worksta-tion. The owl-cam live feed would keep recording, but he was too tired to keep working. After all, this wasn't his livelihood anymore; he had to get up for his lousy day job in just a few hours.

"Goodnight, tiger coyote." He shut both laptops and headed for bed--a futon on the other side of his cramped cabin. "All done with you for now."

"Nope," said Retha Lawson the next morning, between bites of an enormous red apple. "Never heard of a striped coyote before." She was his best friend at work...his *only* friend at work, truth be told. She was also one of the smartest people he knew, which was really saying something.

Because back before The Incident, Matt had rubbed elbows with some pretty big brains. He hadn't *always* been a "picker" in a shipping warehouse fulfilling orders for an online retailer.

"So what do you think this is?" Matt handed her a color hard copy of the fateful frame from the owl-cam video.

Retha kept crunching the apple as she studied the photo. "Hmm." Her brown face scrunched in a thoughtful scowl. "Can't tell." She handed the photo back with a crisp flap.

Matt folded it up and returned it to his shirt pocket. "Can you think of anything that fits the description, at least?"

"Jackal, maybe?" Retha had a Master's Degree in zoology (though she'd dropped out of the field just before completing her PhD), so she knew what she was talking about when it came to animals. "There are a few striped antelopes--the bongo and kudu, for example--but I'd guess they're too big and horny."

"Horny?" Matt grinned.

"They have *horns*." Retha let out a big belly-laugh from the big belly under her bright red polo shirt. "The okapi doesn't, and it's a little smaller...but still. That thing doesn't look like an okapi to me."

Just then, the finder/scanner/timer device in the holster on Matt's belt started beeping, signaling the end of his 15-minute lunch break. Matt pulled the device (which he called "Adolph") out of its holster and switched off the beeper. "Thanks for the ideas, Retha. At least you've given me something to go on."

"No I haven't." Retha took one more bite out of the apple, which was three-quarters finished, and tossed the rest in the trash. "So are you sure your live feed hasn't been hacked?"

Matt frowned. "Why would anyone want to do that? It's just an owl-cam."

"And you're just Mark Mentiroso, famous former science phony," said Retha. "You really need to ask?"

Out in the warehouse, Matt hurried through the rest of his morning at the usual fever pitch. Prodded by Adolph, he filled order after order, grabbing a seemingly infinite variety of items from plastic tubs on the shelves.

This was what his life had come to since The Incident: dildos, diapers, DVDs, bedsheets, yoga mats. He ran from tub to tub--each filled with a seemingly random agglomeration of junk, supposedly positioned by sophisticated computer algorithm for maximum efficiency--and scooped up whatever Adolph demanded. Then, he sent the merchandise off to Shipping, hopefully before Adolph started beeping to let him know he was behind schedule.

After which, he moved on to the next item on Adolph's screen.

Most of the time, it felt like the only job he'd ever known...also a punishment for his sins during The Incident. Other times, like today, he didn't think about it at all. His mind was elsewhere, thinking about tiger coyotes instead of lipsticks or novelty bibs or athletic cups or Ben Wa balls.

The stripes had probably been an optical illusion; he knew that. Yet he still couldn't wait to get home and watch for some sign of the mystery animal on the latest feed from Pliny.

That evening, Matt watched owl-cam feed video on both laptops. On one, he fast-forwarded through the hours of Pliny's feed that he hadn't seen from the night before, the part that had recorded while he'd been sleeping. On the other, he watched the new video streaming in as Pliny grew more active in the gathering gloom of twilight.

Nibbling animal crackers from a jumbo-sized bag, Matt looked back and forth from one screen to the other, staying alert for anything unusual. Both views were much the same for quite a while--murky shots of spindly treetops seen from a lofty perch.

Then, suddenly, the live feed changed as Pliny left the perch. The view swung left, then right, soaring between trees--then punched through a gap between them, out into the open air.

As Pliny crossed a clearing, the shadowy murk brightened; clouds parted overhead, exposing the terrain to the beams of a full moon.

The view turned on its side as Pliny banked, circling the clearing. As Pliny spiraled around the center, Matt caught sight of something moving down below.

In the tall grass of the clearing, Matt saw what looked from a distance like the mystery animal of the night before. It stood stiffly, alert to its surroundings--and there, on its rump, were the familiar horizontal stripes.

Matt's pulse quickened as Pliny looped away from the animal. Just as the shot came around again, the animal ducked out of sight within a copse of trees.

"Damn!" Matt pounded the rickety kitchen table with his fist. "Go after him, Pliny!"

As if Pliny could hear him, the owl shot up above the copse and glided the breadth of it. Up ahead, Matt glimpsed the familiar outline of a rough-hewn wooden roof--his cabin, getting closer.

As Matt watched with wide-eyed fascination, the copse slid past, giving way to the cabin's back yard. There, in the short grass below, trotted the striped animal, heading toward the front porch.

"Holy shit!" Matt leaped up from his chair, knocking it over, and sprang toward the door. He bolted back to grab the animal cracker bag from the table, then dashed out onto the porch.

Thankfully, the clouds were still gone when he got there, and the yard was bathed in moonlight. Because there it was, thirty yards from the right-hand corner of the front porch. Matt was face to face with the animal he'd glimpsed in the blurred frame of video.

"Hello there," said Matt. At the sound of his voice, the animal's ears perked up. "Welcome."

From thirty yards away, the animal looked more like a cougar than a coyote. Its coat was short, not shaggy, and its ears were rounded, not pointy. Its snout was shorter than that of a coyote or wild dog, and its tail, which was canted downward at a 45 degree angle, was long and stiff and straight--perhaps half as long as its body.

It wasn't a coyote, he was sure of that now. On the other hand, that tail, and the striped rump, weren't typical of a cougar. So what *was* it? Matt needed a closer look.

"How about a cookie?" As he dug in the bag, the animal tipped its head, listening to the crinkling plastic. "Here you go."

Matt tossed out a handful of animal crackers, which scattered between ten and fifteen yards away. The creature eyed them suspiciously, then padded carefully toward them.

"Look." Matt popped one of the animal crackers in his mouth and chewed. "They're fine, they're safe."

The creature got to one of the animal crackers and sniffed it. Watching Matt for any wrong move, the creature lapped up one of the crackers and crunched it, exposing rows of sharp white teeth.

"Good." Matt smiled. "I'm glad you like them."

The creature came closer, lapping up another animal cracker and then another. Soon it was fewer than ten yards away, and Matt had his best view yet.

But he still didn't know what it was. It looked like something between a canine and a feline, yet not entirely either one.

"Have some more." Matt tossed out another handful of animal crackers. This time, they landed between seven and three yards away.

One at a time, the creature worked its way through the treats, getting closer, ever closer.

"Good boy," said Matt, though he had no idea what sex the creature might be. "Lots more where those came from." He dug out another handful and scattered them over the last few yards between the creature and the porch.

The creature gobbled them up in short order, licking its chops with its big, pink tongue. When it got to within two feet of Matt, it stopped and straightened, meeting his gaze.

Matt felt a chill up his spine, a quick thrill of fear that he might be on the verge of being attacked...but he pushed it down hard. Whatever this animal was, he didn't want anything to ruin the contact between them.

"What are you, boy?" he said. "Are there more of you around?"

As if in response, the animal tipped its head to one side and made a soft whining sound in its throat.

Matt grinned. "Whatever you are, I'm glad you dropped by."

Suddenly, a shadow passed over them both. Matt heard a flurry of wings from above and looked up.

He was just in time to see Pliny plunging out of the full moon, his wings folded back to streamline his dive.

"Pliny, no!" shouted Matt, but it was too late. The moment of contact was gone...and so was the creature.

Matt did a double-take. The animal had vanished.

Matt was so far off his times at work the next day, he had a feeling his pay would be docked. He couldn't focus at all on picking items from the warehouse; his mind kept going over what had happened the night before.

It didn't help that he hadn't gotten a wink of sleep. How could he, after what he'd witnessed?

Instead of going to bed, he'd spent hours replaying the video feed from the owl-cam. Over and over, he'd watched as Pliny had shot toward the creature...and then, inexplicably, the creature had vanished. It was right there in one frame, then gone in the next.

And that wasn't the only impossible thing about it.

In addition to studying the video of the creature, Matt had searched online to identify it. Now that he had decent images--and clear memories--of the animal, he'd thought he stood a better chance of figuring out what it was.

And he'd been right. His search had led to photos and film clips that had convinced him beyond a doubt that he'd found his creature. Even the whining sound it had made was the same as the sound from an audio clip recording.

He'd identified it quickly, but it was taking him a lot longer to wrap his head around what he'd learned. Because the creature he'd encountered should not have been in his yard in the mountains of West Virginia. It should not have been anywhere at all.

It was called a Tasmanian Tiger--also known as a Thylacine-- and it was supposed to be extinct.

"Any news on the mystery critter front?" Retha asked him at lunch that afternoon. "Did it show its stripy ass on your owl-cam again?"

Matt shook his head and took a bite of his ham sandwich. What had happened last night had been so ridiculously impossible, he couldn't imagine she'd take him seriously.

Not to mention, he still lived in the shadow of The Incident. There would always be a cloud of doubt hanging over him, so how could he get her or anyone to believe such an impossible story?

"Did you check the integrity of your video feed?" Retha gestured forcefully with a nacho cheese Dorito chip from her lunch bag. "Was there any sign it was hacked?"

Matt shook his head again. The video feed was a non-issue now. The Tasmanian Tiger had been right there in front of him, close enough to touch.

"So what's the current theory?" Retha popped the chip in her mouth.

Matt swallowed his latest bite of sandwich and sipped from his water bottle. He'd learned long ago the price for putting unsubstantiated information out there. Talking to anyone without proof in his pocket would burn him in the end. Not proof as in a video recording that could have been faked with computer-generated images; not proof as in anecdotal accounts of encountering an extinct animal with vanishing tendencies.

Proof as in the animal itself.

That evening, Matt set out a box trap a few yards from the cabin's front porch...right where the Tasmanian Tiger had made its approach the night before. He baited the trap with animal crackers and laid a trail of them all around.

Next, he installed a wireless wide-angle camera on the eave of the porch roof, aimed at the trap and surrounding area.

Satisfied with the trap and video setup, Matt double-checked the last piece of his gear--a tranquilizer rifle propped against the wall by the door. The rifle was a must when dealing with an animal that could disappear into thin air.

Preparations complete, Matt sat down to wait. He brought up Pliny's owl-cam on one laptop, maximized the porch feed on the other, and leaned back to nibble animal crackers with his sneakered feet on the corner of the table.

He was alert with the familiar tension of the watch, the hunt, the discovery. It sent adrenaline rippling through his bloodstream, made him feel excited and edgy in a way he hadn't felt in a long time.

It took him back ten years ago, when he'd been a researcher for the Raptor Institute at West Virginia University. He'd been a rising star back then, responsible for a well-regarded study of raptor adaptations and declines in environmentally-compromised habitats. How many nights had he spent during that study, watching incoming data and video streams from birds equipped with sensors and cameras? How many eyebrow-raising results had he assembled in support of his hypotheses and continued research?

Never enough, as it turned out. The original study hadn't managed to sway public opinion against the fracking companies that were wreaking havoc in raptor ranges, tearing up the landscape with hydraulic-injection drilling operations in search of oil and natural gas. Matt had seen the writing on the wall: if something didn't change fast, his precious owls and other raptors would be doomed.

For that reason, he'd brazenly fabricated data, altered findings, and cooked up phony composite subjects for a damning follow-up report on the toll of fracking on raptor habitats in West Virginia. He'd made up fake peer reviews to speed things along, then released the report to the media on the eve of a big pro-fracking vote in the state House. The tactic had worked; the study had gotten nation-wide attention, and the vote had been defeated. Matt had become an environmental celebrity for fending off the frackers and preserving the noble raptors.

At least until the fracking company lawyers had demanded a look at his science, at which time their paid consultants had seen right through his so-called research. After that, the dominos had fallen hard and fast for Matt--job, reputation, career prospects, savings. The Incident had left him a disgraced exile in a cabin in the woods, working by day as an overstressed merchandise picker in a warehouse...watching owl-cams by night in a pale imitation of the work he'd once done at the Raptor Institute.

But maybe all that could change if he captured the Tasmanian Tiger. Maybe, discovering a survivor of an extinct species could finally redeem him and restore his respectability. Maybe, the Tasmanian Tiger was a true life-changing godsend, its arrival no accident.

Assuming, of course, that Matt hadn't lost his mind and halluci-nated the whole damned thing.

Six times, Matt caught the wrong animals in the box trap and had to go set them free. Finally, just before midnight, he saw a familiar striped form approach the trap.

Instantly springing to attention, Matt watched as the Tasmanian Tiger nibbled its way along the path of animal crackers. "Good boy," he said, heart racing with sudden excitement. "Go on in, boy."

The Tasmanian Tiger paused at the door of the trap. For a

moment, Matt wondered if the creature sensed danger and might leave or disappear.

But then it stepped gingerly inside, lapping up more of the animal crackers.

Matt waited till the Tasmanian Tiger had all four paws in the trap, then ran over to grab his tranquilizer rifle. When he saw the animal was about to spring the trap, he yanked the door open and lunged outside.

Just as he ran onto the porch, the door of the trap flipped shut. The Tasmanian Tiger looked back at the sound, its ears at full attention.

Without hesitation, Matt swung the rifle up, aimed at the stripes, and pulled the trigger. One needle-tipped tranquilizer cartridge plunged into the animal's rump, setting off a round of frantic yapping.

The yapping didn't last. With a final pathetic yelp, the Tasmanian Tiger closed its eyes and slumped to the floor of the trap.

Matt watched from the porch for a moment, waiting to see if the Tiger disappeared...but it didn't. It just lay there, limp as any sleeping animal, solid as any scientific proof.

"You're not a good boy after all, are you?" said Matt as he examined the Tasmanian Tiger. "You're not a *boy* at all."

The animal lay on its side on the kitchen table, which was clear except for a few diagnostic instruments, a pen-sized flashlight, and a digital still camera. A video camera shot the scene from a tripod alongside the table, capturing every moment; Matt was determined to document every detail, no matter how small.

"Subject is a female Tasmanian Tiger or Thylacine," he said for the benefit of the video camera's microphone.

Leaning closer, he pried open the pouch between the creature's hind legs. He reached for the flashlight and shone its beam inside the pouch, illuminating its inner details.

At which point, his eyes widened, and his breath caught in his throat.

Snapping off the flashlight, he straightened. "Subject appears to have recently whelped. Nipples are distended and chafed, as if nursing has recently occurred. No pups are present, but tufts of loose fur are visible within the folds of the pouch."

Matt took a few shots with the still camera, then put it down near the animal's snout and considered the situation.

If pups were tucked away somewhere nearby, and their father wasn't watching over them, being without their mother could be disastrous. They couldn't have been out of the pouch for long; Matt doubted they'd be well-equipped to survive in the wild without a parent. On the other hand, releasing the mother would mean giving up a once-in-a-lifetime scientific find and a chance at redemption.

"Where do we go from here?" Matt said it aloud, as if the video camera were a person. "Angel's offspring..." He'd just given her a name on the spot, based on her being a godsend. "Angel's offspring might represent the only breeding population of Tasmanian Tigers in existence. They are this species' hope for the future. But I can't just let Angel go, can I?"

Just then, he caught a glimpse of Pliny's live feed on one of the laptops sitting open on the couch, and he had an idea.

Darting over to the plastic bins where he kept his gear, he fished out one of the owl-cams. A little modification to the strap, and it would fit around Angel's neck just fine.

"On second thought, I *can* let her go," he said, walking over to hold up the owl-cam in front of the video camera on the tripod. "I'll never lose her, thanks to the GPS chip and the video feed of her travels."

Grinning, Matt reached back and patted Angel's flank. Her fine, soft fur felt like velvet to his touch.

"Best of all, she'll lead me straight to her pups," he said. "To our *future*."

Angel's video signal was coming in strong and clear. As Matt watched it on the laptop on the kitchen table, he saw a low-to-the-ground angle captured at the base of the Tasmanian Tiger's throat, bouncing to the rhythm of her footsteps.

Reawakened by a mild stimulant and turned loose from the porch of the cabin, Angel was on the move, heading out on what-ever rounds Matt had interrupted by trapping her. She didn't seem any the worse for wear; if the drugging, blood draws, and sample-taking he'd inflicted had affected her, she didn't show it.

Suddenly, the other laptop--where Pliny's live feed was playing--caught Matt's eye. Looking over, he saw a moonlit view of Angel, seen from some elevated vantage point like a high tree branch.

Then, all he saw from the owl-cam was a deserted forest floor. In the blink of an eye, Angel had disappeared.

"No!" Heart racing, Matt shot his gaze back to the first laptop...only to see that Angel's feed had turned to snowy inter-ference.

Then, just as quickly as the feed had turned to snow, it switched to clear video...but it wasn't what Matt had expected to see. Instead of a nighttime forest scene, the camera was somehow shooting in broad daylight.

And that wasn't the only change.

What he saw on the screen was not a moonlit forest in West Virginia, but a dusty dirt floor bathed in bright sunlight. For a moment, the view dipped and darkened as Angel lowered her head to sniff the ground. Then, she looked up and to the left.

Matt saw a wall of vertical metal bars a few feet away, standing inches apart. Angel turned further to the left, exposing a corner where the first wall of bars joined another. Suddenly, Matt realized what he was looking at.

Angel was in a cage. A high-walled cage, like one in a zoo.

Sure enough, when Angel turned again, Matt saw the lower legs of a man and a woman...but that presented another puzzle. The woman wore a long, puffed-out dress that hung all the way to her ankles; below that, she wore old-fashioned black lace-up boots. As for the man, his trousers were white with black pinstripes, and his shoes were white leather.

Angel looked up then, and Matt got a better view of the people on the other side of the bars. They both looked like actors out of an old movie--the man in a white ice cream suit and straw hat, the woman in an elaborate feathered and beribboned hat and a pale yellow dress that ballooned out over layers of padding.

As Matt watched, the woman opened a yellow parasol over her shoulder and smiled. The man twirled the end of his handlebar mustache with one hand; with the other, he shook a newspaper between the bars--*The Washington Post*. Leaning closer to the screen, Matt could barely make out the date at the bottom of the masthead.

1905.

"What the...?" Matt's mouth fell open.

Was he supposed to believe Angel had traveled back in time to a zoo in 1905? If so, how could he even be watching it happen? He couldn't imagine his wireless tiger-cam's range extended across the time barrier, enabling the transmission of video from over a century ago.

Yet there it was on the newspaper: *1905.*

Suddenly, the tiger-cam's point of view shifted, swinging down and away from the bars. Instead of the old-fashioned people with the parasol and newspaper, Matt saw what looked like a pile of rocks on the far side of the cage.

The video bounced toward the rocks with the familiar rhythm of Angel's trotting gait. Up close, a gap in the rocks was visible, and the tiger-cam slid through it.

On the other side, Angel emerged in a den lit by sunbeams streaming between the rocks. There, in a heap of straw and tufts of fur, was a litter of three tiny Tasmanian Tiger pups.

The camera moved close as Angel went to them. Her snout entered the shot, dipping down to nose the squirming pups.

So there they were--the breeding population of Tasmanian Tigers that Matt had been looking for. The pups' father was absent (foraging through the timestream, perhaps?) but the pups themselves were right in plain sight.

In 1905.

If the video feed from the tiger-cam could be believed, 1905 wasn't Angel's last stop.

Matt watched her tend her pups for a while, letting them crawl into her pouch to nurse. When they'd wobbled back out into the nest, the feed returned to snowy interference.

When the snow became clear video again, Angel was somewhere else, again in broad daylight. At first, all Matt could see was scruffy brush--a thicket of weeds and tall grass. When the brush gave way to a roadside, however, the location took on new significance. A car rolled past, a vintage model with a distinctive chrome nose cone that Matt recognized from classic car shows as a Studebaker. Quickly looking it up online, he saw that exact model was from the late 1940s. The next few cars passing by looked equally classic, all from the 40s or earlier.

Angel gnawed on some road kill on the berm--a rabbit, it looked like--and then the video feed went to snow. When the snow resolved once more, Matt saw that the daylight had disappeared. The view this time was of a clearing in the woods at night; a VW microbus occupied the middle of the clearing, its psychedelic paint job visible in the flickering light of a campfire. Four hippies in beads, jeans, and serapes--two men and two women--sat on the ground around the fire, playing guitars and smoking joints. When Angel eased up to them, they tossed her cheese doodles and pieces of sandwich, which she dutifully gobbled. At one point, she got close enough for one of the girls to tickle.

Then, the feed went back to snow. Matt could only imagine the hippies' reaction as Angel disappeared right in front of them.

The next time the feed cleared, Matt found himself staring at a parking lot outside a bar, again at night. The cars all looked like they were straight out of the mid-1970s, and the outfits on a couple walking out of the place were pure disco-era--gold chains, wild shirts, tight pants, and platform shoes. Angel ignored them and ran straight to the dumpster enclosure behind the building, where she dined on scraps from a bucket.

As Matt watched all this, he couldn't help thinking he was witnessing the ultimate evolutionary advantage in action. An animal that traveled through time would never go hungry; if one food source ran out, the animal could simply travel to another era in which food was plentiful.

The next stop on Angel's eating tour through history was a state park trash can at night in an indeterminate era...then a McDonald's dumpster on a sunny afternoon in the 80s (complete with passersby dressed like characters right out of *Miami Vice*).

But it was the next stop that got Matt's attention the most. He knew it well, because he'd been there.

It was the Raptor Institute building on the campus of West Virginia University.

"Oh my God." Matt couldn't believe what he was seeing on the screen. The tiger-cam was pointing at a squat brick building situated among sunlit, leafy trees.

Upon seeing it, he felt a sharp pang in his gut. He hadn't been there in years, since The Incident, but it was the place he'd loved best in all his life.

Angel circled it at a distance, keeping to an overgrown strip of weeds along the opposite side of the street. Suddenly, she stopped; the camera angle rose slightly and steadied.

The front door of the Institute, which was dead center on the screen, opened inward...and someone stepped out. *Matt* stepped out, a younger version with a fuller head of hair and a bounce in his step.

His older self just stared with stunned intensity, shivering under the skin. He hadn't seen himself that way in so long--that pre-Incident self who hadn't been beaten down by his own hubris just yet.

As Matt watched, his younger self strolled down the front steps and got in a car parked along the street...his cherry red 2003 VW Beetle, which he'd totaled long ago. As soon as he drove off down the street, Angel ran out of the weeds and crossed to the Institute building. She trotted around to the patio out back, where Matt had often sat to do paperwork.

Angel went straight to the weathered gray picnic table on the patio and jumped up to rest her forepaws on the edge. Leaning forward, she plunged her muzzle into a bowl that Matt remembered well. Crumbs dribbled past the tiger-cam as Angel went to town on the bowl's contents. Of all the goodies within her time-traveling reach, these, apparently, were among her favorites.

These animal crackers, the same brand as the ones he'd fed her at the cabin.

The next time the tiger-cam went to snow and tuned back in, Matt saw another familiar view: his cabin, with the box trap sitting empty in the yard.

Angel was back.

Abandoning the laptops, Matt rushed out to the porch with the bag of animal crackers. When he sat on the edge of the porch, Angel came right up to him.

"Well, hello there." He scattered a handful of animal crackers in the grass between them. "You've certainly been a busy girl, haven't you?"

Angel watched him with her round, obsidian eyes as she snarfed up the cookies.

"I guess you must really like these, huh?" He tossed her some more. "You even sniffed them out ten years ago, didn't you?"

Angel looked up and licked her muzzle.

When she'd finished the animal crackers on the ground, Matt held out a handful to see what she'd do. Though he'd trapped and drugged her earlier, Angel came to him without hesitation and ate right out of his hand.

Matt watched with wonder as Angel nibbled the treats he'd offered. According to the video he'd seen, this very animal had just returned from ten years in the past. This very creature had eaten animal crackers from a bowl that the Matt of ten years ago had filled.

Now here she was.

The thought of it filled him with bittersweet longing. If only he could do the same thing Angel had done and travel back a decade to a simpler time...a time before he'd made the mistake that had ruined his life. If only he had her power and could go back and undo that mistake.

If only she could do *anything* to help him. But the truth was, now that Matt thought about it, he realized he was no further ahead than he'd been before he'd found her. No one who put any stock in the scientific method would ever believe his story of the time-traveling Tasmanian Tiger. The video he'd recorded of her travels could have been faked with CGI; even concrete evidence like samples of pollen and chemicals from the past could be called into question...especially coming from someone with Matt's reputation. The live animal would be hard to ignore, and quite a coup...assuming she didn't vanish before he could present her to the scientific community.

Even as he sat there and fed Angel, a terrible sinking feeling came over him. The redemption he'd dared to hope for was unlikely to happen; the miraculous animal, for all her power, could do nothing for him.

Or could she?

As Matt reached into the bag for another handful of animal crackers, he had a thought. Maybe there was a way Angel could help, after all.

"Here you go, honey. Eat up." He grinned as he fed her again. "Now wouldn't you like to take another trip?"

The video on the laptop showed a familiar view of the Raptor Institute. It looked no different than the last time Matt had seen it on the tiger-cam feed--a squat brick building among leafy trees, dappled with sunlight.

Just as he'd hoped, his red 2003 VW Beetle was parked on the street. That meant his plan could move forward...assuming Angel cooperated.

So far, it looked like she would. The shot moved across the street, bouncing to the rhythm of her quick-footed trot. She rounded the building's back corner and headed straight for the picnic table on the patio.

Matt's younger self was sitting there and looked up from a pile of paperwork at her approach.

Future Matt's heart pounded as he watched the scene unfold. He was thrilled that Angel had gone right back to the Institute and found his younger self. Though Matt had let her sniff something of his from those days (an old t-shirt) and something from the Institute (the animal cracker bowl from the patio, still in his cupboard after all those years), he hadn't been sure she'd get the message and go where he wanted.

But there she was, face to face with the Matt of a decade ago. She was one smart animal; she'd have to be, to be able to travel through time the way she did.

Now, all she had to do was what came naturally.

The Matt of ten years ago stared suspiciously...but something about Angel seemed to put any worries he had to rest. He smiled and said something to her, which future Matt thought might be, *Hello there.*

When she hopped up to rest her forepaws on the picnic table, past Matt laughed. Reaching into the bowl of animal crackers on the table, he fished out three and dropped them in front of her. Angel lapped them right up.

Past Matt fed her a few more...and then he frowned and reached toward her. His hand came away with a bit of red ribbon and a rolled-up piece of paper.

Future Matt smiled. He'd put that rolled-up paper under the tiger-cam strap around Angel's neck and secured it with the ribbon. He'd hoped it would reach his past self without getting lost or damaged in Angel's travels.

Past Matt unrolled it and saw it was a twenty-dollar bill. When he looked closer, he would see the year it was minted--ten years in the future--and he would read the message written on the back in fine-point Sharpie.

It was a note from his future self. The authenticity was obvious, as it mentioned a secret only past or future Matt could have known. The rest of it provided a warning in the strongest possible terms...a warning not to proceed with the falsified study of fracking impacts on West Virginia raptors.

After that, it would be in past Matt's hands. The decision to change the future would be up to him.

"Come on, you dumb son of a bitch." Future Matt sat on the edge of his seat. "Do it *right* this time, you idiot."

Matt Mentiroso sat in the high tech command center of the Institute, watching the video feeds on the giant flat-screen monitors arrayed before him. Each feed displayed a different view of the West Virginia forests, the outlines of trees and brush faintly visible in the shimmering moonlight.

"Anything new?" His assistant, Retha Lawson, strolled up behind him, munching kale chips from a snack-size bag.

Matt smiled over his shoulder. "Just business as usual."

"No raptors, I suppose?" Retha leaned against a console and crunched another chip.

It was a question she asked every day, though they both knew the answer. No one had seen a raptor in West Virginia in the past seven years; the owls, hawks, and eagles had been gone almost as long as Matt had been director of the Institute.

Which was why it wasn't the Raptor Institute anymore.

Something about all the fracking had ruined the raptors' habitat, though the frackers still denied it. Maybe, if Matt had come out with that bogus study of his, he could have stopped them and saved the birds...but he'd heeded the advice on that twenty dollar bill he'd gotten ten years ago.

He still wondered if he'd done the right thing.

"No raptors," he said.

"Could be worse, I suppose," said Retha. "At least we still have jobs. At least we still have other animals to study."

"Yes, we do," said Matt.

"Plenty of Tasmanian Tigers out there." Retha owed her career to those particular animals. She'd nearly dropped out of the zoology field, just short of finishing her PhD, when the resurgent Tasmanian Tigers had revived her interest...and led to her job at the Institute.

"They won't be plentiful for long," said Matt. "You know the state's planning a bounty hunt, right?"

"A bounty hunt?"

"To reduce this 'invasive species' to 'manageable numbers.' They keep banging the drum about environmental impacts, as if they even *care* about the environment." Matt snorted in disgust. "I think they want the Tasmanian Tigers to go the way of the raptors."

"So they're really going through with it?"

"Looks that way."

Retha smacked the console. "Well, we can't just sit back and do *nothing*, can we? After all, this is the *Thylacine Institute*, isn't it?"

Matt looked up at the screens, each displaying a different tiger-cam view. What was it about those animals that made him want to study them...want to save them? What inexplicable hold did they have on his heart?

Was it because a Tasmanian Tiger had delivered the note that had saved his career (assuming the contents of the note had been true)? Was it because the Tasmanian Tigers had taken the place in his heart once occupied by the beloved raptors he'd failed to save? Or was there some other, deeper reason he would never fathom?

In the end, it didn't matter. All that mattered was that he had the will to save them. And a plan he'd considered once before, a Hail Mary play that he might be just desperate enough to try. After all, he'd always wondered if things might have turned out better for the raptors if he'd tried it the first time around.

"So what can we do?" asked Retha. "How can we possibly save these animals?"

"You'll see." Matt smiled and reached into his lab coat pocket for an animal cracker. "I'm working on a report that I think will really turn it all around."

AND MILES TO GO AFTER I SLEEP

he Explorers' Club, Now:

"...and at that precise moment," says the furry purple man with the bright yellow eyes, "the giant beast *sneezed*, covering all two dozen of our party in vile, putrid phlegm!"

Every purple male and female in the great meeting hall of the Explorers' Club roars with laughter and bangs his or her cutlery on tables and chairs. Two of the furry purple people even leap up on their tables and dance around hyper-ecstatically, whooping with hilarity at the story they just heard.

It's enough to make the storyteller—Grigri Glee by name—do a little hop-step of his own behind the pulsing green podium thing. The approval of his fellow club members makes his personal parasites twitch and twitter with delight. Reporting on his latest exploration of the Unknownamensity is not only a necessity (as the club funds his travels) but a genuine joy he craves and savors.

"What about the *Jenavenna?*" asks the club Presidex, a tall female named Loga Sabreslake. "You still haven't told us if you found that fabled landform, Dr. Grigri."

"I guess you'll just have to listen a while longer, then." Grigri nods grimly. "For thereon hangs a dark tale of *evil* and *sacrifice* on the great and mysterious *Eastern frontier.*

"All because of a foul *monster* known far and wide as *Craw Cancellakra!*"

The Adventurers' Flock, Now:

"Our *Western* frontier, as you know, is a *foreboding* place," says the six-foot-tall birdlike female with the bright green and gold feathers, red beak, and purple eyes. "It is a vast and unforgiving expanse, traversed only by the *mad* and the *dead*. But the great *Unknownamensity* will someday be conquered, or *my* name isn't *Craw Cancellakra!*"

The vast, domed chamber of the Adventurers' Flock fills with a deafening chorus of squawks, cries, chirps, yelps, and tweets. Feathers of all colors and sizes fly as the hundred-plus members beat their wings in vigorous approval.

Craw, just back from a Flock-sponsored expedition, has them all on the edges of their perches. She's an old hand at this, keeping them in suspense as she spins her tale of exploration at the edge of what to them is the known world.

"It took us a full month to cross the Dry Zone." Craw whistles and wiggles her wings for emphasis. "Those trackless wastes had been reshaped by the elements since our last expedition, leaving us utterly lost and at the mercy of three blistering suns."

This time, the cries in the dome are lower, softer, and simpler—expressions of sympathetic sadness and worry. Some of the bird creatures huddle together for comfort as Craw describes the dark turn of events.

"We dared not take flight, as ravenous *slashdragons* and *aero-squid* ruled the skies. All we could do was continue our doomed march and pray for deliverance.

"Then one day, *b-kaw!* We emerged from our travail! We found paths out of the Dry Zone and into the *Wattlands*, where our sniffers caught traces of the landform we sought—the *Jenavenna*."

The mood in the domed aviary lifts. Craw proceeds to drop it again.

"Unfortunately, that was when we encountered the foul *monster!* That was when the terrible *Grigri Glee* descended upon us!"

The Unknownamensity, Then:

Electrical arcs and streams crackled across the hard, red ground of the Wattlands, zapping occasional insects or small animals in their path. Grigri and his team walked carefully over the plain, trying their best to avoid getting electrocuted.

They'd been in this region before on previous expeditions, so they knew it could be harrowing. Step on the wrong spot at the wrong time, and you could get a full lightning bolt up your ass.

Still, it was the place they had to be for what was coming. No other sector in all the vast and untamed Unknownamensity would do.

"I don't see anyone yet." Hoyga Hoyga Hoga, Grigri's stout and strong-willed female second-in-command, scanned the sparking horizon with crystalline field glasses that glinted in the triple-strong sunlight. "Just a few shock monkeys and a zappa or two."

"Keep looking, Hoyga." Grigri squinted into the distance and tried not to worry. Traveling hundreds of miles through the wilderness, it was tough to time a rendezvous just right.

"There!" The youngest member of the expedition, lilac-furred Kook Achoo, ran ahead, stopped, and pointed. "I see them! They're coming!"

Hoyga swung her field glasses around for a look. "He's right! Raise the banner! *Raise the banner!*"

Kook raced back and grabbed the rolled-up purple banner from the back of the supply-carrying horned white stomp-whale. Grigri, however, didn't wait for him to unfurl it.

Parasites jittering, the expedition leader charged forward on foot, running across the electrified landscape at a fast clip. Even as he bolted toward the newcomers, dodging jagged rocks and sizzle-thistles, one of their number—a bird creature with green and gold feathers—broke away and hurtled straight toward *him.*

Within seconds, they collided furiously—but not in conflict. Grigri and the bird creature threw themselves into an embrace, kissing passionately with purple lips and crimson beak.

"Darling Craw!" Grigri gasped out the words between feverish kisses. "It has been too long!"

Craw Cancellakra pushed him away gently. "And we must wait a while longer. That which we feared most may soon come to pass."

Grigri's eyes widened. "You mean the Jenavenna...?"

Craw nodded. "It stirs. But the power of our love, *b-kaw,* will surely enable us to save this world from the doom its stirring portends!"

The Explorers' Club, Now:

"Tell us, Grigri," says Presidex Loga Sabreslake. "How *awful* is the great beast Craw?"

Grigri spits on the floor dramatically. "*Worse* than you can *imagine.* That *monstrosity* is depraved, sadistic, and *corrupt* in every way. It is a *sickness* in animate, sentient form, endowed with *boundless* destructive capabilities and limitless *appetites.*"

Excited, the purple-furred crowd fills the Explorers' Club with thunderous howls of disapproval.

"The only blessing so far," shouts Grigri, "the *only blessing,* is that this creature has confined itself to the vast wastes of the Unknownamensity...a fact for which you should all be eternally grateful."

The Adventurers' Flock, Now:

The crowd in the great dome of the Adventurers' Flock whistle and shriek up such a storm that the very air seems to vibrate with rage.

"Tell us! What happened to the Jenavenna?" The flock's director, a giant cockatoo creature called Lachrymocha Artifiche, hops up and down on a swinging perch at the dome's apex. "You said this awful *Grigri* creature descended just as your sniffers caught a trace of it!"

Craw nods grimly. "The foul Grigri attacked my team with all the savagery it could muster, *b-kaw*. I tell you, that ravenous beast nearly *slaughtered* every last one of us."

"You fought it face to face?" says Lachrymocha.

"I did." Craw rattles her wings. "In *very* close proximity!"

The crowd squawks and flutters excitedly.

"I gave as good as I got! *Better* even!" shouts Craw. "The monster could not resist my *strength, b-kaw*! Yet neither could I conquer him in that first battle. I soon realized we would have to settle our differences later, when our private struggle finally ran its course."

The Unknownamensity, Then:

Now that they'd made their rendezvous, Grigri and Craw led their teams out of the Wattlands and into a friendlier place. The edge of the Tenderzone lay just a few miles to the south; they and their followers made it over the border in under an hour.

As soon as they crossed over, their moods improved. Gone were the shocks and electrofauna of the Wattlands. Instead of hard red ground and jagged rocks, the gently rolling hills of the Tenderzone were carpeted with soft blue moss and pillowy plushrooms. Warm breezes carried sweet perfumes exhaled by dancing tumblereeds, and herds of tuftaloes scudded by overhead, keeping the skies clear of hostile slashdragons and their ilk.

It was a true paradise, an oasis in the heart of the Unknownamensity...and as far as Grigri and Craw could tell, they and their loyal followers were the only living people who knew it existed.

"Home sweet home." Grigri smiled and sneaked a kiss from Craw. "We've been away too long, wouldn't you say?"

"Always, my love." Craw nuzzled his shoulder and cooed. As usual, they'd been away a year between visits. That long wait made every touch and kiss so much sweeter between them.

"I want to stay this time!" said Kook Achoo as he jogged up beside them. "Please let me stay and keep up Easydoesit!"

Grigri grinned and shrugged as Kook ran off ahead of them. It was a fact that no one ever wanted to leave the retreat they'd built here; Easydoesit was a place where people were free to be as they wished, discovering their truest selves and exploring forbidden loves in peace and safety.

But it was also a fact that except for a chosen handful, they had to leave from time to time to keep the Tenderzone safe. Going back to their respective homelands to spread the word about how *awful* the place was kept the tourists and get-rich-quick-types from charging in and spoiling it. Purple people and bird people alike were greedy and short-sighted, not to mention hateful and bigoted against anyone who was different; there could be no higher calling than keeping those hordes from corrupting this untamed and hate-free wilderness.

That was why, as Grigri and Craw topped a blue-mossed rise on the heels of Kook, they saw the same quaint village nestled among the plushrooms and tumblereeds before them. No one had dug a mine in its place or plowed it under to make way for a noisy, congested city.

Though even Easydoesit would not be safe for long if Craw was right about the Jenavenna stirring.

The Adventurers' Flock, Now:

"You cannot imagine a more terrible place than the depths of the Unknownamensity," Craw tells the Adventurers' Flock. "The land itself is contaminated, the flora poisonous, the fauna aggressive. Never is there a moment's peace or safety."

"What about the people?" asks Director Artifiche. "Surely, there must be *natives* residing even in those extreme quarters."

"Pitiable savages, one and all." Craw wags her head in disgust. "Uncivilized wretches, as you might expect."

Artifiche bobs his head haughtily. "Of course! *Awk awk!*"

"Count yourself lucky you will never need to see *any* of their primitive lot. I only wish *I* could say the same."

The Explorers' Club, Now:

"Each time you send me back there, I cringe," says Grigri. "The Unknownamensity is *that* unbearable. The things and people who inhabit its squalid reaches are *that* repugnant."

"And dangerous!" adds a member of the Explorers' Club.

"Beyond belief," agrees Grigri. "I despise everyone and everything in that reprehensible territory."

"Yet you return again and again," says Presidex Sabreslake. "To hunt for the *Jenavenna*, yes?"

Grigri nods grudgingly. "It has been my only purpose in returning to that blighted land. For only by finding and controlling that fabled landform can I hope to save this world and all who inhabit her. Or so I *thought*. So I was *told.*"

The Unknownamensity, Then:

The Jenavenna was a matter that couldn't wait. There was a small contingent of stay-behind residents—two birds and two purples—and they emerged from their jelly-bubble huts, eager for news and festivities. Grigri, however, hurried things along. He, Craw, Hoyga, and Craw's deputy, Diachotomy Exponenza, left the socializing to others and talked doomsday in the big middle bubble.

"So the Jenavenna," said Grigri. "We know what it means if it's truly stirring, don't we?"

Hoyga frowned. "You're sure it wasn't just another tremor from the Leapfrogging Fields?"

"We're sure." Craw looked at Diachotomy, who nodded in agreement. "We were *nesting* on it at the time, *b-kaw!*"

"Nesting on the *Jenavenna?*" Hoyga sounded stunned.

"We had just trekked out of the Land of Gnash," explained Craw. "Packs of incisorlings and were-cuspids were chewing up the Placid Reach, hunting for us. Nesting on the lofty Jenavenna seemed safest, *b-kaw*, for a short time at least."

Diachotomy, with her rich red plumage, clucked and nodded. "They feared to follow. Soon enough, we knew why."

"The Jenavenna *stirred*," said Craw. "Its gargantuan mass began to *move*. We fled on wing, but even then our jeopardy continued!

Mighty quakes shook and split the ground for miles around, forcing us to stay airborne and pray the stigmata-swarms didn't get us."

"Looking back was *terrifying*." Diachotomy shuddered. "That colossal crystalline *bulk* was *buckling* and *heaving*. The entire landscape was *churning*."

"And then it stopped." Craw stared darkly at each of the group in turn. "For now."

Grigri sighed. "So it's started, then, for real. That means, according to prophecy, the end of the world is upon us."

"The end of the world." Hoyga shook her head slowly and stared into space. "Isn't there anything we can do?"

Grigri was about to answer in the negative when Craw spoke up before him. "Actually, I've had a *dream* about that," she said.

Grigri gaped at her. "When? What dream?"

"It's a hazy one," said Craw. "I had it while nesting on the Jenavenna, when I briefly nodded off." She hunkered down as if reliving the brief nap. "There was a voice, very faint—a *female* voice. I couldn't tell what she was saying, but I somehow knew she was talking to *me.*"

"Where was the voice coming from?" asked Hoyga.

"All around me," said Craw. "I think...I think it was coming from the Jenavenna."

"The Jenavenna is *female?*" Hoyga bugged her eyes wide in surprise.

Grigri scowled. "But you couldn't make out anything she said?"

"No, but I had a *feeling.*" Craw nodded firmly. "I felt as if I might *reach* her if I tried hard enough."

"And then what?" Grigri looked suspicious. "Ask her not to stir?"

Craw shrugged. "I think we have to try, unless someone has a better idea."

None of them volunteered one.

The Explorers' Club, Now:

The purple-furred people listen raptly as Grigri continues his tale. Even the wait staff hangs on his every word, neglecting drink and dessert orders in the process.

"I set off with a small team of fearless, seasoned hands." Grigri steps out from behind the podium and paces the floor restlessly, his body taut with tension. "It was a race against time, for we knew the dreaded Craw Cancellakra was far ahead of us."

"What if the Craw got there first?" asks a waiter, scaly green serving tray hanging at his side.

"I believe the monster's intentions were the *opposite* of my own," Grigri says darkly. "I can only suppose the great beast longed to *end* the world rather than *save* it."

The Unknownamensity, Then:

The team left Easydoesit early the next morning, setting out on their mission with packs and equipment carried by a stomp-whale.

It wasn't long until they glimpsed the towering ridge of the Jenavenna, stretching along the distant horizon. It was visible long before they crossed the border of the Tenderzone, glittering in the light of the world's triple suns.

Just seeing it there was enough to make the fur stand up on Grigri's neck, causing him to shiver with awe...and dread. Now *there* was something truly enormous and mysterious. *There* was something, if the prophecies were true, that could put an end to the world and all who lived there.

"You've been quiet this morning, *b-kaw*." Craw drew up alongside him, affectionately brushing her wing against his shoulder.

"You haven't been that gregarious yourself," said Grigri. "You barely chirped at dawn chorus this morning."

"Maybe I'm saving my voice for later." Craw's eyes fixed on the distant ridge of the Jenavenna. "It could take a lot of wind to get something that big to listen to me."

"I'm still shocked it *can* listen. I never thought of it as *alive* before."

"Who did? But isn't it more *wonderful* that way?" She let out a happy, trilling tweet. "I mean, how often do *landforms* turn out to be *sentient creatures?*"

"Sentient creatures that want to destroy the world?" Grigri shook his head. "Hardly almost never."

Reaching over, Craw held his furry purple paw lightly in her claw. "But that's why we're *out* here, isn't it? The thrill of discovery?"

Grigri gave her claw a squeeze. "The Unknownamensity never runs out of secrets, does it?"

"For people like us, life doesn't get any better. Being stuck in one place for too long would be the death of us."

Grigri turned to her then, as they entered a shady red bower of organ trees, and said something he'd never said before to her or anyone else. "I love you. Oh, how I love you."

She stopped then, though their party was close behind, and kissed him under a tree that was heavy with shiny pink kidneys. Humble bumbles buzzing 'mid the meat hid their fuzzy black faces, embarrassed at the perfectly blatant display of affection.

"Don't die today," whispered Grigri.

"Don't worry, my darling," she said between loving pecks. "It is far more likely that *everyone* will die, in which case neither of us will live on without the other long enough to understand or care."

"Sweet, sweet Craw." Grigri chuckled. "That's about the most romantic thing anyone has ever said to me."

The Adventurers' Flock, Now:

"Legend has it that the Jenavenna is older than the world itself." Solemnly, Craw spreads her wings wide. "Gazing up at its immensity, I could easily believe that."

"The terrible Grigri must have been out of his mind," says Director Artifiche. "How did he imagine he could ever *control* something so massive?"

"Some ancient form of magic, I suspect. Something requiring *blood sacrifice*, perhaps."

"But whom would he sacrifice?" asks Artifiche.

"One of *us*, no doubt." When Craw says it, the Adventurers'

Flock goes wild. "That, I believe, is why Grigri took pains to leave a visible trail through the Bone Zone and Squirmament."

"Such a wily monster!" snaps Artifiche. "Keeping you close so he could *kill* you in the name of whatever hideous dark *gods* he worships. *Awk awk!*"

"Needless to say, we remained on guard against him at all times." Craw clatters her claws for dramatic effect. "And as we approached the majestic bulk of the landform, we guarded against *its* influence as well."

"*Its* influence?" Artifiche sounds surprised. "You make it sound as if the Jenavenna was *alive* somehow."

"Make no mistake, it is as alive as *any* of us," says Craw. "Though its goal, we discovered, is to render all life but its own *extinct.*"

The Unknownamensity, Then:

Two days after leaving Easydoesit in the Tenderzone, Grigri and Craw's party reached the base of the Jenavenna.

After fighting their way through one treacherous zone after another, they paused to savor the beauty of their destination. Sunlight streamed through its prismatic crystalline structure, bathing the explorers and their stomp-whale in shimmering arrays of rainbow-colored light.

Falls of water ran down its scalloped edge, splashing into pools on the ground below. Mosses of every color clung in patches to its sides, puffing out glittering clouds of spore-carrying fairy dust. Fur-covered, many-legged creatures skittered over its surface, calling out in high-pitched, ululating cries that only made sense to others of their own kind.

Grigri exhaled slowly as he took it all in. The scene was stunning beyond what he remembered from his last visit years ago.

"If anything could end the world," Kook Achoo said in a hushed voice, "it would be this."

"It practically *is* the world," said Diachotomy. "They say it has always *been* here. They say the world grew up *around* it."

Kook kept staring up at the distant top, scratching his furry, purple head. "I believe it..."

"Just wait until it stirs." Diachotomy whistled emphatically. "It's like the whole world is shaking at once."

"This time, maybe I can keep it relaxed," said Craw.

Grigri forced himself to stop gaping up at the natural wonder and focus on the business at hand. "Is there any place in particular where you want to set up?" he asked Craw. "Any spot that might be best for...communication?"

"I have no idea." Craw walked straight ahead, picking her way through a tumble of churned-up rock, and pressed her claws against the crystalline wall. "I guess this spot's as good as any to give it a try."

Grigri joined her, keeping a gap between them. He wanted to stay close but not disrupt her concentration. "If anything goes wrong, I'm right here."

Craw nodded. "I'm not even sure how to start." She shifted the position of her claws and leaned closer, shutting her eyes. "Just *reach out*, I guess. Focus on contacting the female entity from last time."

Grigri resisted the urge to touch her, to try to provide comfort and support. The best thing he could do, he thought, was not distract her from her task.

Not that she was faring so well *without* distractions. After a little while, she opened her eyes and drew back, ruffling her feathers.

"Nothing," she said. "I can't feel that presence anymore. I'm not receiving any message."

"Maybe we should move, then." Grigri pointed upward. "I wonder if you might do better on the plateau."

Craw shrugged. "I can fly up with Diachotomy, but it's a long way to climb for you and Kook. Maybe—"

Suddenly, she let out a loud cluck, and her eyes rolled back in her head. Before Grigri could catch her, she hit the ground like an overstuffed feed sack and lay there twitching as if an electrical current had jumped from a shock monkey into her body.

"Craw!" Diachotomy rushed forward.

Grigri intercepted her, holding her back. "Don't touch her! She might be making a connection!"

"Or *dying!*" snapped Diachotomy. "Maybe the Jenavenna is just *too big* for a mind like hers to handle! Maybe she's undergoing killer trauma *right now!*"

Grigri saw Kook moving in Craw's direction, too, and swung up a hand to signal him to freeze. "Everyone stay back! Give her time to adjust!"

As he said it, Craw thrashed and squawked on the ground. Watching it without intervening made Grigri's parasites clench and twist painfully, but he knew it was the right thing to do. *Probably.*

Craw went through another bout of writhing, the worst yet— then suddenly went limp. Nearly in a panic, Grigri dropped to her side and reached out to shake her...only to snap his hands away out of fear that he might do more harm than good.

The Explorers' Club, Now:

"I could not stop the great beast Craw from penetrating the vast mind of the Jenavenna." As Grigri scans the crowd, he sees their attention is more intense than ever. "What happened next would be completely beyond my control. I could only *pray* that the two would not forge an unholy alliance and agree to end the world."

"What about joining the link?" asks Presidex Sabreslake. "Making your case directly to the Jenavenna?"

"Its mind was not open to me," Grigri says grimly. "That reprehensible Craw must have blocked me somehow."

"How awful," says Sabreslake. "Being forced to wait helplessly while the fate of the world was being decided in front of you."

"You should have *killed* the *Craw!*"

When someone shouts it, the whole audience turns suddenly ugly, chanting *Kill the Craw* in unison.

"Hold on a minute!" Grigri hollers over them. "Think about it, my fellow explorers!

"Was *Craw* the one who should have been *killed?*"

465

The Unknownamensity, Then:

Was this what it was like to be dead and face a higher power?

Craw, who had only ever had very mild telepathic experiences before, felt lost and overwhelmed in the vast mind of the Jenavenna. As her own mind drifted through its crystalline latticework, she struggled to find recognizable vantage points—something, anything, to hold on to.

Complicating matters, a female voice roared around and through her, drowning out her thoughts. It was the same voice she'd heard during her last encounter with the Jenavenna, but so much louder she could hardly bear it.

Crying out in her mind, she tumbled and tossed among the glittering facets, straining for purchase. If only she could anchor herself, perhaps she could make sense of the tumult and begin the conversation she had come to have.

Suddenly, then, another voice broke through the madness—little more than a whisper, but it sneaked through and hooked her just the same. She recognized it, longed for it, *cherished* it, and in that strong emotion, she found strength and stability.

I love you, Craw. The voice was Grigri's, talking in the outside world as he knelt beside her body, mainlining into her mind like an arrow into a target. *You can do this, my love. I know you can.*

With the power she got from hearing that voice, Craw was able, at last, to stop her psychic freefall. She was finally able to soften the roar and understand the words that were blasting through the pipeline into her mind. She was able to recognize the softened voice that spoke them as belonging to the Jenavenna.

Where...am...I?

It was a strange question for the backbone of the Unknownamensity to ask. How could something so huge and ancient, something that perhaps predated the world itself, have any doubt about its location?

Craw answered as best she could. "You are in the Unknownamensity, as you have always been."

There was a moment's delay before the Jenavenna's next words.

What is...the Unknownamensity?

"A vast, wild region between the empires of the birds and the purple people. Exploring it, *b-kaw*, is my passion."

And who...am I?

"The Jenavenna, greatest landform in all the Unknownamensity. In all the *world*, even."

That's...not...right.

"Then what else could you *be?*"

A...person. A woman.

How could a landform be a person and vice versa? Or was what she *thought* all that mattered? "You do sound like a person. Well, I'm a person, too. My name is Craw."

Another pause. *Tell me again...what you said* my *name is.*

"You are called the Jenavenna."

Again, a long moment of silence. *I* remember *now. I remember!*

"Remember what?"

My first name...is Jenna. My last name is Venner.

"It is?"

Yes! Jenna Venner. And I remember more than that *now.*

"Such as?"

I've been asleep for a very long time.

And she needs to *stay* that way, thought Craw. "Do you know why you've been asleep that long?"

There was an accident, said Jenna. *I was hurt badly. I've been asleep for years...or at least it feels like it.*

"But you're talking to me now," said Craw.

Because you're part of my dream, said Jenna. *The dream that's been keeping me alive all this time.*

It was Craw's turn to be confused. "You're telling me I'm part of a *dream? Your* dream?"

All the bird people are. And the purple people, too.

"That can't be!"

I built this world to give myself something to do through all the lonely days and nights. Everything in it was created by me.

Craw fell silent. It seemed impossible—but the prophecies had always warned that the world would end if the Jenavenna woke. Maybe it made sense, then, that its mind had *created* the world.

In which case, the stakes of their meeting hadn't changed. "Are you waking up now, do you think? Is that why you're talking to me after all this time?"

Yes. That's why.

"Please don't," said Craw. "You need to keep sleeping if you want to get better."

But it's been so long! It seems like I've been asleep forever!

"What if you wake up and you're not ready?" asked Craw. "You might *never* recover."

Or maybe I am *ready. I haven't felt this alert in a very long time.*

Craw felt a sudden shift of the great mind around her, a shuddering of the vast crystalline latticeworks. There was distant rumbling, too, as if the immense landform was starting to move.

Desperation surged through her like a strong storm wind. "Listen, please! I came here to stop this from happening! To beg you not to wake!"

But I need to!

"This place you've created," said Craw. "If you wake up, if you move, you'll *destroy* it. You'll destroy *all* of us."

Silence (except for the rumbling). *I'm sorry, but...this is a dream. All of you are just dreams.*

"Are we?" said Craw. "Ask any one of us, and they'll tell you we're just as alive as you are, Jenna Venner."

Jenna said nothing for a while, though the rumbling got louder.

But if I stay asleep and die, you'll all die anyway.

She had a point, though Craw couldn't agree with it now. With her entire world and everyone she knew on the brink of extinction, all she could do was whatever it took to save it.

"Please, Jenna," she said. "Please don't wake up. Please let us live our lives a while longer."

But one way or another, it will all end anyway.

"All that matters is that it won't be today," said Craw.

There was another violent shift, and Craw feared she had lost the day. The crystalline structure lurched hard to one side, then the other, as if the whole thing was about to crash apart.

Then, suddenly, the movement stilled. Craw felt the end of things stop like a wind-up toy that had just run out of winding.

As the rumbling ceased, and Jenna's voice remained silent, and the world drifted on as it always had since the beginning of time, Craw felt tears of relief running down her feathered face.

And she felt Grigri's hands, too, as he brushed them away, even as tears of his own fell to replace them.

"Craw!" Grigri's voice was the first she heard as she slowly emerged from the great crystalline mind. "Are you all right?"

"Should we run for the hills?" Kook sounded panicky. "Is the Jenavenna going to stir?"

Craw shook her head slowly as she gazed up at them.

"So you did it?" asked Kook. "You saved the world?"

"We're all still here," Diachotomy said chidingly, "so I guess the answer is yes."

"But maybe we won't be for long," said Craw.

"What do you mean?" Grigri's face was etched with concern. "What haven't you told us?"

"I'll tell you the whole story on the way back to Easydoesit," she said, carefully getting to her feet. "But first, did anyone bring a chisel? I want to take a few samples of the Jenavenna."

"For what?" asked Kook.

"In case I change my mind about something," said Craw.

The Adventurers' Flock, Now:

As the members of the Adventurers' Flock sit hushed, all eyes glued to the front of the chamber, Craw reaches into a red velvet sack.

"You see before you the means of your deliverance!" Slowly, she withdraws a chunk of crystal the length of her forearm and raises it overhead. "Behold! A fragment of the true *Jenavenna!*"

Everyone in the place goes wild at once with cheering cries and squawks and whistles.

Craw's entire presentation has led to this. All the buildup was meant to prep the crowd to receive the glittering artifact in the proper frame of mind.

Meaning *hateful*.

Ever since the day of her link with Jenna in the Unknownamensity, Craw hasn't been able to stop thinking about her. She hasn't been able to stop imagining the poor sleeping woman who gave up her own waking life for the lives of the people in her dream.

Are those people's lives worth any less than those of that comatose woman? Even if you count her as their creator, is her life any more precious than any of theirs?

Maybe, thinks Craw. As much as she has always valued her existence, maybe she wasn't right to demand Jenna sacrifice her own to save it.

And maybe she should do everything she can to repay that sacrifice with one of her own.

"By focusing our combined willpower through this crystal, we can *rid* this world of the monstrous destroyer!" shouts Craw. "The Jenavenna intended to slaughter all of *us*, but *we* can banish her from our own world forever!"

The crowd howls with rage and hatred. Having already touched Jenna's mind twice before, Craw plans to use the fragment of her crystalline manifestation to reach her again—only this time, channeling all the fury of the mob through it. Grigri will do the same with another fragment on the opposite side of the world, also funneling the negative energy of the purple people against the Jenavenna.

Thus bombarded with revulsion from two directions, Jenna will stir with awareness. Realizing the people of the dream world are ungrateful for their salvation, she will take it back...and awaken in her own life after all those years.

At least, that is the hope.

"Focus on the crystal now!" Craw shakes the fragment in her fist as she paces and flaps for the crowd. "Pour all your anger and hatred into it! Tell the wicked Jenavenna to get out of your world!"

Everyone roars at once, their deafening cries bursting eardrums and shattering glasses by the dozen.

If the death of the world is going to happen sooner or later anyhow, if the dream will end when Jenna's mortal life does, then what better time than now to end it? Why not willingly save the woman while she still has a life to save?

That's the only reasoning Craw's conscience will let her accept.

Grigri feels the same way, without doubts or second-guessing. She wishes he could be here now to reinforce it and hold her hand —but he has to be in his own Explorers' Club, far, far away, to make this work. There have to be two poles—one in the land of the purples, the other in the land of the birds—to properly amplify the signal.

And so, along with the mob, Craw shrieks and pumps her darkest feelings into the crystal, serving as a conduit to the sleeping leviathan in the heart of the Unknownamensity.

Even as she sends something else along, too—the slightest undercurrent of thanks and farewell that she hopes will reach her creator through the hurricane of hatred. She hopes and prays that Jenna will always know how much the world she made meant to those who explored it.

Whatever its flaws and dangers, it was certainly unforgettable.

Southern Memorial Medical Center, Atlanta, Georgia, Now:

For the first time in ten years, Jenna Venner opens her eyes and looks out at the world again.

She doesn't know exactly where she is—a hospital room some-where, surrounded by beeping, blinking equipment. She doesn't know what day it is, and she doesn't know exactly why she is here.

No one else is in the room, and the monitors are just in the process of alerting the staff that her condition has changed. For a moment, she lies there in wondrous silence, the calm before the storm of medical attention and doting family and friends that is sure to arrive soon.

In that moment, Jenna remembers the dream from which she's awakened, the dream of a strange world filled with bird people, purple people, and all manner of crazy wonders in something called the Unknownamensity.

But even as she thinks of it, the dream fades away. The harder she tries to hold on to it, the faster it shreds in her grasp, leaving nothing but the faintest impression of colors and light and emotion.

Then, when the nurses and doctor charge into the room, even that is gone, drifting away forever like a ballet of dandelion puffs twirling on a soft summer breeze, never to be remembered again.

Except perhaps, someday, if she is lucky, in another dream.

NOT-SO-FORTUNATE SON

"Here! Catch!" Bunker Buster, with his purple paisley skin and torn green shorts, laughs as he tosses the tractor trailer effortlessly in my direction. "All yours, *Short Bus!*"

Pluribus! The name is Pluribus! That's what I'd say if I had more than a split-second before the truck hits...which I don't. I don't have Bunker Buster's strength level, either, so I do the usual--multiply like crazy.

Closing my eyes, I stretch my arms wide and tap into my power, whipping up dozens of duplicate selves to quickly fill the tractor trailer's landing zone. When the truck comes down, we all raise up our hands and catch it, spreading the impact among all those arms and bodies so it lands harmlessly.

Normally, Bunker Buster would follow up with some smart aleck remark, but he doesn't. The hyper-muscled testosterone farm is too busy fending off the latest squadron of sky-piranhas dispatched by Sticky Wicket.

"Gents, we shouldn't be fighting," Sticky declares in his posh English accent, even as he finishes bashing in the unbreakable wind-shield of an armored car with a massive-headed croquet mallet. "We should all be on the same side, don'cha know!"

"I'm not on *anybody's* side, Stick Figure!" Bunker Buster crushes a sky-ranha between two massive hands and swats another halfway to Poughkeepsie. "I'm out for Number One, and that ain't *either* of you!"

"Suit yourself." Sticky deflects the gunfire of the driver with his mallet, then flings a needle-tipped metal wicket into the man's chest. With the driver dispatched, he operated controls on the dashboard, making the back doors pop open as if by magic. "That's one fewer compatriot who'll need a share of all this *cash.*"

As my mob of doubles charges toward the armored car, Sticky leaps free of the window and skedaddles around the back like his butt is on fire. En route, he pitches more wickets behind him, puncturing one of my clones at the head of the pack. When the lead runner drops, others trample over him--at least until I focus my power and make the first grouping disappear.

Just as Wicket rounds the back of the truck, a big helicopter whips in from the distance. What looks like a huge metal ring hangs suspended from a rig mounted on the bottom of the copter, ready to pick up the armored truck, no doubt.

My doubles and I run harder than ever, but Bunker Buster still beats us to the back with one mighty leap over the top of the vehicle.

And then nothing from back there. When I get to the rear of the armored car, the only sound is the chopping of the approaching 'copter's blades and the footsteps of my running copies' feet.

And instead of Wicket and Bunker Buster, all I see are splatters of bloody gore all over the back of the truck and the street.

"Ah, no." I look away, shaking my head. "Not this."

I'm dimly aware of the helicopter banking and swooping away into the distance. Police car sirens wail in the neighborhood, getting closer.

And I just stand there in shock, shaking my head slowly, and say, "Not this. Not *again.*"

And 25 copies of me shake their heads and wipe away tears of regret for the dead.

"More super-*smearos*, huh?" That's Lieutenant Tank Driscoll making the sensitive comment before the remains of Sticky Wicket and Bunker Buster have had a chance to cool. He's not even *close* to being Isosceles City P.D.'s finest.

But the woman beside him most certainly is. Her name is Detective Bonnie Taggart, and I know her well. "Show some respect for the *dead*, dingleberry." She swats Tank's scrawny arm with her notepad, looking disgusted.

"But there've been so damn *many* of 'em, Fox. I'm startin' to lose *track.*" Tank's eyes bulge, and his pencil mustache twitches with frustration.

"I'll bet you wouldn't feel like that if you'd witnessed as many of these fatalities as *Pluribus* has." Bonnie flashes me an apologetic look.

"Thanks." I watch as crime scene investigators snap photos and take samples of the dead supers' remains. I still can't believe those bloody spatters are all that's left of them after the long and colorful careers they had.

"Ah, what does he care?" Trank lights a cigarette between his bony fingers and puffs away. "They were both *black hats*, weren't they? Pluribus supposedly wears only *white.*"

"They were still part of the superhuman community," says Bonnie. "And as such, they deserve the best investigation we in the Superhuman Protectorate have to offer."

Just as she says it, company of the superhuman variety arrives, swooping down to land alongside us--and I'm instantly on guard again. The two new arrivals aren't exactly what you might call *heroes*.

"Solved yet? Answers?" Headbelly is a higher-up in the supervillain community, a man whose head resides on his ample gut instead of his shoulders. He's also a major pain.

"What do you have for us so far?" Win Chime has night-dark skin, glowing blonde hair, like a mane of fiber optics, and a ravishing figure clad in skintight black and silver spandex. There isn't a man on the hero side of the tracks who hasn't lost at least one fight with her due to extreme distraction.

"Not much." Bonnie's tone is matter-of-fact. "Based on preliminary review of the crime scene, this looks like much the same modus operandi as the other super murders."

"So how many more will it take to finally solve these heinous exercises?" asks Win Chime. "How long until your people get their heads out of their asses?"

Headbelly snickers. "Good one!"

"How long until *your* people *help* solve it?" asks Bonnie. "How long until *they* get their heads front and center?"

Headbelly doesn't appreciate that one. "Protectorate works for *both* sides! We demand answers!"

"Then start by *providing* some," says Bonnie. "We need information on the deceased. Who were their friends and family? Who might have had a grudge against them? What cases were they involved with recently?"

"Just want info to use *against* us," snaps Headbelly. "Want to pin all the murders on *us.* "

"Why?" Tank sneers and leans toward him. "*Should* we?"

"Cut it out!" Bonnie raises both hands, palms facing Tank and Headbelly. "Now is *not* the time! What we *need* is *information*, which will *not* be misused against you or your community. You have my *word* on it."

Bonnie has a rep as a square shooter, and everyone knows it. All of us have at least heard the stories of how she gives *all* sides of the super population of Isosceles City fair treatment.

"Fine." Win Chime sighs and folds her arms over her very ample bosom. "What do you need to know?"

As Bonnie and Tank interview her and Headbelly, I see my chance. When their backs are turned, I snap my finger, quietly raises up another duplicate -- close to my current age and appearance -- and leave him there in my stead as I slip off into the confusion surrounding the crime scene.

As powers go, mine isn't always the most helpful in the thick of a fight, but it sure comes in handy sometimes.

Want to know what a super-hero's best friend is these days? The phone app that lets us summon a car ride anywhere in town. For those of us without the power of flight, you can't beat a ride-hail app when you're stuck on the street in your costume with no way home.

The more seasoned drivers, the ones who've seen it all, just humor me. If they ask, I say I'm on my way to a birthday party, and that's usually the end of it.

This afternoon, I'm not so lucky, but that's okay. When the guy at the wheel asks too many questions, I just crank out a few more duplicates to fill up his car, and that freaks him out enough to shut his yap.

I leave a duplicate to keep him company anyway after I get out of the car around the corner from HQ -- my apartment, that is. As the car pulls away, my copy grins and waggles his fingers at me from the window, already talking the driver's ear off.

As bad of a day as it's been, I can't help smiling at that.

Sending doubles in several directions to frustrate anyone who might be watching, I walk up the front steps of my brownstone and let myself in with a key from the chain I wear around my neck under the costume.

Then I slam the door behind me and head straight for the kitchen. Yanking the hood and mask off, I fling open the fridge, grab a bottle of Guinness, and uncap it.

My hands shake a little as I tip the bottle to my lips.

For exactly the thirteenth time, I wonder what the *hell* is going on. Is another super power manifesting itself? One that draws me to murder scenes when the victim is part of the *powered* community? It's the only thing that makes sense, given how many of those murders I've witnessed.

Which is *all* of them.

That's *fifteen* murders at *thirteen* scenes in *three weeks*. Every last one of them a *super* -- some *white hats*, some *black hats*, some *gray*. And they all blew apart in exactly the same way, the only difference being *when* in the battle they exploded.

Leaving *me* to wonder *why* and *how* this is happening, and why I keep turning up to witness it.

I barely get two sips down before the phone vibrates in my pocket. I see it's a number I don't recognize, but I answer it anyway.

477

"Hello?" The voice on the line is throaty and female, completely unfamiliar. "Pluribus?"

My instinct is to just hang up, but I don't. "Who is this?"

"Someone who wants to help. Meet me in one hour at 315 Grand. Wear civilian clothes."

I scowl at the phone like it smells bad. "Civilian clothes?"

"*I'll* be in costume." The voice laughs once, like a cough. "Just look for the bright green and hot pink spandex."

My heart races as I walk into the church, but for once it isn't because I'm heading into battle or drawn to the probable murder of some powered-up individual. It's because of the giant sculpture at the far end of the nave, looming over the vast body of the Gothic structure. It's a statue of a man, rendered huge, his stern features staring from behind the spiked cowl of his superhero suit.

I knew that man well, *too* well to not be affected by the sight of his likeness towering in the basilica, no matter how many times I've seen it before in the flesh or otherwise.

On the other hand, I'm not sure I'll ever get used to seeing people *worshipping* it. There's a service in progress, with pew after pew filled with super people in spandex costumes, people of immense and varied powers...all of them bowing their heads in humble prayer to the entity represented by that enormous statue.

"In the name of blessed Archetype, brother, I greet thee." The voice in my ear is familiar from the phone -- throaty and feminine. "In this house of Our Super-Lord, thou art *most* welcome."

Looking over my shoulder, I see she has a long face with aquiline features partly obscured by a bright green cowl with hot pink piping. Through the eye-holes of her mask, I see her eyes are deep emerald with a ribbon of gold around the iris, and they're twinkling.

She's as tall as I am, with a well-muscled form that bespeaks a high level of strength and fitness. Depending on her powers, if any, I'm not sure I could take her in a fight...but that's not the most interesting thing about her at the moment.

What catches my eye and holds it is the red-and-gold satin stole slung over her shoulders, reaching down to her thighs. It's embroidered with the symbol I know so well from the ubiquitous Church of the Archetype, the mark of someone highly placed in the hierarchy of this religion.

"Priestess." I'm supposed to bow or curtsy or something, but I don't. "You called?" I hold up my phone.

"Praise be to the Archetype." She keeps her voice low as the service continues. In the chancel, at the massive altar under the statue of Archetype, their god, two priests in brightly colored superhero costumes chant and shoot glittering fireworks from their fingertips.

The whole thing puts me off. I'd hoped never to set foot in a place like this again, to never see that farce in action or hear the crackpot chants or smell the incense cooking down in the censers...yet here I am. Back in a place that reminds me in *so* many ways of the failures and low points of this life that's left me struggling and lonely.

I feel like the loneliest man on Earth, though my superpower is to generate unlimited numbers of duplicates.

"Call me Mother Morning," she says softly. "And it is an honor to be graced by your presence in this most holy cathedral."

She's the one who bows, and it makes me want to leave. "Please. Just tell me why you called me here."

"Because I want to help," says Mother Morning. "I believe I *can* help."

"With what? In what way?"

"With the mystery that surrounds you. The *deaths* of the powered that you've been witness to. I believe I can help you uncover who or what is behind them."

The priests in the chancel float off the floor and come to hover over the crowd. One sprinkles baptismal water on the people in the pews while the other glows like the sun, casting radiant beams in all directions with arms upraised.

"You really think you can help?" I ask Mother Morning.

"I do." She smiles warmly. "My work with the *flock* can be most illuminating at times." She gestures at the worshippers before us, many of whom are drifting up toward the priests.

One more questions nags at me. "And *why* do you want to help?"

"Our brothers and sisters are dying," she says. "Also, it would be a very great *honor...*" She bows again. "...to serve you. The *son* of the great god *Archetype.*"

So it's *that* crap again. "He *disowned* me, remember? I'm *nobody* now."

She bows more deeply than ever. "You will *always* be *His* son, no matter your quarrels."

I sigh. It's *such* a bunch of hooey...but who am I to turn away help in a situation like this? I'm not exactly getting to the truth fast on my *own.*

"All right. Let's see how it goes. But no more bowing."

"As the Son of the God commands, I will..."

"And no more of that, either," I tell her. "Just call me Jack when I'm a civilian and Pluribus when I'm in uniform."

"Yes, Lord." She winces. "I mean Jack."

"Thanks, Mother." The whole congregation glows with blazing light. "So how will this help of yours work?"

"Follow me." She heads for the door, pausing at a wall-mounted holy water dispenser to dip her fingers and make the sign of the Archetype across her torso--lower left, breastbone, lower right, xiphoid process. It forms the shape of a capital letter "A." "There's someone you should meet."

How long has it been since I last visited the superhuman ward of Saint Secret Identity's Hospital? Five years ago, maybe, when one of my body doubles materialized inside-out and couldn't be re-absorbed properly?

But what I think about most as Mother Morning leads me through the doors is *my* mother, who wasn't in the superhuman ward at all the last time she was here. That was more like twelve years ago, though it seems a lot more recent--maybe because I still dream about it so often.

I haven't been the same since *that* day. Mom knew me better than anyone in the world, even my clones.

Maybe even better than I know myself, I still think.

"Right this way, Lo--I mean Jack." Mother Morning guides me through the maze of hallways that leads to the Superhuman Intensive Care department. When we're stopped at the door by a bald, broad-shouldered male nurse, Mother says she's here in her capacity as priestess to minister the sacraments to patients of the faith. I'm a deacon, she says, and that's good enough to get us over the threshold.

"Here we are." Mother Morning leads me into a room and pulls aside a curtain. "This is the person I wanted you to meet."

There's a patient in the bed, but I can't tell if it's a man or a woman. He or she is swaddled in bandages, with raw, scarlet flesh showing in the gaps between them.

"This is Captain Cask," says Mother Morning. "She's one of the Hedonistas."

"I...I..." Captain Cask's voice is a ravaged squeak. "I already...kn-*know* you."

"You do?" The name doesn't sound familiar, though I've heard of the Hedonistas.

"Of *c-course* I know y-you," says Captain Cask. "Y-you're...*God.*"

Mother Morning shoots me a look, so I don't deny it...though honestly, seeing that single bloodshot eye between the wrappings doesn't make me inclined to disappoint the poor soul, anyway.

"Captain," says Mother Morning. "Tell Jack how you suffered your injuries."

"I w-was...stopping a c-carjacking...on Hawthorne and T-Trimble," squeaks Captain Cask. "I was off d-duty...s-so I w-wasn't fully p-p-powered up...but I still st-stopped the black hats." She draws a deep breath that seems to last forever, then releases it twice as slowly, trembling. "Then I h-heard some kind of weird *f-flute* sound and *w-whoosh!* I w-was on f-fire!"

"You don't know what caused it?" asks Mother Morning.

Captain Cask's head twitches weakly, the closest she comes to full-on shaking it. "J-just one p-perp...and sh-she d-didn't exhibit...any p-powers. N-neither d-did the d-driver. Th-they seemed as surprised as *I* w-was."

"And how did you survive?" asks Mother Morning.

"M-my teammate...Flambé...g-got there j-just in t-time...and extinguished the f-flames." Captain Cask lets out a little whimper. "B-but I still f-feel...l-like I'm g-going to...g-going to..." She sucks in another shuddering breath. "There's a *p-pressure*...inside me. I'm f-fighting...t-to hold it b-back...with m-my f-force field powers...b-but it f-feels...like it's g-going...to *l-let go.*"

Her eye closes, and tears squeeze out of it. Her whimpers turn to agonized sobs.

"Shhh," says Mother Morning. "It's okay, honey." She reaches to comfort the woman, then withdraws her hand. The slightest touch to her burn-ravaged flesh could cause Captain Cask a world of greater hurt. "You just keep hanging in there."

"You don't know who or what could have caused it? You didn't see anyone around who might have attacked you like this?" She's so upset, I hate to ask--but I do it anyway. If whatever's pressing at her ever lets go, this might be my last chance to question her.

"N-no." Captain Cask sniffles and shivers. "M-maybe they were h-hiding."

"Do you have any enemies with the power to do this?" I ask. "Anyone who might have threatened you recently?"

"All in p-prison," says Captain Cask. "And n-no threats r-recently..."

"What about the flute sound you mentioned? Was it like a series of notes? A single, high-pitched tone?"

"M-more like f-four...or five n-notes." She barely manages to hum five notes--high, low, high, low, high. "That's it. I d-don't know...w-what they m-mean."

I think for a moment, considering my next question. "What do you know about Bunker Buster and Sticky Wicket?"

"W-who?"

"You don't know them?" asks Mother Morning.

"N-no."

I mention the next two murder victims who come to mind. "What about Wunderbar or Dye Job?"

"I've h-heard of D-Dye Job, b-but...I've n-never m-met him," says Captain Cask.

"What about Metric System?"

She twitches her head weakly and resumes sobbing.

I get the feeling this interrogation has gone as far as it can. "Don't cry, Captain. It'll be all right." I want to make her feel better, but I don't know how, given the circumstances.

"W-will it, G-god?" squeaks Captain Cask. "*Will it?*"

Outside the hospital, Mother Morning pulls out an elaborate-looking e-cig (like something out of a Jack Kirby comic book) and vapes as we walk.

"I think Captain Cask was a target, too," she says. "Her force field powers must have stopped whatever explosive force blew up the other victims."

"Temporarily, at least, from the sound of it." I catch a whiff of her vapor, some kind of orange-chocolate-tinged mist, and I like it. "Should she even be *in* there, if she still might *blow*?"

"I think they're bringing in a super specialist tomorrow." Mother Morning puffs on her e-cig. "I heard them mention the Stabilizer."

My mind is awhirl as we walk onward. The investigation's alive, but not by much.

"We should research any possible connection between Captain Cask and the other victims." I'm thinking aloud as I say it. "She claimed not to know the ones I named, but there are ten others I didn't get to."

"True," says Mother Morning through a cloud of sweet vapor.

"Then there's the *flute* factor. Maybe one of those ten has some kind of connection to flute music or something that *sounds* like it."

"You knew some of the victims, didn't you? Does what she said ring any bells for you?"

I review what I know for a moment and end up shaking my head decisively. "I've got nothing."

"No divine wisdom?" She sounds hopeful, not sarcastic.

It still ticks me off. "I guess all-mighty Archetype must be busy inspiring somebody else just now."

"His grace shall not fail to find us if we but pray with fervent urgency." Mother Morning makes the capital-A sign of the Archetype and ends with a ceremonial double-handclap denoting the two persons in one God: Father and Son.

Me being the Son, for what *that's* worth.

Suddenly, my phone rings, and I grab it in a hurry. When I see the number on the screen, I answer it without delay.

"Pluribus?" It's Bonnie Taggart. "Could you come down to the station right away, please? There's something I'd like to talk to you about."

When I walk in the door of the precinct house, everyone stops what they're doing. Though I changed into my superhero uniform on the way here to preserve my secret identity, I'm rethinking that strategy in light of all the stares.

I should be grateful, I guess. The attention I'm getting in here has nothing to do with my father being a superhuman god. In here, it's all about my recent track record, being present at one superhuman murder after another.

For the super-types in the house, there's the worry that my showing up might mean that more super-murders are soon to follow. Word travels fast when everyone has super-hearing, and I've quickly developed a reputation as a damn harbinger.

For the non-supers manning the station, I'm pretty sure there's another reason for the tension in the air. Because let's face it, as far as the cops are concerned, my being at all those super-murder scenes might not be a coincidence.

Heck, I might think the same thing, if the cape were on the other shoulders.

"Hey, Pluribus!" Naturally, Lt. Tank Driscoll comes out to greet us, the scrawny scumbag. "I heard they got a new code name for you! *Coincidento!* Because it's always such a huge *coincidence* when you show up at so many *murder scenes.*"

Lots of other cops in the room laugh at that one, and I just take it. The jerk is just baiting me, looking for a reason to put me in an interrogation room.

Mother Morning, on the other hand, is not so docile. "Hey!" She marches over and stands toe to toe with tank, snapping off her retort in his knobby walnut of a face. "That is *no* way to address the *son* of the one, true *god.*"

"It is if I smell *murder* on him," snarls Tank. "*Nobody* gets a pass in *my* jurisdiction."

"Funny." Mother Morning presses closer, coming within inches of his face. "That's exactly what *God* says."

Then, she spins on her heel and swoops over, seizing my elbow on the way past. As we head for Bonnie's office, I can't help being impressed and grateful...and a little bit attracted to her. I guess this Son of God bit isn't *all* bad.

Bonnie leads us downstairs to the morgue, which we enter without knocking. The coroner, a tall, gray-haired woman in her 50s or so, is hard at work on an autopsy and doesn't look up.

Her voice, when she speaks, is deep, her words clipped and no-nonsense. "Hello, Detective."

Bonnie gets right down to business. "Where are those DNA results, Agnes?"

"Just arrived from the lab today." Agnes bobs her head at a manila envelope on a nearby counter. "And yes, I've already asked them to run the samples again. There's no *way* those could *not* be in error."

Bonnie opens the envelope and slides out printed sheets, scanning them as they emerge. "What do you mean?"

Agnes lifts the lungs from the chest of the subject she's examining, then drops them on a hanging scale and views the weight on the unit's display. "I mean the DNA results must have been in error or contaminated or both. Each distinct sample reads like it contains fragments from multiple donors, scrambled up and reassembled like I've never *seen* before."

"I see." Bonnie frowns as she reads through the results in the envelope. "And there's no other explanation?"

"None." Agnes shrugs and shakes her head. "It must be some kind of cross-contamination or test error. I gave the lab seven shades of hell when I called for a retest."

"But how do you *know?*" asks Mother Morning. "With all the unique superhuman physiologies out there, how do you know for a fact that the samples *are* the result of contamination or test error?"

"Excuse me?" Agnes doesn't sound amused by the layperson's contribution.

Mother Morning proceeds as if she didn't notice the coroner's haughty tone. "Couldn't it be from someone with an altered physiology? Archetype *knows*, there are some wild power sets and adaptations on the streets of Isosceles City."

Agnes doesn't answer. She and Bonnie both look as if they're deep in thought.

Then, the silence is broken by a male voice blaring over the intercom. *"All units, report to Pendulum Plaza! Ten-ten-ten in progress!"*

"What's a ten-ten-ten?" asks Mother Morning.

"Superhuman battle royal with massive civilian involvement!" Bonnie barks the words as she charges out the door.

By the time we leap out of Bonnie's SUV, Pendulum Plaza is engulfed in superhuman conflict. Civilians run screaming in all directions as a host of costumed warriors unleashes all manner of powers with no apparent regard for non-super-charged life.

"Holy hell!" Tank has his service revolver out but makes no move to set foot in the midst of the action. "This place is out of control!"

"I can't even tell who's fighting who here." Bonnie turns and shouts in my direction. "Maybe *you* have a clue?"

Watching the storm of destruction rage before me, I try to make sense of it all. There are lots of familiar costumes in the thick of it, faces I know from both sides of the fence--but the logic of their struggle eludes me. White hats fight black hats, sure--but also other white hats. Black hats, too, fight each other just as much as they fight their enemy white hats. It's a conflagration without any apparent rhyme or reason, one in which all the rules of engagement in the superhuman community have seemingly and ruthlessly been cast aside.

"I don't know!" I have to shout for Bonnie to hear me over the noise of battle. "Good guys and bad guys are fighting their own allies as well as each other! It doesn't make any sense!"

"I say pull everyone back!" shouts Tank. "Keep our Protectorate forces out of this crap-show and let these freaks tear each other to pieces!"

"We don't even know what the *sides* are, let alone which side *we're* on," says Bonnie.

Suddenly, a male superhero in bright yellow and blue tights crashes into the street not twenty yards away, blasting a crater into the pavement. Another hero--one I recognize, the Mountebank--leaps in after him, swinging a nuclear sword and shrieking with glee.

"It's getting wilder," says Mother Morning. "They're speeding up and fighting harder!"

"Why don't *you* do something, Coincidento?" Tanks asks me. "Call for a super-*time-out* or something!"

I gaze into the maelstrom, mesmerized by the violence. A villain with flesh-molding powers twists a hero with metal breath into a deformed, howling pretzel. Three heroes with power over oxygen, wood, and insects, respectively, hammer two villains with electrical and sound-based talents. A super-speedster and a woman who looks like she's made out of flickering purple light wage a breakneck battle against a giant, fire-breathing sea horse flapping aloft on leathering bat wings.

Even if I thought I could do something, I literally have no idea where to start.

"There must be *something* you could try," says Mother Morning. "Perhaps a special intercession with your father, the great God, Archetype?"

"God is dead," I tell her. "That one, anyway."

Still, maybe she's right that I ought to try something. It strikes me that there's one thing worth doing, whatever the nature of the conflict.

Stepping forward, away from the group, I close my eyes and concentrate on generating duplicates. I feel them popping to life all around me, dozens of clones spun into being by the power-infused heart of me.

Through the magic of my Pluribus gift, they automatically know the purpose for which they were created. I don't have to say a word for them to charge forth and do what I need them to do.

As I watch, they race through the war zone, hauling civilians out of harm's way. I see one of the clones grab a child just as an errant death ray is about to strike her. Another takes a bullet for a young woman on the run, while a fellow clone deflects a hurtling eagle-man from crushing a hobbling old couple as he plunges to Earth.

A team of twelve clones forms a human shield around a group of fleeing parents and children, blocking all incoming fire from turning the innocents into collateral casualties.

The battle continues to rage, but at least more civilians will survive the mayhem. I haven't stopped the fight, but at least I've done that much right.

Suddenly, then, I hear the sound of something plummeting toward me from above, and I instinctively dart away from it. I get clear just in time, as the object rockets into the street on the spot where I just stood, embedding itself in the blacktop.

But it's not an object at all, I see--it's a *person*. It's a gray hat I've worked with before, and brought down on occasion, the one and only Mugwump.

Running back to his side, I see he's mortally injured. The fully-formed villain on his backside is already dead, crushed in the fall, and the hero on his front side is battered and gasping.

"E-Pluribus...," he says. "Y-you came!"

"What's going on here, Mugwump?" I want to help him, but I have no idea what to do at this point. "What started all this?"

Mugwump laughs up blood. "Isn't it obvious?" Reaching up with one shivering hand, he tugs the black cowl from his head, revealing the face underneath.

My face.

My heart races, and the hackles spring to life on the back of my neck. Just then, I hear a series of high-pitched notes, like those played on a flute, and panic rushes over me.

High, low, high, low, high. I know what those notes mean.

"I-it's all about...y-you!" says Mugwump, and then he explodes, leaving a spatter of bloody gore in his place.

It's the exact same thing that happens to every other white hat, black hat, and gray hat fighting in the war zone of Pendulum Plaza, all at exactly the same time.

Leaving me and all my duplicates to be showered by streams of crimson froth falling like a sudden summer downpour from above.

I don't tell Bonnie or Tank what I saw under that mask, but I tell them what I heard...not that it makes much difference in the scheme of things. We're all still splattered from head to toe with the same gruesome slop, all that remains of the dozens of heroes and villains who just waged war in Pendulum Plaza.

The way things go, though, I might not have to worry about being involved much longer.

"Hey, Coincidento!" barks Tank. "You're *banned!*"

At first, I'm not sure I heard him right. "Banned?"

"From active superhuman fight scenes!" says Tank. "And *crime scenes*, too."

"You can't do that!" says Mother Morning. "He's a superhero! Fight scenes and crime scenes are his *workplace.*"

"Yeah? Well, he's bad for business," snaps Tank. "I'm done takin' chances that *maybe* he's not the one makin' our superhuman population go *pop.*"

Bonnie scowls at Tank, then shrugs at me. "It might not be a bad idea to steer clear for a while. At least until we completely rule out any causal relationship between you and the murders."

"Whatever." I try not to look Mother Morning in the eyes as I give up without a fight. "I'll lie low for a while."

"Feel free to give us a call if you get any *funny feelin's*, though."

Tank shoves a business card in the waistband of my tights. "Or if you hear any *flute music* playin' all of a sudden."

"If you'll excuse me." I turn and start walking away. "I really, really need to get cleaned up right now."

"Good luck, Coincidento," says Tank. "Try not to stumble across any more *mass murders* on your way home, y'hear?"

Mother Morning catches up and walks alongside me, brushing goo from her uniform. "I don't care if you *are* the Shirker," she says. "You shouldn't let the cops walk all over you like that."

I glance over at her, surprised to hear that name from her lips...though I shouldn't be. She *is* clergy, after all.

"I'd rather not talk about that," I tell her.

"But it's a central part of the *faith*," says Mother Morning. "Without the Shirker, who refuses to fulfill his Father's wishes, there could be no promised *Compliers*, who shall usher in the new era of glory by *obeying* the Father's commands."

"Well, good for you and the church then." I pull out my phone and start hunting for a ride. "If it gives you all something to live for, more power to you. As for me, I don't want anything to do with it."

"But why deny your destiny?" She sounds worked up. "Why *spit* on the special blessing you've been given by mighty Archetype?"

"Because *Archetype* isn't a *god*. He's just a *man* with *super powers* who set himself up as a *deity* to satisfy his colossal *ego*."

"Maybe it seems that way to you, but..."

I stop walking and turn on her, overflowing with anger that has nothing to do with her. "I haven't seen him in *fifteen years*, ever since I refused to play along with his *phony religion* crap! As soon as I went against him *just once*, he *disowned* me and *disappeared.*"

"That was his *ascension.*" She says it like she's teaching catechism to a six-year-old. "He had to *rise* to the *next level* of existence to pave the way for *superhumanity* after the Compliers deliver them to salvation."

"*Bull.* He had to *run* from his *family* and *responsibilities* because he's huge *narcissist* with a *god complex* and *Peter Pan syndrome* all wrapped up in *one.*"

"Jack," she says calmly. "I understand why your father's abandonment might seem upsetting. I can also fathom why your prophesied destiny might feel oppressive. But the *rest* of the prophecy tells a different story. According to the Book of Futurities, the Shirker will see the light in the end and help make of Earth a paradise." She touches my arm lightly. "If anything, you should *rejoice.*"

"You *don't* understand," I tell her. "You *couldn't.* He's been *gone* for so *long.* Even when he was present *physically*, he wasn't *there* for me...yet I've lived my whole *life* in his *shadow*...having to face the *lies* he's fed his *worshippers.* Like *you.*"

She tips her head to one side and smiles. "You are *just* as he described you in the scriptures. So *slow* to grasp the *truths* that lie in front of you."

Exasperated, is more like it...but I can already tell I'm getting nowhere arguing religion with this priestess. Better, I think, to quit quibbling and get back on task.

"Speaking of truths that lie in front of you..." I turn back to my phone and order a car to come and get us. "I saw something right before the big blast at Pendulum Plaza. Something I didn't mention in front of the cops."

"What was it?"

"Remember the gray hat who crash-landed near me? Mugwump?"

She nods slowly.

"Under his cowl...he looked just like *me.*"

"Seriously? Is that even possible?"

"It *shouldn't* be. I keep track of every clone I *make*, and I snuff them out as soon as I'm *done* with them. Not to mention, my clones don't have *super powers.*"

"And Mugwump did."

I nod. "He could fly, and he had great strength and near-invulnerability. *I* don't even have those powers, let alone my *clones.*"

"So what do you think this means?"

"I have absolutely no idea." Just then, the car I've been waiting for rolls around the corner, and I wave it down. "But maybe I know someone who might be able to help figure it out."

"Do you agree to my terms?" asks the tall man with the narrow, insouciant face and the wispy blond hair.

"Wouldn't be here if I didn't," I tell him. "Whatever information you gain from studying my case..."

He slams his fist down on the living desk in front of him, making it whimper. "...Is *mine* to do with as I please!"

"Of course, Tycho. Goes without saying, old friend."

"Old *enemy!*" Tycho slams his fist down again, drawing a louder whimper from the desk. "Old enemy who *used* to be your friend, but no *longer!*"

"Right." Glancing over at Mother Morning seated beside me, I notice she looks a little shell-shocked. No surprise there. This is her first-ever visit to the Sinstitute and the office of its very volatile super-genius director, Tycho Archimedes his own bad self.

"So what do you think, Tycho? Assuming Mugwump was one of my clones, and *none* of my clones has ever had super-powers, how and why could he have come into existence?"

Tycho leaps to his feet and paces his spacious office. The silvery walls vibrate when he passes, making a soft, tinkling sound like musical wind chimes. The crystalline floor and ceiling glow along his path, and pale smoke wafts from his burgundy smoking jacket, forming elaborate designs and images that hang and dance lightly in his wake.

The whole Sinstitute is like this, elegant and futuristic, a gorgeous, hidden haven of all the latest and greatest in super-high technology put to sinister use. In the past, it's caused me major headaches, backing Isosceles City crime sprees with weapons straight out of a U.F.O. Today, though, I've come in search of answers, the kind of outside-the-box insights I've always thought were best dreamed up by those motivated by unenlightened self-interest.

"*One* possible answer to your riddle," says Tycho from the far

end of the massive room. "Perhaps one of your enemies is perpe-
trating a wildly elaborate hoax to either *frame* you or drive you
insane."

"I guess that's possible." I rub my chin and shrug. "But it still
doesn't explain the existence of the super-powered clone."

"It does if we consider a *shape-shifter* in the mix! A shape-shifter
and *powers-shifter!*"

"Like whom?" I ask him. "Do you know any?"

"Meeting both variables, no." Tycho falls silent for a long
moment. "Of course, you could also be the victim of hypnosis or
some similar form of influence."

"But he never *acted* like he was being subjected to mind control,"
said Mother Morning.

"Well no, he wouldn't. But let's set that aside for the moment
anyway." Tycho paces back over to his desk and perches on the
corner. "Is it possible your *powers* are behaving in unexpected ways,
Pluribus?"

"How do you mean?" I ask.

"You've said the duplicates you generate are under your control
and quickly dematerialize at your command. But *what if* you are
shedding duplicates when you're *unaware* of it? And *these* duplicates
adhere to *different* properties than those you generate *consciously?*"

I consider it for a moment, trying to imagine the possibility.
"You mean I might be generating them *subconsciously?*"

"*Unconsciously,* is what I'm thinking." Tycho leans toward me, eyes
narrowed. "It wouldn't be the first time I've encountered a superpower that behaves differently when its possessor is unconscious."

"Really?"

"I propose an experiment," says Tycho. "If you're not too *squeamish* about putting yourself in my *hands.*"

"He is the son of *God!*" shouts Mother Morning. "What is it you
propose to *do* to him?"

"Relax, my dear." Tycho gives her a sneer that's rife with
strange, unreadable undercurrents. "Think of it as a simple *sleep
study.*" He chuckles and smacks the palm of his hand hard on the
desk, making it yelp. "Only not so *simple!*"

All I see is darkness and the figments of my own imagination. All I hear is the rushing of blood in my ears. All I feel is the warm water sloshing around me, buoying me on its surface.

It's my first time in a sensory deprivation chamber, courtesy of Tycho and the Sinstitute. He claims it will help relax me and isolate variables, allowing us to cut through the normal environmental noise that can prevent clear focus and pure data.

At first, I'm dubious about the relaxation benefits, but my doubts and alertness don't last. I haven't been sleeping well lately, what with the murder scene summonings, and apparently I'm more tired than I realized.

One minute, my mind is roving through the events of the past day, and the next, I'm lost in a deep dream state. Just like that, I disconnect from full consciousness, drifting instead through a series of dreamy vignettes.

Most are drawn from memories, like a scene of me playing with clones of myself in the grassy back yard of the family home. There are seven of us, all identical, playing tag and hide-and-go-seek in the summer sun, running and shouting with delight. Even then, I was only too happy to turn to the clones for friendship--which was the same as turning inward, I see now.

Inexplicably, that scene flows into another from much earlier, when I, as a baby in the crib, was nearly smothered to death by the mob of clones I'd unknowingly generated. It's one of the few moments I remember from infancy, perhaps mostly born out of stories I heard from my parents in later years...but it's a bad one. Panic seizes me as the breath is squeezed out of my lungs, the squirming weight of all those duplicates crushing me beneath them, unable to cry for help.

Next, I'm walking with my mother through Isosceles City as it is now...which is impossible. She's been gone since I was ten years old, and the city has changed so much since then--but there she is, as beautiful as I remember. The wind blows her long, auburn hair, tossing locks of it clear of her sweet, freckled face. Her laugh is like the tinkling of piano keys or bells, and the touch of her hand is soft around mine. Now *this* is a dream I never want to leave, a moment I could be happy reliving for as long as I live.

But then it's gone, and the next dream isn't so much a blissful memory drawn from real life as an improvised nightmare. Instead of the face of my beloved mother, I see an amorphous, faceless mass looming in the blackness. Its only feature is a gaping maw in ceaseless, relentless mastication.

I float toward it, bobbing on the hot, rancid waves of its breath. As I get closer, the sound of a voice becomes audible, if not understandable...a male monotone feeding out ribbons of guttural gibberish.

I begin to rotate on the long axis of my body, turning in circles as I continue my approach. Suddenly, the mass before me divides into two identical masses, which divide in twos again, and again, and again. Soon, I'm confronted with a *wall* of those masses, all faceless and forever masticating.

And then, without explanation, the amorphous shapes resolve into familiar faces. The wall is formed from endless copies of the face of my father, repeated into infinity in all directions.

The male monotone voice resolves, too, becoming the voice of my father, speaking in perfect unison from all those maws. Though I haven't heard it in so very long, I still recognize it instantly--and flinch instinctively.

"MY SON!" says Dad. "YOU WHO HAVE SHIRKED YOUR BIRTHRIGHT!"

I don't know why, but I don't slow down. If anything, my rotation and forward motion speed up as the infinitude of faces speaks out.

"DO NOT FEAR! THE DEATHS YOU HAVE WITNESSED ARE A HOLY CULLING MEANT TO CORRECT THOSE WHO HAVE FAILED EVEN MORE ABYSMALLY THAN YOU!"

I swallow hard, then call out to him/them. "What are you *talking* about? How have they *failed?*"

"REMEMBER HOW YOU REFUSED TO OBEY ME? I ORDERED YOU TO CREATE AN ARMY OF GODLINGS,

BLOOD OF MY BLOOD, TO SAVE THE WORLD--AND YOU REFUSED!"

"You're right! I refused to help you conquer the world!"

"YOUR REFUSAL MEANT NOTHING! I, YOUR FATHER AND GOD, CREATED THAT SACRED ARMY *THROUGH* YOU, WITHOUT YOUR *KNOWING* IT!"

Chills ripple through me at the thought of it. For the first time, I wonder if *this* part is a dream after all.

"BUT PERHAPS YOUR VERY *SPIRIT* AND *MATTER* WERE CORRUPT, FOR THOSE MULTITUDES HAVE *FAILED* ME! THEY HAVE SPLINTERED INTO FACTIONS--SO-CALLED BLACK HATS, WHITE HATS, GRAY HATS...THOSE WHO SEE FIT TO DO MY BIDDING, AND THOSE WHO DO NOT. AND THOSE FACTIONS HAVE GONE TO WAR!"

"Wait a minute!" It's hard to get my head around all this...and the more I understand, the less I like it. "You mean to tell me you've somehow been *using* me to make *duplicates* against my *will?*"

"I AM YOUR GOD! I MAKE ALL THINGS POSSIBLE!"

"But they have *super-powers! I* can't make clones with *powers!*"

"YES YOU CAN! YOU ARE CAPABLE OF *FAR* GREATER MIRACLES THAN YOU HAVE EVER REALIZED!"

I shake my head hard against the information overload. "And now these super-powered clones...they've gone to *war* against each other? My *copies* are fighting my *copies?*"

"THOSE FAILURES WERE MEANT TO SAVE THE WORLD! TO CORRECT THE OLD GOD'S MISTAKE OF LEAVING HUMANITY TO ITS OWN DEVICES! IMAGINE A WORLD IN WHICH GOD HIMSELF IS PRESENT IN GREAT NUMBERS, WALKING AMONG HIS SUBJECTS TO KEEP THEM HONEST!"

If this *is* a dream, Dad is just as deluded as he ever was. "So these clones were meant to be the Compliers of prophecy?"

"INSTEAD, THEY ARE THE RUINATION OF MY DREAM! AND NOW I AM DESTROYING THEM IN ALL THEIR NUMBERS, AS IS MY RIGHT!"

His words sink in like anvils in quicksand. "So *you're* the one who's been killing them off? Making them explode?"

"IT IS THE *LEAST* PUNISHMENT THEY DESERVE!"

"Then why drag *me* into it? Why do I have to witness all that?"

"YOU ARE DRAWN TO THESE FAILURES AS FLESH IS DRAWN TO FLESH. YOU COME TO WITNESS THEM BECAUSE THEY ARE LIKE UNTO YOUR OWN CHILDREN."

"My own children, huh? Then I hope you don't expect me to be thrilled that you're on a mission to *kill* them."

"YOUR FEELINGS DON'T MATTER," says Dad. "WHEN THOSE FAILURES GIVE ME AMPLE REASON, AS THEY ARE *ABOUT* TO, I SHALL SLAUGHTER THE *LOT* OF THEM."

"What do you consider 'ample reason?'"

"ARMAGGEDON! EVEN AS WE SPEAK, THEY GATHER IN THEIR HIDDEN REALM TO BRING THE END CRASHING DOWN UPON THE TOWERS OF ISOSCELES CITY! IT IS THEN, WHEN THEY PERPETRATE THEIR ULTIMATE SIN, THAT I SHALL BLOW THEM ALL TO SMITHEREENS!"

"Wow." As I fight to process all that he's told me, my rotation and forward momentum slow. I start to feel trapped, as if the blackness itself is wrapping tighter around me, pulling me back. "How do I..." I'm having trouble getting the words out. "How do I know...this isn't a *dream?*"

"BECAUSE I GIVE YOU PROOF! IRREFUTABLE PROOF! YOU WILL FIND IT ALL AROUND YOU AS YOU WAKE!"

I feel like I'm choking. "What kind...of proof?"

"YOU YOURSELF HAVE NOT BEEN ABLE TO MAKE SUPERHUMAN CLONES. SO FAR, ONLY *I* HAVE BEEN ABLE TO TRIGGER THIS PROCESS IN YOU!"

"That's what...you've said..."

"REMEMBER THAT AS YOU WAKE FROM THIS DREAM OF YOUR GOD...AND FIGHT FOR YOUR MISERABLE FAILED LIFE!"

"Wait! What about..."

Suddenly, the wall of faces rushes toward me. One of the maws engulfs me, gulping me down, and I can't even scream for lack of breath.

There's a burst of heat and cold all at once, then what feels like a heavy impact--and I'm awake. Or *am* I? Darkness still enshrouds me all around, everywhere I look.

But I feel myself splashing in water, thrashing against the pressure that's squeezing the breath from my body. And I hear a voice then, whispering in my ear.

"Our Father *made* me, Shirker! I am the *proof* of his glory, and I have come to *end* your betrayal!"

Thinking fast, I haul my knees back as far as I can, then pump my legs forward. My feet smash open the doors of the sensory deprivation chamber, and the bright light of the Sinstitute lab floods in.

It's then that I finally get a look at the freshly minted duplicate, the one I had no conscious role in creating. His face is identical to my face, but that's about the only resemblance. His body, like that of a giant boa constrictor, is coiled around me, squeezing me more tightly with each passing second.

I don't have breath enough to talk or even fight--but I *do* have what it takes to deal with this intruder. Closing my eyes, I focus my power and put it to work.

I feel it in my core as it takes effect--and then I see the living proof of it. Three pairs of hands reach into the chamber and haul us out, then attack the serpentine form coiled around me.

Snake Man resists, holding tight, so I whip up three more clones. Six clones strong, my personal rescue squad finally does the trick, unwrapping the rogue clone's body from my own.

He twists and lashes in their grip until one of them finally punches his lights out. Snake Man goes limp, and they dump him in the chamber and slam the door shut behind him.

"Jack! Are you all right?" Mother Morning dashes from an adjoining room and almost throws her arms around me...then thinks better of it.

"I'm...okay." My breath is still short, but not perilously so. I drop myself onto a nearby chair and slump there, fighting to calm my overtaxed lungs and hammering heart.

"Guess what?" Tycho storms into the room, waving a computer tablet overhead. "You *do* spontaneously shed duplicates while unconscious...and they *can* be superhuman!"

"Thanks for...the newsflash," I tell him.

"There *is* a newsflash, actually," says Mother Morning. "While you were in the box, a call came in on your phone from Detective Taggart. I picked up, and she said there's been a development."

"What...kind...of development?"

"Captain Cask broke out of the hospital," says Mother Morning, "and the cops know exactly where she went."

Following the beams of our flashlights, Mother Morning and I trudge through the sewer, knee-deep in the foul refuse of Isosceles City.

"Is super-poop different from regular poop?" she asks conversationally, as if wading through a sewer was nothing out of the ordinary.

"Yes," I tell her, keeping my voice down.

"In what way?"

"Trust me, you don't want to know."

As we slosh onward, I check the tracker app on my phone. It shows a glowing red dot up ahead, two branches away, moving rapidly toward a large junction point.

Good for the cops for tagging Captain Cask in the hospital, injecting a tiny tracking chip under the skin of her arm. Thanks to Bonnie, who wanted someone *other* than Tank to get to Cask first, we got access to the chip's codes and informed of a short cut that would let us outrun Tank in the underground maze of the sewers.

Now, finally, we are about to see where Cask is headed, and the suspense is killing me. Bound up like a mummy, suffering from head-to-toe burns and intense pressure that makes her feel like she might explode at any time, she must have a *huge* reason to make this flight into the sewers.

We make the next turn and walk a little further before stopping. I keep my eyes glued to the app on the phone for a moment, then decide we're finally on the verge of our destination.

"She's stopped." The glowing red dot on the app isn't moving. "She's in a big space up around that corner...some kind of major junction."

"What do you think she's doing there?" asks Mother Morning.

"We're about to find out." I pocket the phone and work my way to the next corner, slowing down and taking care not to make too much noise.

When I reach the corner and peek around it, I'm breathless for a different reason than being strangled by a snakelike doppelgänger.

There, in a vast vault of concrete fed by streams of sewage roaring in from multiple outflows, I see the biggest gathering of clones I've ever seen in my life.

Hundreds of them fill the enormous space, all costumed, all powered one way or another. Some float in midair, while others perch on concrete abutments or ledges. Some I recognize as white hat heroes, while others I know well as black hat villains or gray hats occupying the moral ground in-between.

And just enough of them have their cowls or masks off or lowered that I recognize them as duplicates of me. *Flesh of my flesh*, as Dad called them in my dream-not-a-dream.

Like unto your own children, is how he described them.

My heart hammers, and the hackles on my neck crawl--familiar reactions that can mean only one thing. The end is coming for all of them.

"What's this all about?" Mother Morning asks in a hushed voice. "What are they doing here?"

I point to a figure rising in the middle of the chamber, commanding instant respect and quiet from the crowd. He's one of the greatest heroes in Isosceles City, a multi-powered wonder who goes by the code name Bona Fide. "I think we're about to find out," I tell Mother.

"Fellow superhumans!" His deep basso voice fills the space.

"This war between us has gone on too long! We must *end* it before any *more* of us are struck down by whatever murderous force is stalking us!"

Many of the assembled clones applaud and offer their support with cheers and whistles.

"*Here*, in the underground refuge, we shall *settle* our scores once and for all! Hidden from prying eyes and enemies, we shall *have* the *super-maggedon* that has been too *long* in coming...even if it destroys all of *Isosceles City* in the bargain!"

"No." This is exactly what Dad was talking about in the dream-not-a-dream. This sewer system junction is the "hidden realm" where he said they would gather to bring down the towers of the city. They think they're safe here, tucked away underground, but there's *no* place they can hide from Archetype. There's nowhere on *Earth* where they can get away from God Himself.

And I know all too well what he's promised to do to them.

"Are we *ready* to finish this *struggle?*" shouts Bona Fide. "Shall we *finally* see the crowning of a *winner* in this great *game?*"

Every last white hat, black hat, and gray hat roars with approval.

"The *prepare* yourselves!"

At Bona Fide's command, everyone dons their masks and cowls and starts circling each other. The tension in the chamber grows a thousandfold.

"On my signal!" Bona Fide raises his hands in the air, and they start to glow from within.

"What should we do?" Mother Morning sounds frantic. "What *can* we do?"

It is then that I hear the telltale flute notes--high, low, high, low, high. I know what will happen when hostilities break out.

And I suddenly realize that I can't *let* it happen. Like it or not, those people down there *are* my children, in a way. I might not have *consciously* made them, but I can't stand back and let them be slaughtered by my father.

Clamping my eyes shut, I focus in with every bit of willpower I have, directing my power at a level I've never attempted before. (Dad said I'm capable of greater miracles than I've ever realized, so who knows?)

I feel the familiar burn as clones pop into existence--first a few, then dozens, then *more*. *Hundreds*. More than there are rogue clones in the junction chamber.

Then, as the rogue clones shout and scurry in confusion, I give my *new* clones their call to action...and they take it.

Again, I hear that damn flute playing, but I ignore it. I stay focused on the army I've created and the marching orders they're carrying out.

As, all through that chamber, they grab onto the rogue clones and refuse to let them go.

If the rogues are flying, my new clones climb the rock walls and leap onto them. If the rogues are swimming, they dive in after them.

The new clones double- and triple-team the rogues. If a rogue knocks one or more free, two or three others take the place of their brethren.

Is it because they share the same faces as the rogues that they don't get killed? Or do the rogue clones hold back for other reasons?

In the end, all that matters is that the rogues are restrained. Their super-maggedon does not occur, and the towers of Isosceles City are not laid low.

Though of course that condition won't last forever. Sooner or later, the rogues will decide to break free and restart their war.

Unless somebody talks them out of it.

"Hear me now!" I feel a little like I'm channeling Dad as I call out to the crowd. "I am your *progenitor!* You are flesh of my flesh! And I bear a *warning!*"

"*What* warning?" Bona Fide sounds *pissed*.

"My *father* will *kill* every one of you if you keep fighting this war! Let there be no *doubt*, he can *do* it."

"Your *father?*" says Bona Fide.

"Archetype! Maybe you're *heard* of him?"

Bona Fide just glares in the grip of my clones.

"*I* bring you a *new* commandment! A new way of *life!*"

"Believe it!" shouts Mother Morning, who is beaming at my side. "This is the *son* of God right here, people!"

"Not exactly a ringing endorsement!" says Bona Fide. "So what *is* this new commandment?"

Good question, I think, and then it comes to me. It floats right up to the surface of my mind with all the ease of a bubble in the ocean...a commandment I should have been following from the start, one that would have saved me so much trouble if only someone had thought of it sooner.

One that could still change my life, and all the lives arrayed before me, if only we can manage to make it stick. Maybe change the whole *world,* even--and wouldn't *that* be a poke in the old man's eye? Wouldn't *that* be a destiny I could live with for a change?

"The commandment is this." I clear my throat and smile at all the faces watching and waiting. Dear old Dad tried to force them to do his bidding, to enforce his will upon the world--and he failed. *He's* the true failure in *this* testament.

And all the doubt and self-hatred and loneliness he caused me could have been avoided if only he'd done one thing.

"Love your neighbor as you *wish* you loved yourself," I tell them.

SYMPATHY FOR THE METAL

I am *singing* for all I'm worth as my harpoon grappler lands *POW* in the heart of the speeding slab of silvery metal, sending thrilling shocks all the way through my body and the ship in which I stand.

"And I grab that slab from space and make it mi-ine!" The song is one of *hundreds* I've made up through my many long decades of life as a salvager, telling the tales of my glorious struggles among the stars. I've been singing them as long as I can remember, letting loose with my deep bass voice even though there's no one else to hear it in the cockpit, retrieval bay, smelter, storerooms, or launch bay of this vast ship.

But it would be an outright *lie* to say these songs are the sweetest sounds I ever hear. *Nothing* can compare to the sounds of metal, precious *metal*, as I seize and bend it to my will.

Metal metal metal. Nothing in the universe makes my heart jump for joy like *metal*. It is what I *live* for, what I was *made* for—what I *dream* of.

As I hoist the black carbon-fiber cable attached to my harpoon, reeling in the silvery slab I've caught, the muscles bulge in my arms and back, straining at my filthy gray coveralls. I grin through the sweat and grime all over my face, which is as dark as wrought iron.

This one's a beauty, all right, another piece of hull from another shattered ship in the vast sphere of orbiting junk called the Shardswarm.

Where the fragment came from originally or how it got here, I can't say. The same goes for all the other wreckage spinning around the unseen planet at the heart of the Shardswarm. No two pieces are the same in composition or design; no two *ships* are the same here, either.

Was it the site of some kind of war? A fatal last stand? A wicked double-cross? Or was this just a giant drydock, a resting place for vessels that were damaged or past their prime? If so, why are no two *alike?*

I don't think I'll *ever* know, but that doesn't make the piece of hull any less beautiful to me. The silvery surface flows with a rainbow of colors—bands of miraculous neurocircuitry imprinted in the skin of the ship when it was built.

All *fifty thousand* years ago, give or take *five thousand.*

"*Hand over hand, I bring you to my open arms, your new life just begu-un.*" My heavy-gloved hands keep hauling the black cable in from space, tugging it through the selective force field that keeps pressure and air in the bay. A little at a time, the metal slab slides through the field, crackling as it crosses the threshold. Though it is *at least* the millionth piece I've brought aboard in my life, it feels *just* as exciting to me as the *first.*

Or my name isn't *Tensile,* and my ship isn't the *Lady Alloy.*

"Beautiful, beautiful." As soon as the slab fully clears the field and comes to rest, I let go of the cable and pull the low-grav clamps from the pockets of my coveralls. Stomping over, I slap the clamps on either side of the slab, which is five meters longs and four meters high—over two heads taller than I am. Then, I yank out the harpoon grappler and toss it aside, letting it clatter on the deck plates behind me.

Pulling off one bulky glove, I run my fingers over the slab's smooth surface. The bulk of the piece is intact, aside from the harpoon hole and some damage along the edges. It makes sense, as being disconnected and off by itself is not this slab's natural state.

But as I stare at the jagged edges, I realize something else does *not* make sense. The scorched and broken metal still glows faintly red. When I move my hand close, I feel it shedding heat, as if the damage was only recently inflicted.

Which is impossible. The Shardswarm's orbitals are *ancient.* Except for myself and my ship, I've never come across anything newer than *fifty thousand years old* out here.

I'm about to reach for the molecular analyzer on my belt when *Alloy*'s alert klaxon whoops through the bay. A mechanical voice blares over the whoops, the only voice I've ever heard in my life except for my own.

"Distress signal received. Distress signal received." As *Thot,* the ship's brain speaks—her voice more businesslike and commanding than usual—the harpoon grappler slides over the deck and punches through the field without my help. *"Life sign detected, Metalhead Tensile. Retrieving survivor."*

"What the blark?" Nothing like *any* of this has ever happened to me before. I've been out here as long as I can remember, grown and raised by Thot, whom I've only ever known as a disembodied voice. The closest I've come to encountering any non-mechanical life other than my own are the dead bodies aboard the wrecked remnants of all those ships out there.

"Assistance protocol initiated," says Thot. *"Rendering assistance. Retrieving survivor."*

The carbon fiber cable continues to snake across the deck and into space. The harpoon leaps by remote control into the wall of debris spinning past, disappearing between the glinting hulks and shrapnel like a needle in a junk-storm.

Then the cable goes suddenly taut, and I catch my breath. Something unfamiliar jabs at my mind.

Fear. What if the lifeform turns out to be dangerous and wreaks havoc when it's brought aboard the ship? "Thot! Override assistance protocol!"

"Negative, Tensile. Assistance protocol cannot be overridden."

I clench my fists as the cable reels back into the bay. Watching through the open gate, I glimpse a gleaming silver sphere gliding smoothly toward the *Alloy,* its skin pierced by the tip of the harpoon.

Realizing I can't fight it, I glove up and march over to help with the hauling. I drive the fear further away with each great tug of the line, committing to whatever happens next.

And *singing*, which always makes me strong. *"Life sign...coming closer...life sign...almost here."*

A few more tugs and the silver sphere rolls crackling through the field, its perfect metal skin enough to make my heart skip multiple beats.

I step toward it, reaching for my analyzer, and wonder what kind of life form I'll find inside. More than that, how did it get all the way out *here*, in the middle of nowhere?

"Signaling occupant to exit pod," says Thot. *"Please stand clear, Tensile. Please stand clear."*

I take two steps back and wait as the pod emits a rapid-fire series of beeps and clicks. I want to *touch* its perfect silver skin, and I start to reach—only to jerk back at the last second as the skin quivers and melts away.

In an instant, the sphere is reduced to a silver puddle on the deck, leaving a human male with bright red hair lying, curled up, in the middle of it. His white jumpsuit uniform with the purple piping is streaked red with blood.

He isn't moving.

"Metalhead Tensile," says Thot. *"The survivor is badly damaged. Transport him immediately to the medzone."*

I frown. "But my shift isn't over." I point at the open gate and the spaceborne wreckage beyond. "I've still got *metal* to hump."

"Time enough for that later." Thot can be pretty stern when she wants to. *"If you do not get that man to the medzone fast, he will not be a survivor for much longer."*

"One more piece, all right?" I see a diamond-shaped hunk of gold plating spin toward the bay, and I salivate. I've got to *have* it. "Just one more, and I *promise* I'll take him to the medzone."

"Tensile!" snaps Thot. *"Aren't you curious about who he is and where he comes from?"*

I shrug and steal another look at the gold plating.

"Well, you will never know if you wait another few minutes," says Thot. *"The survivor's death is imminent."*

Sighing loudly, I stomp over to the limp body on the deck.

Reaching down, I scoop him up with both gloved hands, resigned to doing what Thot tells me to do. She *is* the boss, I suppose. She represents Möbius Inc., the legendary human-owned corporation that funded this operation in the first place.

Still, I can't resist one last glance at the gold plating. I just hope I can find and catch it when I get back.

I *do* find the gold plating—but thanks to Thot, I don't manage to grab it.

It's been hours since I took the survivor to the medzone, and I'm back at work. As I scan the passing debris, I finally spot the plating, and it's not far away.

Before I can harpoon it, though, Thot orders me back to the medzone. I try to make her wait, but she won't take no for an answer. I have to go *now*, she says. Something about the survivor being awake and able to communicate, which I guess I'm supposed to care about.

Sure enough, when the medzone door swings open, I see the redheaded survivor staring back at me, lying in the healing bed with his left arm in a cast and IVs and wires attached to his upper body. Blinking monitors mounted around the head of the bed transmit medical data to the onboard auto-doctor A.I., which adjusts medications and therapeutic processes in precisely-calculated increments.

As I approach, the survivor opens his mouth and speaks. His voice is strained, but at least he uses the same language I do. "Where are...the *others*?"

I stop at the foot of his bed, frowning. "What others?"

"The rest of...the Metallurgists." The survivor coughs weakly. "Where *are* they?"

My ears perk up at the sound of a word like "metal." Again, I think of that diamond-shaped hunk of gold plating skimming along the fringes of the Shardswarm, tantalizingly just out of reach.

"Don't you...understand me?" asks the survivor. "Am I speaking...the wrong language...or something?"

"Metalgists?" We might as well be speaking different languages, for all I've understood so far.

"*The* Metallurgists." The survivor coughs. "*You* know. The answer to one of...the greatest *mysteries*...in the *galaxy.*"

I shake my head, already bored. Like a magnet, the wreckage spinning away outside the ship draws me to return to it.

"I have to get back to work." Turning, I head for the door. "Busy day."

"Wait." The survivor raises his voice. "What about *the metal?*"

I pause in my tracks. "*What* metal?"

"*You* know." He coughs. "*The* metal. Enormous *blocks* of it...sailing from deep space...into the inhabited systems of humanity. Arriving for *decades* without explanation."

Slowly, I turn to face him. For the first time, I am more interested in this person than the Shardswarm debris field.

"Humanity has put it to great use," continues the survivor. "Entire *cities* have been built from it.

"But *no one* has ever discovered...the *source* of it...or the *origin* of the fabled *Metallurgists*...who *process* and *ship* it. The only proof of their identity...is the mark of a *Möbius strip*...stamped into the metal. A *figure eight* on its side...with no beginning or end.

"Men have *died* trying to solve the mystery of the Metallurgists. Now perhaps, so will I." He slumps into his pillow and closes his eyes, letting out a long sigh. "And one other may die, as well."

The urge to know more burns within me, nearly as strong as my urge to work metal. "One other?"

"My name is Mezzo," he tells me. "My partner...who already might have lost her life to this quest...is called *Silver*."

I like that her name is a metal. "Lost her life?"

Mezzo opens his eyes and nods slowly. "We were attacked...by the automated defenses...of an ancient ship in the wreckage. I escaped in a lifepod...but Silver went down with our vessel. *All the way* down."

I stare at him in disbelief. "Through the *Shardswarm?* That's *impossible.*"

"But she did it." With his right hand, Mezzo holds up a tiny gold chip that glints in the light of the medzone. "And the proof is on here. Feed it to your computer, and you'll see."

"All that *junk*, spinning in orbit. *No one* can get through it in one piece."

"I'll bet *you* can, being a Metallurgist and all," says Mezzo.

"I don't even know what a *Metalgist* is."

"You might not go by the name...but I'm betting you're *it*. It's the only...explanation. And you..." His eyes flicker shut, and his head falls to one side on the pillow. "You're her only...*hope.*"

I snag the chip from his hand as he drifts off to sleep. Normally, I don't bother with such tiny bits of metal—but this time, I make an exception.

"Thot?" I say on my way out the door of the medzone. "I'm bringing you something to analyze."

Later, I'm back at work in the retrieval bay, feeling good to be bringing in wreckage again. I don't see the gold plating this time, but I spot plenty of other goodies that keep my blood pumping. *This* is what life is all about for me and always has been.

Metal is all that matters to me. It shines, it tingles, it bends, it clangs. It has *weight*.

I *understand* it.

But I still can't stop thinking about what I saw just moments ago on Mezzo's chip: the video of Silver's distress call, played back on a big screen by Thot.

The image of Silver's face keeps coming back to me. There was blood, and there were bruises, but her beautiful blue eyes never stopped shining, and her wavy hair kept gleaming like spun platinum.

Her voice was high-pitched and shivery like the piping of a flute or the tinkling of a bell. Her movements as she spoke were graceful and smooth, her body slender and athletic in her white jumpsuit with the pale blue piping.

Though the message she delivered was anything but sweet and comforting.

"Crash-landed on the surface...of the planet," she said. *"Surrounded by hostile lifeforms. Not sure how long I can last."*

Remembering her words, my heart beats faster. I work harder than ever, pulling cables to haul in wreckage as if my life depends on it.

Since when has anything but *metal* had this effect on me? What do *I* care about some doomed stranger trapped on the planet below?

I've never cared about *anyone*, so why should I start now?

Still, her words continue to replay in my head without fading. *"I don't think I could fly through the orbital debris...even if my ship was operative."* Her voice broke on the next words she spoke. *"There is no way out, and most of my supplies are ruined. Mezzo, if you can't find a way to save me soon, it's only a matter of time until it's all over."*

Hand over hand, I tow an intact engine cowling through the force field gate into the bay. It turns massively heavy when the *Lady Alloy*'s artificial gravity takes hold of it, and I grunt as I struggle to budge it. Sweat rolls down my back as my muscles bulge and strain to the point of bursting.

But no amount of hard labor will burn the memory of Silver's desperation from my brain. Not even a *song*, one of my favorites, will do that.

"Come to me, come to me...from your spinning cemetery." I sing the words as I attach the low-grav clamps to the cowling and lead it across the bay, then load it on the flatbed transport. *"I will melt you into something new...and send you on your way."*

Hard work and metal are always the answer to every problem. I know that. It is why I almost never feel anything other than happiness. It is why I never long for anything other than what I have.

But what if there is *something else* to feel and long for? Something I never wanted because I never knew it existed.

"Mö-bi-us, Mö-bi-us...all these gifts to you will soar. Strength and greatness, they will bring...as you grow..."

My voice cracks as the song makes me think of something other than Silver. A question that has been gnawing at me breaks through to the front of my mind.

What happened to Möbius, Inc.?

If it still existed, the metal I've been sending, stamped with the company's symbol, would not have been a mystery to the rest of the galaxy. Yet Mezzo knows nothing about it. How is it even *possible* that such a giant organization could just *disappear*?

And if it has, what have I been living for all this time? What has it all meant? What have I been missing out on?

As if in answer, Silver's face appears clearly in my mind's eye. My heart beats faster, and I feel the urge to sing.

Since I don't have a song for her just yet, I finish the one about Möbius instead. "Strength and greatness, they will bring...as you grow...forevermore."

But then I frown and bite my lip. Somehow, singing about Möbius just doesn't feel the same to me anymore.

"Please tell me...you're going to help us." Mezzo is sitting up in bed when I walk back into the medzone after my shift—not that he looks much better than before. "Tell me...you'll help me *save* her."

"I don't think I can." I stop alongside him, folding my big arms over my chest. "The planet inside the Shardswarm is cut off by all the orbiting debris."

"But there *must* be a way." Mezzo snaps forward, then grimaces in pain and drops back again. "We can't just leave her *down* there to *die.*"

"*I've* never even been to the surface," I tell him. "And I've lived here all my *life.*"

"What about a small...highly maneuverable craft?" Mezzo grits his teeth against another bolt of pain, then shakes it off. "Surely you've picked up...*something* out here...that could make the trip."

"Even if I *had* something like that, I don't know what's *down* there—except that Silver says she's surrounded by *hostile lifeforms.*"

"Pretty sure *you*...can handle them." Mezzo manages a strained smile. "You're a big guy."

I don't like being pushed, so I change the subject. "How long have you and Silver been partners, anyway?"

"Twelve years...more or less." Mezzo coughs. "We own a treasure-hunting outfit together...though we're down one *ship* these days." He forces out a weak chuckle before the coughing takes him again.

I look at him, and I feel angry inside. They've been together 12 years, while I've been here all alone with Thot and my mountains of metal...and it never even bothered me until now.

"Please," he says. "Won't you at least *try* to help her?"

I shake my head and sigh. "The debris field around the planet is just too *dense*, and it's constantly *moving.* You might get through the first layer or two, but sooner or later, a chunk of debris is going to *impale, decapitate,* or *smash you to* smithereens."

Mezzo wipes sweat from his pale brow with one shaking hand. The longer I stand here, the worse he looks—though I'm sure Thot is doing everything she can for him with the medzone equipment.

"There has to be a way," he says weakly. "We can't just...give up on her. She would *never* give up...on *me.*"

Again, I get that angry feeling. "Get some rest," I tell him as I head for the door. "I have more work to do."

"But there isn't *time.*" He struggles to sit up and swings his legs over the edge of the bed. "Silver could be dead *already.*"

As he says those words, he passes out and falls off the side, crashing to the floor in a jumble of bedsheets and blankets.

Even as I rush over to help him back into bed, I feel an overwhelming urgency at what he last said. The possibility that Silver could be dead—or could still be saved—convinces me of what I need to do next.

All doubts are gone.

"Thot. I need an idea."

I'm halfway across the *Lady Alloy* now, far from the medzone, on the smelting deck—the noisiest, hottest, dirtiest place aboard the ship.

It is also where I do my best thinking and have my best talks with Thot.

"What kind of idea?" she asks me, pitching her voice loud enough for me to hear it over the roar of the blast furnace. "Please be more specific." It's always like that on the smelting deck, which is just how I like it and always have.

"I need to get to the surface and back in one piece," I tell her as I shove the recently retrieved engine cowling into the huge furnace. "And when I come back, I need to bring a passenger with me."

"Mezzo's partner, you mean? But you do not even know her."

"I don't think that matters, does it?" Intense heat belches out of the furnace as the metal slab glows bright red and melts.

"I find this sudden interest of yours unusual," says Thot. "You've never professed to care about anything but *metal* before."

"Can you blame me? Someone's life is at stake."

"Yours will be, too, if you try this," says Thot. "In fact, the odds of you returning alive are so low, they are virtually nonexistent."

I watch as the liquefied metal pours out of a long, black channel and into a cubic form that's almost as big as the furnace. The metal will take the shape of a block when it cools, ready for shipment to the waiting arms of Möbius, Inc.

Or so I have always believed.

"We need to improve those odds," I shout over the sizzling hiss of the pouring metal. "There *has* to be a way."

Thot is silent for a long moment, as if considering what I've said. Then *another* long moment after that.

Finally, her voice booms through the smelting deck again...but she doesn't say what I expect. "Who will do your work if you die, Metalhead Tensile?"

I frown as I shove another piece of wreckage into the furnace. "My work? This work?"

"All of it," says Thot. "Who will retrieve, smelt, cast, and ship the metals of the Shardswarm when you are gone?"

Now it's my turn to think for a moment. My frown deepens as I give the wreckage a last push, then look around the deck from behind my amber-tinted goggles.

"Thot?" I take off my fireproof gloves. "When was the last time you were in contact with Möbius, Inc.?"

She hesitates. "I don't understand, Tensile."

I shake my head. "It's been a long time, hasn't it? A *really* long time."

"A lack of communication with Corporate does not indicate a problem of any—"

"Why didn't you *tell* me? Why did you let me go on thinking nothing had *changed?*"

Again, hesitation. "Do you think it would have improved your life in any way?"

Anger bubbles inside me like superheated liquid metal. "You should have *told* me that all *this* was for *nothing.*"

"Metalhead Tensile..."

"I trusted you!" Pitching the gloves aside, I storm toward the exit.

"Metalhead Tensile, wait..."

The door slides open. "I don't want to hear any more *lies!*"

"Then *listen!*" says Thot.

I pause in the doorway.

"I have a way," she tells me. "I have a way that might give you a chance."

"A chance?"

"Of getting to the surface and back," says Thot. "Maybe."

I glare over my shoulder. "Tell me."

When she's done, I realize how much of a longshot it is. It's probably suicidal, in fact.

But it's also the only chance we have, and I can't afford not to give it a try.

In the hours that follow, I work harder than I've ever worked before, getting ready. I know the window for rescuing Silver is closing, if it hasn't closed already; if we have any hope of saving her, we have to act soon.

I push myself to the limit, hauling block after block of metal to the launch bay. Is it any surprise, as much as I love metal, that it might be the very thing that enables me to rescue beautiful Silver?

The whole time I'm slaving away, I keep singing—and every song's a new one, made up on the spot. Every song is about Silver and her story, though I hardly know anything about her. Every song has a happy ending with a rescue, with Silver and I flying off into the sunset together.

Even though we've never met.

Meanwhile, Thot does the brain work, crunching the numbers and mapping things out. She uses her network of orbital drones to image the Shardswarm and build simulations, calculating the best possible angles and vectors of attack. It's a job she was born to do—manufactured, that is—though it's a brain-buster even for her.

For a while, then, it's business as usual, the two of us working together for a common goal. Maybe she lied to me all this time about Möbius, but I still enjoy teaming up with her. You don't just burn out a lifetime of good feelings for someone like *that*, do you?

"I will miss your songs," she tells me. "If you do not come back."

"Thanks." I grunt as I put my back into hauling another block of metal through the launch bay. Even with the low-grav clamps, it's a strain. "Maybe Silver is a singer, as well."

"It won't be the same," says Thot. "But we'll see."

Mezzo isn't in great shape when I go to see him. He's sprawled in bed, whiter than the sheets, gurgling for breath in his sleep.

When I wake him, his eyes barely open halfway. Moving his head the slightest bit seems to require a major effort. The words "death warmed over" come to mind.

But I treat him like he's perfectly healthy anyway. "I just thought I'd let you know I'm leaving." He's already given me the transponder frequency and codes for Silver's ship, so Thot can pinpoint its location. I have all the information I need...but coming to see him seems like the right thing to do.

"Good...luck." Mezzo tries to smile.

"I'll do my best to bring her back," I tell him.

He takes a long, shaky breath and lets it back out with twice the trembling. "Just remember. If she has any doubts...tell her I said you're one of the *Metallurgists*...we've been looking for. Tell her you'll explain...the mystery of the metal...when you get back to your ship."

"I'll remember." My big hand dwarfs Mezzo's when I reach down to pat it. I'm not sure why I do it at all; touching anything other than metal gives me no joy.

"If I'm dead when you get back," he says, "please promise me you'll take care of her."

"I promise," I tell him. "Don't worry."

Whatever he tries to say next, it comes out as incoherent mumbles. I leave him there like that—I have to, time's running out —and Thot tells me later he was dead before I made it through the doorway.

"Are you ready, Metalhead Tensile? It's time."

I'm standing in the launch bay of the *Lady Alloy* in an orange flight suit, my gloved hands bunched into fists. Looking back, I see the big blocks of solid metal lined up behind me, each mounted with low-grav clamps. Looking forward, I see the speeding wreckage of the Shardswarm through the force field of the open gate, swirling past like a sea of broken metal.

Beyond all that, I know, somewhere far below, is Silver. My heart beats faster when I think of her.

"Ready, Thot!" I shout. "Let's do this thing!"

"Prepare for the first drop, Tensile."

With a nod, I turn and take hold of the low-grav clamps on the corner of the first block in line. Squeezing the grips activates a localized low-gravity field, enabling me to move the block forward, though it's bulky enough that I still have to put my back into it.

When I have the block at the brink, just this side of the force field gate, I call out to Thot. "In position!"

"Stand by," says Thot.

I can tell from the shifting view that the *Lady Alloy* is changing course, adjusting position relative to the racing junk below. Everything has to be just right for Thot's plan to succeed.

"Drop one in five seconds," she says.

I tense, leaning against the corner of the block, keeping the low-gravs tight in my grip.

"Five...four...three..."

I go over it all again in my head. The angle and force of my push can't be the slightest bit off.

"...two...*one.*"

Taking a deep breath, I shove the block for all I'm worth. It slides through the gate and out into space with a good head of steam, its momentum carrying it toward a big, ruined ship far below.

"Next drop coming in 30 seconds, Metalhead Tensile," says Thot.

Turning, I march to the next block, activate the low-gravs, and drag it forward. This one is bigger than the first and harder to wrangle. Each block is precisely sized according to Thot's calculations to serve its purpose in the plan.

"Drop two in ten seconds," she tells me. "Ten...nine..."

When she gets to zero, I heave the block through the gate. Even as it sails toward another wrecked vessel in the Shardswarm, I see the first block crash into the front end of its target, flipping the ancient ship end over end.

The flipping ship collides with another ship, and another, sending them spinning into other craft and fragments. Meanwhile, the second block hurtles into the engine of a huge, cylindrical vessel, which explodes on impact. The blast sends other wreckage tumbling in all directions, setting off new chains of destruction.

"Drop three in ten seconds."

I bring up the next block in line and eject it after the countdown, then do the same for the next and the next and the rest after that. One after another, they leap into the Shardswarm, triggering ricochets and chain reactions that are carefully calculated to create a single end result.

"Your path to the surface is open, Tensile!" shouts Thot. "But it won't stay that way for long."

Without a word, I bolt across the deck to the sleek little craft parked there—a needle-nosed racer I've restored over the years and flown now and then for debris scouting or fun. I've loved darting in and out of the wrecks on those flights, feeling like I was part of the vast metal maelstrom of the Shardswarm.

But this time, the ride will take me somewhere I've never been before...if I'm *lucky*.

"Hurry, Tensile!" says Thot.

I leap into the racer's cockpit, pull on my helmet, and start the engines. The course to the ground is already plotted on the navigation console.

The cockpit hisses shut and the autopilot kicks in, lifting the racer off the deck. My heart hammers in my chest as the nose of the craft approaches the gate, seconds from sliding into space.

"Here we go, Tensile." Thot's voice is in my helmet. "Hold on tight."

With that, the racer flashes out of the launch bay and darts into the one clear passage through the wreckage of the Shardswarm, held open by the chain reactions blowing junk out of the way around it.

For the first time in my life, I glimpse the surface of the planet far below, unobstructed by the churning wall of wreckage all around it. It's a weird feeling, because I've lived in orbit all my life but have never really wondered what it might be like on the other side of the Shardswarm field. Why bother, if there was never a way to reach it?

Until now, that is.

"You are in the planet's gravity well," Thot tells me. "Free-falling into the atmosphere. You will feel the heat of reentry soon enough, Metalhead Tensile."

"Thanks for the heads-up." I'm not worried. The racer has top-notch shielding and an awesome heat dissipation profile.

"Autopilot will bring you in nice and smooth," says Thot. "She will set you down within a hundred yards of Silver's ship. After that, the rest is up to you. But you will have to be *fast*."

"I will." Is it even *possible* that I can get to Silver, explain who I am, load her into my ship, and make it back into orbit before the passage closes? I guess I'm about to find out.

For the moment, I stay focused on the drop, watching wreckage hurtle past me as the racer plunges downward. Every flicker of movement makes me jump, because every piece of wreckage, no matter how small, could end my mission permanently.

"You are almost clear of the Shardswarm orbitals," says Thot. "Another thirty seconds, and you will be out."

She sounds confident, but I know anything could happen. The Shardswarm is close to total chaos; as carefully as Thot planned breaking open the passage, there are multitudes of moving parts that could still act unpredictably and obliterate the racer.

Speaking of moving parts, a massive, mangled carrier ship lurches into the passage below, blocking me. It keeps moving, but I can tell it won't clear the gap in time.

And the racer is flying too fast to stop and has nowhere else to go.

"Thot! I'm on a collision course!"

I'm guessing she doesn't answer because she already knows I'm doomed.

The carrier flashes closer, solid and inescapable. Even as I charge toward it, I can't help admiring its unique structure and the rugged texture of its hull.

Seconds from annihilation, I wish I'd never left the *Lady Alloy*. I loved every minute of my life on that ship, even if Möbius turned out to be a lie, and my life's work turned out to be for nothing.

The carrier's deck rushes toward me. I close my eyes, expecting the impact to wipe me away from the universe forever.

But it never comes.

Seconds pass, and I'm still alive and aware. What I see when I open my eyes leaves me stunned.

"What the blark?" I'm racing through a dark sky toward a rumpled, golden surface far below. There isn't a piece of wreckage in sight.

Not until I check my rear-view screen, at least. That's when I see, receding in the distant heights, the carrier I almost crashed into...and the huge hole in its deck, which I *swear* wasn't there a moment ago. The hole through which my racer must have passed instead of ramming into the metal that had previously filled it.

"Unbelievable." My best guess is the carrier's made of some kind of adaptive metal, designed to flow away from incoming projectiles. I've seen similar things in other wrecks in my many years of salvaging the Shardswarm.

It's still amazing, but I have to look away. The racer's falling faster every minute.

"Thot? Can you hear me?" If she does, she isn't talking. I still hear nothing but silence over the commlink.

And the roar of passing atmosphere in the cockpit as my racer plummets toward the surface of a world I've never visited before.

The racer touches down on a dark plain in what seems like the middle of the night. With so much orbiting wreckage blocking the sun, it must always be nighttime here.

Remembering the tight deadline Thot gave me, I pop the canopy right away. The sensor gauges tell me the atmosphere's breathable, so I take off my helmet and gloves, stowing them under my seat. Then I get up, grab the compact flame-thrower from the seat behind me, and strap it onto my back.

After I climb down and set foot on the smooth, hard ground, I take a look at the tracker watch on my left wrist. According to the blinking red dot, Silver's ship is located less than a kilometer due west from my own (the steady green dot in the middle of the screen).

As I head off in that direction, the glow of the flamethrower's pilot light illuminates my way. The ground casts a metallic, golden gleam, and the rocks strewn over it shine copper, bronze, and silver by the fire's light. With so much metal on display, it looks like my kind of planet; I just wish I had more time to explore and enjoy it.

Low hills obstruct the view, which isn't so great anyway in the darkness. Things I can't make out shimmer and glow in the distance like drifting, living things or mirages.

The air is cold and windy and smells like iron and dust. A low, crackling hum suffuses everything, layered with a keening wail that could just as easily be the wind or something alive.

Or perhaps it's something *dead* instead. This feels like a haunted place, with the darkness and the shimmering, glowing things. It wouldn't surprise me if an actual ghost drifted out of the shadows toward me at any moment.

Around a hill, I finally see what I'm looking for. Silver's ship, battered and broken, lies in a tumble on the hard, metallic ground.

I recognize the craft from a photo Mezzo showed me aboard the *Lady Alloy*—not as sleek as the racer that brought me down out of orbit but streamlined all the same.

As I approach it, however, I wonder if I'm too late. The ship is still and quiet, with no sign of a struggle nearby. There's no trace of hostile lifeforms, either, though Silver warned us about them in her distress message.

Slowly, I proceed toward the ship with my flamethrower at the ready. If any lifeforms spring out of the shadows, I'll be ready for them.

"Silver?" As I call her name, I close the few remaining meters to her ship. "Mezzo sent me."

Because of the way Silver's ship is situated, its hatch is near the ground, giving me easy access. I draw up to it and call her name again, then rap my knuckles on the hatch at eye level.

"Silver?" I raise my voice. "Silver, are you in there? I've come to get you off this planet."

No one answers. There isn't a sound from inside the ship.

I step to one side and raise the flamethrower, wondering if it could melt through the door. I won't get a chance to test the theory, however.

As I'm standing there, the door suddenly explodes outward and blasts off into the distance. Seconds later, a huge pseudopod of bright yellow material plunges out of the open doorway and shoots into the night, twisting and squirming with seemingly blind abandon.

I back away fast, keeping one eye on the snakelike extension and the other on the ship, wondering if Silver is still inside. When the ship rocks violently as more yellow matter pours out, I think there isn't much chance she could still be in there.

Alive, at least.

I run off to the side, dodging the pseudopod and keeping the flamethrower ready for action. The thing whips toward me again, and I feel the intense heat it gives off as I dart out of its way.

Again, it lashes toward me, and I dodge out of its reach. Instead of coming after me again, though, it hurls itself to the ground some distance away—but I'm not off the hook yet. The force of its fall shakes the ground under my feet, knocking me off balance.

I come down hard on the metallic ground, and it hurts. Just as I'm shaking it off, I see the pseudopod rise overhead as if it's about to crash down on top of me.

Instinctively, I let loose with a blast from the flamethrower. The pseudopod dodges the jet of fire, twisting away from it in midair, and rears back to trumpet its victory with a mighty roar.

That's when I hear a familiar voice cutting through the commotion.

"Vod! Leave him alone!"

It's her. I instantly recognize Silver's high, piping voice from the distress video.

And I'm grateful for it. As soon as she calls out, the pseudopod pulls away, sparing me from whatever was coming next.

"Thank you, Vod," says Silver. "Now please let me talk to him."

Sitting up fast, I look toward the voice, and there she is, more beautiful by far in person than played back in a prerecorded video. She strides toward me in her white jumpsuit with the pale blue piping, her bright blue eyes and wavy platinum hair catching the golden glow of the pseudopod hovering nearby.

"Hello there." She walks up to me, exuding cool confidence. "I'm Silver. What's your name?"

"Tensile." I scramble to my feet, trying not to let on how dazzled I am. "I'm your rescue party."

Silver narrows her eyes and tips her head left, taking my measure. "That's too bad."

"Too bad?" I frown.

"You've come all this way for nothing," says Silver. "I'm not going anywhere."

Glancing up at the sky, I can't see the passage home. If it's still there, it won't be for long.

And now the woman I've come down here to rescue is telling me she doesn't want to leave. After all it took me to get here, she's telling me to go home without her.

I don't understand. "But there's nothing here."

"*Vod* is." She gestures at the yellow pseudopod looming over us. "And he's *lonely.*"

So am I, I want to tell her. "What *is* he?"

"The only living thing in the world, other than you and me." Silver smiles up at him. "A being of molten metal, born in the core of the planet. The *last of his kind,* as well."

"How do you know all this?" I ask her.

"He *talks* to me. When I crash-landed, I thought I was under attack by hostile lifeforms, but they were *extensions* of him. He made contact mentally through them and told me his story."

As she says this, Vod slides to the ground and spreads out over it in a slick. Lumps of his yellow mass rise from the slick, taking shapes that have the vague outlines of human bodies but without all the details of an actual human.

Somehow, being surrounded by these humanlike figures makes me more nervous than having the giant pseudopod towering over me. I keep looking around at them, watching for any unexpected movements.

"You said he's the last of his kind?" I ask.

Silver nods. "It's ironic because he's the one who turned this place into a *refuge* for the last members of *other* species."

"What other species?"

"*All* of them," says Silver. "He put out the call through the cosmos, but he didn't expect *how many* refugees he would get. There was a *cataclysm.* An entire quadrant of the galaxy was wiped out, leaving the last survivors of thousands of worlds to come here."

I gaze into the deserted, night-dark distance. *Then where are they?*

"So many came that their orbiting ships eventually blotted out the sun and stars," explains Silver. "Without abundant solar energy, the time came when this planet could no longer sustain life—except *his.*" She sweeps an arm around to indicate the dozen molten figures poised around us. "He has survived like this for thousands of years, trapped in a world of eternal night and emptiness...until now. Until *I* got here."

I see where this is going now. "And he wants you to stay."

Silver nods sympathetically at the nearest figure. "My crashing here was *fate*. I came to investigate the legends of the Metallurgists and instead have found someone even more fascinating, someone in desperate need of basic companionship."

There's a clock in the back of my mind, counting down the approximate time I have left to escape, and it's ticking louder than ever. Soon enough, Vod won't be the only one trapped in eternal darkness and emptiness.

"You can't *live* here, though, can you?" I ask her. "This place looks pretty *desolate*."

"Vod says he can *merge* with me. *Transform* me so I can survive here."

"Would the change be *permanent?*"

Silver nods. "It's a sacrifice I'm willing to make. He *needs* me."

How much time do we have left? It can't be much. An inner voice urges me to leave Silver behind and get beyond the Shardswarm barrier before it's too late. But another voice insists I try harder to take her with me. *Losing* her so soon after *finding* her could be the ultimate tragedy of my life. Maybe talking her out of this is something I need to try.

"Mezzo wanted what was best for you," I tell her. "Before he passed, he told me he thought you should go."

I seem to have struck a nerve. Silver's eyes go wide with surprise and sadness. "Mezzo...passed?"

"We did everything we could, but his injuries were too great." I shake my head. "*He's* the one who sent me down here to get you.

"He said he didn't want you to miss out on the end of your search. He wanted you to study the *Metallurgist* he'd found." I'm proud of myself for not mispronouncing *Metallurgist*. Silver inspires me to want to impress her.

She brightens at the mention of the word. "He *found* one? Where?"

"Right in front of you." I smile and nod. If accepting the title of Metallurgist is what it takes to get her off this planet, I'll do it.

Silver's eyes sparkle...then dim. "I'm glad to know he finally solved the mystery," she says. "But it doesn't change things. I have to stay."

I get the feeling our time is almost up, and I grab her arm. "You *can't*. I promised Mezzo I'd bring you *back* and look *after* you. "

As soon as I touch her, the molten metal figures flow toward us, arm-things extended menacingly. I let go and step back, and they stop in their tracks.

Vod won't let me take her, and *she* doesn't *want* to go. Is there *anything* I can do to get her out of here?

I think hard, knowing full well I might already be out of time...but I can't give up. I've spent my life pulling *treasures* from an orbital junkyard; there *has* to be a way to pull a *human* treasure out of *this* mess, too.

"Thank you for coming all the way down here to help me." Silver backs away as Vod's molten people converge behind her. "But you'd better get going now."

That's when it hits me. "Wait!" I raise a hand, and the molten figures flutter but don't attack. "I have an idea!"

Silver frowns. "What kind of idea?"

"Listen!" My heart hammers with excitement. "I think I know a way for *all* of us to get what we want."

Her frown deepens. "I don't understand."

"We can *all* be happy." Even as I say it, I *believe* it. I *know* it can work. "*None* of us has to be *abandoned*. But we have to do it *now*. "

The needle-nosed racer swoops into the landing bay of the *Lady Alloy*, fresh from its wild ride up from the surface of the planet.

To look at the little craft, you might not know it almost didn't make it through the passage in the Shardswarm, which was closing during the flight. Three times, the racer had very close calls with debris along the passage, nearly getting smashed to pieces in the process. In the end, it barely made it out before the passage collapsed in on itself.

Yet here it is now, lightly landing as if none of that had

happened. The engines wind down, the canopy pops open, and a woman with platinum hair climbs out and down to the deck.

"Welcome aboard, Silver," Thot says over the speakers in the bay. "It is good to have you with us."

Silver nods grimly. "Thank you, whoever you are."

"Her name is Thot." I rise to stand in the racer's cockpit. I've changed a lot inside, but I still look the same on the outside...except for the golden glow emanating from my skin.

"Welcome back, Tensile," says Thot. "Good to see you made it."

"I'm not just Tensile anymore." I—make that *we*—climb down from the cockpit and let the glow flare brightly from every square centimeter of skin. "*Vod* is part of me, now."

"Vod?" Thot sounds surprised.

"A metallic lifeform from the planet," we explain to her. "He needed a change of scenery, and I invited him along for the ride."

"I see," says Thot. "You've joined together, then?"

"Correct."

"Sounds about right," says Thot. "You always *did* have a thing for *metal*, Tensile."

Vod and I turn down the flare, restoring our light to a moderate glow. Looking around gives us an odd feeling—recognition and unfamiliarity at the same time.

But when we look at Silver, we feel exactly the same thing at exactly the same moment. Thanks to our merger, we will share her love equally now, and she remains as perfectly unchanged as ever.

No more loneliness for either of us—Tensile or Vod. Man and metal combined will make up for what we each lacked as separate entities.

"It's good to be back." We clap our hands together and grin. "We're looking forward to getting back to work."

"You and your *passenger* have agreed to work?" asks Thot. "Doing what?"

"Same as always, Thot." We turn to the open gate of the landing bay with its view of the spinning Shardswarm and plant our hands on our hips. "We're going to clear away that mess out there. Only this time, we've got some ideas for speeding things up."

"You want to speed things up?" says Thot.

"Of course." We gesture at the scenic view through the gate. "We want to make the sun shine on that planet down there again. Maybe we can bring it *back to life* if we put our minds to it."

"Great idea," says Silver.

"An ambitious goal," says Thot. "One to be applauded."

"Thanks, Thot." We gaze at the Shardswarm and imagine the planet emerging from its shadow someday. "It sure beats shipping blocks of salvaged metal to a mega-corporation that no longer exists."

"I suppose you'll want to start working right away?" asks Thot.

We turn from the view and shake our head. "I didn't say *that*." When we smile at Silver, she walks over with a smile of her own. Carefully, we slip an arm around her waist, wondering how the touch will be received. Will our merged form make her flinch? Will the heavier, harder arm cause pain to her more fragile human body?

The answers are what we hoped for. She presses close, the heat of her body merging with our own.

In that moment, all fears fled, Vod and I fully recognize the miracle and promise of what we have become. As if by alchemical design, we have done more than simply combine two halves into a whole. The transmutation of flesh into metal and metal into flesh has created something new and unique—an *alloy*, an *amalgam* of the two.

Perhaps that transmutation will include one other person before all is said and done, include *Silver* in this mystical union, and become something even more special and breathtaking in the end. Perhaps all that together will lead to the creation of something or someone *else*, an *offspring*, something or someone that none of us can even *imagine* at this point.

It is enough to inspire Vod and I to start singing a new song on the spot, our most beautiful and heartfelt piece yet. Neither metal nor Metallurgist alone could have sung it exactly the same way, with notes and lyrics you might not think could possibly go together. But they *do*, they complement each other *perfectly*, and that's what makes the song so wonderful. That's what gives it *harmony*.

Because it's just like *this*, just like *us*. It's just like *love*.

THE GREATEST SERIAL KILLER IN THE UNIVERSE

"No, no, no," said Luther James Paraclete, snatching the knife from the alien's tentacle. "Like this."

Lunging forward, he plunged the blade up to the hilt into the soft bulb of the second alien's head. Milky pink fluid spurted out at once, then gushed as Luther sliced the knife across the bulb, tearing a long gash.

The victim creature made a noise like a cross between a sneeze and a shrill whistle. As Luther finished the cut, pink milk poured over his hairy forearm, running off the point of his elbow. The alien's head-bulb drained in an instant and collapsed like a deflated balloon.

The rest of the creature's body followed, slumping to the street. Blue and yellow fluids streamed out of the gash, flowing from lower regions of the corpse to mingle with the pool of pink milk.

"Now *that's* how you kill," said Luther, wiping the dripping blade on his black coveralls. The air was thick with the stink of rotten fish, and he breathed it in deeply. After five killings, Luther was starting to like the rank odor given off by dying Ectozoids.

"Tried," said the first alien, puffing out the word through a fluttering maw on its forehead. "Could not do." The alien's name was

Boraf Zolagorg. Like all Ectozoids, it looked like a man-sized jelly-fish with a lower body of translucent bulbs and tentacles.

And it was Luther's employer for the duration.

In a way, Luther was sorry that the 'Zoids looked the way they did. Killing a creature that looked like something that had washed up on the beach wasn't quite the same as murdering a red-blooded Earthling.

On the other hand, Luther felt a different kind of thrill knowing that he was the first Earthling serial killer to take a stab at an extraterrestrial species. He liked killing what no human had killed before.

Now if he could just get the 'Zoids to do some killing of their own. It was, after all, the reason Boraf was paying him.

"Here," said Luther, holding the knife by the blade and extending the hilt toward Boraf. "Take it. Let's find our next volunteer."

Boraf did not reach out a tentacle for the weapon. The alien's gelatinous head-bulb quivered in the light from the planet's double moons. "Want to," said Boraf. "But no can. Ectozoid no kill."

When Luther stepped up close to the creature, Boraf's bulb dimpled as if pushed in by the human's breath. "You don't have any choice," said Luther. "It's kill or be killed now, right?"

"Still no kill," puffed Boraf.

Luther scowled and shook his head. He was starting to think that the job he'd been hired to do was undoable.

In the three days he'd been on Ectos, Luther had killed five locals, which was history-making and good for his lifetime average, but he'd had zero success in developing the killer instinct in Boraf. Like all Ectozoids, Boraf seemed to lack the ability to kill.

It wasn't that the 'Zoids weren't powerful enough to kill, because they were. As fragile as they looked, the aliens were strong and quick. They were able to generate and discharge bioelectricity, too, though Luther had only ever seen them fire off little zaps of it.

It wasn't that the 'Zoids lacked the motivation to kill, either. They said they expected a hostile invasion in a little over a week and were desperate to prepare for it.

It was just that none of them had the killer instinct. On their happy little world, unlike Earth, all life

co-existed harmoniously. The 'Zoids and lesser species on Ectos shared a low-grade link which was, if not a hive intelligence, at least a limited collective awareness. Organisms ate other organisms for sustenance, but it was more the result of a mutual agreement than a predator-prey competition for survival.

The Ectozoids were simply not wired for killing. In fact, there had never been a murder on Ectos, not even one, until Luther had arrived.

Luther thought that was pretty cool. Not only was he the first Earthling to kill an alien, but he was the first being to commit a murder on the planet Ectos. Every time he thought about it, he got a little kick of adrenaline and couldn't help smiling.

It was a great confidence builder for an aging serial killer whose best years had seemed long gone a long time ago. Now if he could just get the creatures to kill, he knew he would feel like a new man. A new murderer.

"C'mon," said Luther, heading down the street, waving for Boraf to follow. The porous orange surface under his feet pulsed like all the streets and walkways in the living maze of the city. "Let's find you some easy pickings, my friend."

Boraf shuffled after him, its bulbs and tentacles rustling and slapping together as it moved. "Pickings?"

"We're not going home till you kill someone," said Luther. "Get that through your head-bag. This is your big debut, and I'm not letting you quit till you've got something to brag about to your jelly-fish friends."

"Tried," puffed Boraf. "No can kill."

"Sure you can," said Luther, smiling as if he had no doubt that the alien would come through. "Once you get that first one under your belt, you'll be fine."

"Hope," said Boraf. "Hope much."

Luther patted the creature's head-bulb, then wiped the slime off his hand onto his coveralls. As unlikely as it seemed that the alien would overcome its nonviolent nature, Luther still believed that he could bring Boraf around. After all, Luther had had great results with worse wannabes in the past...though, granted, the wannabes had at least been human.

For the last decade or so, ever since his arthritis had gotten bad, Luther had made a living as a serial killer personal trainer. He had trained some of the biggest names of the new generation--Fabersham, Glottal Stop, Chuck Wagon, Father Scalp--and had managed to stay prominent in the serial killer community even though the arthritis had limited his actual body count. Plenty of the newbies had been incompetent at the start; even the great Spay Queen, believe it or not, had been squeamish around blood in the beginning. Once Luther had gotten done with them, however, not one of the newbies had averaged fewer than ten kills a year. Every one of his trainees had done him proud in the end.

Except, of course, for Lech Bomb, the one dark spot on Luther's sterling career. Even Bomb had his good points; no one could criticize his body count, certainly, for he had racked up a solid twenty-two kills in fourteen months. The problem was, Bomb's victims had all been serial killers, which hadn't exactly reflected positively on the man who'd trained him. By the time Sweet Annis and the Unholy Ghost had put down Lech Bomb for good, Luther's rep had been blown to hell. Luther had even been booted out of the Serial Killers Guild...and he was a charter member, yet.

Lech Bomb had pretty much killed Luther's career, but Luther still didn't consider him a complete failure. If anything, he'd been one of the greats, downright brilliant and deadly enough to track down and execute some of the most dangerous killers alive. Luther's confidence had taken a hit because he hadn't anticipated that Bomb would turn on his serial killing brethren...but Luther still believed that his stalled career could be revived.

Once he got the Ectozoids on the road to bloody mayhem, he could return to Earth and the Serial Killers Guild as a hero and a legend. And a wealthy son of a bitch, what with the fortune in precious metals and gems the aliens were paying him.

Excited and impatient at the thought of the rewards in store for him, Luther turned down another passageway...and stopped so suddenly that Boraf bumped into him from behind.

In the pulsing yellow tubeway, Luther saw a lone 'Zoid shuffling toward him from less than twenty yards away. There was no one else in sight, and there were no lights in any of the windows of the surrounding house-mounds.

"Time to lose your cherry," Luther whispered to Boraf. "It's now or never."

"Cherry?" puffed Boraf.

Stepping forward, Luther grabbed hold of one of Boraf's tentacles and pulled the 'Zoid along with him. The other alien kept shuffling toward them, apparently unconcerned.

"Hello, friend," said Luther with a cheery grin. "Wonderful night, isn't it?"

The approaching 'Zoid bobbled its head from side to side but made no reply. Luther wasn't surprised, as Boraf was one of the few locals who understood and spoke English.

The 'Zoid made a burbling sound through its forehead blowhole and kept coming. Pulling Boraf along by the tentacle, Luther moved to one side to let the unsuspecting creature pass.

Then, as the 'Zoid wobbled by, Luther swept a leg through the mass of tentacles supporting it. The alien made a noise like the yelp of a poodle and fell forward, its tentacles and fluid-filled bulbs slapping the street like a mop slapping a floor.

Boraf hung back until Luther yanked it forward by the tentacle. "It's showtime," he said, wrapping the tentacle around the hilt of the knife. "Time for baby's first step."

"No kill," said Boraf, its voice shrill. "Ectozoid no kill Ectozoid."

Boraf tried to unwind its tentacle from the knife hilt, but Luther clamped both hands down hard around it. Arthritis pain lanced his fingers and wrists, but he held on tight. "Brace yourself," he said. "You're about to make history."

Then, he wrenched the knife and tentacle forward, punching the point of the blade through the biggest bulb south of the 'Zoid victim's head. As the tip penetrated, both Boraf and the victim squealed like punctured balloons.

Luther had to struggle to keep the knife moving, as Boraf continued to pull back. Gritting his teeth, the Earthling pressed the weapon deeper into the victim 'Zoid's bulb, then inched the blade upward, opening a gash.

Inky fluid streaked with yellow milk rose from the wound and splashed out onto the street. Luther forced the knife to the top of the bulb, then withdrew it, keeping Boraf's tentacle cinched around the hilt.

"Ta-da!" said Luther. "You did it, Boraf! Your first kill! Way to go!"

Pain shot through his wrists and fingers again, and Luther had to relax his grip for an instant. He loosened his hold on the tentacle and knife just enough to flex his aching joints the tiniest bit.

It was all the opening Boraf needed to free itself. Suddenly yanking backward, the alien jolted itself out of Luther's grasp.

At first, Luther was so surprised and irritated that he didn't notice the tentacle wasn't the only thing that had slipped away from him. "Hey!" he snapped. "Get back here!"

Luther realized what was missing from his hand just a heartbeat before he saw the object flashing toward him, wrapped in Boraf's tentacle.

The knife. Luther had let go of the knife.

While he wasn't worried that Boraf would hurt him, Luther instinctively ducked away from his client. Boraf lunged forward, aiming for the wounded 'Zoid in the street.

Making a sound like a squealing automobile tire, Boraf raised the knife high and brought it down, stabbing the blade into the victim's head-bulb. As pink milk rushed from the puncture, Boraf hoisted the knife back out and up and thrust it down into the head-bulb again.

And again. And again.

And again.

Luther could not believe his eyes. Boraf stabbed with abandon, then slashed the head-bulb into shreds...and took the knife to the rest of the victim's body.

The dead 'Zoid's fluids sprayed Luther, splattered everywhere. Slimy bits of dead Ectozoid flew through the air, blobs of jelly sticking where they landed. Boraf was a whirlwind of motion, gouging and hacking, ripping the corpse to pieces with the blade.

Then, the 'Zoid stopped cutting. Boraf made a sound like

someone hawking up phlegm, then shuddered violently and dropped the knife.

Without hesitation, Luther bolted over and grabbed the weapon. Jumping back, he put some distance between himself and Boraf.

"Killed Ectozoid," said Boraf, its voice high-pitched and reedy. "Boraf killed Ectozoid."

"Congratulations!" said Luther, smiling but staying out of Boraf's immediate reach. "I knew you could do it!"

"Feels good," said Boraf. Its eyes--ten black beads mounted on slender, pink stalks near the bottom of the head-bulb--remained focused on the corpse. "Want more kill."

Then, Boraf swung itself forward and dropped onto the dead 'Zoid. More colored fluids squeezed out of the corpse as Boraf's weight descended.

Gleefully, the first Ectozoid murderer in history rolled around on its victim's body. As Boraf rolled back and forth, its tentacles fluttered, its bulbs glowed with bioluminescence, and a sound like an off-key note from an out-of-tune violin wheezed from its blowhole again and again.

Luther grinned but watched carefully. Once a predictable creature, Boraf had suddenly become capable of unexpected behavior.

Not that Luther was one to look a gift jellyfish in the blowhole, but he couldn't help wondering what had brought about the sudden change. Just like that, as if a switch had been flipped, Boraf had become a killer...and a pretty freaky one at that. The 'Zoid had gone from not being able to bear the very thought of taking a life to totally losing control and getting off on killing in a big way.

"Uh, Boraf?" said Luther, moving just a step closer to the Ectozoid wallowing in the mess of historic remains. "You've gotta tell me what turned you around, buddy. So I know for my next trainee."

Boraf was rubbing his head-bulb with dripping shreds of tissue. "Turned around?"

"You went from 'No kill, no kill' to 'Want more kill,'" said Luther. "What changed? Was it feeling the knife go in that first time with my hand guiding you?"

Boraf stopped rubbing the tissue on his head. "Not feeling knife," said the Ectozoid. "Feeling hand."

"My hand?" said Luther, frowning.

"Before, no want kill," said Boraf. "After touch Luther, want kill. *Love* kill."

Luther turned his hand over, staring at both sides. If, somehow, his serial killer mindset rubbed off on the aliens with just a touch, all the better. It would make his job on Ectos much easier than trying to talk the creatures out of their natural inhibitions.

"How 'bout that," said Luther as a grin spread over his face. "Talk about your magic fingers."

Making a noise like a cross between a horse's whinny and a parrot's squawk, Boraf wriggled off the corpse and struggled to a standing position. "More kill," said the Ectozoid, looping a tentacle around Luther's arm. "More pickings."

Luther laughed as the creature shuffled down the passageway, dragging him along behind it. "Already? But you just killed someone."

Moving out of the passageway and onto the street, Boraf went faster, leaning forward with eager anticipation. "Look," it said, pointing a tentacle at an Ectozoid weaving down the block ahead of them. "Boraf kill that Ectozoid now please?"

Luther chuckled because the alien had sounded like a child asking permission to ride a teeter-totter. "Why sure," he said, holding up the knife he'd retrieved from the last victim's corpse. "Go get 'im, tiger."

One of Boraf's eye stalks swiveled around and spotted the knife. The murderous Ectozoid reached back with a tentacle and latched onto the weapon's hilt.

"Boraf kill two," said the creature. "Want kill more. Kill three, four, five."

"The night is young," said Luther. "Go for it."

By the next morning, Boraf had murdered twelve Ectozoids...and wasn't ready to stop there. Completely exhausted, joints throbbing with arthritis, Luther had to drag Boraf home to get some rest.

Even then, along the way, Luther had to restrain his client from slaughtering passers-by.

When Luther passed out on the sleeping mat Boraf had provided, the Ectozoid was still whistling and pacing around the door, dying to go back out and kill some more. Boraf was still doing the same thing when Luther woke up some hours later; he doubted the Ectozoid had slept a wink the whole night.

Luther rubbed the sleep from his eyes and chuckled. "Man, you need to relax," he said. "An Ectozoid doesn't live on murder alone."

"No relax," puffed Boraf. "Time for save world. Make more Ectozoid kill."

"Later," said Luther, padding over to the locker of food he'd brought from Earth. "Breakfast first. Save world later."

No sooner had he popped open the locker and reached for a packet of corned beef hash than the door of Boraf's house-mound slithered open. Three Ectozoids shuffled in, making whimpering noises as they crowded around Boraf.

"Save world now," said Boraf. "Ectozoids come now for Luther make kill."

Luther sighed and squeezed the tab on the food packet, activating the built-in heating element. In seconds, the packet grew warm to the touch, though the contents inside were heated to a much higher temperature. "Give me five minutes," he said, tearing open the seal and inhaling the smell of the cooked food. "Saving the world's a lot easier on a full stomach."

One of the new arrivals shuffled over and grabbed the packet from his hand. The creature made a sound like a duck as it swung the food out of Luther's reach.

"Make Ectozoids kill like Boraf," said Boraf. "Save world now. Eat later."

Luther tried to snatch the food packet from the 'Zoid's tentacle, but the creature lashed it out of reach. Irritated, Luther tried again, more aggressively this time, but the alien swept the packet up and passed it to another 'Zoid.

Glowering, Luther combed his fingers through his wavy silver hair. He knew when he was licked. "Fine," he snapped, marching past the creatures and out the door. "But if one tentacle comes near me when I'm taking a piss, the world can go to hell."

By the end of the day, 'Zoids were killing 'Zoids all over the place.

From the doorway of Boraf's home, Luther could see and hear plenty of action. Armed with knives and clubs, 'Zoids attacked other 'Zoids down the block, across the street, in neighboring house-mounds. The air was thick with sneezing death-cries and the stink of rotten fish; the pulsing street was strewn with jellyfish corpses and soaked with seeping body fluids.

He'd lost track of how many 'Zoids he'd given the touch, but he guessed it was close to a hundred. They were all out there now, killing like cavemen and loving every minute of it, high on death. Boraf was with them, caught up in the mayhem that only a day ago had seemed so unthinkable.

As Luther stood there, another trio of 'Zoids came shuffling toward him, eye stalks twitching. Before they said a word, he knew they wanted him to transform them like the rest, turn them into murderers so they could join the fun.

But he was out of gas. After the long, exhausting day he'd been through, Luther wanted nothing more than to collapse on his mat and get some deserved sleep. As entertaining and gratifying as the work had been, he couldn't stand the thought of corrupting one more alien jellyfish.

Even as he slipped inside and closed the door, however, he knew that he was screwed. They knew he was there; he knew that they wouldn't leave him alone.

Sure enough, the 'Zoids ended up at the door, coughing and trumpeting and belching his name. They thumped at the door with their tentacles, each blow harder than the last.

Though he knew he would end up opening the door eventually, Luther tried to shut out the commotion for just a moment more. He slipped a cigarette out of the pocket of his coveralls and lit it, inhaling deeply.

And it was then, only then, that he finally noticed how different he felt. As he stood there and smoked, listening to the thumping and sneezing and belching, he realized that exhaustion wasn't the only reason he didn't want to face the creatures.

Up until now, he had been enjoying his adventure. He had loved killing aliens on another planet...loved making a comeback after years of decline...loved being treated like a V.I.P. for doing what he loved to do. He had loved the irony, too, that a serial killer whose nickname was

Bug-Eyed Monster, and whose M.O. included carving crop circles in his victims and arranging their organs like constellations, had become the first Earthling serial killer in space.

But something had changed. The thrill seemed to be gone.

As hard as it was to believe, Luther felt all killed out. He'd never thought he'd see the day when he'd had enough murder, but the day had come.

The next morning, after about three hours of sleep interrupted by Ectozoids whomping on the front door for murder lessons, Luther felt even less enthusiastic about the kill training.

As Boraf shook him awake to face a fresh batch of wannabes, Luther actually felt a wave of dread at the day ahead. Instead of reveling in gleeful anticipation, he wished that the day was over already; the last thing he felt like doing was cranking out another bunch of killer jellyfish.

"Make more kill," said Boraf, coiling its tentacles around Luther's arms and dragging him up to a sitting position. "Save world now."

Angrily, Luther batted off the tentacles and got to his feet. Grabbing his smokes and lighter from atop his food locker, he proceeded to draw out a cigarette and plug it into his mouth.

"Ectozoids need kill now," puffed Boraf, extending a tentacle toward the cigarette. "Now not later save world."

As the tentacle drifted toward him, Luther froze, the lighter halfway to his mouth. He gave Boraf a look that would have killed it if looks could do that...and as dense or inconsiderate as Boraf was, the 'Zoid seemed to get the message. The tentacle wavered for an instant in front of Luther's face, then slowly withdrew.

Luther glared at the 'Zoid for another moment for good measure, then flicked the lighter and touched the flame to the tip of the cigarette. When he released the first lungful of smoke, he was pleased to see the 'Zoids back away; the one thing they seemed to be more allergic to than waiting was cigarette smoke.

If he had thought he could get away with it, and if he had had enough cigarettes, Luther would have stood there and smoked for the rest of the day.

Around his fifteenth conversion of the morning, Luther began to regret his life as a serial killer.

It was a brand new train of thought, one that had never chugged through him on even his worst days. Even when Lech Bomb had gone bad and the Guild had kicked Luther out, he had never doubted his choice of career. It had been a given practically from day one; he had never felt like he could have been anything *but* a serial killer.

So why, all of a sudden, was he questioning his choice? Why did he feel sadness and shame when he looked back at his achievements instead of the usual pride and nostalgia? And why was he jumping the track now, of all times, just when he was at the apex of his career?

As he guided another 'Zoid in gutting another victim, Luther remembered the first human life he had taken. The old woman's face came back to him, looking just the same as it had when he'd thrown the first shovel-full of dirt on her: weeping and blinking and quaking, buried alive. He had thought of her often through the years, always with secret, dark pleasure...but now, the pleasure had soured. When he conjured her image in his mind (Ida Mae Caldwell, that was her name) he felt a brick in his stomach and a wave of dizzying nausea.

Annoyed at this unexpected response, Luther skimmed through his memories of other victims, seeking more familiar reactions. Not counting the 'Zoids he'd killed, he had 276 to choose from over a 42-year period. Normally, recalling them was like fondling rare coins from a collection--admiring them, wallowing in the selfish joy of ownership; this time, he wanted to put them right down just as soon as he picked them up.

For the first time in his life, his murder memories felt unclean.

He flipped from one to the next, hardly daring to glance at them. Each one intensified his feelings of disgust: Number 12, Julie Kefler, age 33, strangled and minced; Number 37, Steve Parrote, age 41, tortured with pliers for three days and hung on a clothesline; Number 108, Abner Lockjaw, age 74, butchered and fed to his dogs a bite at a time; Numbers 246 and 247, Milo Chapel, age 17, and Peggy Brezini, age 16, cut up and stitched back together into one big mismatched body.

And then there was Number 150, which Luther couldn't even bear to think about for a fraction of a second. Once, Number 150 had been one of his crowning achievements; now, it seemed like the most twisted crime of his entire twisted life.

Contrary to what he had thought up until now, Luther realized that he was a sick and wicked individual. His disgust at the memories of what he had done in the past was equaled only by his newborn self-loathing.

How he could ever have imagined that he was a great man was beyond his current ability to comprehend. Would a great man have come all the way out into space and become the first Earthling to set foot on an alien world...only to murder its inhabitants? Would a great man have failed to see that unleashing the killer instinct might cause more harm than good on Ectos?

Would a great man stand by, arms dripping with pink milk from a punctured head-bulb, as one 'Zoid trainee fought another over the remains of a murder victim, playing a savage tug-of-war with the limp mess of bulbs and tentacles?

As the creatures squawked and yanked the corpse back and forth, Luther wiped his drenched arms on his black coveralls. Deciding he had had enough, he turned to walk away.

And before he could take a single step, a third 'Zoid flung itself in front of him.

"Make kill now," the creature puffed from its forehead blowhole. "Now!"

Luther shook his head and backed away. "No more," he said. "I need a break."

The 'Zoid reached out with three tentacles at once, and Luther had to back up fast to evade them. "Make kill," said the creature. "Save world."

Luther wished he hadn't handed over the knife to the other two 'Zoids. "Not now," he said, continuing to backstep as the creature pressed toward him.

"Save world make kill now not later," said the 'Zoid, extending more tentacles.

Luther took another step and ran into a pillowy obstacle. Lurching away from it at once, he spun around and saw that it was Boraf.

The other 'Zoid shuffled closer, still reaching. Its tentacles brushed him as he ducked and darted behind Boraf, putting his 'Zoid host between him and the overeager wannabe.

As Luther got ready to run, the wannabe plowed into Boraf with a sound like wet spaghetti flopping into a colander. The creatures hooted and thrashed around, tentacles intertwining, fluid-filled bulbs sloshing against each other.

One of the wannabe's tentacles squirmed out from between them and twisted toward Luther...but he easily sidestepped it. Another wriggled toward him from below, catching him by surprise, but it only managed to graze his leg before he danced away from it.

Then, the wannabe stopped struggling.

It stood there for a moment, huddled against Boraf, breath whistling in and out of its blowhole. Then, slowly, it uncurled its tentacles from Boraf's and drew back, head bobbing from side to side.

Luther watched, expecting the creature to thrust past Boraf and pursue him. Instead, the wannabe shuffled back, tentacles coiling sinuously, head-bulb quivering.

"Want kill," puffed the creature. "Want kill!"

"I told you, no more for now," said Luther. "You'll have to wait."

"No wait," said the wannabe. "No need human."

The creature turned and wobbled over to the two 'Zoids who had been fighting over the carcass. They had resolved the tug-of-war by tearing the corpse in half, and each was now smearing its slimy prize like a washcloth over its body.

The knife the killers had used on their victim lay forgotten in a pink puddle in the street. Flashing out a tentacle, the wannabe scooped up the weapon...and in the same flicker of motion, swung it around and drove it into the head-bulb of one of the killers.

"Want kill more," sang the wannabe, wrenching the knife from the first 'Zoid and swinging it around into the head-bulb of the second. As both victims squealed, the wannabe ripped out the knife again and slashed it through the air, pink milk flying, to plunge into another of the first killer's bulbs. "Boraf make want kill! No need human!"

Luther stared as the 'Zoid lashed the blade back and forth, hacking up two creatures at once. For the first time that he could remember, Luther felt horrified at watching a killing in progress.

Boraf turned and patted his shoulder with a slimy tentacle. "Boraf make Ectozoids kill now," said the alien. "Luther take break now. Boraf make many kill save world."

Luther just kept staring. Whatever had enabled him to transform 'Zoids into killers--whether it was some fluke of his body chemistry or some warped electrical field in his brain--it had somehow been transferred to Boraf. The timing couldn't have been better, because Luther was sick to death of making killers.

And yet, he wondered if it was entirely a good thing that Boraf had the power. He wondered if it would stop with Boraf, or if other 'Zoids could develop the same ability to implant the killer instinct.

If the killing could be spread by 'Zoids other than Boraf, he wondered what the world would be like in a week. How much of the population would be left by the time the invaders arrived?

And he wondered if it was just a coincidence that Boraf's empowerment had kicked in just as his own murder drive had fizzled.

That night, no one bothered Luther. No 'Zoids barged up to wallop the door of Boraf's house-mound, demanding conversion. Luther figured it was because Boraf--and other 'Zoids, too, most likely--was doing the job just fine without him.

Finally, Luther was alone with time to rest...but all he could do was lie awake and think.

The faces of the many people he'd killed kept drifting up out of his memory, filling him with guilt and regret. Number 150, in particular, kept returning again and again, the worst of the lot.

Number 150, Harmony Duquesne, 18 years old.

The harder he tried not to think about her, the more forcefully she surged back to the forefront of his mind. The man he had become could not believe what the man he had been had done to her.

He wondered how he had managed it, how he had managed any of it. Thinking back, he tried to understand what had driven him, what had enabled him to commit such atrocities...and he couldn't. He had the memories, bright and brutal and real, but no grasp at all of the mentality that had brought them into being.

He was a monster, and he finally knew it. Whatever had blinded him to the truth had been leeched out of him by the 'Zoids; he finally had a conscience and awareness of his nature.

And he wished he didn't.

There was only one redeeming factor, one thing that he might have done right, and he clung to it. By instilling the killer instinct in the 'Zoids, he might have given them the means to save their world.

Maybe (Luther tried to convince himself) this single act could balance the scales for the past...or, at least, allow him to live with the memories of what he had done. Maybe, with this act of redemption and his newfound change of heart, Luther still had hope for a brighter future free of the demons that had ruled him for most of his life.

And maybe, the evil he had done had had a purpose after all, had all been leading up to this...and in saving the 'Zoids, Luther had also saved himself.

Rolling over on the sleeping mat, he reached for his cigarettes and fished one out. As he lit it, he listened to the chaos outside--the yips and whistles and squeals of 'Zoids in frenzy, the splashing of body fluids, the smacking of corpses on the street. It was a round-the-clock madhouse out there, like a vision of Hell...and he had made it.

He tried not to think about how many 'Zoids were dying out there as he smoked, how many had died since his arrival on Ectos. Instead, he reminded himself that the death was necessary for the survival of the 'Zoids, that in order to fend off the invasion, they had to take drastic measures to activate violent tendencies.

Still, Luther worried that it might all fly out of control. Clearly, the 'Zoids were getting carried away with their newfound murderous impulses; Luther expected a worldwide escalation as the killing gift spread around the planet. He thought it was possible that the 'Zoids would get so caught up in their collective rampage that they would be too disorganized or depopulated to fight when the invaders arrived.

Which would cancel out any balancing of the scales for Luther. If anything, it would dump him so far into the negative side that he would never even get a glimpse of the positive side again.

He would be to blame. Conquered, the 'Zoids might have survived, might even have someday overthrown their conquerors. Thanks to Luther, however, the 'Zoids might kill themselves off on their own.

It would have been the ultimate accomplishment for a death-hungry serial killer, a real work of art. Unfortunately, Luther wasn't a serial killer anymore. He wasn't sure what he was, but he knew he wasn't a serial killer.

The next morning, Boraf shuffled in excitedly, dripping with pink and yellow milk and inky fluid. Luther was still up, smoking, but he felt like crap; he was irritated that Boraf was still full of energy after being out murdering all night, and he was further peeved that the entire 'Zoid species never seemed to need sleep at all.

"How was your night?" said Luther, blowing out smoke.

Boraf sniffed loudly and backed away from the cloud that

Luther had exhaled. "Night of history!" it said, voice shrill as a fire bell. "Boraf make many Ectozoid kill. Many Ectozoid make many more Ectozoid kill."

"Looks like you did some killing yourself," said Luther.

Boraf shook his tentacles, spraying fluid all over the walls and floor. "Want kill more," said the creature. A noise like a cross between a fart and fingernails scratching a chalkboard burst from its fluttering blowhole.

"Yeah," said Luther, stubbing out his cigarette. "So anyway, that big invasion oughtta hit soon, right?"

"Invasion two days," said Boraf, tentacles twisting and swaying.

"And the Ectozoids are ready?" said Luther.

"Ready two days," said Boraf. "Make many Ectozoid kill."

Luther sighed. "It just seems like a lot of chaos right now. If there's an invasion coming in two days, shouldn't your people be getting prepared?"

Boraf made a wheezing, oinking sound and bobbled his head. "Ectozoids prepare! Make ships ready kill now. Make troops ready fly ships."

Luther felt relieved. It was the first reference he'd heard to any kind of defense preparations other than Ectozoids killing each other. "So you'll be ready in two days?"

"Ready two days," said Boraf. "Ready save world."

Luther nodded. "That's good. I was starting to think things were getting out of control with all the killing."

Boraf had been fidgeting around, but it suddenly stopped. "Always control," it said. "Ectozoids good control."

Luther smirked. "Except when you're all worked up about killing each other."

"Control killing too," puffed Boraf. "Only kill weak. Only kill lazy."

Luther had been reaching for another cigarette, and he stopped. "You're killing the weak?" he said, staring up at the jellyfish.

"Need strong save world," said Boraf. "Need all strong no weak no lazy."

Luther's stomach twisted. He had never considered that the apparent chaos masked a methodical effort to thin the herd. It had never occurred to him that the 'Zoids were choosing their victims in other than a random fashion.

His newfound conscience shot him full of guilt. Until that moment, he had consoled himself with the knowledge that his brutal influence would at least lead to a redemptive outcome...but now, even that consolation was deflated. The 'Zoids were cleansing themselves of undesirables, and he was responsible for setting the pogrom in motion.

He was no better than Hitler. There was a time when that wouldn't have bothered him a bit, but that time was long gone.

Just when Luther hated himself as much as he thought possible, he found that he could hate himself even more.

He hated the 'Zoids almost as much. Though their crimes had been instigated by him, he believed that the seeds of savagery must have been within them all along. He didn't believe that the notion of systematic extermination of undesirables had dawned on them overnight, springing solely from his influence.

The 'Zoids were just as bad as he was, or as he had been. Looking at them was like looking in a mirror, and he was sick of what he saw.

Suddenly, Luther wanted one thing more than anything in the universe.

"So when do I go home?" he said, grabbing the pack of cigarettes. "You promised I'd leave before the invasion."

"Two days," said Boraf, picking up a fresh knife from a table and shuffling toward the door.

"Isn't that cutting it kind of close?" said Luther. "The invasion's supposed to start in two days."

Boraf slapped the door and its component eels slithered apart. "No worry," said the 'Zoid. "Luther go fast ship. Leave early."

Luther frowned. "You sure I'll get out in time? We had a deal, remember?"

"Fast ship," said Boraf. "Get away go Earth fast."

"Why not leave tomorrow?" said Luther. "You don't need me here anymore."

"Ship ready two days," said Boraf, shuffling out the door. "Now Boraf go make many Ectozoid kill."

As the door closed, Luther lit his cigarette. All of a sudden, he had a bad feeling about his future.

Two mornings later, Luther found himself riding a giant centipede.

He and Boraf sat in a bubble that was either grown from the creature's back or attached there, he couldn't tell which. It was the same type of transportation he had ridden from the spaceport to Boraf's house-mound upon his arrival...apparently, the local version of a taxi.

Sunlight gleamed off the creature's ruby carapace as it scuttled through the streets, neatly winding its segmented length around bends and corners. Giant antennae danced from its head like fishing poles, constantly twitching and flickering in the air.

As the centipede taxi hurried them through the maze of the city, Luther noticed that the mayhem of the past week had finally subsided. The orgy of killing had seemed to die away in the middle of the night, from what he could hear from inside Boraf's house-mound, and now he didn't see a single murder underway anywhere. It was as if someone had given a signal, and all the 'Zoids had stopped killing at once.

Stopped killing and headed for the spaceport, apparently. All along the centipede's route, Luther saw 'Zoids shuffling in the same direction that the taxi was traveling. The further the taxi went, the more 'Zoids filled the streets...until, at the spaceport, the centipede was packed in all around by a vast crowd of jellyfish, all shambling toward the cluster of massive, globular spacecraft steaming on the launch pads.

It got so crowded that the centipede had to slow from a scuttle to a crawl, though it never stopped moving. When the 'Zoids didn't get out of its way voluntarily, the creature simply plowed through them, shoving them aside or nosing them under its hundred-legged bulk.

Before long, the taxi drew up to one of the ships, many times smaller than the other vessels but of the same spherical design. The bubble on the centipede's back rolled open like an eyelid, and Boraf wriggled down the creature's side to the ground.

As Luther handed down his duffel bag of possessions, he squinted up at the mirrored silver skin of the
sphere-ship. It looked identical to the craft that had brought him from Earth, and that ship had made the trip in nothing flat, in less than a day...but he was still worried. In spite of Boraf's reassurances, Luther wasn't convinced that he would escape the invasion.

"You're sure this'll get me away in time?" he said.

"Fast ship," said Boraf. "No worry."

Luther took another look before reaching for his food locker. He started to lift it, but arthritis pain flashed through his arms and hands.

Releasing the locker handles, he hissed breath between clenched teeth and massaged his hands. "Hell with it," he said. "Short trip to Earth, right?"

"Short trip," said Boraf. "Fast ship."

Luther popped the locker open and pulled out a can of chili and a packet of juice. "I'll just bring a snack and leave the rest here."

"Bring snack," said Boraf, extending tentacles to help Luther down the side of the centipede.

Luther held on to a tentacle and slid off the taxi's ruby carapace. He couldn't wait until he was home and would never have to touch another slimy tentacle for the rest of his life.

"What about my payment?" he said.

"All on ship," puffed Boraf. "Plus bonus."

"All right," said Luther, shouldering the duffel bag with difficulty. "Now let's get the hell out of here."

As the ship popped out of the atmosphere like a bubble popping out of soapy water, Luther asked for the tenth time if the invasion fleet was getting close yet.

"All clear," said Boraf, though it didn't seem to be looking at a monitor screen or out a window. "Safe passage."

Luther's eyes were glued to the circular viewport alongside his seat. "Wait," he said, squinting at a distant flicker of light. "Is that one of their ships?"

"No," said Boraf.

"Well, how do you know?" snapped Luther. "You didn't even look."

Boraf floated past, free of the harness that had restrained it during liftoff. "Always notified of danger," said the 'Zoid. "No danger now."

Luther snorted and kept his eyes on the viewport anyway.

He caught a glimpse of another suspicious twinkle and followed it, heart racing...then decided it was just a star and only appeared to be moving relative to the ship. He saw a group of distant lights and leaned so close to the viewport that his nose almost touched the glass...but they were just a group of stars or planets, fixed in the darkness.

Breathing fast, mouth dry, joints throbbing, Luther wished he could light a smoke. Unfortunately, even if the 'Zoids had allowed him to light up on the spaceship, he didn't have any cigarettes left.

Any way he looked at it, he was going home just in time.

Gazing into the blackness beyond the viewport, Luther wondered which of the pinpricks of light was Earth's sun. He wished that he was already there, already breathing the sweet air and moving among other human beings and drinking in the familiar sights...savoring all the things that he had so taken for granted and never would again.

At the same time that the thought of going home excited him, it scared the hell out of him. He was returning to Earth as a new man, free of his old compulsions, remorseful and self-aware. He was already planning to face up to the crimes of his past, to make amends and restitution as best he could and pay the price for what he had done...which would ease his newfound conscience but would be the fight of his life. By the time it was all over, his very life might be the price he would have to pay. That, he was not looking forward to.

And then there was another possibility that was wearing on him.

What if, when he got home, whatever had changed within him changed back?

Suddenly, something caught his eye outside the viewport, and he jumped. Craning his neck, he saw a gleaming silver curve gliding up from the rear edge of the window, sparking in the light of Ectos' sun.

"Boraf!" he said, watching as the silver advanced and expanded...and then, as the word left his mouth, he recognized the shape.

It was one of the 'Zoid sphere ships, moving alongside them. The massive globe floated up from the 'Zoid homeworld, traveling in the same direction as the ship carrying Luther.

He heard a familiar sloshing and rustling as Boraf drifted up beside him. "Killship," said the 'Zoid. "Killship save world."

Keeping his eyes glued to the viewport, Luther spotted another of the giant spheres beyond the first. And then another. Moving in formation, they paralleled his own ship's course and speed, bobbing in the void like enormous silver balloons.

Luther frowned as another sphere pushed up alongside the rest. "We're all heading in the same direction," he said. "Are they escorting us till we're safely away from here?"

"Ships escort," said Boraf.

"Well, good," said Luther, leaning back. "I'd hate to wind up in the line of fire."

Boraf made a noise like the wail of a saw being played with a fiddle bow. "Luther safe," it said, patting his head with a tentacle. "No worry."

As Boraf floated forward to burble at the 'Zoids operating the ship's controls, Luther tried to relax. He felt a little better knowing that his ship had a protective escort, but he still couldn't quite extinguish the foreboding that needled the back of his mind.

After a while, though, when the ships had cruised far from Ectos with no sign of danger, he finally managed to convince himself that he would be okay. Slowly, his nervousness faded, and he actually drifted off to sleep.

Luther awakened to the most wonderful sight: a blue-green world, swathed in clouds of white, with a single pewter moon suspended above it.

Earth.

As he watched his home planet push closer through the big viewport at the front of the ship, he smiled serenely. Whatever awaited him there, whatever trials he would have to face to complete his redemption, he was happier than he had ever imagined possible to be near it again.

He was home.

"We're there already," he said, raising his voice for Boraf to hear.

Boraf was playing his tentacles over the fluttering grassy fronds of a control panel. "Earth," the 'Zoid said simply.

"Thank God," muttered Luther, still smiling. He yawned loudly and stretched, extending his arms overhead and pressing his abdomen against the thick safety strap holding him in his seat.

Staring at the beautiful planet beyond the forward viewport, he daydreamed about the things he had missed most from home...the things that were now within reach. No matter what ordeals he was about to undergo, he promised himself that he would gorge on as many cheeseburgers, T-bones, beers, and pornos as he possibly could.

Then, something caught his attention from the corner of his eye.

He turned to the viewport beside him, and his smile disappeared. His eyes widened and his mouth dropped open.

A chill ran up his spine.

"Boraf," he said quietly, and then he shouted. "Boraf!"

The 'Zoid left the controls and floated over to him, sloshing and puffing. "Luther?"

"Why are the other ships here?" snapped Luther. "I thought they were going to fight the invasion fleet!"

The 'Zoid made a noise like the meow of a cat crossed with the squeak of a hinge. "Fleet no fight fleet," it said. "No make sense."

"No no no," said Luther, gaping at the giant silver spheres outside the viewport. "The invasion fleet! The 'Zoids were supposed to stop the invasion fleet and save the world!"

A gargling sound emerged from Boraf's forehead blowhole. "Only one fleet," said the creature. "One invasion."

Luther's heart raced as he turned from the window to stare at the hovering jellyfish. "One invasion," he said slowly.

"Earth," said Boraf, pointing a tentacle at the forward viewport. "Ectozoids invade Earth."

"I don't understand," said Luther. "You told me you needed to save your world."

"Save world yes," said Boraf. "Ectozoids use up resources. Get new resources Earth save world."

Cold panic rushed through Luther, mingled with rage. "No!" he said, grabbing for the latch on his restraints, trying to pry them open. "You son of a bitch! You tricked me!"

"Luther be happy," said Boraf. "Great killer make greatest kill ever. Kill human species."

Luther battled the restraints but couldn't open them. "No! Don't do it!"

"No worry," said Boraf, ruffling his hair with a slimy tentacle. "Luther safe. Luther special. Luther Ectozoid hero save world."

"Please!" screamed Luther. "I was wrong! I've changed!"

"Congratulations," puffed Boraf. "Luther greatest serial killer in universe."

Boraf was close enough to kill. Luther reached deep, searching for the old murderous fire...but he couldn't even find a dim spark. Even now, the killer within was nowhere to be found.

All he could do was thrash against his restraints and scream like a child in a doctor's office as the gleaming silver globes dropped into the atmosphere of the blue-green planet.

THE MESSIAH BUSINESS

never met Jesus Christ. I followed him around for about six months, making a nice living off him all that time, but I never talked to the guy.

I almost tangled with him, though, thanks to Vashti. It was all her idea, that scumsucking piece of work.

Leave it to her to think of kidnapping an apostle. And leave it to me--Zalmon, dope of the century--to be dumb enough to go along with it.

Before Vashti mucked everything up--and not for the first time, either--the gang and I were doing real well with our chosen field. The messiah business has always been a good one around these parts, but it was never better than when Christ was making the rounds.

I wish I could go back to those days, before things fell apart. Looking back, they were some of the best days of my life...right before some of the worst.

And it was all thanks to Christ. He had a real way about him, you know? Had lots of charisma. And he really knew how to draw a crowd. A *big* crowd, like a flock of sheep swarming around a shepherd.

Which the gang and I would proceed to fleece in every possible way.

People say Christ performed miracles, but let me tell you about the *real* magicians and the good work *they* did.

Huldah wasn't much to look at, a mousey type with stringy black hair and a constant sad look on her face...but she was the best pick-pocket I've ever met. While Christ made his latest inspired speech, Huldah worked the crowd like a shadow, lifting coins from pockets and purses without ever drawing attention.

Asher was our fastest talker, a master of separating pilgrims from their cash with nothing but his good looks and silver tongue. By the time he was done chatting up a Christian, he'd walk away with a nice share of their money or other goodies, giving nothing in exchange but flattery and false promises.

Then there was Naamah, our resident flirt. Red-haired and beautiful, she could charm any man out of his hard-earned shekels in a heartbeat...or just distract him while Huldah picked his pocket.

As for Boaz, he was all about the merchandise. If Christ touched a rock or dropped a crust of bread, Boaz was right there behind him, grabbing it up for resale. Pilgrims couldn't get enough of those Christ-touched souvenirs, authentic or otherwise.

Which brings us to me. I was an information gatherer, finding out important facts and putting our biggest scores in motion. I would find out where certain pilgrims were from, for example, so the gang could rob their homes while they were out being enlightened by Christ.

But that wasn't my original job, you know. In the old days, I was more like Christ--a messiah figure roaming the landscape. Someone had to bring in the crowds and keep the gang fed between appearances by other so-called messiahs, right?

I had a real flair for the work, too. You should've seen me giving my sermons and teaching parables and pulling doves out of my sleeves and such. I kept things rolling during some lean times in Galilee.

At least until the whole thing crashed down around me, which is how I ended up doing the information gathering thing.

Did I mention Vashti set *that* mess in motion, too?

But let's get back to the apostle-napping.

A year after Vashti wrecked our fake messiah scam, the gang and I were living off the crowds that followed Christ around Galilee and the surrounding area. We fleeced the unwary, exploited the pious, and ejected any outsiders who tried to move in on our action.

On one morning in particular, we were going about our business on the shore of the Sea of Galilee. The crowd around Christ was bigger than usual, with lots of new faces, so we had more than enough work to keep us occupied.

Huldah was finding good pickings on the purse and pocket front, and Naamah was stirring up strong interest from the men and boys in the group. Merchandise sales were solid, according to Boaz, and smooth-talking Asher was having his best morning in ages.

My day was looking up, too. I'd overheard enough to know an entire village was sitting empty and undefended, ripe for the plucking.

There was just one thing I didn't count on, and it was enough to wipe the smile right off my face. *She* was, I should say.

The true shape of the day started to make itself known just as I was harvesting the last bits of information about the location of the empty village. "So it's on the *other* side of the valley, then?"

The old man I'd been talking to nodded slowly. "If you do come, you will be welcome." The old man looked past me and gestured toward Christ, who was speaking at the front of the crowd some fifty heads distant. "Perhaps we can discuss today's lesson, yes?"

I smiled warmly, as if I had any intention of doing as he'd said. "That would be wonderful, thank you."

"Good day to you then." The old man edged past me, moving closer to Christ.

Just then, a woman's voice spoke in my ear. "*Chump.*"

Spooked, I jumped and spun around. There she was, as striking as ever--all glittering brown eyes and flowing black hair. I hadn't seen her in a year, yet it was as if no time at all had passed between us.

"Hello there, Zalmon." Her crooked smile made her look sultry and wily...also smarter than me or just about anyone. "So good to see you, my darling."

Dozens of responses flashed through my mind, but all I could manage was this: "Hello, Vashti."

Looking around, she deepened her crooked smile. "I see the gang's all here." She was only an inch taller than I and had to crane her neck to see over the crowd. "Asher, Naamah, Huldah, even Boaz. How sweet." She swung her smile back around to me. "Good to know there are still *some* things I can count on."

"What do you want, Vashti?" I asked her. "Why are you here?"

"Would you believe, to learn at the feet of the master?" She nodded toward Christ, then laughed. "I didn't think so! Would you believe I'm here to rat you out, instead? To tell the pilgrims what you and your gang have been up to?"

I shrugged. "They're Christians. They won't hurt us."

"Maybe." Vashti's earrings--golden diamond-shaped affairs as big as the ears they hung from--flashed in the sunlight as she giggled. "But I bet they'll still *ban* your asses."

She had me and she knew it. I felt an invisible leash snapping tight around my neck, the handle in her hands.

I sighed. "What do you want, Vashti?"

Looking satisfied, she raised her chin. "Get your little pals together and meet me down by those rocks." She gestured toward a nearby jetty. "And don't make me wait."

"You want us to *what?*" Huldah looked and sounded aghast.

Vashti eyed her calmly, squinting a little in the late-morning sun. "You heard me."

"We're not kidnappers." Asher said it with a smile.

"So you're too good to make money now?" said Vashti. "You've got plenty of muscle." Boaz gestured at the pair of bruisers standing behind Vashti--her new henchmen with long, black hair and matching brown robes, whom she'd introduced as Gad and Jabez. "Why not have *them* do it?"

Vashti smirked. "Because they can't get close to the target like *you* people. They haven't been blending in with the regular crowd for the past six months."

"You're talking about an *apostle* here." Naamah's lovely features were crumpled in a scowl. "Kidnapping an *apostle*."

Vashti pinched a thumb and forefinger together. "Just a *little* one."

"The Christians may be peace-lovers and pushovers," said Asher, "but they've got *numbers*." He hiked a thumb over his shoulder toward the crowd. "That's a heck of a lot of *eyeballs* back there. When they're not staring at *Christ*, they're staring at his *apostles*."

"I'm not worried." Vashti shrugged and met my gaze. "You'll figure out a way to make it happen, won't you?"

I didn't look away. I was locked on her, as always--and not just out of hate or fear. Was it possible that part of me had never gotten over her? "You realize, if we do this," I said, "and it goes the slightest bit wrong, it will ruin the good thing we've got going here."

"So don't screw it up," said Vashti.

"We're talking our *livelihoods* here," I said. "I don't want to throw it all away on your say-so."

"I've got news for you," said Vashti. "You will *definitely* lose it if you *don't* help me. I'll go straight to Christ and tell him what you people have been doing, I *swear*."

Just then, a white gull coasted by overhead like a sign. Vashti didn't look up at it, as if she'd been expecting it all along.

Just as she'd been expecting us to fall in line, no doubt. Even after the events she'd brought down upon us a year ago, she must have known she was holding all the best cards.

Not that she couldn't be conciliatory when she wanted to. "Okay, listen." Her voice and expression suddenly turned less imperious. "I've always felt bad about the way things went down last time around. I want to make it up to you, to pay back what you lost because of me. I want to redeem myself."

Good luck with that. Looking around, I could see at a glance that the others felt the same.

But the fact remained: I had to try to make it work. At least until I could think of a way out of this. If I didn't want her to spoil the good thing we had going, I needed to sell her crazy plan.

"How exactly are you going to pay us back?" I asked.

"I can't say just yet." Vashti raised her palms in front of her. "But trust me, it will make up for what you lost and then some."

"*Trust* you?" Huldah snorted.

"What about the *other* question?" said Boaz. "The one nobody's asked yet." He leaned forward, hands on hips, and gazed at her expectantly. "Why exactly do you want to kidnap an *apostle?*"

"Because," said Vashti. "He's the key to making things right again."

We all knew Vashti's proposal was garbage, her promises empty. We knew we'd be idiots if we went along with it.

But we also knew her threats were real. She *would* turn us in if we didn't cooperate. There was also the unspoken threat of the two bruisers by her side; she had enough muscle to rough us all up with very little opposition. Stealth, not combat, was our specialty.

So when Vashti stepped away to let us talk it over, I think most of us were already leaning a certain way. Not that we had to like it.

"This has 'disaster' written all over it." Asher spoke in a whisper to keep Vashti from hearing him, just as the rest of us did. "We all *know* what she did to us in *Nain.*"

"I agree," I said, "but I don't think we have a choice here."

"Sure we do," said Naamah. "We can just *leave,* can't we?"

"But what if she's right about the payoff?" I asked. "What if it really *is* enough to make up for what we lost in Nain?"

"Then I'm sure *she's* planning to get every last *bit* of it," snapped Naamah.

"Don't you think we're smart enough to grab it first?" I asked.

"It *would* be nice if *we* took advantage of *her* this time," Boaz said thoughtfully, stroking his short black beard.

"So let's give it a shot," I said. "Let's find out everything we can and flip this around so Vashti's the one who gets burned. What do you say?"

The gang thought it over for a long moment, then grudgingly agreed.

"His name is Thaddeus," said Vashti. "He's what you might call a *lesser* apostle."

"But he's still an apostle," growled Huldah.

Boaz frowned. "If he is, I don't know him."

"Sure you do," said Naamah. "Little guy, reddish-brown hair, kind of quiet. Usually off to the side sketching while Christ's preaching. He's a pretty good artist, too. I've seen his work."

Asher raised an index finger. "Oh, *that* guy."

"So what do you want him for?" asked Huldah.

Gad and Jabez leaned closer on either side of Vashti, glaring at Huldah. Zalmon guessed they didn't appreciate her curiosity.

"The sooner you bring him to me, the sooner you'll find out," said Vashti. "And the sooner you'll get what's coming to you."

"You're not going to kill him, are you?" asked Naamah. "He seems like a sweet guy."

"Not that it's any of your business, but no." Vashti's crooked smile went away, leaving an unreadable stare in its place. "We're not planning to kill *him*."

The skies were dark that night over the little coastal town of Bethsaida. Clouds obscured the moon and the stars, casting the landscape in a field of spectral black and gray interrupted only by scattered torches and lamps.

If we had to kidnap someone, we couldn't have picked a better night for it. The risk of discovery was lessened by the lack of moonlight and starlight over the shore and the softly lapping sea.

The five of us--my gang, dressed in black hooded robes--trekked in along the shoreline and entered the town unmolested. That was one good thing about the Jesus crowd: it wasn't unusual for strangers to come and go at all hours, joining or leaving the traveling show.

Getting into town was easy. Getting out again with a captive apostle would be the hard part.

"That's where Christ is staying." Asher, who'd done some scouting earlier, pointed at one of the mud-brick houses facing the sea. Lamplight flickered in the windows, throwing glowing golden swaths down on the dusty ground. "The apostles will be right there with him."

"So how do we get Thaddeus away from the others?" I scanned the little town's few buildings, then turned and looked at the fishing boats lined up on the sand.

"Some kind of diversion?" said Boaz. "Set fire to a boat, maybe?"

"That might get them all outside," I said, "but what if Thaddeus stays close to the others?"

"One of us could pretend to be a messenger," said Huldah. "We could say there's an emergency, and Thaddeus needs to come with us."

"Or we could just wait." Naamah shrugged. "He usually goes off by himself sooner or later. He likes to sketch the scenery."

"Why do I get the feeling you like this apostle a little more than you've let on?" I asked.

Naamah's only answer was a noncommittal smile.

But she turned out to be right about Thaddeus. We waited among the boats by the water, keeping watch on the house where Christ was holding court...and eventually, Thaddeus emerged. Alone, carrying a lamp, some charcoal, and a sheaf of parchment, he walked out of the house and headed off down the beach toward a jumble of rocks.

When he was some distance from Christ's location, we followed.

Thaddeus took a seat on one of the rocks, looking toward Beth-saida. He had just started sketching by the time we reached him.

"Hello, brothers and sisters." He said it with a friendly smile. "Lovely night, isn't it?"

"Hi, Thaddeus." Naamah grinned and waved. "What are you working on?"

Thaddeus held up the sheaf of parchment so we could see the drawing he'd started on the top sheet. "'Friends arriving by night,' I call it."

The sketch was rough, but it clearly pictured us--five figures in hooded black cloaks moving furtively along the coastline.

Naamah moved in first for a closer look, and the rest of us followed. "Very nice, Thaddeus," she said.

"We like it so much," I said, "that I wonder if you could come and paint a portrait of our master."

"I'm flattered," said Thaddeus, "but I really can't leave. Perhaps, if he came and visited our crusade..."

"I insist," I told him, taking firm hold of his right arm.

"As do I." Boaz gripped his left arm.

Thaddeus turned his gaze to Naamah. "I have no choice in the matter, do I?"

Naamah took his lamp and shook her head sadly. "I'm sorry, but no."

"You'll have to excuse me," said Vashti as she walked a tight circle around Thaddeus, looking him up and down. "I've never been this close to an *apostle* before."

"There's a first time for everything, isn't there?" Thaddeus shifted his hands, which were bound behind his back. "Being *kidnapped*, for example."

Vashti laughed and patted his shoulder. "We're having fun *already*, aren't we?" She flashed me a nasty look. "And *you* were worried things wouldn't work out."

All I could do was smile and nod. The truth was, things had worked out more smoothly than I'd imagined. Thaddeus had come peacefully, and no one had tried to stop us or raised the alarm.

Unimpeded, we had walked straight to the rendezvous point--an abandoned one-room hut two miles inland from the sea.

Now, we were just waiting to see what was going to happen next...the gang and I just as much in the dark as Thaddeus himself.

"So, Thad." Vashti continued to circle him, letting her fingers drift over his upper body. "Things don't always work out the way we planned, do they?"

"Very true." Thaddeus raised an eyebrow. "Just tonight, I thought I was going to do a little sketching by the sea."

"Exactly." Vashti tousled his shock of red-brown hair. "Now here you are, about to be sold to some friends of mine."

Just as Vashti said it, Gad and Jabez marched into the room. I assumed they were escorting someone else who would follow them inside...

But there was no one else behind them.

"Like I said." Vashti winked at me as she stepped in front of Thaddeus. "Things don't always turn out the way we planned."

Gad, the hairier of the two brutes, was carrying something over his shoulder in a big burlap sack. He put it down on the ground at the base of one wall.

As for Jabez, he said a few words in a language that wasn't Hebrew or Aramaic, and Vashti answered him. As he handed Vashti a leather purse that jingled and clinked with the sound of coins, I quickly realized what language they were using...and I was surprised all over again.

Latin. Vashti and the bruisers were speaking *Latin.*

Suddenly, the game we were playing had taken a dramatic turn. Until that moment, I hadn't suspected the bruisers were anything other than hired Jewish muscle.

I certainly hadn't guessed they were *Romans.*

Vashti opened the purse and gazed inside. "Very nice." She poked a finger at the contents, then cinched the drawstring and dropped it in a pocket of her robes. Stepping aside, she bowed her head and gestured at Thaddeus. "All yours, boys."

Gad and Jabez said something in Latin and stepped forward. Thaddeus didn't flinch in the slightest as Gad's beefy paws closed around his upper arms.

Meanwhile, Vashti glided around behind them. Her crooked smile had a mischievous tilt as she raised a finger to her lips for the benefit of me and the gang.

The Romans drawled Latin at Thaddeus, who seemed to understand what they were saying. Frowning, he shook his head, which led them to talk some more.

Suddenly, a flicker of movement behind the Romans caught my eye. I looked back there just in time to see Vashti leaping at Jabez, lunging a silver blade at the side of his throat. His eyes went wide as she slashed the blade across his neck, instantly drawing a crimson line from his Adam's apple to his ear.

As Vashti dropped away from Jabez, he choked and clutched at the wound. Blood swelled and rushed between his fingers, pouring off the tips of his elbows and down his chest.

Perhaps because of the unexpected nature of the attack, Gad was a heartbeat slow to react. He whipped his head around at the choking sounds, his hands releasing Thaddeus. I could see it in Gad's eyes as understanding quickly dawned...but by then, Vashti was already darting up from behind him with the knife.

Jumping up, she grabbed his long hair and wrenched his head back. Before he could make a move to dislodge her, she was already slicing the blade across his throat.

The rest of us stumbled back as the burly Romans died in front of us. Choking and groaning, they thrashed on the floor, desperately trying in vain to hold their wounds shut. Blood continued to gush out of them, pooling and soaking into the dirt, filling the air with a rusty, metallic tang.

When it was all over, Vashti wiped the blade on Jabez's cloak and slid it into a sheath under the robes at her hip. "So much for Caesar's idiot errand boys." She spat on both bodies and turned to Thaddeus. "You should thank me."

Thaddeus shook his head. "Killing is never justified."

"Even if they were going to force you to spy for Rome?" asked Vashti. "Make you betray your master, Jesus Christ?"

I was intimidated by what she'd just done, but I found the strength to speak. "That's why you were working with them? So you could double-cross them and save Thaddeus?"

"Almost right." Vashti winked. "I also needed them to haul that here for me." She gestured at the big burlap sack on the floor by the wall. "Plus, I needed their money." She pulled the purse from her pocket and threw it to me. "Consider me paid up for the Nain job...plus the rest of the work I need from you."

The purse was fat and heavy in my hands. "What work do you need us to do?"

"Not them." She gestured at the rest of the gang. "Just you." She pointed a finger at me. "I need you to deliver a message."

As the sun rose the next morning, pushing away the grays and blacks of the moonless, starless night, I set out alone for Bethsaida.

After hours of digging, the Romans' bodies were in the ground behind me. My gang and I had buried them deep in a field near the hut where they'd died, then thrown in the blood-soaked dirt from the hut floor after them.

Now, I was on my own. Asher, Huldah, Boaz, and Naamah had stayed behind to watch over Thaddeus...and, presumably, to serve as insurance that I would follow Vashti's orders.

But I couldn't help wondering if even my fear for their safety would be enough to get me to do the job I'd been given.

I was supposed to threaten Jesus Christ himself...and that wasn't the worst part of it. The real trouble would come into play if Christ agreed to go along with Vashti's demands.

Because if he did the one job she wanted him to do, my darkest secret could be revealed.

The secret was this.

A year ago, when things went sideways in Nain because of Vashti, we lost a man. His name was Sharar, and Vashti loved him in ways she would *never* love me.

The gang (including Vashti and Sharar) had been running a fake messiah scam, and it fell apart in Nain. Vashti, our information gatherer at the time, had misinformed us about which homes would be empty in town during the preaching of the fake messiah (played by me). Acting on that information, Boaz, Huldah, and Asher robbed a house, only to have the owner walk in on them. To make matters worse, the owner recognized all three of them as my associates, meaning we all had targets on our backs. A couple of Pharisees got the townspeople riled up, and things turned ugly fast.

The only way I survived was by throwing Sharar to the lynch mob and running like hell. Then I lied to the rest of the gang, who were elsewhere when I did it, and no one seemed to be the wiser.

But that was about to change if Christ paid the ransom for Thaddeus and lived up to his billing.

All because of what Vashti had in that big burlap sack of hers.

As I approached Bethsaida, I could see Christ was already on the move along the coast, accompanied by a huge crowd. If he was worried about Thaddeus, he didn't show it.

The guy was a mystery to me; I admit it. Even after following him around for six months, I still wasn't sure what his game was.

I'd seen some weird things happen around him, things I couldn't explain. Maybe he had some real magic up his sleeve, who knows?

But I'd never seen him work the biggest trick of all, the one that Vashti wanted out of him. I'd heard he'd done it a few times, but I'd never seen it myself, so maybe I would be okay.

Or maybe he *could* do it. Maybe he *could* resurrect the dead.

In which case, he just might bring to life the contents of Vashti's burlap sack...and Sharar himself would crawl out of it, blabbing to everyone that I was the one who'd gotten him killed.

That's what Vashti wanted more than anything: to find out who'd killed her beloved Sharar...and avenge his death. That's what had driven her the whole last year, as she'd gotten away from Nain, hooked up with the Romans, and concocted a plan to leverage Thaddeus for Sharar's resurrection.

It was also what would get me killed if it worked. If Vashti found out who'd thrown Sharar to the crowd, she would cut that person's throat like she had Jabez and Gad's.

I knew this because she'd told me before I'd left to deliver her ransom message to Christ.

It's ironic, when you think about it. Christ, who preached forgiveness and loving your neighbor, could soon be responsible for a bloody act of vengeance resulting in my execution.

Not that I could get close to him anytime soon. The crowd, which was huge from the start, became enormous. Instead of dozens of people, there were soon hundreds...with more arriving every minute. Getting through all those spectators would be next to impossible; it wasn't like I had a special pass because I'd been a regular hanger-on for the past six months.

So the question of what to do wasn't pressing at first. For a while, I lingered on the fringes of the crowd, wrestling with my dilemma. I listened to Christ's teachings and wondered how to get near him, or if I should just run and be done with it.

Still more people joined the crowd as the noon hour approached. Before long, the fringes became the middle; hundreds became thousands, milling around me....even jostling me, in the case of one sharp-elbowed person.

When the jostling continued, I took a look at who was doing it. And my heart sank like an anchor in the Sea of Galilee.

Because it was her. Vashti was there.

Meaning my time had run out.

"What did he say?" Vashti bobbed her head in Christ's direction. "Did he agree to my terms?"

She wasn't going to like what I had to tell her--that I hadn't talked to Christ yet--and I knew it.

My mind flew into overdrive, scrambling for a way out. The best thing I could do, I decided, was lie to her, though I knew it would only get me so far.

"He agreed," I said grimly. "But he won't do more than the one job for you."

Vashti snorted. "We'll see about that. So when do I get to talk to him?"

The words rolled out of me before I realized what I was saying. It reminded me of the way I'd improvised preaching and prophecy and speaking in tongues as a fake messiah. "Back by the fishing boats, in fifteen minutes."

"Then I guess we'd better get back there." She turned and waited for me to lead the way.

Which I did. Still unsure about what I'd do next, I wove through the crowd toward the boats I'd mentioned.

Vashti stayed close behind. "It took you long enough, Zalmon. I was starting to think you might back out on me."

"Not a chance," I told her. "It just took a while to get next to Christ."

"I don't think we'll have that problem again." Vashti laughed. "We might even get to be honorary *apostles* before this is all over."

As we drew toward the edge of the crowd, I was all too aware of the mess I was in. Vashti would never accept my refusal to threaten Christ into resurrecting Sharar. I could just see her killing me like the Romans and moving on to take care of Christ herself.

Which I guessed was why I was leading her to the fishing boats, away from the crowd. Because part of me already knew what I needed to do.

But when we got to that line of boats on the shore, I realized it wasn't enough for what I had in mind. We were about a hundred cubits back from the crowd, and the boats would provide some cover...but we wouldn't be completely concealed. Spectators who happened to look our way might still get an eyeful.

What I really needed was a distraction.

Vashti leaned against the rough wooden prow of one of the boats, watching Christ in the distance. "We'll arrange to deliver the body," she said. "Then we'll hand off Thaddeus as soon as Christ raises Sharar."

"Tonight." As I said it, I looked around at the boats and sand. There was a rock nearby, half-buried, about the size of a human head. "I told him it would probably happen tonight."

Vashti nodded. "The sooner, the better."

Kicking at the sand, I dug out around the rock with the toe of my sandal. "You left Huldah in charge? To watch over Thaddeus with the others?"

"Of course." Vashti grinned. "She's as hard-headed as they come."

Suddenly, the crowd roared. "What's that?" I asked.

"I'm not sure." Vashti pushed away from the boat and squinted into the distance. "The apostles are throwing something into the crowd..."

As the people kept roaring, I realized I had the distraction I'd wanted. "What are they throwing?" Leaning down, I pulled the rock out of the sand with both hands.

Vashti was silent for a moment, straining to see. "Fish! They're throwing baskets of fish at the people!" Again, she was silent for a moment. "And something else..."

Sweat ran down my sides and back as I approached her. This was what I had to do, and I knew it.

Yet I still hesitated. I'd loved her once, and a trace of that love remained in my heart.

But only a trace.

"Bread," said Vashti. "They're throwing loaves of bread, one after another." She whistled softly. "And there sure is a lot of it. Bread and fish both."

Remembering the way she'd murdered those Romans, I quickly squelched the trace of love and continued toward her. Taking a deep breath, I raised the rock overhead.

"Since when does this outfit have such huge food stores?" asked Vashti. "They've got *thousands* of people here, and they don't look they're running out of food anytime soon."

"Some kind of trick, I'm sure." That was what I said before I swung the rock down hard on her skull.

The blow struck diagonally across the back of her head, crashing down with such force that I heard it crack the bone. She was probably dead when she folded to the ground...but I knew I wasn't done.

Dropping the rock, I dragged her by the feet behind the boat, hauling her out of sight for when the crowd's distraction ended. Then, I picked up the rock again.

And I raised it once more over my head.

By sundown, it was all over.

I had finished Vashti quickly and heaved her into one of the boats. After wrapping her in fishing nets, along with some heavy rocks, I'd pushed the boat out onto the water and raised the sail.

I'd expected to feel sad or regretful when I dumped her body overboard, but I hadn't. I'd just dropped anchor a mile out and pitched her into the sea, then sailed for shore. End of story, right?

Not quite.

By sundown, I was walking along the beach in a kind of a daze. Things had happened so fast that they'd left me in a state of shock. I'd shut down my feelings in order to get through what I'd known had needed to be done.

Now, it was all catching up to me.

I'd just murdered a woman I'd once loved in order to hide my blame for another murder a year ago. But that wasn't the only reason I'd done it. After all, I'd been in the messiah business too long to really believe that Christ could raise the dead.

In my heart, I knew the real reason, didn't I? When Vashti had returned after a year's absence, I'd secretly hoped it might be because of me...because she'd seen the light and might be ready to love me back. But even with her lover, Sharar, dead and gone, she'd still preferred him to me and probably always would.

And I'd *hated* her for that.

Now that she was gone, did I feel any better? It was too soon to tell. All I knew for sure was that my life had changed forever.

I had to leave the Christ racket for good. Once the gang realized Vashti wasn't coming back, they would let Thaddeus go...and he knew our faces well. He could point us out if we kept hanging around. None of us could continue getting rich off this particular traveling show.

I would need a new line of work...and new friends, too. There was no way I could keep working with my gang; there would be too many awkward questions about what had happened with Vashti.

So I was on my own for the first time in a while. I guess I deserved it, but the thought of it would take some getting used to.

As I walked along the shore of the Sea of Galilee, I gazed at the bright gold and crimson clouds sprawling over the horizon, mirrored in the still waters below. Something about that sight filled me with a deep longing for what I'd lost...or, more accurately, what I'd never truly had.

It was then that I caught sight of Christ, walking toward me with two apostles. His face glowed as he looked my way, catching the red-gold light of the sunset on his skin.

As I watched, he raised an arm and waved, gesturing for me to come closer.

Suddenly, I was filled with a compulsion to go to him, to relieve the ache of loneliness I felt at staring into that sunset. I imagined a new and better life, one in which I could put the darkness behind me and maybe even find the love I'd never known.

Then, I remembered bashing Vashti's head in, and the compulsion flew away like a gull soaring over the sea.

I offered Christ a friendly wave, then turned and ran away in the direction from which I'd come.

THE ASTEROID THAT STAYS CRUNCHY IN MILK

Perched on the rim of the spacecraft that looked like a silver cereal bowl, Commander Quip, the little pink *Breakfastro-naut*, blasted away with his handheld ray gun at the core of the monstrous, grumpy cloud-beast lumbering toward him.

A determined glare was fixed on Quip's bright pink face, and the rainbow-colored pinwheel sticking out of the top of his bulbous head whizzed so fast, it blurred. His cherry-red spacesuit with the letter Q stamped in green on the chest was charred and torn from his battle with the beast so far.

"How *dare* you ruin a healthy breakfast for the gleeful Gleeblings of Nutrio 6!" Again, Quip squeezed the trigger of his ray gun, and another blinding white *vitaminergy* bolt sizzled into his target with a *zeeee* and a *koooom*. "Take that, foul creature! And *that!*"

The monstrosity's roar echoed through the twinkling darkness of the Yummiverse, making the primary-colored planets wobble in their orbits. Reaching out with one billowing gray arm, the *Grumptor* cloud-beast grabbed the ring from a nearby world and tossed it like a frisbee with furious force.

The spinning ring whipped around Quip's burbling bowl-craft, spinning it fiercely—swinging Quip in crazy circles around the rim.

"Whoaaa!" The bowl-craft suddenly snagged on the point of a

crescent moon, ejecting Quip out into space. As he tumbled across the starfield, the Grumptor thrust out a massive hand and snapped him up, congealing around him like curdled milk.

Quip struggled as the gooey cloud closed in around him, but he couldn't break free. A surge of frenzied action only tightened the smothering glop, encasing him in one last pocket of air.

His strength waned, and his head buzzed. Something in the cloud made him sleepy, and his eyes drifted shut.

Only to snap back open to the wailing of sirens in a very different place.

He was free of the Grumptor but stuck inside the cockpit of a ship. Lights flashed on control panels all around him, and his reflection on the cracked window before him was not at all what Commander Quip would expect.

Instead of a little pink spaceman with a pinwheel sticking out of his head, he was a scruffy, sweating human in a helmeted spacesuit, strapped to the pilot's chair of a ship called the *Paracelsus*.

The truth flashed back to him as it always did, wiping away the breakfast cereal fantasy. Quip was only his great escape from a terrible reality, the only way he could deal with the harsh facts he had to confront.

The facts were these: His real name was Garvey Pope, he was an asteroid miner, and he was already doomed.

"Pope!" A woman's voice over the radio pulled him the rest of the way back from the Yummiverse. Her name was Baker Gillespie, and she was owner of the *Paracelsus* and boss of the ship's mining crew. "I *asked* you if you'd broken the drill free yet!"

"Not yet." Pope fought to shake off the lingering daze he felt. "It's still wedged in the crevice."

"Well, no need to *hurry*." Baker's voice dripped with sarcasm. "It's not like we're running out of *air* and *power* down here by the *second*."

"Right." Pope checked the drill's status on one of the screens on the control board. It was still as stuck as ever, meaning Baker and her team were still trapped in the caved-in mine inside asteroid Q-1X. "Maybe the vitaminergy...I mean if I reverse it again and try easing it out..."

"Hey, asshole!" snapped Baker. "Did you just say *vita*-whatsis? You're not still *hallucinating* about *cereal people*, are you?"

Pope didn't answer. The truth was, he'd been slipping in and out of hallucinations about his favorite retro breakfast cereal for at least 24 hours, ever since his exposure to the strange gray mold they'd brought back from Q-1X. It was a treasure and they knew it, the first lifeform ever found growing inside an asteroid. It was certainly the only substance of value on Q-1X, which was rich in chlorine and not much else.

The crew had been mining the stuff like crazy, everyone but Pope, who'd stayed aboard the *Paracelsus* alone to study mold samples and hold down the fort. The crew all imagined the fortune they'd make selling the space mold to corporations back on Earth. But the side effects were powerful; the mold's composition was biochemically similar to that of "magic mushrooms"— *Psilocybe cubensis*—capable of spawning vivid hallucinations in the human brain.

Once Pope had discovered those psychoactive side effects, he'd decided to test the mold on his own body. Hallucinogen enthusiast that he was, he ingested an extract of the mold in liquid form, soon finding its strongest effects were triggered by stress.

Was it any wonder he'd gulped down a heavy dose when the trouble started? Considering the kind of stress Pope was up against, was it any surprise he'd been seeing crazy shit more often than ever since the cave-in?

Frankly, it was a blessing to him. It fogged his brain sometimes, and he got confused about what was real and what wasn't...but it was the only thing getting him through his panic and fear right now. Not to mention, the mold had powerful painkilling effects, without which Pope greatly doubted he'd be coherent enough to function. He was pretty sure, without the mold to take the edge off, he'd be screaming in senseless agony instead of trying to help his shipmates.

"You didn't take the anti-fungals Doc Spivey prescribed, did you?" asked Baker.

Pope shook his head, though Baker couldn't see him. "I didn't want to risk the possible side effects."

Even if Pope *could* have been cured, there was *no* way he was going without the mold's influence in *this* shitmare. Not considering the lives at stake or the way he'd been sliced in two and was only barely staying alive.

He'd been dead from the waist down since the first incident in his current run of bad luck. While drilling into the rock to open an escape route after the cave-in, flying debris had blown a section of starboard bulkhead inward and severed his midsection. His containment suit was somehow keeping everything in place, but he knew it wouldn't last long.

And he had to get Baker and her team out of the collapsed mine shaft before then.

"Here we go." He flipped a switch on the control board, reversing the direction the drill would spin. It was the third time he'd tried the maneuver, and he prayed this time it would work. "Activating drill."

Pope stabbed a button on the board, and the ship lurched as the drill fought to turn. The vein of super-hard material that had snagged it held fast, gripping it as tightly as Pope was holding on to his life.

He punched another button, ramping up the power, and the ship lurched more violently. Impulsively, then, he flipped the switch to change the spin direction again, hoping the sudden shift would kick it free.

Instead, the ship churned clockwise and broke away. The shaft of the drill had snapped in two.

"No!" Pope's heart pounded as the *Paracelsus* pitched back from Q-1X.

"Pope?" asked Baker over the radio. "What happened? More of the ceiling just caved in!"

Pope didn't have the heart to tell her the truth. Instead, he closed his eyes and let the latest wave of illusion roll him into the brighter world again.

Quip thrashed in the grip of the Grumptor cloud-beast, unable to break free. He was weakening fast, about to lose consciousness and succumb as his last breaths of air ran out.

Just then, he sensed the approach of three more bowl-craft as they zipped up from behind a bright purple planet, piloted by three of his breakfast buddy comrades—Quax, Quazi, and Queg. The three bulb-headed spacemen whooped defiantly and fired away with their *vitaminergy* pistols, pounding the Grumptor with bolt after bolt.

The Grumptor howled with rage and swatted at the bowl-craft, but the blasts kept right on coming. He kicked a bright orange planet at them, scattering their tight V-formation—but the victory turned out to be hollow.

With the Grumptor distracted, Quip rallied his strength and exploded from the monster's grip. Pinwheel whizzing atop his head, he shot out of the gooey cloud curdles with a sound like the tootling of a trumpet.

"The *morning grumps* can't keep me down for long!" Quip reached into a pouch on his bright green belt, pulled out a fistful of glittering yellow cereal—each piece shaped like a five-pointed star—and tossed it into his mouth. "Quantum cereal gives me the quosmic power I need to get a *space-blazin'* start to my day!" he said as he crunched the sweet, vitamin-enriched bits and gulped them down.

Flaring with bright new energy, Quip swooped up and let loose a blistering bolt from his vitaminergy pistol, boring right into the Grumptor's cloudy belly. Quax, Quazi, and Queg followed suit, hurtling up and unleashing blazing bombardments from their bowl-craft.

The Grumptor bellowed its rage to the glittering heavens, then boiled away under the assault. The cheering pink spacemen and their shiny silver bowls zoomed victorious through the wispy gray vapor of the cloud-beast's remains.

"Yay! We did it!" shouted Quax, whose face was flecked with freckles that were known to move around. "The Grumptor is gone!"

"Breakfast is saved!" Cross-eyed Quazi flew his bowl-craft in wild loop-de-loops, leaving a tangled trail of bubbles and sparks in his wake.

"We can finally get back to what we do best!" hollered Queg,

579

with his red mustache and triple head-topping pinwheels. *"Cereal mining!"*

Quip whistled for his silver bowl-craft, which zoomed up to meet him and jolted to a stop, rubbing affectionately against his leg. "The children of the Yummiverse are *depending* on us! So are the gleeful *Gleeblings!"*

"Corn and oats and vitamins!" The four little spacemen chanted merrily as they chipped away with their pickaxes at the golden-grained *breakfasteroid. "Splash 'em in milk and make 'em swim!"*

As Quip and his fellow Breakfastronauts broke away star-shaped chunks of Quantum cereal, their mothership—the *Quaving*—sucked up the chunks with a vacuum sweeper nozzle. The *Quaving* was shaped like a giant Quantum cereal box, with the sweeper nozzle mounted on the box's skinny side.

Just then, the high-pitched voice of their female shipmate, Quizzie, blared from the *Quaving*'s loudspeaker. "Work faster, fellas! Kids are crying all over the Yummiverse because they woke up without a nutritious breakfast!"

"You heard the lady!" shouted Quip. "Triple-time it, guys! Let's fill up the *Quaving* and get the riboflavin *outta* here!"

The spacemen worked faster than ever, their little bodies bouncing up every time their pickaxes swung down into the ore. More and more cereal stars kicked up from the breakfasteroid in a steady stream and were sucked into the *Quaving*'s voluminous hold.

Then, suddenly, a swarm of furry black spiderlike creatures lunged out from behind a nearby green-and-pink-striped planet. Instead of claws or pincers, the creatures' appendages were tipped with gleaming, obsidian spoons.

Quip spotted them first as they went after the stream of Quantum cereal flowing up from the breakfasteroid, and his heart broke. The creatures' ravenous appetite for Quantum cereal was all *his* fault, and now they were a scourge of the Yummiverse. He'd tried to *save* them once with a supply of Quantum cereal during a food shortage on their moon, not realizing how *addicted* or *ferocious* they could get when it came to sweetened cereals. He'd unknow-ingly given them a taste for Quantum, a staple breakfast food of the Yummiverse, and left them hooked for life.

Now, they were going after the *Quaving*'s precious cargo.

"*Starantulas!*" Quazi's crossed eyes spun around on his face like a propeller, the pupils rattling from one loop of the figure eight to the other and back. "A whole *swarm* of them!"

"They'll gobble up every bit of the Quantum cereal!" shouted Quax, his freckles hopping right off his face. "The kids won't get the vitamins and minerals they need!"

"We've gotta do something!" Queg's triple pinwheels spun wildly in different directions, bobbing him up and down like a spoonful of cereal dunked in milk.

"Tell us what to do, Quip!" Quizzie's voice boomed over the *Quaving*'s loudspeaker. "Tell us before it's too late!"

"Have no fear!" Even as Quip drew his vitaminergy pistol, he knew his words were hollow. "I've thought of a way to get you out of there, Baker!"

Quip frowned and cocked his head as the realization of what he'd said sunk in. There was no Baker in the Yummiverse that he knew of.

Then, in a flicker, he was a sliced-in-half human again, strapped into the cockpit of the spinning, drifting *Paracelsus*.

"Pope!" Baker's voice over the speaker was half-panicked, half-relieved. "Thank God! I thought you were dead!"

"Dead?" Pope looked down at his severed midsection. "That's crazy talk."

"You went silent after the last quake!" said Baker. "What happened?"

"Broke the drill." Pope played the joystick, punching buttons to fire thrusters that would stop the *Paracelsus*'s spin.

"You *broke* the *drill?*"

"No biggie." Pope found asteroid Q-1X and plotted a course back to it. "I don't need it now."

"How the hell do you *figure?*"

"I've got a plan." Pope felt a chill ripple through him and pushed it away. How much time did he have left? He had to assume the worst. "Stand by, Quizzie."

"Stand by for what? And who's *Quizzie?*"

"I'm putting 'er down." Pope tugged the stick, tweaking his approach. "Gather up your drones and start digging at the weakest point on the space side of the chamber."

"That's your plan? We'll *never* break through!"

"Send me the coordinates when you have them." Pope felt another wave of cold and goosed the main thruster, pushing the *Paracelsus* faster toward the spinning hunk of rock.

Working with the autopilot, he matched the asteroid's spin and took up a geosynchronous orbit over the area where he guessed the crust was thinnest. Then he went to work prepping and programming the ship's remaining stock of drones, the dozens of digging droids that had stayed behind when the mining team had first descended to Q-1X.

By the time Baker got back to him, Pope was ready for the next step. She read him the coordinates for the weak spot over the cave-in, and he dumped them into the nav-computer without a second thought.

"Geronimo," he whispered as he dropped the *Paracelsus* toward the weak spot.

The ship plunged, and he held his breath. Would the impact jar the severed halves of his body apart? Would it finally shut him down once and for all?

The surface of the asteroid jumped toward him, and he clenched his teeth.

"What's happening up there?" asked Baker. "What are you doing?"

Pope was too busy driving to answer. Watching a host of read-outs, he brought the *Paracelsus* closer, ever closer.

When it hit the ground, the shock knocked him unconscious for a moment. It didn't kill him, though, and he quickly came back around.

The second he could think straight, he smacked the button on the console in front of him, tripping the sequence he'd set up.

Watching the screens, he saw a small army of black digger drones crawl out of the bay on the rear of the boxy *Paracelsus*. The ship was buried almost halfway under the asteroid's dusty gray soil, so the drones didn't have far to go to hit the ground.

Following their programmed instructions, they gathered on the exact spot where the crust was thinnest and went to work scooping out the soil of the regolith.

Pope smiled as he watched the swarm of drones excavate the site. Squat and eight-legged, they reminded him of spiders...or the starantulas of his mold-induced daydreams.

"What was that impact?" asked Baker over the radio.

"I set down the *Paracelsus*," said Pope. "Used the ship's mass to break up the surface dirt and crust."

"But the ship wasn't *made* for that," snapped Baker. "You probably *broke* her."

"Just keep digging," said Pope. "We'll worry about the rest later."

As he said it, alert lights flashed all over the console, and a siren whooped in the cockpit. Quickly, he muted the radio mic and scanned readouts all over the board.

He soon saw what the alarm was about. An engine housing had fractured in the landing. As Baker had feared, the *Paracelsus* was severely damaged.

Pope winced. Even if he freed the team from the cave-in site, he might not have a way of getting them off the rock.

"Pope!" shouted Baker. "Don't you dare go dark on me again!"

"Silly Grumptor." Pope smirked as another hallucination washed over him. "Even *your* grouchiness can't wreck the joy of eight essential vitamins and minerals!"

Quip snapped back to reality—*his* reality—just as the starantulas were devouring the stream of Quantum cereal on its way to the good ship *Quaving*.

His three fellow spacemen were zipping around the swarm, blasting away with their vitaminergy rays to little effect. The black spidery creatures just chortled and kept gobbling up the golden star-shaped pieces of cereal ore that flew into their fanged maws.

Quizzie was in on the action, too, firing extra-strength vitaminergy beams from the *Quaving*'s big cannons. But in spite of their far greater power, even those beams couldn't make a dent in the ravenous starantulas.

Quip knew he had to do something fast, but what? If the vitaminergy rays couldn't stop the starantula horde, what else could possibly make a difference? What other weapons did they have left?

The *Quaving* unleashed another bolt of vitaminergy that sizzled past Quip and crashed into the starantulas. They laughed it off and kept eating—but when Quip looked back at the source of the beam, he got an idea.

It came straight from his memory of one of the daydreams he sometimes had. He didn't always remember those visions, or the strange life he dreamed of leading in a darker, nastier universe, but he did this time.

And he hoped, to the bottom of the bowl, that it would be enough to save the day.

Sticking two fingers in his mouth, he let out a loud whistle, and his bowl-craft came running. Even as he hopped inside and bashed the controls, he was shouting for attention over the whine of the vitaminergy rays.

"Quazi! Follow my lead!"

Quazi stopped shooting and swooped over in his own bowl-craft. His eyes were spinning in opposite directions in their bulging white sockets. "*Lead?* You mean you wanna *dance?*"

Quip shook his head. "Do what *I* do, noble pinwheeled knight-buddy!"

With that, Quip zipped off toward the starantulas. When he got close, he pirouetted up out of the bowl-craft and turned it on its side so the open mouth faced the space spiders.

"Get on the other side of the swarm, Quazi! Then just jump out..." Quip flashed around behind his ship and pressed his shoulder against the base of the bowl. "...and get ready to *push!*"

Quazi followed his usual loop-de-loop flight path and ended up on the far side of the gobbling swarm. He tumbled out of his bowl-craft, flipped it on its edge, and got behind it as Quip had instructed.

"Ready, Quippie ol' pal!" hollered Quazi.

"Start pushing when I count to three!" said Quip. "Go right through the swarm and keep coming toward me till I say stop!"

"Here I come!" Quazi got confused, as often happened, and started pushing without waiting for the count.

Quip sighed and followed suit, driving his bowl-craft forward.

The open mouth of the bowl gathered in the starantulas, scooping them up. The starantulas didn't stop eating Quantum cereal or even slow down, so great was their never-ending hunger.

As more of the spidery creatures collected in the bowl, it got harder to push, but Quip kept going. Straining against the weight, he forced the bowl further, gathering in more and more of the terrible black creatures.

Then, finally, his bowl-craft ran into an obstacle with a *clank* and stopped. Without looking, he knew it had to be Quazi's bowl, meeting his rim to rim.

"Quax! Queg!" shouted Quip. "Seal our bowls together! Do it now!"

The two Breakfastronauts jetted over and let loose with fiery blasts from their pistols, welding together the rims of the two bowl-craft. When they were done, Quip finally let up the pressure and backed away to observe his handiwork.

He grinned when he saw the two bowls were fused into a big metal sphere with all the starantulas locked inside. How long they'd stay there was anyone's guess; the metal was bulging and distending all around as the captives struggled to get out.

Quip spun and called out to the pilot of the *Quaving*. "Quizzie! See that black hole over there?" He pointed at a starless disk of spinning darkness in the distance. "That's your goal, sweet spacegirl! And *this* is your ball!" He swooped down to pat the silver sphere, then darted away.

"You got it, cereal star!" As the echo of Quizzie's voice faded, the *Quaving* lurched toward the sphere. The side panel of the boxy ship swung open, and a giant brown boot swung out, giving the sphere a powerful kick.

The sphere flew past the brightly-colored planets, moons, and suns, winging its way on a beeline for its target. When it got close, the black hole sprouted a pair of huge eyes and a big, fanged mouth with a floppy red tongue. It gulped down the sphere and belched with satisfaction.

Everyone cheered at once, zipping around in wild whirls and spirals.

"We did it!" shouted Quip. "The Quantum cereal breakfasteroid is saved!"

He didn't get to celebrate for long, though, as he suddenly returned to the darker 'verse and again became the man who was split in two.

Pope was shaking off his daze when the *Paracelsus* suddenly slumped, setting off another alarm in the cockpit.

Emerging from his cereal-verse fantasy, he saw that his plan was succeeding. The ship's heavy landing had weakened the ground, and the drone diggers were chipping away at the thin spot from above and below.

Very soon, the chamber where Baker and her crew were trapped would break open. They could get out before the cave-in got any worse.

If only the damn ship were still spaceworthy, they just might be able to get off that moldy rock.

But Pope was at a loss as to how to make that happen. The ship was running every autorepair routine available, yet it couldn't completely fix the broken engine on its own. Without that repair, the *Paracelsus* was well and truly stuck.

"Pope?" Baker's voice over the radio sounded hopeful for the first time in a while. "According to our sensors, we'll break through in a matter of minutes."

Pope flicked on the mic. "That jives with my readings, as well."

"You better get ready for us, then," said Baker. "We've got some hungry, exhausted people down here, dying to get back aboard the ship."

"Hungry for a nutritious breakfast!" Pope blurted out the words as if he were Quip in the Yummiverse. "Quantum cereal will give them what they need!"

He instantly regretted saying it.

"Oh my God!" said Baker. "You've *lost* it! You think you *are* that cereal mascot, don't you?"

"No! I...I..."

Suddenly, a powerful blast rocked the ship. Pope's eyes flew to the monitor screens, searching for the cause—and then he froze, gaping in amazement.

A great gray monstrosity crashed up through the weakened crust, rising from the underground chamber. The thing's body was studded with the bodies of Baker and her crew, embedded in its rippling mass.

Most shocking of all, the beast reminded him of another monster he'd seen recently, a creature he'd battled in his Yummiverse adventures.

"It's impossible!" he said. "That thing can't exist in *this* 'verse!"

But there it was, boiling up from the asteroid, huge mouth spilled open in a silent roar of rage.

Grumptor.

The massive beast towered over the *Paracelsus*, its vast form pulsing with fury. Each time it moved, the spacesuited miners bound up in its mass flowed like driftwood on a cresting wave or river rapids, bobbing and bumping along in the foamy swirls.

Pope squinted hard and shook his head, hoping to disperse the monstrous sight—but it wouldn't go away. However Grumptor had managed to cross over from the Yummiverse in Pope's imagination, the beast wasn't ending its rampage any time soon.

"Pope, help!"

Any doubts he might have had about the reality of the great beast were swept away by Baker's voice over the radio.

"We've all been *absorbed* by this thing!" she said. "You've got to break us *free!*"

Just then, Grumptor booted the *Paracelsus* out of the dirt and across the asteroid. The ship skimmed over the surface like a stone on a pond, finally coming to rest in a nearby crater.

Amazingly, Pope was no worse off than before; the straps had kept the two halves of his body aligned in the pilot's chair. The *Paracelsus*, on the other hand, wasn't in great shape. The ship had lost power when it hit, leaving Pope bathed in the dim red glow of emergency lights.

With the ship more damaged than before, Pope's situation, and that of the captive miners, was grim. Closing his eyes, he gave in to the panic flowing through him, hoping it would kick him back into the refuge of his fantasy life as Quip.

Unlike so many times before, the change didn't come. Instead of bright primary colors, improbable flying spacemen, and a cosmos filled with air and noise, he was still trapped in a dead ship in dark and airless space. Instead of soaring between the stars with an intact and perfect little body, he was still split in two at the midsection, unable to get up and walk.

Of all times for his life as Spaceman Quip to shut down, he couldn't think of one that could possibly be worse than this.

Refusing to give up on escaping to the Yummiverse, he closed his eyes again and again...but every time he opened them, he was back to being Pope. He shut them a final time, then, just to block out reality as best he could.

But Baker's screams and the shaking of the asteroid's surface wouldn't let him stay that way. Opening his eyes, he accepted his reality and set to work on the control board, doing everything he could to restore power—though he didn't know what he could do after that to save his crew from the Grumptor. Unlike the good ship *Quaving*, the *Paracelsus* wasn't equipped with vitaminergy beams to blast a beast. Unlike Quip, Pope had no spacemen pals to fly to his rescue or Quantum cereal to energize him for a fight.

He was going to have to battle a fantastic threat from another reality with resources from one where the laws of physics were far more rigid and limiting.

"Please help us!" howled Baker over the radio. "Do something!"

The power came back on, and Pope checked the Grumptor's status on the monitors. The beast was stomping across the asteroid's surface, shaking its fists at the sky. One of the crewmen shook loose from its arm and plunged to the ground, landing in a motionless heap.

The beast shook loose another man and roared. Pope felt waves of guilt over the deaths, since the creature had somehow material-ized from his own imagination.

But what if it *hadn't?*

Since the creature resembled the Grumptor, Pope had assumed it had come from his fantasies. But maybe the reason that had seemed so impossible was because it *was.*

Zooming in the cameras, he saw the beast's mass wasn't cloud-like at all—it was *fuzzy.* It seemed to consist of a soupy gray material instead of a billowy cloud bank in the shape of a two-armed, two-legged giant.

That gray material was something he knew well. It was the same thing the crew had been mining in the heart of Q-1X, the same thing that had fueled Pope's visions of the Yummiverse.

The alien mold. Somehow, it had taken this monstrous shape that resembled that of the Grumptor. Maybe Pope had ingested so much of the stuff that it had become attuned to his mind and used the imagined Grumptor as a template.

Whatever its motivation, at least he thought he knew what it was now. Instead of some impossible, unbeatable creature that had emerged from his daydreams, it was grounded in the one true reality.

Where, maybe, even a man cut in half had a chance of defeating it.

The *Paracelsus* rose from the crater on thruster power and moved toward the giant mold-beast. The creature wasn't aware of the ship at the moment, but it would be soon enough.

Though one engine housing was still trashed, the thrusters were in working order and could do the trick for now. There would be time enough later for major repairs if the ship and remaining crew were still in one piece...though Pope knew he wouldn't be among them. He had no illusions about that, anyway.

Shaking off a chill, he steered the ship in the mold-beast's direction, preparing to execute his plan. He'd figured it out fast, as if he'd been energized like Quip after wolfing down a bowl of Quantum cereal. Now he just had to hope and pray it worked.

As the *Paracelsus* got closer, he deployed the ship's disposal line—a huge hose used to eject liquid by-products during onboard ore processing. Nosing the *Paracelsus* past the Grumptor, he held position and took careful aim, making sure what he was about to spray would hit its target.

Then, he stabbed a button on the board, and the contents of the ship's cargo hold pumped out in a massive white stream.

It was the only thing more plentiful than mold on Q-1X, and Pope had finally figured out why. He'd used harvester chutes to suck up tons of the stuff into the holding tanks used for liquid storage, then mixed it with water and quickly set out to apply the solution to the creature.

The substance must have been deposited on Q-1X to keep the mold in check, or the mold had been left on that rock *because* the stuff was abundant there. The asteroid had served as a prison for the fungal lifeform held within, and only the substance with its special chemical properties could subdue it.

Just as it now made the mold-beast roar and shrivel as it coated its fuzzy gray mass. Because *chlorine*—otherwise known as *bleach*—was one thing a mold-beast could not survive.

Like a plume of milk, the white liquid continued to blast the creature, breaking it down. The crewmen trapped in its moldy mass popped free of its weakening grip and slid safely to the ground.

Enraged, the mold-beast lashed out in its death throes, catching Pope off guard. Its first swing connected hard, bashing the *Paracelsus* away like a toy.

As the ship tumbled through the sky over Q-1X, leaving a milky trail that arced and looped behind it, Pope fought for control. He wrenched the stick and punched buttons on the board, but the ship was too slow to respond. It clipped the surface of the asteroid and skidded to a jarring stop against an upraised hump of rock.

The impact stunned Pope, knocking him half-unconscious. When he forced himself awake and opened his eyes, he realized things had changed in a big way. In a big, *bad* way.

He was no longer strapped into the pilot's chair, able to access the ship's controls from a seated position. The harness, which he'd loosened to reach the holding tank controls in the rear of the cockpit, had sprung open.

Now, he found himself—the top half of himself—staring up from the floor, unable to reach a single button or switch.

The bottom half of his body was still in the chair, topped off by the slab of bulkhead that had cut him in half and lodged in the padding. Other parts of him were drifting from the base of his trunk in the low gravity; the temporary seal between his severed containment suit and the bulkhead slab had broken in the crash, and his innards were spilling out into the cockpit.

He felt himself growing colder as the blood and organs leaked out of him and his heart slowed. The end was near, and there was no way around it.

Pope smiled. At least he'd lasted long enough to save the others, or most of them. With any luck, they might be able to repair the ship and get off that rock before their fuel and supplies ran out. Maybe they'd even be rescued by another crew; after all, he'd had the foresight to activate the distress beacon before making his final run at the mold-beast.

As for Pope himself, he drifted ever nearer to final unconsciousness and eternal darkness. His eyes fluttered shut, then open, then shut.

When they opened again, he saw four familiar pink faces grinning at him, pinwheels turning on top of their heads.

"Wakey wakey, Quip!" Quazi's eyes crossed, uncrossed, and squirmed around in their sockets. "You know what time it is, don't you?"

"Time to bring a delicious balanced breakfast to the children of the Yummiverse!" Quax's swarm of freckles swam and swirled as he bobbled his head with delight.

591

"Are you ready to get back to work?" Queg's bushy red mustache flicked and riffled as he spoke.

"What do you say, pal?" Quizzie, her glossy blonde shoulder-length hair in a bouncy flip, extended a soft pink hand.

When Pope reached out to take it, he saw his own hand had become like hers. Gazing at his reflection in the cockpit window, he saw he'd become a little spaceman again, his features wide-eyed and cartoony, his uniform cherry red with the letter "Q" in green on the chest.

He hesitated, but not for long. The wonder of the moment filled him, and the possibilities made his heart pound so hard that the shape of it pulsed out of his chest.

Squeezing Quizzie's hand in his own, he beamed at his friends as he floated up from the floor. "You want to know what I say?" His voice rose triumphantly. "*I* say there's nothing like the *vitaminergy* power of Quantum cereal to start the day off *right!*"

Reaching into a pouch on his belt as his friends cheered, he drew out a handful of Quantum cereal. The star-shaped pieces glittered like gold in his palm.

"The kids of the Yummiverse need a high-energy breakfast, and we're gonna give it to 'em!" He gobbled up the handful of sweet cereal, and his body flared with power. The pinwheel on top of his head whizzed so fast, it blurred. "Or my name isn't *Quip*, the *Breakfastronaut!*"

Then, with a joyous whoop, he launched himself into space, whirling like the spinner on a board game or the days of a man's childhood, gone forever.

REVIEWS OF MUSEUM-GOERS BY FAMOUS WORKS OF ART THROUGH THE YEARS

From a 1913 review by *Whistler's Mother:*
Never have I seen such a *hideous* face, complete with bushy brown muttonchop sideburns, a pretentious monocle, a hooked nose, and eyes as dead as pebbles scooped from a riverbed. He never stopped blabbing, trying desperately to impress the young woman at his side, who in turn never shut her own yap. The two carried on a droning "conversation" about the folds of my dress, the pattern on the curtain by my chair, and most of all, *who* was going to do *what* to whom that evening back in their hotel room, far from their respective (and *most* unfortunate) spouses. I give these two buffoons the *lowest rating possible* for their utter gracelessness and the exceedingly bad name they give to *all* works of humanity who pass before the frames of paintings like myself. *Wretched things!*

From a 1948 review by the man and woman in *American Gothic:*
Mother: One particular family spoke volumes to Father and I regarding the human condition. A musclebound young man with mustard or somesuch dappling his navy blue clip-on tie regaled his multiple offspring—all younger than seven, I'm sure—with made-up

stories about us and the house in the painting, spreading *misinforma-tion* to a new generation of poorly-behaved miscreants.

Father: It was quite clear to us that this family was symbolic of human ignorance and the failure to appreciate beauty. So too did I feel there was an undertone of deep sadness to the pieces we observed, a sense of the loss of magic and the descent of the natural world into one of mathematical absolutes free of creative expression or empathy.

Mother: Nevertheless, you must admit there was a certain ironic soulfulness in the arrangement of food and excrement stains on the children's clothes, alluding to the mark of Cain and its extension to all of Fallen Humanity.

Father: I give it five pumps of my pitchfork.

From a 1969 review by the apple-faced guy in *The Son of Man*:

As with all works of humanity, this particular person—a male figure, unless I miss my guess—was only visible in detail from the scalp up and the chin down. Once again, I cannot in good conscience commend whatever bizarre artistic or biological compul-sion has established the *most peculiar fashion* of wearing a *green apple* in front of one's face! Discussing the merits of one's beard (quite shaggy, lice-ridden), clothing (a fringed buckskin jacket over a tattered blouse) and general demeanor (fidgety as a moth 'round a flame) is one thing, but how can this reviewer gaze into the *abyss* of that human's *soul* through an opaque piece of fruit? If there is a message of some kind layered into this piece, I fail to see it (as usual).

From a 1991 review by the screaming person in *The Scream:*

Yes, another uninspired, pedestrian, and derivative human being has gotten the usual reaction from me! Will a person *ever* cross my path who will elicit any reaction from me *other* than a head-clutching *shriek?* WHAT DO *YOU* THINK?

From a 2018 review by *The Girl with a Pearl Earring:*

Sometimes, I wish I could frown or stick out my tongue or at least turn my head and look away from the offensive people-pieces parading in front of me daily. But *then,* something like *this* one comes along and blows me away!

This particular old woman in a black fur coat and enormous, red-framed glasses couldn't put down her phone the whole time she was there in front of me. Not to mention, she put her grandkids on *speaker* with the volume up so everyone could hear their babbling and bickering all through the gallery! On top of all *that,* Granny kept referring to *me* as an ugly boy with hair extensions and a shiny neck goiter!

You just *have* to admire the chutzpah that went into designing and executing such a performance piece! The in-your-face grotes-querie and utter lack of sentimentality came across to me as emblematic of the struggle of suppressed artworks for accurate interpretation throughout history. *Sheer genius, through and through!*

From a 2022 review by *Mona Lisa:*

They all suck. Every last one of them who has ever trod before me for no reason other than *to say they did.* Every artless figure falling over each other before me, bashing each other with their elbows, cameras, and phones as if in a mad crush to curry my favor. And yet, it amuses me to note their inferiority and inability to grasp the true secret behind my so-called famous smile: I do it because *they all suck...you all suck...*and *I* do not.

Zero stars.

TIME, EXPRESSED AS AN ENTRÉE

The rainbow leviathan opened all his trillion trillion mouths at once and gobbled up the next-to-the-last day of the timeline.

Centillions of life-forms screamed at once, but that was background static to the leviathan. All the time in all the universe rushed into its trillion trillion mouths with staggering force, but that was filet mignon with a side of lobster tail to the creature.

Not that filet mignon or lobster existed in this universe-which-was-not-our-own. Not that there was anything precisely like either delicacy in the milky-orange reaches of this alien space, with its red-and-white-striped sun-swarms and its planets like tangled neon tubes in constantly shifting configurations.

The last precious seconds of the next-to-the-last day gushed into the trillion trillion mouths. The "sound" it all made as it died--the simultaneous screaming of a multitude of life-forms across all frequencies, followed by the flushing of an entire universe down the gullet of the leviathan--was what the creature had taken as his name: EeePavoosh.

If the EeePavoosh--a matrix of sentient energy, subatomic strings, and gray matter--had actually had lips, he would have smacked them in satisfaction at the last bites of his food. As it was, he settled for thrashing his light-years-long shimmering rainbow tail through the infinite black void that was left in the wake of the devoured day.

Then, he turned his pale, rippling face toward his next meal. He sensed it beyond the shuddering veil of the void, glowing like a single flickering flame in a pitch black abyss. One last taste of the timeline awaited--one last day, glittering like a perfect jewel.

The EeePavoosh had eaten all the rest, swooping like a shark through what had once been an octodecillion-year timeline, biting off every other day, year, century, and millennium. Now, he was down to one. One more feast of a day, and this timeline would be extinct.

Then what? Then nothing, perhaps. The EeePavoosh had no idea where he would go next. He had gobbled up every other adjacent timeline and could sense no others beyond this one.

Not that he was worried about that. He had been born to eat and move on, to never stop moving. He possessed a simple faith that he would somehow find more food and survive.

And so, with one last triumphant roar in the emptiness, the EeePavoosh plunged into the pristine bubble of the last remaining day.

On the other side of the veil, it was like nothing had happened to the rest of time. Space spread out in all directions, swirling with sun swarms circling planetary bodies.

The EeePavoosh's multi-frequency, infinite-range senses captured every detail of his food, judging the meal's suitability...and any irregularities that could interfere with consumption and digestion. He didn't expect to find any; he hadn't, in any of the other days he had devoured.

And yet, he found one here. He found an anomaly, something that didn't belong in what was left of this timeline and universe.

Like a bird in flight spotting one tiny worm in the earth far below, the EeePavoosh zeroed in on the anomaly and dove toward it. Rainbow tail lashing, he rode gravity waves and solar winds, crossing the sprawling universe in one tiny fraction of the one last day in which it existed.

Arriving at his destination, the EeePavoosh coasted to a stop, gazing at a planetary body of purple and yellow neon tubes. The anomaly occupied one tiny spot on the surface.

Extruding a sliver of his gargantuan body, the EeePavoosh created an avatar small enough to interact with the anomaly. Rainbow colors flickered to life along the avatar's ten-meters-long tail, and dozens of mouths flexed open and closed along its flanks.

Satisfied, the EeePavoosh rode his avatar down to the planet's surface. Emerging from a layer of pale violet clouds, he gazed down with the single multifaceted red eye that occupied most of his face and saw what he had come for. Hundreds of feet below, sitting on green-and-purple-striped stones on the bank of a bright yellow river, was the anomaly.

Specifically, it was a life-form with four appendages, one head, and pink skin. Its head was topped with a soft mane that flowed midway down its back--mostly gray, streaked with dark brown.

The EeePavoosh came to rest near the anomaly, hovering two meters above the ground. For a long moment, the anomaly just stared silently at him with its pair of dull green eyes and its single mouth open wide.

Finally, the anomaly spoke. "Thank God I'm drunk, or this might scare the livin' crap outta me." Its mouth curled up at both corners, revealing a sparse arrangement of broken teeth. "Well, don't just hang there, buddy. Introduce yourself."

The EeePavoosh rotated slowly, considering. The sounds the anomaly made seemed familiar. He had a feeling he had heard them before in some timeline he had devoured...but he couldn't remember where or when.

The anomaly raised one of its upper appendages and shook it back and forth. "I'm Matilda Scanlon. My friends call me Tillie." Tillie leaned forward and narrowed her eyes. "Are *you* a friend?"

The EeePavoosh thought some more, then understood. A run of connections sparked in his gargantuan memory archives, linking similar sounds, facial expressions, and gestures from various extinct species whose timelines he had eaten. None were exactly the same, but they shared enough traits that the EeePavoosh could use them to cobble together a rough translation.

More than that, the EeePavoosh could algorithmically process the commonalities into a set of responses. "Yes." He spoke from his dozens of mouths with dozens of voices, each a different pitch, timbre, and volume. "I am a friend."

Tillie let loose with a flurry of high-pitched stuttering sounds. Comparing them to similar sounds in his archives, the EeePavoosh identified them as laughter (though he didn't use that word).

"Well, it's about time you showed up, friend," said Tillie. "I was startin' to think I was alone here."

"You are not alone." The EeePavoosh's grasp of the anomaly's language was quickly improving. The more he heard of it, the better he understood.

He was also gathering other data on the anomaly. Biologically, it was similar to evolved primates from other timelines. The arrangement of its appendages was even the same as that of certain primates--two arms and two legs, ending in hands and feet which in turn ended in multiple digits. Further, the creature possessed physical traits associated in some primate species with the female gender. So Tillie, as it called itself, was a *she*.

"Let's drink to new friends." Tillie's mouth curled up at the corners again. Reaching into the folds of the loose black garment she wore, she drew out a glass container in a paper wrapper--a bottle in a bag. Unscrewing the cap, she lifted the bottle to her lips and tilted it high. A trickle of liquid flowed down into her mouth, and she swallowed it.

The EeePavoosh identified the liquid as an extract of fermented biological material. Monitoring its passage through her system, he saw it was having an effect on her body chemistry, altering the functions of certain organs. It was a phenomenon he'd observed before: intoxication, an impairment of mental and physical functions which certain species seemed to find pleasurable.

"Nice." Tillie wiped her mouth on the back of one of her hands. "I'd offer ya' some, but there's only a swig or two left. I'm thinkin' I'd better nurse it, know what I mean?" She screwed the cap back on the bottle and stuffed it in the pocket of her garment. "Unless you know where there's a package store around this joint."

"Package store?" said the EeePavoosh. "Joint?"

"If you got one of *those*, that'd be even better." Tillie's laughter started loud, then trailed off. "But y'know what, buddy? I might settle for you tellin' me where the hell I am right now." Tillie spread her arms wide, taking in her surroundings. "What is this freakin' place, anyway?"

"When," said the EeePavoosh. "The question you should ask is *when*."

"Okay then," said Tillie. "When am I right now?"

"The end of time," said the EeePavoosh.

"Huh?" Tillie scrunched her eyes and nose in what looked to the EeePavoosh like an expression of displeasure. "Are you trying to tell me I'm at the end of freakin' time?"

"The end of *this* time," said the EeePavoosh. "The last day of this existence."

"No kiddin.'" Tillie shook her head. "And to think I was just in Pittsburgh an hour ago."

"Pittsburgh?" The EeePavoosh flicked his tail. "Is that a location?"

"Yeah," said Tillie. "It's on the other side of that damn thing." She pointed a finger at what looked at first like empty space. But as the EeePavoosh stared, the space rippled, revealing the outline of a transparent oval disk floating a meter above the purple ground.

Curious, the EeePavoosh trained all his senses on the disk. "The other side?"

"That's right, buddy." Tillie got up from her purple-and-green-striped rock and walked over to the disk. "I walked through it in Pittsburgh and ended up here. Some kind'a doorway, I'm guessin'." Reaching out, she pushed her arm into the oval...and it went straight through as if the oval weren't there. "A *sucky* doorway. I can't seem to go back through it."

"And you *want* to go back through?" asked the EeePavoosh.

"It's funny," said Tillie. "All my life, I wanted to get away from it all. I was just wishin' that very thing when the doorway opened up, in fact. I was homeless and sick and lonely, and I just wanted to get away. But now that I have..." She looked around at the purple and yellow landscape. "...I just want to go home again."

The EeePavoosh glided closer to the disk, picking up the faintest trace of time energy from it...just a whisper. "If it is a doorway, a portal, it is closed."

"Apparently." Tillie laughed. "Just my luck."

"Luck." The EeePavoosh drifted closer, sniffing at the time-trace. Was it a sign of a tiny temporal pocket, a bubble that would barely make a light snack for him...or something bigger?

Tillie hiked a thumb at the disk. "Don't suppose you know how to open it?"

"No." The EeePavoosh kept probing, straining to amplify the trace. "Not yet."

"Not yet?" Tillie tipped her head to one side. "So do you think you could open it eventually?"

The EeePavoosh circled around the portal, sniffing at the whispery signal it was giving off. "Not yet. But yes. I think I could."

Tillie's face brightened. "When? When could you do it?"

"Soon, I think." The EeePavoosh stopped circling and glided through the oval outline of the portal. "It requires more study, but it could be done."

"Ain't that fine and dandy!" Tillie clapped her hands. "You're going to help me? Help me get home?"

"I will open the portal," said the EeePavoosh. "I will access the other side." Even as he spoke to her, the EeePavoosh was busy measuring every characteristic of the portal. Though he had devoured an entire timeline except for one day, he was already hungry for what lay beyond the doorway.

Tillie moved a hand toward him, then caught herself and pulled it away. "Well, thank you, buddy. I'm really itchin' to go back. I was just thinkin' about it when you showed up, in fact. Prayin' about it, for what it's worth." Looking down, she kicked a purple pebble with the toe of her shoe. "Maybe I shouldn't care. I mean, I've never amounted to much. I'm sure nobody even knows I'm gone. But home is home, right?"

The EeePavoosh kept working. "Home is home," he said.

"Maybe I had to lose it to appreciate it," said Tillie. "Or maybe the Lord had a plan in store for me."

"A plan?" said the EeePavoosh.

"For my life to mean somethin'," said Tillie. "I always wanted it to, but it never did. I'm just a homeless alcoholic who can't even help herself. But maybe, comin' here like this..." She kicked another pebble. "Maybe there's still somethin' I'm supposed to do. Whatta you think?"

The EeePavoosh didn't answer.

Tillie watched him for a moment. "You're not an *angel* by any chance, are you?"

"No." The EeePavoosh wasn't sure what an angel was, but nothing in his archives made him think the term had anything to do with him.

"Well, thanks anyway for helpin' with the doorway," said Tillie. "It's been a long time since anyone's done somethin' this nice for me. A *long* time."

"A long time?" said the EeePavoosh. "How long?"

"Years and years." Tillie shook her head. "Decades, even."

"Years? Decades?" Aligning the context with similar semantic constructs from the languages in his vast memory archives, the EeePavoosh became intrigued. The way the female talked about units of time distracted him from his work.

"It's the story of my life," said Tillie. "Sixty years of bullshit, and it feels like an eternity."

"Eternity?" The thought of it distracted the EeePavoosh further. "How do sixty years feel like eternity?"

"Livin' the kind of life I've been livin'." Tillie squinted up at the lavender clouds squirming in the hot pink sky. "Days have a way of feelin' like decades."

The EeePavoosh was having trouble paying attention to his work. "All time is like this on the other side? Days feel like decades? Years feel like eternity?"

"For me, they do." Tillie scrubbed her hands through her stringy brown-and-gray mane. "Some more than others, I guess."

The phenomenon she was describing excited the EeePavoosh. Was it possible, on the other side of the portal, that time was somehow amplified? That it could be extended beyond its usual properties?

The internal structure of the EeePavoosh's avatar shivered with anticipation, and the structure of the parent leviathan in orbit around the planet did the same. "I want to know more."

"I can tell." Tillie smiled. "You're really interested in this stuff, aren't ya'?"

"I am," said the EeePavoosh.

Tillie narrowed her eyes. "Makes you wanna open that doorway faster, doesn't it? To see what's on the other side."

"It does." Even as he said it, the EeePavoosh redoubled his efforts to analyze the portal. "Now tell me more about the longer times on the other side."

Tillie nodded. "Why not, if it gets me home faster?" Pulling out the bottle in the bag, she opened and tipped it to her lips...tipped it high, almost straight up. The EeePavoosh heard a tiny trickle run into her mouth, then nothing. "Damn." Tillie lowered the bottle. "Don't suppose you could whip me up a little joy juice, couldja, buddy?"

"No joy juice," said the EeePavoosh. "Now tell me about the longer times on the other side."

Tillie pitched the bottle, and it shattered against a nearby boulder. "Where to begin?"

The EeePavoosh thought she was asking him a question. "Begin by telling me what makes time longer on the other side."

"Suffering," said Tillie. "That's what makes it longer. Like, for example, the five years I spent married to Ray Coleman. They felt more like *fifty* years than five."

"Married?" said the EeePavoosh.

"When a man and a woman get together," said Tillie, "and make each other miserable for the rest of their lives."

"How does this make time longer?" asked the EeePavoosh.

"Well, it's like this," said Tillie. "When I was a little girl, I used to dream about fallin' in love and gettin' married. I spent hours and hours imaginin' what it would be like.

"I wanted a big, strong man to save me...to take me away from home, so my daddy couldn't get me anymore. And the funny thing is, I got one. A big, strong man." Tillie shook her head. "And he proceeded to kick my ass six ways from Sunday. I went from *one* man abusin' me to *another*."

"This kicking your ass," said the EeePavoosh. "It made the time longer?"

"Longer than you can imagine," said Tillie. "Every day felt like a year. The pain...the helplessness." She sniffed and dabbed at the corners of her eyes. "But the worst part, the longest, was the *waiting*. Waiting for my husband to come home. Then, when he got there, tiptoeing around him, waiting for him to go off. Because I knew it was only a matter of time until he hit me again."

"A matter of time," said the EeePavoosh.

"I remember." As Tillie stared off into space, drops of clear fluid ran out of her eyes and down her cheeks. "He beat me for bein' too pretty, 'cause other men were lookin' at me. He beat me so much, I wasn't pretty anymore." Reaching up, she lightly touched her face with her fingertips. "Then, he beat me for bein' too *ugly*.

"He beat me for gettin' pregnant, too...and then he beat me for losin' the baby." She wiped the fluid from her cheeks and rubbed her eyes hard. "As if I *wanted* to lose the only thing that had ever made me happy."

"And this made the time longer?" said the EeePavoosh.

"God, yes," said Tillie. "Each minute that he beat me lasted a century."

"Each minute lasted a century?" The EeePavoosh couldn't keep the excitement out of his voice.

Tillie nodded. "When it was over, and the bruises set in, the minutes lasted even longer. I'd be doin' the dishes or laundry, and my whole body would ache and sting from what he did, and the minutes would just crawl. I just wanted it all to be over...but the more I wanted that, the slower it went."

The EeePavoosh worked faster. If what Tillie was telling him was true, he couldn't wait to get to the other side of the portal.

"I know what you're thinkin'," said Tillie as she wiped away more fluid from her cheeks. "Why the hell did I stay with him for five years, right?"

The answer seemed perfectly clear to the EeePavoosh. "To continue to stretch out time. And consume it."

"Consume?" Tillie gave him a strange look. "What do you mean, 'consume' time?"

"Ingest it for sustenance," said the EeePavoosh. "Eat it."

The look on Tillie's face deepened. "Why do you say that?" She eased around to the other side of the portal and stared at him through the rippling oval.

"It is how I live," said the EeePavoosh. "I consume time."

"You actually eat it?" asked Tillie. "Hours, minutes, days, whatever?"

"As you understand time, that is correct," said the EeePavoosh.

"Ain't that somethin'?" Tillie gazed at him thoughtfully, pinching her lower lip between her thumb and forefinger. "So, uh...what happens if you open that doorway?"

"When, not if," said the EeePavoosh. "I have completed my analysis. I know how to open it now."

"That's wonderful. I can't wait to get home." Tillie kept staring and pinching her lower lip. "But what about you? What'll you do when the doorway opens?"

"Go through, of course." The EeePavoosh decoded an especially complex network of quantum filaments in the heart of the portal, beginning the process of unlocking it. "I will open the portal soon and go through."

"Then what?" asked Tillie. "Will you start eatin' up the time over there?"

"Yes," said the EeePavoosh. "But if short amounts of time can be stretched into long ones on the other side, my eating will not disrupt the timeline significantly. Minutes can last centuries, correct?"

Tillie pinched her lip harder. "That's true, but..."

"Then there will be plenty of time," said the EeePavoosh. "Now tell me more about how that works, how time stretches on the other side."

"All right then." Tillie frowned thoughtfully. "Let's see." She closed her eyes, then opened them again. "I toldja about the longest five years of my life. How 'bout the longest *month* of my life? How's that grab ya'?"

"Fine and dandy," said the EeePavoosh.

"So okay." Tillie cleared her throat. "So I finally decided to run away from Ray. I finally got up the gumption to get away from him. Basically took the clothes on my back and a little cash I'd been socking away and headed out on foot one night. Headed straight for the bus station." She smiled. "Let me tell you, it was the greatest feeling since I'd gotten away from my childhood home. The air was so sweet and cool. I was free, totally *free*." She slumped and shook her head. "At least till the drunk driving the pickup slammed into me."

"Drunk?" said the EeePavoosh as he unlocked another series of quantum filaments.

Tillie didn't bother explaining. "He did a hit-and-run and just left me there. It took hours for someone to find me. And then I ended up in the hospital for a month with guess who watchin' over me? *Ray*, that asshole."

"Asshole?" said the EeePavoosh.

"Yep." Tillie nodded grimly. "So there I am, layin' in that hospital bed with just about every bone in my body broken...and they're pumpin' me full of drugs, but there's still so much pain...and there's Ray, tellin' me what he's gonna do to me when I get healed and go home. How he's gonna make me suffer and pay for runnin' out on him."

"And this made the time longer?" said the EeePavoosh.

"Oh, yeah," said Tillie. "That month in the hospital was a year to me. *Ten* years."

"A month became ten years?"

"All I could do was lay there and pray I'd die before they sent me home." Tillie turned away from the portal and stared off into space. "The hours crawled...with the pain and Ray's awful voice and the casts and slings keepin' me trapped there. Every minute lasted forever."

The EeePavoosh felt a rush of excitement. "Every minute lasted *forever*?"

"Then, just before I was supposed to go home, a miracle

happened. The nurse came and told me some joker'd killed Ray in a bar fight. I was *free* again." She turned back and smiled. "And that was when time started speeding up."

"Speeding up?" said the EeePavoosh.

"Didn't I mention that?" said Tillie. "Time speeds up sometimes on the other side."

The EeePavoosh suddenly became alarmed. "It does?"

Tillie narrowed her eyes and fixed her gaze on him. "You don't like that, do you? Is it because the time wouldn't be as good to eat?"

"Faster time is shorter time," said the EeePavoosh. "There is less of it to eat."

"You don't say." Tillie nodded thoughtfully. "Well, it happens a lot over there. And here's the thing." She pinched her lower lip. "It might start out longer, but then it gets shorter all of a sudden. You just never know."

"It starts out longer?" said the EeePavoosh. "Then gets shorter?"

"That's right," said Tillie. "Like, for example..." She stared up at the sky, thinking, then looked back down at him. "When I found out earlier this year that I was terminal. I was drinkin' heavy and livin' on the street...and I started coughin' up blood. When I went to the free clinic, the doctor told me I had lung cancer, and it was gonna kill me in six months." Tillie sighed. "The hour I spent in the room with that doctor, when he told me all that, was probably the longest hour of my life."

"The longest hour?" Again, the EeePavoosh grew excited. In a flurry of subatomic space-time reengineering, he unlocked the biggest sequence of filaments yet.

Tillie shook her head slowly. "Maybe I shouldn't've cared after the shitty life I had...but I did. It still ripped my heart out." Droplets of clear fluid again trickled from the corners of her eyes and down her cheeks. "It was like I was trapped again. I wanted to run away, but all I could do was sit there and listen. And there was a clock in the office, an old-fashioned clock that ticked away the seconds...and it seemed like it took an *hour* between ticks."

"A second took an hour," said the EeePavoosh.

"That's right," said Tillie. "But ever since that hour, time's been goin' a million times faster. A *zillion*." She took a deep breath and let it out slowly. "Because it's runnin' out. And the closer I get to the end, the faster it goes."

A wave of disappointment rolled through the EeePavoosh. "Instead of getting longer, time is going faster?"

"You wouldn't *believe* how much faster," said Tillie.

The EeePavoosh thought it over, processing what she'd told him. How could time go faster? It was true that travel at relativistic speeds, those approaching the speed of light, could slow the passage of time for the traveler...but making it speed up was another matter.

Based on the stories Tillie had told, the flow of time must be very different on the other side...and not always in a good way. In some situations, it stretched out; in others, it shrank. How was that even possible?

And then there was an even more important question. "How do you control it? How do you make time longer or shorter?"

"I wish I knew," said Tillie. "I'd stretch out the time I've got left and make it last forever."

The EeePavoosh reached the last few quantum filaments keeping the portal shut. He was almost done with his work. "You eat time, too, then? You consume it as I do?"

"Time eats *me*, is more like it," said Tillie. "Every day, it wears me down a little more."

"And yet, the way you talk about time, you need it to survive."

Tillie nodded. "There's never enough."

"Then we both want the same thing."

"And I can't have it!" Tillie laughed bitterly. "You know what's funny? Most of my life, time dragged because things were so shitty. I just wanted it to speed up so the shittiness would end. But ever since I found out about the cancer, I just want it to slow down. I just want more of it."

On the verge of throwing the portal wide open, the EeePavoosh paused and gazed at Tillie through the rippling oval. More droplets ran down her cheeks; those droplets, and the way the breath was catching in her throat, had more to do with sadness than any kind of joy.

It was a sadness the EeePavoosh could identify with--the sadness of hunger. The sadness that came when there wasn't enough time to feed the ferocious craving that kept him alive.

Suddenly, a strange feeling took hold of him--a feeling of alignment, of connection with a living being. How many life forms had died screaming when he'd gulped down their timelines? And yet here he was, surging with affinity for one tiny creature from an alternate reality.

Here he was, an avatar of a light-years-long leviathan accustomed to straddling universes and devouring epochs, and he actually felt sympathy for one little anomalous female primate. Because just as she was running out of time, he'd been running out of it, too...with only one day left to devour in all the known feeding grounds.

At least until she'd shown him the portal and told him about the other side where time stretched out in ways he'd never imagined. Thanks to her, he stood on the threshold even now, ready to plunge into those rich new feeding grounds and gorge himself on the time they had to offer.

"I am ready to open the portal now," he announced.

"Wait a minute." Tillie scowled and pinched her lower lip. "Didn't you hear what I said about time speeding up? What if there isn't enough for you?"

"Hopefully, the stretched-out, longer time will make up for it," said the EeePavoosh.

"What'll be left when you're done?" said Tillie.

"When all time is devoured, nothing remains," said the EeePavoosh. "But if time can be made longer on the other side, there is nothing to worry about. If a little time can become a lot, the timeline will survive."

"That's true, that's true." Tillie shuffled her feet nervously. "But, uh, what if time doesn't work exactly the way you expect over there? If it runs the same as it does here, and it can't be made longer, you'll eat up all the time a lot sooner, right? The timeline won't survive."

"Theoretically," said the EeePavoosh.

"Then why take the chance?" said Tillie.

"Because I must feed. I must have more time in order to survive."

"Okay, listen." Tillie moved to stand between him and the portal. "Please don't do this. Don't go to the other side."

"I must," said the EeePavoosh. "I am hungry."

"So go somewhere else," said Tillie. "This is my home we're talkin' about here."

"There is nowhere else to go. Nowhere that I know of."

"Please," said Tillie. "For me. Don't do it."

"I must," said the EeePavoosh.

"Wait." Tillie threw her hands out in front of her. "Remember when I talked about my life meaning something? That maybe there's somethin' I'm supposed to do? What if this is it? Why I came here. To save my *world*."

"You should not care," said the EeePavoosh. "Your life was shitty."

"Not all of it, though," said Tillie. "There were good parts, I swear."

The EeePavoosh thought for a moment, gazing into her eyes. To ensure his survival, he could not do what she asked...yet the pull of his alignment with her was strong. The sympathy he felt for her demanded he do *something*.

Something, perhaps, that would repay the debt he owed her for leading him to the new feeding grounds. Something that would give her back the time she was running out of.

"Then tell me about one of the good parts," said the EeeP-avoosh. "If you could make one time of your life longer, which would it be?"

Tillie frowned. "Will that make you not go to the other side? Will that save my world?"

The EeePavoosh thrashed his tail. "Just answer the question, Tillie."

The air shimmered in a corner of the dimly lit hospital room. A rectangular outline appeared from floor to ceiling, traced in soft silver light...and then the space within the outline flashed, and Tillie stepped through.

She blinked hard, adjusting to the low light. Then, as the portal vanished behind her, her eyes went straight to the room's one bed. She couldn't see the occupants, because they were surrounded by a huddle of women with their backs turned to her...but she knew who they were. She knew exactly who was in that bed.

Instantly, a smile spread across her face. Tears ran from her eyes, and she didn't bother to wipe them away.

"Go ahead," said a soft voice from the shadows. "Go to them."

Turning, Tillie saw that the voice belonged to herself...another version of herself. And there were more besides, many more crowding around the room as well as huddling around the bed.

"Don't be afraid." One of them moved out of the shadows and took her arm. "There's nothing to be scared of anymore."

Tillie stared in wonder at her other self, the one holding her arm. The EeePavoosh had told her it would be like this, yet it was still so very strange seeing her mirror image staring back at her.

"This is your first time through the loop, isn't it?" said the other Tillie.

"Yes." Tillie nodded.

"We're all here for you." The other Tillie smiled and squeezed Tillie's arm. "We just keep coming, but there's always room for one more."

"Thank you." Tillie felt a welling-up of warmth, a deep, abiding comfort that she'd never felt before. Other hands touched her, reaching out from other selves, and she closed her eyes.

It was then she thought of the EeePavoosh. Where was he now? Off devouring the rest of the timeline, no doubt, bringing the end of time to the universe Tillie called home. She hadn't been able to stop him, back on the purple-and-yellow planet, or even delay him much. Her stories of stretched-out time, which she'd told to entice him to open the doorway, had made him want to cross over; by the time she'd realized her mistake and switched to stories of speeded-up time, it had been too late.

But it didn't matter anymore, did it? The EeePavoosh had been grateful and set aside this one hour for her, this hour forty years in her past which had now become her present and her future as well.

It was the first thing the EeePavoosh had done after coming

through the portal. Tillie had told him about this one time in her life, this one good hour that she'd make longer if she could. Then he'd brought her back to it. He'd given it to her for helping him find the portal.

And she was going to spend the rest of her life here.

"Come on," said the other Tillie who was holding her arm. "You want to see this, don't you?"

Tillie opened her eyes. "Are you kiddin'?"

She shivered with anticipation as the other Tillie escorted her across the room. The women who were huddled around the hospital bed--Tillies, every one of them--slowly parted to make way for her.

Heart racing, tears flowing, she stepped forward. The last few Tillies moved aside, giving her the place of honor at the head of the bed.

"Hello," said the woman lying in the bed...the brown-haired twenty-year-old girl looking like an angel in her white hospital gown.

Her green-eyed gaze met Tillie's, and Tillie melted. Had she really been so beautiful forty years ago? Had she *ever* been so beautiful?

"Her name is Michelle." Young Tillie looked down at the newborn baby in her arms...so tiny and frail, she seemed to be fading into the little pink blanket in which she was wrapped.

The truth was, she really was fading. She had exactly one hour to live.

That one hour had been the happiest of Tillie's life. And it would be again, and again, until she faded out, too. Until the cancer took her.

Because the EeePavoosh had created a loop. At the end of the hour, after Michelle died, Tillie would go back to the start and live through it again. Every hour that remained before Tillie's own death, she would spend it here, stringing together a lifetime out of this repeated hour like a strand of glittering pearls.

Each time she started the loop again, she coexisted with past and future versions of herself who'd also entered it. All the Tillies from all the hours she had left to live were sharing that precious fragment of time and space...but somehow, the hospital room didn't seem crowded. They were all in this together; even the twenty-year-old version, to whom this experience rightfully belonged, didn't seem to mind the company.

"Would you like to hold her?" asked young Tillie.

"Yes, please." Tillie nodded and reached out.

When the tiny bundle touched her hands, it was like a bright new star blazed to life in her heart. It didn't matter who the baby's father was or how much pain he'd caused; it didn't matter why the child was sick or that she had less than an hour to live.

All that mattered was that this was *Tillie's* baby, her precious lost Michelle miraculously restored to her. And they would never be apart again for as long as they both lived.

Dozens of Tillies crowded around, beaming and cooing, but the moment belonged only to those two at the head of the bed...only mother and child, brought together after an eternity apart.

The baby squirmed, and Tillie trembled. Cradling Michelle in her arms, she bent down and kissed her softly on the forehead.

And Michelle, as sickly as she was, as fast as she was fading, opened her tiny green eyes and looked up at her. Their gazes met for the first time in forever.

And they both smiled.

ABOUT THE AUTHOR

Robert Jeschonek is an envelope-pushing, *USA Today* bestselling author whose fiction, comics, and non-fiction have been published around the world. His stories have appeared in *Clarkesworld, Galaxy's Edge, StarShipSofa, Pulphouse,* and many other publications. He has written official *Star Trek* and *Doctor Who* fiction and has scripted comics for DC, AHOY, and others. His young adult slipstream novel, *My Favorite Band Does Not Exist*, won the Forward National Literature Award and was named one of *Booklist's* Top Ten First Novels for Youth. He also won an International Book Award, a Scribe Award for Best Original Novel, and the grand prize in Pocket Books' Strange New Worlds contest.

Visit him online at www.bobscribe.com. You can also find him on Facebook and follow him as @TheFictioneer on Twitter.

Subscribe to the Blastoff Books Newsletter: http://newsletter. blastoffbooks.net/

www.ingramcontent.com/pod-product-compliance
Lightning Source LLC
Chambersburg PA
CBHW070536030726
47505CB00001B/58